THE TREE
OF LIFE

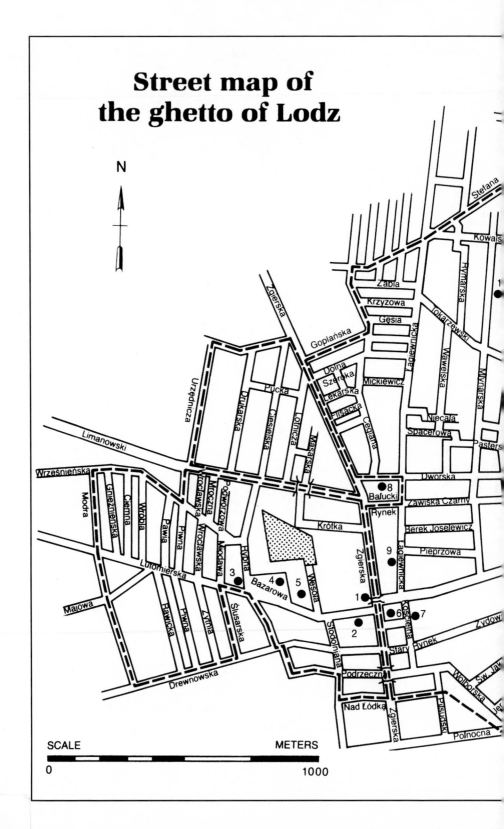

Street map of
the ghetto of Lodz

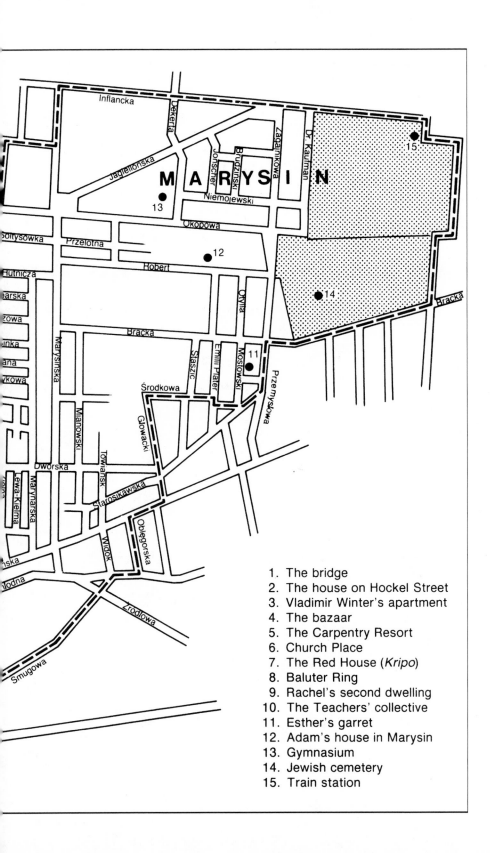

1. The bridge
2. The house on Hockel Street
3. Vladimir Winter's apartment
4. The bazaar
5. The Carpentry Resort
6. Church Place
7. The Red House (*Kripo*)
8. Baluter Ring
9. Rachel's second dwelling
10. The Teachers' collective
11. Esther's garret
12. Adam's house in Marysin
13. Gymnasium
14. Jewish cemetery
15. Train station

In memory of my parents
Sima and Abraham Rosenfarb

THE TREE OF LIFE

(A Trilogy of Life in the Lodz Ghetto)

Book 2: From the Depths I Call You, 1940–1942

Chava Rosenfarb

translated from the Yiddish by the author
in collaboration with Goldie Morgentaler

The University of Wisconsin Press
Terrace Books

The University of Wisconsin Press
1930 Monroe Street
Madison, Wisconsin 53711

www.wisc.edu/wisconsinpress/
3 Henrietta Street
London WC2E 8LU, England

5 4 3 2 1

Printed in the United States of America

Library of Congress Cataloging-in-Publication Data

Rosenfarb, Chawa, 1923–
[Boym fun lebn. English]
The tree of life: a trilogy of life in the Lodz Ghetto / Chava Rosenfarb; translated from the
Yiddish by the author in collaboration with Goldie Morgentaler.
p. cm.—(Library of world fiction)
Reprint. Originally published: Melbourne, Australia: Scribe, c1985.
Contents: Bk. 1. On the brink of the precipice.
ISBN 0-299-20454-5 (pbk.: alk. paper)
1. Holocaust, Jewish (1939–1945)—Fiction. I. Title. II. Series.
PJ5129.R597B613 2004
839'.134—dc22 2004053592

ISBN 0-299-20924-5 (volume 2)

Terrace Books, a division of the University of Wisconsin Press, takes its name from the
Memorial Union Terrace, located at the University of Wisconsin–Madison. Since its in-
ception in 1907, the Wisconsin Union has provided a venue for students, faculty, staff,
and alumni to debate art, music, politics, and the issues of the day. It is a place where the-
ater, music, drama, dance, outdoor activities, and major speakers are made available to the
campus and the community. To learn more about the Union, visit www.union.wisc.edu.

Acknowledgements

Many people assisted me in preparing this book for publication. I thank them all full-heartedly. But I especially want to thank my daughter, Dr. Goldie Morgentaler, for her love, for her selfless hard work, her dedication and devotion to me in all my literary endeavors.

Ch. R.

"Love thy brother as thyself."

Rabbi Hillel

"Die Erstellung des Ghettos ist selbstverständlich nur eine Übergangsmassnahme. Zu welchen Zeitpunkten und mit welchen Mitteln das Ghetto und damit die Stadt Lodz von Juden gesäubert wird, behalte ich mir vor. Endziel muss jedenfalls sein, dass wir diese Pestbeule restlos ausbrennen.

Der Regierungspräsident
gez. Uebelhor.
Lodz, am 10 Dezember 1939"

("It is self-evident that the establishment of the Ghetto is only a transitory measure. I reserve my judgment on the point in time and the means by which the Ghetto, and with it the city of Lodz, should be cleared of Jews. In any case, the final goal should be to relentlessly burn out this pestilent boil.")

BOOK II

The Years 1940–1942

Chapter One

Michal Levine,
Litzmanstadt,
February 9, 1940.

Dearest Mira:

This is the fourth letter that I haven't mailed to you. In my breast pocket I have the other three and this one will share their fate. They lie on my heart, warming it. Who knows, perhaps this is the best way of corresponding with you. Reason mocks me, but my hand grabs the pen without consulting my reason. No doubt I am writing not as much for your sake as for mine — for the preservation of my self. Perhaps one day I will show you all these letters. But that day seems remote and for the time being I am talking into a void — or talking to myself.

This whole week has been terribly cold. But today it is mild, miraculously mild. Warm winds scour the city and I can already feel the promising fragrance of flowers which will break into bud any day now. The snow is melting rapidly, vanishing from the streets; it has left only a bit of glass-like mud here and there as a warning that the winter may still return. But the overflowing gutters mock this warning. They run over and inundate the sidewalks, washing and rocking a newborn sun in their wavy mirrors. Water drips and drops from roofs and pipes and the hazy rain-covered windows seem to be smiling through tears. On the clothes-lines, the laundry waves like white flags; warm winds play with the ballooned shirts and flap the behinds of airy underwear. And the bare trees in the parks and on the sidewalks, their branches lifted towards the sky, look like brides waiting to slip their arms into the sleeves of their flowery bridal dresses. Above their heads, the city birds circle like swarms of busy attendants, filling the air with their housewifely twitter as they gossip about the arrival of spring.

So, dear Mira, it is indeed nice outside — and the Jews of Lodz are moving into the Ghetto.

It was supposed to happen systematically, according to the plan which the *Polzeipräsident* Herr von Strafer and his special staff worked out so elaborately. Every hour another hundred "heads" were supposed to be ready for the march. They were allowed to take any clothes and "family souvenirs" with them, provided they could carry them without using any special means of transportation. The apartments which they abandoned had, of course, to be left in the best order, windows closed, doors locked; the keys had to be handed over to the janitor or to a representative of the German authorities. In a word, this was the plan of a genius, a perfect work of precision which only a logical order-loving mind could have concocted so as to make the impossible, possible; namely, the resettling of two hundred and fifty thousand Jews in the *Wohngebiet* Baluty, which I doubt could shelter even a tenth of this number.

However the plan had one single flaw. Its realization would take too long, weeks, perhaps months. And since Herr von Strafer and his collaborators do not belong to those people who stick to a plan only because it is a work of ingenious precision, but rather possess enough flexibility to adapt themselves to the requirements of the moment — they decided to annul their plan. The orderly resettling is over. Tomorrow all of Lodz is to be made *Judenrein*, actually today, since it is 4 a.m. already. I am unable to sleep; everything is packed and the bundles on the floor look like apparitions. They stare me in the face, mockingly; they ask me about my "ideals", my "philosophies", neither of which I can remember any longer.

Shafran sits beside me at the table, pretending to read. It is he who brought the news yesterday. He was at a meeting of the school board with Herr Presess Rumkowski, where they debated the problem whether Rumkowski should sign the report cards as "The Eldest of the Jews", or "The Leader of the Jews". But it was not given to the Presess to decide this question. There was a massacre going on in town.

Guttman is not asleep either. While we were packing, he stood by the stove, tearing up and burning all that was left of his paintings. I have stopped questioning him. All topics are finished. Mira, I have a new inner face but do not recognize it yet. I am not weak, neither physically, nor morally. I am getting ready to fulfil my duty as a doctor, perhaps my mission, but something is freezing within me. I sit in my undershirt, dripping with sweat. Guttman's burning of his art has made a hell of a heat in here. The stove is glowing red — and yet I am so very cold, Mira — although I still love you . . .

Michal

✦   ✦   ✦

It was the last day of the *Übersiedlung* and the city purged itself of the Jews. Arriving from the suburban districts, from the wealthy city centre, from the market places and from the industrial quarters, they inundated the entire city. Through all the streets and alleys they moved in black swarms, dragging on like an endless funeral cortege. It seemed that not even the houses would remain stationary, but would soon be carried away by the torrent of people, were it not for the citizens looking out of the windows who served as anchors to hold them back. Once in a while, a face in a window would light up with a broad smile, and it was difficult to judge whether it was one of delight at the beautiful day, or delight at the fact that a huge invisible broom was sweeping the Jews out of every nook and cranny of the city, gathering them in the distant dumping ground called Baluty.

The road led uphill. The wheels of the buggies squeaked and grated over the wet cobblestones. Tens of thousands of shoes soaked with mud shuffled and sloshed in monotonous rhythm. Later in the day, the road became drier. The many shoes had sucked in the mud while the wheels of the wagons had ground out the last remaining drops between the stones. Or, perhaps the street had dried up under the heat of so many bodies. The sun shone on the beet-red faces as if they were cobblestones, moving on, stone after stone — uphill.

Rachel walked in the crowd, asking herself whether there was a pair of All-Seeing Eyes somewhere, looking down from above and taking in the entire awesome spectacle; a pair of Eyes watching, as a people marched forward in history while walking back in time — towards the ghetto. She wore her new blue suit and winter shoes with woollen socks, her dress a mixture of summer and winter, just like this day. She walked bent under the weight of the knapsack on her back. It pressed down on her shoulder blades and cut into them. Her hair was glued to her forehead. Beside her walked her father in a new striped suit which he had not, until today, had the occasion to wear. On his back lay a huge sack tied around his arms with cords. Both of them, Rachel and Moshe carried a pack of bedding between them, and in their hands each held bags full of dishes.

Moshe's lips were swollen, cracked and covered with dried crusts of blood; an extinguished cigarette butt stuck to the corner of his mouth. This morning, while he was transporting the first load of his belongings, the janitor's son had knocked out his two front teeth, because Moshe had wanted to take along the sofa on which Shlamek slept. The janitor's son caught him in the gateway, punched him with his fist and forced him to put back the sofa, warning him that he would "bring a German". Before the war, he would come up to the apartment to repair the electricity. When Rachel met him alone, he would ogle her, chatting with her like a dandy. On Sundays he would stand within the gate, a white scarf around his neck, white gloves on his hands. When Rachel passed him, he would doff his hat, greet her chivalrously and then whistle after her like a love-sick canary.

Rachel was amazed at her father's composure; he did not seem to mind the two knocked out teeth. Even this walk, now that they had left their home for the last time, did not seem to depress him. Does he not regret anything? She asked herself. Does he not recall the years they had lived in the old apartment, the important moments of their lives which had taken place there? She glanced at his profile. His lowered eyelids, red and without lashes, were heavy with the usual dream-like sadness which she knew from before, a quiet sadness, far from the despair and anguish of late; almost an optimistic sadness. What makes him so calm? She could not understand. But she was too tired to think much. She was impatient to free herself of the burden on her back, of the crowds around her and of the clamour, the screams. From all sides people pressed against the pack of bedding which she and Moshe were carrying; she had to grip the cord tightly so as not to lose the bundle. Her hands were cut and they burned at the fingertips.

At length, they pushed themselves through to a wall, leaned the weights on their backs against a window sill, and rested. Moshe wiped the sweat from his face and neck. "So, daughter," he said, "another bit of road and we shall be home." He caught the question in her eyes. His gaze became clearer, more playful. "Home means where your mother is, where we are all together." Rachel had to answer him with a smile, not because his words brought her relief, but because she felt like his child again. He raised his eyes to the windows across the street. "They're watching the spectacle . . ." He shook his head. "They, you see, have one 'home'. If you chase them out of it, they perish. But we can make our home anywhere. They call it 'Jewish endurance'. This is it. That's why we don't disappear." Rachel did not believe her ears. Moshe had never spoken like this before. "We" and "they" had never existed for him; he had so much loved the word "humanity". He added, "We shall be together with all the Jews. It will be better."

A stocky man, laden with parcels, who was just passing by, caught Moshe's last words and turned to him with a guffaw, "Sure, sure. Together with the Angel of Death!"

Moshe let him pass, then sighed optimistically, "Great tragedies, daughter, befall strong people, and great calamities befall strong nations. Never mind, we will survive." He straightened the straps of her knapsack, puffed on his dead cigarette butt and asked, "Shall we go?"

The sky was almost white. Light flooded the city which they were leaving. Both the light and her father's optimistic pathetic words increased the gnawing in Rachel's heart. Only one thing was good: her father was the same as he used to be. It was good that he was walking here at her side, in her bewilderment, in her dark nagging fear, in her anxious curiosity about what was to come, and in the sadness which devoured her soul — for all which was past, for her childhood. She knew that she was walking away from it forever.

Someone shoved her aside so vigorously that she screamed out in pain, turning her head around. She saw no face, only a curly unkempt knot of hair and the sweaty rim of a forehead. The man did not react to her scream. He was pulling a table, its legs up in the air. The table lay on a sleigh which screeched unpleasantly on the dry cobblestones. A thick cord was wound around the legs of the table, holding together a pile of packages, sacks and bedding. At its very top, surrounded by heaps of books, sat a heavily bundled little girl, holding a doll on her knees. Behind the sleigh walked a woman who pushed it; her face was bent towards the stones. "He almost knocked me over," Rachel pulled her father aside to let the man with the strange caravan pass by.

Moshe pointed his chin in the direction of the sleigh. "I know him. A young writer. Berkovitch is his name."

A father and a son, both neatly festively dressed, passed them, carrying a huge trunk. The father talked to his son in a loud voice: "Now we will have to prove whether or not we deserve a country of our own. The ghetto will be for us a trial homeland."

✦   ✦   ✦

(David's notebook)

If it were not so tragic, it would be quite comic. I mean the people with their twisted faces, carrying their strange packs and sacks, with their "brilliant" inventions which helped them make the walking and load-carrying easier. For example, instead of carrying bundles of clothes, most of us wore them, and the richer one was, the fatter one appeared.

I was pushing a baby carriage with our belongings (the carriage, a broken piece of junk found by Abraham in a heap of garbage), listening to people talk. This talking, a chapter by itself. They dragged their luggage, panting and philosophizing about Jewish fate, or they talked "normally", casually, and both kinds of conversation sounded equally weird. Near us a woman, thin and scrawny, was walking with a hump of bedding on her back. She looked like a camel; she kept mumbling to herself, "Oy, Kreindle is not a *mentsch* any longer. Oy, Kreindle is not a *mentsch*." The repetitiousness of her mumble was so catchy, that I could hardly refrain from joining in with my mumble, "Oy, David is not a *mentsch* any longer . . ."

Or for instance, the couple walking on our other side. She, petite, plump and red like a piglet; he, huge, broad-shouldered and bull-like. She, the wife, carried nothing. Instead, she was surrounded by six kids and held three of their hands in each of hers. In the meantime, she was engaged in a quarrel with her hubby as they moved on. "Oy, may the ground swallow you, Isaac," she squeaked in a thin child-like voice. "Why didn't you take along the *treyfa* basin, why didn't you? You'll bury me alive, you'll bury me."

The man pushed ahead as he bent down to her with his clattering paraphernalia. "Ay, Gittle, did you say something?"

"And for whom, my Angel of Death, did you leave the coal box?" she said something. "And watch the pails! Oy, calamity! You'll drop the dairy dishes, heaven forbid!"

The pails on the man's back tilted even more as he bent down to his wife, "Ay, Gittle, did you say something?"

And behind me, they were speaking Polish. A woman's voice, the voice of a girl, a man's voice. "I am sure I won't survive amongst this rabble," cried the woman.

The girl commanded, "Stop crying, Mother!"

The man consoled his wife, "I swear, darling, I checked the latrines myself. The cleanest in all of Baluty."

The woman was inconsolable. "I will go out like a candle at this stinking stove!"

The girl warned, "If you don't stop crying, Mother, I'll go away!"

The woman became even more hysterical. "Go, go. All the world is leaving me."

The man proceeded soothingly. "Don't cry, darling. The devil is not as black as they paint him. The neighbours assured me that the mice and rats come only to the lower floors, and we, my pigeon, will live under the very roof. It will be airy."

Then we witnessed a skirmish that was not funny at all. The two men who fought each other looked like quite sober-minded middle-aged citizens. They struggled clumsily, as if wishing to spare each other, yet each jabbed the other in the "seventh rib". The wives and children also fought among themselves. And the reason for this war was a handcart. Between the smacks and blows, the men, women and children of one family tried to push off the belongings of the other and load the cart with their own possessions. My brother Abraham, naturally unable to watch such a spectacle with indifference, said that he was going to make peace between the two parties, and the next thing I knew, he was in the very centre of the action, working with his fists among the brawling children. The passers-by also tried to intervene both with their hands and with a bit of moralizing, "Feh, brethren, it's a crying shame!" But who heeded them? And so the knot of scufflers was left behind in the middle of the road like a rock between two strands of a current, and the crowd streamed on.

Abraham also consented to move on. I was tired and nervous, worried about Mother who had remained in town. She had gone to see the milkman to give him our address in case Father was set free. This morning Mother scribbled a note to Father and put it in the table drawer. How silly! Didn't she know that as soon as we left, the entire apartment would be emptied.

I looked up. On a window sill there stood a flower pot which reminded me of the one I had seen at summer's end, when I had run away from Lodz before the

Germans came. The azalea will bloom again, I thought. It is the same one that I saw then. Only I have changed during the time it shed its flowers and now. That road in September led me through here as well. But then I was a frightened boy, escaping from an enemy that I had only heard of, or read about. Now I am the "head" of my family, and I know the enemy. And another thing: then, the entire city had walked with me. Now a part of the city looks on through the windows and gates as the enemy drives out the other part.

A group of Jews, in long frock coats with swaying sidelocks and skull caps on their heads, came abreast of us. A few of them carried together something wrapped in white on their shoulders. "The Holy Scrolls are being carried into the ghetto," a whisper went through the crowd. I was surprised by the admiration I felt for the Scroll-carriers. They were able to care about something like that, while all the rest of us were so busy with ourselves. I recognized a familiar Jew in this group. He was pushing a white cart with a sign "*Lody*" painted on it. I pushed my carriage closer to his, noticing that the cover of his cart had been removed, and in it were stacked books; huge black books, arranged in rows, one on top of the other. "How are you, young man?" He shook his wispy beard at me. "Do you recall the church outside of Lodz? You slept leaning against me."

"You're alive!" I called out, stupefied.

"As you see, I have lived to go through the chapter *Lech Lecho*, and I shall survive this too, with the Almighty's help." A large crack opened in his beard; it smiled with red toothless gums. "We are, in a way, related to each other, young man, don't you think? I'm not out to say that we are relatives in the normal sense of the word. But people who look Death in the eye together share a kind of kinship. A common grave awaited us, eh? Surely. But His Holy Name intervened. Now we'll share a common life. Yeah, even if . . . one of us should, heaven forbid, leave this world, the one who remains will continue the partnership, not so?"

"It must be hard for you to push such a load," I remarked.

He shook his head. "Hard? It is hard for him who tears himself away from the Holy Scriptures, not for me." He threw restless glances about him as he talked, "At least I settled the little ones, thank heaven. They are in Baluty already. But the wife . . . vanished, and that's that. If a woman walks looking backwards and wailing all the time . . . 'Sarah', I said to her, 'what are you staring at behind you? At the great happiness you've left? You will become just like Lot's wife who looked back at Sodom!' So perhaps she really has turned into a pillar of salt?" He looked at me and I could see how sad his eyes were. "You may laugh at me, young man," he continued, "but according to my calculation, it must be His Holy Hand that is behind our moving to Baluty. He assembles us in order to protect us against the punishment he will send upon Sodom."

I noticed Marek, my friend of the "Flying Brigade", one of our trio (he, Isaac and myself), walking with his parents and his Aunt Sonia, who is not a real aunt but his mother's friend, a spinster with a romantic revolutionary past. It was she who gave Marek his intellectual upbringing. Aunt Sonia noticed us and called us over. I wanted to say good-bye to the ice-cream vendor, but could no longer see him.

"I am talking here with Marek about our people," Aunt Sonia said, leaning towards me. Her tone of voice, as usual, was that of a teacher or a preacher. "The Jewish people are a people of hope. Look at their faces. Look at how they walk. They sigh, of course. They cry and curse. But they are not broken. I am sure that each one of them is trying to figure out how to make a living. Look at this woman here. She probably is thinking how to make her new living quarters more comfortable. And this man here, with his two youngsters, nice sidelocks they have; he must be thinking about a *heder* for them. And this is what I am discussing with Marek. You have to start thinking about your education." At that moment Simon and Ber, comrades from our organization, came abreast of us, both of them loaded with sacks and suitcases. I was glad to meet Simon. For the last few days I had had no idea what was going on in the world and Simon was just the person to give me some solid information. Aunt Sonia greeted them, throwing worried glances at Marek who did not utter a word. She said to Simon, "We were discussing the Jewish people just now, with Marek and David . . ."

"The Jewish people have always been the scapegoat of reactionary powers," said Ber who likes to use newspaper phraseology.

"We were saying," Aunt Sonia went on, "that Jews are great optimists." Again she threw a stealthy glance at Marek.

I asked Simon what was new. After he gave us some unimportant information about Finland, Marek spoke up for the first time. "There is not one single bit of cheerful information to take into the ghetto, is there?"

Immediately Aunt Sonia was there to console him. "To me one thing is clear," she said. "If the dark powers win, the world will perish. And this cannot happen."

"Sure, in Germany itself things might change," I wanted to help her out, since I felt that Marek's gloom was beginning to work on me.

Marek made a face. "Are you waiting for the German people to come to their senses? In the meantime you are going into a ghetto."

"Why are you so afraid of the word 'ghetto'?" Aunt Sonia exclaimed. "We say 'ghetto' because we know of ghettos in the Middle Ages. But times have changed. Even if the Germans wanted to torture us, as was done to us in the Middle Ages, they would be afraid of public opinion, of the rest of the world. Don't fear the ghetto so much," she begged, taking Marek's arm. "The news that freedom has come will reach you in the ghetto too."

Marek shook off her hand. I knew that he felt like running away. I felt the same. His black mood took hold of me. As usual, in such moments, I evoked Rachel's face in my mind. One good thing was certain: our friend, Shalom, had found a place for her and her family, as he had for us, in his backyard on Hockel Street.

✦ ✦ ✦

Simcha Bunim Berkovitch did not feel the sweat running down his face. His black winter coat was unbuttoned. The prickly hair of its collar was stiff; to each hair there clung a dried ball of mud. His eyebrows were also pointed and stiff, the mud on each hair resembling the head of a pin. He kept his head bent as if he were counting the footsteps on the pavement. Had he raised his head, he would have seen little more than the packs, sacks and faces of his nearest neighbours on the road. Nevertheless, he saw the entire picture, sharp and clear. It weighed on him heavily, brutally, as if he, Bunim, were taking with him not only his belongings and his own wife and child — but the entire street, the city, everyone who was walking here, everyone who was already there or who would follow behind. It was as if he were dragging all of their lives, their childhood and youth, their maturity and old age toward a yawning abyss. And he felt guilty. Because what he had foreseen and feared had happened. He had been aware of its coming, yet he had not warned them. He had done nothing even to save his own flesh and blood, done nothing even to save himself. True, he had not known exactly what to warn them against. It even seemed that it would be better like this. The Jews would be rid of the sight of the Germans, of the Poles; they would live together, brethren sharing the same fate; they would suffer, yet live a clean honest life, with dignity. Yet he felt something ominous waiting for them there, in the heart of Baluty. He was afraid, not knowing whether his fear was related only to his own fate, or to the fate of the entire community. Both were now inseparable.

An old man with a prayer sack and half a loaf of bread under his arm trudged along beside him, boring him with endless quotations and proverbs. "Yeah, brethren, a free people suffers little and complains much. An enslaved people suffers much and complains little. Yeah, we shall survive everything except death. *Koheleth* says, 'God seeks the persecuted'. The question is, when will he finally find them?"

Miriam begged Bunim to stop for a minute so that they could catch their breath. He refused. He hurried and wondered why. He was anxious to begin this new life, to face it as soon as possible. He felt that if he were to stop in the middle of the road, something would happen to him.

"Is it still far, *Tateshe?*" Blimele called from the top of the sleigh.

"It is only the beginning . . ." he mumbled to himself without answering the child.

"We are almost there," Miriam assured Blimele, as she pushed the sleigh from behind.

"Where, there?" Blimele asked. "How is it called, this, this . . .?"

"Our new home," Miriam replied patiently.

"Ghetto," Bunim mumbled, feeling as if he were throwing this new word at the child, so that she could play with it on the road.

✦   ✦   ✦

Esther carried just a small knapsack, and in her hand, the suitcase with Hersh's manuscripts hidden among her clothes and dishes. This meant that she could walk faster than the others, but she was in no hurry. The fact that she had no room did not worry her. She knew that her feet would lead her on to Hockel Street and to Uncle Chaim's apartment, and further than this she did not think.

The stream of people carried her along and she felt comfortable and safe. Often she helped those walking beside her, arranging a knapsack on someone's back, holding a child or leading an old man. No one thanked her, and she expected no thanks. People looked at her with familiarity, and somehow her own fate seemed light to her, so light, that it was almost unimportant. This indifference to herself was a consolation, not at all like the kind provided by her comrades. With them she always felt clearly and explicitly her self. With them she thought of the gift of her life as something she was ready to offer for the benefit of the masses. But now she was dissolved into the masses and hardly felt that she had a life of her own. Even her longing for Hersh, which used to be so sharp, both in her despair and in her hopefulness, had now become less acute, more vague. She did not know how this change had come about so suddenly, as she was walking. She felt that only now was her heart opening up with generosity; that only now, here, was she learning what "humanity" and the "masses" meant, and she was learning what it meant to make their "sentiments" her own.

She noticed a gray cart with one wheel, the kind that janitors carry garbage in or that gardeners use. The cart rolled on with its one wheel at the back; the short shafts pointing to the front were pulled by a woman. On the cart, upon a layer of bedding, lay a man covered so that only his face was visible. It was wan and sallow, the nose pointing towards the sky; the chin shook as if he had a fever. From out of the yellowness shone a pair of eyes with a moist nebulous sheen; yet they were sharp, as if there were a fire burning behind their mist. The eyes fixed on Esther. She bent down to him, and asked loudly, as one asks a deaf person, in order to make herself heard above the noise, "Do you want something?"

"Pull up the cover," she heard him say. He was well covered, so she moved her hand over the blanket, pretending to adjust it.

The woman pulling the cart turned around. Esther saw a worn face, a mask of wrinkles and sweat, and a pair of ugly lips smeared with stains of lipstick which resembled crusts of blood. Only the woman's eyes were young and lively; they seemed familiar. She leaned the shaft against her knees so that the sick man would not slide down from the cart and asked Esther in a hoarse masculine voice, "What does he want?"

"He's shivering!" Esther called back to her.

The woman puffed, "Can you understand that? To shiver in such a heat?"

A shout was heard coming from somewhere in front of them. A tall broad-shouldered fellow, who carried two sacks over his shoulder, halted in the middle of the crowd and waited for the cart to reach him. His dishevelled head, covered with black spiral-like locks, glistened. A pair of full lips of a brownish red parted to emit an unexpected guffaw. "What is he lacking, your bundle of joy?" he asked the woman at the shaft. The air around him seemed to vibrate with his restlessness, his strength. There was only one such figure alive in Esther's memory: Valentino, the Prince of the Toughs who had lived in Uncle Chaim's backyard. She recognized him, although he had grown older; no, not older but stronger, more magnificent, more bursting with life. He called out to the sick man, "Friede, look, the sun is shining! So, why are your teeth chattering as if you had malaria? You are a scribbler, aren't you? How can a scribbler be cold when the sun is shining?"

A smile hovered over the corners of the sick man's mouth. "Cold from its heat, Valentino . . ." His glowing eyes indicated Sheindle, Valentino's wife, who was the woman at the shaft. "It must be hard on her . . . Are you mad at me, Valentino?"

"Sure, I'm mad. She's more your wife than mine. If you were a *mentsch* like the others, I would have broken your bones a long time ago. Believe me, you're better off like this."

Valentino straightened up and walked beside the cart. Esther wanted to say something to him, to feel at least for a minute his hot eyes on her, but instead, she moved to the other side of the cart, opened her suitcase, pulled out one of her blankets and covered the sick man with it. When her hand reached his face, a thin white finger appeared beneath his trembling chin, lightly touching her hand. It was like the touch of hot glass. "You have green eyes," the sick man whispered.

Esther cheered up, "If you can still notice the colour of someone's eyes, your condition can't be so grave." She bent down to him, "What exactly is the matter with you?"

"The proletarian disease," he replied. After a pause, he asked, "Why are you wasting your time with me?"

"I have no reason to hurry." She shrugged her shoulders. "I am all alone." It gave her pleasure to say this. She smiled, "Are you warmer now?"

"Yes, I am warmer . . . from your red hair, the green eyes and the pink blanket. And I become warmer still when I think that only last night it covered your beautiful body. Now it covers me. Such a blanket could cure." He looked at her searchingly. "You feel offended? Don't hold it against me. I am a Jewish writer you know. I didn't mean my remark in a banal sense, believe me. My name is Friede. You've probably never heard of me."

"Of course I've heard of you," she lied.

"Really? How come?"

"I'm interested in literature."

He had no intention of questioning her. "So tell me, what am I lacking? A beautiful day, a promenade in a coach through the city, and a girl with red hair and green eyes who has heard of me. If it is so, you must tell me your name." She told him her name. He played with it, repeating it. "If I had to choose a name for you, it would have been Esther too . . . Do you hear the sound? Silk, velvet, delicate sad Jewish charm. You know, Esther, I have a book of short stories ready. It was to go into print, when the war broke out. Now I'm glad it didn't. I will dedicate it to you. I will write, 'To Esther, with the green eyes and red hair, in thanks for the pink blanket'. Do you think I have the manuscript with me? I am not so stupid. I left it behind, locked in a drawer. Let it at least be sure of a tomorrow. Right? I hope I won't miss it. You see, for a writer, his work is like a woman he always wants to be close to. That's why publishing one's work is a joy; but at the same time it's a loss. As if the beloved becomes a . . . Everyone is profiting from her beauty, but she leaves a feeling of regret in the author's heart, a void. That's why the best period is now, when the manuscript is ready, but the world hasn't seen it yet. This is the honeymoon, and my manuscript and I must spend it apart."

She was amazed at the attention with which she listened to his feverish chatter. Tears filled her eyes and she could not understand why. The street, the road, the people around her, they all vanished. She was alone with this face which swayed near her, so close to the earth. And suddenly she felt weak and very tired of her compassion, of her loneliness. She noticed that the sick man was quiet. Sweat had broken out on his forehead. He kept his eyes shut and nibbled on his lips which were twisted in a painful grimace. She bent down to him, "You don't feel well?"

With difficulty he lifted his eyelids. "You see," he panted, "an impossibly early spring has arrived . . . to console us, while such a spring can destroy me. Isn't it scandalous? Me, a singer of beauty . . ." he caught her glance. "But your presence does me good. Yeah, with all this I am fortunate. People are good to me. You see her?" he pointed his chin at Sheindle. "A street walker, and her man, Valentino, the Prince of the Toughs of Baluty. They both came to fetch me. So, shouldn't we believe in man? Do you believe in man? You doubt whether I know where we are going? Don't worry, I do. Where we are going will be very cramped, and I . . . Actually I like humanity only when I sit at my desk. Otherwise I am afraid of it. The lonely person, you understand, feels lonelier still in the crowd."

"And I am just the opposite!" she said in an overly loud voice. "I feel good with the masses!" Suddenly she was full of reproach. "You are a writer, you said. So where is your social conscience? Where are your ears and eyes? Why don't you look around at what's going on here? It would be better for you, believe me, if you lived through this experience, instead of shutting your eyes to it, preoccupied only with yourself!" She noticed the last bit of colour draining from his face.

"I have the right," he mumbled, "to be busy only with myself. You shut your eyes first to your surroundings, before you . . ."

Ashamed, she did not catch his words. "What did you say?"

"I said that you have beautiful green eyes."

He did not look at her eyes. The painful grimace disfigured his clay-like face. A helplessness overcame Esther. She bent down very low to his twisted mouth, feeling his hot breath on her cheek and her voice rattled in her throat, broken, dull, while from within her it called out imploringly, "You . . . Mr. Friede, do you want to be my friend?" It sounded childish, silly, yet she could not control herself. "We could be good friends. I am also lonely, walking here all alone. Open your eyes, Mr. Friede. I am serious."

"Are you?" He did not open his eyes.

"Yes . . . Yes!"

"Then go and help Sheindle pull the cart."

She pushed herself ahead towards Sheindle, took one of the shafts from her hand, and hitched herself up beside her.

✦ ✦ ✦

Miss Diamand carried, along with her basket, the deluxe edition of Slowacki's poems under her arm. With her other hand she held on to Wanda. They were supposed to have taken leave of each other some time before, but they were unable to part, postponing it from one corner to the next and finally from one house to the next. Wanda wanted to come along to the ghetto, but Miss Diamand refused to hear of it, although she could not explain why, even to herself. She was certain that they were doomed to part. "You have to stay," she kept on repeating to the crying Wanda. "It won't be good for us to be together there. There, Wanda dear, you will not only be with me, but with all of them. Look," she nervously pulled her friend by the sleeve, to indicate the preoccupied trudging crowd. "Besides suffering, nothing binds me to them. They have a different style of life . . . They take joy or sadness differently. Even their language is repulsive to me. Listen to them. What do you feel? Strangeness, that's all. But I belong to that strangeness. The question is no longer whether or not I like them . . . And I am afraid, Wanda dear, that with you there, I will loathe them even more. Because I will be ashamed . . . Because, Wanda, I am not supposed to . . ."

Wanda would not stop weeping. "You hurt me. You hurt me so very much."

"I am hurting myself. You see, I have always seen beauty and greatness in the ancient Biblical Jew. In my heart of hearts, I was proud of him. Yes, now I can tell you this. But I won't survive if I don't rediscover something of that in these people. And here they are so backward, so fanatical, so remote from everything near to me . . ." Miss Diamand burst into sobs as well.

Wanda put her arm around her. "Let me come along. That is the easiest solution for both of us. I will adjust, you'll see. I will do everything as you do."

Miss Diamand shook her head. "To adjust, to copy, are external things. It's a question of the heart. That's what it is."

"Don't you trust my heart? Do you believe that I can hate people who suffer?"

To this Miss Diamand had no answer. Yet she held firmly to her decision. "I know and I feel that this is a road which I must take without you. Perhaps someone else wouldn't go alone, but I must. I am going back to my people who are on their own road of suffering with no one to accompany them. When I say this, I feel already bound to them and . . . this doesn't mean, Wanda, my dearest, that I am alienating myself from you."

"You have alienated yourself already. You don't realize it, but you are no longer the same. You are confused, tormented. You don't know what you are saying."

Miss Diamand felt cold. She wrapped herself tighter in her shawl. It was true. Wanda was still at her side, yet she felt alone already. "No, I don't know what I am saying," she mumbled.

"I will go in spite of you!"

"You won't. But you can come with me in a different way. Go to your school, your children, tell them . . ."

Wanda released a sigh of despair. "That means . . . the end."

"The end? Heaven forbid. Not of my friendship with you, nor of my beliefs. I believe that what we have sown has remained somewhere . . . will always remain. We may be separated, but we will be together in a higher sense. Wanda, Wanda . . ." Miss Diamand repeated her friend's name and as she did so, she realized that she was still holding on to the arm of the only human being close to her. "I will teach in the ghetto, you will teach on the outside. We will say similar things. We will find each other . . . somewhere . . . above the dirt and chaos. It sounds pathetic. Life can sometimes be more pathetic than any words. Look around . . . the people walking here . . . Ugly, aren't they? Sloppy, pitiful, noisy. Yet in fact, this is my people walking bravely to meet its fate. A great day today in Jewish history." Miss Diamand would not stop chattering, losing herself again and again in the same circle of thoughts. Tears kept dripping from her eyes. "Once I told you, not long ago, that the Germans made a Jew out of me. So I have to credit them with one good deed. Because I now think that in truth I have served our ideal wrongly. How I used to talk to Jewish children! How could I have reached their souls if I preached to them to abandon their own selves? If one leaves one's own people, is one not like a picture without a background? And if each people is an instrument in a great orchestra and the finer and clearer each instrument plays, the richer and better the concert, then why did I wish that mine . . . the Jewish fiddle, should be quiet?" Her face shone through her tears. "We shall meet in the Overture which all of humanity will intone when freedom comes." Ashamed of her pompous-sounding words, she began to stammer. "Why does everything I say sound so awkward?" They stopped, both of them trembling with cold. Then their hands met, clinging to the volume of Slowacki's poems; two pairs of old hands, wrinkled like dry autumn leaves, finding support against a ravaging storm — on the still fresh covers of the book. "I thank you for him . . . for Slowacki," Miss Diamand said, her voice choking.

Now, awkward strange words poured down from Wanda's salty lips, with despair, with hope, like a question, like an affirmation. "We will meet here . . ." she indicated the book and tore her hands away from it. She turned away from Miss Diamand and let the waves of the crowd slowly wash around her.

Miss Diamand climbed the steps of the house nearby, watching Wanda vanish into the crowd. Then she wrapped her mauve shawl more tightly around her neck and pressed the volume to her chest. She flung her bird-like head high, as if searching for room to soar away.

✦ ✦ ✦

There was a dog going to the ghetto as well: Sutchka, who belonged to Adam Rosenberg. Of all the creatures filling the street, Sutchka was, in a sense, the most privileged. Firstly, she did not wear a Star of David; secondly, she had enough space in front of her, because the other walkers apparently believed in the rule that if one sees a Jew with a dog, there are two possibilities: either the dog is no dog, or the Jew is no Jew. Since there was no doubt about the doggishness of the huge bitch, there remained some doubt about the Jewishness of her master. And on this road it was wiser to keep away from any kind of stranger or goy.

Adam's pate shone with sweat. His forehead was beet-red, as was his neck which hung over his collar in a few loose parallel rolls, like half-baked bagels on a bagel holder. The skin on his face which had once looked healthy and firm drooped from his jawbones in loose pouches. He puffed and panted. His coat, his jacket, his sweater, thrown open by a desperate gesture of his hand, revealed the bulk of his huge shaking belly like layers of leaves reveal the heart of a head of cabbage.

Samuel Zuckerman led him by the arm. Adam did not see him. Nor did he see anything that happened around him. He felt like a man condemned to death; for he was sure that he would die, over there, in Baluty. He saw himself lying somewhere in a dark room, giving up the ghost. He saw his wailing Sutchka at his side, licking his face. He evoked this tragic image constantly in his imagination. For this one moment he did not fear death. On the contrary, he found a strange satisfaction at the thought of it, a pleasant feeling of revenge, he did not know on whom. But a moment later, he was back in the throes of despair.

For the last few months he had felt all the sap of life dripping out of him. He had no will, no plans, no thoughts. He felt as though he were a pricked balloon from which the air was slowly escaping. He would have vanished a long time ago, if not for the weight which tied him to the ground: his fleshy body. The only pleasures remaining to him were his cigars and his food, the last pleasures of the condemned. He had no other desires. The world existed no more. Only nightmares were left.

Adam stared at the cobblestones, seeing in their stead a pavement of numbers, as if the street were one long paper roll, out of a counting machine, counting his treasure which had been so brutally squandered. Now and then, he lifted his eyes from the cobblestones to Sutchka. He sighed. A thought began to persecute him. What would happen to her when he was no more? He saw her howling, wandering around a snow-covered cemetery, alone, sniffing, searching for a trace to him — until she found his grave under a mountain of snow and buried herself alive in it. Tears rolled down his cheeks and he did not know whether he was bemoaning his own fate or that of his dog. Something stuck in his throat like a hard morsel of food, refusing to move. He raised his head as if in search of help, and only then did he remember Samuel and feel the latter's hand around his arm.

✦   ✦   ✦

Samuel carried nothing except the pail in which the parts of his disassembled radio were hidden. He wore a light casual suit, since Wojciech, the servant, was transporting the rest of his belongings in a wagon. The wind was playing with Samuel's pitch black hair which had already begun to thin at the temples. His lean figure seemed leaner still beside Adam's; his pale face, paler still in contrast to Adam's redness. He looked around every now and again to check whether there were any Germans in sight, but in fact, he was not afraid. In the enormous density of the crowd there was little chance that someone's glance would fall on the pail with the "unkosher" radio.

He, unlike Adam, was acutely aware of what he saw around him. The faces of the traditionally-dressed Jews reminded him of his grandfathers, of his father; the older, well-dressed women — of his grandmothers, of his mother. The sight of the buildings at the side reminded him of his own houses, the old one on Novomieyeska Street and the new one on Narutowicz Street, both houses fused in his thoughts into one. He was surprised at the coldness with which he remembered these two places in town where he had spent his life (the factory and his shop did not enter his mind.) He wondered why he did not miss the objects to which he had been so attached. It seemed to him that everything which was of any real value he was carrying with him.

As he strode on, observing the streams of people, it began to seem to him that the air, vibrating with talk, with sighs, with curses and lamentations was also carrying tremors of another kind. He heard piano music, deep penetrating tones; a music capable of dissolving everything material and tangible, and transforming it into a brutal and yet transparent beauty — which hurt with a kind of consoling pain, which consoled with a kind of hopeful sadness. It was as if that music sifted itself through him, reaching to the core of both the earth and the sky. The tones of this dark invisible piano fused everything together into one, yet it resounded with an additional echo. Samuel told himself that this additional echo was borne by the march of all the generations of Jews from Lodz who were now accompanying their children into the ghetto. It dawned upon him that he was indifferent to his old homes because the house on Novomieyska, for which his grandfather Shmuel Ichaskel Zuckerman had fought so bravely, was now a hollow lantern of brick and clay; because his beautiful house on Narutowicz Street was now an empty ruin. The spirit of the Zuckermans hovered here, in the accompanying music above the street leading to Baluty. Never before had he felt such closeness to his ancestors. It was as if they were holding him by the arm, leading him, just like he was leading tired Adam. Thanks to them his steps did not falter and he felt light and self-assured. The deep fears which had been gnawing away at him since the beginning of the war had left him as if by magic. It was as if he needed this long march to release all those cramped dark feelings, to cleanse himself of the *dybbuk* of weakness. The street seemed like a bridge leading from weakness to strength.

He looked up. It occurred to him that for years he had not looked at the sky with such familiarity, not even at the spas, not even when he came into contact with the most enthralling landscapes. He could not soar towards it because dry shallow thoughts, petty worries dulling all the senses had held him chained to the earth. Now he flared his nostrils as if inhaling the entire sky, and as a result, the darkness of the earth also seemed to have brightened up.

Adam stared at him. Unable to understand Samuel's composure, he felt all the more depressed and irritated, overcome by an impulse to destroy the latter's light-heartedness. "Abandon all hope ye who enter here!" Adam uttered a philosophical sigh. Then he licked his dry lips, exclaiming, "Zuckerman, who knows how much cigars will cost up there! I cannot do without them."

Samuel grinned, "You'll have to get used to many things, and to that as well. Don't worry, one gets accustomed to things easily if there is no choice."

"I have a choice, I still have some money!"

"You do? Then you should begin saving it for more important things. Difficult times are coming upon us, Adam."

Adam was still choking on something in his throat. No, he did not want a quarrel with Samuel now. Not for such a purpose had he made up with him that very morning, not for that reason did he today cling to Samuel. What he needed from him was solace, at least a grain of support. He moved closer to him. "Listen," he panted. "I have a presentiment that I will die in the ghetto."

Samuel's eyes twinkled mockingly, "A presentiment is not a sure thing."

"Don't laugh at me. Better listen to what I am telling you. As long as I live, I want to have my bit of food and my cigars. That is all I want."

"Fair enough."

"Don't interrupt me. I am serious. I want to tell you what no one in this world knows. You are my only friend. If something happens to me . . . If I fall ill . . . I have hidden some money in town, in a wall, just . . . like you have." He swallowed a few times to rid himself of the knot in his throat. "I am being frank with you. I know that you have hidden money in town."

Samuel stopped. There was no longer a trace of mockery on his face. "Wojciech told you?"

"Why have you stopped?" Adam pulled him by the sleeve. He shook his head. Such was human friendship, good only for balls and jokes; in a moment of calamity man was lonely and abandoned anyway, each man thinking only of himself. "I don't need your money. That low I haven't yet fallen."

Samuel was boiling with rage. "How do you know about my money?"

"Samuel, I beg of you."

"Speak!"

"All right . . . I was digging in your cellar . . . building an underground passage to the backyard, so that if the Germans attacked the house I could escape. You know how afraid of them I was. Wojciech, he helped me . . . but he has no idea . . ."

"What have you done with it?"

"Nothing, I swear. I buried the box again. You'll find it easily. Look . . . I could have kept silent, but I think that you should have told me yourself, just as I am telling *you*. It is better that we know about each other's money, in case something happens to one . . . the other will find a way . . ."

Samuel's first impulse was to run back to town, dig up his little treasure and take it along. His second impulse was to throw himself at Adam, the repulsive, disintegrating creature who was now preaching friendship to him. But gradually his nervousness subsided. What had happened after all? The only thing that had happened was this walk to the ghetto. Had he, Samuel, while walking here, thought even once about the jewellery box? Had it not ceased to exist, along with everything else he had left behind? And what actually was Adam's sin? He had dug in a cellar which was not Samuel's any longer anyway. It was good that no one was guilty, good that Adam was frank with him. Samuel did not like to discover falsehoods or bear a grudge against anyone.

He flared his nostrils again, as if trying to sniff out the previous music that Adam had destroyed with his talk. But Adam would not permit him to remove himself with his thoughts. He continued talking on to Samuel, forcing him to promise him something, repeating words . . . words about money and numbers. So this march was no longer as light and as elating as before, but Samuel still felt the presence of his ancestors near him. He still heard the rhythm of the march into the ghetto. He had a premonition of his own, which was both pacifying and painful: he felt that in the ghetto he would write his book about Lodz and that there he would finish it with this last chapter. It was clear to him that the history of the Jews in Lodz was approaching its end, and that whatever followed would call for a new beginning.

He did not notice that he and Adam had left behind the wagon with the luggage and the members of both their families. Far behind them walked Matilda and Yadwiga, along with Professor Hager, Mrs. Hager, the Zuckermans' daughters and Mietek.

Mrs. Hager carried a small basket, while the Professor carried a briefcase in his hand. Mrs. Hager wore an elegant black hat which went well with her carefully arranged hair. Her wrinkled face was powdered, her lips covered with a discreet layer of lipstick. The Professor also wore his best hat and his coat was buttoned up. On the hands which held the basket and the briefcase they wore gloves, but the hands by which they held on to one another were bare, the fingers knotted and tangled. There was solemnity in their gait, as if they were following the funeral hearse of a distinguished stranger. They did not stop talking for a moment; they constantly squeezed each other's hands, inclining their heads towards one another, and the Professor's lips, fringed by the stiff hair of his neat beard, now and again touched his wife's cheek.

Yadwiga and Matilda were unable to remove their eyes from the old couple. "Look, Mrs. Matilda," Yadwiga blinked in the direction of the Hagers. "Like pigeons . . ." On Yadwiga's tongue a half-dissolved candy danced, shiny and red. She licked the tips of her freshly manicured nails, tilting her head closer to Matilda. "What does such an old couple still have to talk about?" she tittered.

"He is consoling her," Matilda replied apathetically, not too eager to converse with the lively Mrs. Rosenberg.

Yadwiga, accustomed to one-sided conversations, took Matilda's remark as an invitation to carry on. "So, is that a reason to isolate oneself from the rest of the company? We are one family, aren't we? They lack tact . . . Two old egoists, that's what they are!" Matilda was ready to agree with her, but she was aware that she envied the old pair. "And look at her coiffure," Yadwiga chattered on. "See with what chic her hat matches her hairdo? You see, Mrs. Matilda, that's what I like. A woman should never neglect her appearance." A wave of heat swept over Matilda's face. She understood Yadwiga's insinuation. She, Matilda, had terribly neglected herself during these last few days. She wore no make-up and had not even packed her corset but had left it in the bedroom. She had been unable to pull herself together from the moment it became apparent that she would have to leave her home. Seeing Matilda ill-at-ease, Yadwiga remarked cheerfully, "I didn't have you in mind, Mrs. Matilda . . . You look quite well this morning." Matilda made an effort to move away from her. "Mrs. Matilda, you are just like a child. You mustn't be offended by something I did not intend."

Matilda tried with all her strength to control her nervousness. "Please, Mrs. Yadwiga, I have a headache." Yadwiga dropped behind and unwrapped her bag of candies. The road was boring and it was particularly exhausting in her high-heeled shoes. It seemed impossible to pass the time in silence. Slowly she approached the young Poles who were helping Wojciech pull the wagon.

Now Matilda could watch the Hagers undisturbed. How jealous she was of them! How much she wanted Samuel to walk by her side, and not leave her alone. She was no longer the brave and strong Matilda of recent times. She was now a dethroned queen, going alone into exile beside the remnants of her ravished kingdom. Her heart swelled in painful rebellion against her husband and her children. "They don't need me. I don't exist for them," she whispered to herself. She felt estranged from everything around her and from herself as well; the cold estrangement of a corpse which still possessed a live aching heart and a pair of living eyes filled with tears. Time and again, as she looked at the Hagers, she re-awakened the moment in her memory which had so brutally cut her off from life, the moment when she had left her home.

The thought of her past home led to the thought of the place that she would have to call home from now on. She recalled how a few days ago, Samuel had taken her down to a mouldy cellar on Hockel Street, to a carpenter he had known and who had introduced them to a baker upstairs. The baker's room was filled with the smell of bread and of spicy garlic dishes. The sight of the half-blind baker, with his black pointed little beard and his grayish white apron, made her feel nauseous. Alone with Samuel in the room which the baker wanted to sublet to them, Matilda had grabbed her husband by the hand, wailing spasmodically, "My beautiful house! My beautiful things!" She broke down altogether and Samuel, frightened, had run off to Mr. Rumkowski to beg him for assistance. That was how they had gotten the landlord's house in the very same backyard, a completely isolated building with big rooms and a treasure, a toilet. Samuel was happy, but Matilda, although she said nothing, had no idea how she would survive even here. Now, as she walked on, she noticed her two daughters and Mietek in the crowd. She had the feeling that she was taking her beautiful flowers, the fruit of her womb, so lovingly raised, uphill, to be sacrificed on the altar of a brutal god, of Moloch.

Mietek led the girls by the arms. Junia whistled, throwing coquettish glances at the boy. The day was so bright that she felt like flying. She pressed to her bosom an "expensive" flowerpot in which a little bag of jewellery was hidden. She laughed, "Why should we worry about a ghetto if the sun shines there too? Right?"

"Nonsense! On a day like this I'd rather take my motorcycle and go out on the roads," Mietek countered.

"Why do you have to poison your life with what you are unable to do? Do what you can do. Breathe! Yes, breathe with both nostrils!" Junia expanded her chest, inhaling deeply.

"I need something more than just breathing," the young man did not share her enthusiasm. "I'm not poetic enough to sit around and stare at the sky."

Junia wagged a finger in his face. "Don't worry, you won't sit there and stare at the sky."

Mietek turned to Bella, "And you, what will you do in the ghetto?"

Junia giggled. "It won't make any difference to her, ghetto or no ghetto, she will go on burying her nose in her books. She's a dreamer, don't you know?"

Mietek, pretending to be serious, pressed Bella's arm, "'Wake up, wake up, Deborah!' We are not going to a place designed for dreamers. You must face reality, to be able to protect yourself against it."

Bella felt like biting her nails. "Thank you for worrying about me," she muttered confusedly. "And do you know how much reality you will be able to take yourselves? When you feel really bad, where will you escape? You'll see . . . you will create, like I do, such . . . such little boats of dreams and jump into them." Mietek and Junia laughed at her strange words. She was laughably ugly at that moment.

Suddenly a deep silence fell around them. Carts and people moved to the side of the road. A horse was galloping in the crowd. Behind it shook a black lacquered droshky. The coachman, a mighty man with a broad red face, held a whip not above the horse, but over the heads of the throng. He called out to let him pass, and with curses chased the people towards the walls. Inside the droshky sat an imposing man with a flying mass of gray hair, darting majestic glances from behind his thick eyeglasses; his mouth with lips tightly closed was in constant motion. He wore a gray summer suit and his hands held on to his hat which lay on his knees.

"*Ave Cesar, morituri te salutent!*" Mietek called out, raising his hand in a Roman greeting.

✦ ✦ ✦

Mordecai Chaim Rumkowski felt his heart fluttering in his chest. A nerve vibrated at the left side of his neck in time with the rhythm of his pulse. Not only the nerve, but everything throbbed within him with the same restless beat, the beat of his galloping thoughts, of his galloping excitement. He was tense, overwhelmed. He was both proud and weak in all his limbs. He was on his way to take over his kingdom, riding in a black lacquered droshky to meet his fate. He was aware of the greatness of the moment and hardly had enough strength to bear it.

He heard the murmur of the crowd, saw the eyes . . . eyes turning to him from everywhere. They made him drunk with their submissiveness. They looked up at him from below. A sea of faces. It seemed to him that the droshky was not riding between them but above them, soaring like a winged phaeton. And it appeared to him that the hammers that pounded within him, the rhythms that pulsated, were forging in his heart, as on an anvil, his mighty feeling of love for his people. He promised himself that he would do everything in his power for them. He would be their father and protector, their judge and teacher, and already he saw another procession of the same Jews, but going in the opposite direction, leaving the ghetto. He saw himself not in a droshky, but on the hands of the crowds. On their hands they would carry him out of the ghetto and millions of Jews from all corners of the world would join them. They would carry him to Eretz Israel, put the reins of a Jewish homeland into his hands and beg him, "Be our coachman! Here, lead us! Reign over us, because you are blessed by God, annointed by Him to be a leader, a father, a King of Jews!"

He wished for two things simultaneously: he wanted this ride to last as long as possible, so that he could satiate himself with the great feeling, with the beauty of the moment. And he wanted to be there in Baluty already, because his body nagged at him. He was tired of the drunkenness, of the great emotions. He was thirsty and craved for a glass of cold soda water. Besides, he was impatient. There was so much to do in the ghetto. "Hurry up this nag of yours!" He prodded the coachman with his walking stick.

The coachman indicated the crowd with his whip. "I can't, Mr. Presess. They're rolling under our feet!"

"It's an order," Rumkowski said mildly. The coachman flicked his whip in the air, yelling in all directions. People began to scatter. Rumkowski held on to the droshky with both hands because the street was badly paved and the wheels shook. Suddenly, the nag hit something with her hoof. The coachman stopped the droshky and jumped to his feet. A scream rose from the crowd. In the middle of the road lay a broken white cart with the inscription "*Lody*" on its sides. Between its collapsed walls and under the wheels of the droshky lay a pile of black bound books, some opened, with the pages flapping, others face-down, their pages in the mud. A little man kneeled bent over the heap of books, reassembling them carefully, closing them, cleaning and kissing them, his wispy beard caught between their pages. The coachman heaped curses on the little man's head. Mr. Rumkowski, who had stood up behind him to see what happened, shook him angrily, "Shut your mouth! You're a *schlemiel*, not a coachman!" The people around nodded their agreement and with great respect waited to see what Rumkowski would do now. What he did was to step down from the droshky, helped by a few men in the crowd. They cleared a way for him, so that he might approach the little man. "Are you hurt?" he asked loudly, as if the little man were deaf. The onlookers, impressed by the Presess' expression of care, moved closer, to feel more familiar with him. The little man, as if he were indeed deaf, did not answer or interrupt his work. "An idiotic coachman. Doesn't see where he's going," Rumkowski said, embracing the crowd with a paternal glance. The people nodded their heads in agreement. He bent over the little man, "He might have killed you, a little fly like you."

The little man arranged the books in small piles. Without raising his head, he said, "Please help me, Mister. These are precious volumes, *Gemaras, Mishnas.*" He raised his hands as if in prayer, but let them fall immediately. His face twisted. "You are the rider of the coach, aren't you? Over the dead and the living you ride, don't you?"

Mr. Rumkowski chewed on his lips. The little Jew had offended him in the presence of so many people. "Get up when I talk to you!" he commanded, hardly able to control his nerves.

The little man handed the books to those in the crowd who had begun to help him out. "Who are you in our town that I must get up and stand in front of you?" he asked, not speaking directly to the Presess but addressing his words to the air.

A murmur passed through the crowd. "This is the Presess Rumkowski, idiot," they explained. "Come on, get up!"

The little man behaved as if all this had nothing to do with him; he continued to gather the books and then finally got up with the last few in his hands. Someone took the books from him; a few sleighs and carts were now covered with the assembled volumes. Only the broken ice-cream cart remained folded, like a house of cards, on the cobblestones. Mr. Rumkowski felt ill-at-ease. Everything was boiling within him, but he knew that the scene must end with dignity. He cast a last glance at the ice-cream cart and then turned toward the droshky. Climbing in, he faced the preoccupied little man, saying loudly, almost apologetically, both to the little man and to the crowd, "It is difficult to ride uphill . . ."

The ice-cream man straightened up and raised his head; his wispy beard split in two, revealing a pair of red gums that looked like a cut. He smiled bitterly, "Uphill, you say you're riding? It only appears so to you. You are riding downhill, my dear Sir. Hurry, hurry, the road before you has been greased and smoothed!" Mr. Rumkowski did not hear him. He was already sitting in the droshky, ready to move on. "*We* are climbing uphill." The little man turned his misty eyes toward the crowd. "That's why it's so hard for us."

Mr. Rumkowski prodded the coachman with his stick, "Move on!" The coachman cracked his whip. People began quickly to move aside. The droshky swayed. Mr. Rumkowski held on to it with both hands.

Chapter Two

"THE JEWS OF BALUTY are privileged. They don't have to move into the ghetto," Sheyne Pessele said to Itche Mayer who was busy taking apart his working table. She herself was packing the bedding into ash-gray pillow-cases. The beds had already been disassembled and the chairs were covered with clothes, utensils, books, picture albums and Sheyne Pessele's bare "heads", a reminder of her old profession as a wig maker. The big wardrobe, the "coffin", as Itche Mayer used to call it, had also been taken apart, and its thin walls covered the floor, one on top of the other.

Moving was for them a simple enterprise. The important things had not been taken out of the knapsacks after the family's return from Glovno, and the less important things were missing. Gone also were Yossi's football shoes and Shalom's trumpet. Sheyne Pessele had not stopped deploring the loss of the "priceless" trumpet which was worth a "fortune" and of the brand new football shoes "which one could not buy even for money nowadays". She had refused to be consoled by Itche Mayer's argument that they were lucky to have returned to the cellar at all. But ever since it had become clear to her that she was, thank heaven, moving out of the cellar, she had ceased to talk about the theft and now, while packing, it did not even enter her mind.

All three unmarried sons — Shalom, who returned with his parents from Glovno, Mottle who had also tried to flee through the "belt" to his comrades, and Yossi, who had set out into the world with no particular aim — were now back home, helping their parents move into the new apartment. But although the moving was not a big enterprise, and the new apartment was in the same backyard, the moving, in Sheyne Pessele's words, "dragged on as long as the Jewish diaspora and one could not see an end to it".

Sheyne Pessele knew perfectly well that neither her sons nor Itche Mayer had their minds on the job. Every time they went out with a bundle, they ended up procrastinating in the backyard, talking with the new neighbours who had arrived from town, and helping them perhaps as well, instead of minding their own business. That was the type of people her men were: providers for the world, "all-the-town-on-my-head" fellows. But Sheyne Pessele was not in the mood this day to make an issue out of these things. She consoled herself with the thought that she had lived in the cellar for nearly thirty years, and a few hours more would make no difference to the calculation. The main thing was that at last she was going to a new dwelling, which had a bright room with a kitchen, and two big windows through which the daylight shone so long and so fully that the electricity could take a rest until evening came. And this tremendous change had come about, strange as it might seem, thanks precisely to the craziness of the world which boiled like a kettle of miseries and catastrophies, playing havoc with human destiny.

Their good luck consisted of the fact that of all the neighbours whom the Germans had evacuated from the backyard, only a small number had returned. Apartments stood empty and the yard was desolate. At first it had not entered the minds of those who returned, to exchange their bad apartments for better ones. They had smuggled themselves back into their own apartments and lived in constant fear that the Germans might again raid the backyard and discover that those who had been evacuated had returned, and who knew what might happen then? — How, in such circumstances, could it occur to anyone to open the apartments of others? But when the Jews from the town began pouring into Baluty, and the establishment of the ghetto became a fact, and people did indeed begin to open doors as if they had no owners, then the old residents said to themselves that if things were as they were, they, more than anyone else, deserved to pick a better dwelling.

Sheyne Pessele, who knew that whoever comes too late to the table is liable to find only bones, came to her husband with the same question: If everyone else was doing it, why not they? And even before he concede the point, she ran out, and before long she announced to her family that they had, thank heaven, a new domicile. And what a domicile! A palace, the like of which she had long ceased even to dream about. It had once belonged to the teacher Mermelstein and legends about it used to circulate in the yard. Sheyne Pessele, who had seen all the apartments in the backyard with the exception of the one in question, where she had never before set foot, was immediately attracted to it.

And no wonder. When Itche Mayer broke the lock and they entered, Sheyne Pessele held her breath, enthralled. True, with the exeption of two beds and a mirror, the apartment was bare, but the walls were covered with wallpaper of a flowery design and, more important, the apartment had a red lacquered floor. Sheyne Pessele fell in love with this floor on the spot. At the sight of it, she felt as excited as a little girl. She even felt a tickle of a desire to sit down on the boards and slide around on them in order to feel their smoothness.

People passed by the window of the cellar. From the backyard there came a clamour. Carts squeaked, people yelled, quarrelled. Sheyne Pessele knew that the female neighbours in the yard, those who had come back with her from Glovno, were all outside, watching the arrival of the city slickers, and some of them undoubtedly taking delight in the fact that they had lived to see their hour of vengeance on the rich, who must now move to the slums of Baluty. But she, Sheyne Pessele, had no such feeling of vengeance. She herself felt like a nouveau riche, a person who possessed two rooms and a red lacquered floor where no mud would be oozing up between the boards, even if one jumped or danced on them.

Of course Sheyne Pessele's good mood did not show. She did not want to expose herself to people's laughter. That was her nature. She was always a bit ashamed of herself when she was in a good mood, which in any case rarely happened. And for that she had a remedy, namely, when she was well disposed, she tried to hold on to a sad thought in order to dampen her cheerfulness. Of course, these days she did not have to search too long for a sad thought. It was the thought of her first-born who had left Lodz with his wife and child in search of his parents, and had never returned. The last news she had had from him was that he was in Warsaw, and nowadays this was comparable, in Sheyne Pessele's mind, to crossing the ocean. With this thought in her mind, the joy of the new apartment was easy to bear and easy to bury. Nevertheless . . .

Sheyne Pessele raised her head from the depths of the pillow-case in which she had packed the bedding. She had a sudden idea and pondered for a while whether she should share it immediately with Itche Mayer, or whether she should wait until he was in a better mood. But she was impatient today. "Itche Mayer," she said, "I have a plan." She noticed the sourness on his face, and mustered her courage to further explain the proposition to him. "If you agree, we will take the teacher's beds for ourselves and we'll give the boys our own cots. They will surely enjoy sleeping on them and we, the two old ones, will get a taste of life in our old age . . . straighten our bones out. Have you seen the mattresses upstairs?"

"I've seen the mattresses," Itche Mayer grumbled.

"So what do you say?"

"I say mattresses for kings. But I will sleep in my own bed."

Hands folded over her breast, she approached the two cots, shaking her head at them with disgust and revulsion. "This you call a bed? These miseries full of bedbugs? Since beds have been beds, there has never been a bed like this. This is an inquisition, not a bed. Have you ever spent a smooth night on it? Have you ever gotten up in the morning without aching bones? Let's not kid ourselves, Itche Mayer."

"They are mine," he growled.

"And if they are yours, where is it written that you have to sleep and torture yourself in them all your life? Never mind, a grave one doesn't change, but with a bed, change is permitted."

"Of course, when I buy myself a pair of new beds."

"The teacher's mattresses are just like new. Never in your life have you tasted the pleasure of such a mattress. It doesn't squeak, it doesn't pinch. It's butter, not a mattress." She cast a hate-filled glance at the sunken cots and grimaced. "Where have you ever seen such bumps, such holes? The beds in Sodom must have been more comfortable."

Itche Mayer could not bear the prosecution of the beds any longer. "It's enough, Sheyne Pessele. I refuse to sleep in a stranger's bed." His eye fell on the two iron cots. He felt no resentment towards them. On the contrary, the sight of them made him sentimental. He sighed. "How many years have we slept in these, Sheyne Pessele? They must know by heart every little bone of our bodies. Why are you forsaking them, eh?"

"Because I have had enough! Because I also want to have a taste of life. I want to sleep in the teacher's bed and that's that."

"Aren't you afraid that the teacher and his wife will come to haunt you in your dreams at night?"

"You're crazy!"

"So I'm crazy. And if you want to know, I can't at all understand how people can break into apartments that aren't their own and say: It's mine."

She favoured her husband with the same kind of look which she had bestowed on the beds a while before. "Don't be such a saint!" she exclaimed. "Go out, have a look in the backyard and you'll see how many apartments have remained empty, waiting for their owners to return! Luckily I came to my senses in time. If not, we would have to go on living in this grave forever."

"I don't build my happiness on someone else's misfortune," he stuck to his argument.

"Do you know already that this is your happiness and someone else's misfortune? Perhaps the teacher has it better than you? Perhaps we shouldn't have returned either, but should have left for Warsaw to be together with Israel. Who knows what is better? But in the meantime, Itche Mayer, in the meantime the teacher is not here and we are. If we hadn't opened the apartment, someone else would have. And another thing." Her husband was surprised to see a tiny smile appear on her face. "You're afraid that the teacher will haunt our dreams? What if he haunts our sons' dreams? Will that be all right?"

Itche Mayer could not understand what was happening to Sheyne Pessele. "My goodness, wife, you have become a regular philosopher."

She put her dark worn hands on his shoulders, and looked into his face, while he looked into hers. It was creased and ashen and in it he could clearly read his own past. Only in her eyes did he see something which did not agree with the face, but which was also familiar to him: something like a cry of longing, a call from the young Sheyne Pessele of the distant orchard in Konska Vola. "Don't be so tense." She shook his shoulders. "We are getting rid of the cellar."

"If we had gotten rid of it in the proper manner, I wouldn't mind," he sighed, feeling strangely soft and warm inside.

"Every manner is proper, Itche Mayer. We aren't, heaven forbid, going to kill anyone. Why should you have so many scruples? Can't you see that you won't save the whole of humanity anyway?" She shook him again as if to shake off his heavy mood. At the same time, moved, she began to cry, sniffling through her wet nose. "So what do you say, Itche Mayer?"

Itche Mayer, completely conquered, spread his hands out. To him a woman was wrong so long as she did not cry. The moment she started crying she was immediately right. "Yes, a woman may be no more than a broken shard, but she can shred the strongest man to pieces. I won't divorce you because of that, Sheyne Pessele," he muttered.

He embraced the cellar with his glance. No, he could not be as carefree as his wife. The other night, when the Germans had come to transport them to Glovno, it had been like a cut with a knife and he had not had time to regret then what he was regretting now, in this voluntary abandonment of the cellar. It was strange, because he was unable to explain to himself what he was so upset about. He knew that Sheyne Pessele was right in everything she said, yet he felt with all his senses that the cellar was dear to him and the new apartment strange and cold. A room with a kitchen, a wall in between. He could not imagine how one could live in two rooms at the same time. Here it was cramped, but everything was together. At night he could raise his head and see the heads of his sons sleeping on the work table and listen to them breathe. He could lie in bed in the mornings, and watch Sheyne Pessele cook breakfast.

Itche Mayer slung the boards of the work table over his shoulder and went out. In the corridor he ran into his youngest son. "Father!" Shalom called out excitedly. "The Zuckermans are here already!" He removed the boards from Itche Mayer's shoulder and flung them over his own.

Itche Mayer looked at his son. Now, he could not understand what had happened to *him*. "So what's the great excitement all about?"

"You're in a lousy mood, Father."

"What other mood do you want me to be in? Jews are going into a ghetto. Is this a celebration for you? Do you realize what this means?"

"And you, you do? Have you ever been in a ghetto?"

"Oy, such sons I raised!" Itche Mayer sighed. "So go, don't stand there and stare at me. Mother wants to put an end to the moving."

However, Shalom had to tell him what was on his mind. "At the moment, Jews are assembling. That is what I see. The backyard is empty no longer. That is what I see. And that is not so terrible." He added, "Zuckerman stopped to talk to me, and do you know what he told me? 'We will be neighbours,' he said to me, shaking my hand."

Itche Mayer turned away from Shalom and, dissatisfied, returned to the cellar. As soon as he opened the door, he met Sheyne Pessele's eyes, with their strange little flame. "Itche Mayer, if you agree . . ." she immediately said, "I have another plan."

He scratched his head. "What now?"

"Listen, husband," she approached him. "What do we need all these old beds for? How can you put a child on such a ruin full of bugs, tell me? If you agree . . . Yes, take the boys right away, put together a few boards and, one-two-three, fix up a place for them to sleep. We can put a lot of bedding on it and get rid of the bedbugs at the same time. So, what do you say?"

She was really beginning to get on his nerves. "You absolutely want the pleasures of the rich, right now, on the spot, don't you, wife? Show me one house on the entire Hockel Street that has no bedbugs. Show me such a house in all of Baluty."

"That's what *you* say. And I can swear that the teacher had no bedbugs."

"Swear and you will be a liar. What do you think, that bedbugs are afraid of intellectuals? May I have as many years in my life as there are intellectuals whom they've bitten!"

"I said that they are afraid of intellectuals? I say that they are afraid of cleanliness. And don't worry, husband, you won't make such a pigsty out of your home any longer. Every Sabbath we will wax the floors and polish them with rags. Mirrors I will have, not floors!"

"Oy-vey," Itche Mayer rubbed his hands against his face. "Perhaps it would have been better if Adam had died with all of the ribs intact in his body."

Sheyne Pessele loaded his arms with clothes which she picked up from the chairs. "Go and don't talk so much," she pushed him out. At the door, she held him back, "And with the old beds, it will be as I said."

He stared at her. "You're going to throw them into the garbage?"

"Are you out of your mind? I should take a pair of good beds and throw them into the garbage?"

"What then? You'll sell them?"

"One we can sell. Many people are arriving from town without beds. And the other we will give away for charity. Uncle Henech told me that Valentino is bringing a sick man from town. So there will be a bed for him. Poor soul, coming to inherit this cellar. May our enemies inherit nothing better."

"And you're going to offer the sick man such a piece of furniture?"

"You have something better to offer him? Without a bed, he will be more comfortable? So go, find the boys, fix up a good sleeping place in the new apartment and come back to clean up the garbage. It's a crying shame to let a person move into such a pile of dirt. And let there be an end to it once and for all."

✦   ✦   ✦

In the backyard on Hockel Street the wagons and carts loaded with furniture, bedding, packs and sacks were surrounded by swarms of adults and children. Like ants, men, loaded down with heavy packs, went in and out of the dark entrances which were like the depths of hidden canals. The open downstairs windows, which revealed the gray torn walls of the apartments inside, were now used as doors as well. Through them too people went in and out, carrying packs of clothes and pieces of furniture. Children crawled along the sills, or used them for dangling. From each open window, as from a gaping mouth, there issued a series of yells, curses and wails. Through one of these open windows could be seen a dark room crammed with people fighting over some packs and suitcases. They were quarrelling over the ownership of the room. In front of another window there stood a crowd of people, motionless and quiet, listening to a scream which came from inside, different in kind from the others; it was a tearing, howling yell. A woman was giving birth.

The short walk through the backyard, through the chaos and hubbub appeared more depressing and tiring to Rachel than the long walk uphill to Baluty had been. She searched with her eyes for some escape and noticed a fence in the distance. Against its background, like a sketch, appeared the contours of a tree, its trunk half-buried in the snow. Only its branches looked in their nakedness like bent bony fingers stretched towards the sky — towards her? They seemed to be inviting her to imagine how they would look when they were covered with leaves and buds. With her mind's eye Rachel saw the greenness. The memory of this colour was refreshing.

She climbed the wooden steps along with her father and entered a long corridor. The two of them shuffled along it, holding on to the walls. Although the corridor was not completely dark, because the open doors let through some rays of light, Rachel and Moshe kept their eyes shut. There was smoke coming from a kitchen somewhere, which made their eyes burn. Moshe's foot hit against a shaky cupboard and there was a sudden clatter of tin utensils and dishes. Heads poked out from open doorways. Rachel saw her brother Shlamek. He helped them enter the room and deposit the packs.

She ran immediately to the window. "Shlamek, come here!" she called. "What do you see there, at the fence?"

He leaned against the window. "What should I see? I see snow."

"Can't you see a tree?"

"Sure, I see a tree. So what?"

"We'll have a tree at least." She turned and faced the room. It was divided by a thin cardboard wall covered with wallpaper. In the wall were two openings, one served as a passageway, in the other stood a huge stove. In both parts of the room there stood large heavy cupboards of a dark brown colour. The beds were wooden, heavy and also dark-brown. This dark-brown sombreness bespoke an unbearable gloom. "This is home from now on," she told herself, unable to fully grasp the fact. She began to unpack her dresses and took the boxes with photographs and souvenirs out of her knapsack; then she opened the brown doors of the wardrobe. Her glance fell on a pack of books inside. She picked one up and flipped through its pages. It was a Psalm book. She picked up another one, a prayer book. Then she found a pile of unbound torn booklets. "Czarska's romances," she said to Shlamek. "There was probably a girl living here, who loved Czarska's stories."

They sat down at the table and ate their first meal in their new home. Familiar dishes stood on the familiar tablecloth. Seen through the steam coming from the hot plates of soup, the furniture looked less depressing, but an ache still gnawed at Rachel. She thought about the people who had lived here, about the girl who had read Czarska's romances. "Shalom told me" she said, "that in this apartment there lived a hosiery maker."

"A large family," Blumka remarked. "You can tell by the size of the pots they left."

The soup spread through Rachel's body, warming her limbs. In her imagination, she saw the people who had lived here wandering on distant roads. Then she saw the home that she herself had left that morning. She bent her head to hide her misty eyes.

✦ ✦ ✦

Inside the gate of the house on Hockel Street, stood Blind Henech, the baker, his wife Pearl and their cat Perelka. As soon as the "caravan" carrying the invalid Friede appeared, the gate filled with Valentino's cronies and with Itche Mayer and his sons. They surrounded the cart, scrutinizing the sick man. Esther felt a pair of eyes watching her with strange insistence. She smiled faintly, as she recognized Shalom. It was he who as a boy had helped Blind Henech pull the *cholent* out from the oven on the Sabbath.

The men lifted the sick Friede. Limp, heavy, as if he had no backbone at all, he let himself be carried into the house. His face was twisted into a painful grimace and his eyes were closed. Sheindle, Valentino's wife, prevented Esther from leaving. "Thank you very much," she said. She turned towards Pearl and indicating Esther, explained, "She helped me pull the wagon."

Pearl squinted in the manner of her almost blind husband. "A familiar face . . ." As she turned her little head, the loose wig she was wearing became separated from her skull and followed it somewhat belatedly. "I would swear . . ."

Esther turned away from them and headed in the direction of Uncle Chaim's apartment. The backyard looked the same to her as in the old times, full of noise, full of people and children. It seemed that any moment the head of one of Uncle Chaim's daughters would appear in the upstairs window. "So many have returned, but not they," she thought with regret and bitterness, considering it a kind of personal punishment. Upstairs in the corridor, noise came from behind all the doors, just as in the old times, yet its rhythm was not the same. Esther had the feeling of being aboard a swaying ship on a stormy dark night. Her head swam. She had to stop in front of Uncle Chaim's door. For a moment she had the impression that she was hearing the sound of hosiery machines. She shut her eyes, afraid of what she would find, then pushed open the unlocked door.

In the room four people were sitting at a table, eating. Esther stopped on the threshold; her gaze met four pairs of eyes. Someone rose from the table and approached her. Was this a hallucination again? Who was this girl who stood in front of her, watching her with such astonishment? "How did you know that we live here?" Rachel stammered, not knowing what to do with the visitor. Her experience with Esther, something she hated to recall, came back to her. She cast a glance at the suitcase in Esther's hand, "Is this the precious valise she wanted me to hide for her?" she asked herself.

Moshe looked at Rachel with reproach. "Why don't you take the suitcase from your guest? Why don't you ask her to sit down?"

"Don't bother," Esther mumbled. "I'm not a guest." She moved slowly ahead, as if hypnotized, unable to rid herself of the strange feeling of unreality. Her green eyes like nebulous projectors wandered along the walls of the room, along the windows. Again it seemed to her that she heard the sound of hosiery machines. From the stove the clank of dishes reached her ears. Was Aunt Rivka preparing soup for someone? Esther sank into a chair.

Blumka approached her with a steaming plate of soup and placed it in front of her. "You must be hungry," she said, handing her a spoon.

Rachel smiled an awkward hostile smile. Esther felt like repaying her with the same. How she hated her! How she hated all of them at this table! She could not bear the coziness of the room, the cheerful sound of cutlery. But as soon as she had taken the first spoonful, a warmth spread through her empty stomach. It was weeks since she had tasted a warm meal. Burying her face in the plate and unable to raise her eyes, she sipped the soup quickly and avidly. "Where did you meet, the two of you?" she heard the man's question as if from far away. Was he speaking to her? Not important. She was unable to utter a word. "He is sitting in Uncle Chaim's chair," the thought was gnawing at her.

"We know each other from the library," she heard Rachel's voice.

Blumka asked, "More soup? I always prepare a little more . . ."

Esther's eyes became mistier. Aunt Rivka also used to cook a little more for the beggars, she recalled, and answered, "No, thanks." An urge to get up and run out overcame her, but she remained seated, glued to the chair, unable to move a limb. She drank tea with Rachel and her family. She sipped eagerly, stubbornly, feeling its good taste on her palate. Then, words began to pour out of her mouth. They streamed without a stop from her moist warm lips. "I used to live here. I grew up here, in my Uncle Chaim's house." She sipped openly now, her words, her tears and her tea. "I thought I would be able to settle here. You see the windows? My cousins worked there. Uncle was a hosiery maker. And here, at this table they repaired the socks. There, at the stove, stood the spindle that my aunt worked at . . . The candlesticks there in the corner . . . My aunt used to bless the candles . . ."

The tea had been finished for some time now, but she went on sucking from the cup with eager lips, between one sentence and another. She hardly knew what was happening to her, hardly heard what was coming out of her mouth. It was clear that this was not what she wanted to say, what she wanted them to understand, and her words brought her no relief. At length, her shame and her pride both grew until they helped put an end to her talking. She jumped up from her chair. Those at the table looked at her in silence. She snatched up her valise and started towards the door. She felt Blumka's hand touching her. She had to turn around, at least for a moment, so that the hand would stay on her shoulder for a little while longer. "I have come all alone into the ghetto . . ." This was what she wanted to say, but she did not.

"Come back for a minute," said Blumka and threw a questioning glance at her family. "I mean . . . you have the right. And you probably have nowhere to go."

Now Moshe also stood beside Esther. She felt the pleasant weight of his hand on her other shoulder. "Stay," he invited her.

"Never felt the taste of having a father . . ." Little lights of sorrow and self-pity went on and off in Esther's mind. She wished the man would put his hand on her forehead and stroke her hair. How strongly she longed now for a father and a mother! How sick she was today with that longing! The taste of the sweet tea was still on her palate; the taste of having a home, of being a child. "Stay . . . stay," she heard a voice coming from the depths of her weakness, of her fatigue. She was afraid to look into the faces of these two people who stood in front of her, afraid she would feel weaker and more tired still. So she turned her gaze to the other two, to Rachel and Shlamek — and the sweet warm taste vanished. Two pairs of eyes commanded, "Go!" She shook off the hands from her shoulders and without another word, left the room.

In the backyard, she sat down on the water pump, buried her head between her arms and shut her eyes. Around her all was clamour. The water pump screeched and squeaked. Water was pouring into pails, drumming upon her heart as if trying to call forth the strength in her and not let her be inundated by despair. Friede came to her mind. She recalled her walk to the ghetto, her good mood. "I am going all alone into the ghetto," she had said so cheerfully to the sick man. If she could only stop thinking about herself, forget herself, dissolve into someone else's fate and let herself be carried away by it . . .

Shalom, the carpenter's son, sat down on the well by her side and observed her with unpleasant tenacity. "You have probably been to your uncle's room. I put my friends there." He said this shyly, with an uncomfortable smile. "Come, I have a room for you too," he added, got up and took her suitcase. She followed him in silence. He led her into an entrance and they climbed three flights of stairs. The room he opened for her was tiny, with only an iron bed and a little table in it. "This is the only room they did not grab. They've overlooked it," he smiled a bit more courageously. "I kept it locked, in case a friend arrived who had no place to go. Here is the key." It seemed as if he expected a word of thanks from her. She took the key, waited for him to put the suitcase down and walked to the door. "Where are you going?" he asked, surprised. But then he understood. "You are probably going to the sick man. They've settled him already in our cellar. We live on the first floor now."

She went down into the backyard with him and left him there. He looked after her, devouring the flame of her red hair with his eyes and tracing the outlines of her slim nimble body with his gaze. He could barely grasp that it had finally happened, that today, for the first time in his life, he had spoken to the girl about whom he had dreamed all the years of his youth. It was an extraordinary experience.

✦ ✦ ✦

(David's notebook)

So we are in the ghetto. The funny thing was that I was unable to find Rachel, although I knew that she was supposed to be living in the same backyard. But this is not a normal backyard, it's an entire city. In all the hoo-ha I finally caught hold of Shalom who showed me Rachel's windows. I called her down and we went out into the street. It was dusk already but people were still coming in from the city. The streets were bulging with the crowds, streaming in all directions, people . . . people everywhere.

"The entire ghetto looks to me like one noisy backyard," said Rachel. Our walking step did not agree with the rhythm of the street and unfriendly eyes looked at us as if to say, "So you found time to go for a walk?" Someone even cursed us, shoving us into the gutter. We approached Zgierska Street. From a distance, we noticed something which did not fit into the surrounding colour. These were the green Tyrolean hats of a group of Germans who stood in the middle of the road, near the church. One held a map spread out over his briefcase and drew something on it with a finger as he talked to the other Germans who surrounded him. Two of them measured the sidewalk with long metal measures. Around them the street was empty; this part of it looked like a white pate on a black head of hair. Above, in the niche of the church stood the blue snow-covered figure of the Holy Mary with her hands piously folded, as if she were blessing the Germans at her feet, who were drawing the borders of the ghetto.

I recalled that once, in the country, I had seen an ants' nest, an entire kingdom in the forest. I watched the ants carry dry pine needles and hurry about busily. "Perhaps they are laughing and playing around in their own way," I thought. I held a brick in my hand. "They don't know that with this brick I will soon crush them." And in the meantime I teased them, blocking their passages, mixing up their canals, killing a few of them and observing how the others reacted. Then I got bored with the game and I crushed them with the brick. This was the time of my childish "scientific experiments".

Rachel lifted her head towards the church tower, indicating the clock with her eyes. "Do you see what time it is?"

I looked up. "Ten minutes to ten."

"The clock has stopped."

I pulled her by the sleeve. We turned back. At the gate we stopped. We stood at a distance from each other and people passed between us. The clamour roared in our ears.

"I'm going upstairs," Rachel said. "I have no time."

"Neither do I," I replied with a lie to her lie.

Later on, she came up to our room to show me a poem she had written. It began more or less like this: "Ten minutes before ten, the clock stopped and the world abandoned us . . ."

✦   ✦   ✦

The Zuckermans could have had the entire seven-room apartment to themselves. Matilda could have gotten rid of the Rosenbergs with whom life had become unbearable; she could have freed herself of the Hagers who were as quiet as pigeons, but hurt her with their amorous displays, feeding her jealousy. The pleasure of living alone, however, was not given to her, and this was Samuel's fault. He simply believed that it was a sin, in the cramped ghetto, that four people should live in seven rooms. And he added, that in time they would in any case have to take in strangers to live with them. What would she, Matilda, do then?

The apartment had a large rectangular corridor from which all the doors gave off. The Zuckermans took up two rooms. The Rosenbergs another two. One was left for the Hagers and one for Reisel, the cook. They, of course, all shared the kitchen and the bathroom.

Reisel agreed to cook for all of them on condition that each family paid her separately. She let them know that she had a big family living not far away, a bunch of sisters, nieces and nephews who expected her help, and that she did not intend to let them die of hunger. In general, Reisel became a transformed person the moment she arrived in Baluty. She forgot the word "Madam", and became familiar with everyone. Twice she even yelled at Matilda that Matilda "did not put her hand into cold water", by which she meant that her mistress did nothing but get into her way. The sight of Yadwiga or of old Mrs. Hager was completely unbearable to her. She grumbled and snapped at them and whatever they did or said displeased her. In one word, the aura around her mistress and the guests had vanished, and Reisel at last had a chance to free herself of the resentment she had hidden for so many years under the veneer of servile submissiveness.

Reisel waged a particular war against Sutchka who felt drawn towards the kitchen. She was unable to chase her away, and all the curses that Reisel did not dare heap on her mistress' head, she would pour out on the dog's head. Moreover, every time she looked at Sutchka, she was reminded of Barbara, the cat, who had spent her life with Reisel and who had been left behind. This especially Reisel could not forgive the dog.

The only person who pleased Reisel was Junia. The girl lent a helping hand with the work. She even helped her scrub the floors and did the job deftly as if she had spent her whole life doing nothing else. "You are a *mentsch*," Reisel praised the girl, "and all the rest of them are a bunch of spoiled brats, your mother included." She felt a soothing pleasure in kneeling and scrubbing the floors together with the rich man's daughter. Reisel was even more delighted when Junia forbade her to enter her own room, telling her that here, the girls themselves would see to their own needs.

The girls had the largest and brightest room in the house, the room with the balcony. As they arranged their things, they talked about the summer days that they would spend outside. This new place, the new life filled them with impatience, with tension. The work they did by themselves and Matilda's helplessness made them feel grown-up and responsible. Junia was excited by this feeling of maturity which smelled of freedom. Bella however felt unsure of herself. She longed for a moment when she would be able to shut herself off, book in hand, from what was now called life. The word "life" loomed in her mind as awesomely frightening, although it also excited her and kindled her curiosity. She forced herself to converse with Junia. What Junia actually said was not important. The mere sound of her sister's voice had a calming effect on her.

But Junia's gay chatter was often interrupted. Sometimes Reisel would call her, at other times Mrs. Hager would ask her to help the professor. Even the Rosenbergs asked her for help when the other men were gone. Samuel had vanished somewhere and as soon as they arrived, Mietek had run out into the street, unable to take the chaos in the apartment.

Adam Rosenberg gathered together all the money which the members of his family had carried hidden in their clothing, and for the first time in their life together, he asked his wife's advice. Both of them decided that they would hide the money in their room, but that they would leave the two cigarette cases which were filled with less valuable jewellery in the suitcases, for which they found a place in the bathroom. They reasoned that it would occur to no one to break open suitcases which stood in such an open place. They worked together, both of them realizing that this was actually the first time that they had done something jointly. When they had finished, Adam felt, to his own surprise, a whim to take his wife into his arms and kiss her. He did not mind that the washroom was not exactly the most romantic background for a love scene. After all, she was his wife, in spite of the fact that he had not touched her for quite a while. Nor did Yadwiga mind. She clearly felt that a new era was beginning in their relationship. She busied herself in their two rooms, constantly humming a little song. Adam's friendliness intoxicated her. She did not worry about a thing, determined to look at the situation from the positive side, and everything made her laugh.

The backyard seemed particularly funny to her. She observed it through the window, amusing herself at the sight of the swarming people, each of whom displayed a different expression of his face, each of whom was bent in a different way under the weight of the load he was carrying. The women, wrapped in thick plaids, scarves on their heads, especially aroused her curiosity. She was sorry that the windows were shut and she could not hear their shouts and chatter. The activity of the backyard seemed to her like a grotesque performance put on especially for her benefit. Time and again, she would run into the kitchen and, oblivious to Reisel's sour face, ask her questions about the people, the backyard, amusing herself with the cook's comments.

Nor did Adam know why he felt so much better as soon as he arrived at the house. The doom-filled thoughts left him. He looked about his bright comfortable room and it did not seem probable that he would die here. He too looked out through the window, and tiny plans and schemes began to take shape in his mind. The backyard, bulging with people, led him to think of the crowded ghetto, a town of thousands who would need things to buy. He began to play with the thought of a business, a small one at first, and he decided that he must go out into the streets that very day.

The thought that he would be able to walk the streets without fear made his heart light. Here no one would catch him for labour, no one would slap him. No, he had not arrived at a prison; rather he had come out of one. It was not a very comfortable freedom, but it was freedom. He felt a certain fervour; he was not so old yet. There were still years ahead of him to survive and to live. The large amount of his capital in Switzerland lost its depressing power and began to smile at him. For the first time in months he spoke to Yadwiga as sweetly as in the old times.

Samuel remembered well his lessons at the radio technician's. He lay on the floor of the little shed near the washroom, carefully unpacking the disassembled parts of the radio which he had carried in the pail. He had a plan for later of how to hide the radio and disguise all the traces of it. For the time being, he made everything work, in order to hear that night the first tones of the Fifth Symphony which preceded the newscasts. He tried to work quietly, so as not to be heard outside. He still had doubts whether or not to let the people in the house know about his secret. A flashlight illuminated his long slim hands which shook somewhat. The thought that here he would some day hear the news that the war was over was overwhelming.

He worked quickly. He had come here a few times when the apartment was still empty, to prepare a "home" for the radio; and now all there was left to do was to assemble the pieces. At last the electric wires were tied and the little light in the apparatus went on. The whiteness of Samuel's trembling hands became brighter; the shed's contours appeared discreetly in the darkness. And then — he heard the warm voice of a woman: "*J'attendrai . . . le jour et la nuit . . . J'attendrai toujours.*" A melancholy smile lit his face. He recalled when he had heard this song for the first time. It had been the day he had brought home the radio which was a gift from the Hagers. It even seemed to him that the same female voice was singing. However, the meaning of the song was no longer the same. It was not just the love song of a woman in distant Paris. In the darkness of the shed, the words and the tune took on another significance. Now it meant that the enslaved world, and he, enslaved Samuel, were singing the song to freedom, "I shall wait for you, day and night I shall await you."

Apparently it was too late for the newscast. He turned off the switch and covered the radio with the pail. Crawling on all fours, he moved to the little door and put his ear to it. It was quiet outside. Carefully, he slipped through the small opening. Still on all fours, he noticed a pair of feet on the threshold of Adam's room. When he stood up, Adam put both hands on his shoulders as if to reassure him. "So, you've hidden it here? Not a bad place. Perhaps I too should hide my most valuable things inside?"

Samuel sighed with relief. "It's not good to have everything in one place." In his mind, a nagging thought arose that the hiding place for the radio was not as sure as he had thought. He tried to free himself from Adam's hands. "I'm going out."

Adam's face lit up, "You are reading my thoughts, I see. Perhaps we could do something together . . . a little business."

"You don't feel like dying any longer?" Samuel, nervous, asked ironically.

Adam smiled, "The road up here seemed so desperate, but a human being struggles. I want us to start something right away. Let's go out and look around."

"I am going to look for work."

"What kind of crazy idea is that? What work do you want to do? Sweep the streets? Clean latrines?"

"These too are jobs which need to be done."

"Don't make a fool of yourself. Have you ever worked in your life?" Adam asked. Samuel stared at him. Adam's baggy cheeks, shaking with weird laughter, tempted him to slap them. Quickly he stepped outside. Adam followed him, "So, where are you going?"

"To see Rumkowski."

"That beggar?"

"Now I am the beggar. I'm going to beg him for a job." Running down the stairs, he turned to Adam, "Do you want to come along?"

"Not I! I wouldn't stoop so low!"

"Stop pretending you're royalty. Remember that the world has turned upside down!"

"That's right! And the garbage came up to the top!" Adam hurried down a few steps after Samuel. "He will never live to see me! You hear? Not me!"

In the backyard, Samuel's daughters caught up with him. They asked him to take them along to show them Baluty. They wandered through the noisy streets, halting on their way home in front of the church. They looked up at the clock on the tower for a while. The immobile hands covered one another, pointing at the number ten. They resembled a knife which had cut off the time in the ghetto from the pulse of the rest of the world.

✦ ✦ ✦

Back at the gate to their own backyard, Samuel and his daughters noticed Miss Diamand. Strings of unkempt gray hair protruded needle-like from behind the mauve shawl that covered her head. She held something in her clenched fist as she looked about her forlornly, her eyes tearing with the cold and with fatigue. Bella let out a cry of surprise. Samuel, his heart quickening at the sight of her, stretched out both arms to the old woman. He had completely forgotten that it had been he who had provided a room for her in the same backyard. She blinked at him, "Perhaps you know where I could buy a few potatoes?"

He was on the point of inviting her to his house for supper, but he was afraid of Matilda and Reisel. It was wiser to avoid unexpected invitations today. It was Junia who took it on herself to supply the teacher with a few potatoes. She took the money from her and dashed off into the street. Samuel bowed nonchalantly to the teacher and to Bella, hurrying back toward Church Place and Mr. Rumkowski's office.

It seemed to Bella that fate was not as brutal after all, as she had imagined. She came closer to the old woman — who was constantly blinking her eyes as if she were trying with her eyelids to wipe out the fog between herself and her surroundings — and said in a whisper, "I'm glad we will be neighbours, Miss Diamand. There will probably be a *gymnasium* here and you'll teach me again." Miss Diamand nodded in agreement. Encouraged, Bella asked, "Will you allow me to visit you?"

The old woman's pale bird-like face approached Bella's, "Not yet, my child . . . First I must make order . . . around myself . . . within myself . . ."

Bella's heart was filled with love for the teacher. "You came alone?" she inquired.

"Alone, child, yes . . . But I have you . . ."

Junia returned with a bag of potatoes; she handed it to the old woman, exclaiming, "I bought it from a boy in the market! Don't they speak a funny language!"

Junia seemed to have called the bemused teacher back to reality. Her voice became clearer, her gaze sharper. She lifted a finger at Junia and mildly admonished her. "You must not mock them. Have they chosen their language willingly, my child? Is it a person's fault that he is lame?" Miss Diamand nodded to the two girls and shuffled away from them.

"What an oddball!" Junia exclaimed in amusement.

"She was my favourite teacher," Bella felt offended.

"No wonder. She and you make a real pair!"

They went upstairs to finish unpacking.

✦ ✦ ✦

Presess Rumkowski plunged into the sea of activities and duties like a brave captain who knows his destination, sure that no blizzard, no stormy chaos will cause the ship entrusted into his hands by fate, to stray from its appointed course. He worked with a clear head, with order and a plan, in total composure.

First of all, he had to deal with the problem of Jewish institutions, which ones to liquidate and which to take over and continue in the ghetto. Then there were meetings to be held with Mrs. Feiner and her staff from the *gymnasium*, as well as with the boards of the elementary schools which he had reopened while still in town; and there was the problem of food provisions for the children in general. The rest of his time was spent in conferences about finances. There was the urgent necessity of creating an independent source of income, by opening some factories or Work Resorts as the Germans called them, which would give the people an occupation and establish a more solid base for the existence of the ghetto.

Despite all this work, the Presess was in high spirits. And in spite of his many obligations, he managed to treat himself to a substantial dinner and his beard to a second shave. He put on a clean shirt, (lately he wore only white shirts, changing them as often as possible.) Afterwards, dressed up in his new suit, he examined himself in the mirror. He was pleased with himself. The hard work did not show on him at all, it seemed rather to suit him. He contemplated his gray head with self-respect. This was how he ought to look. Only the eyeglasses with their cheap frames needed to be changed for better ones. He also decided to see a doctor, not because he felt ill, but because with the help of modern medicine he might perhaps regain his former strength. He, who once had cared so little about his health, decided to protect it here, in the ghetto, like a treasure. Before, it had been only the health of an old director of an orphanage, he objectively explained his case to himself, now it was the health of a great man, of the leader of all Jews in Litzmanstadt-Ghetto. He purred contentedly, as he put on his new stiff hat. He also remembered to put a white handkerchief in the breastpocket of his jacket.

He drove through the streets which teemed with people. He had ordered the coachman of the droshky to put up the hood, but people recognized him. They raced after the droshky, yelling, "Herr Presess! Herr Presess!" begging for favours, for work, for charity. As he passed a corner, someone raised a fist, calling out to him, "We are starving!" He was kept busy brushing off the letters and notes people threw at him. He thought about hiring two muscled body-guards who would accompany him everywhere.

The corridor to the office was bulging with people who had waited for hours to see the Presess. He nodded to them as they greeted him in a chorus and moved aside to let him pass. He waved to his secretary, Miss Blank, who had once been his ward in the orphanage. She replied with respect, informing him, "Thirty people have appointments to see you, Herr Presess."

He screwed up his face. "Thirty? I saw a hundred. Throw them out. From now on everyone who wants an appointment must write a petition and wait until we call him." He added mildly, "Once the militia begins to work properly, we'll have no trouble. Come here, you must take a letter."

They worked carefully and slowly on the letter. Chaim Rumkowski, as a rule impatient in his writing, was meticulous when it came to his correspondence with the authorities. The letter finished, the time had come for the interviews. He arranged the glasses on his nose, buttoned his jacket and sat up straight. He had mixed feelings about these daily interviews which he had introduced while still in the city. He was pleased with the submissive politeness, in particular of those who, before the war, had kept him waiting for hours in their own waiting rooms. He enjoyed the whining of the well-dressed women, the scent of powder and perfumes which issued from them, as well as the servile flame in their eyes. It was as if they were pledging something in exchange for a good position for their husbands or for themselves; he made a mental note of the most attractive amongst them, to make use of in calmer times. But what he was unable to bear was their syrupy narrations of personal tragedies, as if they were the navel of the world. Nor could he stand it when he detected an undertone of demand in their humble pleas, as if he, Rumkowski, owed them a debt which they had come to collect.

As he signed to Miss Blank to call in the first supplicant, she remarked, "A good friend of yours is waiting outside, Herr Presess. Mr. Samuel Zuckerman. Should I let him in first?"

The Presess was ready to nod, but he restrained himself. A cunning smirk appeared on his face, "There are no privileges here. Let him wait."

Miss Blank called in the first person on her list. A woman entered. She was blond, tall and quite young. She wore a buttoned-up raincoat, with the collar turned up, and carried a big black pocket-book under one of her arms. She sat down and put her hands on the top of the Presess' desk. "I am a representative of the Bund," she spoke up composedly. "You refuse to meet our delegation officially, so I have come privately." He cast a stealthy glance at her hands, wondering how they could be so shapely and feminine, when the purpose of her visit was so practical and unpleasant. Her head covered with a pelt of blond curls and her narrow glowing eyes reminded him of a lioness. She was tempting, powerful; this made him feel less sure of himself. "The ghetto is starving already, Herr Presess. People have no work," she went on calmly.

"If they will let me carry out my plans, they won't starve, nor go without work." He had no courage to reply in the manner she deserved. "Tomorrow a few public kitchens will be opened."

She puffed out her cheeks with disdain. "Charity kitchens? There you want Jewish workmen to go begging for food? The Jewish proletariat of Lodz knows of better traditions."

Now his blood was beginning to boil. "Don't you knock me on the head with your traditions-shmaditions! What do you want me to do?"

"Meet a delegation of the workmen and we shall confer jointly on how to introduce social security, public works and how to initiate an economic scheme. Discuss these problems with us, then the responsibility won't rest entirely on you."

"Never mind, it suits me quite well that it rests solely with me. The Jews of Lodz need me, not you!" He became master of himself at last.

"We demand that you receive a delegation of workers."

"You came to make demands on me?"

"I also came for the ten thousand marks of relief money sent to us by the 'Joint' of America. We need the money for our sick comrades, our schools and our nurseries."

Now the Presess unleashed a real counter-attack. "It's time that you stopped caring only for your comrades, great socialists that you are! All people are equal to you, aren't they? If you want to know, I am a better socialist than all of you! For me there is no difference between one Jew and another. We are all in the same boiling kettle! And you are a bunch of egoists, that's what you are! Each of you thinking only of himself, his family, his affairs! Who do you think has the entire community in mind? Of the entire ghetto, I alone! There is no money for 'comrades'!" he concluded, certain that he had conquered this powerful female.

She rose, her voice remained calm, only her eyes pierced him with a dagger-like gaze, as she said, "That is the law of life, Herr Presess. A person cares first for his family and friends, especially in the middle of chaos, particularly when there is danger. Had life in the ghetto been arranged on a different basis, had we indeed met and organized ourselves, we, our party, would surely have renounced this money for the benefit of the entire community. But you refuse to convene with anyone and have set out to rule the ghetto like a . . ." She did not finish the sentence, but headed for the door. There she halted, turning her face to him. "I shall report our conversation to my comrades. And you should know, Herr Presess, that the ghetto will soon stir and become restless."

The Presess had to master himself before he could receive the next supplicant in the proper frame of mind. The most important thing in which he had to train himself was to refrain from becoming overwhelmed by irrelevant incidents, by unpleasant and meaningless human reactions. So he finally managed to establish a fatherly composure that evoked respect for his person, both in himself and in the petitioners during the next interviews. People bowed before him, thanked and praised him. When Samuel Zuckerman's turn came, the Presess stopped Miss Blank, and the cunning smile reappeared on his face. "Enough for today," he announced.

✦ ✦ ✦

Michal Levine,
Litzmanstadt-Ghetto,
February . . . 1940

Dearest Mira,

Here I am to report to you. I have my first patient already. He is (was) a writer. His name is Friede. The same man Guttman and one of his friends had in vain tried to "deliver into my hands" before the war. A lonely soul. Neighbours take care of him. Can there be anything more awful than to be hopelessly sick and alone in the ghetto? Perhaps I should be cynical and say that it is better like that?

We are already settled. Mother and I will keep one room and Shafran and Guttman the other. Housekeeping will be a joint affair. Guttman wants to be our "Minister of Economy". Fine, but for the time being we have no "economy" worthy of the name.

To be honest, my relationship with both my friends is still pretty strained. We scarcely talk to each other. What we all need at the moment is to escape from life, while at the same time we need to give meaning to it, through work. But we are, each one of us, each in his own way — still lame . . .

In the meantime, only one thing can save and console me: you. Dearest, from now on I shall not call you Mira, but Mirage.

✦ ✦ ✦

Simcha Bunim Berkovitch occupied the "latrine man's hut", as it used to be called. One of its walls leaned against the big brick tenement, while another, bordered on the latrines. The hut, one large room and a shed which served as a kitchen, was a country-style structure with an entrance into the yard and with shutters on the windows. As soon as they arrived, Miriam closed the shutters, to prevent the smell from the latrines from penetrating the hut. They turned on the electric light and Bunim told himself that in this way had begun the long night in their lives.

He helped Miriam unpack their belongings, reproaching himself for not having found a better place. He also knew that he should go out immediately into the streets to find a job, since he had arrived in the ghetto with only five marks in his pocket, but something kept him from leaving the hut. Instead, he took the pail and the scrubbing brush from Miriam and knelt down to scrub the floor.

Miriam was delighted with his diligence, oblivious to the inner agitation propelling his movements, unaware that he was purging himself of his pent-up rage. His hands moved back and forth over the boards, in a hard staccato rhythm. He had the feeling that he was engraving a poem in the floor, a poem without words, one which flowed with the streams of water along the cracks, sinking into the wood, then inundating it with new streams. Miriam watched the dirty mud-covered boards reappear, bright and clean. This restored her tranquillity. It was evident to her that precisely here Bunum would be closer to her than ever before. Now and then she pointed out a stain on the floor that he had overlooked. He obeyed her, correcting his mistakes. Sweat washed down his face. Its taste was good. Miriam spoke to him as if she wanted to calm his conscience. No, he did not have to rush into the streets today. They still had some barley and potatoes in the house; there was also some kasha left for Blimele. She wanted him to remain at her side until she became used to these foreign walls.

Only when Blimele was asleep and Miriam was ironing the curtains for the windows, did Bunim wrap himself in his coat and go out into the backyard. His face was hot; the stiff collar scratched unpleasantly against his sweaty unshaven neck. He inhaled the fresh air deeply, and with it, the smell of the latrines. Briskly he walked away from the hut. The backyard was empty. Above it hung a deep dark rectangle: a slice of the evening sky. Somewhere in the sky a pallid fringe of the moon could be seen behind a cloud, a nebulous eye gazing into the backyard. Faint rays of light peered out through the cracks between the blackout curtains and the windows, searching for the light of the moon, as if they were trying to convey a message to it — but could not reach it . . .

He glanced at the snow-covered corner near the fence. There, its trunk half-buried in the snow, stood a short naked tree. Then he looked up at the windows. Somewhere nearby a child was crying. Elsewhere people were quarrelling. He could hear a girl's laughter. A dog barked behind a door. In the dark, patches of torn paper, rags and dirt twirled in an inaudible dance, led by the fingers of a sharp cold wind. The sweat on his back began to freeze, pricking him with icy needles. He quickened his steps, pacing faster and faster through the empty yard. Within him a voice was screaming. He raised his head to the pale misty shimmer of light in the distant slice of sky. "God!" he called out.

Chapter Three

WINTER RETURNED with full force. Blizzards followed one after another, veiling the streets and the houses with cobwebs of snow and frost. Even the old people could not recall such a long cold winter. And when, at the beginning of March, the cold finally subsided, it was replaced by endless rain. The winds became even more biting. The streets of Baluty formed one swampy sea, and where the sidewalks were unpaved one was almost likely to drown. The mud covered not only the streets and the backyards, but filled the entrances to the houses and crept into the dwellings themselves. Like cold sticky worms it crawled everywhere, seeming not to have come up from the ground, but rather down from the heavens.

With the mud, starvation crept into the ghetto. At first, it was a quiet sort of starvation. One could detect it only in people's faces, in their eyes; but as time went on, it became louder, screaming with increased strength and arrogance out of their mouths as well.

At night the mud stopped crawling. Then it lay under the hard claws of the frost, forged into a parched glaze. But the worm of hunger knew no rest. People went to bed without a warm meal; they turned and twisted restlessly, listening with alarm to the nagging rumble of their empty stomachs. They counted the hours until dawn, when they could set out into the streets, to try and fight this new affliction and find some food to fill the emptiness inside.

All day long the streets teemed with people. The houses were abandoned, their inhabitants having poured out of them like thousands of ants, to swarm about in the mud. There was tension, fever, fretfulness in the bustle of the people, and, for most of them, also aimlessness. They scurried from one street to the other, around and around, back and forth, not even taking pleasure in their freedom of movement. They no longer had need to fear assault, nor a voice calling, "Komm Jude!", nor being caught for forced labour. They were now protected by the inscription on the posts in front of the ghetto: "Achtung! Seuchengefahr!" But what pleasure could there be in looking upon a sea of faces, in knowing that they were all brothers tied to each other by similar fates — if one had become the reason for the other's hunger; and the existence of one deprived the other of his crust of bread?

Those who stood at the street corners, selling whatever they could afford to sell, fought over the customers. As for the customers, they spent their last groschen on a piece of bread or a few potatoes, and considered the vendors to be parasites, "capitalists", and in turn wished them no good. And all of them together turned envious eyes on the better-dressed passers-by who did not seem to be suffering from the new affliction. While they, those who still had

41

reserves of food, of money or jewellery, were the most desperate of all. They realized with anguish that what had meant "a lot" in town, melted away between their fingers here. The starvation which was about to knock on their doors was so unfamiliar, so alien to them, that their fear of it was even greater than the fear of those who had known it before; especially because it threatened in this forsaken place, in the dirty backyards with the smelly garbage dumps, in the badly paved streets full of commotion, of foul language, and because they felt so unaccustomed to living among this rough mannerless mob.

So they, the "haves", felt more bewildered, more confused, than the "have nots". They scurried about, as if lost in a nightmare, going from one office to another, struggling for the few more or less valuable positions that were available. They searched for someone to intercede with Presess Rumkowski, for connections with his secretaries, with his helpers. In the waiting rooms and corridors of the new men of power, where they congregated, each of these "has-beens" regarded the others like wolves ready to tear each other apart over a meagre bone.

Only the children were content. They did not as yet feel the hunger so badly; their parents saw to that. If they did begin to feel it, their strange new life made them forget it. The long vacation which they could not fully enjoy in town, for fear of the German boys, now acquired the taste of true freedom. The ghetto was one big marketplace, full of adventures, true ones, not imagined. They could play all kinds of games, for their parents were busy with their worries and had relaxed their vigilance. The children could even play at being adults, gather firewood, carry pails of water and learn to cook. When they tired of that, they could scamper through the streets and watch the workers build the fence around the ghetto, or rush to Baluter Ring where wooden structures were being erected and encircled with a barbed wire fence — a spooky place where the Germans installed their offices. Over there, there was a constant commotion, wagons and freight trucks coming and going. And since people were saying that the Presess was moving heaven and earth to prevent the children from running wild in the streets and that he would soon be ready to open the schools, the youngsters hurried to make the most of their carefree days.

✦ ✦ ✦

Then, unnoticed, spring awoke in the streets, in the backyards and alleys. Until the month of April no one in the backyard on Hockel Street paid any attention to the cherry tree. It stood far off and shrunken near the fence, looking like a pencil sketch against the gray background. But in April the meagre tree transformed itself into an imposing presence. Overnight it became covered with a delicate, almost transparent green; its tiny budding leaves were like the silken-soft skin of newborn babies, while their rustle was akin to the sound of baby chatter. It took a few more days and the leaf-tubes unfurled, their skin became thicker, their green deepened. A few days later the boughs themselves became invisible, concealed by the tree's frizzled green headgear that rippled and swayed, exchanging whispers with each passing breeze. Between the leaves a swelling of an indeterminate colour appeared, tiny and round, which burst open one night like a well-kept secret come to light at last — and greeted the backyard next morning with a sprinkling of pinkish whiteness.

Then everyone noticed the tree. Its bright festive appearance was in such contrast to the commonplace grayness of the yard, that there was no adult or child who did not, at least for a moment, glance at the white and green blot in the distance. It seemed strange, almost abnormal, that a tree should burst into bloom in such surroundings. And this marvel which bordered on the miraculous, filled people's hearts both with hope and with a kind of philosophical resentment — that the world, that Mother Nature carried on as if nothing had happened.

During the daytime, people would only cast but fleeting glances at the tree; everyone was too busy, too preoccupied with his own worries. Even the children had no patience for the tree during the day. But in the evening, after curfew, young and old alike would stream out from every nook and cranny towards the tree. The ground beneath it was carpeted with a small patch of grass and there were even a few ferns and bushes which grew cuddled against the tree's trunk, as if they wanted, by its merit, to claim their own right to exist. There, the neighbours would gather together to catch a breath of fresh air. One day, Valentino and a few of the yard's strong men rolled a dozen flat stones up towards the tree. There also appeared some basins and pots, which, turned bottoms up, served as seats for the old and weak. The rest of the crowd would stretch out on the sparse grass, or stand around chatting.

Sheyne Pessele, into whose mind the thought of the tree had surely not entered all day long, would, at night, become the central figure among the tree's visitors. She would take care of the tree as if it were a pregnant woman, giving lectures to the people in her vicinity on the nature of cherry trees. Patting the trunk, winding bandages of rags around its broken bark, she would rage against the unknown vandals who had hurt the tree.

"It's like tearing the skin off your body. How would you like to be skinned like that? And it is the nature of a tree that if too much of its bark is peeled off, the juices cannot reach the branches, understand?" If, at such a moment, she noticed a youngster lift his hand towards a bough, she would break into a shout with the warning, "Remember, I'll tell your father!" And if the father happened to be around, she would face the sinful neighbour who had raised such an irreverent offspring and reproach him, "Why do you sit there like God in Odessa, without saying a word? If things go on the way they're going, there will soon be neither tree nor fresh air. Are you aware of that fact?" Then she would turn back to her audience, prophesying the abundance of the cherry harvest that year.

There no longer existed a neighbour in the yard who was ignorant of the fact that Sheyne Pessele was the actual "mother" of the tree, that it was she who had planted it many years ago. For this reason both the women and the men — the latter demonstrating a sudden unexpected interest in the nature of cherry trees — would pay her due respect and lend an eager ear even when she digressed to tell them about her orchard in Konska Vola. The neighbours, in particular the children, would listen to her with their mouths watering. The youngsters were not afraid of her, they rather respected and admired her for her knowledge. Born either in Baluty or in town, few of them had actually had the chance to see how trees flower and fruits grow. According to their experience, fruits grew in the baskets of the merchants in the market.

Thus, thanks to the cherry tree, Sheyne Pessele became, during that spring, the queen of the backyard. And the neighbours inferred, on the basis of her knowledge about trees, that she was knowledgeable about people as well, about human diseases, human problems and in general — about everything. Under the cherry tree, they would turn to her for advice. Mostly, they were grateful to her for not considering the tree her private property, but a common treasure, a blessing for the entire backyard. They loved this cherry tree, which they called the Garden, with all their hearts, because more powerful than their resentment of nature for going its natural way, was their desire to read a promise in the flowering of the tree, that as long as the tree was alive and thriving — there was still hope. At night, the cherry tree would look like a lighted *menorah*; the blossoms peering out between the leaves were like blinking swaying flames of candles.

The people sitting around the tree were by no means a homogenous lot. They separated into groups, the women sitting with their own kind, the men with theirs. The young would gather with the young, the old with the old, the Zionists with the Zionists, the Bundists with the Bundists, the communists with the communists, the observant with the observant, the intellectuals and the Polish-speaking with the intellectuals and Polish-speaking, and the toughs would cluster with their cronies. They would sit or stand around, shoulder to shoulder, back against back, but they rarely mixed. Only when they stared at the cherry tree, or were engaged in discussing it, would they merge into one congenial gathering.

This would also happen when they turned their attention to the balcony of the "landlord's palace" that stood nearby. Apparently the *shishkas*, as people began calling the bigshots, those who had made it in the ghetto, were also attracted to the cherry tree. Every night the door of the balcony upstairs would be flung open and the members of the upper crust would present themselves. They would then sit down, the better to enjoy the fresh air. As soon as they appeared on the balcony, all the talking under the tree came to an abrupt halt; all attention became centred on these personages, as if the crowd were a theatre audience that had been entertaining itself with conversation until the stage performance began.

◆ ◆ ◆

To those sitting below, the "characters" on the balcony seemed always the same. In reality, however, they had undergone a formidable metamorphosis.

From the day that they had arrived in the ghetto, the Zuckermans' money and jewellery began melting away much faster than they could ever have imagined. Not a single day passed when Samuel did not have to take some of his valuables into town to sell. That became his sole occupation. He learned the art of "making a deal" and wasted half of his days bargaining. When he did succeed in extracting the sum he wanted from a buyer, he was elated, but also exhausted, as if he had spent the entire day at hard labour. At the same time, the meals at home became deplorable, the portions shrunk and the menu was monotonous. Reisel walked about grumbling that they must save food, that they should not allow themselves too much, and would bring half-empty plates to the table.

The Zuckermans took their meals with the Hagers. The Rosenbergs ate alone. This came about as a result of Reisel's efforts to prevent Adam's plateful of meat from teasing the appetites of the others. Though Reisel served each family with equal devotion, she began to treat Adam as if he were the actual master of the house. She also began to show respect for Yadwiga; moreover, she even became chummy with Sutchka, letting her into the kitchen and seeing to it that she got her plate of bones on time. Sutchka lacked nothing. She shone with energy and good health. So did Adam shine again with energy and good health. He recompensed himself for the days of deprivation when he had sat locked up in Samuel's cellar. Now he spent his days wandering through the streets, listening to people's talk, catching snatches of news, information, and storing them in his mind. He did not establish a business of his own, but rather became a go-between in the commerce plied by the Jews with the Germans and Poles who visited the ghetto. The money he brought home helped him to regain his self-respect.

At first, he was amazed at how quickly he had acquired a new sense of values; a new concept of money and its worth. He was surprised at how he could so easily be satisfied with such pitiful earnings and still be in good spirits. Tomorrow, which he used to consider synonymous with the future, a projection into the expanse of time to come — implied here, in the ghetto, only the following day. And as long as this tomorrow in the ghetto was provided for, one had every reason to be content. At the same time, Adam did not fail to observe that along with this new attitude towards tomorrow came a new approach to life in general — an ability to take it with more ease. Sometimes it seemed to him that the light-heartedness of his youth had come back to him and with it, the lust for the pleasures of bygone times. They too were easy to come by. A slice of bread, a little bag of sugar would work wonders. And Adam soon became an expert in providing himself with whatever he craved.

At the same time, his family life became more serene and harmonious than ever before. Yadwiga was, as usual, sweet and kittenish. But now he sensed an attachment and devotion hidden behind these superficialities, of which he had never thought her capable; daily, she waited for him at the window. Then there was Mietek, who also became more of a son than ever before. He held a job in the newly created militia, looked manly and imposing in his policeman's outfit, while at the same time he became more warm-hearted, more cheerful and also more talkative. Now, instead of taking their meals in complete silence, the three of them would engage in a light and lively conversation. Consequently, if Adam had not been afraid in such times to admit it, he would have said that in some strange incomprehensible manner he was happy now.

Little wonder then that Reisel sensed the master in Adam, in particular since her own master, Samuel Zuckerman, had completely lost his lustre. It became impossible to feel towards him what she had used to feel, or to treat him as she had used to treat him. There was no need to "put a finger into her mouth". His luck, poor man, had reversed, and had fallen "with the buttered side down".

Samuel had applied a few times for an interview with Presess Rumkowski, however, the latter could never seem to find time to receive him. The many hours spent in the offices of other important dignitaries also came to nothing. He would run from one pre-war acquaintance to another, but the acquaintances had turned into people with weak memories. True, they were not stingy with good advice, but the "connections" they had to save for themselves and for their own kin. To have "connections" or good "backs" meant to possess a treasure which was not to be wasted recklessly. Yet Samuel was optimistic. And it was easier for him to sustain his hope thanks to the support which he had: the radio. Like a child seeking solace in a secret place by hugging a favourite toy, Samuel would sneak into the little shed every evening.

One day on his return home, Samuel ran into Adam who had been waiting for him. Adam dragged him into his room. "I know what you're hiding in the shed!" Adam wheezed. "Do you realize what you're doing? It is not just a question of myself, but of you too, of your wife, your children."

Before Adam managed to find the proper tone for his moralizing sermon, Samuel grabbed him by the lapels, "If you let out so much as a peep about it, I swear to you that you won't leave the ghetto alive!"

That very same night Samuel rushed down into the yard with the radio and cleared away the rubble from the entrance to an abandoned cellar. Once inside, he buried the treasure under a heap of sawdust and sand. The following day he found himself in the grip of panic, pursued by the fear of the great unknown approaching his threshold, in particular by the fear of starvation. It was true that hunger was God-like, all people were equal in the face of it, but he also knew that for him and his family the descent into its pit was more difficult, more dangerous than for thousands of others.

Then, one day, Junia gave Samuel the idea of firing Reisel. For weeks now she had been playfully and jokingly spying on the cook, and it did not take her long to discover that Reisel was smuggling food out to her family of sisters, nephews and nieces. Junia liked Reisel well enough, she enjoyed her down-to-earth wisdom, her sayings and expressions. She also remembered her former devotion. Moreover, it did not even occur to Junia to label Reisel's appropriations as theft. It was quite understandable that Reisel should want to help her starving relatives; but it was just as understandable that she should be prevented from doing so at the Zuckermans' expense. And this Junia told Samuel. They both carefully suggested the same to Matilda who, to their surprise, did not object. Reisel's *hutzpah* and aggressiveness had begun to fill Matilda with disgust; the discovery that Reisel stole food from the house, where she had for so many years found a home, evoked such resentment in Matilda that she could no longer bear the sight of her. She refused to spend even one more day under the same roof with her.

The idea of firing Reisel did, however, meet with resistance from other quarters. Adam refused to hear of it. He knew how to protect himself against her stealing: the food must be kept under lock and key, and they must watch what she put into the pot and what she dished out of it onto the plate. So they resolved that Reisel would no longer serve the Zuckermans or the Hagers, but would become the exclusive possession of the Rosenbergs.

The transition from the old masters to the new happened in the most natural manner. Reisel forgot whatever debt of gratitude she owed the Zuckermans and did not take the issue to heart. On the contrary. Although she openly complained about her previous masters for whom she had sacrificed herself for so many years and who now had left her "on the water" — it was as clear as day that she was extremely satisfied with the turn of events. Before long, she was quarrelling with Matilda about whose turn it was to cook at the stove, or about scrubbing the floors. Her face shone with delight when she saw the sloppy clumsy Matilda doing the work on which she, Reisel, had wasted a lifetime.

Matilda was drowning in work. She had to stand in line for food, do the washing, the house-cleaning and the mending. Samuel and the girls helped her out occasionally; the truth was that they were busy with their own affairs. The burden of responsibility fell on her shoulders. The first weeks she would sob herself to sleep on her pillow, night after night, and walk about the following day with swollen eyes, apathetic and sulking. Samuel and the children were kind to her, exaggeratedly polite, and they never refused her requests, but she knew that they were acting out of pity. So, although she yearned for a warm word, for a caress, she was careful not to give herself away, for she knew that they would condescend to her needs as a charity. She may have been down on her hands and knees, scrubbing floors, but she was still not a beggar.

Dejection and fatigue began to line her face with deep red furrows. She looked ten years older. But little by little a kind of stubbornness began to cement itself inside her. Her bitterness, up to now more or less concealed, surfaced through her complaints and reproaches. Samuel and Junia would sometimes put their ears against the kitchen door and listen with satisfaction to her disputes with Reisel; her rage against the ungrateful cook was bringing her back to life. She would not however, spare them either. There was no pleasure in sitting with her at the table, or in being with her in the house. She always found a reason to reproach her family, to criticize. She snared them into her gloom; often in the middle of the tastiest bite of food she would burst into hysterical sobs. Samuel and Junia, each in his or her own way, protected themselves against her. Samuel, with calm reasoning, with the warmth with which he managed to soften his voice; Junia, with her laughter and caresses. Only Bella, who again took to biting her nails, did not try to protect herself, and Matilda's explosions of anger were mostly directed against her. Matilda could not bear the idea of Bella shutting herself up in her room, buried in her books. She seemed to derive pleasure from calling her away from them and assigning chores to her. "You're lazy, lazy! The only thing you're capable of doing is biting your nails!" she nagged at her. Bella's willingness to obey only served to irritate her more.

With Samuel she would get even at night, in bed. During the day she proudly, stubbornly avoided him, but by nighttime she felt ready to beg for affection. When he had neither the courage nor the strength to accommodate her, she would reproach him mercilessly, painting him as a monster, an inquisitor, the cause of all her miseries. If, overcome by a tide of compassion, he did respond to her, their embrace would be like that of two strangers who had briefly crossed each other's paths, only to part again, each going off in his own direction. Then, dissatisfied, shamed and humiliated, she would erupt anew with bitterness and complaint.

Then the day came when Samuel no longer had any valuables to take into the streets to sell. All day long Junia followed him like a shadow, coming up with a new idea by the moment. Samuel was too confused to heed her, so she decided to act on her own. The two suitcases in the bathroom had for a long time aroused her curiosity, and during this critical day she felt drawn to them like to a magnet. That same night she broke their locks and discovered the silver cigarette case full of diamonds, earrings and gold chains. Thus on the first day of what should have been their time of hunger, Junia appeared in the house with half a bag of potatoes, a bag of sugar, a bit of flour and a few onions. The members of her family stared at her flabbergasted as she informed them, an innocent smile on her face, that she had successfully mediated in the sale of a pack of wool. From that day on, every time their supply of food was on the point of vanishing, she would appear in the house loaded down with new provisions.

One day Yadwiga's screams were heard coming from the corridor. The inhabitants of the house who gathered around her found out that the Polish workmen, who had recently fixed the water pipes, had stolen the Rosenberg's treasure or rather, a part of it; for, to everyone's surprise, the thieves were people with compassion in their hearts. Junia listened to Yadwiga's story without blinking an eye.

A few days later Samuel received an invitation to go for an interview with the Presess.

The moment he saw Samuel walk into his office, Presess Rumkowski stretched out both hands to him; it was a greeting of sincere friendliness, "Why haven't you come by before, Zuckerman? Others run after me, tearing at my coattails." Warmed by these words, Samuel chuckled, telling the Old Man that he had been unable to get through to him, that weeks before, he had submitted a written request for an audience. "A written request?" Rumkowski guffawed. "You need to write requests in order to see me? God, what a fool you are! You should come in and ask to be announced, that's all. My door is always open to you. Remember that, Zuckerman." And to demonstrate his trust in Samuel, the Presess drew out a letter from an envelope which carried the seal of the *Polizeipräsident*. "Here, read what arrived today."

Samuel read:

To Herr Rumkowski, *Älteste der Juden* in Lidzmanstadt.
Dear Herr Rumkowski:
   According to the order of the *Polizeipräsident*, all the inhabitants of the ghetto are strictly forbidden to leave its premises as of the date of April 30, 1940. I hold you personally responsible for the prompt execution of this order. I also oblige you to apply all the means necessary to establish an orderly community life in the district of Jewish domicile. In particular I consider it your duty to secure order in matters of economy, work and health. You are entitled to issue orders and take the appropriate measures as well as to receive assistance from the militia subordinated to you, for all purposes necessary. I entitle you to immediately open registration centres through which, by means of lists, the inhabitants of the ghetto might be reached. The lists in question, five copies of each, should reach my desk before the date of May 30, 1940. All communication, business or otherwise, with the German authorities must be conducted solely through you, or through a representative assigned solely by you. All Jewish properties which are, in accordance with the laws of the Reich's government, considered confiscated, you must assemble, register and secure. You are entitled to draft all Jews to unpaid labour. All measures of an essential nature which you deem necessary to undertake require my written approval . . .

While Samuel read the letter, Rumkowski knotted and unknotted his fingers, nibbling on his underlip, as he studied the expression on Samuel's face. As soon as the latter raised his eyes to him, he cried out, "Do you understand? There is not a thing in this letter that I haven't done before he ordered me to. Take the militia, for instance, or the Work Resorts. Who do you think planted those ideas in the Germans' minds?" Dramatically, he stretched out his hands to Samuel. "I need you, Zuckerman. You must help me. I am surrounded by enemies. I trust no one. You I trust, you hear?"

"I will gladly help you, Herr Presess," Samuel felt elated. "That's why I came to see you. I must find work."

The Presess' face immediately changed, turning cold. "You're all the same, only seeking your own gains. But to worry about the good of the community wouldn't enter anyone's mind."

Samuel was flustered. "What should I do? I have a family. I must take care of the Hagers. The savings have melted from between my fingers. My family is not used to that kind of life. Matilda is not the same . . . Mr. Presess." He straightened up, and offered the Presess an apologetic smile. "I'd gladly do anything in my power to help you . . . to help the ghetto, Herr Presess. But could one not combine this . . ."

"Yes, yes, we will combine it," Rumkowski nodded. "Go home and tell your wife that she won't lack a thing. I'll hand over all the carpentry Resorts to you. As soon as they will start to work, I'll thumb my nose at the whole world. The *Yekes* will have to feed us and that way we will survive the war. Come to see me next week. I should have assigned all the Resort commissars by then."

Samuel wavered. "I know nothing whatsoever about carpentry, Herr Presess."

The Presess offered him a paternal smile. "I know that I have better carpenters than you, but I want you to be the boss, to manage the factories. That's the kind of job you know, isn't it? That's what you will become, a boss, and you'll keep an eye on everyone . . . How do you like your house? You said the Hagers are living with you?"

"The Rosenbergs too, Herr Presess."

"Rosenberg? You mean he's in the ghetto?" Rumkowski burst out gaily, as if hearing good tidings. "If he catches the cholera in the ghetto, believe me, I wouldn't mind." He stood up, shaking Samuel's hand. When Samuel was already at the door, he remarked mildly, "Your coat is covered with mud on the back and your leggings too. It doesn't suit for you to walk around like that, Herr Commissar."

Once back on the street, Samuel intended to hurry home to announce the good news to his family, but there was too much chaos in his head, and he did not want to face his family in such a condition. He slowed down and began to wander about the streets, trying to figure out what awaited him now. The threatening shadow of starvation had vanished from his mind, but it was replaced by a new kind of anxiety. The new job — what would it mean to be a boss in the ghetto? Surely not the same as it had meant before the war. But he would be able to build something; he liked to create something out of nothing. And he would be able to help; to help Rumkowski serve the ghetto and the Jews. Samuel had no idea how he would accomplish this, what possibilities he would have. Yet it was something positive, aside from the positive gain of having a secure life, free from hunger. Nonetheless, the feeling of anguish refused to let go of him. This time it was not a fear of external circumstances, but rather a fear of himself.

At home there was a surprise awaiting him. A messenger boy had brought a parcel of food sent by the Presess. And when Samuel announced the good news to his family, an air of jubilation descended upon the house; even Matilda livened up. Then Junia had the "ingenious" idea of celebrating the happy event with a visit to the "Restaurant of the Intelligentsia". Matilda rubbed some vaseline onto her hands; she unwrapped her hat, while everyone else busied themselves with their own toilette.

In the "Restaurant of the Intelligentsia", a barley soup was the main course on the menu and there was a *tzimmes* of turnips for the second course. Though turnips had overnight become an important food item in the ghetto, the Zuckermans could not get used to eating them. The sharp sweet smell of watery straw that lingered in the mouth made them all feel nauseous. So they consumed their soup, leaving the *tzimmes* on their plates.

A slim elegant lady approached their table. She drew a tin cup out from her magnificent purse, asking politely whether she could take the *tzimmes* for her little dog. At the sight of her, Matilda blushed. She recognized her as an aristocratic acquaintance, a pre-war patroness of many charity organizations. Bella also recognized the lady and blushed. She felt humiliated, as if it were she herself who was emptying the plates. She felt still worse when she noticed the lady, who was hiding between two open doors, take out a spoon from her magnificent purse and devour the pot's contents.

Then they went to Karo's Cafeteria. Here a pre-war atmosphere still reigned. Well-dressed men and women sat around neat tables, conversing in Polish and smiling politely at each other. It seemed as if the little cafeteria had flown out from the ghetto and landed back in bygone times, in the very centre of noisy and gay Piotrkowska Street. Matilda met acquaintances. Now there was no reason why she should not approach them and let them know about the position awaiting her husband. Samuel had nothing against her spilling the good news. It was pleasant to be surrounded by people again, to be addressed with respect. Someone even mentioned the popular saying to him, "One hand washes the other". Already, there was someone eager to use Samuel's "back".

The girls also met friends at the cafeteria. They chatted about the *gymnasium* that was supposed to open soon. They talked and talked — the entire Zuckerman family — as if they wanted to make up to themselves the long weeks they had spent in solitude. They talked hurriedly, but ate slowly, to savour the pre-war *Napoleonkis* which required a certain reserve in their consumption. The Zuckermans were intoxicated with the sudden pre-war atmosphere that surrounded them.

That night as well as the nights that followed, Samuel slept very little. In the cellar where he had hidden the radio, he arranged his new receiving station. He worked slowly, cool on the surface, but inwardly impatient, anxious to connect himself with The Brother in the distant world.

✦   ✦   ✦

Each of the neighbours who gathered around the cherry tree in the evening had his favourite "actor" or "actress" on the balcony stage. For instance, the older women liked to watch Mrs. Hager and her husband, the bearded professor. They scrutinized the old lady's nicely arranged hair, her comportment, the aristocratic smile on her thin lips and the sparkle of her earrings which swung discreetly when she whispered in her husband's ear. When the professor, who was so spontaneous in his expressions of affection for his wife, occasionally stroked her arm, the women downstairs would hold their breaths in suspense. Similarly, the middle-aged women liked to observe Matilda. There was no doubt in their minds that she was the actual queen of the "palace"; true, a sad and broken queen, but one who still carried her head proudly raised, as if she were wearing an invisible crown. Consequently, the teenage girls would look upon Matilda's daughters as if they were princesses.

One particular group of women in the yard could not take their eyes off Yadwiga, who in actual fact was the most interesting personage on the balcony. Although the others acted their parts in character, so to speak, they lacked a sense of theatricality. She was the only one who knew what was expected of her. Every half hour or so she would appear wearing a different outfit. Her shapely hands with their red pointed nails were in constant motion, while her made-up face with the red lips never wore the same expression. Or she would suddenly exit, keeping her audience in suspense, until she reappeared with a cigarette in her mouth, exhaling the smoke with infinite grace. Seeing her with a cigarette in her mouth, the older women would, of course, curse and spit a few times to ward off evil spirits, but the younger ones would see in her smoking, in her dress and in her bearing, the embodiment of the coquettishness and charm of their sex. Nor did the men in the yard, except for the very pious, mind casting a stealthy glance in Yadwiga's direction. But her greatest admirers were the tough guys. As soon as Yadwiga appeared on the balcony, they let loose their unpolished vocabulary.

As for the higher-class men, those with a "head on their shoulders", those who were self-respecting and practical, they preferred to observe Yadwiga's husband, the renowned pre-war "millionaire" and world merchant. It was an honour and a privilege to have such a personality for a neighbour and to be able to watch him from so close. Even Adam's pate evoked reverence, as did the rest of his corpulent form. But more than anything else it was the fat cigar, protruding so arrogantly from between his fingers, that underlined his glory.

Even the youngsters had a "hero" of their own on the balcony, although he seldom showed up. This was the smart-looking policeman, Mr. Rosenberg's son, Mietek. They admired his colourful hat, his armband and especially his shiny boots.

The personage who had the least luck with the public was Samuel. Many of the neighbours knew what an important and influential Jew he had been before the war, but as an "actor" he was of no interest whatsoever, and the fault was entirely his own. He mixed too much with the people in the yard, who ran into him at the house committee or when fetching the food rations. He was chummy with Itche Mayer the Carpenter and his sons, and would often come down to the cherry tree to chat with the painter Guttman, the teacher Shafran, or the lame doctor Levine. He would even converse with the distracted fellow who lived in the "latrine man's hut" and who, according to rumour, was a "scribbler". All this deprived Samuel of any theatrical glamour. On the contrary. It was as if his presence pulled the entire balcony down to earth.

The balcony was a good introductory topic for the revival of memories related to the past. From there it was only a cat's leap to talking about the good pre-war years which otherwise seemed so remote. The balcony served as a jumping-off point to a discussion of the business and trade world of former times. Each ex-businessman imagined that he had once been just as great a millionaire as Mr. Adam Rosenberg, while every woman imagined that in her home she had once been as regal as Matilda and as coquettish as Yadwiga, and that her husband had loved her as well as the professor loved his aristocratic wife. And from these thoughts it was not far to the most important thought:

food — the dishes one used to savour, the chickens, the ducklings, the cracklings, the good fat roasts, the *cholents* and the preserves.

By the time the neighbours abandoned these sweet ruminations, it was usually late at night. The cherry tree, its colour dissolving into the darkness, seemed enormous, as if the cupola of the sky were its crown. The white blossoms seemed like stars while the moon — like one huge flowering blossom. The people under the cherry tree began to feel very close to one another. The balcony too had lost its contours and appeared to have descended to the cluster of people downstairs. Peace and tranquillity reigned in the empty yard with its shut gate. There were no Germans, there was no war. There was only this night, this dreaming earth, and spread out upon it, cuddling up next to it was a flock of tired sleepy children.

Chapter Four

WHEN ESTHER FIRST NOTICED the cherry tree suddenly covered with green, she thought of it as a sister to the one that lived on in her memory. If the tree attracted her attention, it was because its beauty stood out against the background of gray surroundings, but it was a sight which gave her pain rather than pleasure. She never sat under the tree.

It took her a long time to become accustomed to her new life. The room in which she lived was not a home, only a place to rest her head. For a long time her things remained in her suitcase. Her bed was not made and coils of dust gathered in the corners of the room. She swept them up only when they began to cling to her shoes. When she slumped down on her bed, her eyes would meet the bare window which stared at her in the darkness like a blind eye without eyelids.

She was glad that she cared so little about her room. This was a sure sign that she no longer cared about herself, and this was what she wanted. It became more and more apparent to her that before the war she had not been ready for the communist movement, that for all her devotion to the ideal, she had first of all been seeking personal gratification, that the sacrifices she had been ready to make for the good of humanity had basically been a means to please herself. It had been a kind of game, a test of her will power and its victory was more significant to her than the good she hoped to bring about by her actions. She tried to convince herself that now it was different, that she had really changed. The proof was that she never sat down under the tree, that she did not care what she wore, or how she looked; she did not even own a mirror. She, who had been so proud of her red tresses, had recently cut them off, leaving only a short crop of hair. And the fact that she had ceased to miss Hersh, that he had become a kind of impersonal memory, and the fact that she thought of her dead child more frequently than of him, and that even her thoughts of the baby were cold and indifferent — was this not proof enough that she had ceased to exist as a "self"?

As for the pangs of hunger, she felt them all right. They made her realize that her body cared for itself against her will. She developed however the ability to walk around without having eaten for days. She pretended not to mind. Often she would feel uncanny at the sight of her body with the protruding ribs, the bony hips, or at the vast emptiness under her loose dress. But at the same time she was glad that her body was vanishing, that her clothes hung on her as on a skeletal mannequin. She tightened the leather belts she wore, constantly punching new holes in the buckle, and threw herself, like some kind of wilful sheep, at every new day as if it were the open muzzle of a wolf.

She became involved in her party work body and soul. The feeling of inferiority had gone from the comrades; the helplessness and confusion which had overcome them after the dissolution of the Polish Communist Party had vanished as soon as they had passed the threshold of the ghetto. Here it was apparent to everyone how right this decision had been. Here, like Esther, all the other comrades realized how little they had been prepared for communism and how many bourgeois, middle-class weaknesses they all harboured. Now they felt free of these weaknesses and thus worthy to call themselves communists again. They felt reborn; their devotion to one another and to the ideal surpassed all that they had felt before the war. However, Esther's relationship with the party did not follow a smooth path. Here her wish to become one with the group was thwarted.

It began with an honour that the leadership wanted to bestow upon her. Now, that most of the experienced activists were in the Soviet Union and the Party consisted mostly of a younger element, Esther suddenly found herself in the ranks of the veterans. It was therefore only natural that she should take over one of the responsible party posts, and even before the advent of the ghetto, she had been co-opted by the board. Now, however, instead of accepting her assignment to the executive, she resigned from the board altogether. She was ready to do everything that was required of her, but she wished to remain a "gray sheep". She refused to become a "personality".

The comrades could not understand her behaviour. Not even Comrade Julia who, along with Comrade Baruch, led the Party and was the sister and the mother to every communist in the ghetto, understood her. They all began to look at Esther either with reproach and resentment or with suspicion and distrust, almost as if she were a traitor. In fact, Esther herself could not understand why she behaved the way she did. She only knew that her decision was stronger than her reason or her will. She therefore applied herself with even more diligence to the tasks which she took upon herself. She liked to visit the homes of her comrades and help them out; she took care of their little ones, nursed the sick and disabled; or she would willingly discuss a comrade's problems, sitting somewhere at the edge of a dirty table. To communicate in that manner was easy. Everything was clear, tangible and concrete. And this was reassuring. She felt that she was achieving her goal and was about to reach the shores of serenity and peace.

✦   ✦   ✦

But there was Friede who was so very sick. Merely stepping over the threshold of his cellar destroyed all Esther's delusions. She was drawn to the cellar against her will. Down there, at Friede's bedside, she felt her own self with such perspicacity, with such awareness as one can feel only in a nightmare. Here she knew clearly that she was deceiving herself, that it was a lie that she did not exist as a person. Here she felt her existence as never before — not through delight and pleasure, but through a biting pain, through the gnawing compassion that took possession of her whole being. Here she was aware that she would never be able to keep herself frozen and indifferent to the call of her body and soul. Here, in the cellar, she knew that she was alive. Here she hated Friede for the power he had over her — for his sick body. Here she loathed death, feeling that her desire to offer herself derived not from resignation, but from her vibrant nagging femininity which, while in the act of giving itself, still sought gratification and fulfilment for its innermost cravings. Indeed, at Friede's bedside she more than once felt the desire to perish with him; yet even that desire was nothing but the expression of her desire for life. She grasped this with her senses rather than with her reason.

Friede was being consumed by fire, spending entire days lost in fever. Breathing required the effort of his entire heaving chest. He mumbled delirious incomprehensible words. However, even in this state of unconsciousness, he maintained a sense of reality with regard to Sheindle. He recognized her, and when she fed him, he would faintly stroke her hand with one finger. If she left his room for a while, he would call her, not by name, but with a groan which only stopped when she reappeared.

He did not recognize Esther. When she sat at his bedside, he would look through her with staring nebulous eyes as if she were transparent. Esther felt at a loss because of this strange form of non-existence. She let her eyes wander around the cellar, over the wet walls and the dusty electric bulb which day and night cast a shadowy circle of light on the cracked glistening ceiling. It was then that her feeling of living in a dream was most acute. It was a dream that tormented the mind with the clarity of its visions, a dream from which one struggles to wake up, in which one screams while one's mouth remains shut, a dream from which there was no escape.

During one especially critical evening, Esther was sitting with Sheindle at Friede's bedside. His breathing was heavy and staccato. It sounded as though a rusty machine was working in his chest, wheezing away its last bit of strength. His eyes were shut. On the hairs of his short sparse eyelashes hung two partly formed tears, too weak to slide down his cheeks. Sheindle was biting her lips, her body swaying as in a trance. "What shall I do?" she repeated over and over again. There was such anguish screaming from her eyes, that it penetrated Esther's stupor and made her look up at Sheindle in amazement. "Had I kept him in my house," Sheindle continued swaying, "it would never have come to this . . . Oy, Valentino," she cried, "may you sink ninety miles into the earth! Who says that I have a husband? I have a cutthroat, a bloodthirsty bitter murderer! He didn't want to live with a consumptive, he said. His sister, he said, has small children, he said. As if the disease could jump on top of them! And what shall I do now? I'm asking you something. Give me some advice." She caught Esther's distant bewildered gaze with her eyes. Unable to sit still any longer, she jumped to her feet and threw her hands up into the air as if aiming at Esther. "What are you sitting there for, like a hen on her eggs, goggling like this? Can't you see that the man is at the end of his tether?"

Esther stood up and took a step forward. "What should I do?" she muttered.

"You should get out of here, that's what you should do!" Sheindle twisted her tear-stained face. Then she burst into profuse sobs, embracing Esther and pressing her to her bosom. "Oy, what do I want of your life? What would I do without you, Esther my crown?" She leaned down to Friede and placed her palm against his forehead. "Take a look. He's boiling!" She put her mouth to his ear. "Friede," she whispered, "Friede, can you hear me?" The moisture gathered in Friede's eyes now formed into two heavy tears, which slid down his hollow cheeks towards his ears and from there mingled with his sweat to drip down onto the pillow. Sheindle stood there helplessly, her arms spread wide apart. "It's no good. No good!" she shook her head, biting her lips.

Esther could not remove her eyes from Friede's clay-like face, from his red swollen lips and the white pointed nose. Overcome by a morbid curiosity, she wanted to know what was going on behind Friede's pale forehead, to see the images he was seeing. She wished to break through to the soul that fluttered somewhere inside him. She saw Friede as a being whose body was consumed by fever, but who yet remained apart from its decay. She felt sick and feverish; her lips were swollen just like his, her bosom rose and fell just like his. Her mind too wove nightmares, while her heart galloped to encounter the sick man's heavy breath which was wheezing out through his locked mouth and trembling nostrils. She had no faith, no courage to fight for the life of this stranger who had become so close to her. But like all the other times when she had seen him, she felt ready to drown together with him, to sink with him into the abyss that was waiting for him.

Then Valentino came into the cellar, and as soon as he appeared, the entire room was full of him. His enormous frame, the long heavy arms, the powerful legs, the dark-skinned face, his whole figure seemed to extend the walls. It was as if he sent a fresh lively breeze wafting through the cellar. Suddenly Esther felt wide awake and freed from her nightmare, as if Valentino were a magician. She eagerly listened to him bellowing at Sheindle to go home. It seemed to Esther that it was for her sake that he shouted so loudly, that he wished to shake her out of her stupor. Valentino's gaze, the fire in his eyes, which were stealthily aimed at her, was burning through her, but it was also there to help her, to save her. "Go with him, Sheindle," she said. She accompanied them to the entryway, jealous of something, although she did not know what.

During those critical days Esther and Sheindle did not leave Friede alone for a moment. Sheindle stayed with him during the day, while Esther stayed at night. The first few nights Esther would lie down on the table or stretch out on a few chairs placed together, or else she would sit through the night at Friede's bedside. Then, one evening, Valentino appeared in the cellar with a deck-chair in his hand. "Here, Esther," he called out, "I brought you this piece of furniture so that you can sleep like God in Odessa!" He set up the chair for her and invited her to lie down on it. Then he drew out from his pocket a chunk of bread wrapped in a piece of old newspaper and handed it to her. "This is for your dinner!" She refused to take it. So he unwrapped the package, grabbed her by the waist and pushed the chunk of bread into her mouth. With the touch of his hard arms around her body, the touch of the bread against her lips, everything in Esther began to stir. She bit greedily into the crust of the bread, although she barely felt its taste, barely knew what was happening to her.

While Esther devoured the bread, Valentino devoured Esther with his eyes. His face, which was brown like polished leather, beamed. He rubbed his hands against the pullover he always wore and which emphasized the impressive expanse of his torso, and began to take such massive steps about the cellar that the loose boards in the floor shook, sending strings of mud out along the cracks. He stopped at Friede's bed. "How are you, Friede?" he inquired. Friede did not hear him. His head moved rhythmically from one side to the other; the sweat dripping down from behind his ears left wet blotches on both sides of his pillow.

Valentino fixed his burning eyes on Esther. "What is he to you that you have buried yourself alive with him in this grave?" He approached her, still staring. She had to lower her eyelids because of the heat radiating from him. The bread stuck in her throat. Her head swam. "Someone like you . . . with such a head . . .

such eyes!" she heard him say, and saw nothing but his large full mouth with the dark lips. He put his heavy hand on her shoulder; it seemed to her that his hard fingers were cutting into her flesh. "Beware of me, Esther! Every time I see you here, in the cellar, by his bedside . . . You hear? I could swallow you!" His hands slid down her arms, manacling her wrists. He placed her palms together; between them she clasped the remainder of the chunk of bread. "Eh, you're too pretty for me . . ." he whispered, "and too good too." He noticed the piece of bread between her hands and guffawed, ill-at-ease. "I don't let you eat, eh? Eat! Eat!"

She came back to herself, grabbed him by the hand and pushed the piece of bread into his palm. "Get out of here!" she heard herself order him.

Valentino wrinkled his forehead. "Esther, may my lungs collapse if I meant anything . . . May I be spared all the evil . . ." he looked guiltily into her eyes. "I don't know what happened to me, Esther, I swear . . . May I get an apoplexy here, on the spot, if I ever step over this threshold again, I swear to you . . . Every time I see you here, in this cellar, by his bed . . ."

"Get out!" she pointed to the door.

Valentino bowed, holding out his hand to her with the remainder of the bread in it, "I beg of you, Esther, do me this favour." There was such a funny clumsiness in his doubled-up figure, in the servile expression on his face, that Esther's hand, as if by itself, reached out for the piece of bread. "Eat, eat," he sighed with relief. "I'm on my way."

As soon as she could shut the door behind him, she threw the bread on the table and knelt down at Friede's bedside. "Friede, help me . . ." she clasped his hand in hers. Then she wiped the sweat off his face and his bare bony ribcage. She poured cool tea between his lips. He groaned. She knew that he was calling for Sheindle. Nightmarish cobwebs again held Esther in their nets. She paced along the wet glistening walls of the cellar, letting all the unshed tears pour out from her eyes. Sobbing, she returned to the piece of bread and devoured it along with her salty tears. Only then did she sink down into Valentino's deck-chair. Gradually sleep came over her. In her sleep she saw Friede's bed. On it lay someone who was both Friede and she, who had the body of a motionless newborn baby. "Its name was supposed to be Emmanuel," she complained to someone. She heard a voice calling her, "Mother!" Then she saw the tiny motionless body rise, stretch and become a large body which grew into a magnificent tree. It embraced her waist with its boughs which were like warm strong arms. She opened her eyes and saw the dusty bulb blinking down from the ceiling. "His name was supposed to be Emmanuel," she whispered to the sad circle of light on the ceiling.

"Mother . . ." Friede groaned.

Occasionally, there would be a day when Friede's forehead was cool, his gaze clear. His breathing, although heavy, was regular, without the accompanying screech. He would recognize Esther and motion to her with his thin finger. "Good morning," he would say, even when it was late at night. His clear tired eyes would blink. If Sheindle were also around, he would look up at the two women and smile at them as if he were a traveller who had just returned home from a difficult journey. "Go to your Valentino, go . . ." he would say to Sheindle, and she would excitedly leave nursing instructions with Esther and with a light heart go to join her Valentino.

Then Esther had Friede to herself. She boiled an egg, warmed up some milk and fed him. Her heart sang with delight when she saw him empty his plate; she felt satiated, as if she herself had savoured the delicious food and drunk the milk. How grateful she was to Valentino for having provided Friede with all these expensive delicacies. It was for her that Valentino had done this, to make her feel strong.

After the meal, she and Friede would sit looking at each other in silence, letting their faces talk, letting their eyes communicate. Sometimes Friede would whisper to her, a faint smile on his face, "You are my life . . . Do you know that?"

She replied with stubbornness in her voice, "I'll bring you back to health."

With a finger he would stroke Esther's blanket which was stained with sweat, its pink colour long since faded, and he would shake his head, "Yes, I'll write a book, 'The Diary of a Blanket' . . ." He expected her to smile back at him and so she did. At such moments she did not fear Dr. Levine or his prophecies. She was sure that she had the power to keep Friede alive; and this made her jump to her feet and hurry to prepare something else for him to eat. She knew that he could not taste the dishes she cooked for him, that he was forcing himself to chew, like a wise child obeying his mother for his own good. When the plate was empty, they would return to the conversation with their eyes, scrutinizing one another, until he again said, "Esther, I am beginning to believe . . ." Sometimes he would remember his manuscript. It seemed to him that his book was about to appear. "The first copy will be for you," he would say. Sometimes he mentioned the name of his friend, insisting, "Bring me Berkovitch!" Esther would look at him, at a loss to understand. Who was Berkovitch? Friede, however, soon forgot about him. At other times he would start to tell her a story from his childhood, then interrupt himself and lose the thread of his tale. He would look up at her, "You are beautiful," he would mumble.

He never wondered what she was doing in the cellar, how it came to pass that she was taking care of him. He never asked her about anything and she, who so strongly wished to open her heart to him, could only speak with her gaze, through the slivers of her green eyes, "You must get well, Friede." But then his breath would become irregular and heavy once more, his eyes foggy. He would stare at her with increasing estrangement. It seemed as if someone were standing at Friede's bedside, dragging him off, taking him away from her. Beads of sweat would spring out on his forehead and drip down onto his pillow. His head would begin to fall from one side to the other. She would grab hold of his hand as if she wanted to hold him back. "Help me, Friede," she would implore him, but he no longer saw nor heard her.

In her despair, she became obsessed with the thought of finding Friede's friend, Berkovitch. It seemed to her that what she was incapable of doing for the sick man, his friend perhaps could. Sometimes she fancied that Friede's health depended on whether or not she could find Berkovitch. But when she asked Sheindle about him, Sheindle shrugged her shoulders, "Go and find a grain of sand in the desert. And if I saw him, do you think I would recognize him?"

✦   ✦   ✦

Soon Esther experienced an encounter she had long since ceased to even dream about. It happened in the morning, after a night spent by Friede's bedside. She had left the cellar and was trudging home, when she was confronted by a Jew with a prayer bag under his arm. At first she thought he was part of a dream she had dreamt while asleep in the deck-chair. The next thing she knew she was in the arms of Uncle Chaim.

As soon as they both recovered from the initial shock, they each began to talk at the same time. "You don't look good, Esther," Uncle Chaim said.

"And the aunt, the children, where are they?" Esther inquired.

"The boys . . . as if they drowned in deep water . . . Not a trace . . . Your aunt has had a notion that they were here in the ghetto and we came back . . . miraculously. So, go upstairs to see your aunt." She stared at him transfixed. "Have you forgotten where we live?" he smiled crookedly, unnaturally. She noticed how changed he was, how gray and sparse his beautiful beard had become and how many deep furrows ran down from his hollow cheeks into his beard.

She ran ahead, making straight for the familiar staircase. The next moment she was in the arms of Aunt Rivka. Around them stood the flustered cousins. They made Esther sit down on one of the big brown beds. Aunt Rivka looked aged and pale, but the same familiar mildness shone out of her face. The cousins barely resembled the same girls whose faces had lived on in Esther's memory. Their conversation did not run smoothly. There was too much to tell, too much to ask. The aunt bemoaned the fate of her sons who had left for the war and vanished as if "drowned in deep water". Esther tried to change the subject.

"I know the people who live with you, the Eibushitzs," she remarked.

The aunt sighed, wiping her eyes. "We fell down on them from the blue sky. They've moved into the kitchen." She leaned over to Esther. "The trouble is that your uncle is eating his heart out. He cannot watch our neighbour walking around with his head bare. I ask him 'Chaim, what business is that of yours? Will you have to answer for him in the Other World, in a hundred and twenty years from now?' But with your uncle it's like throwing peas against a wall. I say my thing and he says his. 'Why should a Jew behave like a goy?' he keeps asking me. 'It's because of him and his like,' he says, 'that this terrible bitter tragedy has befallen us.' Or, all of a sudden he pities him. 'A decent man,' he says, 'why should he be a sinner? In the Other World they'll burn and roast him for his sinful deeds.' So I say to him. 'In the meantime you, my good Jew, have been thrown into the same frying pan with the bad Jews and you're being roasted and burnt together here, in this world.' As for myself, you see, Esther, I don't care. She, the wife, told me the good news right at the start, that she doesn't keep kosher. So we don't mix the dishes and that's that — as long as we get along. You should know, my child," the aunt whispered confidentially, "that a person may behave as he pleases, so long as he is a *mentsch*. And you should also know, as it is written somewhere in the Scriptures, that if God doesn't build a house, the builder's labour is in vain, and if God doesn't guard a city, the watchmen guard it in vain . . ."

Every day Esther found time to pay a visit to Uncle Chaim. The first days she did so in a festive frame of mind, overjoyed at having all of them near her again, but before long she became used to their presence. And so, little by little, her former feelings returned to her. She felt that she had nothing in common with them. Thus she began to spend less and less time with them as the days wore on. To calm the pangs of conscience aroused by her neglect, she would tell herself that she could not bear the presence of the Eibushitz family, since her aversion to Rachel now extended to embrace the girl's parents as well. She considered them a family of egotistic petits bourgeois, proletarian only in their outlook, not in their hearts and souls.

Although the return of Uncle Chaim and his family did not alter Esther's way of life, a few changes did take place in it. Firstly, she began to care about her room; she even hung a piece of curtain up on the window. She did not want her aunt or her cousins to infer the state of her life from the state of her living quarters. Secondly, her cousins obliged her to come down to the Garden. They were eager to talk to her, for in reality they had changed a great deal and not only in their looks. Before the war, Esther would have welcomed their curiosity. Now she sat with them on the grass, without a speck of enthusiasm explaining to them those same problems about which they had refused to listen before the war. She, who was such an excellent propagandist as far as strangers were concerned, did not apply a fraction of her power of persuasion when it came to her cousins. She could not help it. Between them and herself cheerlessness and boredom had set in, and although they had become dearer to her than ever before, she considered the time spent with them a total waste.

Once, as she was sitting under the cherry tree, she saw her favourite teacher from the orphanage in Helenovek, Mr. Shafran, walk by in the company of Dr. Levine, the doctor who had delivered her dead child and who was now taking care of the sick Friede. The very first time she had met Levine in the ghetto, she recognized him, although he seemed to have doubled his age during the three quarters of a year since she had seen him last. He now walked with a limp and his back was slightly bent. As soon as she had seen him at Friede's bedside, she knew that there was no hope for the sick man. How she detested this man with the instrument bag! To her he had become the messenger of misfortune. Whenever she met him, she was sure that something bad was about to happen to her. She was glad that he had not recognized her and had no idea who she was. So, rather than give her pleasure, her meeting with Mr. Shafran in the presence of Dr. Levine filled her with dread.

From that time on, however, Shafran took to visiting her in her room. Once, she told him about her life, not really knowing how she had started on the confession. They were sipping chicory water from tin cups and between one sip and the next she blurted out her story. "And now I don't exist any longer," she concluded.

Shafran asked softly, "Do you want to die, Esther?"

The question enraged her. "You don't know what you are talking about, Mr. Shafran."

He did not seem offended. "Why don't you find work? Why don't you go to see the Presess? He is helping all the children from the orphanage." It was then clear to her that Shafran had not the slightest understanding of what was happening to her. She felt ashamed and humiliated.

Shafran would not leave her alone. He would often come to see her uninvited, or he would visit her in the cellar, accompanying Levine on his professional call. Before long, all that she had felt for the doctor she began to project onto Shafran as well. His presence made her feel uneasy and jittery. At the same time, he began to bore her to tears.

She was also bored by another visitor who often came to see her: Shalom, Itche Mayer's son. He would come up to her room, on one pretext or another; he would ask her whether she wanted him to fix something or to bring her something. She had nothing to talk to him about and would, out of boredom, turn the conversation to the topic of politics. They would work themselves into some excitement, until she became so weary of him, that she had to hint that he ought to leave. She could not bear him and was even more annoyed with him for his stubbornness and for never taking offence.

There was only one person who did not bore her, one person whom she did not tire of seeing and whom she nonetheless also chased away: Valentino. He had not kept his promise. Often, late at night, when she was about to let herself sag into the deck-chair, she would hear his heavy rapping on the door. She always dressed completely before letting him in. He would appear before her with his enormous frame, his brown face shining with health, with ripeness and with power. The gaze of his black eyes caressed her, stroking her figure with its heat. He would stretch out his hand and offer her a little parcel wrapped in creased paper, "For you, for your dinner . . ." She never refused him. His presence always aroused her craving for food. They would sit down at the table and he would watch delightedly as her teeth bit into the bread.

One evening, as she sat across from him, eating, she burst into a ringing laughter, then became frightened of its sound and covered her mouth with her hand. Puzzled, bemused, she took a big bite — and became more afraid of her own self than of Valentino. "You're a good man," she said, looking away.

Melting with pleasure, he crossed his arms over his chest. "Me? Good? Do I give you from my portion . . . little cow that you are? I have so much grub . . . up to here." With a finger he made a cutting motion across his hairy neck.

She laughed her unnatural strange laughter which she detested but could not control. "You are good," she repeated.

"First time in my life I hear such a thing! May I live so long in good health, you hear? First time!" He kept on licking her face with his hot eyes; his gaze darted over her boyish crop of red hair. He insisted on catching her glance, she, on avoiding his.

"Let me be, Valentino," she chased him out. "Go home."

He began to implore her, "Why do you turn me out like this? What am I doing to you, little cow? Let me look at you a little longer."

"You're stupid," she giggled. "What is there to look at and what is there to see? Nothing but skin and bone." She showed him her skinny arms.

"I'd crush you to pieces!"

"Get out!" she ordered.

After he left, she felt hot all over. She opened the window and let herself sink down by Friede's bedside. She sat there for a long while, wiping his face and pouring tea between his lips, until the tension subsided inside her and she slumped into the deck-chair.

Esther finally consented to Mr. Shafran's pleas and asked him to persuade the Presess to give her work. She was assigned to the post of a *wydzielaczka*, a distributor of soups at the window of a public kitchen. In truth, she was ashamed of herself for having made this sudden decision, ashamed of the post itself. Freed of the pangs of hunger, she was sorry to see that her dresses fit her again. With how much regret she extended the belts around her waist! At the same time a childish joy kept somersaulting within her; her healthy body exulted, although she refused to acknowledge its triumph. As usual, she sat at Friede's bed, and nurtured the wish to perish with him.

In the beginning, she saw nothing of what went on around her at work. All she saw was the kettle of soup before her. She would stir it with a huge ladle and dish it into the canteens, pots and pans that the people in the line outside of her little window held out to her. She made an effort to distribute the soup equally and give the same number of potatoes to each person. Only when the hand stretched out to her was that of a child, did she add a few more pieces to the soup and then lean out through the window, curious to see the little face light up.

Little by little, she came to realize that the kitchen consisted of more than her window and her kettle of soup, that she was working with a staff of cooks, porters, potato peelers and vegetable washers. She noticed that the relatives and acquaintances of the manager and the office people would often come in, nosing around the kettles of soup and loiter in the potato warehouse, and that these visitors usually vanished through the back door loaded down with pots of food. She also noticed that at their little windows the other *wydzielaczkas* had the habit of exchanging meaningful glances with some of the people in line outside. She protested, overcome by an urge to introduce justice into the affairs of the kitchen. She threatened, she warned, she quarrelled. The manager and the staff shunned her. The fact that she was under Rumkowski's protection did not add to their esteem of her, only to their fear. She had no one to talk to, she felt uncomfortable and counted the hours to the end of the working day.

Nevertheless, as time wore on, Esther gradually became chummy with the other *wydzielaczskas* and had her own secrets with them. At Uncle Chaim's, lack of food was becoming the order of the day. She was ashamed to visit the family on a full stomach and she finally asked the youngest of her cousins, to come with a pot to her kitchen window. Thus the wheel began to turn in the opposite direction: it was now Uncle Chaim's household which lived off of Esther's kindness. Aunt Rivka now greeted her with such reverence that Esther would blush. At first, she just gave little Bina good soups. Later, there would be more potatoes in the pot than soup. After a while, Esther's comrades also began to show up at the window. She chose the most hungry and the most needy, but she ended up doling out a few more pieces of potato to every acquaintance that she noticed in the line.

The soup in her kettle became watery. No matter how much she stirred it, she still had nothing of substance to pour into the remaining canteens handed to her. She would watch the people leave the window, draw their spoons out of their pockets and stir their soups, frowning. The more aggressive would approach her and show her their canteens. "Plain water!" they would say bitterly. Others quarrelled with her, imploring her to add a few pieces of potato. Some cursed her, spitting at her and raising their fists, "Exploiter! Blood-sucker!" Their screams pierced her like needles.

Friede's cellar became her refuge.

Esther no longer accepted Valentino's "dinners", but this changed nothing. The more often he came down to the cellar at night to see her, the more daring he became. He would take her into his hard arms and exclaim, "Here in this cellar . . . by his bed . . . I could eat you up."

It seemed to her that he already was "eating her up". She felt all her limbs ready to submit to his touch. But her will was on the alert and protected her against both herself and him. "I don't know what you want of me, Valentino," she would mumble, tearing herself away from him. "Can't you see that there is no life left in me?"

He would bare his shiny big teeth and pucker up his eyebrows. "In you?

Good heavens! You're nothing but life!" He would let himself down on his knees, awkwardly spreading out his hands in ecstatic adoration. "May I die this minute, Esther, if I would not bare my neck for your sake! I beg of you . . . Let me only . . ."

She would not let him. She would look down at him, not knowing whether she should laugh or cry. She decided to complain about him to Sheindle. But Sheindle shrugged her shoulders. "I know that he is getting the cholera for you . . ."

"Don't let him come in," Esther begged her.

"So, what would that help? It would be worse. You don't know my Valentino."

"He is your husband."

"Husband-schmusband! Are you going to take him away from me, or what? He won't divorce me, don't worry."

"What should I do? I can't drive him away."

"Do you want to? Go to bed with him and put an end to the whole story."

"Are you crazy?"

"May I live so long, how sane I am. That is the only way to get rid of him."

"Aren't you jealous, Sheindle?"

"Jealous-schmealous! In my profession you laugh at such things, even if your insides turn upside down. What do I have to be jealous for, tell me? Are you one of ours? Can't you see the ceremonies he goes through with you? What do you think? That he does it with all women? Not on your life! Only with you . . . You are to him . . . the Holy Mary, that's what you are to him. That's why I'm not jealous. Have you ever met anyone who was jealous of the Holy Mary?"

Esther realized that she would have to solve the problem on her own. The next time when Valentino came to pay her a visit in the cellar, she lashed out at him, "Listen, you have to rid your mind of all this . . ." He did not immediately grasp the meaning of what she was telling him and she had to increase the tone of severity in her voice. "Leave me alone, understand?" she shouted.

She saw his face changing. A fierce light came into his eyes. "What's the matter? Don't you fancy me?" he thundered.

"I fancy you all right." She looked him straight in the eyes. "But I don't love you."

He stayed where he was, his mouth open, his eyebrows taut. "Either . . . or . . ." he stammered, bewildered.

"It's not either-or, Valentino."

"May I be cleansed of all evil, Esther, if I don't have your good at heart," he muttered confusedly. "I swear to you by all sacred things . . . a *dybbuk* has got into me. Can't you see for yourself?"

"I don't want to see you, Valentino, ever again . . ."

He began to pace the cellar like a caged lion. All the boards of the floor swayed under his steps. The mud oozed out from between the cracks and the boards squeaked like the insides of a broken musical instrument, as if they were accompanying the last notes of Valentino's love song. Finally, he took a leap towards the door and turned to her with a growl, "But remember!" he waved a finger at her. "One day I may do something to you or to myself. Keep this well in your mind!"

✦   ✦   ✦

It was a bright Sabbath day. The sun reigned over a completely cloudless sky, stroking the houses with its brilliant rays. The streets were quiet, washed with light, an air of repose prevailed in every corner. The yards were full of clean neatly-combed children in their Sabbath clothes. The adults were also carefully dressed; men and women stood around in knots, chatting and inhaling the delightful air. Those who still had some food at home knew that today they would have a particularly good meal. Those who went hungry all week long usually arranged matters so, that on the Sabbath they would not be too bothered by the pangs of hunger. And those who could not do even this, still took delight in the Sabbath day, hoping that the new week might hold some good luck for them. The ghetto was catching its breath today; not only the ghetto — but God's entire world.

The yard on Hockel Street was permeated by the holiday air. Groups of women, wrapped in checkered plaids, with neat colourful scarfs on their heads, stood around in front of their entrances or sat on the thresholds. The water pump was besieged by conversing male neighbours. On one side they surrounded Blind Henech, on the other, his nephew Itche Mayer. Both of them had their permanent public. On the window sills on the ground floor sat rows of girls whispering and giggling amongst themselves, their necks and shoulders bared to the sun; they resembled big talking dolls. The young men strolled past them, absorbed in their own heated discussions. They belonged to various organizations and vehemently defended the "platforms" of their respective parties, thus trying to make order in world politics. In the middle of the yard the younger girls skipped ropes or played hop-scotch. Urchins gambolled all over the yard.

And then there were the cherry tree's visitors. The tree was already shedding its blossoms. A pink-white snow was falling from its boughs, covering the grass. It seemed that no one wanted to miss this last day of its beauty, and the tree was beleagured with guests today. People sat on boxes, on chairs, on broken pots; they lay on rags and plaids, sunning their backs. Women warmed their blue-veined legs, their socks rolled down in "bagels" around their ankles. Little girls in their Sabbath dresses trotted among the bodies spread out on the ground, collecting the fallen flower petals. They did not actually know what to do with them, yet could not resist picking them and holding them in their palms; they were so beautiful.

Friede felt well today. His eyes were clear, his face smooth. As soon as Sheindle came in, still dressed in her flowery housecoat, her hair dishevelled, she began to dress him in a clean shirt. She changed the covers of his bedding and left. When she returned, she was wearing a blue décolleté dress which hung crookedly around her legs. Her hair was combed, her lips and cheeks covered with lipstick and rouge. She could not keep her mouth closed for a moment. She invited in the neighbours, the new ones, those from the city — who did not know her profession and thus, unlike the old neighbours, did not shun her — and showed them how well Friede looked today.

In the afternoon Friede still felt fine and Sheindle decided, "Today we take him into the Garden. The fresh air will do him good and allow the man to see a bit of the world as well!" She caught Esther's eyes staring at her in amazement and guffawed, "What are you popping your eyes at me for? Can't you see that the crisis is over?"

Yes, Esther too believed that today Friede's illness had taken a turn for the better, but for that reason she wanted to have him to herself. He clung to her. Only today had words begun to tie between them the threads of understanding which had previously been tied only by their occasional glances. There was so much light within her today, so much wonder. The radiance of the day so meagrely stealing into the cellar seemed more enchanting to her than the light outside.

Sheindle, however, stuck to her decision. She opened the door wide and called in a battalion of strong men with Valentino in the lead. "Careful! Beware!" Sheindle ordered the men as she helped them carry the bed outside. "Take him to the Garden! To the Garden take him!"

When the procession with the bed reached the cherry tree, a great commotion started around it. People moved over with their rags and plaids, with their boxes and chairs. The bed was placed near the tree trunk so that the sick man would get some shade. A white snow of flower petals began to fall on him. All around him sat the people, enclosing him in a circle — as if they were all one family surrounding a sick, tired son. Esther sat close by, but her heart was in the cellar, at the empty spot left by Friede's bed.

By dusk, when he was brought back from the Garden, Friede's mind had resumed roaming through distant worlds. In the cellar, the day was over. The circle of light on the ceiling, cast by the electric bulb, seemed to mourn the lost daylight with its sad glow. Esther and Sheindle listened to Friede's breathing. The rusty machine in his chest seemed to be working with every last bit of energy. His eyes were shut. On the tips of his short eyelashes hung a few tear drops. Sweat trickled from his hair down onto the freshly covered pillow.

Sheindle, distraught, set about preparing food for Friede. Soon she was standing at his bedside, a bowl of soup in her hand. She stirred it with the spoon and blew at the steam while swallowing her tears. "Friede," she whispered, "will you eat something?" Her hoarse masculine voice acquired the softness of velvet. Friede did not stir. Sheindle pressed down her eyelids, trying to dam up her tears. "Friede, have pity on me," she implored him, pushing the spoon between his tight lips. "Open your mouth, Friede, please, open it . . ." The soup spilled into the crack between his lips, streaming down from the corners of his mouth through the grooves around his chin, onto the pillow. It had a reddish colour. Sheindle scooped it up from his chin with the spoon. Two streams of blood, thin and as clear as red threads of silk, wound their way from his mouth down to his neck. Before long, the pillow-case was coloured a moist fiery red. Sheindle puckered her eyebrows, glaring at the sight. She stopped her mouth with her fist. Finally, she let out a scream, "Look! Like a Jesus! Woe is me, what shall I do now? The man is dying!" She swooped down on Esther and shook her violently. "What are you sitting there like a *golem* of clay for? Why don't you run outside to call the neighbours, for heaven's sake!"

Esther struggled to stand up, but her legs refused to obey her. Soon she heard Sheindle's screams coming from the yard. The cellar filled with people. The women bent over Friede, rags in hands, wiping off the blood that oozed from his mouth. Some put cold compresses to his forehead, others put wet towels to his yellow chest from which every bone protruded. Sheindle stood amongst them, hysterically tearing the skin of her cheeks with her nails. Men gave advice to Blind Henech who stood on the threshold, his half-blind eye wide open, the visor of his cap pushed back over his forehead. He nervously scratched the palm of his hand. A few dressed-up children pressed their skinny bodies through the crowd at the door and whispered among themselves. Their glowing eyes darted over the faces of the people in the cellar, halting at the bed with curiosity. Their faces expressed fear as well as a strange kind of delight.

Soon Itche Mayer arrived flanked by Dr. Levine. The people made way to let the doctor approach the bed. He cast a long glance at the sick man and checked his pulse, while his eyes stared into the distance. Sheindle hung on to his arm. "Save him, Mister Doctor! Darling dearest Doctor!"

Levine snatched the edge of a wet rag and wiped Friede's face with it. His eyes wandered over the faces of the people surrounding the bed. "Where could we get some ice?" he asked.

A hush passed through the room. Then Blind Henech began to give orders to the young men. "You run to the soup kitchen on Zgierska! You try the drugstore! You rush over to Karo's Cafeteria!" In spite of his bad eyes he noticed that the doctor was annoyed at the crowd of people in the cellar; he rushed over to the women at the bed and began to shove them all towards the door. The cellar was emptied.

Sheindle hung on to the doctor's arm again, "Do something, Doctor! What are you standing there like a *golem* of clay for?"

The doctor looked around as if he were looking for help. The forlornness of a child peered out from his eyes. At length he drew a box of needles out from his bag, handed them to Sheindle and asked her to boil them. "I'll give him an injection," he muttered. "He's haemorrhaging, as you can see."

Sheindle wavered, not knowing whether she should immediately rush to the stove or nag at the doctor some more. She did both, hurrying to the stove and steadily imploring him, "Doctor, dearest, don't let him go out like a candle. He felt so good today. I swear to you . . . If you had only seen him this morning before we took him out to the Garden."

"How did you carry him?" the doctor asked.

"What do you mean how? As he is, Doctor darling, on the bed . . ."

"The shaking . . . perhaps also . . ."

Sheindle stared at the doctor for a while as if he were a madman whom she did not understand. Then she clasped her head between her hands, crooning in a frenzied singsong, "Woe is me! Woe is me!" Then she began to howl shrilly, "Oy, I killed him myself, oy, by my very own self! What a cow I am! What a cursed miserable cow!"

◆   ◆   ◆

Simcha Bunim Berkovitch spent all that Sabbath day poring over a rare book which he had bought from a man in the street for ten pfennig. He sat at the closed window and the light of the day fell on the yellowing pages covered with partly faded print. It had been a long time since he had felt such peace inside him. It seemed as if a mysterious hand had led him towards this precious book, so that he might salvage it from destruction. He delighted in deciphering the words of the religious verses in it, repeating the lines over and over again, humming them with a tune of his own.

Miriam spent the whole day on her bed, reading the book Bunim had acquired as an addition to the sacred volume. It was "The Sorceress of Castilia", by Shalom Asch. She had set her mind on finishing it that same day; while doing so, she forgot that she was hungry, and she was also saving energy. Blimele, her daughter, spent the entire day in the Garden, playing with the other children. It was quiet and neat in the hut. The noise from the backyard penetrated the walls, reaching the ears of husband and wife with a subdued pleasant sound.

Late in the evening Bunim stepped out into the yard to get a breath of fresh air. The yard was empty. There was no one sitting under the cherry tree. Its leaves were rustling with the secrets of the night. A breeze was picking the flower petals, scattering them around the trunk. Bunim let himself sink down onto the grass and looked up to the sky. He noticed the neighbouring building. His boss from the factory where he had worked before the war, Mr. Adam Rosenberg, lived there; the fact no longer had any meaning. Bunim observed the empty yard. The peace within him was gone, gone with the Sabbath, gone with the moment he had set foot into the yard. That was how it always happened. The minute he stepped out over the threshold, he felt it — the lurking gnawing dread. Even this quiet evening, this silent yard had the power to evoke it.

A last flower petal fell on his face. He picked it off, brought it to his lips and then to his nose. He looked at it as it lay on the palm of his hand: a fleck of beauty, a piece of perfect harmony. His heart winced with compassion for man who seemed to be the most disharmonious and most awkward work of creation. His own inner disseverance, the disseverance of every single soul, the entanglements and contradictions of the human character ached in him. A vague craving drummed at his heart: to be like a tree, like a leaf, like a flower petal; to exist without being aware of one's existence, to live without torment, to wither without fatigue.

Suddenly, someone emerged from the gateway and hurried through the yard. Bunim stood up slowly and walked in the direction of the shadowy figure. A tall thin man with a pointed little beard stopped him. "Come," he said, "we need one more person to make a quorum." Bunim wanted to ask something, to say something, but his tongue got tangled between his teeth. The figure of the Jew walking by his side, the silver of the moon as it washed the cobblestones in the yard created a white eerie reality at which one could only stare mutely.

They descended into the cellar. On the floor lay a body covered with a dark blanket. Candles burned by the dead man's head. Like a reflection of one of the candles' flames a woman's red head of hair burned in the distance against the wall. Nearby was another head of hair — a black flame. The black head stirred. Bunim recognized Sheindle. Awareness rose within him with such clarity that it seemed unreal. "Friede," he said to himself in a loud voice. He did not know whether Sheindle recognized him or not. In her glassy eyes, he read her guilt, his guilt, God's guilt.

All around him, men chanted the psalms, swaying to a monotonous rhythm. The words issuing from their mouths fell on Bunim's head like drops of a long rain. Someone threw a prayer shawl around his shoulders. He felt enveloped — like the corpse. But around the corpse candles flickered, embracing the prostrate body with a circle of light, a circle which divided and separated forever. Bunim tried to penetrate this circle of light, to join his soul with the soul of him who had been a man, a friend. But the circle rejected him. He belonged to another world — to the world of those who still suffer.

Chapter Five

(David's notebook)

Today is the first of May. From today on we are really trapped, locked up in the Ghetto, hermetically sealed off by a net of barbed wires. I have heard it said that the Poles who live on the other side near the wire fence will have to move. Their houses will be demolished, so that besides the fence and the German guards, we will also be "protected" by a strip of "no man's land". There will be no way out — except through the sky. The sky is bright today, so bright that it grips you. Today is the Day of Freedom. One ought to feel united with mankind. Do they know anything about us? Do they care? Will anyone come to help us, to save us?

At times it seems to me that we are not in the middle of a big town, in the centre of a country, in the middle of Europe — but that we are stranded on an unknown island in the middle of a stormy sea where no ships pass. We are in the hands of cannibals. We may not light a fire so as to be seen from the distance, we may not wave a flag or call for help. The question is whether it would make any difference if we could.

I wish I were a pious Jew believing in a God who protects us, who guards us, before whom we can unburden our hearts; someone who at least hears us out.

I am now working as a teacher in the school where I was once a student. For this I get a soup. Mother will probably soon start working too. She is scouring around, seeking "connections", "protections", "backs", as we call it, in one word — contact with the Old Man. In the meantime I go around hungry, but I bear it somehow. The truth is that nothing interests me; I am apathetic.

There are only a few hours in the day during which I liven up somewhat: when I visit the barber shop. There I read the *Lidzamstädter Zeitung* which the barber smuggles in through Baluter Ring. Whatever I read, I explain to the men who come in, eager to hear some good news; they nag me to find at least a tiny hint between the lines about German defeats. I read about the low instincts of the Jews and about how Hitler has finally found the means to get rid of that "boil", first from Europe, then from the entire world. My listeners laugh when they hear this. "*Yeke* idiot," they say mockingly. "He will first meet his Maker, before he wipes out the Jews from the face of the earth!" I laugh just like they, but what's going on in my heart is a different story. This is my "intellectual nourishment". The rest of the day I spend running around, fetching the food articles on our rations (the main items are always missing). Then I tidy up the room and peel potatoes or turnips. I have become a first class cook. We have an electric kettle and in it I cook our soup: water with salt. The salt adds a soup-like taste to the water, giving the impression that we are indeed consuming a tasty dish. At night I dream about Father. My dreams bring me back to our country house. I see myself sitting at the table on the sun-bathed veranda, eating a plateful of noodle soup. In the morning I don't feel like getting up. Mother has to shake me hard and remind me of my duties as a teacher. The three teachers left over from the old staff are proud of me, their ex-student. Yes, it could have been interesting to share whatever one knows with others, but I just get it over with as fast as I can.

Even in my attitude towards Rachel I am no longer the same. I cannot bear being with her longer than a half an hour or so. Sometimes she asks me what's wrong with me. I hate these investigations. I get the impression that she wants to see me break down. And on top of it all, spring is here — to mock at us; a spring blossoming not with flowers, but with hunger and fear.

However in our backyard there stands a true witness to spring: our cherry tree. Often, on the Sabbath, I go to sit under it. On the balcony of the building nearby, two girls sometimes appear, Rachel's friends. One smiles at me, the other has slow languorous movements. I always see her reading something. Her figure, her head against the background of the sky make her seem like a cloud that has stopped before my eyes. I long for her as I would for a cloud, or for the sky. Eh, fiddlesticks!

In the past I used to dream about becoming an astronomer, a seeker for the stars. I used to dream of laboratories and telescopes. My motto used to be: "Knowledge is might!" This strikes me now as an idiocy. Knowledge is not might, but powerlessness. The less you know, the better. Better to be an ass or have a head full of sawdust. This is the mental level I have almost achieved. I am a *schlemiel* par excellence! Abraham is much better at peeling potatoes than I am. He can sweep the floor in five minutes, while it takes me "a year and a Wednesday". He is craftier, smarter, more agile than I. Only in appetite am I on a level with him.

I think that we will have to divide our bread ration into three portions, because from one day to the next we leave a smaller portion for Mother. We rob her of her bread. When Abraham takes a slice of bread, I catch myself measuring it with my eyes.

Yes, everything I jot down here is "sour and bitter", but never mind. It does not show on me. I act the happy clown. There are, however, days when my feelings of gloom and doom really do let go of me. Today for instance. In accordance with an order from the party leadership, we walked from house to house to visit Bundist comrades and sympathizers, reminding them that today is May Day, that they should not despair, that "We shall weather the storm and survive!" (This is the slogan of our party.) Again I am asking myself: Is it dishonest if I, depressed and pessimistic as I basically am, encourage people, telling them that the war will soon be over, when I don't believe it myself? In each home we visited, we gave an account of the latest political events — we, that is my trio of the "Flying Brigade". We told the people the truth, one hundred percent of it, but we so decorated and dressed up each piece of information, that it almost convinced everyone that we would be liberated if not today then surely tomorrow. Luckily, our listeners were not too critically inclined. They pumped our hands gratefully. I will not deny that this made me feel great. It is pleasant to console people and watch their faces light up. Like a child who makes up a fairy tale and then believes in it, so I began to believe in my own stories.

But is this right? Is it not better to look the truth in the face, bitter as it may be? The Germans hold all of Europe in their fist. We are imprisoned who knows for how long, and who knows what is still awaiting us. That is the truth. But such a truth is liable to deprive us of the will to struggle. The lie does the people more good. It gives them courage in their fight for existence. So the question is, what should be done with a truth that does no good, and with a lie that does? Should we here, in the ghetto, renounce the love of truth, the search for it? And where is the border that a lie should not be permitted to cross? Truth has no degrees or borderlines. Truth is either complete or it is not truth. With a lie the story is altogether different. The question is also whether it makes sense to live in an unreal world of groundless hopes, even if they are beneficial at the moment? Will the bare truth not pop up sooner or later anyway, catching us unprepared? Then it might indeed crush us. So what is the way? As I said, I don't know. On the other hand, perhaps I do, but am afraid to concede. In spite of all I know and read — I too wrap myself in an illusion. I cling to the bluff because I cannot do without it.

In the afternoon we strolled in the streets. No one wore a coat. On each of our chests was, on one side, the Star of David, on the other — a tiny red bow. Behind me and Rachel walked my Brigadeniks, Marek and Isaac, with a bunch of girls in colourful summer dresses. Other comrades, young and old, passed us by. We exchanged glances and smiles, greeting each other: "Good *yomtov!*"

Then we went up to a comrade's room to celebrate. Simon, our leader, made a fiery speech. According to him, the victory of the Allies was so close that the Western Armies might at any moment march past the window. The truth is: the German army has penetrated the Fjords near Oslo, they have landed in Narvik, and Quisling is already sitting pretty in his saddle. The entire defence fleet of the English and the Polish-French armies has been broken up and the Allies have decided to withdraw the armies which protected Norway and make them useful elsewhere. If Simon was able to deliver such an enthusiastic speech on the basis of these news items, he is indeed the greatest artist in the world.

After his speech, we worked ourselves into a mood of exultation. We sang our precious songs about the days of "love and peace". Why should I kid myself? I felt just as jubilant as the others. (My theory is that hope is just as contagious as fear.)

In the evening I went for a stroll with Rachel. The ghetto seems to be quite big, yet we encounter barbed wire at every step. Perhaps I see so much of it because it attracts me. It seems as if it has not only cut the ghetto off from the town, but also from the sky, from the air. I felt like grabbing Rachel by the hand, breaking through the barbed wires and fleeing with her into the night. My Rachel. How well she understood me in my muteness. Why then am I unable to talk to her? Why do I so often feel like running away from her? Is it because she reminds me of the past?

It is night now. I am going to bed, praying that freedom will pay me a visit in my dreams.

✦   ✦   ✦

Yesterday I was at a wedding. Yossi, my friend Shalom's brother got married. The girl, his bride, is also a Zionist. Her name is Aviva, which is supposed to mean spring in Hebrew. The name suits her, but she is a contrast to Yossi who is a lively talkative fellow. He did not keep his mouth shut for a minute, constantly laughing, shifting in his chair, kissing the bride and joking with the guests at the table — then he embraced the bride again and pressed her against his chest, so forcefully, that I was afraid he would break her in two.

The two of them appear to love each other, but is it the kind of love which can resist the dirt and degradation of life in the ghetto? What gives the two of them the courage to undertake such a step? Is it courage, or is it thoughtlessness? I felt Rachel's gaze on me, and I knew what she was thinking: how strong is our love? Would its "sacredness" not drown in the dirt surrounding us? She leaned over to me and whispered, "The ghetto is a good test for love, an exam. Don't you agree?"

I told her that I did not agree. "It is not a real test," I said. "Even the most sacred love could be crushed here."

"Ours too?" she asked. I did not want to hurt her, so I said that our love was too precious for me to submit it to such a test. With that I made things worse. "You don't love me anymore," she said. For the first time we were speaking about not loving one another.

I was irritated, as if by my anger I wanted to silence the questions which had begun to nag at me. Perhaps she was right. I did not feel that I loved anyone but myself, with a bad animal-like love. "You're imagining things," I lashed out. "If I don't love you, then I don't know how to call what I feel for you."

There was an air of gaiety all around us. Itche Mayer and Sheyne Pessele were celebrating doubly. Firstly, on account of the marriage of their son Yossi; secondly, on account of their son Israel's return from Warsaw. He has come back alone, without his wife and child. How he smuggled himself into the ghetto remains a riddle. A few days ago he came up to our place, bringing regards from Halina. He told us that she is pregnant. Shall we ever see this new member of our family?

At the wedding, we sat at a big long table covered with a white tablecloth. (All the furniture was taken out of the apartment for the occasion.) There was no food or dishes on the table, but the whiteness of the tablecloth alone created a festive mood. To the right of the bride and groom sat Sheyne Pessele and to the left, Itche Mayer. (The bride's parents are not in the ghetto.) Around the table sat only young people, the girls in their prettiest dresses, the young men wearing white shirts. I wore one too. Mother had ironed one of Father's white shirts for me. Before the "official" part of the celebration began, Mottle and Shalom placed glasses and cups on the table, telling us that wine would be served. Someone said that the wine in question was actually borscht. Someone else said that it was cherry juice from last year's cherries. There were still others who thought that it could not be anything else but tea with a few drops of lemon. Even when we later tasted the drink, we still argued about what it was and Sheyne Pessele and her family refused to reveal the secret.

At length Itche Mayer rose from his place and began the "official" part of the ceremony — with a speech. He looked oddly young. His hollow cheeks were so pale that they seemed blue, and his eyes reflected the whiteness of the tablecloth; his pupils were red. His jacket hung limply on his shoulders; the long sleeves covered his hands up to the tips of his fingers. It made him look like someone who had dressed up to act the part of buffoon, especially when he smiled. And today he smiled a lot.

"My children," he called out at the top of his voice. "We have gathered here today to celebrate our son Yossi's wedding. Had we lived in another time, this table which you see here would not have stood empty." He let his fists drop on the table top — with a bang. The table, consisting of the boards on which his sons slept, jumped into the air on the opposite side. Those who sat there were treated to a "caress" on their chins, dealt by the loose boards. There was also a *mazal-tov* to a few broken glasses.

A general outburst of laughter followed, whereupon Sheyne Pessele, gathering the crockery and adjusting the tablecloth, said to her husband with pretended anger, "Perhaps you'll talk without the help of your hands, Itche Mayer?"

Itche Mayer pushed up his "fallen" sleeves. "At other times the table which you see here would not have stood empty." He now placed his hands on the table very daintily.

However, Sheyne Pessele heckled him again, "It won't stay empty today either!"

"In other times, the wedding celebration of one of my children would have looked different!" Itche Mayer eyed Sheyne Pessele, to check whether she now understood what he was trying to say. She nodded and he concentrated on his listeners. "We would have taken a dance hall. Fish and meats, tarts and cakes would have been served, and we would have hired a first class orchestra, such as my Yossi likes. However, my dear guests, I tell you with my hand on my heart, that in spite of the fact that we don't have all these nice things, a wedding in the ghetto is a more important celebration than before the war, and a greater *mitzva* at that! To marry in the ghetto is to spit in the face of all our enemies, may their names be cursed! The best, the most magnificent spit in the face! And we show them a fig!" Here Itche Mayer thrust the thumbs of each of his hands between two fingers, in a sign of defiance, flinging them in the direction of the window. Applause followed, but Itche Mayer, carried away by his own fervour, had no patience to wait for the bravos to die down. "The Jewish people, my children," he continued, holding on to the edge of the table, evidently having difficulty in standing on his feet, "Our Jewish people are stronger than the Germans, may their names be erased! And we shall survive them all!" Unsteady on his feet, he began to sway back and forth, his voice turning hoarse. "We shall live to see the day when we take the barbed-wire fences apart! All the barbed-wire fences in the entire world!"

"And we shall have a country of our own, Father!" Yossi laughed, raising his fist in the air as his comrades applauded.

"And we shall live to see the day when we will all dance in the streets!" Itche Mayer responded. "And Yossi, my son, and Aviva, my daughter," he turned to the young couple, tears bursting from his eyes. "May this be a lucky hour! Love each other, my children, to spite our enemies! And I, your father, wish that you live to see the great magnificent hour . . . And your children . . ." Itche Mayer began to struggle with his voice which suddenly refused to serve him. He fell into Aviva's arms, crying as he kissed her.

A scene followed. The remaining members of the family joined them, thus creating a closed, weeping, kissing and hugging circle. From all sides you could hear bravos and shouts, "*Mazal-tov! Mazal-tov!*" Then Shalom and Israel, both very moved, disengaged themselves from the family group and set about filling the glasses with wine. Israel called out, "*Lechaim!*" and this was the moment when we tasted the mysterious potion. Sheyne Pessele was on the point of rushing into the kitchen, when she noticed Itche Mayer, shaken and preoccupied, take up his previous post at the table, as if he were at the verge of speaking again. She raised both hands into the air and waved them at her husband, "Itche Mayer, don't you think you have talked enough?"

"Today I'm allowed to speak as much as I please, right or wrong?" Itche Mayer faced the public.

"Speak! Speak, Itche Mayer!" came the shouts from all sides, encouraging him.

Sheyne Pessele would not hear of it, "You'd better sit down right away and not say another single word! I want to have a father for my children, understand?"

"And what am I for your children, an uncle?" Itche Mayer asked facetiously.

"I don't want you to wear your heart out. Enough speeches, right or wrong?" she in turn appealed to the audience.

Thereupon the groom himself jumped to his feet, grabbing the bride by the hand, then by the waist, and with his empty glass in his other hand, he intoned in a hoarse voice, "Oy, Oy, *Hosen-Kala, mazal-tov!*" We all joined in and Sheyne Pessele set out for the kitchen, nodding approvingly to the rhythm of the song.

Soon she reappeared, accompanied by a bunch of girls with plates in their hands. The singing began to wane. Curious eyes lit up. Fish was being served. A new ghetto dish. It consists of everything one normally puts into the pot when cooking fish — except for the fish themselves. For the second course we were served slices of turnip with coffee cake. The latter is also a new food article. Apparently one can prepare all kinds of belly-stuffing dishes out of the dregs of Ersatz-coffee, which is in fact not coffee but the refuse of burnt grain. There were also cookies made from mashed potatoes, and each of us received two candies. On top of all this, we were served lemonade, that is, water sweetened with saccharine. In a word, we had a real ball.

Warmed by the delicious dishes, we resumed the singing with real zeal, initiating a kind of political singing-contest between the Zionist and the socialist guests. The groom himself joined in with both factions and conducted the choir, a teaspoon serving as his baton. During the livelier parts of the songs he danced on the chair on which he had jumped, so that the "choir" could see him. After a while, he pulled his bride up onto her chair and things really began to swing. Yossi was called upon to do a solo, and he gave us his personal rendition of all the Polish hit songs we suggested to him. He made the appropriate grimaces and gestures, rolling his eyes, pretending to kiss the seam of Aviva's dress, and grabbing hold of his own heart. We roared with laughter. Poor Aviva was no longer smiling shyly, but holding onto her tummy as if afraid that she might burst from laughing.

After the concert, the table was disassembled, its boards taken out, and the floor was cleared. Before long, Yossi and his crowd formed a circle with him and Aviva in the centre, and they led off in a *hora*. My comrade Shalom refused to join in, declaring aloud, that as a matter of principle, he was against *horas*, and that it was against his principles to betray his principles. However, since it was his brother's wedding, he would condescend to sing and clap his hands to the beat. But Rachel and I betrayed him. Without ceremony, the twirling dancers grabbed us by the hands and swept us along into their circle. Sheyne Pessele implored us to have pity on her and not holler so loudly because of the barbed-wire fence being so close. But who cared to listen to her?

On top of that, a new bunch of guests arrived. Itche Mayer's cronies. Sheyne Pessele grabbed herself by the head. She jumped up to them, begging them, as if they were robbers, to go home, and telling them that today the party was only for the young, and that they should come back next week when she would repeat the celebration for the older people. Valentino consoled her with his thundering voice, "Don't worry a bit, Sheyne Pessele. Next week we will come again, with God's help." He pushed himself through the circle towards Yossi and Aviva and joined them in their twirling frenzy. Blind Henech leaned against the wall, clapping his hands to the rhythm and shaking his goatee. It was he, people said, who had supplied the bottles of the mysterious wine we had savoured, it was apparently his own production. The famous cashbox thief, Lame King and a few horse thieves, pre-war neighbours, were also present, having come along with Blind Henech who would not think of taking a step without them. Then a tall fat fellow came in who, they said, works as a porter in the food storehouses of the ghetto. He brought a wedding gift, a cake made of one hundred percent pure flour (stolen from the storehouse, of course). The dancing stopped. A racket started up. Sheyne Pessele counted the heads a few times before cutting the cake, and then shut everyone up by stuffing their mouths with slices. Rachel took a bite from her piece, then wrapped the rest in a piece of paper to take home. I took a bigger bite and did the same, so that Mother and Abraham might also have a reminder of how a pre-war slice of cake tasted.

Afterwards the crowd poured out into the yard. It was late in the evening, but the yard was packed with people. Sheyne Pessele came down and distributed the remainder of the candies to the children. Itche Mayer who looked dead drunk, stumbled from one knot of people to the other, so that everybody might shake his hand.

The moon came out, the cobblestones shone with light. Human faces looked pale and unreal. I held Rachel's hand as we strolled towards the cherry tree. The silver of the moon seemed to hang from its rustling leaves. A last blossom petal which looked like a piece of the moon, fell on Rachel's head. It looked like a beautiful hairpin. I put my arms around her and kissed her. Her cheek remained on mine, her hands, in mine. My heart began to pound, my knees shook. I wanted to touch her body.

✦   ✦   ✦

A few hours ago, while I was busy washing dishes, Rachel rushed into the room all worked up and begged me to go down with her for a few minutes. But even in the street she refused to talk. To all my questions she replied, "Let's hide somewhere." She led me over to the empty Bazaar. There she told me that Sutter of the *Kripo* had paid a visit to our yard this morning. He was going from floor to floor, searching every apartment. After they had searched her room, she had leaned out from the window and had seen Sutter about to enter our staircase, when a German came running, whispered something in his ear and they took off. At that time I had been quietly eating my lunch.

Sutter has been pointed out to me a few times already. He is a *Folksdeutsche* from Lodz. He looks like a bulldog, short and broad-shouldered, with a round flat face. His nose is red and looks like a potato, his lipless drooping mouth is like that of a frog. He has small shrewish eyes. He is never angry, nor does he raise his voice at anyone, behaving quite chummily when talking to Jews, as if he were one of them. Even in the *Kripo* House where he invites those "customers", about whose foreign currency or hidden merchandise he has found out — even there he is well-mannered. And so, politely, he sends people down to the torture chambers which are already going full steam.

At Rachel's place, he first turned the entire room upside down, pulling everything out from the cupboards and closets and mixing everything up on the floor. He found a hosiery machine at Chaim the Hosiery-Maker's, so he ordered him to present himself at the *Kripo* tomorrow morning. Then he gathered all the neighbours in one apartment, asking the men to go into one room and the women into the other, to undress. One neighbour, Rachel told me, an old decrepit bachelor, came in, holding the cover of a pot pressed against his stomach; he has an ulcer. Sutter found a photo camera in his room and asked him too to report at the *Kripo* tomorrow morning. The despondent man kept on repeating, "But I am a master tailor, Herr Sutter!" The fool wanted to be excused because of his great importance to the ghetto. The more he whined, the more cheerful Sutter became.

He ordered them to form a line, each with his bundle of clothes in his hand. The hosiery-maker's daughters were unable to unbutton their dresses in their confusion and fright. One of them yelled at Sutter that he should shoot her rather than make her undress. Sutter calmed her down, telling her that she had better undress if she wanted to see her father come back. He took the underwear of each woman and scrutinized it against the light, in case there were money bills sewn into it. When Rachel's turn arrived, she looked him in the face and asked, "*Sind Sie ein Mentsch?*" Sutter smiled at her kindly, paternally, and asked her in turn if she absolutely wanted him to take her along to the Red House. Her mother and the other women hung on to her, covered her mouth with their hands, imploring her to have pity on them and not bring about a tragedy with her talking.

"I had to tell you this," she said as if she were apologizing. She looked at me. I knew she expected me to say something. Cursed creature that I am, I did not know what to say. I only felt that if I saw Sutter at that moment, I would scratch his eyes out. Whether I really would do so is another question. The coward in me would probably lame my hands. I let Rachel go home. I wanted to be alone as soon as possible.

What is happening between Rachel and myself puzzles me. Has one of us changed? Who? I am sure that I love her; a certainty which I have no need to analyze. However, there are only rare moments when a veil does not hang between us, cleaving us asunder. Even when we are close, it is not the same as it used to be. It is more powerful, but also more undefined. And it is so short-lived and happens so rarely.

Chapter Six

THE GHETTO HAD the appearance of a miniature town. Although it was divided into three parts, each part separately enclosed with a fence of barbed wires — thus leaving outside the major arteries which united Lodz with the rest of the world — the ghetto, thanks to the gates which led from one part into the other, presented an entity. Its major streets, located in the largest enclosed section, linked the two central squares which lay in that part of the ghetto as well: Baluter Ring and Church Place. There was still a third square, the bazaar, but it was located in one of the smaller sections of the ghetto, near Hockel Street. Although it was the centre of the black market, the bazaar was often empty.

An important role was played by the two main squares. Baluter Ring, separated from the rest of the ghetto by an enclosure of barbed wire of its own, was the headquarters of the ghetto management, the *Gettoverwaltung*, headed by Herr Hans Biebow. Also the highest Jewish officials led by Presess Rumkowski had their offices there. Through the gate of Baluter Ring, food supplies and everything "imported" from the city had to pass and undergo the required inspection before being admitted into the ghetto. Here also was the delousing and disinfection station, for all those who, due to their positions or functions, circulated between the town and the ghetto. The inspection of all the merchandise and manufactured articles, which began to leave the ghetto as a contribution to the German economy and to the pocket of Herr Hans Biebow, also took place here.

Church Place was the square around the Church of the Holiest Virgin Mary which had been included within the ghetto. This was the most historic corner of the ghetto and an air of distinction and beauty hovered over it. It had what could be called atmosphere.

The Place was, of course, dominated by the red brick church. Massive and majestic, its towers and steeples rose above the entire ghetto. Across from it, in a luscious garden, stood the monastery and parsonage. Before the war the monks would wander about here on the carpets of grass, reciting their prayers and meditating on Jesus and his love of humanity. Now, both the monastery and the parsonage were occupied by the *Kripo*, a department of the *Kriminalpolizei*. The construction of the building, its division into upper chambers which were spacious and comfortable and narrow lower cells, did not require any particular adjustments in order to serve the purpose of the *Kripo*. The investigation offices and the torture chambers were located on the upper floors, the prison cells, in the basement. In this sacred locum certain selected Jews of the ghetto were invited to confess — under the influence of whippings or of more modern means of torture — where they had hidden their dollars, their diamonds, their merchandise or furs. Those amongst them who had no treasures to speak of, hidden either in town or in the ghetto, or had already "eaten up" what they had kept hidden, paid for their sins with broken bones, cracked ribs, disjointed limbs, or simply with their lives. Jews were forbidden to walk the street in front of the *Kripo* or the Red House, as the ghetto Jews called it, or along the garden fence. This was the only stretch of free space in Church Place which otherwise teemed with people. The houses around the Place harboured many institutions as well as the *Einkaufstelle* where the Jews "voluntarily" traded in their fur coats or other objects of value, in exchange for a sum of paper bills, the ghetto money, called *rumkis*. Also the gate leading to the smaller part of the ghetto was strategically located here.

In Church Place the central streets of the ghetto originated. They were made of cobblestones, intersected by shiny streetcar rails which lay unused. A great many stone buildings stood here, still displaying their pre-war signs above the stores which now served as dwellings. In these streets, vendors of all kinds were clustered against the walls. Further up, these central streets, cut through by countless little sidestreets, grew narrower. The sidestreets were either partly paved with crooked cobblestones, or not paved at all; the sidewalks were barely broad enough to allow two people to pass simultaneously. The houses here were wooden and old, covered with mildew, tightly squeezed together, as if to give each other suport so that they would not collapse. The colour of all these huts was a mouldy green and a brownish gray, here and there covered with black patches of rotten wood. Nor were the single steps leading into these huts straight, but rather they were partly chopped off, worn smooth by the shoes which had stepped over them for so many years. The shutters over the windows hung askew, on loose hinges. The windows were small, divided into quarters; here and there a missing pane was replaced by a dark piece of rag. This increased the resemblance of these huts to half-blind hunched-up old men.

These narrow sidestreets of the ghetto reminded one of a poor Jewish *shtetl*, without the *shtetl's* charm, or its pastoral beauty. In the poor *shtetl*, the expanse of a clear sky, the fragrance of the air coming from the neighbouring forests and fields would hover over the rotting roofs. There, the mildewy dwellings were surrounded by the bounty of trees, of fields and of flowers. Here, in the ghetto streets of Baluty, there were no trees growing; here and there only a few stubborn blades of grass would succeed in springing up between the crooked cobblestones, or in sprouting out of the ground near the rubbed-out stone steps.

The backyards behind these huts were sandy and dusty. In their middle, there stood a water pump, either with a long handle or a crank, while in a corner stood the whitewashed latrines, their framework, for decorative purposes, painted black. Nearby were the huge communal garbage boxes, the marketplaces of the rats and mice. The fences which had divided one backyard from another had been disassembled right at the beginning of the ghetto, by some lucky neighbours who used them as firewood. The result of this was the formation of one common backyard for all the huts on each side of each street. This was quite convenient for the inhabitants of the little streets, because many water pumps refused to work, and the lack of fences made it easier to carry pails of water from the good pumps to one's home. The main advantage was, however, that people could spend many hours after curfew here. Here they would sit, chatting or studying the Scriptures. Here they exchanged bits of news, or heard "ducks" hatched in people's minds, or they speculated about the date of the German defeat. Here they learned the recipes for new dishes, what dish could be concocted out of the Ersatz coffee, how to make a compote of radishes, a soup of parsley leaves, or cutlets out of beet leaves. Here from morning until night youngsters played ragball, ghetto police, or war. And here, they could follow the clouds with their eyes and see the birds flying by, gliding from the town to the fields — from freedom to freedom.

The ghetto resembled a town in miniature even more when a suburb was added to it. The suburb was called Marysin. It lay on the border of Lodz, so that this part of the barbed wire fence surrounding the ghetto stood in the middle of a field. The fence looked casual, as if it were dividing one pasture from another. Even the green uniforms of the gendarmes pacing in front of the fence resembled patches of field in motion; the guns over their shoulders seemed like brown boughs, particularly when seen from a distance.

Although the houses in Marysin were also made of wood, they had no resemblance to the shabby old huts of Baluty. They rather looked like solid country houses. They stood apart from each other, surrounded by little gardens. There were flowers and even a few clusters of needle trees. The air was delicious and whoever happened to wander into this region might well believe that the ghetto with its clamour and smells lay some thousands of miles away, or was perhaps a bad dream altogether.

As soon as Marysin was included into the ghetto, Presess Rumkowski came over to take a walk through its paths. The houses, recently cleared of their Polish inhabitants, stared at him with their shiny window panes, as if they were still full of life. He peered into the little gardens as he tickled his nose with a bough of withered lilacs. The lilac reminded him of the garden at his orphanage in Helenovek and his heart contracted with sadness. He knew that the surrounding silence would soon be banished by the hullabaloo of the ghetto, that the fences would be taken apart, the flower beds trampled, that garbage and dirt would lie scattered under one's feet.

Then he had his great vision: Marysin would become a paradise for the children, the orphans. Here he would settle them, build schools and hospitals for them. Here they would live and grow. The Presess was suddenly overcome by a powerful longing for his youngsters. Yes, it had once seemed to him that leading a people would come to him as easily as leading an orphanage. How wrong he had been! Only children could be grateful for what was done for them, only they were honest and sincere. Adults were false and mean, always expecting additional benefits. Therefore he, Mordechai Chaim Rumkowski, would create a refuge from the grown-up horde. The chidren's colony would become his pride and his solace.

The moment this extraordinary idea flashed through his mind, he no longer had the patience to waste his time dawdling in Marysin. He ordered the coachman to take him back to the ghetto, and immediately he invited his devoted advisor, shrewd minute Mr. Zibert, the Zionist activist, to supper. Basically, he could not bear Mr. Zibert, but he liked to test every new idea against the latter's sharp mind, especially when he was in a hurry. And Mr. Zibert liked this idea, he even became enthusiastic about it. So it happened that during the supper meal the plan expanded, becoming even more beautiful than at the moment of its conception.

Since Mr. Rumkowski's projects always bore the mark of his impatience; and since the crafty Mr. Zibert, who matched Rumkowski as far as determination and energy were concerned, had on his part a particular interest in the project — Marysin was very soon populated with children and youths. First, the three thousand orphans were settled there, then the colonies and schools for the other children were organized. Apart from that, the enthusiastic Mr. Zibert founded exemplary *Hachsharot* there, preparatory farms where Zionist youths trained to become useful members of the *kibbutzim* in distant Eretz Israel, where they hoped to emigrate one day in the very near future.

Thus the beauty of Marysin remained not only intact, but was actually enhanced. To the songs of the birds was added the laughter of children.

◆ ◆ ◆

The *gymnasium* of the ghetto was also located in Marysin. It occupied the only brick house in the district, but since the structure could not accommodate all the students, the higher grades were settled in the surrounding houses, amidst a tiny "forest" of needle trees.

Rachel enjoyed her walk to school. Hockel Street was still steeped in silence. A few sleepy street vendors stood against the walls lazily enumerating their wares, there were as yet no buyers. A few Jews hurried to the prayer houses, a few office workers to their offices, now and then a man with a canteen in his hand would pass by, and the rest were all school children. The church was still wrapped in a shawl of nightly shadows around its belly, only its head of towers was bathing in the sunlight. The crows inhabiting the turrets and eaves had already begun their workaday search for food, crowing gaily, as they communicated with each other and with the depth of the sky. Nearby, a few men were already working away at the construction of the bridge near the barbed-wire fence. This bridge was to replace the gate and serve as a passageway from one part of the ghetto into the other.

Rachel chose the most out-of-the-way sidestreets. More than ever she needed the solitude of her morning walk. It was her only opportunity to be alone, to find a kind of accompanying motif within herself. Even if this motif were not joyful, it nevertheless deepened her sense of being alive, allowing her to get in touch with her thoughts and reveries, to discern every nuance of her own moods, every shade of her own emotions.

The windows of the classroom stood wide open. The air outside had already begun to warm up and the needle trees stood motionless as if painted onto the sky. The net of their boughs allowed the sun's rays to sift through and paint streaks of gold on top of the benches. At the front of the room stood Mrs. Feiner, the directress of the *gymnasium*. Her specialties were mathematics and physics, but today she was replacing the teacher of German, Mrs. Braude, who had been taken ill with dysentery. Mrs. Feiner started her lesson with one dry laconic sentence. "My dear girls," she said, "the German people have trampled their only great treasure. Let this be their loss, not ours." She picked up the book that lay before her and swiftly flipped through its pages. Then, proudly raising her grayish head, she announced, "*An die Freude*", by Friedrich von Schiller."

A commotion started up in the classroom. A girl in the back of the room began to hum the tune of the Ninth Symphony and was joined by other girls accompanying themselves with their pencils. Mrs. Feiner listened to the singing and smiled wisely. At length, she raised her hand to quiet the class. She took the comb out of her hair, combed it energetically and straightened up. With controlled pathos, she read the poem slowly, powerfully, letting each word take shape on her lips before uttering it:

> "Freude, schöner Gotterfunke,
> Tochter aus Elisium,
> Wir betreten feuertrunkend,
> Himlische dein Heiligtum."

Rachel sat at her desk stiff and aloof. She had decided to treat the German lessons with the utmost indifference. She did not listen to Mrs. Feiner reciting the first stanza; she looked through the window and noticed a little bird with a yellow belly swinging on a tree.

> "Your magic binds again,
> What fashion has strictly divided,
> All people become brothers
> Wherever your soft wing flutters."

Something began familiarly to drum against Rachel's ear. "All people are brothers!" The slogan of her party, the dream of her comrades? The symbol of her wishes? Had someone been mocking her, or her friends, or proud Mrs. Feiner herself? These words, uttered in this room, in the ghetto, in this language, sounded brutally false, eerie. A heavy pounding against distant doors resounded in her ears, "*Raus! Alle Juden raus!*" She heard the stamping of boots against the pavements, and another piece of poetry: "*Wenn Judenblut vom Messer spritzt.*" The same rhythm, the same number of syllables, the same language that cracked like a whip, that was ground between teeth, that roared with the laughter of the Devil.

> "Be embraced, ye millions,
> This kiss for the entire world!
> Brethren, above this starry tent,
> A kind Father must be dwelling!"

Instead of hearing, "Be embraced, ye millions, this kiss for the entire world!" Rachel heard, "Be effaced, ye millions, a death kiss for the entire world!" Then she thought about the "*Sternenzelt*", the starry canopy. Had not the Germans "evacuated" the kind Father from His "tent", emptying the skies of any God, of any ideal? All this sounded so outrageously funny, that she had to cover her mouth with her hand, so as not to explode into cynical laughter, or scream out with anger.

Outside the window, the bird was still swinging on the bough, against a white patch of sky. It resembled the white of an eye with the bird as its pupil, peering into the room. Rachel was overcome by a powerful wish that there should be someone who could see, could listen in from outside, from far beyond, and provide a comment. But she knew that the eye was an eye which could not see, that out there was only a void which could not listen. There was no one who, looking in from the outside, would provide an explanation. Abruptly, she turned her head towards the teacher. She wanted to see the expression on her face, to know what Mrs. Feiner herself felt while reciting the poem. Perhaps she had chosen to read it in order to underline the irony?

The teacher was not looking at the class, nor into the book. Her gaze hung above the girls' heads as if she were staring into a boundless distance. Her face was motionless, only her lips moved, like lips in devout prayer, the lips of a woman in love. Rachel had never seen such an expression on the face of down-to-earth, matter-of-fact Mrs. Feiner. It was through this face that Rachel, in spite of herself, suddenly became caught up by the melodiousness, the rhythms, the words of Schiller's poem. The other rhythm was gone, gone also was the other language. There was no language, no words at all. There had once lived a man whose heart so overflowed with compassion for humanity, with the passion of love, that its flames reached up to here, to this room, leaving Mrs. Feiner's lips not in the form of words, or music, but as something which was beyond both.

In her mind's eye Rachel saw the cherry tree bursting into bloom in the backyard on Hockel Street. Mrs. Feiner was like the cherry tree; she flowered amidst the dirt and muck, blooming with a white untarnished love. Rachel's heart expanded, overflowed with tenderness. A dazzling thought struck her mind: here, in the ghetto, there was only one way to set oneself free and thus escape annihilation: Love. No, not the soft submissive and forgiving love, but a strong, healthy and wise love, like Mrs. Feiner's. Rachel wished she were as strong as the cherry tree, as Mrs. Feiner . . .

She looked around and noticed Bella Zuckerman who sat leaning forward, her head resting on her arms. Bella's homely face with the irregular features was contorted into a grimace of pain.

> "Yes, whoever could call one other soul
> his own, on the round of this earth . . .
> But he who could not, let him steal himself,
> weeping, out from this bond."

Two tears began slowly to roll down Bella's cheeks, dripping onto the black top of the bench where they were transformed into two tiny crystals, in which the light of the day searched for its own reflection. The moment was too complete, too dazzling. The bird with the yellow chest was still swaying outside, on the bough. Now it seemed to Rachel, that the patch of blue revealed by the bird, was a blue tray upon which the heavens were serving her a treat of joy.

It seemed that the teachers had taken it upon themselves that day to fill their students' hearts with hope. Miss Diamand who took over the course of the Polish language and world literature decided here, in the *gymnasium* of Marysin, to discard Shakespeare with whom she had so determinedly begun the school year in town, and to regress a number of centuries. She declared to the class that the ghetto was the most appropriate place for the study of Greek Tragedy. "Because Greek Tragedy," she said in her pearly voice, "deals with the basic passions of man; man stripped of all the inessentials, as he stands facing Fate. Here it will perhaps be easier for us to grasp such a reality. For here, in the ghetto, my children, man, his soul stripped naked, will in the end remain to face his basic passions: love, hate, hunger and the will to live. Here man will emerge from his shell, as he is, without embellishment. Here he will stand against the forces which are out to destroy him, against the *Moiras* over which he has no power — he will stand majestic and small, pitiful and heroic."

"Yes, and here too a *deus ex machina* will arrive!" A girl called out sarcastically from her seat, cutting off the rustling flow of the teacher's words. "The Nazis will solve our problems with Fate!"

The teacher, her mouth still open, stood there like a bird suddenly faced by a devouring beast, but she pulled herself together and energetically shook her head. "Let's leave the Nazis to themselves, children. They have nothing to do with our subject. And do you know why? Because they have no say over our inner life."

"That's not so!" Rosa, a girl with an open round face and clear eyes, who usually set the tone for the class, exclaimed. "Take me, for instance, Miss Diamand. My parents were taken away during the raid. Do you think that this has nothing to do with my inner life?"

Miss Diamand's voice took on an imploring tone, "Let's get on with our work, children".

She had not changed much in appearance. The same old dress, resembling a Greek tunic, hung loosely on her fragile body; the mauve shawl was draped around her neck. Her sparse gray hair, fluffy like eiderdown, was gathered at the nape of her neck with a few black pins. Her childishly innocent gray-blue eyes blinked, often filling with tears.

She chose to begin the course with "Prometheus Bound" by Aeschylus. Now she held the book with one hand and pointed the other at the class like a conductor ready to begin her concert. She often interrupted her reading, commenting, asking questions, quoting. It seemed that she had completely forgotten Rosa's remark, but her eyes were fixed precisely on her, on the student who had raised this disquieting question, as if pleading with her to find the answer between the lines that she, Miss Diamand, was reciting. For homework she asked the girls to write a composition entitled, "Prometheus in the ghetto".

During recess the girls poured out into the yard. Their dresses with the Stars of David fluttered colourfully between the trees. From the other wooden houses, there exited a crowd of male students, and from the brick building, came the youngsters of the lower grades with their teachers. Mrs. Feiner appeared on the front stairs, and the students gathered around her as she called them to assemble. She made a tube of her hands, and through it announced in a cheerful voice that the students would receive soup at school every day, and that they should provide themselves with fifteen pfennigs and a canteen.

An air of gaiety swept through the yard. The young people spread out over the green grounds, filling every corner, every path with their boisterous laughter and shouts of excitement. They seemed to race along with the shadows after the gold of the sun, after the breath of the breeze. The earth, mossy and luscious, seemed to spread under their feet like a mattress or a trampoline, lifting them up in the air with every leap. The sky rocked before their eyes like a huge bell with the yellow ball, the sun, in its middle. The world was an airy inflated balloon. It seemed that it was not carrying the children within it, but rather that the children were carrying it on the tips of their fingers, bouncing it lightly, back and forth, between themselves.

Among this merrily bustling crowd of young people, Miss Diamand walked about, her arms spread wide, as if she herself were entangled in the dance of the young feet. Here she tried to catch one youngster, there another. But they swept her by, brushing against her shoulder, almost tipping her over; they neither saw nor heard her. And so her feet, in the black shoes with the loosely tied shoelaces, took tiny steps around and around. A smile played on her lips. Her watery eyes appeared more bewildered than ever. They were full of wonder, enchanted with the beauty they beheld. A girl lost her white scarf. Miss Diamand, supporting her hip with one hand, bent down to pick it up. She ran after the distraught girl, calling her and waving at her from the distance with the scarf, but in vain. Then another girl, her braids undone, passed her by. Miss Diamand grabbed her by the hand, and began to braid the brown tresses. Before she had managed to tie the ribbons into a bow, the girl was gone. So the ribbons and the scarf became an accessory to her own dance as she circled the yard.

At length she began to walk amongst the teachers who were watching the youngsters. She struck up a conversation with them, although she knew that no one was listening to her. She had long been outside the circle of interest of these young men with gray hair and shiny pates, of these young women with waterbags under their eyes and with wrinkled foreheads. In this respect nothing had changed. She was old, she was alone, she was an outsider. She did not mind that they were not listening to her, just nodding at her as they stared over her shoulder into the distance, as if she were thin air. She continued with her chatter and stopped only when she herself realized that the conversation was over. Then she went back to rejoin the children. Now she was even more aware that it was to them that she was related, aware that as long as she was amongst them, she would stay alive.

Rachel and Bella Zuckerman were strolling arm in arm, away from the clamour in the yard. When they reached the other side of the school grounds and emerged on the sandy road leading to the *Hachsharot*, the preparatory *kibbutzim*, Rachel asked Bella, "Why did you cry when she recited Schiller?"

Bella's face flushed. She broke off a twig from a tree, chewed on it, then answered in a whisper, "She made me miss my piano . . ."

Rachel squeezed her arm. "A good sign. I'm missing something too . . . I never played the piano, but it seems to me that today, if I sat down at one, I could play." She elbowed Bella cheerfully, "It seemed we might go stale here, didn't it? Now, I think . . . Something is budding inside me that has nothing to do with the body, with bread or with any conveniences. Perhaps Miss Diamand is right?"

Bella remained serious, "I need the keyboard. A craving . . . It almost hurts."

"Yes, a kind of hurt . . . of joy. A sort of painful enthusiasm. Perhaps it is because of the summer, or because we are young, but who needs to look for reasons?" Rachel too broke off a twig from a tree and brushed it against Bella's nose, "Inhale, resin . . ." She added jokingly, "A lover will soon take the place of the piano in your heart. You'll play Chopin etudes on him."

"Don't laugh at me." Bella seemed even more disturbed.

"I'm not. I am laughing to you."

"Let me be. With someone who looks like me, they should do what they did in Sparta. Ugly women should be thrown off a cliff, as they used to do there with the old and crippled."

"There are no ugly women!"

"Is that so? And how many women are never noticed? People open up their hearts easily at the sight of a petty girl. They smile at her, they're always ready to accommodate her. They pay homage to her for her beauty as if it were her personal merit. And not only men behave that way, women do too."

Rachel refused to succumb to Bella's gloom. "You see, it never occurs to me to think about all that. And look at the beauty that I am!"

"If you are not forced to think about it, then you are a beauty."

"You are beautiful, Bella. Your soul is . . ."

"Even if that were so, people would not see it. They see the nose, the face."

"And I am telling you that the man who deserves you will recognize your beauty."

"There won't be such a man, certainly not the one for whom I care. He does not belong to those who discover Sleeping Beauty in the Ugly Duckling."

"But it is good to be in love . . ." Rachel remarked, becoming serious and somewhat unsure of herself.

"Not always."

"Not always, and yet . . ."

They became silent, watching their shoes shove away the gravel on the road. Bella spoke up, "Sometimes I think of joining an organization. It's becoming difficult to live only with books. In an organization all these things probably don't matter much."

This remark kindled the spark of the propagandist in Rachel. Perhaps it would not be so difficult to win Bella to her ideal, after all. But she was unable to find the right words. On the contrary, her words undid her purpose. She said, "Sometimes I think of what the organization means to me. It is a feeling which satisfies me only superficially, I would say, physically; it is like having an extended family. But very often I do feel better when I am alone." She laughed. "I am awfully complicated, Bella. I don't really know what I want, to be with the group, or to stay away from it. They, the group, have such a healthy optimism. They think in a straight line, without becoming confused from seeing everything from a thousand points of view. And they are devoted to the ideal and to one another. It comes to them naturally. I am not like that, not at all. I don't know, perhaps socialism means something else to them than it means to me." She eyed Bella from the side. "Does this word still scare you? What do you think now about socialism?"

Bella spread her arms, "I don't think about it".

"What do you think about?"

"About myself. Yes, sometimes I think about Palestine. It would be nice to have a country of our own, to be free from hatred. I imagine Jewish towns and villages . . . streets with the names of Jewish heroes. But in general I still feel that the crowd in our backyard, let's say, belongs to another world, and this is not only a physical estrangement . . ."

"But you dream of a Jewish state!" Rachel called out with a note of irony in her voice. "This is your first feeling of being part of a community at large. Bravo!" She pressed Bella's arm affectionately. "You see, in the ghetto, we may allow ourselves . . . If we wish for something, then let it be for the highest, the all-embracing . . . for the well-being of the entire world . . . the vision of Isaiah. That's why it is not enough to be a Zionist. If we dream, let us dream the most beautiful dream . . ."

A group of young people approached them, running noisily from the direction of the *Hachsharot*. "Junia!" Bella pointed to a girl who was racing towards them with a bouquet of acacia flowers in her hand.

Junia fell into Bella's arms and burst out, "They've accepted us into the *Hachshara*, all of us! If you want, you can register too, and you too, Rachel! Come, I'll go back with you!"

A youth clasped Junia's hand and admonished her earnestly, "They have to arrive at such a decision on their own, otherwise it doesn't make sense."

They walked home from school together, a big noisy bunch of students, Junia barely able to step normally. Impatient and excited, she plucked the petals from her bouquet, roguishly ogling the young man at her side. "He loves me . . . He loves me not . . ." The bouquet fell from her hand, petal by petal, flower by flower. The rest of the group was just as excited as she. The tails of their jackets, the skirts of their dresses fluttered animatedly in the air, as if they were participating in the heated discussions of those who wore them.

As they reached the crowded streets, they suddenly noticed that the people were moving faster than usual, that the entire teeming street was in a hurry, excited and impatient as if it were filled only with school children. People were laughing, pumping each other's hands, exchanging shouts across the sidewalks. At first, it seemed natural. Were they, the bunch of *gymnasium* students themselves, not carefree and gay today? But then they noticed the same commotion at every step, people embracing, wiping their eyes, heaping good wishes on each other's heads and talking with a stammer as if choking with joy. It became obvious that something had happened, something unbelievably important. Junia stopped a boy who was waving his hand at everybody.

"We're getting out of the ghetto!" the boy yelled.

A group of people stood talking in a knot. "We are going over to the Russians!" someone said. And so the further the students moved on, the clearer the situation became, although it was still far from being clear. The gist of it was that the Germans had signed an agreement with the Russians about restoring the borders of 1914.

In the backyard on Hockel Street there was quite a to-do. The air boiled like a kettle, bubbling with talk. Rachel noticed her parents and Shlamek standing in a knot of neighbours; Moshe's eyes were misty. Someone embraced her from behind. She found herself in David's arms. They kissed. Then they all poured out into the street, eager for news. Their arms linked, they ploughed ahead. Little Abraham stopped every single passer-by, calling out, "The borders of 1914!" Through the barbed-wire fence, near Church Place, the stupefied gendarmes peered in, as they watched the ghetto go insane.

That evening no one thought of food or of sleep. After curfew, people moved from the streets into the backyards. In some windows red pennants or red pieces of rag appeared. Here and there revolutionary songs were heard. Valentino and his wife, who had an illegal shop, came out with a bag of candies into the yard, and distributed them free of charge. The crank of the water pump squeaked incessantly. The people had become thirsty from their great exultation and excitement.

The following day the continuous shooting into the ghetto through the wire fence began. People predicted even worse decrees than those of the past, because the ghetto inhabitants had disregarded the curfew laws, had blacked out their windows negligently, and worst of all, they displayed red flags in their windows. No one was able to tell whether the "duck", which had hatched in people's minds the day before, had been a provocation, or just a news item issued by the ghetto station IWIT, the initials of "I Wish It Were True".

Chapter Seven

Dr. Michal Levine,
Ghetto Hospital,
July . . . 1940.

My Dear Mirage:

I have not written to you for a long time. My pen is full of ink, but my well of words dries out from time to time.

I want to ask you a foolish question: should we let the people stuff their stomachs with the strange grains of I don't know what, and with the rotten vegetables which wreck their digestive systems, or should we forbid them to eat this garbage, and ask them to starve? The question is only theoretical, since they would not obey me anyway. A hungry stomach must be filled. Anyway, in this manner we have more vitamins. Why is it that when eating the same kind of grains, some people become sick and others not?

About me personally you should not worry. As Mother would say, "I wish it on all the children of Israel." I receive good food rations. I belong to the privileged. I wear a black cap with a red brim and a band with a red cross around my arm. People look at me with awe, they step aside to let me pass and follow me with their eyes. I wonder whether they admire me for my fat face or my lame foot. Since arriving in the ghetto, I have delivered seventeen babies.

I have become close to a woman. After the accepted laws of morality I am deceiving you. It is twenty-five months and an eternity since I made love to you last. Have I waited too long, have I done it too soon? Why am I still writing to you? My answer is, that you have become both less and more important to me than you were before. In the image in which I see you, I love you with a love which no one can destroy. It will be your choice to accept it or reject it — if I still live to see the day of your judgment.

She is a "nurse". I write it in quotes, because she is just as much a nurse as I am a dancer. She was looking for work, so it occurred to her that since there is a need for nurses in the ghetto, she would register as such. And since she had to choose her specialty, she chose midwifery. She felt closer to this branch of medicine because she had recently given birth.

The first day when I watched her at work, I unloaded all the bitterness in my heart on her head. Afterwards she caught up with me in the street, and begged me to have pity on her and not squeal on her. So I had pity on her and let her drag me up to her room. There, I listened to her story, from the day she was born, up to when her baby girl was born. Her husband is one of the smart alecs. He managed quite well here, buying hams from the farmers who entered the ghetto. She — Nadia is her name — would cook the hams and sell them. Then he somehow got hold of an entire transport of English materials. He removed

87

the floor of their apartment and hid the treasure beneath it. But of the money they both earned he gave her barely enough to buy bread. When it was time for her to go to the hospital — this was before they closed the ghetto — our smart alec took whatever he could with him and vanished. She came home with the newborn baby, all alone. "If I need money," she told me, "I sell a few metres of material and have enough to live on for a time."

"Then why do you have to work?" I asked her.

She stared at me with the eyes of a beaten animal. "Do I take it away from anyone? Aren't they looking for nurses? That way I can get a bit of fresh milk. What will I do if I'm not able to nurse the baby?" Do you want to know what made me stay with her? There is something in her helplessness that attracts me. I don't even know whether she is pretty. But her eyes follow me, submissive, frightened eyes that beg, "Don't leave me alone." Her baby, no more than ten weeks old, has the features of an old man. When you watch the smile of such a baby, kindness begins to grow within you. There is no hair on its head yet, and its bare skull and the pulsations you feel when touching the still soft fontanel give you the impression that you have touched human frailty itself with your fingers.

Do you know when I think of you most? Precisely when I lie in bed beside Nadia. I try to imagine how our life together would have shaped up, how our children would have looked. Sometimes I imagine that it is you lying at my side, that the baby making its first sounds is the new being that is both you and me. As you can see, I am deceiving not only you, but Nadia as well. But if you think that my conscience bothers me, you are wrong. I have found a peaceful corner; perhaps an abnormal peace, an awkward dishonest one — yet I cherish it because it gives me strength for my work, if you want, for my calling. It sounds exaggerated? Life in the ghetto is full of exaggerations, yet this does not prevent them from being true.

I work about fourteen/fifteen hours a day. Our health department is on quite a high level, fine practitioners, first class specialists. For the time being there is no lack of medicines — nor is there a lack of patients. Besides the normal ghetto disease, tuberculosis, we have a seasonal disease, dysentery, in full bloom at the present. I see about thirty, thirty-five patients a day. I should figure out one day how many stairs my lame foot has to climb up and down daily, so that you could have the right idea about my work.

I am a rare visitor at home, but Mother does not worry about me as long as I have my puffed cheeks and a good appetite. Her two adopted sons, Guttman and Shafran, are still devoted to her. Shafran works at the orphanage in Marysin. Guttman does nothing, officially that is. All day long he scours the streets in search of food and in the evenings he paints. He has come back to it. He set up his atelier in a corner of the kitchen and there he spends half of his nights at if possessed by a *dybbuk*. Before he finishes one painting, he is already at another. Some other time, he says, he will finish them, now he has to grab his inspiration by the hair. Sometimes he brings a model up to the room: a boy from the backyard, a street vendor or an old Jew. Lately he began a portrait of our neighbour, Mrs. Matilda Zuckerman, in whose home I met him at a New Year's ball, once, many centuries ago. Sometimes he grabs his palette and the paint box and dashes out of the room, returning with a partly completed painting of the church, or with the sketch of a funeral. For Presess Rumkowski he has already painted three portraits. These, he says, are garbage; he does them, he says, only to earn a living. One of these portraits represents the Presess, full length, surrounded by a forest of children.

The three of us have unwound our tongues at last. Often we sit through the night, talking. It both tires me out and fortifies me. Most frequently I quarrel with Guttman, while Shafran acts as the peace maker. For instance, I told them that those who are hopelessly ill will soon have to be left to die. You should have seen Guttman explode! He told me that this is not in accordance with Jewish ethics, nor with human ethics. I conceded that this is against medical ethics as well, but that in the ghetto we must surrender to different laws and different ethics. Now, that we are hermetically enclosed, we will soon run out of medical supplies. So whom should we help then, those who can still recover, or those whom the drugs will not help anyway? May it never come to such a situation. Apropos, I have noticed that in the homes that I visit, there is a tendency on the part of the family members to give away their entire rations of sugar, butter, or meat to the hopelessly ill, and as a result the rest of them fall ill. All right, in the homes this is a private problem; no one has the right to tell people what to do with their food. But a hospital cannot allow itself to be guided by sentiment.

Do you realize how cold and logical I have become, Mira? I, your romantic Michal? My profession keeps me close to bare reality and every spark of romanticism that medicine held for me has evaporated. Even delivering babies does not give me the same feeling as it used to. On the contrary. I consider it a crime to bring children into the ghetto-world. Here, every birth celebrates not life, but death — and not the easiest kind of death. When I see Nadia's little girl, guilt burns me, although it is not I who gave her life.

Here is an episode that happened a few days ago. It was daytime. A suffocating heat. Everything seemed about to melt from the fire coming down from the sky. The people with sweaty faces, hazy eyes and bare wet necks barely moved in the streets. I was dragging myself from one patient to another, conquering the many steps in the suffocating houses like a mountain climber conquers the Everest. I was personally grateful to those patients who happened to live downstairs. On my entering an apartment, I was attacked by heat permeated by the sharp smells of sweat and urine. On the messy beds lay the sick, looking like raw chunks of meat — powerless, half naked. Barefoot women sluggishly attended them and the children crawling on the dirty floors. But where it was the woman who was sick there was a kind of restlessness, a panic in the air; the children were noisier and the men more agile in their despair. This supports my opinion that in the ghetto the home depends much more on the woman than it once did. Without the woman the man in the ghetto is doomed to disintegrate; and only the man who learns the woman's self-discipline, her home-discipline and orderliness will be able to bear the life here.

Here and there I asked for a drink of cold water, which would immediately evaporate with the sweat of my body. I would have gladly walked around without the jacket, but I had no Star of David sewn on to my shirt. Everything within me longed to stretch out in a cool cellar somewhere, on a stone floor, and shut my eyes. Finally, I could take it no longer. Although I still had to see one more patient, I decided to drop off for a moment at Nadia's apartment. I wanted to see her baby. Like a wanderer through a desert, who in spite of exhaustion musters all his energy at the sight of an oasis looming in the distance, I accelerated my steps. It seemed to me that a mere glance at the little creature would refresh me more than all the glasses of water.

I had forgotten that Nadia was at work. I knew that she usually left the baby with a neighbour, but which? Then I heard a kind of bleating and realized that it was the little creature I wanted to see, crying. I rushed up the stairs to the top floor. The next moment I stood in front of a large wooden bed where the naked baby girl lay on a diaper, whining, the tremulous little fists against its mouth, from which the nipple of a bottle of sugar water had slipped out. I rearranged it properly. The crying stopped. I felt light. A fresh breeze fanned my back.

Now I looked around the large bright room. To my astonishment, the walls were covered with paintings. "You are Dr. Levine, aren't you?" I heard the owner of the apartment ask. I noticed a quaint-looking crooked frame of a man with a huge hump on his back. Above the hump, as if supported by it — a large head, with an enormous forehead fringed by a black artistically-long mane of hair in a "Polka" cut. The face was dominated by a pointy nose that cast a shadow both on his hollow cheeks and his shapeless mouth. His sharp hot gaze restlessly jumped over me, uncertainly, but with curiosity. We shook hands. I felt the unpleasant touch of his cold wet fingers. "Nadia told me about you . . ." he said, then noticed the paint splotches he had left on my hand with the handshake. "Oh, forgive me," he grinned, rubbing a corner of his artist's cape against my fingers. "I am in the middle of something." He pointed the tip of his nose in the direction of the window. There stood an easel, and on it, a canvas with the unfinished outlines of a boy's face, surrounded by multicoloured patches of paint. Only the eyes in the face seemed completely finished. They stared at me with both a deep earnestness and a childlike charming shyness. I approached the painting; the little man hurried ahead of me. "This boy has been intriguing me for quite a while now." He guided his finger over the surface of the canvas. "A genius. Fifteen years old. A second Einstein. The greatest professors of mathematics have tested him. Usually I paint him downstairs, near the dried-out water pump. That was where I noticed him for the first time. The way he was sitting, the inclination of his head, the expression of his eyes, looking into a book and at the same time beyond its pages, the shape of his body, the shape of the water pump and its wheel . . . Do you understand? A fantastic harmony in the dissonance."

I looked out through the window. Before my eyes there rose another fantastic sight. I saw the town outside the ghetto: the churches, the streets, the tramways, and nearby, the barbed wire fence, a snake striped with poles running past the very front of the house. I leaned out and saw a green uniform, the muzzle of a gun, a helmet. It occurred to me that the German soldier must be unbearably hot, dying for a drink of cold water. With even more delight I inhaled the air of the spacious room. I asked for a glass of cold water. I did not feel like leaving yet, wanting to rest at least for another few minutes. The little man caught the glance I cast at his old-fashioned padded armchair.

"Do sit down, please," he said with animation and handed me the glass of water.

I sat down. From the paintings on the walls faces stared at me, ghetto types, ghetto scenes. At the side, leaning against the wall, stood an enormous painting of Presess Rumkowski. It seemed as if the Old Man was soaring above the houses, above the landscape of the ghetto. I was surprised at how much this painting resembled Guttman's portraits of the Presess. When I had scrutinized the other paintings, however, I immediately realized the difference in his style of painting and that of Guttman. Guttman is more traditional, more realistic, more a story teller, a draughtsman, whereas the paintings on the wall in front of me had an air of restlessness, of search. They were more poetic, rather symbolic and they all seemed wrapped in a mist that blended form, colour and mood into one. Only here and there I noticed a sharp, screaming, almost painful line of colour. Some paintings seemed familiar to me, I did not know why.

"It looks funny, doesn't it?" he asked, his restless eyes following mine, "that I hung them all up like that? To whom could it occur before the war to cover the walls with his own paintings? But here . . . This way it is easier to keep oneself company."

"I live with a painter. Guttman." I said. "Do you know him? I'll give him your address."

"Don't bother. He has my address, but he won't come."

"Why are you so sure?"

I insisted that he tell me and he did. He blinked his small sharp eyes. "I don't make a secret of it. I fell ill last winter. It burns me out. You're a doctor, so you should know that the only thing that can save me is to eat well . . . and I must paint." He slumped onto the little sofa, seeming even more shrunken and hunched than he was before. His face turned gray, the sharp nose completely overshadowing his shapeless mouth. "I work for the *Kripo*. Don't get frightened. I'm not a stool pigeon. The Germans give me photos of their wives or sweethearts and I paint portraits of them. I don't harm anyone, and if I can smear on a face on a canvas for them, to save myself, then I do it. Do you understand, Doctor? I must live. I'm a good painter. They provide me with as much paint as I want, and with canvases too. I'm in their hands. But don't forget, I'm no different from those who work for them in the Resorts, and if you want to know, not different from you, Doctor. Because, let's not kid ourselves, by bringing a Jew back to health, you only fix a machine that works for the Germans." His eyes did not seek condemnation in mine, they sought approval. He was nervously combing his long mane with his fingers. "If my colleagues have abandoned me for that reason," he concluded, "then let them. I shall pay the price." He cut off his monologue and moved to the edge of the sofa, closer to me. "What could it be, Doctor, that I constantly run a high temperature? And I perspire. Pails of water pour down from me." I remembered that I still had a patient to visit and stood up. "I don't mean, heaven forbid, that you should examine me." He also jumped to his feet, blocking my way. "It was only a question. You don't have to answer me."

"Get undressed," I ordered, annoyed, apathetic.

Within a moment, his bare hunched back flashed before my eyes. I pressed my ear against it, then against his chest. His pulse was racing. I did not know whether out of nervousness, or because of his fever. Nor did I like his breathing. His pointed nose was already against my face; the glance of his veiny eyes nervously danced over me. I did not know what to tell him. "It isn't That, is it, Doctor?" He smiled crookedly, while slowly dressing. It seemed unnatural to me that his underwear was so clean.

"I'll come to see you again." I shook his hand. I stopped for a moment as I passed the bed where the baby slept, its fists relaxedly raised above its head. I envied it. At the door I turned to my host, "Your name is . . ."

"Winter, Vladimir Winter," he introduced himself. As I left him, I recalled having seen his paintings at exhibitions in Warsaw during my student years.

Now comes the second part of the episode.

I trudged down the stairs, feeling nothing, thinking about nothing. The heat and the sultriness of the yard smothered me. As I passed the gate, I took out the note with the addresses of my patients. The last one's address was not far from where I was. I recalled that upstairs, looking out through the window, I had seen the barbed-wire fence and the guard. It was precisely to that street running alongside the fence that I had to go. The streets near the fence have lately become dead and desolate because of the guards' frequent shooting at passers-by. I turned back. Surely there was a passage through the backyards through which one could reach the house I needed to go to, I thought. And indeed, I soon noticed such a passage in the distance. What a convenience people have created by tearing out a few boards, or by cutting out a hole in the walls dividing one yard from the other. It is better for the evening life, for avoiding crowded streets, or as a short cut and a safety precaution.

As I marched past the yard, the first thing I noticed was Vladimir Winter's young model. The backyard was hot and empty otherwise. It seemed that there was no life even in the apartments. But there he was sitting on the boards of the water pump, just as Winter had described him — bent over a book, beside the wheel of the dry well. Is he indeed a genius as Winter claims, I wondered. However, I was not curious enough to observe him from a closer range. I walked along the walls where there was some shade, and so proceeding, looking and not looking at the boy, I realized that there was something amiss with him. He was sitting half-naked, his narrow boyish shoulders raised, casting a shadow on the book and on his bare knees. He wore nothing but a pair of shorts; the sun shone directly on his shiny tanned back. It dawned on me: he wasn't wearing a Star of David. I had to smile to myself. I concocted an invention in my mind for the purpose of fastening the Stars of David to one's bare body. I was thinking of a special gummed paste sometimes used at the hospital. I weighed all the pros and cons in my mind, imagining myself walking about the streets half-naked, without having to wear the jacket or the sweaty shirt. What comfort!

I noticed the gendarme at his post. He was standing opposite the gate of the adjoining backyard, on the other side of the barbed wire fence. Again I pitied him, and recalled the boy sitting on the water pump only in his shorts. How much more comfortable he was! I began to think about how much the gendarme's helmet must weigh, about how much sweat he was collecting inside it. I thought of the gun weighing down his shoulder. I even thought of his boots, comparing them to my light sandals. I almost felt guilty that he had to stand there because of us. And as I kept watching him from the distance, his green uniform looking as if it were sliced up by the rows of barbed wire — it seemed to me for a moment, that it was he who was the captive, the one who was fenced in, peering in our direction, where freedom was. His green helmet sparkled before my eyes, reflecting the sun's rays. Now I was so close to him that I could see his face, although I was unable to discern his features. I saw a raw mass of red flesh, like the face of one of my patients, or of the passers-by in the street. He removed his gun from his shoulder. I sighed with relief for him. He leaned the gun against his forearm, as if wishing to ease himself even more. His finger manipulated the trigger while he raised the gun and neared it to the fence.

A shot was heard. All the windows in the yard filled with heads which vanished immediately. Around me all was quiet. I turned my head and there he was again — the boy. He lay on his side, stretched out on the boards of the water pump as if he were sleeping. I made a dash towards him. My lame foot was slipping in its sandal. I almost fell. I have become a miserable runner.

The first thing I noticed were the open eyes and the thin lines of his brows. How well Vladimir Winter had caught his child-like yet knowing glance! The boy's forelocks were shining through the sun's rays and looked like a silken ball. From the head of the genius oozed a fat red stream. In the sand at his feet lay the book he had been reading, its title page facing the sun. "The Forty Days of Musa Dagh", by Franz Werfel, I read. Strange what we are capable of noticing at such moments. The boy was dead. I had nothing to do there, yet I had no will to move away from the spot. I felt that the last bit of my strength had left me. I caught myself observing the scene in front of me with Winter's eyes: a dry water pump, the shape of a young body lying at rest, a red stream of blood and an open book in the sand. Form, colour, atmosphere. How had he said it? Harmony in the dissonance.

I heard a double scream. From one of the entrances there appeared a barefoot man wearing only his pants. He was followed by a woman. Both approached the pump with a kind of dancing step. Their screams recharged my energy. I raced out of the yard in the direction from which I had arrived. I wandered about the neighbouring backyards until I finally found the house where my patient lived.

Now, the epilogue of the episode.

Yesterday I went to see Winter, in order to examine him. I found him huddled up on his plush sofa, staring at the window, as if he had not noticed me come in. When I approached him, he jumped to his feet and grabbed both my hands, "Dr. Levine, *shalom aleichem!*"

"I want to examine you," I told him. "Get undressed."

He puckered up his eyebrows as if he had not understood what I said. "I feel wonderful . . ." he mumbled. I noticed the red borders around his eyes and the haze in his pupils. "You think . . . because I was lying down for a while . . ." he laughed eerily. "Firstly, I deserve the rest after standing on my feet for three days and three nights. Secondly, this is the best spot from which to observe my work. Come!" he pulled me by the sleeve towards the window. There I saw him again — the youth on the water pump. He lived again, a life which was beyond life — in a reality beyond reality. There he was, the child with the brain of a genius, with the charming wise eyes — the Jew without the Yellow Star. I saw the sun embracing him, kissing him, filling him with strength; I saw him growing, his muscles strengthening. The glare of Winter's eyes attacked me and drew me into its orbit, hurting me to the point of losing my breath. He spread out his skinny fingers as if to embrace the canvas. "If you only knew in what a hurry I was!" I asked him again to undress. He replied defensively, "Not today, dear Doctor. Today I have no body. Today I feel nothing. Only an hour ago I put away the brush. Do you know what kind of feeling that is? Let me enjoy it. Come, sit down with me for a while. Let's talk. You are indeed a physician, but apart from that, you must have some feelings within you for the person himself, for me, not so?" His eyes burned through me. "You'll do me a favour. I'm not asking you for an opinion about the painting. I don't need any criticism at this point, no praise or condemnation . . . About this I don't ever want to hear a thing. No comments. This is not a work of art, understand? It is . . . I don't know what . . . You should have seen me these last few days. You'd have understood me better. So . . . Sit down." He moved the old-fashioned armchair to the window, opposite the painting.

I sat down, waiting for the torrent of his words to pass. Then I repeated, "I want to examine you."

Disappointment rippled through his face. "That's what you've come for," he groaned.

"I consider it my duty," I said as if apologizing.

"And apart from your duty," he exclaimed, incensed, "is there nothing within you . . . for the person . . . for the soul? for me? Do you know . . . Can you imagine what I lived through before I could digest that death on the water pump, before I could conquer it?"

Did I really have to apologize to him? I had an afternoon off and had thought of him. Surely I could have done him the favour and sat down with him for a chat. But chatting is not my profession. And if I was going to chat, then it was a choice between him and my dear ones. My free time is so pitilessly limited. Here I had come only to work. "Undress!" I ordered him, annoyed.

He let himself down on the sofa, stared at me and shook his head with disdain. "Doctors! God's assistants on earth! Fixers of lives! How little you really know about human beings!" He made a face, calling out, "So I won't let you examine me today, and perhaps never! May the devil take you!" He drew his legs up on the sofa, folding both hands under his cheek as if he had finished with me and was ready to sleep. Huddled up in this position, he looked like a grotesque unearthly creature. I waited, my patience hanging by a hair. "Our relationship is over before it even started," he added, shutting his eyes and refusing to look at me.

I stood up. "You're throwing me out," I remarked coldly. "I came to see you, with your good in mind."

"With that indifference?" He gave a jerk.

"If I were indifferent I would not have come."

He opened one eye, then the other. He darted a searching, inquisitive look at me. At length he stretched out his hand to me, "Forgive me." I felt the unpleasant touch of his moist cold fingers. "Believe me, I don't know what I am saying. I have not slept for so many nights . . . and then, this cough bothers me . . ." He undressed while telling me in great detail about his condition. This time I had no doubt that it was tuberculosis. I gave him a prescription for an X-ray. He kept his eyes fixed on me for a long while. "It is not That . . . eh?"

"You have to eat well and . . . to paint," I said. "You are a fine painter."

He understood. We shook hands. I went up to Nadia's. Once more I warned her not to leave the baby in Winter's room. I ate supper with her. That is another advantage of being with her. I can join her in a meal without overcharging my conscience. I played with the baby.

I recommend a good book to you, by Franz Werfel, "The Forty Days of Musa Dagh". It is a very popular novel in the ghetto, but it can be enjoyed as well outside the ghetto.

Chapter Eight

SIMCHA BUNIM BERKOVITCH'S frantic search for work was not crowned with success. Day after day he would stand in line at all possible departments and each interview would end with the official telling him to apply in writing. Every move in the ghetto had to begin with a written application.

Bunim's applications were, as a rule, longer than they should have been. This was perhaps because of their author's literary inclinations, or because of his desire to make his situation as clear as possible to his reader, to prompt those in power to help him as soon as possible. In any case, the unknown officials received, not applications, but long letters from him, in which he described with vivid imagery and poetic language the hunger for food which he, his wife Miriam and his three year old daughter, Blimele, suffered. He also noted that he was a writer, a creative person, and as such, deserved the special care and attention of the community. He also took care to point out that his present domicile bordered the latrines, and expressed the wish to be assigned to better lodgings. Using many profound Talmudic quotations related to the situation of the Jews in general and to his own in particular, he closed with his best wishes for the good health of the official to whom the letter was addressed and with the hope for a quick and positive result.

Whenever he finished writing such a petition, he immediately felt like tearing it up. He had the feeling of having stripped himself naked in the middle of the street. With no courage to reread what he had written, he nevertheless sat over it for a long time, biting his pencil, before, abruptly and with disgust, shoving the letter into an envelope and running out to deliver it.

In time, he worked out a better, briefer style of application, hoping that the brevity of the text and the conciseness of the content would evoke the official's interest in the author. This too was of no avail. After a while he threw away his chewed-up pencil as if he never wanted to see it again.

He had no work. Days passed without a warm meal, with a few thin slices of bread in the morning and before bedtime, and with countless cups of Erzatz-coffee and saccharine. At first the pangs of hunger did not so much bother as surprise him. He would observe himself with curiosity, like a scientist observing the object of an important experiment. He noticed that he was more aware of his body, of its inner side, which was always attuned to the rumblings and the gnawings of his stomach. Most stubborn and unpleasant though these naggings of the body were, he could subordinate them to his will, calming them by offering his teeth the least morsel to chew on. On the other hand, he noticed that his mind had become freer, more sure of itself, that it overpowered his entire being. To his great amazement, he realized that his thoughts had acquired

95

a new clarity. He could now recite entire pages of the Talmud without difficulty and recall verses that had not entered his mind for years.

When it was not too hot outside, he would aimlessly roam the streets along with the other inhabitants of the ghetto, conducting scholarly disputes with himself. In his mind he would bring forth proofs and counter-proofs about the meaning of Jewish suffering, about sacrifice and *kiddush hashem*, about salvation and the Messiah. He was oblivious to what went on around him, noticing no faces, hearing no sounds, so carried away was he by his tangled thoughts which he so easily, almost playfully unravelled. His mind, which had always seemed to lead a life apart from his body, was now tied to it, lifting it in its weightlessness to its own heights. It seemed to him that he was thinking not only with his head, but also with his hands, with his legs and even with his rumbling stomach.

His clothes became loose on him. And the lighter he felt, the clearer was his awareness that life and death created an entity. The borderline between the two was erased and he could see one as a part of the other, but not as an equal part. There was more death in life, than life in death. And from that he inferred that death was more essential in the universe than life, because it was infinite, eternal; because it was the before and the after. Therefore Bunim saw the tremendous meaning of life itself. There was a mission that all which was alive had to accomplish, while it was alive. He asked himself what that mission was and came to the conclusion that God Himself had made conscious a part of his creation, supplying it with senses, with body and mind, so that it could become aware of the greatness of His work, of which it was a part. God, in whom Bunim had long since ceased to believe with the faith of his own father, appeared to Bunim here, in the ghetto, to be the great spirit of a lone creator, who, having no admirer of his work, continuously awakes a part of this very work — so that it can admire itself, criticize, judge and take delight in its being. And miracle of miracles! He even endows some of the awoken existences with a part of His own talents — so that they can, with the motes of beauty which they themselves create, deepen and enrich God's world, God's work.

This was how Bunim thought of himself, the human being, the artist. There was no doubt in his mind that man had been created to make as much use as possible of his physical and spiritual potential. This was man's mission — the meaning of life. Indeed, never before had Bunim felt so attached to life as now. Never had he been so enthusiastic, so worshipful about it, as here, behind the enclosure, on an empty stomach.

Summer was nearing its end. Its days, ripe and bright, lingered in the streets, scattering its gold in the gutters. Bunim felt the end of the summer, as if it were his own love declaration to existence. He wanted to live as never before. As at the beginning of the ghetto, he still had the premonition of the suffering in store for him. But now these feelings elated him, enhancing even more the charms of life in his eyes. His torment had the biting sweet taste of the torment of someone helplessly in love with an enchanting but unattainable woman. Because of his suffering, she became even more beautiful and alluring; because of it, he hoped to win her for himself.

He would not view the agony of his people as meaningless. He saw the Jewish people prostrated on one great altar, in the very centre of the world — a collective total sacrifice; all the Jews as one Isaac. And deep down, within him, he had the conviction that God would refuse to accept this sacrifice, just as He had refused to accept that of Isaac; that He only wanted to bring about the purification of the world, through the suffering of the Jews; that the Jews would demonstrate their greatest heroism in their endurance of life on its most debased level, not in order to perish, but in order to rise from the altar and lead the world out of its confusion. Because man, Bunim mused, had not grasped the meaning of his mission. Man was wasting all his gifts, doing not what he was destined to do, but just the opposite: rendering ugly the work of creation. The purpose of the Jewish trials was to open man's eyes, to make him embrace the true meaning of his humanity. Indeed, that kind of chosenness against which Bunim had once, at the beginning of his road, used to rebel, he now accepted with the humility of a lover.

However, now and then something deeper, something suppressed would surface in his consciousness, whispering in his ear with the cutting rage of bygone days, that in fact all these thoughts were only a superficial shield to protect himself against what was more profoundly hidden within him: against fear. He sensed that surer than anything, truer than anything was the inevitability, the decisive verdict executed by the demonic hands of the same God — the "hands" which are called "man". And this very voice from his depth also indicated to him who it was that stood behind all his hopeful reflections. He saw a round little face, a pair of velvety innocent eyes. It was for Blimele's sake and because of her that he had such thoughts.

In reality, he lately avoided Blimele as much as he could. It seemed as if the child were no longer his own, as if he could not bear the sight of her. Her ringing voice irritated him. He could not bear to watch her play with her doll, Lily, and most of all he dreaded meeting her gaze with his eyes. He would grow angry with her for no reason at all — and she became frightened of him. She would hide in a corner close to Miriam, when he was home. She would look at him stealthily, as if wondering whether this was her real *Tateshe*. In her mind, she imagined that her true *Tateshe* was gone somewhere, that a stranger was wearing his clothes, talking in his voice, and replacing him until his return. Sometimes she would listen at the door for the steps of her true *Tateshe*.

Bunim's manner of "escaping" was not new to Miriam. She had never understood what happened to him when suddenly, although physically close, he became estranged from her and the child. She ascribed that kind of behaviour partly to his habit of "making an elephant out of a fly" — of blowing every experience out of proportion and brooding over it ad nauseam; a characteristic which had always annoyed her. But she thought it also to have some relation to his being a writer, and she tolerated his moods with a kind of awe: icily, jealously, forcing herself to be patient and wait for him to "come home". She knew that this time she needed much more patience, but it was precisely now that she had less patience than in the past.

Bunim seemed to have given up his search for work and Miriam did not know what to do. When she tried to reproach him, to shake him up with angry words and bring him back to reality, he would dash out of the house. She realized that she would have to manage by herself, and she decided to become a street vendor, selling bars of soap, men's socks and second-hand trousers. She placed herself and her merchandise not far from the church, on the closest side of Hockel Street, so that she could run home every now and again. Customers were scarce and she had ample time to converse with the neighbouring vendors, or to watch the Jewish workers who were busy constructing the bridge which would connect the two parts of the ghetto, and to observe the Germans who were supervising the works, moving the poles of the fence and stringing the barbed wire.

Miriam would not have thought about the poles and the barbed wire so much, if it were not for the heavily wrapped woman, a stooped old saccharine vendor, who stood beside her and considered it her sacred duty to jump over towards Miriam every few minutes and elbow her, "You see, they're putting a noose around our necks, building scaffolds for us, each single pole's a scaffold for another Jew." So Miriam saw the rows of poles every night in her dreams, feeling that they and the barbed wire were winding around her, strangling her like a cobweb strangles a fly. She would scream in her sleep, waking Bunim, but she never told him of her recurring nightmare.

Every day the tension between Bunim and herself grew. She could not forgive him for his behaviour. Was it not clear as day that it was he who should be caring for their livelihood, not she? He knew this too. He knew that the chore of feeding Blimele, of tidying up the room did not belong to him, yet this was precisely what he did. And as soon as it was done, he would grab Blimele by the hand and dash out into the street with her, always heading in the direction away from where Miriam was standing with her merchandise. He dragged the child along in great haste, as if he were afraid of arriving somewhere late. Blimele would take tiny steps beside this stranger of a *Tateshe*, too frightened to lift her head. The Yellow Star on her coat danced before his eyes and he felt his guilt more acutely than ever. But the guiltier he felt, the angrier he became with Miriam. He could not bear her determination and envied her ability to adjust to every situation. The more strength he discovered in her, the more he raged against her.

When they met in the evening at the table to eat their bowl of soup, they would avoid looking at each other. But when he discovered that she had given him the thickest part of the soup with all the pieces of potato, leaving only water for herself, all hell would break loose. "Don't sacrifice yourself for me!" he would shout, beside himself with anger.

She answered him with screams and reproaches for having neglected the child and the house, as if to prove to him that it had not even entered her mind to sacrifice herself for him. They would stare at each other with hatred, neither of them hearing the heated words they spat out; their wrath sizzled too loud for that. And the more they screamed at each other and hurt one another, the heavier their hearts became, the more difficult it became for them to stop the torrent of words. Only when they realized that the child was fluttering between them like a trapped bird and running, frightened, from one to the other, her eyes overflowing as she implored them, "My tummy is pounding . . . *Mameshe*, kiss *Tateshe* . . . *Tateshe*, kiss *Mameshe* . . ." would they press their lips together, replacing words with a loaded silence. At night, hungry for her body, he would smother Miriam in his arms with brutal passion. Some strange force brought them together against their will, in spite of their will. They would cling to each other, mumbling words of devotion. The bed became their blessed escape.

The days filled with craving for food and with wrath, the nights filled with passion sapped them of all energy. Silvery strings of hair began to frame Miriam's face. She still had her full rounded cheeks and her skin looked fresh; only under her eyes was her face puffed and swollen and the eyes themselves were blurred, misty, encircled with red borders. The clothes hung loosely on her and her once full bosom vanished behind the folds of her garments.

A morning arrived when both Miriam and Bunim awoke with the knowledge that not only they, but also Blimele would be deprived of a hot meal that day, since Miriam had sold nothing for the past few days. That morning Bunim suddenly became aware of the sight of his wife. In the light of day her appearance cut into his heart like a scream — and in the blink of an eye, he was back with her and the child. He jumped out of bed, hurried on his clothes and grabbed the bag of merchandise from Miriam's hand. "I will go today," he blocked her way out, "You stay home."

He placed himself near Miriam's spot and without much thought began calling the customers, enumerating his wares. He called out with arrogance and anger. Like the other vendors, he accosted the passers-by, showing them the good quality of the used trousers he had for sale, and waving the pairs of men's socks in their faces. In his heart of hearts he felt proud like a man and humiliated like a beggar. People avoided him, turning their heads away, or they pushed him aside. Perhaps none of them needed men's socks or secondhand trousers, and perhaps they were repulsed by his manner, by his demanding tone of voice.

After two hours of shouting, his zeal cooled. Exhausted, he moved back to the wall and leaned against it, while he stared in front of him. He ceased looking at the faces passing him by. The street vanished, flowing past him like a muddy river. He was lost in himself. Nevertheless, it did not take long before he heard a rhythmical pounding which reached him from somewhere within or without, and cut off his thoughts: it was the sound of hammers against stone, against wood. He noticed the workmen at the bridge at the same time as he felt the nagging pangs of hunger in his stomach; his dry tongue craved something to chew on. He listened both to his rumbling belly and to the sound of the hammers, nodding his head to their beat — and saw the fence's gray-green poles transform themselves into loaves of bread, long and tasty, fresh from the oven. He felt like biting into them with his teeth and swallowing them along with the barbed wire.

That day he sold a few bars of soap and Blimele had a hot meal. He and Miriam drank countless cups of coffee and their teeth got something to chew on: a few slices of the last quarter of a turnip.

The following day he took up the same position on the street. When he grew tired of calling out his merchandise and leaned against the wall, he no longer became lost within himself. His mind had ceased to function. Pages of the Talmud no longer came to his mind, nor would he immerse himself in lofty questions and speculations. He was nothing but a stomach. The thought that he would not have a warm meal that evening increasingly extended his stomach-ego, making him one with the nagging emptiness of his insides; an emptiness which reached up to his mouth, setting his dry tongue in motion and making his teeth gnash.

It was nightfall. The sun was still shining, taking apart every stone of the sidewalk with its light as if it wanted to warm every speck of dust. The wall against which Bunim was leaning was mildly warm. It seemed to have become softened by the setting sun's tenderness. Bunim had not sold even one bar of soap, nor one pair of socks or trousers. He was tired of screaming, of the scream within him. As he pressed his back against the wall, he felt jealous of it, of every stone in the sidewalk; his limbs secretly wished to turn to stone, to become part of the wall, so that he could stand, unaware that he was standing, be warmed by the sun, unaware that it was warming him, so that he could become unaware that he was being.

Suddenly, he was struck by the sight of a cart passing through the middle of the street. A heap of potatoes and turnips flashed by before his eyes, stirring up a noise within him. A band of Jewish policemen flanked the cart on both sides. They were working their clubs, shooing off the beggars who were following the cart from behind, in the hope that they would catch a potato or turnip that rolled down from the heap. Bunim's heart began to flutter in his bosom at the sight of every potato that he saw wobbling at the top of the heap.

Before long, he found himself in the middle of the road. The beggars beside him were yelling, throwing themselves from side to side. They followed the falling potatoes and picked them up from the gutters, from under the oncoming wagons. They fought over them. Bunim did the same, but he never managed to pick up the treasures, since he always bent down too late. Sweat poured down his forehead. He cursed his heavy winter coat whose fur collar pricked and stung his neck. He shoved its tails apart, but they bothered him even more, tangling between his legs as he ran.

Through the thickness of his coat he felt a blow on his back. One of the policemen was giving him a going over, trying to chase him away from the cart. He found himself very close to it now. With stiff trembling fingers he rolled down a turnip from the heap and shoved it into his bag. Fists attacked him from all sides. Now the heavy winter coat shielded him like armour. The more blows he received, the quicker his hands reached out to the heap, rolling down the wonderful edible balls. Someone grabbed him by the fur collar, someone else tore at his flying coattails. He was clamped in. A heavy blow on the back threw him off his feet. The cart was moving away. Bunim was being dragged off, pulled by his arms. He tried to free himself with one hand, while with the other he held on to his bag. At length he tore himself out of the clamp and started to run. The policemen raced after him, shouting at him to stop; but his feet had wings. He felt so strong and light as if his coattails now too were a pair of wings.

At the gate on Hockel Street a woman wrapped in a plaid blocked his way, as if she had been waiting for him. "Give me at least one potato," she grabbed hold of him. He shook her off his arm.

The next moment he was home. Miriam looked at him with wide-eyed astonishment, "So soon?" She noticed the swollen bag in his hand and her face lit up. Solemnly, she approached him, patting the bag's belly. "Turnips?" She drew out a turnip, weighed it in her hands and beamed at him, "You've sold all the merchandise?"

He looked around him searchingly and saw Blimele. He swept her up into his arms and buried his sweaty hairy face in her body. "Let me go, *Tateshe!*" her voice trembled. But he did not let go of her. He stroked her hair with dirty fingers and kissed her forehead, her eyes, her chin, with eager lips. He held her tightly as if he wanted to press her into himself. "*Tateshe*, you're wet, you're hot!" she defended herself against him. In her tearful eyes there was however the awareness that her *Tateshe* had come back.

Miriam peeled a turnip. Yellow and clean, it looked like a chunk of the sun. Soon the tablecloth appeared on the table, and on it — three plates. They sat down. Miriam cut three slices of turnip, putting one on each plate. "In the past only pigs would have eaten this," she remarked, energetically biting into the slice of turnip with her teeth. Bunim looked at the tablecloth. Even here Miriam had not lost her ability to transform every meal into a ceremonious ritual. It seemed as if Miriam had the verse *Birkot* of the Talmud in her blood, where it was written that as long as the Temple in Jerusalem existed, its altar would bring salvation to Israel; but nowadays a man's table was his altar. Yes, eating the slice of turnip was not just eating, but a sacred service, a prayer, a song of praise to life. He listened to the crunching, munching sounds issuing from their mouths. There was a sweet juice on his tongue and palate, flowing down into his bloodstream, healing his soul. The joy of eating was great.

Thus Bunim ran every morning with his merchandise to take up his place in the street, accost the passers-by and offer them his wares. If Miriam still had some food at home to put on the table in the evening, he would, after having shouted himself hoarse, lean against the wall, rest, and then start all over again. However, if her supply of food was about to give out, he would, after noon-time, set out to scour the streets in search of a cart with turnips, potatoes, cabbage, or even coal. He did not always have the same luck as that first time. Sometimes the carts were so well guarded by the Jewish policemen that he could get nothing but blows from the escapade. At other times the carts were nowhere to be found.

He was already so familiar with his occupation, that his former indolence now appeared strange to him. When he took a rest, leaning against the wall, he had no thoughts, hopeful or desperate. All that he felt was that he was a part of the street, a particle of the ghetto. With his ears he would catch the shouts, the clamour raised by the throngs, while his eyes drank in the colour of the air, of the distant sky that would change with the passing of the hours. It was as if a spectacle was being put on for him with the sun as the star performer. He would look up and hum along with the tune of the little saccharine vendor at his side who called his ware with a girlish voice:

"Saccharine, saccharine, original stuff!
One hundred pieces for a *rumki* and a half!"

Bunim hummed that tune to the sun, as if he were offering it the little vendor's saccharine. He would alter the tune with the tone of a lanky youth whose voice was changing:

"The good, the best, the extra delicious!
The big, the biggest, the size of *knishes*!
Candies! Toffees! Toffees!"

Sometimes he would offer the sun his own merchandise, the trousers, the socks, the bars of soap. For he had his own tune with which he tried to attract customers. This importunate tune had become so much a part of him, that often he did not know whether he was singing it aloud, or it was just singing within him.

The ghetto had begun to breathe within him and he ceased to provide it with commentaries. All that would take the shape of a thought in his mind revolved around the hot meal, around an hour of the evening when they, the three of them, would sit down at the table, and take the spoons into their hands. All that would take the shape of a thought in his mind would revolve around the question of how to procure a few pieces of wood to cook the meal. All that his mind was aware of was Miriam's bony hips and vanishing bosom and Blimele's cheeks, still rosy and fresh.

Now both he and Miriam had dreams. He too would see poles and barbed wire, barbed wire and poles in his sleep. But in his dreams they would be transformed into the bars and nets of a cage. He would see himself trapped inside it. Like a beast chasing its own tail, he would howl and roar, throwing himself at the net of wires and springing away from it. But he never knew what kind of a beast he was. Was he a clumsy bear, a leopard, a wolf, or simply an ape? The only thing he knew was that in his craving for food he was ready to bite off his own tail. And from outside, through the bars of the cage, a green face peered in with green eyes. A green hand thrust a gun through and tickled the exasperated beast, while a voice exclaimed enthusiastically, "*Gott, wie gross ist dein Tiergarten!*"

When he woke from his sleep, he had the dim awareness that he still breathed the air of his dream. The feeling of being in a cage stayed with him. The narrowness of the cage no longer seemed circumscribed. It was huge, endless, immeasurable. The feeling of being a beast also stayed with him — a raw clear self-image. Total dullness. Given the level of life at which he now found himself, he accepted this dullness as a blessing.

✦ ✦ ✦

Once in a while he experienced moments when his dormant self was teased by a need for something more, something spiritual. Once this occurred when the painter Guttman, whom he had met on a Sabbath in the Garden, came over to him and pumped his hand for a long while, overwhelmed by the discovery that they were both living in the same backyard. From him Bunim learned that the poetess Sarah Samet was also living in the ghetto. The very same evening Guttman took him along to visit her.

The poetess received them with a sad, barely visible smile. It was not a note of pleasure they heard in her greeting, but rather a compassionate tenderness and regret, as if she were saying, "So you are here too." Bunim noticed that she seemed to have shrunk, her small face still smaller than he remembered it; her hair was sprinkled with gray. She invited them to sit down on the bed. Her husband was busying himself in the kitchen, preparing tea. Bunim was curious as to how the couple was managing, but did not inquire. He did not want to talk about the ghetto. His relationship to the poetess was not ghetto-ish; he felt this from the moment his eyes met hers. Here he wanted the animal within him to be silenced, at least for a while.

At length the tea was served and Bunim mustered the courage to propose that the poetess read some of her poems. She read in a hushed prayerful voice, and the softer her voice became, the noisier became the voice within Bunim. She was reading poems about the Sabbath days of her childhood in the *shtetl*. In his mind's eye he saw his own home, his parents, his sisters, not as they looked now, in the ghetto, but as they had looked in Lynczyce. They looked up to him with so much hope, so much expectation. Guilt grabbed him by the throat, suffocating him. It was not the guilt of the old times, the guilt of having left his parents' home. It was the guilt of the present. Of course, he visited them in the dwelling they had found after their return from Glovno. He would let his mother offer him a bowl of soup, or a slice of bread and devour it without asking from where she had gotten it. Sometimes, when he succeeded in his attacks on the vegetable carts, he wanted to run to his parents' place with a turnip or a few carrots. But he always rushed home first, after which it was impossible to give any of the little treasure away.

Sarah Samet interrupted her reading a few times. She did not want to impose with her poems, although reading them evidently gave her a great deal of pleasure; her face seemed like that of a mother in whose face the serenity of the Sabbath was reflected. Her visitors would not allow her to interrupt her reading. And the longer she read, the milder Bunim's sorrow became, his guilt feelings — not erased, yet more bearable. While this calm descended upon him, his heart began to pound more forcefully. A craving ran through his veins, through his entire being — to write . . . write. He wished to take the chewed-up pencil into his hand, find a piece of scrap paper and fill it with words. He caressed this craving in his mind, feeling that he was nurturing a way back to himself. With the pencil in his hand he would become a giant; the beast within him would have no power over him; he would become complete again.

On the way home there was his conversation with Guttman. "You know, Berkovitch," Guttman said, "before we came into the ghetto, I got rid of all my paintings. But lately I've picked up my brush again. It seems to me that here we could stop stammering. And do you know what else I think? I think that it is a duty . . . Take me, I am for active engagement in fighting for freedom. If you want, my chapter Spain is my greatest achievement. Here, after the Germans came in, everything inside me was on fire. The spirit of Spain was calling. I ran about the town like a madman. Everyone laughed at me, Poles and Jews alike, even my old battle companions. How could I compare the situation in Poland to Spain, they asked. So there was only the choice of personal action open to me. But what could I have done? Kill a German or two at the most. And the artist within me, yes, the dead artist who had destroyed everything he had created, was not too excited about that kind of arithmetic. Even here, before I began to paint, I more than once had the impulse to throw myself at a gendarme at the fence. But since the moment that I started painting again, this does not even enter my mind. Do you understand me? This is an essential struggle: The duty to immortalize. The same is true of you. You know what a great opinion I had about your writing, even before anyone else recognized you."

Bunim grumbled, "Do you think that I lack duties, without that?"

"Everyone has them, but you must have the strength to carry one more. You can write."

"What of it? Do you think that even the greatest master would be capable of handling such a topic?"

"Each can produce only in accordance with his own abilities."

"Nonsense!" Bunim waved his hand, yet he felt grateful to Guttman for his words. Yes, he felt that kind of calling within him. Writing could give sense to his life. He said good-bye to Guttman and walked through the backyard with vigorous steps. He knew what he would do that night.

When he entered his hut, he met Miriam's worried gaze. The child was sick. For the last few days Blimele had had diarrhoea. There were quite a few people in the backyard who suffered from it, and the neighbours said that it was due to the diet of strange grains which were being eaten with their skins intact and were therefore difficult to digest. Blimele was running a high temperature and Dr. Levine had diagnosed dysentery.

Days and weeks of worry about Blimele's health passed by; weeks of being preoccupied with her stools, her temperature, with selling bread and sugar in exchange for a little bit of rice. A few neighbours in the backyard died of the dysentery, but Blimele recovered after a while. Bunim became more stubborn, more aggressive in trying to attract customers. Nonetheless, he was forced to sell his and Miriam's piece of butter and their allotment of honey from the ration, so that he could buy an additional piece of bread for the child. Of his visit with Sarah Samet and of his desire to write he had completely forgotten. He had fallen back into his stupor.

The second time, he was pulled out of it by a neighbouring vendor in the street. An air of restlessness was sweeping over the ghetto. Hunger demonstrations against Rumkowski followed each other in rapid succession. Bunim was exasperated, tortured by the rumbling emptiness in his intestines. When his craving for food met with the fuming hunger of the throngs, it multiplied a thousandfold and became wild and unbearable. There could be no question of running off in search of the vegetable carts. The work was now being done at night, when the ghetto was asleep, for fear of the raging mob which would attack the carts and snatch up all of their contents.

As Bunim watched the demonstrators, he felt like leaving his place to join them, yet he stayed put. Here he had to stand. To wrestle with both his hungry insides and with his guilt was too much. Then, a tiny man with a whispy beard came over to him. A flat box with a glass cover was suspended from his neck by a cord. Under the glass lay an assortment of homemade candies. Unlike Bunim, he did not call out his wares in a loud voice, since he evidently did not have the strength for it; he had nevertheless a tune of his own. He sang it with a soft, drawn-out lilt. Bunim knew the tune by heart, just as he knew the tunes of the other vendors. The little man would sing out monotonously while repeating one single phrase: "Children of Israel, resuscitate your hearts with a candy, sweeten your lives with a toffee!" He accompanied himself by drumming a finger against the glass top of his box.

The little man leaned against the wall beside Bunim and raised his chin with its thin beard to him, "No carts to chase after today, eh, neighbour?" Bunim gave him a hostile glance, ready to tell him to mind his own business. The little man was not discouraged by Bunim's stern face. "I noticed that you haven't earned a pittance yet today." Fatherly compassion radiated from his face. "You know," he went on, "you never say a word to me, but I watch you a great deal. I listen to the tune by which you call your buyers. I mean, when you're not screaming at the top of your voice. I've heard this tune somewhere. It's the tune of a prayer, isn't it?" Bunim shrugged his shoulders. "You don't know what kind of melody it is? Don't you listen to your own singing?"

"Singing you call it?" Bunim could no longer control his irritation.

"Ruler of the Universe!" The amazed little man turned his head from side to side, his long wispy beard following. "And what singing!" Never mind, such a tune doesn't get lost. There are ears that listen. A Jew in the ghetto may pray in such a manner too. The words are not the most important . . . the tune is. And not even the tune itself, but the soul behind the tune . . ."

There was something in the little man's words that caressed Bunim's heart, a feeling like that which he had experienced when visiting Sarah Samet. However in his fretfulness his tongue could utter only bitter words, "Do me a favour and don't knock me over the head with such idiocies. Here, inside me, there is nothing, nothing!" Bunim hit his fist against his chest. "If I have a soul, it is the soul of a devil. If you think I'm praying, it's the prayer of a beast for a full stomach! Secondly, there is no one to direct one's prayers to. God has been fenced off from us with barbed wires."

The little man gave a short laugh, "On the contrary, neighbour! Just the opposite! It is not we who are fenced off from the world, but the world from us. They are the ones behind the barbed wire, and we are free. Surely, this is the way with every fence, every enclosure that divides. Where the inside or the outside is depends on how you look at it. As far as I am concerned, the Ruler of the Universe dwells here, not there. Let's presume that you found yourself on the other side, do you think you'd feel any better? Worse, I'm telling you. A thousand times worse. Because on the other side is the real trap, the real hell. The world is tearing out its hair, wallowing in evil, in viciousness. From there, you see, there is no escape. But here? Here people still walk around with faces like yours, for instance."

Bunim looked at him, "What's wrong with my face?"

The little man raised his hand as if he wanted to stroke Bunim's cheek, "A face like yours, carrying torment and pain like that . . . showing such soul in its eyes . . ."

"What do you pick on that darling of a word, 'soul' for? I have no soul, what do you want of me? Who needs a soul to get a piece of cabbage, a slice of turnip? And it's better like this. With time there won't be a soul in the ghetto who has a soul."

"Eh, don't say that," the little man implored. "One must take care of one's soul. Only it can show us the way."

"Yes, to the cemetery."

"And I'm sure that it is just the opposite: To life, to real true life!" Something stirred within Bunim. It seemed that the sun in the western sky was putting its fiery seal on the little man's words. Hope, however, did not become intimate and close, but alien and cold. "I say this," the little man continued talking. "The Germans have shut us up in the ghetto, this goes on their account and they will receive their judgment for it. But what happens to us here, is our problem. For what we do here with ourselves, we will have to answer. And even if it were true what you have said, it is still better . . . wherever we should go . . . that we go with it, rather than without it."

"With what?"

"With the soul. Don't forget that we are Jews."

"There are those who see to it that I don't forget."

"No, it's your business to see to it. Why do you think the Almighty allows all this to happen? For the sake of the world. So that we should become its mirror, so that it should, through us, see its true face. We are the Chosen Ones. This is not a tale sucked out from one's finger, it's not a delusion."

"Thank you for the privileges."

"You may like them or not. But this is fate and to change fate is not in our power. We can choose, either to shut our eyes and refuse to acknowledge our calling, or to keep our eyes open and carry out this mission with great pride. And this could help us, us and the world, you hear what I am telling you?"

Bunim shrugged his shoulders; he had had enough. "Please," he said with weariness in his voice, "Let's leave that alone. What sense is there in all that chatter? When I was on the first level of hunger, so to speak, I had similar thoughts. It depends on what's going on in your stomach. When you don't have a warm meal for your child, you cannot talk so smoothly about all these things."

"And how do you know on what level of hunger I am?" The little man felt offended.

"From the way you're talking. Simple as that."

"In that case you're wrong. How many children have you got, may they be in good health? One? Two? I have got nine sparrows, dear neighbour, may they be strong and healthy. And they cannot help me out either, because I don't want to take them out of the *heder*. The wife is helping me out. Out of our food rations she makes the candies, out of mine and her allotment of sugar and honey. So, that gives you some idea, doesn't it? And since we are on the subject, you'd probably like to know how I have come to this business in the first place. Why candies and not something else? So, you understand, there is a reason behind that too. I like to deal in sweet things. Before the war, I was in a related field. I used to sell ice-cream. I liked to watch children's faces light up when I handed them a cone, how their eyes would begin to sparkle with delight. It is a physical delight, but with children every physical delight transforms itself into the delight of their little souls. And we, the Jews of the ghetto, are like battered children. A candy in the mouth makes us feel good, body and soul. Do you understand me? One must offer people solace. You ask why He, the Almighty, doesn't bring solace, don't you? But what do you expect — that He dress up like a person of flesh and blood, walk about the ghetto and pat everyone on the shoulder, saying "Cheer up!" He has His own ways. He comes to us through our own selves; in the good we do one another He Himself is present." The little man began to busy himself with the cord of his box, finally he took it off his neck. "Well, well," he sighed. "It will be enough for today." He waved his hand at Bunim and waded through the embittered crowd.

The air around the place where Bunim and the little man had been talking seemed to vibrate with their words both spoken and unspeakable. The pining to hold the chewed-up pencil between his fingers again gnawed at Bunim's heart. The chord which he thought had burst and vanished, had again been struck and it vibrated deep inside him. At the same time he was pushed and jostled from all sides. The crowded street was bulging with people who poured into it from all the side streets. He noticed that they were all streaming into the gate next to that of his own yard. "We demand work and bread!" he heard a shout above his head. The street responded with a loud multi-voiced echo. Bunim had no idea of whether he had torn himself away from his spot, out of his own free will, or whether he was merely being swept along by the crowd. He allowed himself to be pushed through the gate of his own backyard, towards the broken fence in the back, past the passage to the adjoining yard where the newly created fire brigade was stationed. Here the crowds swayed in waves like a turbulent sea. People were standing even on the firemen's wagons.

This was not the first hunger demonstration, and the crowds had already had some experience in chanting their slogans and raising their fists. Entire families were taking part. The children in their parent's arms, or sitting on their shoulders, curiously watched the performance their parents were putting on for them. Their faces expressed amazement at the sight of their fathers and mothers raging not at them, the children, but at someone else for a change, though they did not know exactly who that someone was. The youngsters were also raising their little fists, laughing, echoing the incomprehensible slogans and mimicking their parents. Here and there a little creature, frightened by the entire spectacle and by the twisted faces of its parents, burst into howls.

Bunim was pounded by the crowd. Just like it, he knew of nothing beyond his rumbling stomach. Only a short while before he had forgotten about his hunger, while he discussed lofty issues with the Toffee Man and longed for his bitten-up pencil. Now his face was twisted into a grimace; his crumpled forehead was covered with wisps of his graying hair. With one hand he held on to his bag, while the other was raised high, in a fist. He was yelling, his yell a thousand times more powerful than his own voice; just like the collective hunger was a thousand times stronger than the hunger of each individual.

But then, amidst the clamour, amidst his own screams, Bunim heard a voice which was not yelling, nor shouting — but singing, really singing with words. The voice was thin, girlish, clear and gay — a funny little voice. Bunim turned his head in the direction from which it was coming and noticed a youth in a black gaberdine with a round little cap with a visor on his head, standing on one of the firemen's wagons. The youth was lanky, pale, with the face of an old man, the eyes of a child and the voice of a girl. And the childish eyes were laughing, the girlish voice danced down from the pale lips, the old face was twisted into constantly changing masks. He continuously wiped his lips with the sleeves of his gaberdine and looked around with his sharp eyes, as he measured his success. The people surrounding him were staring in amazement, some shrugging their shoulders, others eyeing him scornfully. The youth did not take their reaction too much to his heart. When one song did not evoke sufficient enthusiasm, he cut it short, and switched to another:

> "Such are the times, no use making a noise,
> No use crying, such is the golden rule.
> We Jews of Lodz are but the whipping boys.
> Every wise guy today is nothing but a fool."

The listeners became more attentive. For a moment they forgot to join the screaming crowd or to raise their fists. The singer repeated the refrain, "Oy, oy, every wise guy today is nothing but a fool." A child sitting on his father's shoulders burst into a little laugh. As if this were a signal for the others, the faces of the audience relaxed and a low chuckling could be heard coming from all sides. The youth's mouth spread into a broad smile; gratefully he displayed his tiny decayed teeth. He pushed his round little cap towards his left ear, then pointed his finger at the firemen's wagon on which he was standing and intoned a new song:

> "I have an uncle whose name is Lemel.
> He is commander of the fire chaps.
> He moves his belly like a sleepy camel,
> Fighting a fire with his bottle of schnapps."

The crowd, which had already made the acquaintance of the short, fattish, red-nosed chief of the fire brigade, could not hold back any longer, and burst into laughter. Further up in the yard, the people kept up their shouting and raised their fists, but here, in this corner, they forgot about their hunger for a moment. But only for a moment. In the very middle of one of his couplets, the singer cast a glance deep into the yard and cut short his singing. As soon as he did so, all the others turned their faces in the same direction. Silence descended upon the firemen's wagon and on the entire backyard.

On the first floor of the building that stood between the two backyards there was a little open window. In it appeared a figure, or rather a pair of hands, because the man himself, swallowed by the darkness behind him, could not be seen from the yard. Two fists stretched out to the mass of people. Itche Mayer the Carpenter began his speech to the hungry masses.

✦ ✦ ✦

This was not the Itche Mayer of bygone days, not even the Itche Mayer who belonged to his wife Sheyne Pessele or to his sons. This was both a sick and a renewed Itche Mayer whose existence had become dissolved in the general tragedy, who took upon himself the duty of doing something for his brothers in "work and want". After he had lived for so many years as a sympathizer of the Bund, as a reader of all sorts of tales about heroes and revolutionaries, he now suddenly felt the Bundist and revolutionary, the fighter who had for so long lain dormant within him.

He could no longer sit in his new apartment, chatting with his wife. He could now be found wherever people gathered, distributing bulletins and handwritten leaflets. He marched through the streets, seeing to it that out of the chaotic mobs a disciplined demonstration was formed. He directed the masses through his own backyard into the neighbouring larger one, where he was sure of the protection of Valentino and his gang. It was he who had found out that the little window in the stairway of his house, near the entrance to his apartment, faced the firemen's yard, and it had been he who had removed the casements with the panes, so that he might address the crowd from there. Thanks to him the little window became the grandstand for all the hunger demonstrations in the ghetto.

Itche Mayer never worried beforehand about what to say to his brothers and sisters of "work and want". As soon as he appeared at the open window, words would begin to pour out from his mouth by themselves. He would let them fly down from his lips as if they were threaded on an endless string of sorrow and bitterness, winding out from his heart towards the crowd below, which would swallow them eagerly. He himself would not listen to his own words, or his own voice. Somehow it seemed to him that it was not he who was speaking, but that his son Israel, the fiery orator of past May Days, of meetings and demonstrations, was the one who was delivering the speech, and Itche Mayer listened with delight to Israel's voice, not to his own.

Now Itche Mayer raised his fists and took a deep breath of the cool evening air. With hazy eyes he embraced the sky upon which dusk was spreading its shadows, then he allowed his gaze to swoop down upon the darkness of the human mass beneath him. "Brothers, Jews!" he cried out, hearing a voice, not his own, bounce back from the silence in the yard with a pleasant muffled echo. "Our situation is a bitter one! It cannot go on like this and it must not go on like this! We must not let ourselves be starved and tortured to death! We cannot silently look on as our children suffer! And this is only the beginning! Imagine what still awaits us, if we don't resist right away! Presess Rumkowski does nothing to alleviate our plight. He and his clique of parasites of the ghettocracy are having the time of their lives. They don't know the meaning of war. They live out their days in the same luxury as before! We have been silent for too long and this silence must come to an end right here and precisely here! We won't tolerate anyone feathering his nest on our account, nor will we tolerate protectionism and boot-licking! We demand a just distribution of the food arriving in the ghetto! We demand that many public dining rooms be opened! We demand that the Presess recognize the representatives of the workers and convene with them. Let the Old Man not think that he is dealing with a blind mass of people, which will let itself be led by him like a mindless flock of sheep. We are the Jewish workers of proletarian Lodz! We don't want any dictators! We refuse to be doubly enslaved!"

Here Itche Mayer had to interrupt himself, in order to gather some strength. He inhaled deeply and listened to the murmur of general approval sweeping through the crowd. He was aware that the people below refrained from exploding into a thunderous roar of protest, on account of the barbed wire fence nearby.

"Brothers, Jews!" he began again. "There is one thing you should all know. If we want to survive the war, if we want to live to the day of freedom, we must stick together, all for one and one for all, and we must organize ourselves. Only then will we be able to resist our inner enemy. Brother Jew, brother proletarian, let us take a resolution now, not to leave this yard until the Presess himself shows up here and listens to our demands!"

The crowd was apparently no longer able to restrain itself and a "Hurray!" thundered through the yard. "We demand the Presess!" was heard from all sides.

Itche Mayer raised his hands as if to gather all the shouts into one. "Yes, my brothers!" he went on. "We demand the Presess and we won't move from here until he arrives . . ." The last phrase did not slide smoothly from his lips, but came out like a cock's crow. His throat was dry. Undisturbed, he continued in his crowing voice, as the sweat washed down his face.

Sheyne Pessele pulled him by the tail of his jacket, imploring him, "Itche Mayer, for heaven's sake, when will there come an end to your talking?" He was not disturbed by her pulling or nagging. His voice may have been hoarse and rasping, but what he had to say was clear and sharp. Sheyne Pessele was beside herself. "Itche Mayer, remember, you'll scream your gall out, heaven forbid," she shook her finger against his back. Ever since he had begun his speech, she had been standing behind him with a glass of water in her hand, ready to offer it to him at the first opportunity. "At least take a sip of water to revive your heart. Have pity on me, Itche Mayer!" But he would not interrupt his speech for one moment. This time he only gave a jerk, as if he wanted to shoo away an irksome fly. He had no idea what she wanted of him. But he saw his three sons, Mottle, Yossi and Shalom down there in the crowd. In their faces raised to him, in their proud satisfied glances he found the reassurance that he was speaking well and forcefully.

Then something forced him to tear his gaze away from his sons. He saw a horde of Jewish policemen, clubs in hand, pouring into the yard. His heart began to pound hastily. He screamed out, "Look whom the Presess is sending us! The police with their clubs! He is going to offer us blows instead of bread!"

The mob became restless, huddling tighter together; some tried to make it to the exit. The policemen stopped for a moment. They looked at one another as if wondering what to do. Then they plunged into the crowd, swinging their clubs over the heads of the people. "Disperse! Disperse!" they bellowed.

"You, policemen!" Itche Mayer yelled beside himself. "Don't you dare raise your hands against your own brothers! Go to the Presess! Bring him here!"

"We demand the Presess!" the mob burst out with renewed courage.

There was a commotion behind Itche Mayer's back. He could explicitly hear Sheyne Pessele talking very loudly, but he had no time to turn his attention from what was going on before his eyes.

Sheyne Pessele was squabbling with Mietek Rosenberg, the young policeman who was standing at the top of the stairs, trying to get past her outstretched arms to reach Itche Mayer. "Darling neighbour!" Sheyne Pessele implored him as she pushed him away from her. "Let him be. You'll see that in no time I'll take him away from there. He has almost finished. So go in good health, dear neighbour, I beg of you!" Then it occurred to her that she was perhaps offending him by calling him "dear neighbour" and she corrected herself, "Mister policeman, be a *mentsch*, please, have pity on an old man and leave him alone!"

Mietek Rosenberg, amused by the woman's funny way of talking and by the scene in general, was wrestling with her more in fun than in earnest. He had volunteered to remove the speaker from the window, hoping that while he was disputing with Sheyne Pessele, Itche Mayer would vanish and the problems would be solved. "I have an order to arrest him!" he warned her, making a serious face.

The moment she heard this, Sheyne Pessele rushed towards Itche Mayer, shouting, "Itche Mayer, did you hear that? They are going to lock you up!" Now she hung on to Mietek's lapels with both hands, "Policeman dear," she implored him, "You wouldn't do such a thing as locking up your own neighbour!"

Mietek was beginning to worry that Itche Mayer's presence at the window might cause him embarrassment in front of his colleagues. It was time to act and prove that he was a policeman and not a milksop.

Itche Mayer had heard distinctly the words "lock you up" coming from behind his back. He gave a shout to his sons below, "Mottle, Yossi, Shalom! Your mother is fainting!" Seeing his sons leave their places and dash off, he regained his composure and lowered his head to the confused crowd, "Don't let yourselves be chased away by these scoundrels! We demand the Presess!" This was the last thing he said. He felt a heavy blow in his back. That was the first blow that Mietek had ever given a Jew in the ghetto, and the blow was well measured. Itche Mayer's heart constricted. With both hands he hung on to the sill, his head swimming. He felt Sheyne Pessele's arms around his waist. She threw the glass of water into his face and dragged him away from the window. As they passed the stairs he managed to notice Shalom and Yossi evening out the account with the policeman. Those were the first and last blows that the policeman Mietek Rosenberg received from a Jew in the ghetto.

Mottle, the communist, the oldest of Itche Mayer's unmarried sons, replaced his father at the little window. As Itche Mayer lay in the comfortable bed which he had inherited from the teacher Mermelstein, he listened to the voice of his son. The blow he had received did not bother him at all. He felt good. After Mottle, a few other speakers followed. The policemen were unable to handle the embittered crowd. They waited for the people to tire and disperse. The police chief had apparently rushed off to the Presess for advice and orders. The crowd felt encouraged and did not leave the yard. It was better to stick together. They waited for the Presess. Someone brought the news that in exactly ten minutes he would arrive. One half hour passed and then another. It was nightfall and the Presess had still not shown up.

At long last, instead of the Presess, a green armoured car arrived. Four German soldiers with guns in their hands jumped out of it. The crowd froze in place, paralyzed. The next moment people began to dash wildly in all directions. A shot rang out. The four Germans returned to their car, its engine started up; it vanished. Their appearance and disappearance happened so quickly, that they seemed to be the hallucination of a mob gone mad. However, in the middle of the empty yard, a wounded man lay in a river of blood. The little window on the first floor, empty and dark, stared down at him like an eye covered by a black monocle.

✦ ✦ ✦

Bunim waited for a long time at the locked door of his hut. After what had happened, the backyard was desolate, empty. He ran through it a few times, looking out into the street which was also empty. He walked in front of the gate, nervously wiping his glasses. Then, gradually, the yard and the street began to fill with people again; they gathered in islands and eddies, talking in a whisper. He rushed from one knot of people to the other. He was sure that nothing had happened to Miriam and Blimele, yet fear choked him; a hard hoop pressed around his heart. He was angry with Miriam for not being at home and prepared himself to greet her with a storm of bitter words. At the same time he felt with all his being how attached he was to her and the child. He longed for their faces to appear before him. The later it grew, the darker became his anguish.

He was inwardly calling them by their names, humming them with the nagging tune which he used to attract his customers, when they both emerged from a cluster of people approaching in the street; emerged so naturally, winding themselves out from the distance so imperceptibly, that he stared at them for a long while before he realized that he was seeing them. They walked slowly, holding hands. Blimele was taking little jumps as she walked. Miriam waved a finger at her, admonishing her about something. Bunim embraced them with his gaze, his heart calm and comfortable again. He no longer felt like scolding Miriam, nor did he feel like rushing forward to embrace them.

They stopped in front of him in the most natural manner, and he, as if nothing had happened, took Blimele by the hand. The light of her big eyes beamed up at him, "*Tateshe*, I will go to school, ask *Mameshe!*" she said, taking little jumps.

He turned to Miriam, "Without even asking me?"

"I had this idea," she replied, satisfied with herself, "So I went with her to the kindergarten." She took him by the arm, looking devotedly into his eyes. "Don't get mad today, Bunim, please."

"I want to have the child at home," he grumbled.

"*Tateshe*," Blimele tried to help Miriam appease him. "It is very nice there, you have nothing to be afraid of." Noticing that her father's face would not clear, she rose up on her toes and said confidentially, "There is some good food ready for you at home. Today is your day, *Tateshe*, you mustn't get mad."

Mother and daughter exchanged meaningful glances. Miriam turned to him, saying warmly, "You'll see, the child will love it. She won't have to spend her days in the dirty yard, and let her learn a few songs, where's the harm?"

"I too have some say in this matter, don't I?" he cut her short.

"It's better for the child. Other parents would be happy to . . ."

"I am not other parents!"

"Bunim, I beg of you, let's have at least one good evening."

He did not answer. He felt no strength within him to be separated from the child for half a day. The kindergarten was in the other part of the ghetto. True, one could freely pass through the gate connecting the two parts. However, there was always the possibility that the passage would be blocked; that between Blimele and himself there would stand the unsurmountable barbed-wire fence. The moments of anguish that he had experienced a while ago were not to be repeated; it was too much to bear. And he was very surprised at Miriam. Had she not waited for him, all aflutter with worry, during the first days of the war? Did she think that life in the ghetto was beyond any danger? But then it occurred to him that he could rely on her instinct; perhaps she knew better than he when danger lurked and when it did not. At length he cheered up and pressed Blimele's hand in his, "Will you at least sing the new songs to your *Tateshe?*"

At home a surprise awaited him. Miriam had made a *cholent* in honour of his birthday. He was thirty-two years old today. They spoke very little during the meal. Even Blimele was quiet; she sat bent over her plate, absorbed in eating the delicious *cholent* made of turnips. This was a real feast. Their bellies were full with food, while their hearts brimmed over with peace.

That night Bunim found his pencil. As soon as Miriam saw that he was looking for some clean sheets of paper, she felt so happy that she drew out a few old balls of unravelled wool and sat down to knit a sleeveless sweater for him. Blimele was asleep in her bed, both arms resting spread out above her head. A part of her left foot peeked out from under the cover. The colour of her heel was a delicate warm pink.

Bunim sat on his bed, supporting himself on his elbow. He was overpowered by the feeling of satiation, something he had not experienced for a long time; it had taken hold of every cell of his body, of every recess of his mind. He wanted to resist it, but could not. It had conquered him; it possessed him completely.

Filled with the delight of his belly and the dejection of his spirit, he let his pencil run over the blank sheet of paper, "I am afraid of you, God . . ." Anger seized him. He crossed out the line, put down a few other ones, then crossed them out as well. He stretched out on the bed, shut his eyes and heard a voice within him, "You are no poet, no writer, Simcha Bunim!" He turned to the wall and buried his face in the pillow to escape that voice. But it continued to pursue him, calling after him, "Forget your language, forget your alphabet. You are no longer human . . . no longer a soul . . . You are a beast trapped in a cage, that's what you are! A beast that has had its fill of food today! A beast who is thirty-two years old today! Then roar and laugh . . . howl and wail . . ." He buried his face deeper in the pillow and pressed his lips together, trying to control the twitching of his shoulders, so that Miriam, who sat at the table knitting him a sweater, would not notice.

Chapter Nine

IT APPEARED THAT LIVING in the ghetto inspired Itche Mayer's sons in a particular way. They became romantic. Despite the hunger and the long hours they devoted to their party work, they found time to carry on love affairs, but such love affairs as led directly towards practical results, namely marriage. In the spring this had happened with Yossi. Now it was Mottle who had found himself a "comrade from the movement", and one fine morning he announced to his family that he was going to "live with her".

His parents looked at him as if he had gone out of his mind. "What do you mean?" Itche Mayer puckered his eyebrows, observing his son closely, to check whether the latter was in his right mind. "Neither one of you has work, or a place of your own to live. What will you live on? Where will you live?"

Mottle laughed, "Don't worry, Father, we'll go hungry together. It'll be more fun. And as for a place to live, this is also only a pre-war habit. We'll get a corner for ourselves somewhere, rely on me."

Sheyne Pessele saw right away that the issue had already been decided on and that there was no use wasting another word on it. Did she not know her Mottle, the most stubborn of all her sons? So she wanted to save something at least. "Why do you have to look for a corner to put your head down with strangers? Don't you have a home? Is somebody chasing you out? Make a partition in the kitchen, and live there till you're a hundred and twenty." She bit her tongue, realizing that on account of the great news, she did not know what she was saying. She corrected herself, "I mean, till the war is over."

Mottle shook his head categorically, "I want to be on my own."

"Not for my head to understand this," Itche Mayer put a finger up to his temple. Suddenly he felt very tired, and trudged off to lie down on his bed. The trouble with Itche Mayer was that he was feeling increasingly tired. The reason for that, in Sheyne Pessele's opinion, was the grain which they ate for lunch every day. The grains were of an unusual sort that had never before been seen in Lodz. While being cooked, they would colour the water a dark red and cast off their shells. There was no way of getting the shells out of the pot so as to leave only the grains. One either had to throw the soup out altogether, or to eat both the grains and their shells. Indeed, one would have to be out of one's mind to throw away a bit of food which, in spite of everything, filled the belly and quenched the pangs of hunger; so people kept on eating it.

The grains did not agree with Itche Mayer's stomach. Not that they really made him sick, but he had to "run". To "have to run" was nothing new in the backyard, or in the ghetto in general. Eating all these turnips and weeds, along

113

with these new grains, with only a rare piece of meat or slice of bread, had turned many people into "runners". But as long as it was not dysentery, Itche Mayer would not let himself be bothered by it. He had more important worries on his mind. Nor would he spare a thought on the fact that there was no trace of his former "potato belly", that the hair on his head was gone and that his eyebrows had become white. He could still laugh at his reflection in the full-length mirror which the family had inherited with the apartment. He would compare the skin on his face to an old rag, stating that the freckles on it, having joined into large brown blotches, made him look unwashed. His only problem was that he felt increasingly tired and was drawn towards his bed the moment he stepped over the threshold of his apartment.

Mottle stood at the bedside staring at his father reproachfully. "Can't you at least wish me good luck, Father?"

Sheyne Pessele burst into tears, not "dry ones" as was her habit, but true sobs in which her whole being seemed to dissolve. Not in such sadness had she imagined her children leaving her, not so mundanely. She knew from her experience with the oldest, Israel, that she would feel hollow inside after their marriages. But she also expected to feel joy, which would sweeten the sadness, to feel satisfaction at having lived to see the moment when she had successfully accomplished her task of bringing up her children in such hardship and misery, and making fine healthy people out of them, people with a trade "in their hand" and not ignoramuses either. Hadn't they both, Itche Mayer and herself, lived for their children? Deprived themselves of many a bite of food for them? She did not, heaven forbid, expect any thanks. She could not imagine what she would have done in this world without her children. But at least that tiny bit of pleasure she wanted to have, the good feeling that they were leaving her, going out into the world to build something for themselves, to achieve something. With Israel she had had that feeling, and at Yossi's wedding she had deluded herself that she had it. However, with Mottle she could not even delude herself. All she felt was an ache in her body and soul.

At length she pulled herself together. Mottle was right. At least she could wish him all the happiness she wanted for him; at least she could heap her blessings on his head, as she had done for each of her sons from the moment she had taken them into her arms for the first time. So she wiped her face with both hands and approached the bed where Mottle stood waiting for his father to give him his blessings. She embraced her son, kissing his manly face with the same passion with which she had kissed him twenty-three years before, when he had lain in his crib, and she would, prodded by a surge of love inundating her heart, tear herself away from her "heads", or from the washtub full of laundry, and rush to pick up little Mottle, to cuddle him in her arms and press him to her bosom. Now, as she was wetting his face with saliva and tears, the young man's stiff taut body became softer, yielding to her embrace. He threw both arms around her neck and pressed his mouth to her gray hair. He returned her kisses, a thing he had not done since he had attained the age of reason. Sheyne Pessele, feeling the son's kiss on her head melted so in the overflow of emotions, that a new stream of tears began to wash down her face. It seemed to her that she had already been rewarded with everything she had wished for herself: cold Mottle, the stubborn mule, the choleric, the doggedly spiteful — her Mottle — loved her.

Now Itche Mayer, who had always been particularly sensitive to Sheyne

Pessele's tears, felt a tickling beneath the Adam's apple in his neck. With great effort he put his feet down on the floor, sat up and stretched out his arms to Mottle who snatched his father's hands and pumped them awkwardly. Then he bent down to the little shrunken man and kissed him on the cheek. This outpouring of affection was apparently the highest degree of tenderness to which Mottle was capable of rising, because he hastily let go of Itche Mayer, walked past Sheyne Pessele as if he no longer noticed her, and approached the knapsack in which he had packed all his belongings.

"If you need something, don't be afraid to come home," said Sheyne Pessele, following him and talking to his back. "And tell her . . . that she does not have to feel like a stranger with us. Don't let me wear out my eyes looking for you, do you hear me?"

"Am I going abroad or what, Mother?" Mottle tightened the cord around his knapsack and put his arms through the straps. Then he passed through the kitchen where Israel and Shalom had been sitting with pricked up ears to catch what was going on in the other room. He shook their hands and listened with a crooked smile to their jocular blessings.

As soon as he left, Sheyne Pessele entered the kitchen, followed by Itche Mayer clumping in his slippers. He felt the need for a "conference" with the remaining members of his family. "Wants to be on his own! It does not even suit His Majesty to live with us!" Itche Mayer still could not forgive his son.

"And you, did it suit you, to live with your parents after your marriage?" Sheyne Pessele asked. "Just try and remember."

"You call that a marriage?" Itche Mayer guffawed helplessly. "He gets up, leaves the house and that's that?"

Israel also took up Mottle's defence. "Is it his fault that there is a war on?"

Sheyne Pessele sighed, "If there had only been something to save, I could have managed to fix up a bit of a celebration for him too. If you, my husband, were in good health at least. He has no luck, Mottle, being let out from his home so dryly, so coldly."

"Don't take it to heart so much, Mother," Shalom consoled her. "He doesn't need any celebrations."

"What human being doesn't need some celebrations in his life? What are you talking about?" she asked reproachfully.

"He knows quite well what he is talking about," Itche Mayer said, fuming. "Mottle is not a family man. And do you know why he is leaving? Because he doesn't want us, that's the whole story."

Sheyne Pessele eyed him with disdain. "You should be ashamed of yourself, Itche Mayer. That's how you talk about your child, your own flesh and blood?"

Itche Mayer became even more heated. "What I wish for him may become true for me, you hear, Sheyne Pessele? But that's what it is. He knows quite well what's going on at home, that I can barely drag my legs around . . . One fine bright day we'll remain alone, Sheyne Pessele, so prepare yourself. We might give up the ghost, and still there would be no one . . ."

Israel fixed his serious eyes on his father. "Father, you of all people, talking like that?"

Shalom's face flashed a dark red. He hit his fist against the table with such violence, that the few empty glasses and plates standing on it jumped up in the air. "Father, I swear to you that I won't leave home! I will stay with you and Mother. I swear it to you right now!"

"For heaven's sake!" Sheyne Pessele called out. "Are you out of your mind or just crazy? God forbid, Shalom! How can you swear like that?"

All four of them fell into silence. Israel approached the bread cupboard where five equal portions of bread lay on five plates with differently coloured rims, so that each would recognize his portion. "Mottle did not take his ration," he remarked.

Sheyne Pessele walked over to the bread cupboard. "Poor child, in the confusion, he forgot which world he was in. He didn't even say where he was going." Shalom waited for Israel to cut his slice of bread, and took the knife from him. But instead of using it, he broke off a half of his bread portion with his hands and stuffed it quickly into his mouth. Seeing this, Sheyne Pessele reached out to tear the chunk of bread away from him. "What will you eat tomorrow and after tomorrow?" she yelled at him.

He wrestled with her, then, with his mouth full, made a dash for the door.

+ + +

To tell the truth, Shalom, just like his brothers, had become infected with the same fever. He was in love — a sweet, painful, hopeless love, a condition about which no one had the faintest idea, least of all the object of it herself.

From the moment he had seen Esther in the backyard, from the day she had arrived in the ghetto, everything within him had stirred violently, as if something had exploded inside him. He felt with his whole being that it was she, not Flora, or anyone else in the world, who dwelt within his heart. Of course there was very little in Esther's looks that could remind him of the blooming lightfooted girl with the red curly hair who had lived on in his memory — perhaps only her eyes which she squinted charmingly, or the little vein that had become larger, a blue streak to the left of her forehead. Of course she had changed, but so had his love. There was nothing in it of the dreaminess of bygone times. Now, when he saw her in his dreams, it was not only her face, but her entire alluring body which he longed to touch. It was the mystery of her being, her soul — a kind of physical soul — that he wished to join with his.

Just as he had done in the past, he began to "spy" on her, to collect pieces of information about her, to find out where she was and what she was doing during every possible hour of the day. But now he was no longer afraid to talk to her. When he saw her pass by, he would stop her and exchange a few words with her, just to hear the sound of her voice. Since he had provided her with a room, he felt entitled to knock at her door. In her room, he could see her from close up, at arm's length. Sometimes when she spoke to him, her lips were right across from his. And yet he knew that she was infinitely distant; that although she was talking to him, she did not really see him, did not know and did not want to know anything about him. And the more he saw of her and talked to her — the more unattainable she appeared and the more he longed for her.

At first he made an effort to get her to notice him. Before visiting her, he would check his shirt, his nails, his shaven face. He would help her with her daily chores, stand in line in front of the shops for her, to take out her food ration; he had often come down to the cellar, when Friede was still alive, to inquire whether she needed anything. Having noticed that the only time she would show him any interest was when he discussed politics with her, he would discuss politics with her, although, in that case, this was the most painful topic for him. He would grow heated as he argued with her, not as much in defence of his own convictions, as out of pleasure at seeing her so lively, so attentive. Her liveliness did not last long, however. The light in her eyes would quickly fade, and he knew that she wanted him to leave.

At the beginning, he would hate himself for his heavy clumsy body, his short arms, his crooked legs, his face. He was ashamed of his ignorance, his lack of education. With a desperate stubbornnesss he would try to correct his shortcomings. He read whatever came into his hands, in order to show off to her later on. But little by little he grew tired of dressing up in a skin not his own. He had to remain what he was, and only as such could he love Esther. As soon as this became clear to him, he regained his pride. He gave up scrutinizing himself before he went up to see her and gave up reading the books which did not interest him. It was not in his nature to read books. He had no patience for them. Never mind, he knew enough about life without having to read about it. And a mind of his own he also had, and his heart was certainly in the right place. He had nothing to be ashamed of.

At the same time, however, he became more submissive and humble in his love. There was no longer the will to win Esther — only the pleasure of serving her. He cared about how she looked, what mood she was in; he could easily guess whether she was rested or tired. After Friede's death, his heart would hurt at the sight of her passing the yard, broken, her mind transported into distant worlds. He would embrace her red curly head with his eyes and kiss her tired squinting eyes with his glance. His heart was engulfed by so much warmth, so much tenderness, that he felt almost like weeping. Indeed, he felt capable of prostrating himself before her with all his pride, with his entire being — so that she would stride across him as on a padded sidewalk, in order that life might not hurt her so much.

As she recuperated, as her sunken cheeks became fuller and rosier and her twig-like arms became more rounded, as her bosom and hips began to give shape to the clothes on her body, his heart filled with gratitude, yet also with a new kind of uneasiness. Now when he saw her appear before him, his hungry body would swell with such desire, that he was barely able to control himself. He had once wished that she would become so intimate with him, that she would allow him to sit in a corner of her room and watch her without having to talk politics with her, or making any other effort. He only wanted to breathe the air that she was breathing. Now he knew that he would never be able to bear such intimacy.

It never came to that anyway. Their relationship had not changed much from the moment they had met, and their lives, although so intertwined on account of Shalom's feelings, headed in different directions. He was an optimist by nature. He believed that his father would get well, that more Resorts would soon open and he would find work; he was sure that the war would come to an end soon and that socialism would arrive. Only in one respect was he a pessimist. He despaired of a future for his love of Esther.

As a rule, an optimist by nature becomes panic-stricken when it comes to handling an attack of despair. It is like discovering a foreign body within himself; a discomfort of the soul, a disturbance of the mind liable to destroy the inner core. Thus Shalom's explosions of uncontrolled anger' repeated themselves with increasing frequency. He would yell and storm for no reason at all, and at whoever happened to be at hand. At other times he would attack the bread cupboard, stuffing himself without measure or self-control; and he felt himself capable of doing worse. Until he decided that he could no longer go on like that, that he had to feel the ground under his feet again — find work, hard physical work that would exhaust not only his body, but also his despair.

He began to pass his days in the former butcher shops where the workers would gather according to their occupation. It was expected that many work Resorts would open any day now. Nothing happened however, and he began to go to all kinds of storage places, or to Baluter Ring, in case someone with strong hands was needed to deliver a load, or to unload a truck. He would also walk from house to house with his carpentry tools, inquiring whether people needed something fixed. It was a futile search. To whom would it occur, in such times, to spend a penny on fixing doors, or windows, or pieces of furniture?

So things went on until the "chicken blindness" smelled Shalom out, "soaping him in" at home in the evenings. Barely able to see in the dark, he could no longer await Esther in the yard and would seldom see her. He was glad. Firstly, because the doctor had prescribed a ration of liver, as the best remedy for the disease. Sheyne Pessele sold the liver and bought a bit of flour and some potatoes for it. Secondly, Shalom hoped that along with the "chicken blindness" he would cure himself of his "blinding" love for Esther. The "chicken blindness" was also lucky for him, because it brought him closer to Valentino who would often come in to "have a word" with him — until they talked themselves into the idea of finding a job for Shalom.

During those days Valentino was indeed in his "feathers". He and his cronies were the "power behind the house committee" and he would pace the backyard, hands in pockets, the undisputed master and ruler of the yard. He wore massive boots which loudly announced his arrival, and if the boots did not do it, his voice did. Even when the yard was full of people, Valentino would stand out with his tall build, with his head full of wild black locks, his muscular neck and his dark skin that shone like brown polished leather. Since the backyard was his estate, he would accost whomever he pleased, starting from the children to whom he sometimes threw candies from his pocket, up to Mrs. Yadwiga Rosenberg, whom he would address in a Polish full of rolling r's and mistakes on every second word. He was always well disposed, cheerful. Yet everyone knew that even while laughing, he was capable of knocking a man out "between a yes and a no", so that the latter would not be able to stand up on his feet with all his bones intact. In particular lately it had entered no one's head to start up with him. The entire yard was aware that Valentino was hiding a wound behind his smile. He had his Achilles heel.

The neighbours often saw him in the evenings looking up at a particular window on the third floor. They could hear him whistle under the cherry tree like a lovesick canary. They would spot him standing at the entrance to Esther's stairway, so that she should at least brush against his arm as she walked by, because she had long since stopped speaking to him or even greeting him. He would make himself the laughing-stock of all the neighbours when he placed himself in front of her in the yard, not letting her pass before she said a word to him. Of course nobody laughed at him openly. They were all as careful not to tease him, as one is careful not to tease a wounded lion.

Valentino chose none other than Shalom to be his confessor.

Valentino's apartment was downstairs. There, together with him and Sheindle, lived his sister and her half dozen children, whom she had had with a half dozen different gentlemen. The apartment also harboured the store where Valentino traded in smuggled merchandise while the ghetto was still open, and with stolen wares, after the ghetto was closed. Valentino had his cronies in the "white guard", the army of flour porters who made "golden" business, as well as in all the other departments of food provisions, including the meat storages, the dairy storages and the Vegetable Place. His store was of course illegal, but well greased.

After Shalom was cured from the "chicken blindness", Valentino invited him to his kitchen for a cup of coffee. Along with the coffee a substantial slice of buttered bread and a piece of *baba* cake of a pre-war taste appeared on the table. At the "cup of coffee" Valentino proceeded with his confession. He, Valentino, looked on Shalom with the kind of awe one has for the lackey who guards the entrance to a palace. He knew that Esther was talking to Shalom, that she let him enter her room, that she stopped to talk to him whenever she met him in the yard. So he asked Shalom silly little things about her, which apparently had a particular meaning for him. It was clear that Esther's seductive image reigned in his mind. He would look into Shalom's eyes as if he were begging him for something. "You hear, Shalom, as long as I live I have never gone through such a thing."

Shalom understood that the mighty Valentino was imploring him to intercede with Esther on his behalf, and Shalom was amused. It was pleasant to listen to Valentino talking, and conjure up Esther's image in his own imagination, to fondle his own great secret in his heart, a secret which no one in the world knew — and at the same time to feel so much superior to the powerful Valentino, so much stronger and, of course, smarter than he. Valentino's passion for Esther seemed so funny, his hope to conquer her "by her own good will" so ridiculous, that it made Shalom think of a dwarf trying to reach for the sun. Valentino's mighty figure pining away in its melancholy despair was so laughable, that Shalom sometimes found it hard to control himself and keep a serious face. He patted him on the shoulder and looked cockily up at him, saying "Feh, Valentino, time that you knock this craziness out of your head."

Valentino spread his hands out forlornly. "Easy to say, knock it out. And if you smashed and crushed me into pieces, you think it would help? As I am a Jew . . . I've tried everything in the world, you hear, Shalom? But what can I do? There is no one else like her."

In his heart of hearts Shalom readily agreed with him. There was no one else like Esther in the whole wide world. So he offered Valentino another argument, "You forget that you have a wife, Valentino?"

"So what if I have? What does one have to do with the other? Sheindle herself says that Esther is for me like the Holy Mary. That's what she is. A god! Do you think that I would be in such a dither over any other of her kind? So, you're wrong, brother. Every other hen falls into my hands even before I open my mouth, you hear? But not Esther. Maybe if I weren't such a know-nothing . . . if I became a *mentsch* . . ."

He asked Shalom to talk to him about "intelligent things", to enlighten him in geography, to tell him the latest news about events at the fronts, and to teach him the exact names of all the generals and important strategic locations. He became interested in the political parties in the ghetto and wanted none other than Shalom to enlighten him about the communist program. Shalom, however, poured "pitch and sulphur" upon Comrade Stalin's head and on his pact with Hitler. And the confused Valentino could in no way connect Esther to the caricature of an idealogy that Shalom sketched for him. This being the case, Shalom took advantage of the occasion to paint the noble superiority of his own ideal for Valentino, trying to recruit him for his own party. "Do you remember that before the war you were almost a *Hasid* of Bundism?" he nudged Valentino.

Valentino shook his head. "What are you knocking me in the head with your Bundism-shmundism for? I want to be a red. If Esther is red, justice must be red too!"

"That doesn't even begin to be true," Shalom argued all afire. It was painful for him to remember that Esther belonged to the enemy camp. "Even she can be blinded by the fancy words they preach. She herself probably believes in communism sincerely, but let her go and live under their dictatorship, then we'll see what she thinks of it!"

"Dictatorship is fine, first class!" Valentino pounded his fist against the table. "A strong hand, a hard law, that's what is needed so that we, the proletarians, can have our say."

Shalom grimaced, "Since when did you become a proletarian?"

"I will become one! I'll go to work and become a *mentsch*. Let them only open the Resorts. Now go and tell her that I want to register in her party."

Shalom looked at him resolutely, "Not on your life. I don't recruit members for someone else's party. If you want to, go and tell her yourself!"

They parted as enemies and for a while avoided each other in the yard. Until one evening Valentino grabbed hold of Shalom's sleeve and pulled him into his kitchen. "I am going to become a red!" He looked into Shalom's eyes, evidently moved. "I talked to her, maybe for half an hour. She'll send a young man over. Twice a week he'll come to give me lessons. You know," he became sentimental. "I owe you a debt. If it were not for you, it would never have come to this." He placed his big heavy hand on Shalom's shoulder. "You see, you are the kind of friend that is worth having. Wouldn't I jump into the fire for you, you think? So, do you want a kilo of flour? A bag of sugar? A basket of vegetables?" Valentino was changed beyond recognition. A grimace of painful determination twisted his face.

"I need nothing," Shalom stammered, unable to disguise his amazement over what had so unexpectedly happened to the fellow.

"What do you mean you need nothing?" Valentino insisted. "You think I don't see how your father looks, and you yourself . . . A man wants to do something for you, why don't you let him and stop holding your nose up so high in the air? Where is your bit of humanity, great Bundist that you are? Only villains don't accept favours, you hear? That is my territory!"

"Theory you mean," Shalom corrected him, his heart aching with regret. Valentino could have become more of a *mentsch* in the Bund than with the communists. Yet Valentino was right in what he was saying and Shalom gave in to him. "Find me a job," he said.

That particular demand was quite daring. Not that Valentino's good intentions did not reach so far, but his possibilities in this respect were limited. He did have connections in every important department, but to the official "high windows" from which one could get an honest job, he was unable to reach. Therefore it took some time before he managed to figure something out. "You're a carpenter, aren't you?" Valentino began to draw his plan before Shalom. "So, fix yourself up a hand cart, a strong one, and take yourself a partner, so that one of you can pull it from the front and the other push it from behind."

"And what is it that we will push?" Shalom asked.

"Garbage."

"Are you making fun of me?"

"God forbid. And if you think that you can so easily get such a job, you're wrong."

"Not just anyone can become a garbage collector in the ghetto, eh?"

Shalom wanted to leave, but Valentino blocked his way out. "You think I don't know what's on your mind?" He placed his large hand on Shalom's shoulder. "You say to yourself that I, the bigshot Valentino, your dear friend, could afford to provide you with a better fish and fry. So, the thing is that I can't. If you wanted to walk my alley and become one of ours, that would be another story. But you don't want to do that, do you? Then, being a garbage collector is the cleanest job that there could be. The Sanitation Department is paying, mind you, and the thing is only that you have to be acquainted with the janitors in the yards, because they give the garbage to whomever they please. In that respect, you see, you can rely on me. You are assured of the whole of Hockel Street, and as for the other streets, don't worry. You just have to do one thing. Get a permit from the Sanitation Department because to them I am no bigshot, and you have yourself a ready-made job."

A few days later Shalom found himself the necessary partner, a neighbour from across the street, a bookkeeper by profession, a small middle-aged gentleman who wore thick glasses to match his pallid intellectual face, a father of two *gymnasium* girls and the spouse of a very bony Polish-speaking lady. Mr. Wiseman had acquaintances in the Sanitation Department, and it was not difficult for him to acquire the necessary document.

And so their collaboration began. Mr. Wiseman fitted himself out in a pair of brown coveralls and Shalom dressed up in a pair of old pants with a threadbare jacket. One day Shalom acted as the horse and harnessed himself to the shaft, the other day it was his partner's turn. Shalom was satisfied with his partner who was an industrious man, meticulous and exact, bookkeeper-like. Every garbage dump they emptied was picked clean and not a speck of paper or refuse escaped the attention of Mr. Wiseman's bespectacled eyes. Mr. Wiseman had only one single weakness, namely, he loathed rats, and before the two garbage collectors could approach the loaded trash boxes, Shalom first had to shoo off the freeloaders. He did not mind this, since he had been familiar with the species for as long as he could remember, having practically grown up with them. Consequently, this weakness of Mr. Wiseman had no bearing whatsoever on their harmonious collaboration.

It was in general quite pleasant to be in Mr. Wiseman's company. They would never discuss their work; there were more interesting topics to discuss. Mr. Wiseman was an educated man and there was barely a subject about which

Shalom would ask, that did not inspire him to relate an interesting story. Only one subject did not interest him: politics. He had never occupied his mind with it and here, in the ghetto, he avoided it like the plague. "That is black magic!" He would shake off a political question with such revulsion, as if he were suddenly surprised by the sight of a fair of rats. "You can see where it has brought the world, can't you?" No matter how vehemently Shalom insisted, explaining to him how important it was that people knew what kind of stew was being cooked in the Upper Kettles, it was to no avail. Even to the news of the battlefront Mr. Wiseman lent only "half an ear", nodding, as if he had known the results all along.

He and Shalom spoke Polish to each other. It was not that Mr. Wiseman had any difficulties with the Yiddish language, but he probably felt that the fact of conversing in Polish elevated in some way the profession of garbage collector to an aristocratic height which excluded any feeling of shame. And Shalom did not object.

Thus Shalom finally found the ground under his feet. It was delightful to lift the rake, to feel one's muscles move, to feel the blood circulate livelier in one's body. Even his head worked better, clearer, and the pangs of hunger had an orderliness and patience about them. Only his thoughts of Esther did not allow themselves to be fitted into the pattern of regularity. Sometimes they attacked him unexpectedly, pricking him like needles. He protected himself against them as well as he could. He lifted the rake more vigorously or became entangled in the conversation with Mr. Wiseman in a silly awkward manner; just like someone who feels an attack of illness approaching and tries to drown it in noise, in order not to feel it burn inside him. Sometimes he succeeded in forgetting himself, at other times he did not. It also happened that in his self-assurance, in the strength derived from working his muscles, he would call Esther's image to his mind and think of her with a leisurely tenderness. Then his heart would feel warm, enveloped in his love as in a soft silken shawl. Yes, here, at the garbage dumps, he was occasionally capable of such moods. He would try to hold on to them as long as he could, but the rake would finally rake them, too, away.

✦ ✦ ✦

It was a good day for the ghetto. Placards had appeared on the walls, announcing that the Presess would pay nine *rumkis* per head allowance for those families where no one was working. The streets were full of clamour. People clustered in front of the placards. Total strangers would stop each other in the street and discuss the issue at hand as if they had been neighbours of long standing. Even the children abandoned their games and moved between the groups of grown-ups; they caught one word here, another there, and bridged them with their own comments. It was they who carried the news around to those who had not learned of it yet, and that included Shalom.

Shalom realized that he had to see such an announcement with his own eyes and he left Mr. Wiseman with the cart, to go and read through the placard point by point, thereafter sending off his partner to take a glimpse at it. "For nothing in the world will I leave the job," Shalom was the first to speak as they resumed their march down Hockel Street.

As far as Mr. Wiseman was concerned, he was not so sure. "Garbage collecting is something you do out of necessity, when the knife is at your throat," he said.

Shalom shook his head. "It makes no difference to me. Let it be garbage, but never again will I go around idle, with nothing to do."

The same day however became exceptional for them precisely on account of their garbage collecting. As they were marching along with their empty cart, they heard someone call after them. Turning their heads, they saw two Jewish policemen waving their hands at them from the distance, indicating that they should stop. "Be so nice, gentlemen, and make an about turn," ordered one, as soon as he came abreast of the garbage collectors. Both policemen seemed preoccupied and excited.

Mr. Wiseman cast a stealthy glance at Shalom, "To jail?"

The other policeman pinned Mr. Wiseman by his overalls, "That's right! Straight to jail!"

His colleague calmed them down, "We are only going to pay a private visit at the private residence of the Chief of the Prison. Carry on!"

In the yard where the chief of the ghetto prison lived, Shalom immediately recognized the fleshy face of the *Kripo* man Sutter in one of the windows. "A search!" he whispered solemnly in his partner's ear. Following the instructions of the policemen, the garbage collectors approached the wall with their cart. Herr Sutter leaned out of the window, politely indicating the exact spot where to place the cart, so that it would stand straight below him. After a while a rain of little soft packages wrapped in shiny silver paper began to pour down from the window. They fell almost soundlessly into the wagon. Shalom and Mr. Wiseman picked up those that missed. "Tea!" Shalom let out a sudden suppressed shout. A little package rustled dryly between his fingers.

Strange thoughts began to inundate their minds. It was clear that with such a cartful of tea one could survive the war, dancing. Mr. Wiseman's eyes behind the heavily rimmed glasses began to jump from Shalom to the policemen, from the policemen back to Shalom. His cheeks turned white, his lips turned blue, and he shook as if he had a fever. The policemen too, when they saw the treasure pouring down from the window became deadly serious, their eyes grew big and round, the pupils full of greedy stupefaction.

The cart was three quarters full, when the rain of silver bags stopped. Herr Sutter leaned out from the window and glanced at the cart. He raised his hand, signalling to someone behind his back. Now he held tiny bottles in his hand. They were in various shapes, some tied with coloured ribbons, others with thin golden cords. The little bottles began to fall into the cart, on top of the soft heap of the tea packages. This happened in slow motion. Herr Sutter aimed carefully, so that he would not miss the cart. After a while, however, there was a light clink of glass as something hit against the edge of the cart. A crushed bottle fell into it, splashing its content over the heap of tea packs.

The world around Shalom began to smell like a rose garden, like an alley of lilacs, like a field of hyacinths, since some of the following bottles broke as well. Shalom's head began to swim from the mishmash of intoxicating fragrances. It seemed as if a wonderful, a heavenly spring had suddenly burst into bloom.

"*Donnerwetter!*" Herr Sutter was heard cursing upstairs.

The little bottles stopped falling. Soon Herr Sutter himself appeared in the yard, followed by a German wearing a Tyrolean hat. Both had their pockets stuffed with little bottles. Herr Sutter buried his short hands in the cart and fished out the pieces of glass. He felt the wet tea packs with his fingers, then threw about twenty of them to the ground. He blinked at the two garbage collectors, addressing them in a homey Yiddish, as he pointed to the ground, "This is for you and for you!" With a smile of his broad froggish lips, he took a minute bottle in his hand, looked it over, weighed it between his fingers and with a generous gesture handed it to Mr. Wiseman, "And this is for your women. Let them divide it between themselves and tear each other by the hair." He laughed with a croak to his companion in the Tyrolean hat. Shalom and Mr. Wiseman thanked him. Herr Sutter gave a sign with his hand and the two garbage collectors harnessed themselves to the cart. They passed the two policemen whose faces expressed the disenchantment of cheated children. And thus began the procession through the ghetto in the direction of the *Kripo*.

This was some march and these were some garbage collectors! From their pockets such an aroma was released into the air that passers-by had to stop and inhale, hard-pressed to believe that such a smell was coming from a garbage cart. Of course they would have immediately assaulted the cart, had it not been for Herr Sutter, his companion and the two policemen who followed behind. So the passers-by kept at a distance, eyeing the heap of silver packages as they wondered and pondered what it all was supposed to mean.

After unloading the cart in the storage cellars of the *Kripo*, Shalom and Mr. Wiseman roused themselves and headed for their homes in a rush. They pulled the empty cart, running with their arms linked, like two drunkards. People looked after them; stunned by their smell, they tried to accost them. But the two garbage collectors were barely aware of what was happening around them. All they felt was the soft touch of their swollen pockets against their hips. They were dizzy, their heads swimming in clouds of perfumy aromas. "We're rich!" Mr. Wiseman said in a choking voice.

"We're rich!" Shalom repeated after him with a stammer.

As they approached their respective homes, Mr. Wiseman composed himself somewhat. "And the perfume we'll sell to a *shishka*, eh, Shalom?" he proposed practically. "Which of us needs perfume, eh, Shalom?"

Shalom was struck by a great idea. "I'm buying off your part of it," he proposed.

Mr. Wiseman beamed, "You have a fiancée?"

"No, not a fiancée."

The transaction was made.

When Shalom entered his apartment, he was met by a confused Sheyne Pessele. The story of the allowance had knocked her off balance. And here was Shalom swooping down on her with the announcement, "Mother, we are saved! Look what I have!" Nonchalantly, he tossed the tea packages on the table and a spring-like intoxicating fragrance began to permeate the air of the entire room. Sheyne Pessele was stunned. It was a long while before she could utter a word. Now she was really undecided about what to do with the problem of the allowance. Should Shalom give up his garbage collecting job or not. Because now, for instance, it came out that salvation might unexpectedly come precisely through garbage collecting, and who knows whether Shalom might not one day arrive with such a treasure, that one could peacefully survive the entire war thanks to it. Shalom slumped into a chair, spread his legs and called out, "You know what, Mother! You first brew us a kettle of tea and let me have something to eat, and then we shall see . . ."

Sheyne Pessele agreed with him. First of all a person had to eat, then he could talk. Before she served Shalom supper, however, she went into the other room to fetch Itche Mayer who had been lying on his bed. She told him the good news and he trudged after her into the kitchen. Sheyne Pessele boiled a kettle of water and tore away the silver paper of a tea package, with shaking fingers. Not since the outbreak of the war had any one in the household tasted a decent glass of tea. "A few glasses of strong tea a day may put you back on your feet, Itche Mayer," she said to her husband; then she turned to face her son, "What is the price of a package of tea on the black market nowadays? And how many packages should we sell, and how many should we leave for ourselves, eh, Shalom?"

Shalom made a wide gesture with his arm, "As many as you want, Mother."

"And maybe we shouldn't hurry, and keep everything as a remedy for Father?"

"All right, let's leave everything for Father."

"A half of it we'll sell and a half we'll leave," she decided. "A bite of meat and a piece of bread should not be shrugged off either. And what have you put into the drawer there?"

"Nothing."

"What do you mean nothing? I saw with my own eyes that you put something in there."

"A little bottle of perfume, that's all. Sutter gave it to me."

"A pretty nothing!" Sheyne Pessele beamed. "Little thing! Do you have an idea, Itche Mayer, how this is perfuming the whole room? And what's the price of perfume on the black market nowadays, eh, Shalom? This, you see, you can turn into money here, in the yard. Ask the vamp with the manicured fingernails who lives in the Landlord's Palace."

Shalom cut her off, "The perfume is mine."

Sheyne Pessele stared at him questioningly, "For whom is it, if I may ask?"

"For nobody. I'm going to sell it and contribute the money to the fund of the Youth Movement."

"Your end will be that you'll marry your movement." She rumpled his hair affectionately.

They ate hurriedly. In comparison with the tea, today's meal had lost some of its importance. And as they were eating, their nostrils became increasingly aware of the sharp breathtaking aroma issuing from the steaming teapot, an aroma not of tea but of perfume. At length Sheyne Pessele began to pour the tea into the waiting glasses. She did it slowly, unsurely. At the sight of the tea colour filling the glasses she felt reassured. "It smells good." She eyed Itche Mayer, slightly disconcerted. "Take a spoonful of sugar with it."

"It pricks in the nostrils," Itche Mayer mumbled, keeping his eyes fixed on the magnificent colour of the glass. Shalom was the first to take a sip. He was sipping not tea, but amber-coloured perfume. Itche Mayer and Sheyne Pessele also took a sip. A light steam rose from the hot glasses. Its wonderfully sweet and flowery smell permeated the air with an indescribable sadness. Itche Mayer shoved away his glass. "A spoonful of sugar wasted."

Sheyne Pessele sighed and with feigned pleasure forced herself to take another sip. "I like it," she said, "Tea with alcohol is healthy."

Shalom also pushed his glass away. Avoiding his parents' glances, he approached the drawer, took out the little bottle of perfume and left the room. Of all his hopes only one ray remained: to hand over the gift to Esther. Impatiently he paced about the backyard. The problem was that a celebration devoted to the works of Sholom Aleichem was supposed to be taking place at the youth *dzialka*, the camp organized by the party on the plot of ground it had received in Marysin. All week Shalom had promised himself that he would hurry to the *dzialka* right after work, to help his comrades with the preparations, but offering Esther the gift could not be postponed. He imagined what she would say, what he would reply. In his mind, he saw her opening the cork of the tiny bottle and pouring perfume over her red curly hair. He saw her enveloped in the same fragrance which only a short while before had chased him out of his apartment. Only through Esther could it rehabilitate itself. Only through Esther could it restore his equilibrium.

At dusk she arrived. The grayness of the backyard lit up with the light of her hair. He stepped forward to meet her, and as he approached her, he pondered whether to push the tiny flagon immediately into her hand and leave her, or whether he should accompany her to her room and then hand it over to her. His heart aflutter, he observed her unbuttoned coat, the colour of her light dress, her slim bare legs and her feet clad in the light summer shoes. It occurred to him that she was dressed too lightly for the time of the year. Her eyes squinted, blinking at him with familiarity as she shook his hand, not intending to stop with him. "May I come up to your room for a moment?" he muttered.

She looked down at the ground, "I am busy."

"Only for a second." She did not reply but allowed him to follow her. As soon as they stepped over the threshold of her room, he drew out the flagon from his pocket and handed it to her. "A gift for you!" he cried out with a triumphant ring in his voice, while his hungry eyes scanned her face.

She lifted her thin eyebrows. A charming, a curious kind of smile played on her lips, "Perfume?"

"Real perfume!" He watched her as she looked at the tiny bottle and touched it to the tip of her nose. "Pour a bit over yourself," he encouraged her.

He heard her ringing laughter, warm, thin, both childish and wise. "What do I need it for?" He looked at her, lost, speechless. "Don't you know yet, Shalom, that I'm not one of those women who uses this kind of thing? I know it's not nice to refuse a gift, but . . ." She handed him the little bottle and took off her coat, standing there in her sleeveless light dress, thoughtful, as if she were not aware of his presence. Then she fetched the empty water bucket. He remained glued to his place confounded, until he caught himself, took the bucket out of her hand and before she could utter a word, he rushed down the stairs. He felt his heart pounding in his bosom; he felt that she must take the perfume from him. As he turned the wheel of the water pump and watched the streams of water drum against the bottom of the bucket, he saw rivers of perfume, cascading springs pouring over Esther's red head.

Soon he was back in her room again. He noticed that she was no longer wearing her dress but a light ankle-length fitted housecoat which revealed the outlines of her shapely figure. Above its round collar her head looked like a curly multi-petalled flower with red smiling lips. She wanted to take the bucket out of his hand, but he would not let her, putting it in its place himself. He breathed heavily, with his gaze embracing her beauty which hurt him so much. "Take the bottle," he implored.

She laughed, "What's come over you, Shalom?" She busied herself, filling a basin with water, preparing a towel, a piece of soap. "It doesn't make sense," she added. He panicked, afraid that now she might discover his secret. He rushed to the door. "Thanks for the water!" her voice followed him.

As soon as he reached the street, he flung the little bottle into the gutter with the same movement of the arm as he had seen Herr Sutter use that morning. He set out at a run in the direction of Marysin where the Solom Aleichem celebration was taking place

◆　◆　◆

The Bundist *dzialka* was a solitary island in the sea of Zionist *dzialkas* which took up a large part of Marysin. Mr. Zibert, who had so enthusiastically supported Presess Rumkowski's idea of creating a children's paradise in Marysin, was by nature a practical man. He was of the opinion that to offer a substantial plot of land to the Bundists was equal to taking a slab of gold and throwing it into the sea. The Bundists did not in any case support the idea of emigration to Eretz Israel, or think of joining the *kibbutzim* and working on the land — so what good was there in wasting a good piece of land on them, when it could serve Zionist children to learn agriculture on, and thus serve the Zionist ideal? But to Mr. Zibert's chagrin, the Bund was a force in the ghetto with which the Presess had to reckon; they were a threat to his endeavours because of their manipulating the "starving ghetto proletariat". And he felt obliged to throw them a bone once in a while.

The trees on the Bundist *dzialka*, however, flowered and gave fruit just like the trees on the Zionist *dzialkas*. And although here, in the evenings, Yiddish songs and songs of the liberation of all mankind were sung, and there, Hebrew songs were sung, *horas* were danced and one would dreamily long for Eretz Israel — the children felt with all their senses that the earth was everyone's mother, and they treated her with respect. They, the youngsters of Marysin, had grown to become full-fledged experts on trees. They diligently studied agronomy and invented increasingly better means of improving the growth of whatever they planted. And across the "political" fences they shared their experiences, offering each other advice, each group boasting of its own harvest.

There were forty young people in all on the Bundist *dzialka* which was called "The Ninth Socialist Children's Republic", implying the continuation of their summer camps of the past. And they conducted themselves as in a republic, electing their own council through a parliamentary voting system, collectively deciding on the sowing, the planting, or on who should be the main speaker at a gathering. They had their own drama circle, their own wall-newspaper with the camp news and the ghetto news, with editorials, poems and stories. They had their own library; they studied political economy, sociology and history; and they shared a common meal prepared from food provided for only twenty-two people.

As Shalom entered the orchard, he saw the whole gathering at once. Although the air was already cool, autumnal, they were sitting outside; they looked like strange, motionless plants rising from the beds of soil. The pale cool sun was reflected in their faces. All eyes were fixed on the performer who was standing in the centre of the group. Their gazes seemed to hang on to his mouth in the expectation of a funny line, of a clownish grimace; their mouths were open, ready to explode with laughter. When the laughter came, it exploded chorally, gratefully, embracing Shalom with warmth. They made room for him on the edge of a box. Among the invited guests sat his brother Israel, waving his hand at him.

Mucha, the leader of the drama group, a dark young man whose eyes burned with the unquenched desire to become an actor, was mobilizing all his talents, in order to give the spectators a perfect rendition of Mottle the Orphan's adventures in Menashe the Barber-Surgeon's orchard. Here, in their own orchard, it was easy for the youngsters to understand Mottle as he lay on the roof, greedily watching the fruits on the barber-surgeon's trees. Here, in their own orchard, he seemed much funnier, much nearer to their hearts than ever before. And here they also felt superior to Mottle, because they were not afraid of a barber-surgeon, nor of his dog. They themselves were the owners of an orchard.

Shalom heard his own laughter among the chorus of voices. As he laughed, he imagined his parents in the orchard in Konska Vola; he saw his own cherry tree; and as he laughed, he began to feel like crying. He did not know whether it was on account of his mother who craved to drink a glass of real tea, or on account of his father who was becoming steadily more ill, or on account of Esther who would not respond to his love. He jumped to his feet and dashed out of the garden.

He was slowly pacing along the sandy path when he felt his brother's hand on his shoulder. "Why did you leave?" Israel asked, although his wise gray eyes seemed to know the answer; there was so much of Shalom's sadness reflected in them. "Stay," Israel took hold of his arm.

By the time they were on their way home, it was already dark. They marched arm in arm, in disorderly rows, arguing about what Sholom Aleichem's greatest work was, and whether one could reconstruct the image of life in the *shtetl* purely on the basis of his works. They deplored the fact that there was no Sholom Aleichem living in the ghetto, that if all the Jews perished at the hands of the Germans, there would not remain even a single work immortalizing life in the ghetto, or depicting the *dzialka*, for instance, or a type like Mucha who so badly wanted to become an actor.

Shalom's arm was linked with Israel's. The ache in his heart was still present, but seemed milder. How well Shalom now understood the meaning of brotherhood, of friendship. How near all his comrades were to his heart! He felt capable of doing so much for them. Never before had he felt such "boundless devotion to the Bund".

Chapter Ten

TO ADAM ROSENBERG happiness began to mean nothing more than the breathing space between one tragedy and another. The deeper the abyss of misfortune, the higher the moment of happiness. Before the war, the worst thing that could have befallen him was an attack of the liver, or the flu, or Sutchka's indisposition, or a slump on the stock market. For this reason he had hardly ever experienced the sensation of happiness. What he knew was a pale sense of satisfaction, of well-being, which he accepted as a matter of fact.

It was different in the ghetto. Here he savoured the taste of happiness with his whole being. Its power surprised him. It fed on so little, on things he would have considered rather tragic before the war. How could the pitifully few German marks that he earned on his transactions with those Germans or Poles who visited the ghetto compare with the profits he had once made every day? How could Reisel's "cuisine" compare with the meals in Feldman's restaurant? How could the German "straw" he now smoked, and which it cost him so much trouble to procure, compare with the cigars he had once smoked? And yet, he had never derived as much enjoyment from life as now. Not only were the women in the ghetto, whom he would buy for a piece of bread or a few marks, capable of giving him moments of ecstasy, but even his family life provided him with new pleasures. For all the spaciousness of his house in town, for all its glitter and comfort, the coldness and emptiness would nevertheless drive him away. Now, however, life felt warm and cozy in the two rooms that belonged to him. They were home.

Yadwiga, who had changed so little in her looks and still indulged herself in such silly ways, now slowly revealed the hidden recesses of her soul to him. She needed him and clung to him as if her life were in his hands. Only now did he feel that she belonged to him. Only now had she become a real wife. And he, his heart overflowing with generosity, no longer felt so repulsed by her sagging breasts, by her protruding hip bones, by her lean dry body. His physical disgust, his boredom with her yielded to his kindness. Once in a while he made love to her and her gratitude would elate him.

His son Mietek also became more approachable in the ghetto. He had matured, become muscular, manly, No longer was he the son who noticed his father only when he needed a few zlotys. Now he was a comrade, a companion to whom one could turn when in need, who knew what was going on and who could teach his father a thing or two. Mietek so readily put his policeman's earnings on the table, with such satisfaction did he bring home his additional food rations, that Adam sometimes felt ashamed and guilty. It seemed to him that basically he did not deserve such devotion, and he accepted it as a gift from heaven.

But above everyone and everything else, there was his devoted Sutchka, the brown bitch with the drooping ears and the round brown eyes with their wise gaze. To her Adam had been attached even in the other life. It was to her that he would rush home impatiently, bringing treats and walking her. There had been no vacation for him without her, in spite of the difficulties he encountered in foreign hotels and guest houses. Yet it had never occurred to him that he loved her. This dawned upon him only here, in the ghetto. It was like a revelation: He, who loved no one in this world, who juggled with the word "love" both at home and in the outside world, he who in reality hated so many, feeling even towards his best friends a mixture of disdain and aversion — he loved an animal, a dog. And he rejoiced in that feeling and nurtured it. It occurred to him that all his life he had been emotionally impotent, and that only Sutchka had taught him to love, had helped him to discover that treasure within himself without which life seemed to make no sense.

The fact that a dog could accomplish a feat, which a human being could not, did not surprise Adam. For a long time he had harboured the conviction that the dog belonged to a higher species than man; that although the dog had not been created for great achievements and was not endowed with the wisdom or intelligence of man, it was beyond a doubt also free of man's deviousness and cruelty. What was the dog's devotion, if not the truest expression of its being, its essence? Egoism, the overload of the human soul, was alien to the dog. Thus Adam would look down at Sutchka, but with respect, with admiration and gratitude. Every day after supper, he would brush her, a chore he had previously left to his chauffeur. And while brushing her, he would converse with her, not with silly words as one usually uses to a dog, but with his gaze. What they exchanged were no longer banalities. Expressed aloud, they would have sounded funny, ridiculous; conveyed through silence, they were perfect. The conversation could flow the richer, the more expressively between them, because it was not forced to fit into the strait-jacket of the spoken word.

His favourite moments of the day were when he took his daily walks with her. Together they would roam the streets, side by side, tied to each other by a cord of speechless understanding. Later, when the abyss of misfortune again yawned before him, when he felt that he was slowly being swallowed by it, he would wander off with Sutchka as far as Marysin. There he would unhitch her from the leash, finding solace in the sight of the dog's freedom. He would sit down under a tree with her, and feel her chin against his lap. Looking into her serious brown eyes, he would forget about his worries, about the hidden fears that were beginning to haunt him again.

This occurred after the ghetto had been hermetically sealed off from the rest of the world, and the Germans and Poles were no longer allowed to enter and trade with the Jews. Adam lost his meager earnings; he could only occasionally mediate in small deals in the ghetto proper, where there was not much left to deal in. The daily raids on the houses by the *Kripo*, or the ghetto police had left behind empty hiding places, and whoever did manage to salvage some valuables, held on to them as security against the darkest hour. Those whose darkest hour had already arrived, hurried to Rumkowski's Trading Post where they would exchange their treasures for *rumkis*, with which one could immediately buy food.

A few days before the ghetto was so tightly closed off, Adam, in a moment of panic, sent a Pole to retrieve part of his treasure which he had left hidden in town. After paying the Pole his share, Adam realized that his capital was quite substantial, even for the ghetto. Apart from that, if bad came to worse, there was still Mietek with his earnings and his additional food rations. And since Adam had acquired the habit of living in the given moment, he tried to remain calm and pretend not to notice that his bowl of soup was becoming more watery with each passing day. Fear, however, lurked beneath the surface.

He tried to loosen the grip of panic by talking, fast, uncontrollably, and to whoever happened to be at hand. He considered Samuel, however, to be the most suitable assistant in his escape from fear. Adam would watch for him at the window, and as soon as Samuel appeared on the threshold, he would step forward, making it appear that they had met by accident. He greeted him with feigned indifference, then waited impatiently until Samuel finished his meal. Only then would Adam knock on his door and whether or not Samuel was willing, he somehow persuaded him to come into his own room.

The inhabitants of the apartment no longer lived like one big family. Now they were more like neighbours who had known each other before the war. They kept the doors to their rooms shut and locked them when they left the house. In the kitchen, the hours for eating and cooking were divided (the quarrels between Reisel, the cook, and Matilda had stopped as if by magic.) Each family had a few cupboards to itself. The food, however, was kept not in the kitchen, but in the private quarters.

The two women, Matilda and Yadwiga, no longer felt they had anything in common. Yadwiga had found new companions who suited her better. They were the wives of two great smugglers who constantly commuted between Lodz and Warsaw. With her new friends Yadwiga could play a good game of poker (of them and others like them a recently composed song said: "In their gardens they're working hard, sipping wine and playing cards."). With them, she could chatter and gossip away the hours, discussing everybody who was somebody in the ghetto; they also occasionally offered her a shot of vodka. So for what did she need the flabby sloppy housewife Matilda, with her chapped hands and broken nails? Not even for a moment did it enter Yadwiga's mind that she might one day come down to Matilda's level. She had no idea of what was happening to her husband. His sudden loquacity, his meekness, she accepted as proof of his renewed love for her, and in all other matters she relied on him as she always did. To her it seemed impossible that Adam should ever run out of money.

The only person, who was truly aware of the direction in which the wheel of luck was heading, was Reisel. She noticed quickly enough that Adam had stopped being the great "sackblower and bigshot", while Samuel had begun to climb the ladder of glory. There was no need to put "a finger into her mouth". It was true that Adam still had enough "to fiddle with", but Reisel was farsighted and wanted to secure for herself a livelihood until the end of the war. She not only stopped quarrelling with Matilda, but clearly played up to her, doing her little favours, even calling her Madam once in a while, as if by mistake.

Reisel was aware of her position and was proud of it. Like her Madams, she never mixed with the women in the backyard; she thought of herself as belonging to the "higher windows". She had always paid great attention to cleanliness, yet it had never occurred to her to dress nicely. Before the war, she had always been too busy, nor had there been anyone for whom to dress up, as far as she was concerned. In the ghetto, however, the situation was different. Here there were the womenfolk in the backyard, in the street, or in her sisters' backyard where she was considered a charitable lady. Besides, in the ghetto one could come by the most attractive dress with a hat thrown into the bargain, for one single bread ration. So, nowadays, Reisel took to dressing up. She would buy the dresses of the fallen aristocrats, choosing the silky materials in the most screaming colours. And when she "put herself together" in a dress and hat, with a purse under her arm, and faced herself in the mirror, she looked, in her own eyes, to be thirty-five, or forty at the most. And as she stood there, she was more than once overcome by a desire which she herself considered sheer madness, but which was stronger than herself, namely, the desire to get married. There was no doubt in her mind that she, with her position and income which many an aristocrat might envy, could get herself the finest husband possible, an intellectual who spoke Polish and read books. She figured that by that time she would have gone back to work for the Zuckermans, and she could wheedle a high position for her husband out of Samuel, something in office work or bookkeeping. That way, she really would become a "better woman" and truly enter the "upper windows". Indeed, the ghetto was capable of blowing up people's imaginations, feeding them dreams which they had never before dreamed of dreaming.

Reisel would not let herself be fooled by Matilda's downcast face, or by her reproachful bitter words to Samuel and her daughters. Reisel had seen the clearest indications that Samuel was surpassing the heights of his pre-war glory; she saw signs of this not only in the sacks of potatoes and flour, of sugar and barley which were hidden in great secrecy in his bedroom, but also in Matilda's looks. Matilda, who had always had a tendency to obesity, had lately grown in width. Her body had become round and flabby, and since she was rather short and no longer wore any corsets and had in general become negligent in her dress, she looked like a moving bag full of water. Her round face acquired a double goitre, and what, on other faces, might be considered a chin, looked like a moonshaped crease on hers. Her features had lost their soft delicate expression to a combination of sadness and irritability which shimmered in her eyes. She looked years older than her age. It was precisely these looks, however, which convinced Reisel that it was not on account of misfortune that a woman in the ghetto might look like Matilda.

In Samuel's comportment Reisel also perceived the symptoms of grandeur. True, he was as lank as he had always been, his back was now even bent a bit, and his pitch black hair had thinned considerably, but he wore boots, and along with them he had acquired a way of marching through the house which stamped out any speck of doubt as to the importance of his position. Moreover, although he was now gayer and more carefree than ever, he experienced moments of short temper when he would scream and fume in such a manner, that Reisel, her ear against the closed door, would wonder whether it was he or not. Only a master who held the fate of others in his hands was entitled to roar like that. At such moments Reisel's respect for him rose to unsurpassable heights. Indeed, these explosions, although short and rare, sufficed to make all the other inhabitants of the house fear and revere Samuel. As soon as his bootsteps were heard on the stairs, the whole house entered into a state of suspense.

Adam was of course aware of these facts too, although he still conversed with Samuel as an equal. He had the strange notion that he would survive the war only thanks to him. So, although he harboured the same kind of disdain for Samuel as he had had before the war, he felt that now, more than ever, he needed this man whom he called his friend.

Samuel would enter Adam's room reluctantly. He had no patience for him and considered his presence in the house a nuisance. He even planned to move his family into another house, to avoid being spied on by his co-inhabitants. He was also weary of the fear that Adam might again discover the radio hidden in the abandoned cellar. Samuel wanted to enjoy freely the good life that he had begun, and reproached himself for postponing this decisive step from one day to the next.

One day, Adam nervously grabbed hold of Samuel's arm and dragged him over to the only armchair in his room. He pushed him into the seat and offered him a cigar. "Here, have a taste from the pre-war times!" He tried to force the cigar into Samuel's mouth.

Samuel had weaned himself from cigars and he pushed Adam's hand away. "How many times must I tell you that I don't smoke cigars?" His annoyance with Adam surfaced, "What do you want of me?"

Adam took the cigar from Samuel's mouth and lit it for himself. "How is business?" he asked with feigned concern. "How many people do you now have under you?"

Samuel quickly came to the crux of the matter, "I can still take you in as a *Meister*."

Adam's sagging cheeks flushed. "Do you think that you always have to underline your superiority to me?"

"You know that I have no right to assign managers. That's in the Old Man's power. Even to make you a *Meister* is not as easy as you think."

"For the time being I can survive without a boss over me."

"Then what do you want of me?"

"Nothing. I want nothing of you. Can't you believe that?" They scrutinized each other until Adam became aware of his moral superiority over Samuel. "What happened to you, Zuckerman? Have you forgotten that friendship is based on more than doing favours for one another? I just wanted to talk to you for a while, man to man . . ."

Wearily, Samuel surrendered, "What do you want to talk about?"

Weariness overcame Adam as well. He moved away from Samuel, slumped down on his bed and stared at his visitor with sad eyes, his head hanging sideways on his chest. This caused him to acquire a resemblance to his devoted Sutchka. "What will become of me?" he sighed. "Life seems to strangle me. Such a senseless existence. The little money I have left is melting between my fingers. My end is approaching. Oh, Samuel, if you only knew what I am going through. Of course you're not familiar with such feelings. They attack you suddenly, they grip you by the throat, as if you were caught in the fist of an enormous monster. They fill you with such fear that your heart stops. Then you feel as if the Angel of Death were flapping its wings above your head. I want to escape from my own self. I feel my reason leaving me. You have no idea . . ."

Samuel gave him a glacial stare. "Go to work," he said.

Adam reacted as if he had not heard. "If you only knew what it means to get up in the morning not knowing what for . . . how long a man's day seems when the clock drags the leaden hours with no aim, no purpose."

"Go to work!" Samuel exclaimed. Unable to bridle his impatience, he jumped to his feet.

Adam stared at him, shaking his head, "Become a *Meister* in your factory? Will this give sense to my life?"

"Are you searching for a sense to life in the ghetto? The only sense is to survive the war!" Samuel planted himself in front of Adam, raging openly now, "And what sense did your life or mine have before the war, tell me? We saved up thousands on bank accounts, gorged ourselves on food, drank ourselves to oblivion, while blabbering niceties and juggling with phrases which barely scratched the surface of our souls. If you want to know, we needed our little ghetto. A good school, a splendid school!" Samuel waved his finger in front of Adam's face. "Go to work, Rosenberg. Sweep streets, collect the garbage, but do something! Not only can work save us physically, it can prevent us from disintegrating . . . Do you hear what I am telling you?"

Adam was deeply hurt that his confession had been received in such a manner. He again shielded his wounded heart with bitterness. "The Old Man is talking through you," he hissed.

"Because he is right. He knows what he is talking about!"

"Sure, sure, you have become his lackey. You don't even feel what he has made of you."

"You would have been wise to fall at his feet and beg him to make a lackey of you too!"

Adam smirked proudly, bitterly, "Not on his life! That old *shnorrer* won't live to see the day when Adam Rosenberg goes begging to him!"

Samuel left the room. Before long Adam heard him joking and laughing with the new friends who now came to visit him daily. The pressure around Adam's heart tightened and there was no one else to whom he could run for relief, but Sutchka, the most devoted, understanding, wisest of all God's creatures. He embraced her neck and felt her moist tongue lick his cheek, lick the poison from his heart, lull his fear and calm him. He looked searchingly into her pupils and was sure that she was the only one who knew the meaning of all this. He gave himself over to her wisdom like a blind man. As long as he had her, he was sure that he would not be defeated, that somehow he would get through this difficult stretch of road.

✦ ✦ ✦

Then came the order to hand over all domestic animals to the authorities. Adam sank into a state of mind that could only be compared to the nightmares of the insane. He stopped eating, stopped sleeping, stopped counting his daily ration of cigars, but puffed on one after the other all day long. His son Mietek, the policeman, was his only salvation and Adam was not ashamed to implore him with tears in his eyes, to save Sutchka. Confused, Mietek, who in his own way loved the dog, tried to intercede on her behalf, but to no avail. Adam had the idea of running to Baluter Ring, to Rumkowski, to plead for her life; he was even ready to throw himself at Herr Biebow's feet, but Mietek held him back. These actions would have meant Sutchka's sure end.

There was nothing to do but hide the dog. When the fateful date arrived, Adam locked Sutchka up in his bedroom, then rushed down into the street to see what was going on. He saw children and adults carrying their pets in their arms. He observed the double pairs of eyes, of man and beast, perceived the pain of parting in their heads and limbs glued together in a last embrace. At the gathering place he was struck by the sight of the mewing, barking, fenced-in creatures. Their owners standing around in knots, watching from a distance, were oblivious to the rain that soaked through them — for it rained that day, as if autumn in its sorrow were weeping both for the animals who weep without tears, and for the people who were ashamed to bewail the fate of the animals. As soon as he had taken in that sight, Adam hurried home. He sank down by Sutchka's side, and told her all the things he had never brought to his lips, because it had seemed ridiculous for a man to say all that to a dog.

Thus the hellish days with Sutchka began. At first it was only Yadwiga who tormented Adam. The other people in the house, who were not directly touched by the decree, knew that the dog would have to go, but it had occurred to no one that the last date to deliver her had already passed. Yadwiga had always had a strange feeling towards Sutchka, a kind of jealousy, as if the bitch had been robbing her of something. This rivalry with the dog had never made her feel very proud of herself. But now that Sutchka did not move out of the bedroom, and Adam's fear of losing her had increased his tenderness towards her, making him forget that there was a Yadwiga in this world at all, she felt so hostile to the bitch, that she was unable to bear the sight of her. Adam's way of talking to Sutchka, his feeding and fondling her, his fussing over her irritated Yadwiga to the point of madness. She could no longer even sleep, because the miserable shut-in dog, having lost its bark, as if in the fear that barking could bring misfortune upon her, had acquired a mew-like whine which continued through the night and pierced the marrow of one's bones. This whine stopped only when Adam climbed down from his bed to pat her. Half awake, Yadwiga frequently chased him out of bed to calm the dog. After a time, Adam spread a blanket on the floor and spent most of the night at Sutchka's side.

Apart from this, the room was becoming permeated by a smell so unbearable, so foul and biting that it did not allow Yadwiga to breathe — Adam refused to open the window for fear that the dog's whining might be heard outside. At length, Yadwiga insisted that Adam move her bed into Mietek's room. Adam's submissiveness, his readiness to meet her every demand gave her some satisfaction; for the first time in their life together she was ordering him around. However this was marred by the bitter awareness that he was doing all this for the sake of a dog.

The first one to realize that something was brewing in the Rosenberg household was of course Reisel. Before long she knew everything. She forgot about her loyalty to her new masters, and one day she stopped Matilda in the kitchen and asked, "And what does Madam say to the story of the bitch that Mr. Rosenberg refuses to deliver to the *Yekes*? She is the only dog left in the ghetto. We might pay dearly for that. Does Madam think that the *Yekes* care to whom the dog belongs?" This said, Reisel knew that she had put the "stew on the fire". There was no need to add a single word, otherwise she would have done so. For the crux of the matter was that her relationship with Sutchka had already passed its honeymoon period. Reisel could not refrain from counting the number of Jewish children who could be fed on what Sutchka consumed in one day; it seemed to her that Sutchka was feeding on her, on Reisel herself.

At first Matilda wanted to order Adam to give up the dog immediately. She still considered the house as belonging to her, and the other families to be living there thanks only to her and Samuel's generosity. But instead of turning to the Rosenberg quarters, she burst into the girls' room, exclaiming to Bella, "Do you realize that the deadline for delivering the dogs expired long ago?"

"Poor Sutchka," Bella mumbled, biting her nails.

Bella's pity for the dog exasperated Matilda. "You fool!" she exploded. "You live like some princess in a glass palace!" She rushed out into the corridor and pushed open the door of Adam's room. "Out with the dog!" she roared as if with someone else's voice. Adam, stupefied, was at the dog's side in the blink of an eye. "We can't risk all our lives for the sake of your dog!" Matilda's goitre shook. "We are in a ghetto, Mr. Rosenberg! It's time you woke up. We don't live in glass palaces. The dog has to go before this day is over!"

Adam let go of the dog and with his arms spread out wide, slowly, carefully, approached Matilda, like a circus trainer ready to appease an irritated lioness. "Hush ... Matilda ..." He awkwardly raised his hands to her as if in self-defence. "This is not just a dog, darling," he whispered imploringly. "This is our Sutchka." He pointed in the direction of the armchair where the exhausted listless dog was lying.

Matilda shook her head, waving her fists in the air. "She must go today! If not, you will all have to go. I won't risk anyone's life for the sake of a dog!"

Bella dashed out of her room. "Don't shout, Mummy, please." She embraced her mother, sobbing.

"Bella, my child," Adam hung on to her, "She wants to get rid of our Sutchka ... to send Sutchka to a sure death. Don't let her ..."

This enraged Matilda even more. There she was, standing before them like a yelling brutal witch, she, the sensitive, long-suffering Matilda. Were they all insane? Was she insane? Beside herself, she exclaimed, "I am going for the police!"

Yadwiga emerged from Mietek's room. She touched Matilda with one of her manicured fingers. "Why do you have to go for the police? Mietek is a policeman. Wait until he comes home." Nonchalantly she flung her head up, glancing at Adam out of the corner of an eye. At this moment it was appropriate to display her devotion to her husband and family, since the dog's fate was in any case decided.

There was indeed no better solution at that moment, than to wait for Mietek and Samuel. They came home at the same time. Junia, who lived on the *Hachshara* in Marysin, also arrived to spend the evening with her family. A muffled commotion started in the house. Sounds of nervous conversation could be heard from behind closed doors. These were broken by long moments of silence during which Samuel's boot-steps thudded through the house. Back and forth he paced in the bedroom where his family had gathered.

Junia sat on the bed, her feet shaking rhythmically to the sound of Samuel's steps. She was frantically searching her mind for a solution to the problem at hand, and was unable to find one. "Don't be so hard on them, Ma," she turned to Matilda. "You talk as if you had no heart."

She should not have said that. Matilda jumped to her feet. "Of course I have no heart! I am a block of ice! Because I want to protect you. Because you refuse to realize what this might bring down on our heads! Sutchka is nothing but a dog, a bitch . . . Do you want to risk our lives for her? If you want that . . . If you want . . ."

Junia stared sadly at her mother, wondering whether this was really the same woman whom she had once loved so tenderly. She said nothing more. Samuel also kept silent as he continued to pace the room. He was thinking, comparing the meaning of having a hidden dog with that of having a hidden radio, and asking himself which risk had more justification. These were burdensome thoughts. He realized how tense the atmosphere in the room had become. It was difficult to breathe. He stopped pacing and looked at the three women who, though so close to him, had lately become such strangers. He burst out with an overly loud laugh, "Look at this air of gloom and doom! Come on, first we eat!"

The rest of the day passed uneventfully, and was followed by a few similarly uneventful days loaded with tension and nervousness. Matilda stopped greeting the Rosenbergs, turning her head away whenever she met one of them in the corridor. At night she was unable to sleep. It seemed to her that she heard steps on the stairs, that the police were arriving to fetch the dog and that everything was finished. She could do nothing, however, to bring about an end to her torment. Samuel had forbidden her to even mention the question of the dog. Nor did Samuel take any decisive steps, postponing his confrontation with Adam from one day to the next. It seemed strange, ridiculous, to have a problem with a dog in these circumstances, and to feel so paralyzed in doing something about it.

One evening Mietek called Samuel down into the backyard. The tall, broad-shouldered young fellow in his policeman's uniform looked like a little lost boy. His head hanging, hands in his pockets, he was distraughtly kicking pebbles with the tip of his boot, as he said in an unsure pleading voice. "Talk to Father, Mr. Zuckerman, please. I don't know how to tell him this . . . Sutchka is my dog too . . . I was still a child when we got her . . ."

When Samuel entered Adam's room the same evening, he found Adam changed almost beyond recognition. He saw an old man before him, whose head hung sunken between a pair of drooping shoulders, his face wrinkled like a dry apple. It seemed to Samuel that the dog's sorrow peered out from Adam's eyes. So alike were the dog and its master that Samuel, unable to bear the sight, averted his eyes and stared at the window. An autumnal haze had deprived the panes of their transparency. The room seemed cut off from the world; the anguish hovering within it was stifling. "It's getting cold," Samuel mumbled. "Winter is coming." In his mind, he mocked his meekness, his inability to attack the problem head on.

Adam, in his slippers, shuffled closer to him. "If you have no pity on her," he motioned in Sutchka's direction, "then have pity on me."

Samuel was doggedly staring at the window panes. "It is your problem, your responsibility." Again the thought about the radio entered his mind. "In this situation you're risking not only your own head, Adam."

A long silence followed. Then Adam straightened himself. "All right," he muttered. "I will leave the house with her."

A wave of sincere compassion for him surged up in Samuel's heart. "So many people are getting killed at the front . . ." he mumbled. "So many Jewish tragedies. And who knows what our own fate will be? In view of all that . . . what meaning is there . . . I mean, after all . . . a dog . . ." He was unable to continue his consoling words. Disdain so disfigured Adam's face that Samuel had to leave the room immediately.

+ + +

The autumnal rains came down on the ghetto with pitiless monotony, washing the sidewalks and sweeping them with prickly brooms of dull grayness. An eerie sadness enveloped the houses; the windowpanes, like eyes, incessantly shed fountains of tears. It seemed as if the ghetto were suffocating under the cover of low clouds. The people, wrapped in their soaking gray garments, moved through the streets, passively surrendering to the downpour, with an indifference that made them appear related to the gray stones of the pavement, to the gray walls of the houses, to everything that existed but had no will.

Adam would disappear from the house every morning, returning only to eat and feed the dog. He would change into dry clothes, hurry back into his dripping coat and again set out in search of a hideout for the dog. Finally, one evening he came back and planted himself in the middle of the corridor. "Hear me, hear me, my honourable friends and neighbours!" he called out. "Tomorrow you shall be rid of me!" He gave a strange guffaw and waited for Matilda to come out to congratulate him. But instead, Yadwiga appeared before him.

"What are you talking about, dearest?" She smiled forlornly.

"Tomorrow morning, my love," he replied, copying her kittenish tone of voice. He left her and shut himself up in the bedroom.

He was planning first to transport the dog into the hideaway, then to move some of his things. He would come back for his meals, so there was no need to take leave of anyone. Nor did he have to go too far, only to the other end of Hockel Street, where he had found a little room which belonged to a pre-war rag collector. The room was dark and filthy, but Adam was not choosy, he was not looking for conveniences now.

Outside, dawn was dozing like a blind beggar woman wrapped in a rain-soaked plaid with dripping fringes. Adam approached Sutchka, put his hand on her head and let it slide down her ears. "Come," he whispered. His heart quaked as he noticed with what difficulty she rose to her feet. He embraced her thin body with a despondent gaze. She had not touched her food lately and she had stopped her sad mewing whine as well. Adam consoled himself that there, in the remote blind alley, he could take her for a breath of fresh air every night and bring her back to health. He hooked the leash on to her collar and without looking back, opened the door.

Downstairs, in the entrance, he stopped to compose himself. Like someone ready to plunge into the sea from a high diving board, he deeply inhaled the cool air and dashed out. He had planned to pass the road through the backyards. The darkness of dawn and the rain were good protection. The ghetto was still asleep and there was little chance of encountering anyone. Yet suddenly, after he had run only a couple of metres through the yard, something flashed past his eyes in the distance, from the direction of the fire station: something reddish, pinkish, like the colour of a face, or a policeman's cap. For a moment he thought of Mietek. But Mietek was asleep upstairs, in his bed. Adam jerked at the leash, urging the dog to run faster.

"Halt!" he heard a voice behind his back.

"Run, Sutchka!" Adam goaded the dog on, as he ran.

He felt a hand touch his shoulder. "Stop!" Sutchka was still pulling ahead. The fresh air had evidently invigorated her, awakening her need to move her legs, but the leash around her neck tightened as Adam came to a halt. He saw a policeman's cap; streams of rain were pouring down from its wet visor onto a pale young face. The policeman swung his rubber club. "Where are you running to?"

"No ... nowhere," Adam stammered. The coloured stripes of the policeman's cap circled before his eyes, joining the circling rubber club in a vertiginous dance.

The policeman swung his club with more vigor. "Don't spit in my eyes, old man. Out with the story!" Suddenly his hand stopped moving; his eyes grew huge, goggled; his whole body became motionless, stoned with surprise. "A dog ..." he mumbled, as if he only now realized what he was staring at. "How do you still come to have a dog?"

"Yes, a dog ... mine ..." Adam began to babble without hearing his own words. "My son is also a policeman, my friend. I have had him for years ... I mean her ... Sutchka. She was really tiny when I brought her home. I am Adam Rosenberg. You know who I am, don't you? I had the biggest factory in town. You've probably met my son, Mietek, your colleague ..." He took a step forward with Sutchka, however the policeman's hand remained pinned to his sleeve. "Look at how she's shivering." He made a helpless gesture in the dog's direction. "She will catch a cold ... such rain ..." His eyes were imploring, begging for pity, and the expression on the young face softened, becoming friendlier, although there still remained determination painted on it.

"Give me the leash, Mr. Rosenberg," the policeman said gently, "I will hand her in. No one will know a thing, I promise you. I'll say I found her in the street. You won't lose a hair of your head, so help me God."

Adam sighed with relief. "You are a fine young man. Please, just let me cross the few backyards with her and forget that you've seen us. Mietek will always remember you for that. I have good cigars. How many do you want? Perhaps something else? Just tell me what ..."

The policeman politely yet stubbornly shook his head. "You can run, but without the dog. I'm on duty, Mr. Rosenberg. I cannot let such a thing pass ... for your own good."

"But no one is watching ..." Adam pleaded with him as he took another step with Sutchka.

The young man followed, swinging his club. "I'm warning you, Mr. Rosenberg. I don't want to get you into trouble. The dog goes with me."

For a second, Adam weighed something in his mind. Then he abruptly unhitched the leash from the dog's collar, exclaiming, "Save yourself, Sutchka! Run!" The bitch did not move. She turned her nose to Adam and looked at him as if asking whether it was worthwhile. "Escape!" Adam called out again, tearing himself away from the policeman. Now Adam and the dog sped ahead. The confounded policeman remained planted in his place for a while, wavering, undecided about whether to chase Adam or the dog. "Run! Run!" Adam, beside himself, goaded the bitch. Breathing heavily, he kept his hand pointed to the distance. At length she obeyed him, letting herself dash ahead with the leaps of a hunting dog.

The policeman decided that he would eventually get Adam anyway, and he set out after the dog. Thus they were three, running through the rainy haze of dawn: the dog in front, the policeman after her and the racing half-insane Adam behind them. They found themselves running along the barbed-wire fence. The dog increased her speed, perhaps irritated by the presence of the barrier at her side. She began to bark. Her barking replenished Adam with energy. How long had it been since he had last heard her bark? Her barking sounded like a beautiful hymn to freedom. Indeed, he himself began to feel free too, as if a leash had been taken off his neck. He was already lagging far behind the two racers, but he would not stop running. Every now and then the dog turned her head back. Adam waved his hand at her, pointing to the other side of the fence. "Get through! Get through!" he roared, not with his own voice. "Get out, Sutchka! Out!" After a while he saw her coming close to the fence. She stopped, lowered her graceful body and slid beneath the barbed wire. "Free! Free!" Adam clapped his hands, unaware that the rain washing his face had become salty and hot.

A shot was heard. Sutchka made a somersault and collapsed in the middle of the road, her raised legs quivering for a moment. The rain poured into her wide-open eyes.

The gendarme on guard behind the fence motioned to the approaching Jewish policeman. They both strolled down the street for a while, the knotty wire fence between them. Then the policeman halted and turned back, setting out at a run towards Adam who was standing glued to the spot where the sound of the shot had reached him. The policeman came at him with a leap, grabbed him by the coat with both hands and dragged him into the nearest gateway. He pressed Adam against the wall and brought his wet pale face close to his. The young man's entire body was shaking; the fear he had just experienced was still screaming from his child-like eyes. "I saved . . . saved your life, you son of a bitch!" His voice was hoarse with fury, and yet seemed near to sobs.

Adam snarled, exposing his gold-covered false teeth.

✦ ✦ ✦

Two days later, Mietek was informed of the whereabouts of his father. He interceded with the chief of police and received permission to free Adam from jail. The man whom Mietek brought home had only the external features of his father.

In the house, the inhabitants sighed with relief. Sutchka belonged to the past. Before the week was over no one remembered or mentioned her. Only in Adam's mind did she live on in a peculiar manner. He no longer loved her. Every spark of love he had harboured in his heart had been extinguished by the sound of the shot which had killed her. She lived on in his mind with her last bark, barking on within him, with disdain and hatred for man on both sides of the barbed wire fence.

Chapter Eleven

GHETTO AND AUTUMN — what a wonderful match they made! How harmonious their embrace; how perfectly they complemented each other, revealing the essence of each other's nature. And how securely the swarthy child of their union, black-eyed despondence, played in their arms. How tenderly they caressed its dark locks — the kinky spirals of subconscious awareness, of gnawing premonition! That first autumn in the ghetto, with its eternal rains, winds and fogs, with the cobwebs of grayness that wound and wove themselves around houses and fences, around sidewalks and cobblestones, around carts and people, stitching everything together with the invisible threads of destiny. Who has enough words with the thinness of needles, with the heaviness of rocks, with the snarls of swamp weeds to describe the soul of a ghetto Jew during that autumn? And who has violins of non-existent nuances and dimensions of sorrow, and who has a palette with so many shades of shadow — to paint the ghetto during that autumn?

There was no sky. And even on the earth everything was washed out, faded. The church's towers seemed like amputated necks, their tips swallowed by the clouds. A tongue of cloud incessantly licked the clock and its dead hands, erasing it like a sponge, then revealing it, then erasing it again as if it were a nut which refused to pass down the cloudy gorge. Every contour, every form had lost its solidity, dissolving in the mist and leaving only threads of lines behind, or rather a suggestion of them. Every colour in the streets and backyards had trickled out to the merest speck, as if some substance had sucked out all its brightness, leaving behind only one colour, the queen of colours: gray upon gray. Even the fence encircling the ghetto no longer suggested division but, as a part of the all-embracing cobweb, became woven into its net-like design and was barely seen from the distance. However its dissolution into the grayness of the surroundings by no means gave the illusion of freedom. On the contrary. It gave the feeling of being cut off from life by more than barbed wire; of being suspended in a boundless void. That was why the people in the ghetto felt so inhumanly lonely that autumn.

For this same reason perhaps they liked to climb the newly constructed bridge. It rose above Zgierska Street, which had been excluded from the ghetto, and served the pedestrians as a crosswalk from one part of the ghetto to the other. During those days, the wooden bridge looked like an imaginary contrivance. Its colour was also gray, but at close range the grayness took on its true stair-shaped form, suggesting heights. It was leading upwards, as if only its foundation were rooted in the nebulous abyss, while the rest of it possessed the power to "lift one up". Each of its stairs was a note higher on the scale, every shoe which clopped against it sounded a pulse of hope, a cry of longing for freedom. And so, from morning until night, the shoes clopped against the wooden stairs, rhythmically, measuredly, a clop-clop, a tick-tock of revived clocks, of awakened hearts mounting ever higher and higher. On the other side, the church would seem to be moving downwards with its towers, the clouds peeled away from its swallowed tips which descended lower and lower. The surrounding houses also began to sink, while the feet kept climbing, as if they were about to soar above the ghetto to leave it behind; as if they were about to miraculously escape the bottomless swamp below.

When the foot remained suspended in the air, finding no more stairs to climb, its owner disappointedly put it down on the landing and caught his breath. Inhaling the air of the heights, he slowly moved along the platform towards its centre. From there he peered for a second into the foggy depths of Zgierska Street, meeting the distant city eye to eye. But to linger there was dangerous; a stolen pleasure. At the foot of the bridge stood the green uniforms with guns pointed upwards. So the climber had to move along the platform to the stairs leading down. Only then did he feel how tired his legs were. Each step caused him to sink a level lower, all the stairs having turned into the black keys of a piano playing a descending scale, which pulled downward like a magnet. Then the pedestrian felt doomed to remain below forever.

Miss Diamand also enjoyed crossing the bridge, particularly in the mornings, along with the workers of the newly founded workshops, along with the office workers and school children. Her black boots, tied with knotted laces, did not lag behind the many other boots that were rhythmically clopping against the wood. And as soon as she reached the middle of the landing, she would stop and face the depth of Zgierska Street; her eyes lit up. She looked longingly through the low cloudy sky, to where Wanda lived, so far away, yet so close, to where she walked the streets, a pack of books under her arm, just like Miss Diamand. Miss Diamand would feel her friend's breath in the air, would see her face as clearly as if it were close enough to touch with her hand; she would hear Wanda's voice in her ear. Miss Diamand had to remove the glasses from her watery eyes, and move on. The sight of the distant city would become increasingly blurred, swirling before her tired gaze. In vain did she try to recapture the feeling of closeness to her past which was again becoming remote and unattainable.

She would walk down the stairs with more effort then she had climbed them. What she had experienced a while before, remained up there, along with her thoughts about Wanda. Just as a starved person forgets about food after he has been satiated, so Miss Diamand immediately forgot about her friend. Instead, she worried about her shoes, overcome by anxiety for their survival.

They were still shining nicely. She polished them daily, and their laces, although torn, were securely tied in knots. However, their soles were as thin as paper and she could feel the wood of the stairs through their middle. The interminable rains, the mud of Marysin had done them no good. They were practically finished, and Miss Diamand knew that it was only a question of days. Her wet stockings made her heart freeze with fear. How could she go to work without shoes? From her food rations she bought only bread and potatoes, saving every pfennig that she could, although she knew that before she managed to save up the money for a new pair of soles, even rubber soles, the thin old ones would crack open.

Once arrived at Marysin, however, exhausted, soaked by rain, splashed with mud, her polished shoes sticky and disfigured, Miss Diamand forgot about her shoes as well. Here were the children, and with them were spent her happiest moments of the day. She refused to profane even a fraction of her time with them. No, Wanda would not re-enter her mind for the rest of the day. Things had not turned out as she had imagined they would on her way into the ghetto, when it had seemed to her that while standing in front of her students in the classroom, she would feel Wanda's closeness, and would salute her in her mind. The truth of the matter was that the experience of standing here before students in a classroom was so unusual, so different from what she had known in the past, that there was nothing to lead her thoughts back to her friend.

The children of the ghetto, the growing, maturing youngsters — when she saw them streaming through the rain-soaked streets and muddy fields towards Marysin, each with a clinking canteen in one hand, a pack of books in the other — seemed unlike any other school children in the world. When they sat on their school benches, their bony pale faces lifted towards her, their teacher, she felt as if they were devouring knowledge like food; with such greed, with such a physical sensual enthusiasm did they throw themselves upon whatever she offered them. And when, during recess, she saw them lining up in front of the soup kettle and then seek shelter on the stairs and under the roofs where the rain could not reach them, when she heard them clink their spoons against their canteens and smack their lips — it seemed to her that they were swallowing knowledge, drinking down wisdom, life. That in stirring their soup with their spoons in pursuit of a piece of potato, they were stirring the chaos of the world, in search of a grain of truth, of a comment on their fate, of the meaning of existence in general. If there was still a ray of light in Miss Diamand's days, it came from these children. If there was a ray of hope for the ghetto, they were its source. She worshipped them. She served them like a priestess, praying for them with every pulse in her veins, with every breath of her sunken withered chest, with every flutter of her eternally longing heart. Her life was in the hands of the *gymnasium* students of the ghetto. And how grateful she was to the gray-haired Old Man with the splendid face of a prophet, to Presess Rumkowski, for having created this world of Marysin where her life could still make sense.

She walked the way home from Marysin in total oblivion to her surroundings. She was digesting the day which had just passed, thinking about each of her students separately, weighing and measuring his or her progress and making notes in her mind. She thought about the lectures she had to prepare, the books she needed to look over, the essays waiting to be corrected. She did not notice that she was climbing the bridge, and did not think of Wanda on her way up, nor of her shoes on the way down. She passed the clusters of neighbours in her backyard and greeted them mechanically, with a distant smile that still belonged to her students. She did not notice their curious, somewhat mocking glances follow her. In her dark coat with the mauve shawl, with her proudly raised gray head, her absent eyes gazing into the distance, she would glide through the backyard like a strange comet whose origin or destination no one knew.

Only Sheindle the street walker had taken an obvious liking to Miss Profesorka who, as she passed the yard, greeted her too with her faint distant smile. And it was Sheindle indeed who fetched Miss Profesorka's food rations and kept her informed of the changing amounts on the food cards, how much more or how much less sugar, barley or marmalade there was, than on the previous ration; how much coal was alloted each person, or what kind of dishes one could concoct out of the Ersatz-coffee.

Sheindle never stepped over the threshold of Miss Diamand's room. She revered the old lady too much and considered herself too lowly, with her broken Polish, her thick hoarse voice and her low profession, to move any further into the room than the doorway. There she would stand and recite the most recent news while she waited for Miss Diamand to give her her food cards. When she returned with the food, Miss Diamand received her with the same remote smile, and rather than thank her, she would stroke Sheindle's hair, as if the street walker were a student who had done her homework well. Moved by her touch, Sheindle would feel innocent and clean all over. Then she would rush down to her apartment, cover her face with a fresh layer of powder and rouge and unbutton her dress to give it a proper décolletage. She would sit down on her tabouret in the corridor to await her guests, her spirits as well as her skirt uplifted.

One day in late autumn Miss Diamand invited Sheindle into her room for the first time. The teacher's shoes had finally been bitten through by the mud. Her feet had begun to slip about in a cold prickly wetness which climbed up her stockings and reached her ankles. Every morning she would stuff her boots so thickly with pieces of cardboard, with wax paper or with rags, that her feet hurt with every step she took. But this insulation at best lasted only until she reached Marysin, where the mud attacked her feet through all the layers of rag, cardboard and paper. This continued until one day when, along with the wetness, a frosty shudder began to climb up Miss Diamand's body. She developed a fever and the following day had no strength to pull on her boots which, in spite of the fact that she had put them under the stove to dry, were still soaking wet. She was too weak to do anything but look at them from her bed with helpless rage and speechless reproach, at their surrender to the mud. And the boots with their twisted soaking snouts seemed to apologize, while reminding her that they had always served her faithfully, that in the city there had always been the hand of a shoemaker to renew them with care, to put them back on their soles; that the ghetto could suck the marrow out even of boots; that they were, alas, so far gone, that who knew whether even a shoemaker could help them now.

That day, when Sheindle appeared in the door, Miss Diamand motioned to her with a finger to come in. Sheindle stared at her with a pair of big eyes, not daring to cross the threshold. "What's the matter with you, Miss Profesorka?" she asked, worried.

Miss Diamand beckoned to her again, "Not with me . . . with the shoes."

The next moment Sheindle was standing at the bed. "Perhaps Miss Profesorka will let me touch her forehead? I'm good at judging temperature." And without waiting for permission, she pressed the palm of her hand against the old woman's forehead. "Good gracious!" she exclaimed. "You're as hot as a baking oven!"

Miss Diamand removed Sheinle's hand from her forehead. "The shoes . . . Go, child, bring them over. Let's have a look at them."

Sheindle cast a glance towards the stove and saw the two twisted muddy boots, with their worn knotted laces dangling at their sides. At the sight of them, she lost all her shyness and walked over to them, lifting them into the air with the two fingers of one hand. She turned them over, soles up, and met the two holes in their centre eye to eye. "Oy, I'm going to faint!" She bit her lips. "A pure disease!"

Miss Diamand spread her arms out over her blanket, as if she were completely giving herself over into Sheindle's hands, "What should I do?"

Sheindle put the boots back under the stove. To her it was clear as day that the boots were finished, firstly, because new soles would not stick to them; secondly, because even if they did stick, such new soles cost almost as much as a pair of brand new shoes; and thirdly, because a pair of brand new shoes was too expensive for Miss Profesorka's pocket, judging by the price of her own new shoes, the leather for which had been stolen for Valentino from Rumkowski's warehouse. So Sheindle stood there, confused, staring at the cold burners on the stove, her back turned to the old woman. Then it occurred to her that she did not have a speck of reason in her head. Here lay a sick person and the stove was not even lit, and who knew whether Miss Profesorka had even had any food in her mouth today. Sheindle immediately began to search for a few balls of peat with which to start a fire. "I'll cook a *soupka* for you," she announced without turning her head.

Miss Diamand's face took on the same expression as it did in class when one of her students was not behaving properly. "The shoes . . ." she groaned impatiently.

However, Sheindle knew that a sick person should not be given bad tidings, so she said, "I'll cook a bit of cereal for you. *Roggenflocken*," she added, in order to prove that she was not a total ignoramus. "Oh, you still have a bit of *farbrokechts* too!" she exclaimed, noticing a carrot and parsley. The Yiddish word *farbrokechts* stuck out like a scarecrow from the shockingly lame Polish sentence, but this Sheindle could not help. How should she know how to translate such a word as *farbrokechts* into Polish?

The word grated on Miss Diamand's ear with strange unfamiliarity; its sound evoked all her contempt for those lowly people and their droll language. The presence of the woman pottering about in the intimacy of her room became unbearable. She could not forgive herself for having given in to her weakness, and allowing that stranger to cross her threshold. "I don't want to eat," she stammered nervously, helplessly. "I only wanted some advice about the shoes."

Sheindle had already lit the stove. Cutting up the carrot over a little pot, she turned to the sick woman, her warm eyes smiling. "First of all a person must be healthy, Miss Profesorka. A healthy person needs shoes . . ." Her warm gaze made Miss Diamand feel even more uncomfortable, but she lacked the courage to ask Sheindle to leave. "In the ghetto, Miss Profesorka, the slightest thing can, heaven forbid, lead you straight to the cemetery!" Immediately it occurred to Sheindle that old people did not like the word "cemetery", even in Polish, and she corrected herself. "I mean, you can, heaven forbid, catch *Te-Be-Ce*," she shot out, proud that she could show off with her knowledge of the modern name for consumption.

Miss Diamand who was closely following Sheindle's struggle with the Polish language was not even slightly amused by the oddities to which she was listening. All she felt was revulsion. When Sheindle had used to stand at the door, mumbling a sentence or two, Miss Diamand had not had the opportunity to realize how badly the woman crippled the beautiful Polish language. Only today, when she was speaking freely, did she make Miss Diamand feel really and truly sick.

Sheindle stood before her, stirring a bowl of soup with a spoon. "Tastes like heaven!" she said in Yiddish, forgetting herself completely. She did not notice the teacher's tormented face, the expression of impatience and helplessness on the withered lips. She helped the rigid sick woman to sit up. "Like that!" she laughed, displaying the holes in her mouth left by two missing teeth. Miss Diamand took the bowl from her hand and waited for her to leave, but this Sheindle had no intention of doing. "Blow! It's boiling . . . It's cooked on fire!" she called out facetiously, trying to encourage the old woman. She felt as much at home in that room as she had felt in Friede's room. Now, that she had busied herself in it a bit, she had the impression that she too was related to the books on the shelves, to the piles of writing books on the table, to the inkpot and the red pencils. Perhaps it was not true that she had never gone to school and could not even sign her name properly; it was enough to inhale the air of this room, in order to feel intelligent and learned. She caught herself, realizing that the sick woman was not eating. "I'll feed you," she proposed, sitting down on the edge of the bed. "When a person is sick, it is hard to lift even a spoon. I can take care of sick people. I've a knack for it," she boasted. Miss Diamand, surrendering to her like a lamb to the sacrifice, let her take the spoon out of her hand. "And you must get well very soon, Miss Profesorka," Sheindle continued talking, because the sick woman seemed like a child whom one had to distract, so that it would not notice that it was eating. "All the students are waiting for you."

As she said this, an idea lit up in her mind. She saw the muddy, torn boots under the stove transformed into a pair of wooden ones, of the kind that had lately, with the opening of the *Holtzshue Resort*, become fashionable in the ghetto. Sheindle was, however, not sure whether it would suit a person of Miss Profesorka's stature to wear wooden shoes. For how could she put up with a situation in which she, Sheindle, would be clad in leather shoes, while Miss Profesorka would clop around wearing such cheap monstrosities? But the idea was not to be discarded with the wave of a hand. She, Sheindle, could easily get a pair of wooden shoes through Valentino; nor would the money to pay for them be too serious a problem. Suddenly she stood up, and leaving the teacher with the bowl in her lap, dashed out of the room.

She returned in the evening, entering the room without waiting for a formal invitation. Within a moment she was standing at Miss Diamand's bedside, and within another, a pair of white wooden boots appeared in the palms of her hands. "*Holtzshue!*" she announced. "Everybody will be wearing *Holtzshue* sooner or later. You'll be able to go to your students in Marysin!"

A thin bony hand with bent fingers reached out for Sheindle and for the shoes in her hands. The old fingers began to run over the wooden soles, over the thick white canvas fringed with strips of leatherette. "Give me my glasses, child," the teacher pointed to the table.

With both hands, Sheindle carefully picked up the glasses, opening them piously, and handed them to Miss Diamand. The old woman put on the glasses and turned them towards the shoes, and from there, towards Sheindle. The eyes behind the glasses darkened, the always present mist in them became thicker. "I don't know how to thank you . . ." She wiped her cheeks with a corner of her blanket. "If you only knew how desperate I was . . ." She raised her head to Sheindle who stood frozen in her place, flabbergasted. "Don't laugh at me . . . I'm crying. Old people cry easily, like children. Come here."

Sheindle, stiff like a stump of wood, moved still closer to the bed. Suddenly a feeling of such blessed fullness swept over her, that she bent down, grabbed the sick woman's hand, raised it to her mouth which was smeared with lipstick, and kissed it. When she had come to herself, she pulled out an old sweater from her shopping bag, and the next moment she was standing on the window sill stuffing a hole in the pane with the sweater.

Miss Diamand lay on her pillow, the new shoes by her side. Sheindle's pottering around the room no longer bothered her. This was no stranger who had intruded into her privacy. This was her child who was taking care of her sick mother. Miss Diamand could not understand how a pair of wooden shoes could set off such emotions within her, entirely reversing her state of mind and her mood.

"Now you'll know what comfort means, Miss Profesorka," Sheindle had become talkative. "And they are big too. You'll be able to wrap your feet with rags. So what if they clatter when you walk. Let them clatter in good health. And so what if they aren't too fancy? It's no hole in the sky. Where does one go in the ghetto, after all? On parades? As long as you don't have to fear the cold . . ." She spoke quickly, as if she wanted to free herself of the overflow of joy; she had not even noticed that she was no longer speaking Polish.

Miss Diamand, however, had noticed, and was surprised that this rough grating language spoken in Sheindle's hoarse masculine voice sounded so soft, so caressing to her ears. Miss Diamand could not understand what was happening to her. "You, you," she shook her head, trying to copy the sound of Sheindle's Baluty dialect. "What's your name, child?" she asked.

"Sheindle. But if Miss Profesorka so wishes, she may call me Sheina."

"Do you know, Sheina, we won't throw out those old shoes. Fine shoes. We'll polish them and put them away for the summer, if we're still in the ghetto. And I'll go to work tomorrow in the new shoes."

Sheindle was already at her side, bending down to her, "Don't be silly, Miss Profesorka, forgive me for saying that, but you're burning like a baking oven."

"A few cups of coffee will help. Will you make some coffee?"

"First I'll run for the doctor, that's what I'll do."

Miss Diamand caught hold of Sheindle's hand. Only now did the old woman, to her great astonishment, see a face before her which did not at all resemble the faces of her students. A creased mask hung suspended above her; only the eyes in their bed of wrinkles were young, warm. Miss Diamand peered into those eyes. "You are a treasure."

Sheindle felt good, clean. "Don't say that, Miss Profesorka."

"A good angel peers out from your eyes."

"I'm garbage, Miss Profesorka."

"You're a pearl."

Confused, enchanted, Sheindle exclaimed, "I'm going to call the doctor! The sooner you call him, the sooner he comes." She tore herself away from the bed, but on her way out, she stopped, held back by a sudden important idea which could be expressed only at the present, most suitable moment. "Would you teach me a bit, Miss Profesorka? A bit of Polish? Give me lessons? Not for free, heaven forbid . . ."

Miss Diamand caressed Sheindle's figure with her eyes. There was indeed nothing in Sheindle which resembled her students. Sheindle was an adult, more grown up even than she, old Miss Diamand herself. "You . . . you better teach me Yiddish . . ." she mumbled.

✦ ✦ ✦

It was precisely through her acquaintance with Sheindle that Miss Diamand began to discover what she took to calling "the Jewish soul". She was not sure what this term actually meant. It was a label for something which could by no means be precisely defined, but which clearly indicated a particular quality of perception. It came to the fore even through Sheindle's crippled mish-mash of Yiddish and Polish, through her strange expressions and sayings, the meaning of which Miss Diamand sensed rather than understood. Sheindle pulled Miss Diamand down to the earth and its inhabitants. And this very ghetto earth, although it had not ceased to be repulsive to her, became more familiar, and in a sense, more sacred, more "Biblical".

In a way, Sheindle had an influence even on Miss Diamand's attitude towards her students. Although Miss Diamand had known their day to day problems, she had not liked to hear about them. She had always tried to lift her students' spirits above the mood of the ghetto. Recently, however, she had come not to mind dealing with these topics, devoting all her attention to them when they would come up for discussion in the classroom. In that manner she not only found a new contact with her students, but teaching itself became more meaningful to her. Recently, as she analyzed her workday on the way back from school, she also began to keep her eyes open to the life pulsating around her. From all sides the hodge-podge of talk in that ugly strange language attacked her ears. Yet, instead of grating on them, it slowly began to caress them with its soft singsong, its warm lilt. She did not notice when she herself began to cripple that language, overjoyed that she could make herself understood.

All in all, now, that she had recovered from her illness, she saw little of Sheindle. Sheindle liked to come when she was needed. Of course every once in a while she felt the urge to inhale the "educated" air of the teacher's room, but this she could do from the threshold. And imperceptibly, their conversations did become richer in content. Miss Diamand no longer stared into the space above Sheindle's shoulder, absent-mindedly shaking her head as Sheindle spoke. Now she would listen and ask questions. It was as if she were learning a subject on which Sheindle was the one authority whom no number of books could replace.

Indeed, Sheindle's "breaking" into the privacy of Miss Diamand's room had left its lasting trace. Miss Diamand could no longer shut herself up within its walls as completely as before; it was as if her door were now always ajar. So it happened that her two students, Bella Zuckerman and Rachel Eibushitz, who had rarely visited her before, now came to see her more often. She never accepted any help from them, but held strictly to her role as their teacher.

Miss Diamand was the only person before whom the girls could, without any restriction or shame, relieve themselves of the restlessness that was tearing them apart, of the worries that gnawed at their hearts. Miss Diamand was close, yet completely outside of the tangle of their days. It was as if they relieved their hearts to a diary, as if they were confessing to themselves. But the relief and the sense of renewal that followed were of the kind which no diary could provide. Although so very impersonal, Miss Diamand possessed a pair of ears in which their voices resounded, a pair of misty blue eyes in which their tormented gaze was reflected with acute sensitivity. That was what they were seeking: the undivided attention, the impression of someone else's soul having moved into theirs — so that through it they might see themselves better. It was as if the girls were undressing before a mirror which X-rayed them, took them in, while at the same time it left them outside; it took them apart, in order to put them together; it twisted them around, in order to straighten them up; it plunged them into darkness in order to strengthen their inner light.

Miss Diamand became such a mirror to her students during that autumn when she herself had changed so much. True, the change within her was not radical; it had little to do with her basic character. Her renewed interest in life, her acceptance of its daily reality was after all nothing but a kneading of that reality into another, which was also spiritualized, also poeticized. However, the bit of actuality of which she had become truly aware had the right measure; it allowed her to come in touch with others who shared her fate, something she had previously been unable to do. A thin fragile thread began to link her lofty inner world with the abysmal world surrounding her, and this put an end to her loneliness. "Nothing human is alien to me. I am you and you are I," she would tell her students with her gaze, encouraging them to make use of her closeness.

Bella Zuckerman usually stormed into the teacher's room. This was the only place where she was not shy. She did not ask the teacher whether she had the time or was in the mood to receive her. Breathing heavily after her race through the backyard, she would slump into a chair, put a finger into her mouth, bite her nails, or grab whatever came into her hands and twist it about distractedly. Before the teacher managed to sit down beside her, she would begin pouring out words in chaotic disjointed sentences, like someone pulling out the pins which held together a tightly-packed bundle. Tears began to drop on the table, as her monologue became increasingly passionate.

"It's strange," the girl complained. "I'm leading the most normal, pre-war-like life. I even eat chocolates. And yet the presence of the barbed wire drives me mad. When I first came to the ghetto, it seemed to me that here too I would live in my own world which would not depend on the one surrounding me. But it is not so . . . And this is not because of the suffering going on around me. Sure, it makes me want to help. But the slice of bread I offer someone, or the soup which I give away at school can calm that discomfort . . . but not the other. I feel trapped, as if I were choking . . . At first I buried my nose in books, studied languages. I'm still doing that, but I can no longer lose myself in it. I cannot tear down fences with it . . ."

Miss Diamand embraced the girl's ugly twisted face with her gaze, observing her restless fingers with the bitten nails. She gave her all her attention by now, and forgot completely about herself — even more thoroughly than during that night when the same girl's father had sat before her, drunk, telling her his life's story. How much easier had it been then, when all that had been required of her was to hear him out. Now that was not enough. Bella was asking for a reason and a remedy for her fears, for her sadness, her restlessness. "It is the effect of the ghetto . . . hm . . . plus the autumn . . ." Miss Diamand chose her words with effort. "The union of the two . . . against your youth."

The girl who listened to her was not the obedient, tactful student she knew in the classroom. "That is poetic phraseology!" Bella grimaced.

"It is your youth that is rebelling within you." The teacher's voice flowed slowly past the girl's ear. "You are perhaps more sensitive than other young people, so your longings, your cravings are more powerful too. If you were not in the ghetto, you would feel something similar, certainly not to the same extent as you feel it here, but basically . . . not different. In the ghetto you are more acutely, more painfully aware of your youth, because you see the barbed wire which has cut you off, not only from space, but from time as well. Your need to soar into the future meets with a barrier . . . For who lives as much in the future as a young person? And then . . . you observe, you feel the rawness of life here, even if it does not touch you directly. And it is too prosaic, too ugly to nourish your present."

"No, it has nothing to do with that," Bella protested, annoyed. However, her voice was beginning to lose its shrill tone, as if it had been softened by the teacher's soft words. "Perhaps it is rather the fault of my home. Rather that! Yes . . . my mother, Miss Diamand . . . she's not the same. I don't mean in her appearance. On the contrary. She has become fatter than ever; she's as round as a barrel. It is rather her heart that seems to have dried up. Understand? If you only knew how much good the mere sound of her voice would do me. Now she doesn't stop screaming. Madam Zuckerman yells like a slut. And when she yells, everything freezes inside me. Sometimes I embrace her, kiss her, as if I wanted with tenderness to melt the frozen mother inside her. But I remain hanging on her neck, myself turning into an icicle. And with . . . with Father, it is also . . . He wears heavy boots, stamping, marching up and down the house. I shiver at their sound. And all he talks about seriously is 'his' factory, his special food rations, or the number of times the Presess has invited him to lunch. And when he is not being serious, he laughs. I used to like it when he was gay. Now I dread it. Because his laughter, Miss Diamand, doesn't seem to be his own, as if he too, just like Mother, had vanished. And there is nothing between the two of them. Absolutely nothing. I can't bear it. I cannot bear the sight of the two of them together. Such coldness, such frozenness. It seems to me that the foundations of my life have collapsed. I am buried under the ruins of my home, suffocating . . . Yes, Miss Diamand . . . Nor do I have a sister now. She lives on the *Hachshara* and has become a pious Zionist. I don't recognize her . . . She begs me to join her. I can't. All that is alien to me. And he too . . . Mietek. I have loved him for a long time. Sometimes when he is drunk, he tells me about his parties. Sometimes he tries to kiss me. Often I feel like shutting my eyes and letting him. But then I become disgusted with myself, afraid that I might give in to him just because I want to escape from the trap . . . Then . . . What would become of me then, Miss Diamand? And . . . How come they have all become such strangers?" Her face was wet, twisted, her nose pointy and red. Strings of moist hair, freed from her stiffly plaited braids, fell over her face and neck.

Miss Diamand covered the palms of Bella's hands with both of hers. "They are not more estranged from you than they were before, Bella. The ghetto has not changed our essential nature, it has only revealed it more clearly. It won't be long before we all appear before each other . . . with our souls bared. There will be no way of masking ourselves as we did before the war. Of course there are some truths which hurt when discovered."

"You mean to say that my father . . . that all of them really are what they are now?"

"No, in the kettle into which we have been thrown, everything within us is now boiling over. But with time we shall emerge from the chaos with our true faces . . ."

"You speak as if the ghetto were to last an eternity, Miss Diamand!"

"Heaven forbid, child. I only wish that after it is all over, we should not go back to the blindness with which we used to face each other."

"But, Miss Diamand, you talk so abstractly, so . . . I don't know how . . . I've told you a thousand times that all that has no bearing on my life, that for the time being I lack nothing, that we live like kings!"

"You've said that you do lack something," the teacher smiled softly. "Perhaps they are lacking something too? Your father must now be prouder of his achievements than ever before, of the fact that he has emerged a winner in this wolfish struggle for survival. That's why he laughs. Or perhaps he laughs . . . instead of crying . . . with shame. Because to be a winner in the ghetto, Bella, may also mean to be guilty. And as for your mother . . . She must be miserable. In spite of her eating so much, she must be very hungry. What do you know of your parents, child? Or of your sister?"

Bella blinked her tearful eyes. "It's true. I think too much of myself," she admitted with a sigh. "If I had my piano at least . . ." She fell into silence, then added in a whisper, "Mother must be missing the piano too. Life without music is unbearable."

Rachel Eibushitz's visits at Miss Diamand's were different. Rachel would not admit even to herself that she was looking for anything but the teacher's assistance with her homework. Although she too would burst into the room as if driven by an uncontrollable impulse, she did not surrender so easily. She would try to keep alive her resentment of the teacher, to remember that the latter belonged to the enemy camp against which a struggle was still going on. Most often she would test the teacher, to find out the latter's reaction to her, Rachel's approach to literary problems as she saw them through the prism of life in the ghetto. Surprised by the teacher's interest, by the understanding she read in her eyes, she would finally burst out with words whose only purpose was to negate any possible bond between the old woman, who never seemed troubled by hunger, and herself.

"Today my father made a scale out of pieces of string and two jar covers. On these covers he put our bread rations and weighed them. He cut off a slice from one and added to the other, took a few crumbs here and put them there. His hands shook, his eyes protruded, saliva dripped from his mouth. Those were moments of justice." Avoiding Miss Diamand's gaze, she wandered about the room with her eyes, jealous of its comfort, its spaciousness. It seemed like paradise. Here lived one person, all by herself, while her own family was occupying a corner of someone's kitchen. Embittered by this comparison, she continued to tease the teacher. "And once the bread is divided, do you think it stays that way? After justice is given its due, my parents add some bread to my brother's portion and to mine, so that we won't notice, of course. But don't we? Thirty deca of bread doesn't look like thirty-five. Sometimes I catch myself on the second or third day. I see that my portion hasn't diminished . . . And this is done by Father who devours the bread with his eyes whenever he divides it. I protest. I pretend." Rachel's gaze unwittingly immersed into the hazy blue of the teacher's eyes. This would make her anger melt, "When will all this end, Miss Diamand?" she asked helplessly, lost.

The teacher replied in her rustling voice, "You'll live to see the day, child. It will all be as it used to be."

This answer again inflamed the girl. "I don't want it to be as it used to be!"

"Wasn't it better than it is now? With food, with freedom?"

"If I get out of the ghetto, I want to get out into another kind of freedom. Do you think that before the war people didn't suffer from hunger? If I get out from here, I want our highest ideals to materialize. If not, then what sense is there to our suffering now, or to the suffering of other nations?"

"What are your highest ideals, Rachel?"

"You know quite well, Miss Diamand. I am a socialist."

"Explain to me what that means."

Rachel became thoughtful. This was a suitable topic to help her avoid the other, the more intimate one, that was clamouring to be brought out. "Socialism is not my highest ideal, it's rather the most basic . . . When I was small I used to repeat after the others that all people are equal, that when socialism arrives, everyone will be happy. That's silly. All people are not equal and not all problems can be solved by socialism. But the physical, material needs of people ought to be satisfied equally. No one was created to live in wealth or poverty. The idea of socialism . . . it sounds prosaic, not intellectual enough, but here, in the ghetto, we can see best how much the human spirit depends on the conditions of life." She went on in this strain for a long time, discussing socialism and freedom, clinging to the topic, until she heard the teacher's voice sliding into the flow of her words.

"You are sad, Rachel." The girl froze in her seat, silenced, overpowered. "You are sad not because you are starved for food. That only makes one irritable and bitter, as you were a while ago. Sadness is the luxury of the satiated. Do you understand, child, your body is starved for food, but you are satiated. I mean full of feelings . . ."

"Yes, full of hatred."

"Really?"

"Yes, the more I love those I love, the more I hate those I hate."

"And yet it seems to me that you are aware of how much soul energy it deprives you . . . of how destructive hatred is. And you also know that your enemies don't deserve that you give them so much of yourself. This . . . the wealth within you . . . this fullness stems from the fact that you love more those whom you love, than you hate those whom you hate," Miss Diamand smiled softly. "How is your boy friend? How come I don't see him at school?"

Rachel blushed. She looked as if the teacher had caught her in the act of committing a great crime. "He lives here, in the yard," she mumbled. "He has to support his family. He eats up his bread ration the first two days, then he goes hungry for the rest of the time." She bit her tongue. She would not reveal her most intimate, most painful thoughts. Never mind. She was strong enough to deal with them on her own. Now there was only one way out of the uneasiness she felt. Was it a way out? Automatically, her hand, as if deciding for her, reached into her pocket and pulled out a sheet of paper. "Lately," she mumbled, "I've begun writing a bit." Miss Diamand stretched out her bony hand for the sheet of paper. She adjusted the glasses on her nose and began reading:

Light up the night in my soul, in my being,
and tell me, My Fate, who am I?
Am I all goodness, or am I all evil?
Angel, or devil, who am I?

Am I with God or myself in collision,
a fighter in lonely anger,
who only on paths remote and entangled
could find the food for his hunger?

Have I been begotten for joy or for sorrow?
Why am I here? for what reason?
If a sunlit shore awaits me tomorrow,
why that storm where I drown in my prison?

If peace with people will be my salvation,
why am I an alien, a stranger?
Why when my time calls for loving and praising,
do I curse, daily dreaming of vengeance?

Light up the night in my soul, in my being,
let me know, am I dying or greening?
If I am a quivering string of a cello,
throw a ray on the tune I am spinning.

✦ ✦ ✦

Thus, in the sixty-fifth autumn of her life and her first autumn in the ghetto, Miss Diamand discovered her new vocation. She considered it to be an extension, a continuation of her work at school. At the same time she was aware that she had taken a completely new mission upon herself, which made her feel for the first time that there was indeed something more important to do in the ghetto than lecture on Polish or World Literature. These new activities gave her a kind of satisfaction and inner peace which differed from what she felt as a teacher. Here was an experience which had a direct bearing on her personal life. She forgot herself completely as she listened to the confessions, and this cleansed her and brought her relief. She even found a name for it: "vicarious catharsis".

Therefore that autumn which affected everyone so negatively became for her a kind of spring, of blessed renewal. Even physically she became stronger. She began to pay more attention to what she was eating, listened with more interest to Sheindle's news from the food co-operatives and noted down, half in jest, half in earnest, the recipes for the new dishes that people had concocted. She allowed herself to play with her food rations, on her own inventing treats and "refreshments" for herself. To her great amazement she noticed that the more she ate, the stronger her craving for food became.

It had all started with Bella and Rachel. But before long her other students also started to visit her, as did the teachers, her once so proud and aloof colleagues who had rarely noticed her before. It is possible that this change was brought about by that autumn which so filled people with anxiety and sorrow, that they desperately sought any means to relieve their heavy hearts. And it is also possible that the change occurred because of Miss Diamand herself, who having lost so much of her "transparency", had become more approachable, more down-to-earth. Indeed, she did not need to look for visitors now. They came by themselves. Sometimes she would humorously view herself as an amateur psychoanalyst. However, deep in her heart she considered her function to be more important than that. In her new awareness of reality, she realized that she was one of the few individuals in the ghetto who had a keen interest in the struggle of others for survival. This gave her the feeling of being unique, useful; more useful than a teacher could be and more than a mere expert on the human soul — that she was needed as a person, and as such was irreplaceable.

The sole person whom she expected to see and who never came to see her, was Samuel Zuckerman. The conversation they had had during that memorable night, when she had opened her heart to let in another, had really been the first of its kind. Up to then there had been only Wanda and herself, which to her present way of thinking seemed like doubled egotism. So, even though she regretted his present indifference, she was nonetheless grateful to Samuel.

However, it was only to Sheindle, the illiterate woman with the withered face and the raw language, that she felt a clear uncomplicated feeling of gratitude. Paradoxically, it had been Sheindle who was the real cause of the change in Miss Diamand's life. Indeed, it was in just such an unexpectedly strange manner that Fate juggled people's lives in the ghetto. How breathtaking, how exciting this might be, thought the old woman, if it were not so tragic.

So Sheindle's turn arrived as well, although it took her a long time before she dared to tell Miss Diamand about herself. She was sure that as soon as "Miss Profesorka" found out about her profession, everything between them would be over. Miss Diamand, for her part, refrained from pulling Sheindle "by the tongue". She approached her new function without a trace of curiosity. She was old enough and, with the addition of her recent experiences, had time to realize that human lives all reduce themselves to the same general patterns, marked only by greater or lesser deviations. She was not curious about the deviations. She wanted to help those seeking to relieve themselves of their inner burdens and nothing else.

One rainy evening, Sheindle was standing on the threshold of Miss Diamand's room, telling her how the Jewish policemen had behaved at the butcher store, how as soon as the doors were opened, the policemen had rushed inside and loaded themselves with many kilograms of the best meat, so that when they began to let in the people waiting in line, there was only enough meat left for a few, while the rest had to go away empty-handed. Sheindle was waving her fist in front of Miss Diamand's face, "May the cholera take them, forgive the expression, Miss Profesorka . . ." She had long ago given up worrying about her language when she conversed with Miss Diamand, but she always remembered to apologize. "They're a pack of scoundrels, of blood-suckers! Do you think, Miss Profesorka, that I depend on the meat they give? If I did, I would have kicked the bucket long ago. But I can't look at their dirty tricks. A hellish fire burns inside me . . . forgive the expression . . ." Here Sheindle interrupted herself, "Give me your food cards. They're distributing fruit tea". She grabbed the food cards from Miss Diamand's hand and took a big step to the side, in order not to touch Rachel Eibushitz who had come up the stairs; then she ran off.

Rachel entered the room, looking at the teacher with wide-eyed astonishment. "Miss Diamand," she whispered. "You've given her your cards? But she's stealing from you!"

A smile appeared on the teacher's thin lips, "She is my guardian angel."

Rachel furrowed her brow. She had to warn the naive helpless woman. "She . . . Her husband belongs to the underworld. That pair needs nothing better than someone like you, Miss Diamand. Who knows how much food you're missing from your ration. They have a store of stolen food and merchandise in the yard. Whenever I ask you whether you need something, you say no, but her you trust . . . And do you at least know that she is one of those . . . a full-fledged prostitute?"

Miss Diamand slumped into a chair and buried her head in the palms of her hands. "How strange . . ." she mumbled.

When Sheindle reappeared on the threshold the following evening, the two women stared at each other as if they had just met for the first time. Sheindle entered the room and approached the window. She leaned her elbows against the sill, her back turned to the teacher. "You know, eh? About my profession, eh?" She shrugged her shoulders. "And if you think that I do it out of need . . ." Her hoarse, masculine voice sank an octave lower, sounding rougher than usual, yet there was an undertone of pride to it. She had no reason to be ashamed of herself. "You like your job, don't you? I like mine! You were born a 'ristocrat and I a whore, so?" She did not apologize for the expression. "Is that why I deserve that you should be disgusted with me? Believe me, there is worse evil going around . . . And if you think that I avoid meeting anyone at your door for my own sake, you're wrong. I do it for your sake. May I live so long in good health, that I do it only because of you!"

Miss Diamand's mind was racing through a maze of thoughts from which she was unable to extricate herself. Sheindle's profession was so repulsively alien to her whole being, was so ugly, so incomprehensible, that she could barely believe or imagine that Sheindle, the very woman who was now talking to her, was a part of that sordid world. Indeed, even in literature, Miss Diamand had found it difficult to read about prostitution, to understand the psyche of women or men who were involved in such a business. Even in literature, every description of that world appeared cheap and pornographic to her. Of course, she had been aware that such a world existed, but she had never wanted to come in touch with it, not even through the mediation of the greatest masters. And now, how could she imagine Sheindle "at work", if she could barely visualize the course of any sexual act. Her body, withered for so many years, could not even assist her imagination. All she was able to remember was the taste that had lingered in her memory of an exaltation of her body and soul in the presence of a beloved man. That, however, had to do with the lofty ideal of the beauty of man. Here, on the other hand, was Sheindle, speaking the very words which locked all the doors of understanding, depriving Miss Diamand of the possibility of forgiving her. What had this woman said? "You like your job, Miss Profesorka? I like mine!" Some comparison! Some analogy! Oh, how much Miss Diamand wanted Sheindle to leave, to vanish from before her eyes! But Sheindle, the good angel who dwelled in that sinful body, could not be so easily discarded. If she forgot Sheindle, Miss Diamand would also have to forget the day when Sheindle had brought her the wooden shoes, when she had fed her and nursed her. What entanglements life in the ghetto could create!

"And if you want to know, Miss Profesorka," Sheindle sat down on the sill, her legs dangling above the floor, her face turned directly to the shrunken old woman. "If you want to know, my profession made a *mentsch* out of me. So it is! You think I mind the women turning their noses up at me, or that they're afraid to stand too near me, as if I were a leper? Believe me, they sell themselves to their husbands more than once. That's why they can't bear the sight of me. I give them competition. Don't worry, Miss Profesorka, I have lived some life in this world, I have! I've seen and I've heard, believe me! As you see me here, I've tasted my share of poison. From the day, may it be cursed, when my mother the bitch, may the cholera take her, brought me into this world . . . Do you think I even saw her face, or knew her name? Not on your life. I was a foundling, I was. Grew up a bit with one family, a bit with another. They didn't keep me for free either, heaven forbid. They made good use of me, and when they didn't need me anymore, they threw me out like a dog, even in the winter, even in the frost . . . naked and barefoot, with only the clothes on my back. Even before I had a brain in my head, men would take me. And I didn't mind a bit, you hear? I didn't care for the chocolate or even for the money they'd give me. But for that one moment . . . I was a piece of garbage, but a piece of garbage that was needed. Yes, only later, much later, my Valentino came around . . . He went for me. Piece of garbage that I was, Miss Profesorka, I had a body like marble, I looked like a queen. As they say, a rotten apple is pretty on the outside. And only then, when I had my honey years with Valentino, was I bored with the profession. But the wretch cooled off pretty soon. Now he only needs me as a housekeeper, nothing else. So I realized that there was nothing to live for, if not for men. Later there was one, Friede. An important person, Miss Profesorka. So I gave him my soul and my body. But then he left this world because of me. That's the kind of luck I have. And that's that. I'm back at my profession again, and this time for good. Because here the profession is not like it was before the war. Here, when a man comes to me, I know that he's carrying a rope around his neck and that no one in this world can loosen it except me. The men in the ghetto make me feel like a human being. Believe it or not, they kiss my hands; they cry and wail when they're with me. So I'm not useless, I'm not a rag. I have some use in this world. Yes, me, Sheindle!" She interrupted her monologue and sat there with her mouth open as if she were waiting for a new flow of words to reach her lips.

Miss Diamand's misty eyes blinked. She shuddered at the thought of the similarity between herself and the woman sitting before her; a kinship which was there against all reason. Evidently Sheindle knew what she was talking about, when she had compared herself to Miss Diamand. How could she defend herself against such a repulsive bond? Did she even have to defend herself? The feeling that one is needed, that one is not useless in this world — does it not give some sense to life? Had this not been her own great triumph over loneliness? Suddenly her heart began to swell with compassion for Sheindle, for herself, for every single human being who wanted to belong, to be related, to find his own worth in the worth he had for another, and thus free himself of the sense of meaninglessness that accompanies man along his earthly path. Viewed through the eyes of such compassion, Sheindle's profession ceased to be repulsive. Every kind of aversion vanished into the softness of feeling. Now only the good angel, Sheindle, was present in the room.

With her hand on her hip, Miss Diamand shuffled slowly over to the window and put her other hand on Sheindle's knee. "Let's brew some fruit tea and see how it tastes," she proposed.

✦ ✦ ✦

Miss Diamand's parting from Sheindle took place for an entirely different reason. During the week when the first snows fell and a light frost began to harden the mud, officials from the Housing Department began to pay Miss Diamand daily visits. They would measure the length and width of the room and solemnly note everything down on paper. They paid no attention to the frightened old woman, as they whispered among themselves and calculated, ignoring her questions. One gray morning an eviction notice arrived. Her room had been assigned to a family of five, while she was to be transferred to a room on the other side of the ghetto, to an apartment already inhabited by a family of total strangers.

When Miss Diamand showed her the eviction notice, Sheindle exploded with rage. She dashed off to the Housing Department and threateningly pounded her fist against the officials' tables, but to no avail. Even Valentino, whom she gave no peace, could do nothing. He had no "protection" in such a "dry" department.

On the specified date, Sheindle helped Miss Diamand to pack her belongings and loaded them on the same garden cart which she had once used to bring Friede to the ghetto. She transported the teacher's things, not to the assigned address, but to the house of Miss Diamand's colleagues, Professor and Profesorka Lustikman.

As they walked along, both pulling the cart, Sheindle cursed the officials of the Housing Department along with all the other *shishkas* and bigshots who "commanded the world". She could not forgive Miss Diamand for not having taken advantage of the "protection" of the *shishka*, Samuel Zuckerman, who was after all the father of Miss Diamand's pupil. She gave the old woman endless instructions of how a person should behave in the ghetto in order to survive. Sheindle swore that she would visit Miss Profesorka and not let her out of her sight, after which they both cried. They knew that in the same strange manner as the ghetto could bind people's fates together, it could also cut them apart.

Chapter Twelve

MORDECAI CHAIM RUMKOWSKI was bathing. The water in the bathtub, mild, soft, embraced him like a flowing blanket. He rubbed and scrubbed himself energetically, and the redder his skin grew, the better he felt and the more he groaned with delight. He enjoyed soaping himself with the perfumed soap which was rounded like an egg and slippery as the breast of a woman. It was so pure, so free of dirt that it invited one to bite into it, to swallow it and feel it cleanse one's insides. Here, in the ghetto, taking care of his personal cleanliness had become a kind of holy ritual for Mordecai Chaim, a substitute for prayer. The soaping and scrubbing seemed to cleanse not only his body but also his soul. After each bath he felt newborn.

He flexed his arms and checked for his muscles. It seemed to him that they had grown. His body was less flabby than it had used to be; only his goitre was still loose, folding under his chin. With satisfaction he observed his belly protruding from the water like a bare island, and he lightly pinched one of its folds like a merchant expertly inspecting a piece of material. There was no doubt in his mind that he had regained his vim and vigor. He had been taking hormone and vitamin injections for a while, and their beneficial action was beginning to show. He was convinced that the older he got, the younger he would feel. He remembered how rundown he had been the last few years before the war. Like an old man he had used to fall asleep in the middle of whatever he was doing. He smiled to himself, recalling the fierce slap in the face he had given a young policeman the week before, when the latter, not having noticed him, failed to salute him. He vividly recalled the mark all his five fingers had left on the fellow's cheek. Lately, he had been seriously thinking about doing exercises every morning, of hiring a good instructor. He envied the Germans of Baluter Ring. They moved about as if on springs, their chests protruding and as hard as armour. And how splendidly they carried their shoulders, stiff and straight, in one line with their backs! He wanted to walk like they did. Such a way of walking could be awe-inspiring.

He continued to reflect about how negligent his attitude towards himself had been in the past, as if he had not been worth a broken pfennig. That had been his great fault. Since he had had no respect for himself, no one else had respected him either. Indeed the ghetto had become an excellent school for him. Not only had it put him on his feet and straightened him up, but it had put a crown upon his head. Of course the Jews called him "King Chaim the First" behind his back, mockingly, cynically. But never mind, he felt the spark of royalty within him, and the Jews felt it too. Even the Germans, although they looked down on him, betrayed a concealed respect, even awe. They were aware of his superiority. Now that he had acquired their cleanliness and punctuality, their discipline and endurance, he even surpassed them, because he possessed the *Pintele Yid*, the dot of Jewishness, the Jewish mind, the prophetic spirit. And that put him, Mordecai Chaim, above Hitler himself who with all his power was after all nothing but a German *Kraut* head. There might still be a doubt whether or not Hitler would win that war, but there was no doubt that he, Chaim Rumkowski, would fulfil his mission. He rarely allowed himself to reflect on this mission, since he did not want to weaken his brain with mere dreams. He knew that each day he climbed a step higher on the ladder of glory, and that looking down from a height was not healthy; his head might begin to turn, which would make him shakier rather than more certain in his climbing.

He cast a glance at the frozen pane of the bathroom window. The frost looked like a white froth of soap. He smiled sentimentally. He liked the ghetto in the winter. It looked neat. The snow covered all the holes, all the ruins, all the garbage boxes and latrines; it gave the ghetto an almost festive appearance. Even the people looked more decent as they ceased walking around in such sloppy, negligent attire. So many idlers and *shnorrers* had been filling the streets with their flying coattails, their unkempt heads, twisted faces and hungry eyes! The clamour which pierced the ears had made the ghetto resemble a market place to such an extent, that it was a disgrace before the people in the streetcars which passed through Zgierska Street. Now there was an end to all that. Now the Jews rushed through the streets without stopping, without loitering and looking about. That had been achieved thanks to the winter and thanks to him, Chaim Rumkowski. The ghetto now ticked like a German clock.

It occurred to him that the half hour allotted for his bath had already passed and he reluctantly prepared to climb out of the tub. Discipline was discipline. He was tempted to call in his aide-de-camp to help him climb out of the slippery tub, but he gave up the idea. A man of his importance should not expose himself to others in his nakedness. It deprived one of respect.

Slowly, he lifted his body out of the water and stepped out onto a little blue carpet which was embroidered with white swans. Shivering, he put on his glasses and wrapped himself in his red bathrobe. He had picked out the robe and the little carpet himself in the *Verwertungsstelle*, the trading post in the ghetto. They served him for decoration during the ritual of his ablutions. He faced himself in the mirror on the door. He looked regal in the red robe, as he stood on the blue carpet with the white swans. His hair, with its whiteness of swan down, together with his silken white eyebrows, his glasses in gilt frames, and his high forehead crossed by deep furrows contributed to the image of majestic dignity and patriarchal serenity that he saw before him.

He opened the door and immediately his tall, broad-shouldered aide-de-camp, the *Cerber* who watched over him day and night appeared before him. The fellow saluted, "Dinner is ready, Herr Presess. And your brother has already arrived!"

The Presess dressed in a hurry. He did not like to let his brother wait too long. True, he was keeping him at a certain distance, but he was careful not to let the distance grow beyond its prescribed limits. For this reason he had raised him to an appropriate position, by making him the head of the Health Department, the ruler over all the eggheads whom he so detested. The fact that his own brother had the say over the doctors in the hospitals, in all the important medical decisions, gave him great satisfaction. After all, Joseph was his own flesh and blood, also a Rumkowski, and the glory of royalty therefore rested on him too. Indeed, in the ghetto, Rumkowski had come to like his brother somewhat better than he had before. Having dinner with him was relaxing, comfortable, a mood which only the presence of Joseph's wife, the Countess Helena, as the ghettoniks called her, could disturb. She was a bit too "Blue-blooded"; the polished manners which Mordecai Chaim no longer minded in his brother irritated him in her. It was good to appear with her at banquets, during evenings of entertainment, or at the head table at conferences. She had a matronly beauty, she always dressed with taste and was wonderfully presentable to the public, but he preferred to dine with Joseph alone. It was easier and he did not have to be careful with every word.

✦ ✦ ✦

Joseph was busy studying the portrait of the Presess which had just arrived and was waiting to be assigned a place on one of the walls. The portrait showed the Presess wearing a violet coat with flying tails and a high collar. His figure seemed to rise from behind the structure of the ghetto bridge. Beneath it were the outlines of many hands and arms raised towards the Presess who towered above the bridge, against the background of the sky. The entire portrait was in a subdued tone of autumnal haziness, which all the more clearly emphasized the light of the Presess' face, the white of his hair and the blue of his eyes with their glowing metallic gaze; a gaze which was both soft and warm as well as cold and harsh, in a word — prophetic. It was the portrait of a king into whose hands one could safely entrust the lives of a people.

Above the portrait which leaned against the wall, there hung another very similar one, also by the painter Vladimir Winter. Here the Presess was presented as hovering above the entire ghetto. The colours were bright and gay. The ghetto seemed to be a smiling peaceful little world above which the Presess' face glowed with fatherly love and tenderness, like a sun illuminating every nook and cranny.

Mordecai Chaim took in his brother's figure at a glance. If there was one thing about Joseph which he could not bear, it was his gentile appearance. Joseph was slim, straight, his shoulders almost as stiff as those of the Germans on Baluter Ring; his face, lean and hard, reminded Mordecai Chaim of a typical intellectual, not a Pole, but rather a German. He had grayish blue eyes, like Mordecai Chaim, but Joseph's were smaller and more watery. They did not betray the *Pintele Yid*, the little dot of Jewishness. In addition to that, he was taller by a head than Mordecai Chaim who was forced to look up at him. Mordecai Chaim sometimes thought that if he had had his brother's build, his posture and manner of walking, in addition to his own magnificent head, he would have had the perfect appearance.

As soon as Rumkowski took up his seat at the head of the table, his brother turned around and sat down by his side. "Good paintings," he remarked.

Mordecai Chaim cast a quick glance at his portraits. "Tell me, which one is better? You're supposed to be the connoisseur in the family, after all."

"I prefer the one on the wall. It's more cheerful." Joseph pointed his slim delicate finger at the wall. "It's more like you."

Mordecai Chaim was flattered. He had a kind face in that portrait. However, in his heart of hearts he wished that Joseph had chosen the new one, which so vividly brought out his messianic qualities. But he understood. It was true that no one could be a prophet to his own family. Joseph could see only the brother in him, see only his kind heart. Joseph was too close, too subjective in his view. Mordecai Chaim forgave him that. "I won't argue with you," he groaned benignly, indicating to his brother that he should fill their glasses with schnapps. "Perhaps I have just as good an eye for beauty as you do, but since you're considered the authority on the subject, let it be as you say. Lechaim!" They clinked glasses. Mordecai Chaim took one gulp and closed his eyes. That was all the alcohol he needed. "You're still all right, eh, Joseph? You drink like a goy," he smirked, watching with envy as his brother emptied the whole glass of schnapps into his mouth. "And what's new apart from that?" He tucked his napkin behind his collar.

Joseph attacked the food. "Everything under control."

"Ticking like a German clock, isn't it?"

Joseph, his mouth full, smiled. He was not an overly talkative man and Mordecai Chaim appreciated that quality in him. He disliked garrulous people. However, during their meetings, he quite enjoyed a bit of small talk intertwined with their silence.

They kept silent throughout their consumption of the chopped liver entrée and the potatoes with *borscht* which had always been Chaim Rumkowski's favoured dish. He needed no conversation to accompany it. But when the beefsteak was served and his false teeth begged for a pause, Mordecai Chaim contentedly spoke up again. "You see, my reasoning is almost prophetic." He raised the hand which held his knife to his forehead. "My mind tells me things which no one in the world would fancy happening."

Joseph asked through a full mouth, "For instance?" ·

"For instance, the Germans themselves had no idea whether the ghetto would last or not. Only in October did they realize that they had no other solution. But I knew it all the time. Only now are they beginning to go at full speed, building work Resorts. But I said right from the start that the ghetto would work and live from its work. If only the Jews themselves understood me. But don't worry. One day they'll bless me for the ghetto. True, it's no paradise, but here we'll be protected against the bombings and all the other plagues."

"So it is," Joseph agreed, nodding.

"Everyone was shouting that the ghetto had no financial basis." Chaim continued. "Well, doesn't it? Whose idea do you think it was to introduce ghetto money? The *Bürgermeister's?* The President's of the *Reichsbank?* No, it came from this little head!" Again Rumkowski raised the hand holding the knife to his forehead. "They only approved what I invented. That's how we got in five million marks, pulling out all the money from Jewish nest eggs. A tragedy? So they have paper notes. What do they need money for? They need food. And if you ask me, it has its value too. It raises our prestige. Our own Jewish money called by my name, carrying my likeness, like in a real state, with a state treasury. And like a real state it shall be. And if, on top of it, people begin to work, then things will start rolling as they should. No one will die of hunger in my ghetto."

"Except those who are already dead," Joseph, half-drunk, blinked at him.

"So, is it my fault?" Mordecai Chaim grimaced. "Do I have to explain to you too that I did what I could? They're stealing behind my back. I'm surrounded by crooks. That is the tragedy. But an end will come to that too. I'll root them out, hand them over to the *Kripo*, evacuate them. Justice will reign here, you'll see."

Joseph gulped down another glass of schnapps and moved his plate of carrot *tzimmes* closer. "I know that you have good intentions."

"I certainly have!" Mordecai Chaim shoved away his plate of carrot *tzimmes*. He was full. "Tea!" he called in the direction of the kitchen, and as if she had been waiting behind the door, the housekeeper entered with a silver tray in her hands. Mordecai Chaim deeply inhaled the aroma of the tea, took a toothpick, and after he had picked his teeth thoroughly, pointed the toothpick at the heads in the foreground of the painting that was leaning against the wall. "They don't appreciate a thing. All I hear day and night are their grumblings and complaints."

Joseph also glanced at the painting. "Yet they shower you with gifts . . . with portraits."

"Some gifts! This painting here cost me two loaves of bread."

"Quite a bargain. After the war it will be worth thousands. You'll hang in the museums."

"Big deal! The truth is that they cannot bear the sight of me. Every one of them, from the bigshots down to the *shnorrers*, is corroded by his hatred for me. As if I were the one who led them into the ghetto, as if I made this war. Honestly, sometimes I am disgusted with that whole lot of Jewry, with their reproaches, their behaviour, with their wild manners, their lies and falsehoods and with their market-place clamour. Sometimes I'm simply ashamed of being a Jew, I'm disgusted with my own self." A grimace of disgust appeared on his face. He took a sip of his tea and grunted. His face relaxed. The groan that followed was rather pleasurable. "On the other hand, between you and me, what would I be without them, and what sense would there be to my life? If one is doomed to be a Jew, there is nothing one can do about it. And after all, it is a pity. They're going through hell. One ought to help them. One ought to lead them like a lost herd of sheep." He took another sip of his tea and added, "And yet, we have more brains in the nail of one finger than the *Yekes* have from head to toe."

Dinner was over. Slowly, leisurely, Joseph rose and walked over to the sofa as if he were giving his brother time to observe his long legs in the black boots which outlined the shape of his muscular calves. Mordecai Chaim tried to imagine how he himself might look in a pair of boots. They would make him look taller no doubt, yet they would not suit him, they would not agree with his bearing. He would look ridiculous. Nevertheless, he decided to order a pair of high boots for himself.

"The Germans have lost three thousand airplanes," Joseph said, since this was the time which they usually devoted to discussing politics. "Which means that Hitler has nothing to fiddle with in the air. England is still standing strong."

"Rely on Hitler," Mordecai Chaim interrupted.

Joseph lit a cigar. "General Wavel pushed Mussolini back until El-Geila. Look it up on the map of Africa and you'll get the idea. Twenty-four thousand prisoners. The fortress Bardia which Mussolini declared was untakeable has been surrounded and you'll see the English march in there yet."

The Presess leaned over in Joseph's direction. "All this good news interests me as much as the speck of dust on my left earlock, you hear. What is there to twist our thumbs about? Hitler will conquer the world, rely on me, and all I care for is my people, the rest of the world may hit their heads against the wall." His face grew animated. "Did you mention Africa?" he smiled. "Do you know what Biebow told me the other day? He said to me: 'Herr Presess, we have to co-operate to keep the ghetto going.' I nod and he confides to me: 'There could be difficulties. General Gubernator Frank has declared that Poland will be *Judenfrei*. As soon as boat transportation becomes available, all the Jews will be shipped over to Africa, into the desert, among the black cannibals.' Yeah, that Biebow always thinks that he can outsmart me. If they were going to ship us off to Africa, they would not have ordered factories built here. But he wanted me to willingly give him two hundred Jews for deportation, do you understand? That's why he said that we ought to collaborate. In order to keep the ghetto going, it should be worthwhile for me to give him two hundred Jews. And so it is. No hole in the sky. All in all, only six hundred Jews have left up to now. Except for that, the ghetto as a whole has been left intact. That, you see, is what I call politics. The rest is not worth even a broken pfennig." In a sudden surge of energy, he jumped to his feet and marched over to his desk with a vigorous step. "Time to get ready," he declared, drawing out a wad of notes from his pocket. He began to write down the agenda for his meeting with the Resort directors and commissars who were soon to gather in his study.

A young maid entered the room, trying to make the least possible noise with the dishes, as she loaded them onto a huge tray. Carrying it in both hands, she left the room, looking around forlornly. She had been told that the Presess required every door to be immediately shut, and here her hands were full, and to her added chagrin, someone was knocking at the front door. She stood there for a moment before deciding to put the loaded tray down on the floor. The sight of the crystal and porcelain dishes made her head turn. After she had safely lowered them to the floor, she carefully shut the door of the dining room and rushed to open the front door.

A young man stood before her. He was wrapped in a black coat with a huge hairy fur collar that allowed her to see nothing of his face but a pair of heavily rimmed glasses. He was covered with snow from the visor of his cap to the tips of his shoes. He blinked his eyes behind the thick glasses which he wore, and as soon as he asked, "Is the Presess at home?" a piece of melting snow slid down from his visor straight onto his lips. The girl was completely at a loss. The stranger might be one of the beggars who pursued the Presess everywhere, and she had been strictly forbidden to let any beggar across the threshold. On the other hand, the stranger might be an important person, judging by the thickness of his glasses. Seeing her uncertainty, the young man solved the problem for her by entering the corridor. "I must speak to the Presess," he whispered resolutely.

The girl gathered her courage and fluttered off in the direction of the dining room. Left alone in the corridor, Simcha Bunim Berkovitch was dazzled by the sight of the tray on the floor, by the crystal and porcelain dishes filled with the leftovers of the Presess' meal. He took one step and knelt down in front of the tray, immersing his hands in the jumble of plates. He picked up a spoon and dipped it again and again into the dish of carrot *tzimmes* which the Presess had left untouched. He swallowed hastily, without chewing, without even managing to savour the taste of the delicious dessert. Shiny little cubes of carrot slipped down onto his chin, onto this fur collar, while the snow slipped down from his visor, from his hair and shoulders, and dripped into the glittering dishes. Gorging himself, his eyes protruding, he sensed rather than saw the few yellowish slices of *halah* framed by a well-baked shiny crust. He grabbed them and pushed them down into his pocket.

The maid reappeared. With one glance she took in the sight of Bunim bent over the tray and of the mud puddle around his shoes. He stood up and tried to brush off with his sleeve the orange pieces of carrot that stuck like confetti to the fur of his collar. "The Presess wants to know what you want," she stammered.

He swallowed the food in his mouth. "I'm a writer. I brought a poem for him."

As soon as she had vanished again, he continued frantically to work on his appearance, trying to get the stubborn pieces of carrot out of his collar with his nails. He grabbed a white napkin from the tray and rubbed his coat with it. The girl came back and told him that the Presess wanted him to come in. He wiped his face with the napkin, then he stuffed it into his pocket. He removed his cap and with the look of someone about to throw himself over a precipice, stepped forward. The light of the chandelier in the dining room blinded him for a moment. He reached mechanically for the serviette in his pocket to wipe his glasses, but caught himself. He had the impression that he was alone in the room and he moved ahead more courageously. He noticed the Presess' head at the desk and then, a pair of black boots and a cigar near the sofa. He bowed.

A paternal smile spread all over the Presess' face. The agenda for his forthcoming meeting was already securely fixed both on paper and in his head. The same with his speech. It was supposed to be a powerful speech. Production at the factories had to be raised. He also had some news to tell the commissars and the managers. It would be good for the Jews. He would order additional soups for the heavy workers, for the good foremen, and for the directors he was planning to open a special "diet shop". He motioned to Bunim with a finger, the way he had used to invite one of the children of his orphanage to recite a poem. "Well, let's hear . . ."

Bunim inhaled deeply. This was the moment on which Miriam's, Blimele's and his own life depended. The last chance. Indeed, Mother Luck had been smiling on him today. For weeks the Presess' aide-de-camp had chased him away from the door.

"Are you really a writer?" the Presess asked, as he waited for the young man to overcome his stage fright. He enjoyed it when people were flustered in his presence.

Bunim nodded, "I write . . ."

"Have you gotten any great works to your name? What do you write?"

"Poems, Herr Presess . . . poetry."

The Presess exploded into a hoarse laugh which sounded like an attack of whooping-cough. He raised his hand and pointed to the ceiling, "Do you hear, Joseph? He writes poetry!" The Presess was far from being an admirer of that particular genre of literature. "You see, and they tell me that Jews are suffering in the ghetto! Here you have a Jew writing poetry! I should take him along in my droshky and parade him through the streets, eh, Joseph? Let the Jews see that things are not all that bad."

Bunim mastered himself. "I haven't written one word yet in the ghetto, Herr Presess."

The Presess' smile froze on his lips. "Why?"

"Because, when life is bitter one can still write, but when it becomes worse than bitter . . ."

"Is writing about me the only thing you're capable of? So, let's hear your poem. I'm holding my breath."

Bunim ran through the room and stopped in front of the Presess, bowing. "Save me, Herr Presess!" he sputtered hoarsely. "I can't bear it any longer. It's almost a year now that we're starving. Give me some work. My trade is of no use here. I'll do anything. I have a little girl, Herr Presess, a beautiful child of four. You love children, Herr Presess . . ."

At the sight of the Presess' overcast face, Bunim felt his courage collapse. He strained his memory to recall the text of the plea which he had so carefully prepared. Not a word of it came to his mind. In his panic, he began pouring out words over which he had no control. He took another step forward, stopping very close to the Old Man. An inner voice goaded him, prodded him to fall to the Presess' feet. But his legs refused to bend, his body disobeyed him, his spine stiffened. And standing so rigidly he went on talking into the blue depths behind Rumkowski's glasses.

"Herr Presess, I beg of you. I must work. I am a writer. Granted, I have written nothing in the ghetto, but the creative struggle is alive within me . . . I only need the strength to hold a pencil in my hand. The few marks from the allowance melt between my fingers. The child has become weak. I have to sell the bread of the ration, sometimes the potatoes too. You can help me. Kindle the flame, Herr Presess. I feel my characters inside me. They grow, they ripen, they demand, they nag me to bring them to life. I want to write a great poem about the ghetto . . . a saga . . . I want to seal . . . to give an artistic expression of our tragedy . . . No, not artistic . . . something altogether different. I want to hammer out my characters, hew them with my pen . . . as one hews in stone . . ." As the stream of words continued, Bunim caught himself, realizing that the spittle from his mouth was hitting the Old Man's face. He noticed the Old Man leaning back in his chair, wiping his cheeks in disgust. But Bunim was no longer capable of restraining himself. "Herr Presess," he spluttered, "Fate . . . I feel it in my flesh and bones . . . You should understand. You have been singled out by fate. The people look up to you. So . . . So you ought to hear me, Herr Presess, to have ears for my cry. I'm ready to do anything, to accept anything with love. Herr Presess, I beg you, take upon yourself the role of the High Priest. Kindle the *menorah*. There is darkness within me, Herr Presess." Suddenly his voice became stuck in his throat and ceased to serve him. He saw the Presess stand up and march over to the sofa where Joseph was sitting. Without thinking, Bunim followed him, watching the rosy skin of the Old Man's neck stick out from between his finely cut silvery hair and the white collar of his shirt. Gradually, arrogance and pride began to burn within Bunim. "I am a modest man, Herr Presess," he said. "But I am entitled to demand from you . . . I feel that within me, within my blood."

They stood face to face. The heavy cloud which had gathered on Rumkowski's face was now ready to burst into storm. Sparks of rage lit up his eyes like lightning. Rumkowski cut the tension with a mocking little laugh. He bent down to Joseph and shook his knee, "Listen to that! Did you hear? He demands! He has the right to demand from me, the louse! He feels it in his blood! You see, Joseph, these are my lovely little Jews," he pointed at Bunim. "Simultaneously arrogant and crawling on all fours, beggars with pretensions, *shnorrers* with conceit. And this one is a writer! Just go and carry him around on your hands! He has a child, the big achiever, and he has a mission too! He's going to erect a monument!" Rumkowski raised his finger into the air. "No more, no less! A monument for all the generations to come, and I must help him hold the pen in his hand, so that he can describe me as the villain, the traitor, the devil and who knows what else. I must help him spit in my face, help him sit in judgment on me, eh?" He prodded Joseph in the knee. "How do you like that?"

Joseph, who saw that his brother would not remain too long in a composed frame of mind, turned to Bunim, "Mister, recite your poem to the Presess . . ."

For a moment it was quiet in the room. Then Bunim spoke up, "I have no poem."

Joseph rose to his feet as well. "You said yourself that you came to recite a poem for the Presess."

"I wanted to get in." There was such emptiness, such darkness in Bunim's mind, that he did not feel any despair. At the same time, someone else, another being who sat inside him, was experiencing a weird compulsion to discover who the Old Man really was, to smell out the seed of humanness within him. His eyes followed Rumkowski's every move. "I write no panegyrics," he added.

Rumkowski was no longer able to master himself. He had an impulse to imprint on Bunim's cheeks the same kind of finger marks that he had left on the policeman's cheek the other day. He felt cheated, mocked by the pitiful wretch of a man; but he kept his hand in check. "To tell lies, of that you are capable, eh?" he exclaimed. He turned around as if seeking his brother's assistance. "That's what they are, Joseph! In addition to all their other good qualities, they're shameless liars! Is there any wonder that the world hates us?" A strange light surfaced in Bunim's eyes, glowing threateningly. With a measured step he strode towards the door and from there turned his head to the Old Man as if to assure himself that his burning gaze had reached its aim. Something happened to the Presess at that moment. "Wait!" he called out, approaching his desk. He hastily jotted down something on a scrap of paper and came over to Bunim with it. "Here, you'll be an usher at the Vegetable Place." A mocking smile expressing conceit and vengefulness played on his lips. As soon as Berkovitch left, he turned to Joseph, "I gave him what he wanted! But don't worry, that job will give him the taste of my yoke. That, mind you, is psychology."

◆　◆　◆

There was one person in the ghetto whom Mr. Rumkowski truly respected, in spite of the fact that this was a young man of less than thirty years of age. Rumkowski would listen to his young friend's advice as a student listens to his teacher.

Herr Schatten was a German Jew. He had come to Poland via Zbonshyn. However, despite the one hundred percent Jewish blood in his veins, he considered himself a German. He was of the opinion that all the misfortunes that had befallen him, such as the humiliation of being exiled from his fatherland and imprisoned in the ghetto, were the fault of the other, real Jews, who on account of their ugly deeds, of their swindles, had brought the ire of the Führer upon themselves, while at the same time making him, Herr Schatten, an innocent victim. Therefore Herr Schatten lived in the ghetto, with only one purpose: to avenge himself for the abuse he had suffered, to punish the real culprits responsible for his torment, the *Ostjuden*, the ghettoniks.

He was a slim sportive young man with a handsome, partly boyish, partly manly face and a pair of agile muscular legs which expressed strength and energy in their every move. He had a good mind and his German was polished and elegant. He had won the Presess' heart without difficulty, securing a key position for himself in the hierarchy of the ghetto, by becoming the Presess' confidant, his personal advisor as well as his official representative to the authorities. Apart from that, he had another, not at all official function. He had taken upon himself the task of providing the Presess with young girls of a particular physical type. He had quickly discovered that the Presess liked thin nimble girls, half-women, half-children, nymphets with innocent delicate features and big sad eyes that carried the promise of smiles and mischief in their depths. Herr Schatten did not have to make too great an effort in order to find these girls. This was his extremely satisfying manner of expressing his gratitude to the Old Man. Indeed, even in the ghetto, life had its charm for young Herr Schatten, and were it not for the fact that he was trapped between barbed wire, he would perhaps have stopped longing for his *Heimat* where, despite all the good things it had to offer, he could never have climbed to the heights he reached in the ghetto.

It was late in the evening. The Presess' meeting with the factory directors had been over for a long time. The maids had already cleaned the room; Joseph, the Presess' brother, was gone. The Presess sat at the dining room table, fidgeting with a cup of cold coffee. He was satisfied with himself. The meeting had been successful and had passed in a congenial atmosphere. A few of the commissars, those nearest to his heart, he had invited, at leavetaking, to attend a modest New Year's party in his home. It gave him a particular pleasure to invite Samuel Zuckerman. "Two years ago, we celebrated at your place," he chummily patted him on the shoulder. "This year it will be at my place."

Samuel pressed the Presess' hand gratefully, "As long as we have survived to celebrate another New Year. And it's all thanks to you, Herr Presess." The Presess was delighted. He would never have believed that he was capable of having such influence, not only on people's lives, but also on their characters. How that Zuckerman had changed! There was not a trace left of his pre-war aristocratic loftiness, of his elegant salon mannerisms, nor did he any longer display his flexibility and tolerance of other people's opinions. Initially, the Presess had been somewhat worried about him. He had entrusted him with a high position because of his devotion, but he doubted whether Zuckerman would be capable of carrying out his job with a strong hand, without letting himself be led around by the nose by the *Meisters*, or by the workers. For that reason he had kept a close eye on him, until Samuel had become thoroughly disciplined and fit for his role. Nowadays it was a pleasure to be with him. His good mood was infectious. The Presess congratulated himself on his pedagogical victory, which for some reason seemed to be a victory over Samuel himself.

As the Presess consulted his watch, Herr Schatten burst into the room. He looked fresh, with his cheeks flushed from the cold. Rumkowski's face lit up.

How healthy that fellow looked, how crisp! "The frost is burning outside, eh, Schatten?" he asked and with a gesture of the hand invited him to sit down on the sofa.

Schatten was too full of energy to sit down. "I like it, this kind of weather," he laughed, displaying two rows of strong teeth. "It's healthy, it improves the circulation." It was the Presess who moved over to the sofa and slumped down on it, not because he was tired, but because from that vantage point he could better observe his visitor who was pacing the floor, both hands in the pockets of his riding pants, his head with the brush hair-cut raised high. It was a visual delight to watch that firm body in the tightly-fitted tailored hunter's suit move about so gracefully. He admired him the way a loving father admired a son. Herr Schatten unbuttoned his jacket, fanned himself with his hand, and indicated the glowing stove. "Why do you heat so much, Herr Presess?" He thrust aside his jacket tails and pushed his hands into his pockets. The dark tie on his brown shirt seemed to cut his chest in half. "Not a breath of fresh air in this room. How can you stand it, Herr Presess?"

The Presess purred guiltily. "Do you think I am a young stallion like you?"

"Come off it, Herr Presess," Schatten laughed. "You have young blood, don't we both know that?" He halted in front of the Presess with his legs spread apart. "I have something for you ..." he bent down to him, "Ready for immediate consumption. The problem is that she's a bit too bony ... even for your taste. But does she ever have a pair of eyes! Good heavens!" The Presess hung his head. While making this kind of transaction with Schatten, he preferred not to meet his eyes. "And even though she is a bit too lean, you'll enjoy her. I promise." The young man hit his fist against his chest, "I would have tried her myself, but as you know, Herr Presess, I don't like to deliver used merchandise to you. She's waiting outside ... the poor child."

The Presess was not precisely in a romantic mood. He was not tired, but his mind was rather drawn at the moment to working or thinking. He had so many problems to attend to in the morning. However, the thought of a girl's body shivering outside, in the frost, kindled the fire within him.

Gaily, Herr Schatten leaped out of the room and before the Presess could manage to arrange his thoughts and put himself in a proper frame of mind, the young man was back, exclaiming, "All set!" He fixed his tie, buttoned his jacket and stretched out his hand to Rumkowski, "The way is clear. Your *Cerber* is in the kitchen and I too will leave you. Get up and go in there, it's good for the circulation. Bon appetit!"

On the bed in the bedroom sat a shrunken figure which resembled an old woman rather than a young girl. She was wrapped in a thin coat, her head covered with a shawl. From beneath it, something of a silken golden colour shone out, winding snake-like down her back in two long strips — two braids, the only trace of brightness in the entire figure, and the Presess' gaze was drawn towards it.

The figure jumped to its feet. A pair of huge deep eyes glared at Rumkowski. He immediately recognized them. He failed only to recall whose they were. He was sure that they had already glared at him like that before, frightened, despondent and imploring. He came close to her and tore the shawl off her head. Yes, he had known those long silken tresses. He moved his face closer to hers, "What's your name, child?" She did not answer. Her shoulders moved and the light coat she was wearing slid down to the floor. As she stood there before him, shaking, he heard her teeth chatter. She really was too skinny, even for his taste. By the many folds of her loose dress he was able to judge how skeletal her body was; her dry bare arms and the fingers of her hands were thin as sticks and hung limply at her side. She was still staring at him with her large deep eyes, when he was overcome by a wish to see them light up with the gaiety he detected in their depths — a readiness for joy crying out to be released. He wanted the girl's mouth to open, so that she could show him her teeth. He was sure that he had once felt them through her lips. He took hold of her finger, then caressed her under the elbow. "Don't be afraid, child," he encouraged her. "What's your name?"

A sigh escaped her mouth. That sigh was a name, "Sabinka."

The name told him nothing. His curiosity grew, while her frightened eyes began to pierce into his heart, releasing all the hidden sources of tenderness within him. Lightly he glided the palm of his hand over her ash-gray sunken cheeks which were as smooth as a wet bar of soap. He touched her head, letting his hand skim down along the gold of her braids. He played with her fingers which were thin, cold, and yet soft and submissive to his touch; it seemed to him that he was holding a pair of icicles that could be kneaded in his hand. "How old are you, child?" he asked.

This time a groan issued from her mouth, "Eighteen."

"And why are you so skinny? What does your father do?" The sadness in her big eyes began to rock, kindled by a familiar little flame both of surprise and mischief. A faint smile shimmered on her thin blue lips. "You don't recognize me, Herr Presess?"

"I do, but I don't remember where I've seen you." He laughed a fatherly hoarse laugh, happy that the smile on her lips was widening.

"I am Sabinka . . . from the orphanage . . . Luna Park . . . Really I'm only sixteen."

"Oh!" he exclaimed with relief. He remembered: the lilac, the bare knees shining down at him from beneath a ballooning dress on a carousel . . . the cherry-shaped lips, the cool meadow and the shouts "dirty Jew!" or something of the sort that had chased him out of the park. The joy that took hold of him now was so great, that he could barely catch his breath. Her leanness no longer bothered him. The dryness vanished. All that was left was the presence of youth, of virginity. She had come back to him like a pigeon that had been stolen from his cage. Now no one would be able to take her away from him. That made him patient. It was sweet to feel one's power, one's potency. The feeling filled his heart with mildness, with kindness. "Why have you never come to see me, child? You know that I do everything I can for my orphans."

She hung her head. "I was scared, Herr Presess. I ran away from the orphanage and . . ."

"And what else?"

Her eyes filled with tears. There was such beauty in that girlish-childish weeping. He embraced her thin waist with both arms and pressed her lowered head against his chest. A gnawing tune, both familiar and alien, began to resound within him. "I'm scared," she stammered.

Carefully, he placed his hand on her breast. "Of me?"

"I want something to eat."

He scratched his head and looked around uneasily. Then he caught himself and opened a drawer in the night table near where they had sat down. "Here, eat a piece of chocolate!" She grabbed it out of his hand. He barely noticed when and how the whole chocolate bar vanished, leaving a brown film of saliva on her lips. He pressed himself tighter against her. "Now you're not scared of me anymore, are you? Say it, child, say it," he begged her.

"I have no one but you, Herr Presess." Her lips moved like those of a doll, revealing the pearly whiteness of her teeth fringed by the brown chocolate marks.

He wanted so much to see her laugh, with those tempting shiny little pearls in her mouth, fringed with the brown borders. But he was patient. "How did Herr Schatten find you?" he asked tenderly, slowly gliding his hand down her back.

"He took me from the line . . . He said he had work for me."

He slowly leaned her back onto his lap. She lay in his arms, tortured, submissive. The golden tresses hung down from his knees like two bright snakes. He felt capable of sacrificing a great deal in order to see a spark of satisfaction in her eyes. He touched her face with his rough cheek. "With me you'll lack nothing, child," he whispered. "Your torments are over. I'll bring you back to health. I'll make you strong. Look at me, child . . ." She looked at him. "Did you hear what I said?" She nodded. "You'll flourish in my hands . . . like a lilac bush." He kissed her cheeks, her forehead, her lips. "Well, repeat what I've said to you," he playfully touched her lips with a finger.

"Finished . . ." She moved her lips like a doll.

"Yes . . ." he was delighted. "Then put your little arms around me. Yes, like that, and give me a tiny smile. I want to see your teeth."

The whiteness of two rows of teeth bordered with brown lit up before his eyes. With his mouth on hers he sucked up their sweetness. When he at length removed his lips from hers, she was still smiling. "More . . ." she whispered. "More chocolate . . . please."

✦ ✦ ✦

The last night of the year 1940 was dark and frosty. It was not snowing, but the sky was covered with heavy clouds which merged with the darkness of the air and the earth. It seemed that the snow-covered houses were frozen into that blackness. Icy gusts swept through the streets, tearing at the roofs and fences as if determined to shake them out of their frozen stupor. Here and there, they succeeded and a broken fence would crackle and groan, shaking its boards like chattering loose teeth. Tar papers, like black hands in white gloves, slapped at the houses whose frozen windows looked like the lowered eyelids of corpses. With the white perseverance of death the windows defended themselves against the wild gusts. But the winds whistled through them into the rooms which, unheated and defenceless, surrendered to their will, letting them sweep across the floors and around the furniture. Their eerie breaths howled in the chimneys, somersaulted in the cold pipes of stoves and danced a devil's dance under the beds and above them.

In the beds lay the people, wrapped in whatever had the power to keep them warm. They lay huddled in each other's arms, as if each were the other's little stove. With the blankets over their heads, they warmed the air beneath with their breaths. But it did not always help. In some beds, people lay shivering, unable to abandon themselves to the good hands of sleep. Alone, deserted even by those closest to them, who had managed to remove themselves into the world of sweet dreams or biting nightmares, they stared at the frozen window panes, reading white frightening letters on them, letters written with a frosty pen. Babies cried, unable to satisfy their hunger at their mothers' empty breasts. Half-dressed mothers jumped out of bed, barefoot, and hurried to the cots where their children slept, to check whether they were well covered. Then they returned to their own beds, the winds pricking the nipples of their breasts and filling their hearts with gnawing premonitions. Here and there also lay someone who did not shiver, who was neither asleep nor awake; someone for whom the last night of the year 1940 was the last night of life and the first night of eternity.

Only in a few houses in the ghetto was it warm. There, a thin, barely perceptible light broke through the covered windows, along with the sound of merry voices. In the Red House of the *Kripo* the unmarried officials on guard duty had organized a party for themselves. Glasses full of beer and schnapps clinked, while the sound of drunken singing escaped through the windows, to reach the waxen ears of the Holy Virgin Mary in her niche. That night was also a holiday for the Jews imprisoned in the cells of the *Kripo*. They could, in peace and quiet, hug their own wounds, their disjointed limbs and bodies, and their fears.

Further on, inside the ghetto, a few *shishka* houses were also enjoying a night of merriment. Here the people gathered by clans, the common policemen separately and their superiors separately, the managers of the Resorts separately and the office managers separately. The nouveau riche of the ghetto celebrated together with their old cronies of the underworld. The Jews who worked for the *Kripo* celebrated with their colleagues, the stool-pigeons. And Mr. Rumkowski saw in the New Year at a gathering of the chosen few.

The party was a great success. Mr. Rumkowski was in an excellent mood. He had started the evening by assembling his guests and giving them a long speech in which he proved that they, just as he, had every reason to enjoy themselves tonight, because the ghetto was ticking like a German clock. Because orders for work were coming in and because he was planning to open several new factories. He good-naturedly shared his plans with them about the publication of a newspaper in the ghetto and about opening a hotel, a vacation resort where each of the deserving dignitaries would be able to spend a few weeks. Everything he said was received with "Hurrah!" and with exclamations of "Long live the Presess!" They sang "May he Live a Hundred Years" in his honour, and drank "*Lechaim* to Presess Chaim!"

Mr. Zilbert, whose thin short figure looked very funny in the high boots he wore, lay half-drunk, stretched out on the sofa, telling racy jokes. The crowd gathered around him responded with laughter, but the Presess listened to him with only one ear. He had no patience to hear out a joke to its end. Moreover, he was not sure of the *kashrut* of Zibert's jokes, and he wanted to keep the party on the aristocratic and dignified level that befitted both his position and the dignity of his sister-in-law, Joseph's wife, whom the people called Countess Helena.

Samuel Zuckerman had not joined the merry group surrounding Zibert. He was busy entertaining a bunch of office girls whom their bosses had brought along, in addition to their wives. Samuel danced with them, exchanging partners with Herr Schatten. Samuel was not less agile than the younger man, and the girls, flushed, half-drunk, clung to him, attracted by his flair for mischief and by his boyish charm.

Matilda sat at the patephone. As soon as she had entered the room, she noticed the patephone and had hurried towards it. After that she refused to budge. First she put on a record very dear to her heart, a tune which seemed to irritate Samuel, since he went over to her, offered her a glass of schnapps and told her to play something more lively. So, Matilda, already drunk, chose records with increasingly livelier rhythms to match the increasingly livelier dancers. She laughed aloud and followed Samuel with her eyes. Now and again she put her round face into the patephone's tube, so that it might be washed by the music.

After midnight, when the guests had all wished each other a Happy New Year, no one listened to Zibert any more. Now they were all dancing, whirling past Matilda's eyes along with the walls, the floor and the ceiling — a kind of vertiginous fast-spinning wheel at whose centre she saw Samuel holding a girl with a snake-like body in his arms. The image looked so funny to Matilda, that she was unable to control her tears as she laughed. She felt so carefree, immersed in a pain which somehow did not hurt, that she wished that the night would never end. This was also the wish of the other guests, but of course, not of the Presess who never wished time to stop. In spite of his delight in the moment, his mind was eagerly looking forward to the coming day.

Dawn of the first day of the New Year arrived. The guests took leave of the Presess, thanking him for his hospitality. As they all poured out of the warm house into the cold of a gray morning, they heard singing coming from the street. Wooden shoes rhythmically clopped against the cobblestones. The Presess' guests saw a group of youngsters with red frost-bitten faces approach them, marching in closed ranks. They were the members of the "Ninth Socialist Children's Republic". Mr. Zibert had finally achieved what he wanted. The "republic" had been liquidated and its members were now marching back into the ghetto. When they came very close, the Presess' guests could clearly hear the words of their march song:

> "We don't need any favours,
> nor charity from Rumkowski's hand."

After a while, the guests met with another group of ghetto inhabitants, also marching, but with chaotic wobbling steps: a team of sleepy workers, shovels in hand, on their way to the cemetery. It had become necessary to speed up the burial of the ever increasing number of corpses, for which there were not enough graves.

Chapter Thirteen

WHEN MIETEK HAD BROUGHT his father home from prison and Reisel saw his face, which no longer displayed even a trace of conceit, but seemed rather like a twisted mask of dejection, she understood that Sutchka's departure had been the signal that the wheel of fortune had turned for the Rosenbergs full circle. She realized that the time had come for her to return to her former masters, on whom luck was now smiling with the best promises of surviving the war. As soon as she had made her decision, Reisel's devotion to the Rosenbergs went out like an electric bulb at the touch of a button. One wintery morning, as the hour dawned when she had to get up and light the stove, she instead gave in to temptation, and turning to the wall, drew the blanket over her head and went back to sleep. Today she had no master, and since this meant that she was in "no man's land" for the time being, she could allow herself the luxury. When she finally woke up, she got out of bed energetically, hurried on her old winter coat — she now had a new one with an Astrakhan collar and a hand muff — and stepped out into the corridor.

But instead of entering the kitchen, she put her ear against the door of Mietek's room and triumphantly shook her head. If she did not wake them, they would go on sleeping. Without great ceremony, she burst into the darkened room and approached Yadwiga's bed. She shook her ex-mistress' curled-up body, and leaned over that part of the cover under which Yadwiga's ear was supposed to be. "If you want to eat, Madam," Reisel shouted into Yadwiga's ear as if the latter were deaf, "then you'd better get out of bed and cook for yourself!" Terrified, Yadwiga emerged from beneath all the pillows and covers, ready to spring out of bed. But as soon as she met Reisel's threatening gaze, she sighed with relief and smiled like a spoiled kitten. "I won't work for you any more!" Reisel proclaimed. She turned on her heel, rushed out of the room and entered the kitchen. She stopped in front of the table where the Zuckerman family was having breakfast. "Do you want to take me back to work, Madam?" she faced Matilda, speaking in the tone of by-gone days.

Matilda was not one to forget a wrongdoing so easily, and she seized the opportunity to avenge herself on the unfaithful servant. She replied coldly while staring into her plate. "I don't need you."

Reisel remained standing with her mouth open. This response she had not expected at all. In her mind she saw herself going down the stairs with all her belongings, lost, doomed, just like all the other common ghettoniks. She could not forgive herself that, with all her cleverness, she had thrown out the dirty water before making sure of having the clean. At the thought, as if at the touch of a switch, a stream of hot tears poured down her face. "Is that the reward for my devotion?" she stammered, letting her tears drip undisturbed down her cheeks.

Matilda smiled ironically, "You stole from us."

Matilda's words burned through Reisel. That was how the rich were! They would rather choke on their opulence than share a crust of bread with the poor. She forgot that when she had sneaked out the pots of food from the Zuckerman household, they themselves had been almost poor. She grabbed hold of her head, "Woe is me! I stole from you? I? I gave away my own bite of food to sick weak orphans! That you call stealing? Sweet Father in heaven! Where shall I go? I'm all forsaken in this world. How can you have such a heart of stone, Madam? I'll go out like a candle, that's how I'll go out."

Pretending indifference, Matilda sipped her soup, keeping her face buried in her plate. "One does not go out like a candle so quickly," she said. "And why are you so unhappy? Thanks to the ghetto you're no longer a servant. You're a madam just like myself." She wanted to continue the game of humiliating Reisel, but noticed the expression on Samuel's face and bit her lips.

Samuel was restless and irritable that morning. Matilda's talk almost made him jump to his feet. Why should she, his fat wife, mind if Reisel took a bit of soup out of the house, or a few potatoes? Did Reisel throw it away? Did she, Matilda, who sat at home and had no worries, lack anything? And even if Reisel refused to work any longer for others, they had no right to throw her out of the house. And besides, wasn't he trying to get a house of his own in Marysin? How would Matilda, who had remained a terrible cook, be able to prepare the meals for the visitors he would invite? "Reisel belongs to the family!" he snapped, impatient and angry.

At that point Yadwiga entered the kitchen. She was fully dressed and carefully combed; a sufficient layer of powder and rouge covered her cheeks. But her painted face was changed. Her tiny sleepy eyes stared at the gathering in the kitchen; her habitual kittenish smile was absent from her lips. As if she were blind, she stretched her hands out in front of her, "Reisel, I beg of you . . ."

Matilda stood up. Casting a fleeting glance at the stupefied Yadwiga, she commanded the cook, "Wash up the dishes!"

Yadwiga approached the stove and stared at it with fear, as if she saw a wild beast in front of her. From a distance, with the tips of her fingers, she picked up the raking iron and removed the rings of the burner with it. Samuel's eyes met hers. Overcome by rage and by a jealousy of Adam's freedom, he shouted at her, "Wake up your old man. Let the great lord help you out a bit!"

Samuel's daughters were waiting for him (Junia had come home from the *hachshara* for the winter, on account of her pernicious cough, and she was again going to school). As they went down into the yard, the biting cold embraced them. The snow near their house was piled up high and it took them a while before they could scramble out of it. The girls held on tightly to Samuel. Junia raised the tip of her little nose to him. "They say that the Presess is going to liquidate all the *Hachsharas*. He's afraid that revolutionary elements will breed there." Samuel did not hear a word of what she was saying, but he muttered a few sounds in reply, pretending to pay attention.

The street had already assumed its daily rhythm. Children were hurrying to school. Men and women wrapped in heavy clothes, wooden boots on their feet, clinking empty canteens in their hands, were rushing to the Work Resorts. Here and there a few people, shopping baskets in hand, were running to place themselves early in a food line. Tiny children wrapped in scarves, with plaids tied over their coats, were sleepily playing with the snow in front of their gates. In front of one of the gates stood a black hearse overloaded with corpses. From another gate came someone's hoarse wailing. Or perhaps it was only the wailing of a frozen water pump?

Samuel took leave of his daughters at the foot of the bridge and followed them with his eyes, as they mingled with the crowd streaming down into the other side of the ghetto. The clopping of the countless pairs of wooden shoes against the snow-covered stairs resounded in his ears with a dull echo. A dull ache began to gnaw inside him: a sense of dissatisfaction, of bitterness. He was quite aware that this was not only the aftermath of the home atmosphere, which he could hardly bear, but also a premonition of the unpleasant day that was awaiting him.

Without his usual eagerness, he let himself go in the direction of his favourite factory. This was one day when he was not going to the only place in the ghetto where he could forget himself. Today the Work Resort was threatened by a strike which he could not allow to happen. He had to see to it that the heated squabbling and the tensions were calmed down, so that he could preserve his own equilibrium. Because he liked the factory. It was his work, his baby. It added zest to his life, rekindling his old passion for building, for constructing. He did not care that he was building for the Germans. He was building for his own sustenance. Without it, he would have perished and the Germans would perhaps be more fortified by his extinction than by the wood products which the Resort fabricated for them. Yes, he wanted the German defeat just like all the other Jews did, but sabotage was dangerous, first of all to himself. What his factories produced had to be good, useful, though it be for the devil himself. He could not live without creating useful things.

Of course he was fully aware that there was an essential flaw in his reasoning, something that erased and annulled it completely. But he refused to think about it, just like he had lately refused to think about many other things. Indeed, he well understood the workers, who were demanding not to be deprived of the additional slice of bread they were receiving at work. He knew that on an empty stomach they could not accomplish the work expected from them. With the Presess it was the opposite. Him he did not understand, although he wanted to. He could not grasp why Rumkowski, who was convinced that the existence of the ghetto depended on the workers, refused to meet their demands.

His resentment against the Presess was an unpleasant feeling. Samuel believed in him and was ready to subordinate himself to him. Here, in the ghetto, in the chaos, when all foundations seemed to have collapsed, the authority of the Presess was a blessing. It was stimulating to work, if one's achievements found approval in the Presess' eyes, as if his recognition or praise added meaning to one's efforts and gave value to one's days. Samuel stubbornly refused to listen to all the gossip, to all the "ducks" hatched in people's minds, with the sole purpose of discrediting Rumkowski. Samuel wanted to help him, and through him, to help the ghetto. He rejoiced in the Old Man's accomplishments, in the order and discipline he had introduced, in his creation of an economic organism out of practically nothing. Granted, Samuel sometimes thought that his acceptance of Rumkowski's power was partly due to the fact that it allowed him, Samuel, to relax, to surrender to his own weaknesses and avoid many problems. But what was wrong with that? He wanted to have peace of mind and a sense of security and he could only acquire these by collaborating with the Presess.

What, in addition, had begun to incline him negatively towards Rumkowski, was Samuel's attitude towards Zionism. It had become a passion which, against his will, took hold of him and gave him an altogether different kind of support. In his mind, Eretz Israel was no longer only a solution for the hungry Jewish masses. It had become a solution for all the Jews, himself included. No longer was Poland his homeland and Lodz his hometown. He had been uprooted in this country and transplanted into a Jewish land. For the time being it was an insecure, pain-giving homestead called ghetto, but in his imagination he saw it carried over into the Promised Land which would heal it. Zionist thought had become Samuel's dream thought, his music of redemption, his vision of the future. He would toy with these dreams during his sleepless nights, or during the moments that he spent in the cellar with the radio receiver. With them he regained his dignity, with them he resisted the oppressor. As a Zionist, he, for the first time, began to feel his real adherence to a community, an adherence which was morally obliging. It alienated him from the Presess and brought him closer to the workers in the Resort. It made him feel uneasy in the role of a *shishka*, and prevented him from approaching the strike of the carpenters in the ghetto in the same manner as he would have in his factory before the war. This frustrated him, filled him with anxiety, and made his steps so hesitant as he walked to work this morning.

How he longed for the days of his natural, unperturbed gaiety! How irritated was he by the fact that all he had tried to escape was now imposing itself on him. He hated his workers for forcing their problems on him. He resented the Presess for refusing to remove these problems. At the same time he hated himself for wanting to free himself from any responsibility, for refusing to think independently, for having changed so much during the one year in the ghetto, for his alienation from Matilda, for the wall that had sprung up between his daughter Bella and himself, and for having forgotten about the book he had intended to write about the Jews of Lodz. Yet, he saw no other way, than to carry on in the same manner and to go on clinging to the Presess today, in order to reach redemption tomorrow.

He pulled his fur hat over his ears and thrust his hands into his pockets. The cart laden with corpses passed him by. Starvation and the cold had joined forces to annihilate the population, so that the Germans did not need to "put a finger into cold water". For a moment Samuel tried to imagine what it meant to die, not of any disease, but of hunger; what it meant to freeze to death. These strange thoughts made him shiver. He stared at the posters on the fences and walls. One of them announced the new food ration. He stopped to have a look at the amount of meat promised for the next ten days. In spite of the special rations he was receiving as a *shishka*, he had begun to experience an uncontrollable craving for meat, as if whatever amount he consumed were only an entrée to tease his appetite.

A crowd of people was clustered in front of the placard. Men and women, pencils in their frozen hands, were copying the entire text, word for word, onto scraps of paper. They dictated the decagrams of sugar, of horsemeat, of butter, to each other, comparing them with the last ration, or the one before the last. The children expertly corrected the mistakes of the adults. They had better memories of the exact weights and measures of past rations than the older people, and the latter listened to them respectfully. As for the neighbouring poster, with its warning that the ghetto population had better behave properly, no one bothered to read it through.

Samuel had just managed to find what he was looking for on the placard, when a great commotion started up around him. A black mass of people was approaching from the depth of the street, a crowd of dishevelled women, children by their sides. Big and small clenched fists rose into the air to the accompaniment of clamorous voices: "We are starving! We want food!" The fists waved threateningly against the faces of the Jewish policemen who, clubs in hand, were shoving the crowd in all directions. With great effort Samuel plowed through the knots of people, accelerating his pace. He knew that he was leaving the shouts and chanting behind, only to meet with other shouts and screams, this time raised against himself. Before he entered the yard of the factory, he had one last thought: how well the Germans had succeeded in transforming the Jews into the monsters which they claimed the Jews were. How easy it would be to destroy them, without any pangs of guilt; for the Jews were no longer human beings but a pack of hungry rats, and rooting out rats is a good deed.

In the yard of the factory, he noticed clusters of workers standing around, whispering among themselves. A crow was perched on the snow-covered fence. Strange that it wore no Star of David! It occurred to Samuel that the black crow was perhaps more clever, more knowledgeable than every single Jew of the ghetto. Perhaps it had been listening behind a window on the Hermann Göring Strasse, where letters from Berlin were lying upon marble desk-tops, on how best to throw mud in the eyes of the ghettoniks, how best to entice them against each other, according to the principle of *divide et impera* — so that the Jews would not realize what was being done to them. Had not the Germans declared openly that it was convenient to let the Jews "cook themselves in their own sauce"? Were the Germans not the best psychologists in the modern world?

✦ ✦ ✦

There was someone else who was watching the same crow, while following an altogether different train of thought. It was Shalom, Itche Mayer the carpenter's son, who was employed in the factory. Leaning against a huge box, he was waiting for the return of his brother Mottle who had left with a delegation for the other Resorts to check strike preparations there.

Shalom pondered whether the crow had flown into the ghetto by chance, or was part of the crow population which occupied the towers of the Church of the Holiest Virgin Mary. It occurred to him that his father would perhaps recover more speedily if he had a daily soup of crow meat, followed by a tiny leg of crow. If one could only catch such a black bird every day, he mused — and became aware of the fact that his own intestines were as frozen and stiff as his hands and feet. But if the frozen state of his extremities was more or less bearable, the internal frost was devastating, burning and pricking in the emptiness of his stomach. He heard Samuel greet him, but his internal stiffness did not permit him to reply.

"Why is everyone outside? Samuel asked.

"Because the strike has begun, Herr Commissar!" Shalom hissed through his clenched teeth. Emphasizing each word, he intended also to underline that at the present moment the two of them had nothing in common, that now they were neither neighbours nor good friends.

Samuel dashed into his office. The crow sitting on the fence spread its wings. If it had come as a warning, no one heeded its message. As if in disgust, it dropped something behind as it soared into the air.

The group which made up the delegation appeared in the yard. "Everyone is on strike!" Mottle informed Shalom.

"Have you seen Israel?" Shalom inquired about his eldest brother.

Mottle spat through his teeth. "He's still standing behind the Old Man's door. The whole leadership is nothing but a bunch of idiots, *shnorring* for an interview while the Old Man refuses even to look at them." They entered the factory building. The unusual silence inside seemed odd. Were all the machines really still, or were Shalom's ears blocked? They passed the empty halls and arrived at the one where the meeting was to take place. The hall was packed with workmen. "All the Resorts are on strike, comrades!" Mottle called out, facing the crowd. There was no boisterous response to his announcement. The pale yellowish faces, tight with determination, responded with the defiant gaze of desperados. The silence was broken now and then by the weird tingling of the workers' canteens.

Unexpectedly, Commissar Samuel Zuckerman jumped onto the boxes which made up a kind of rostrum. There he stood high above all the heads, unprotected against the hundreds of poisonous glances aimed at him. At that moment he forgot about Rumkowski, forgot about the factory. All he felt was the hatred in those eyes. He was all alone and lonely. "Brothers!" he called out, immediately realizing how strangely that word must sound in the ears of those who stood at his feet. "Workers!" he corrected himself, mustering all of his courage. "I am not standing here as your enemy. I am a ghettonik just like you, and I want you to trust me and to hear me out. Believe me that I have your own good in mind. Believe me! ... Believe me!" he repeated a few times, then stopped. He was a pitiful orator. What he had to tell them he had already told them, with his outcry. However, something was still buzzing in his head, a torrent of phrases which he must not bring to his lips. He knew well that they were the Presess' phrases, but he would not surrender to them. At this moment he was mature; he was standing on his own two feet. Suddenly he called out, "Against whom are you fighting? Against whom?" Was that his own voice, or that of the Presess? At that exclamation the crowd stirred. The spark had come and kindled the fire.

"Against Rumkowski!"

"Against you leeches, who are sucking our blood!"

"We refuse to be doubly enslaved!"

"Why don't they take away the extra rations from the *shishkas*, instead of robbing us of our additional slice of bread?"

"We are hungry! We want better soups!"

"Down with the ghettocracy! Down with Rumkowski and his clique!"

Samuel raised both hands in the air. "Quiet!" he thundered, feeling himself sinking lower and lower. No one paid any attention to him. The clamour resounded in his ears along with the orchestra of clinking, clattering canteens.

Raw, twisted faces like ghostly apparitions were coming up against him, ready to devour him. The managers of the departments joined to help him. A few of them scrambled onto the boxes where he was standing and they too began to shout, their fists raised against the fists of the mob.

Then, suddenly, riding on the shoulders of his two brothers, Israel emerged above the heads of his comrades. He had given up waiting behind Rumkowski's door. As soon as they caught sight of him, the workers became silent. He did not raise his fist in the air, nor did he shout. Samuel was stunned. That common carpenter had power over the crowd, and he, Samuel, felt even more helpless. It was not a helplessness caused by jealousy. It was the helplessness of a stranger among strangers. None of the men assembled here were his brothers; they belonged to an alien race whose language he did not understand.

Israel's voice, calm, controlled, reached Samuel's ears, "We shall not move from this place before you, Herr Zuckerman, and the Presess hear our demands. We declare a sit-down strike from this moment on."

"Against whom?" Samuel exploded with helpless rage. "You forget that we are fenced in, in a ghetto. Aren't we all, the Presess included, in the hands of the Germans!"

There, in the centre of the hall, was Israel smiling shrewdly. "Perhaps you go to the Presess, Mister Zuckerman, and remind him of that. There is no need to tell us about it. Go and bring him here. Let him come and talk things over with our delegates."

"That's exactly what I'm going to do!" Samuel lashed out, to his own surprise. "I'm going to the Presess!" With these words he jumped down from the box and left the hall.

The next moment he found himself in the arms of the frost and the wind. Although he wore nothing but his jacket, he felt the biting cold within him rather than without. "Who am I?" his heart hammered. "Am I that carpenter's pawn? His messenger boy to Rumkowski? Or am I a boy running to his father to beg for protection?" He saw himself talking to the Presess and felt himself torn in two. One part of him was promising to submit obediently to his protector, promising to help him master that wild hungry monster, the mob. The other part was demanding leniency on behalf of the hundreds who waited in the factory, imploring the Presess not to deprive them of their slice of bread, to hear them out and negotiate with their representatives. And between those two divided parts — where was he? Had he become ground into dust? He wondered why he was running so wildly as he had never before run to anyone. "For whom and for what?" he asked himself, and answered himself, "For my own sake, my own survival . . . for my peace . . . for me . . . me!" But who was that "me"? Where was it? Was it indeed he who wrangled and struggled so? Did that really make any sense? As he ran, he noticed a slogan scribbled on a wall, with chalk, "Death to the Presess!" A voice within him hollered: "Death to Samuel!" The air above his head was filled with crowing. A flock of crows was circling the church's tower. "Cha-cha-kra-kra," they laughed. There was a warning in the flapping of their wings.

Out of breath, he climbed the bridge. The shiny boots on his feet weighed tons and dragged him down, towards shame, towards abuse. A painful longing for the secret light in his cellar lit up within him. He felt drawn to his radio receiver — the desire of a prisoner for his beloved. In his mind he saw himself sitting by the radio in the pitch darkness of the dirty cold cellar. Down there he knew who he was. There he felt his "I". There he was powerful: an armed soldier on the Western Front, a pilot, a commander of airplane formations, a commander of tank units, a strategist, a bayonet fighter. Down there he had his dignity. There he was a Zionist and a Jew. There he savoured the brotherhood of people, not of rats.

Someone grabbed him by the arm, calling, "Whereto are you speeding like that, Zuckerman?" It took him a while before he recognized the manager of the Printing Resort. "I could swear you're running to the Presess!"

"Yes," Samuel panted. "The workers refuse to calm down."

The man shook his head derisively, "Call the police, idiot. Call them and you'll get an extra ration of food and a caress from the Old Man. Learn from my mistakes. Zuckerman!" Samuel shook off the man's hand and dashed off.

In the Presess' waiting room he met the commissars and directors of the other Resorts. He knew that these people had the same worries as he, so he avoided them. He pushed himself through to the Presess' secretary and asked her to announce him. Before long he found himself in Rumkowski's office.

Mordecai Chaim Rumkowski was drinking tea with lemon. If there was a spark of nervousness or excitement in his eyes it was that of a passionate card player who reads victory in his hand of cards. "What have you come for?" he asked with reproach in his voice.

Samuel, uninvited, sank into the chair beside the desk. "You have to do something, Herr Presess," he muttered.

The Presess raised himself. "And you have already done your share? I've told you time and again, Zuckerman. You must learn how to act. I trusted you with my factories, so that you would help me, not the opposite."

"Why don't you meet with their representatives?" Samuel asked in the tone of a scolded child.

"Why? Because I won't dance along with their pre-war idiocies. Here no one will tell me what to do. I am the boss here! Do I have to knock that into your head too, Zuckerman?"

"But why . . ."

"Stop why-ing me!" The Presess jumped to his feet. He approached Samuel and looked down at him from under his glasses. "Do I ask the Germans 'why'? What do you want me to do? Let this riff-raff take over the leadership of the ghetto? I am responsible! I alone! And I know what I am doing. They must start working right away! And you are going back to make them work! Tell them that I will call the Gestapo. Go and tell them that!" Samuel stood up. He felt a dullness all over him, as if his mind had become frozen. But here, unexpectedly, the Presess' face relaxed; his voice became softer. He asked in an almost paternal way, "Why do you stare at me like that? I've told you that I'm taking everything on myself. Eh, Zuckerman, I thought that I had gotten you out on the right road. You should know that a man, wherever he puts himself, must stand there with both feet, not one foot here and the other there. Yes, take me for instance. I want to save the Jews of Lodz and I will do so, with or without their good will. And you will help me." He pushed Samuel towards the door, adding. "Since you've asked me, I don't mind telling you, that the bread I'm taking away from the workers will be distributed amongst the entire population. I make no exceptions. Tell that to the managers who are standing behind the door, too. Tell them that I've ordered them to go back to their posts and make order right away. They're incapable of doing anything besides consuming their extra rations and living it up. Tell them that whoever comes again to ask for my intervention will be publicly slapped in the face!"

As soon as Samuel left the Presess' office, he picked up the receiver of the secretary's telephone and called the police. On the way back he did not run. He marched with strong measured steps. His boots no longer seemed heavy. On his way, he stopped at two smaller carpentry Resorts. There the strike was practically over. The police were chasing the workers into the street.

In his favourite factory the workers were still gathered in the hall, waiting for him. Again he was standing, raised above them, while all their eyes were fixed on him. "Workers!" he began without any introduction. "I order you to go back to your work immediately!" Before he could manage to utter another word, the storm erupted anew. This time, however, he was determined to master the situation. The dullness within him had power. He raised both his fists into the air and thundered, "The delegations of the workers will not be recognized by the Presess! The Presess will not allow any mediation! We are in a ghetto. We're working for the Germans! We're working for the *Wehrmacht* and any strike will be considered an act of sabotage!" He was quite aware that it was the Presess' voice that was shouting through his mouth. He did not mind. "I give you ten minutes!" He cast a quick glance at his watch, repeating, "In ten minutes I want to see you all at your work benches. That is an order!" He jumped down from the box and hurried into his office.

The sound of singing voices reached him from the hall. It hardened his heart against the stiff-necked mob. Now he knew where he stood and he stood there with both feet. He called the police again, then he called the Presess, because the singing had begun to be mingled with a stampede of wooden shoes, with the sound of raked and broken furniture. It sounded as if the building were about to tumble to the ground.

He saw the police through the window. They marched into the yard in an orderly formation. He recognized the police chief, and realized that it was not the regular police but the special *Überfallkommando* that had arrived to liquidate the strike. They halted in the yard as their chief addressed them. Samuel's breath stuck in his throat. He felt incapable of coping with the situation any longer. The screeching of the broken furniture seemed to drill holes in his head. Somewhere wooden planks were being shoved about and broken up, split up, sawn up. The workers were constructing barricades, and to Samuel it seemed that they were encasing him within a wall of furniture, of wood, the same wood out of which he had wanted to make useful things. Now they were about to strangle him with it. Not only they, but also the Presess. It seemed to him that it was precisely Rumkowski who had joined forces with the workers against him.

A wild howling reached his ears, pierced by the voice of the police chief, a cold metallic voice barking orders in German. At the sound of that language a frosty shudder crept down Samuel's spine; millions of tiny worms seemed to crawl down his skin. That language made the experience totally unbearable. Through the window he saw the members of the *Überfallkommando* dragging out the workers one by one from the first floor. He sighed with relief. Within a few minutes all would be over. However, the clamour inside and outside of the building did not cease, nor did the stampede of wooden shoes on the stairs. Somewhere furniture was still being shoved and broken up. Wood was struck against wood, hammering with dull blows against Samuel's head.

Those workers on the first floor whom the police had not managed to seize had climbed up to the second floor and again barricaded themselves inside. They blocked the open door half way with a wall of furniture. Through the free part above, they threw down the frames of cupboards, drawers, legs of beds, of dressers, of tables — against the oncoming policemen.

Shalom was standing up on the very top of the barricade. Like his comrades, he was hurling down the stairs anything that was handed to him. He was not excited, nor was he particularly overcome by a fighting spirit. But the sense of defiance which had taken hold of him made him feel good. Of course he knew that he was not standing on top of a revolutionary barricade, just as his comrades knew it. Yet just standing where he was elated him. At that moment he even forgot that he was hungry; forgot that his father was sick. Slinging down pieces of broken furniture loosened the tightness around his heart. His hands were carrying out a double mission. The old furniture, gathered here from abandoned Jewish homes in order to be renewed for the Germans, seemed to be grateful for being demolished, while the furniture made of new wood seemed to rejoice, in solidarity with the old. Wood was joining wood in brotherhood. Wood was joining wood in an act of vengeance. Because the Jewish police chief who was barking his orders in German was not a Jew, nor were the Jewish policemen of the *Überfallkommando* Jews. In the eyes of Shalom and his comrades they were Nazis. And to fight against a Nazi who had such a visible, such a familiar face was a delight. It was easy to unload one's bitterness, one's hatred of the diabolical enemy whom one felt but never saw, who held everyone's life in his black fist — by attacking these attainable concrete foes. They, the workers, knew very well that they had not the least chance of victory. Yet they were experiencing victory during the present moment of reckoning.

The police chief ordered his men to withdraw, in order to give them new strategic instructions. On the stairs leading to the barricade the broken pieces of furniture, of splintered mirrors, of drawers, of doors, of seats, of chairs and the many many legs of tables, beds, cupboards were strewn about in heaps. From downstairs the voice of the police chief could be heard yelling. He was giving the workers five minutes time to clear the building, if not there would be a blood bath. The workers used the five minutes to increase the stacks of wood. They divided themselves into groups. One group raked and crushed the furniture, the other collected drawers, doors and chairs. A third broke the legs off of every piece of furniture. They had decided to save the legs for the last, to arm themselves with them when there would be no choice left but to surrender.

After five minutes, the policemen launched a new attack. Hunched over, they scrambled up the stairs, each covering his head with one arm, while the other, wielding a rubber club, was stretched in front. Pieces of wood came flying down on top of them, accompanied by a hail of nails, locks, screws and hinges. Each trace of blood on a policeman's head was greeted with laughter from upstairs, with curses and triumphant cheers. The sturdy policemen were crawling up the stairs, then sliding down on all fours. Their faces were red with rage and shame. They snarled like bloodthirsty animals. Here they were, the bigshots, stuck between hammer and anvil: between the pitiful barricade upstairs, facing these wretched corpse-like monsters who reminded them of the

Angel of Death, and the beet-red furious face of the police chief downstairs, who barked at them, goading them on from behind. They withdrew a few times in order to rush up the stairs again and storm the barricade. Every time they were forced to retreat, the expression on their faces became less human. They too had now forgotten against whom or for whom they were fighting. They too felt a savage delight in being able to release their pent-up rage. True, the barricade had not yet been taken, and there was no longer a policeman without a gash on his head, or on his back. But never mind. They knew, as did those behind the barricade, that the supply of "ammunition" up there would soon run out and that the moment of revenge was sure to come.

Shalom, standing on top of the barricade, was leading the attack together with Mottle. They were both shouting encouragement to their comrades, every now and again striking up the song of the Internationale, about the "last decisive fight", although the words sounded somewhat odd here. Actually, both brothers were craving to express themselves through a fist fight, through a hand-to-hand encounter with the enemy. And the closer that moment seemed to come, the more fiercely, the more defiantly they sang.

At last, the heap of ammunition beside the barricade diminished to the last pieces of wood. Shalom and Mottle grabbed the last box of nails, locks, cogs and hinges, and poured it out over the heads of the approaching policemen. There was nothing left to do but take apart the barricade, and hurl it down piece by piece. After a few minutes, the barricade was gone and the door was free. "Grab the legs!" Mottle called out, throwing himself on the heap of the previously prepared wooden legs.

They could already feel the blows of the rubber clubs on their backs. The policemen filled the hall, throwing themselves upon whoever came into their hands. The room turned into a battlefield. Groans and screams filled the air. The entangled bodies of the workers were shoved towards the door, then down the stairs, where two rows of policemen stood ready to receive them with blows and kicks as they rolled down. The stairs were stained red. Some of the maimed workers fainted, blocking the way down for the others who also became stuck, while the blows they received increased in number as well as power. Finally one of the stuck bodies slid down, pulling along the entire heap.

Shalom would not let go of the wooden leg he held. He flung it left and right, trying not to let himself be pushed to the exit. All of a sudden, he lost sight of Mottle and became frightened. Mottle was not the same as he had used to be. His legs had become swollen and he had difficulties in breathing. Shalom called him, but in the hullabaloo, he was barely able to hear his own voice. Then the wooden leg was kicked out of his hand. He slid down the stairs under a torrent of blows. He forgot about his brother. All he wanted was to speed up his way down without losing consciousness. Downstairs, while still on the ground, he recognized a familiar face under the visor of a police cap. "Moshe Grabiaz!" he called out beside himself, as he scrambled to his feet. The policeman, a neighbour from Hockel Street, a pre-war horse thief, recognized Shalom too, and removed his club from the latter's back. "You . . . You too begrudge us our piece of bread?" Shalom roared, then spat at him.

"Run before I kill you!" Moshe Grabiaz wiped the spittle off his face with his sleeve.

"So kill me! Come on, kill me!" Shalom aimed with his knee at Moshe's groin. He could barely keep himself on his feet and the policeman easily evaded the kick. He twisted his arms backwards, then pulled him outside and pushed him into the crowd of battered workers.

He shrugged his shoulder, "What have you got against me? The Old Man promised a whole can of conserved meat. Did you want me to refuse it?"

Two policemen were carrying a body out from the building. A bleeding mass of flesh, of dangling legs and arms. It was not Mottle. It was an elderly carpenter who had been working on the first floor. The policemen laid him out on a heap of snow. With that they had finished cleaning up the building. They began to drive the crowd together and gather it near the fence. A cold biting wind was sweeping through the yard, tearing at the bruised bodies. The workers huddled in their light jackets and blew on their fists.

"Who are the leaders?" The police chief bellowed into the crowd. After a moment of silence, the three delegates stepped forward. Shalom noticed Mottle among them. He wanted to rush over to him, but the policemen pushed him back. The three were arrested and led out of the yard, while the rest of the strikers, guarded by the police, remained behind to wait for Commissar Zuckerman to address them and pronounce his sentence. Cold and hungry, the workers squeezed together to keep warm. The ambulance arrived. The orderlies loaded it with the more seriously wounded. Finally, it was announced that the strikers could disperse, since Commissar Zuckerman would not address them; he would let them know when they could resume work.

On his way home, Shalom came abreast of Samuel. They were both hurrying in the same direction, to the yard on Hockel Street. "Do you remember, Mr. Zuckerman," Shalom turned to him, "that when we got acquainted, you asked me if I would ever be capable of killing you? The answer, Mr. Zuckerman, is yes, I would."

"So why don't you?" Samuel asked him coldly. "You hope that the Germans will do the dirty work for you, don't you?"

"You're a louse!" Shalom turned away from him and crossed the street onto the opposite sidewalk.

✦   ✦   ✦

The strike had done Samuel a lot of good. At last he had become a complete man, just as Mr. Rumkowski wanted him to be. His indecisiveness was over. His party work, the Zionest ideal, the moments of elation at the radio receiver belonged to another Samuel, who was as much related to him as dreams are related to a person fully awake. They were separated from him as the day is separated from the night. And that made his life easier. He almost felt as if he had recovered from a grave illness. Now his good mood came back to him, and since the ghetto as a rule heightened the intensity of people's feelings and moods, his good mood was often transformed into exuberance and gaiety. He was now capable of sucking the pleasure out of every favourable moment, and if the favourable moment did not arrive on its own, he would set out to look for it or create it for himself.

He now managed the factories with ease, almost playfully. The only question which weighed on his mind was how to raise production and thus get more praise from the Presess. With enthusiasm he devoted himself to the expansion of the factories, enjoying the sight of the new furniture produced for German houses and offices, as well as of the boxes for ammunition. All these finished products were of the highest quality as far as both craftmanship and design were concerned. Samuel had grown to like wood, its roughness, its smell, the way it surrendered to the machines. He also came to like the good workers, the diligent ones, who so deftly transformed the wood into all these useful objects. He favoured the healthier, the better-looking workers; he gave them special privileges and joked with them when he passed their work benches. But he despised the others, the pallid ones, those barely able to stand on their feet, who gave the impression that any minute they might be swallowed by their machines. He loathed those who conserved their strength, pretending to work only when a *Meister*, a manager, or Samuel himself was around, as they followed the sabotage slogan of T.I.E. — Take It Easy. Samuel did not hesitate to give such lazybones a few blows or a slap on the face. Slapping someone on the face had become for him, as for the Presess, a kind of conditioned reflex. As soon as he noticed such a *klepsydra* face with ashen fallen cheeks, with water bags under the eyes, his hand began to itch. He could not bear the resemblance these unfortunates bore to death masks, and he had to push the sight of such a face away from him, to erase it. This he could accomplish only with a slap.

But most of all he hated those who stole from the factories, sneaking the wood out from behind his back. It seemed to him that by doing so, they were mocking him, and most of all he feared being ridiculed, as he had been during the strike, or on that day in Rumkowski's office. One of his favourite duties was to stop at the checking posts by the exit, and attend the searches. In spite of his irritability, he would often be amazed at how ingeniously and inconspicuously workers stuffed their pants or covered their chests with wood. After the stolen wood was pulled out, their clothes would shrink like balloons, collapsing as if the bodies were no more than clothes hangers. Samuel would fume, threaten and deal out the appropriate punishment. Only when the thieves were foremen or *Meisters* would he pretend not to see a thing, thus buying their devotion.

He would personally dispatch cartfuls of wood to the homes of the managers and commissars of other factories. These men were his friends. They did him favours too, reciprocating with sacks full of flour, or vegetables, with suits, dresses or shoes for his family, depending on which department each of them controlled. He was bound to them by common problems with the workers, with the Presess. With them he could also enjoy a few hours of relaxation and forget himself completely. He did not carry on any highly intellectual conversations with them. They, like Samuel, shunned "high-calibre" thoughts. His conversations with them were light, full of the carefree daily concerns of animals who had a warm lair and enough food to eat. And although they intrigued against one another and begrudged each other's successes, although they were far from being ready to stick their necks out for each other, this was nevertheless a brotherhood to which they could cling.

Samuel took to shunning his former acquaintances and friends. If, however, one of them succeeded in reaching him and asked for a favour, for a bit of "protection", he would help immediately, in order to be rid of the "friend" as soon as possible. He behaved in the same manner towards his party comrades. He would do all he could for them, but he refused to have anything to do with them socially. He also helped out the neighbours who lived with him. Adam and Yadwiga Rosenberg were completely defeated by circumstances. Adam would do nothing but pace about the house like a lunatic, while Yadwiga, who had to run to the food lines and do the cooking and washing, had finally given up her lively chatter. As a matter of fact, she had completely stopped talking. She would smile a dull bewildered smile and follow her husband like a shadow. Behind her back Reisel called her "Sutchka". Samuel avoided the pair as much as he could, but once in a while he would send over a sack of wood for them with Mietek. He also supported Professor Hager and his wife who had become alienated from him, isolating themselves in their room. Although they never asked for anything, he sent in during every meal a bowl of soup and a slice of bread for them. Old Mrs. Hager would accept the gift with trembling hands, with words of thanks on her lips; but there was resentment rather than gratitude in her eyes. Samuel wished that their faces too would vanish from his sight. He could barely wait for spring, when the Presess had promised to give him a home in Marysin.

As far as his life at home was concerned, it had now assumed the form, the outlines of which had been traced months ago. Nothing bound him to Matilda any longer. The reproach he read in her eyes was unbearable, the sight of her face, fat, flabby, twisted with pain, the face of a martyr, froze his heart. But he had stopped venting his anger against her and pretended not to hear her bitter words. He used his gaiety like a shield to protect himself against her. He also tried to avoid Bella, even refusing to allow the thought of her to enter his mind, as if she were no longer his child.

He had only Junia. She who had once been in constant rebellion against him had now become his only true friend. She admired him. She was proud of him for the tireless work he did for the party, for the kindness and humanity which he displayed during every campaign of help for needy comrades. She would tell him this, praising him, and boosting his self-esteem. If, at the same time, he felt a certain inner discomfort, he denied it. And he reciprocated, because he was no longer capable of accepting anything without reciprocating. He shared his secret about the radio with her, taking her down into the cellar to listen to the newscasts. Moreover, he allowed himself to be persuaded to let her take notes and bring them to the meetings of the party youth. Because of Junia and the increased danger created by her distribution of the news, listening to the radio acquired even more meaning for him, while the fear of being discovered, which sometimes attacked him, became more bearable. Now he really was resisting the Germans.

In the cold cellar, after the broadcasts, they would let themselves go and set their imagination free. "When the war comes to an end," Samuel dreamed aloud, "we won't wait even one day, but immediately leave for our Land. No bitter cold there. There, the sky hangs low and the stars are huge and clear. I'll buy a comfortable house, only for ourselves. And you, Junia, what will you do there?"

"I'll fight to make the Land ours," Junia whispered. "But do you know what I think, Papa? I think that the fight for Eretz Israel ought to begin here. We should help the armies of the world. We sit here doing nothing, while they are dying for our sake."

"You're talking nonsense, daughter. What could we achieve when we haven't the slightest contact with the outside world? Not even one piece of ammunition? We are helpless."

"Jews are always helpless."

"Well, imagine that we are armed with whatever there is. We kill our guards, cut the wire fence and escape . . . we, a community of thousands and thousands of Jews. Can you imagine the massacre? And even if some did manage to hide, wouldn't they be betrayed by the Poles? And if they avoided even that, what would they do? Where would they run to? How would they fight? No, our sole achievement is to survive. Only that could become our victory. If all that remains of us is a mountain of corpses, of dead heroes who had the courage . . . what would come of it? We ought to fight for life, not for death. Even the most beautiful death is nothing but a defeat."

After a while they gave up on this unpleasant subject and resumed their play of imagination. In their minds they skipped over the unknown nebulous period of transition, the borderline between Here and There, and imagined how it would be when the Promised Land was liberated. "No, Papa," Junia concluded. "We won't buy any houses there, nor become rich through any private means. The whole Land will be our wealth. We will join a *kibbutz* and live in equality. Who needs money, or jewellery, or other silly things? We need to be happy. With money you can't buy happiness."

Samuel laughed softly, "And I always thought that you were practical. How come you're so naive? Our land needs wealth, capital." He forgot himself and spoke of the Jewish State as if it were already a fact. "I won't join any *kibbutzim*. What would I do there? Work the land? Plough and sow, day after day, week after week? Not for me. I want to build, I want to construct large factories, enterprises that will bring the capital of the world to us. We will become mighty. No one will ever again be able to break us, no one will dare to rise against us."

"But Papa," Junia rejoined. "We don't want to have power over others. We want to be left alone. We want to teach the world how to live in peace."

"In order to teach the world, you first have to be strong, daughter. No one listens to the weak."

They went on arguing, dreamily, with childish seriousness. When they tired of that, they would again warm their hearts with soothing sunny images of Eretz Israel. Finally, they became aware of the stiffness in their limbs and stood up from the heap of sand and sawdust that covered the radio receiver. Holding hands, they crept through the darkness towards the exit. Samuel bolted the door of the cellar, at the same time bolting a cellar door deep inside him, behind which he buried both the conversations with his daughter and his dreams — that were never to rise to the surface of his workaday life.

Chapter Fourteen

YOSSI, ITCHE MAYER'S SON, saw the Presess every day. He worked on Baluter Ring, in a place where the old furniture arrived from the city to be remodelled and renewed in the Ghetto. Since the Presess had recently become unable to stay in his office and roamed about the factories and institutions to see how the work was going, he quite often also visited the Jewish workmen on Baluter Ring. In particular, during the last week when Yossi had been working on reconstructing the Presess' office, adding a room for the Presess' archives, the Presess often stopped to talk to him, each time asking his name, address and his father's occupation before the war. The Presess especially liked to stop with Yossi, because Yossi had a face which was ready to smile at the least opportunity, a face which, when compared to the majority of the ghetto faces, looked almost radiant.

Yossi himself experienced no particular excitement in the presence of the Presess. To him the Presess was a Jew like all the other Jews, slightly nervous, a bit absentminded, but also diligent and able. Yossi chatted with him freely, in his natural manner, with the same respect that he accorded the older neighbours in his backyard. If the Presess were well disposed, Yossi was certainly glad; but when he was ill-tempered, Yossi did not take it to heart either. It did not occur to him to interpret the Presess' every mood, as the other ghettoniks did, as a sign of whether things were going well for the Jews or not, of whether they could expect a better food ration or, heaven forbid, an evil decree.

It had never entered Yossi's mind to beg the Presess for any particular favours. Firstly, he found it repugnant to exploit a person's friendliness; secondly, like his brothers, he resembled his father. Begging words were alien to their lips. What they considered themselves deserving, they demanded; and if they could not demand, they kept their mouths shut. Besides, Yossi had no reason for complaint. He and his young wife lived better than many other people. He did not want to become rich in the ghetto; and as for helping his relatives, he did what he could, bringing home special food for his sick father and sharing part of his salary with his brothers. Anyway, he knew that it was not in his power to satisfy their craving for food. With all the luxuries he enjoyed, he was himself always walking around hungry.

Now, however, Yossi was faced with a dilemma. His brother Mottle, who had been arrested during the strike along with the other delegates, had still not been released from prison. At first the managers of the factories as well as the representatives of the parties tried to intervene on the delegates' behalf, but the

Presess warned them that anyone who came to bother him with the issue would get slapped in the face. The workers and their leaders had to be taught a lesson, so that they would for ever lose their appetite for striking.

Sheyne Pessele did not let a day go by without wailing before Yossi. She could not fathom how one brother could refuse to save the other. Yossi did not respond to her pleading and reproaches, but every morning he woke with the resolution: "Today I'll do it. I'll ask him to free my brother. I'll beg him." Then if it happened, as he was working, that the Presess stopped to talk with him, Yossi's hands would begin to shake. He was unable to look the Old Man in the face. The latter was no longer like a neighbour with whom he could joke and chatter at ease. He was the mighty master who held the life of his brother in his hands. And so Yossi's face ceased to shine and began to look drawn and worried, just like the other faces in the ghetto. The Presess stopped noticing him. And Yossi's task became even more difficult. Moreover, because of his confusion, he became restless and unable to work. He began taking out passes for an hour or two, to wander aimlessly about the ghetto.

The ghetto through which he wandered seemed as tired as he. The houses seemed barely able to stand on their foundations, as if they were being pulled down by Yossi's wish to sink into the ground. Long black blotches like weird black fingers ran from the snow-covered roofs down the walls. Dirty windows, smeared with snow and mud, reminded him of his father's hazy tired eyes. Some of the windows, their panes broken, the holes stuffed with dark rags, seemed like blind eyes. He peered into the empty backyards. Only where the water pumps were not frozen was there a stream of people arriving to fetch water. Yossi heard the music of the water pumps reaching his ears with their squeaking grating tune. An ice-cold sorrow seemed to stick in their pipe-like throats; it prevented them from bringing forth a full stream of water, and allowed through only a trickle of thin tear-like drops. Like transparent beads the water fell into the pails, drumming against their tin bottoms as if helplessly trying to wake someone who was already dead. Yossi had an urge to tap-dance to the rhythm of the water pumps' song of sorrow, but it gave way to a wish to slump down in the very middle of the road and remain there forever. Such wishes frightened him and he hurried back to Baluter Ring, grabbed his hammer or plane and resumed work.

Then came the days of big orders for the factories, especially for the carpentry Resorts. The Presess was beaming. In general, these were the days when he celebrated his personal victory. He had finally conquered all those whom he had envied all his life, those who had the masses behind them, those who had used to shove him aside, who had turned him into a second rate activist, a pitiful philanthropist, a petty merchant, an insignificant insurance agent. Now he could show them who he really was. Much good it had done all those party bosses, the great achievers from before the war, when they had finally joined forces against him and tried to incite the mob in the ghetto. He had overpowered them thanks to his iron will, his prophetic far-sightedness and his gift for diplomacy. Now he was convinced that there would be no more demonstrations or strikes. The additional slice of bread of which he had deprived the workers and promised to distribute among the general population, had not been restored. He gave the population nothing more than before, and he had no pangs of conscience on that account. He had been forced to resort to such manoeuvres in order to isolate the strikers from the rest of the population, for the common good. He had to behave like a father who refuses his children a pleasure which he would gladly grant them, did his wisdom not forbid it. Instead, he fed them with new forecasts of larger food rations, which made them immediately forget the promises he had not kept, for they were like children who forgot to cry when they were promised a candy.

Since his collaboration with the populace had become so harmonious, he felt he could allow himself to play at democracy with them. He organized a Social Committee of all those who owed their successes to him and allowed them to elect a government. He assured them that all their decisions would become law, if he approved them. He invited them to a private banquet in honour of the first anniversary of the ghetto's existence and accepted with great humility the praise showered upon him. He accepted gift albums of artistic, symbolic drawings, depicting the productivity of each factory. On the leather bindings, engraved in gold letters, were inscriptions such as "Long live the Father of the Jews of Litzmanstadt-Ghetto!"

As if to underline his victory, big orders for work began to arrive. Happy and excited, the Presess did not stop telephoning, conferring, calling in the directors, the commissars and the police. He gave speeches to announce all the good news. In Baluter Ring he rushed through the halls, issuing orders to prepare everything for the great movement of merchandise and raw materials that would soon begin to go in and out.

It was then that he noticed Yossi again and stopped to talk with him. "A whole wagon of wood is due to arrive soon!" The Presess panted excitedly. "Apart from that, we've an order for three thousand military uniforms . . . three thousand military caps . . . seven hundred pairs of winter shoes . . . a thousand pairs of summer shoes!"

Yossi was thunderstruck by the unexpected attention and by the confidence that the Presess showed, by telling him the great news in such detail. Something began to stir within him and he had to smile at the Old Man. Yes, he agreed with him. It would be good for the Jews. And as soon as Yossi smiled, he no longer felt as ill-at-ease, as he had lately felt in the Presess' presence. He realized that this was the moment . . . that now it would be easy. He blinked at the Presess in his old amiable manner, and said, "There will soon be a lack of working hands in the ghetto, Herr Presess."

The Presess beamed. "Of course, I will have to introduce two shifts, one for the day, one for the night. And even that may not be enough."

Yossi leaned over to him confidentially, as one leans over to a friend one is about to serve with advice. "I don't understand you, Herr Presess. Do you know what could happen in a few days' time? You won't have enough carpenters. Yes, each carpenter will soon be worth his weight in gold, and here you are letting three first class carpenters rot in jail?"

The Presess caught himself right away. "You mean the strikers?"

"What do you think, Herr Presess? Will you be able to replace them with some *schlemiel* who has learned the trade in the ghetto? If you think so, you're wrong. If you search through the whole ghetto, no, through the whole of Poland, you won't find such good carpenters as they are!"

The Presess mulled over the issue in his mind. It now seemed ridiculous to fear strikes or the party politicians. At this moment he was incapable of thinking about anything but the good craftsmen who were rotting in jail, when they were needed at their work benches. No doubt this lively carpenter fellow knew what he was talking about. He gave Yossi a fatherly pat on the shoulder. "I'm going to call . . . right away!"

Yossi had to lay away his hammer and sit down on a box. Such a weakness had come over him in his joy, that he had the feeling that he was about to faint. What was happening was dazzling, miraculous . . . How effortlessly, how playfully Mottle's fate had been decided.

Later on in the day, the Presess halted once more beside Yossi. "Are you still a bachelor?" he inquired.

Yossi was unable to look him straight in the eye. "No, Herr Presess, I got married in the ghetto."

"Did I officiate at your marriage, or did the *rav*?"

"No, it was my father. At that time you weren't yet officiating at wedding ceremonies."

The Presess grinned as if he had just heard a good joke. "Now I do. Go and register. You deserve it. Next week I'll have fifteen couples. You'll receive your wedding ration. And don't forget to bring along the bride!"

In his great confusion, Yossi failed to laugh at the joke. He also forgot to thank the Presess

✦ ✦ ✦

At last the frost let up and monotonous rains fell on the ghetto. They were received with a sigh of relief. Between the rain and the frost, the rain was the lesser evil. People still shivered from the cold in their homes, but the air outside was not so biting. Little by little the rains began to wash away the heaps of frozen snow and thaw the piles of garbage, allowing the janitors to clean up the yards and sidewalks with their long wet brooms. The people themselves also began to thaw, moving about in the rain as if newly awoken from sleep. The noise, which had been muffled during the winter, began to pierce the air, especially around the lines in front of the food and bread co-operatives. The wind which spread the smells of the partly-demolished latrines also began to carry a discrete fragrance on its wings — the promise that the sun would soon be dispensing a warmth that was neither rationed, nor at the mercy of either the Germans or the Presess. For the time being, however, the sky was still low and gray, covered with swiftly running clouds which rolled into each other like billowing plaids. Night still fell quite early.

Although it was already dark outside, the work in the Carpentry Resort continued at full speed, superficially that is. The glare of the overhead lights joined the light coming from the huge furnace. On the furnace sizzled a few pots with the remainder of some workers' soups, kept warm there in order to save firewood at home. The owners of the pots were busy at their work benches, their watchful eyes running from the oven to the door and back. They were keeping an eye out for *Meister* Berman who was of the correct opinion that whoever warmed his pot on the furnace had the pot on his mind and not his work. He was Commissar Zuckerman's pet, because he watched out for the good of the factory.

Meister Berman was tall, all skin and bone. He had a yellow face with loosely drooping cheeks which bore witness to the fact that his face had had a completely different shape before the war. Now his eyes were just two slivers set in a blown-up, ballooning mass. Before the war he had been the owner of a furniture store, thanks to which he had now reached the position of a carpenter *Meister*.

Meister Berman did not let anyone steal, nor did he steal himself. He was that kind of person. He carried out his work one hundred percent. And he did indeed keep an eye on everything and everyone. As weak, as marrowless as he seemed, he was agile on his feet, unexpectedly springing up to yell at a worker, so that the latter would jump into the air with fright. For that, the workers made him pay dearly. They did not share the news about the war with him, even though *Meister* Berman was dying to hear a bit of news, dying to become a part of the workers' brotherhood. He was a lonely man with whom even the other *Meisters* refused to have anything to do, on account of his "straightness".

The end of the work day was approaching. The foremen were walking between the working benches, keeping their eyes on the windowed door through which *Meister* Berman kept an eye on the hall. "Time to prepare the Hannas," the foremen whispered. The expression "Hanna" originated with the foremen themselves. When they saw the old pieces of furniture from Jewish homes brought into the factory to be remodelled for the Germans, and found Yiddish papers, prayer books, letters and photographs in their drawers, they would imagine the Jewish women who had taken care of them. Every time, before taking the pieces apart, they would sigh, "Look at these Rivkas, at these Hannas". And so the name "Hanna" was transferred to the portions of wood and sawdust the workers were sneaking out daily from the factory. Now, as long as *Meister* Berman was busy balancing the production, the workers could quickly cover themselves with wood, or fill their canteens with sawdust.

Mottle and Shalom helped each other prepare their Hannas. When they had finished, they remained in their places and pretended to work, while waiting for the bell. Usually at such moments, they chatted a bit with each other about what each of them was going to do during the upcoming free hours, before they went to sleep. But today all that was unimportant. Their father was approaching his end. It had made no difference that Yossi sent home the best of his food rations, nor had the daily glass of milk that was bought for him from a *fecalist*, a latrine cleaner that is — produced any change. Itche Mayer's stomach was incapable of holding any kind of food. He was suffering from a mysterious disease, of which the doctors had never heard and which in the ghetto was called a "shrunken stomach". So the sons ate up their father's bread rations and sipped the soups which Sheyne Pessele cooked for him, and which he did not touch. And the most painful thing for the sons was to realize that they were relieved that their father felt no hunger, that while he desperately attacked the food offered to him, he was unable to keep it down. "My reason is hungry . . . the stomach needs nothing," he would explain to the sons, while they burnt with shame because of the delight they felt on their own palates.

The last resort was to try the medicine well-known in the ghetto: Coramine. Coramine were actually drops for the heart, and Sheyne Pessele convinced her sons that Itche Mayer was probably unable to eat because his heart was too weak, and the man simply had no energy left for chewing. Although Dr. Levine insisted that Itche Mayer's heart was quite healthy, Sheyne Pessele persisted in her own theory. Israel would buy the little bottles of Coramine on the black market and Itche Mayer would empty them, not by drops, but by spoonfuls. And since his stomach did not reject it, it was a sign to her that this was the sole possible remedy; especially since a hospital bed for a non-contagiously ill person was impossible to come by, and both Sheyne Pessele and Dr. Levine were of the opinion, each for his own reason, that a hospital would not achieve much more. So they kept up the Coramine, the sons doing anything they could to provide the money for the little bottles which, with their father sipping the contents by spoonfuls, emptied very quickly.

In fact the little bottles of Coramine were a remedy for the family too, morally. They all felt better when a new little bottle appeared in the sickroom. It seemed to them that they were doing something tangible for Itche Mayer, that they had not abandoned him, that they were not just helplessly watching him expire. And Itche Mayer himself also liked the little bottles. He was calmer when they were there. They would stand on the little mahogany table by his bedside, and the family would look at them as if they were a life-giving elixir.

Shalom stared at the rain-washed windows of the factory hall, shuddering at the thought of going home. During the day, when he was at work, and in the company of his comrades, the conversations and discussions, the work itself, allowed the thought of his father to fade, so that it only occasionally gave his mind a prick. Now, however, the moment was approaching when he would have to step over the threshold of their nice new apartment and see Sheyne Pessele's green face and the face of the man who had come to bear only a remote resemblance to his father. Mostly Shalom dreaded the night when he had to lie down beside Itche Mayer and feel the touch of his hot bony body, smell its sharp ugly smell and listen to his heavy snoring. He had been sharing his father's bed ever since his own cot had gone for firewood a long time before.

He envied his brothers Mottle and Yossi who came in for an hour every day, then returned to their homes where no one was sick; where, in bed, there waited for them not the disintegrating body of a father, but the body of a young woman. He envied his oldest brother Israel who, although he lived alone, was involved in party business from morning until late at night. It was easy for a person to care only for a community and not be entangled in the worries of his family circle. And Shalom also painfully resented Esther, because she, the only light in his life, never noticed him. Sometimes he felt within him the urge to force her to love him. Because it was unfair. Because he felt so cold and despondent.

Staring at the mat dark window panes in the hall, he wrote Esther's name on them with his eyes. He recalled how she had looked that evening when he had met her in the gate; she had been soaked from the rain, but her face still shone with her alluring beauty. Under the fitted coat fastened at the waist with a wide belt, her bosom, full and enticing, had moved up and down. She had just run in from the street and she was holding on to the wall with one hand, while with the other she shook the water out of her shoe. He stared at the foot she raised in the air. The wet stocking clearly outlined its shape. His breath got caught in his throat at this unexpected encounter with her perfectly sculptured sole. She called out to him, "I hear that your father is sick." She balanced on the other foot and shook the water out from the other shoe. He wished that she were leaning against his shoulder rather than the wall. "Come up to my room for a moment," she invited him. He followed her.

"The cherry tree will soon be budding," she pointed with the tip of her chin to the tree. On the stairs she removed the wet shawl from her head and shook out her short red hair that waved at him with the promise of spring. "When it gets warmer, your father will feel better," she added. They entered her room. A brightness welcomed him. There were curtains on the window. The floor was neatly scrubbed, the table covered with a flower-design tablecloth. Everything was right with the world and with life. Esther was well disposed. She was satisfied. He saw it in the way she talked, the way she looked, the way her room looked. Turning her back on him, she stood at her little stove, in her unbuttoned coat and the wet stockings, pouring the soup from her canteen into a few pots. She handed him one of them, "For your father . . ." His ears began to burn. He did not stretch out his hand for the pot. "Take it. I can spare it," she encouraged him.

"No," he pressed out from between his lips.

She put her hand on his shoulder. Her face was close. All he could see was her mouth, alluring and fresh. "I won't insist," she said, "but tomorrow you must come to the kitchen where I work. Bring a big pot . . ." She shook off her coat, gliding her hand over her wet stockings. She wanted him to leave and everything within him prodded him to do as she wished. Yet instead, he slumped down on her bed, buried his head in both his hands, and broke out into wild sobs. He forgot where he was; he forgot about Esther. Everything within him dissolved in this impetuous lament. He felt her hand on his head. She was saying something softly, but her voice did not reach him. Instead, he heard another voice within him, his own, which made it clear to him that as he was sitting there like that, with his hands on his face, something was breaking inside him; that the fact that he was crying before her was a sign that it was all over; that the fatigue of so many years of giving without getting anything in return, had overcome him. But he feared the sign. No, he could not live without Esther, without what she represented to him, not now, that his father was so sick. After all, she was innocent. She had no idea about his feelings. He must tell her that he loved her, tell her — not today, but tomorrow, after tomorrow, in a calmer frame of mind. He jumped to his feet, and without turning to her, left the room.

Lost in his own thoughts, Shalom had not noticed that an ominous whispering was going on among the workers at their work benches. Then he caught himself: Mottle was standing beside him, his eyes laughing. "The Soviet Union has declared war! Everyone's talking . . . The diplomatic game is over! It's not the kind of news anyone would dare to suck out from his finger."

Usually Shalom liked to set free his imagination when he heard of a "duck hatched in people's minds". But now he was not in the mood. He did not feel like playing with illusions. He looked at his brother with pity. For Mottle, the fiery communist's sake, he wished that the "duck" were true. A wreath of workers surrounded him and Mottle. With such a piece of news they could "whistle" at *Meister* Berman. "Soon we'll be taking apart the barbed wire and going home," a worker stated. The others nodded, rubbing their hands enthusiastically.

Meister Berman, however, was not one to allow workers to "whistle" at him. Through the glass in the door he could see very well what was going on in the hall, and realized that some important information was being discussed. Unable to continue keeping his mind on calculating the production, he dashed into the hall and waited for a while for someone to rush up to him with the good news. When this did not occur, his furor carried him off towards the furnace. He raised his hands and with all his strength shoved all the warming pots onto the floor. The air began to crack and sizzle. Those who had been burnt began to scream, while the owners of the pots fell down on all fours, trying to save some of their treasure. "If I see another pot on the stove," Berman roared, "I'll see to it that you don't get your soup for a whole week!"

"Don't forget to sell the 'duck' to the controllers," Shalom said, elbowing his brother. That was the only use of a good "duck", to tell it to the controllers and in return not be searched so thoroughly.

The search booth was crammed with people, pressing and shoving each other. The controllers yelled, pushing back the line whose collective pressure hampered their work. They were not calm people, but were always busy with their own sins, with their fear of the manager or of the Commissar himself. "I'm too loaded down today," Mottle whispered in Shalom's ear.

"You sell him the 'duck' and he'll let you through," Shalom tried to calm both Mottle and himself. The controller would have to be blind not to realize, at the sight of the stiff fat figures of the brothers, what was going on inside their clothes. At length, they parted, each of them choosing a different controller. Shalom arranged the bits of political news in his mind, according to their importance, and when the controller placed his hand on Shalom's canteen, he quickly whispered in the man's ear, "The English have taken Bardia!"

The controller's hand, as if at the sound of a magic formula, removed itself from the canteen. "Where is Bardia?" he asked, proceeding with the search.

"Africa. Libya." The controller was now patting Shalom's hard chest. Shalom stopped him with the announcement, "Tobruk and Bengasi have fallen!" The hand forsook his chest, only to descend on a flat board on Shalom's back. "The English are having continuous victories in the air!" The controller let go of the board and allowed his hand to slide down Shalom's hard belly to the leggings of his pants. Underneath the material, a few logs of the best burning wood were tied to his calves with wires. Shalom, overcome by the fear that the wires might loosen, quickly exploded, "The Russians have entered the war!"

The controller straightened up like a puppet jerked by a cord, "A duck!"

"One hundred percent true, may I live so long!" Shalom tore himself away and dashed out. In the street he adjusted his load. He immediately noticed that Mottle was much thinner than before the search.

"He didn't want to believe me," Mottle shook his head sadly. Silently they walked on in the pouring rain, tired of the day's work, of the day's thoughts. At the sight of the gray, unchanged ghetto, the news about Soviet Russia seemed more and more like a "duck". Shalom's stomach was rumbling, but he would not hasten his steps. The rain washed down his face and dripped onto his neck; it drummed against the tin of the canteen in his hand. He constantly bumped against someone as he walked. The street was teeming with workers who were hurrying home from the Resorts. In the rain and the dark they looked like shadows or like coiling black clouds. "I don't have a chip of wood to sell," Mottle put up his collar, folding one lapel over the other. "I cannot contribute anything for a little bottle today." The rain dripped down from his nose. He looked like a corpse. Shalom felt both pity and anger towards him. Mottle, the strong-headed, the stubborn, let his party suck the marrow out of his bones. He was devoting his evenings, his nights and his last bit of vitality to it. "Why do you trudge like that?" Mottle asked.

Shalom did not answer and Mottle finally left him behind and vanished into the darkness. Shalom slowed down even more. People turned their heads to look at him. The touch of him and the shape of his figure seemed odd. It was difficult to walk with his load, but his reluctance to go home was strong, although he knew that Sheyne Pessele and Itche Mayer were watching the clock, waiting for him. The thought of that enraged him. Of all their sons they leant most strongly on him, attaching themselves to him as one attached a cord to a dog; and he was unable to break free and escape. He could not look at his father's face. His insides turned at the sight of it. He felt like vomiting, like fainting. He could not look at Sheyne Pessele, could not listen to her talking. Whatever she said, whatever she implied would burn inside him. He was doomed. Dead inside. Even his pangs of hunger subsided when he thought of home. He tried to keep his mind on the "duck" about the Russians in order to regain some courage. But what meaning could all this have if his father was lying in bed, dying?

He raised his eyes to the windows of the houses. Here and there a thin sliver of light shone through the blackout papers. He knew that in most homes it was now the most beautiful moment of the day. Families were gathering, sitting down at the tables. The stoves were being lit. While consuming their food, they would enjoy the cosiness of the few hours, when the fears of the day were gone and those of the night had not yet begun. They would tell each other the news and allow their dreams about the end of the war and about the good times that would follow, to blend into the steam from the hot bowls. Each spoonful of soup was a full spoon of hope, a promise that they would survive.

He found himself at the barbed-wire fence and dragged himself along the street. Raindrops dripped from one wire onto the other like the notations on a page of sad music. He thought he heard a shot and turned back. Somewhere in the distance he caught sight of a policeman's cap. Shalom entered a passage between two houses and came out on a narrow street. The wood under his clothes unbearably restricted his every movement. He pulled up his collar but immediately put it down again. The collar was soaking wet. He had no idea what was happening to him. He felt alien to himself, afraid of himself.

As he passed one of the gates, he ran into a boy wrapped in a thin gaberdine. Heavy drops were streaming down the broken visor of the boy's round cap. The youngster was wiping his dripping nose with his hand. "You're soaking, Shiele," Shalom said to the street singer.

Shiele's face lit up. He quickly blew his nose. "Want to hear my new song?"

"Who needs your song, Shiele? I've a cacophony in my stomach."

"And you think that my stomach is full? With what? With rain? I need twenty pfennigs. Someone in the yard wants to sell me a soup with eight pieces of potato in it. Listen to my song." He grabbed Shalom by the lapels but immediately let go. "Why are you so hard?"

"I practise boxing," Shalom pounded his fist against his chest.

The youngster blinked his eyes mischievously. "I have a song that will fit you like a glove!" He struck a theatrical pose, wiped his nose and taking a step away from Shalom, broke into song:

> Who knocks at the door so late at night?
> It's the ghetto's pangs of hunger.
> Open, open, dear store of supplies,
> you'll make me feel better and younger.
>
> How can I open my door for you?
> The Old Man is watchful and leery.
> Don't fear, I shall hide your tasty supplies
> deep in my tummy, my dearie.

Shalom gave Shiele a few pfennigs and left him. As he approached his own gate, he heard another kind of singing. The vendors of candies and saccharine were enumerating their merchandise in a singsong. A little man, a flat box suspended from his neck, pulled Shalom by the sleeve. "Buy a remedy for the heart," he pointed to the toffees under the glass of his box.

Shalom freed himself of his hand. "I don't need any remedies for the heart."

The little man followed him. "Your face tells me that you're dying for a candy. Take one. It'll sweeten your mouth and make things lie easier on your heart."

Shalom was sorry for him, "Are you asking for a handout?"

"What gave you that idea? Customers buy up the merchandise from under my hand. The sweet taste of my candies remains in the mouth for a whole day."

"If so, then give me three," Shalom gave in.

"That I understand." The little man lifted the glass cover of his box. "And give your father a candy. It'll be a remedy for him."

"Do you know my father?"

"What do you think? I know you and I know your father, and whom don't I know?"

Shalom left him. Out of habit he raised his eyes to Esther's window as soon as he entered the yard. There was no light in it. He entered his stairway, forcing a cheerful smile onto his face. Sheyne Pessele had apparently heard his steps, because she came out on the landing to meet him. "Where have you been, for heaven's sake?"

"Don't ask, Mother. A policeman was after me."

She helped him take off his wet clothes and pulled out the pieces of wood from under his jacket and pants. In a moment the floor around Shalom was covered with a considerable heap of wood. "You carried all this around!" She shook her head in disbelief. "And how dear is wood on the black market today?"

"The rain is knocking down the price. It's getting warm." He sat down at the table.

"But will there be enough for a little bottle?" She followed him with her eyes as he began to sip the boiling liquid from his bowl. As soon as she noticed him turn towards the bread cupboard, she stood up and shielded it with her body. "Not on your life, you don't! This is for tomorrow morning. I prepared meat balls for you." she hurried to the stove and returned with two black balls made from the dregs of Ersatz-coffee. Shalom attacked them greedily. At last his teeth were biting into something tangible, chewable. He did not feel the taste of coffee in his mouth, but rather the salt and the bit of oil which gave the balls the taste of meat.

"As you see me here, Mother, I could swallow at least twenty dozen more of these little meat balls," he remarked.

She smiled faintly. "I don't doubt it. You have a stomach without a bottom." She sat down opposite him. In the light of the electric bulb her white head shone before his eyes. He saw the pink of her scalp between the sparse strings of hair. He took the jug of coffee that she offered him and sipped from it slowly, economically, letting each saccharined gulp dissolve in his mouth. He wished that the coffee in the jug might never reveal the bottom, so that he would not have to get up from the table and enter the other room. "Have you heard about the new food ration, Mother?" He was trying to postpone the crucial moment. "A whole loaf of bread to a person, a kilogram of sugar, five kilograms of flour, half a kilogram of butter, a full jar of marmalade, and a hammer."

She stared at him. "What is the hammer for?"

"To knock it all out from your head." The coffee was finished. Sheyne Pessele looked at him with a gaze that explicitly told him what he now had to do. He stood up heavily. On his way, he remembered something, went over to his wet coat and took out the piece of paper with the three candies. "Here, have a remedy for your heart," he offered her one and threw another into his mouth.

Itche Mayer's small shrunken face looked like a yellow blotch on the pillow on the bed. The face, with its greenish lips, its half-lowered eyelids, the loose cheeks that inflated and shrank with every breath, reminded Shalom of a frog. He felt that all the food in his stomach was struggling to come back into his mouth. He sucked vigorously on the candy and approached the bed. A foul acrid smell attacked his nostrils; a smell that pursued him through the day and held him in its power at night. He bent over the sick man. The heavy eyelids were drawn up slightly to reveal a pair of nebulous pupils. "Are you asleep, Father?" Shalom asked, knowing very well that Itche Mayer was awake. How many times had he inwardly prayed that his father should fall asleep or lose his consciousness at least for a few hours, so that one might be rid of his painful presence that seemed to fill every corner of the room.

The lips which had been pressed together parted and sipped in a bit of air. "Why are you angry at me?"

Shalom guffawed noisily, gasping. "Why should I all of a sudden be angry at you, Father? Can't you see that I came in as soon as I ate up?"

"You've been here for more than an hour," the lips rustled.

Shalom sat down on the edge of the bed. "Father," he called out merrily, "the Russians have entered the war!"

"You don't have to feed me lies."

"Father, I swear to you, the whole factory was buzzing with the news. Tonight we'll know for sure."

Itche Mayer sighed. "They're drawing out our souls."

Shalom took Itche Mayer's sigh and his remark for a good omen. "Summer is coming, Father." He lightly patted the sick man's yellow hand. "Summertime something always happens. And have you heard . . . the new food ration? A whole loaf of bread per head, a kilogram of sugar, five kilograms of flour . . ."

"Yes, I heard . . . and a hammer."

Shalom laughed falsely. "Not a bad joke, eh? Here, I brought you a candy." He pressed the brown lump into Itche Mayer's mouth. As Itche Mayer sucked it in, one of his loose cheeks became pointy and swollen. He let out one sigh, then another, then the candy behind his cheek stopped moving, as if he had grown tired of sucking on it. Shalom could not bear the sight of the immobile swollen cheek. "It does you good, doesn't it Father? I bought it from the Toffee Man. He sends you greetings. 'Itche Mayer?' he said to me. 'Who doesn't know Itche Mayer? Small thing!'" Instead of replying, Itche Mayer pointed with his finger to the mahogany table where the little bottle with the Coramine drops was standing. Sheyne Pessele who had been watching them from the door nodded and Shalom approached it, took the reddish little bottle and held it up against the light of the electric bulb. "We'll have to buy a new one any day now," he said.

The sick man's thin lips moved, "Buy right away."

"I have to sell the wood first, Father."

"Sell it."

Sheyne Pessele wrapped herself in her plaid. "I'll ask Valentino. Maybe he'll take the wood." She left, and Shalom knew that she was running out of the room in order to relieve her heavy heart somewhere.

After Itche Mayer had taken his drops, the candy under his cheek began to move again. He seemed to look better, more lively. He motioned to Shalom to sit down at his side. "You don't eat . . . you don't rest . . . I know," he shook his head.

The false smile reappeared on Shalom's lips. "If you had seen the meal I just devoured, you would be talking differently."

"It would be easier for you without me . . ."

"If you go on talking like this, Father, I'm going out."

"Let me . . . What do you care? Let me say what I think. I will not surrender, understand? This is the only way I have of fighting the *Yekes*. And some help I am entitled to accept from you. I mean . . . You have my bread ration, my sugar ration . . . That is my contribution for the drops. I want to see the beautiful world that will be built after the German defeat. It will be another life, Shalom dear . . . This is the last and decisive fight . . . All my life I have waited . . . I want to see with my own eyes . . . I may not be so sick, after all, if the doctor doesn't send me to the hospital."

"That's what I keep telling you, Father."

Itche Mayer smacked his lips. "These are really good candies. Maybe I'll be able to swallow something today . . ."

"I'll call Mother. She'll cook something for you."

Itche Mayer lifted himself on the pillow. "Why do you want to run away from me?"

"What are you talking about, Father?"

"You could have bought yourself a piece of bread for the wood . . ."

Uncontrolled rage exploded on Shalom's lips. "Will you never shut up?" he yelled. "What do you think we are, we, your four sons? What do you want us to do, let you die?"

"Why are you yelling at me?"

"Because every time I come home you start up with the same thing."

"Why don't you understand?"

Shalom bent over Itche Mayer. "A man who can talk as much as you is not so terribly sick."

"I have a lot to tell you. I want to tell you that I want to survive the war."

"You've just told me that."

"I've struggled with the Germans for a whole year in the ghetto . . . I did not surrender."

"This I know too."

"I brought up four fine sons . . ."

Shalom smiled crookedly, "This we also know."

"I want to enjoy them, see them in the New World. But Shalom dear . . . On the other hand . . . even if I die, the Germans will not have conquered me . . . Because I'm leaving four beautiful sons behind."

Shalom jumped to his feet. The air in the room seemed to strangle him. He began to pace, wishing he could break down the walls, break the windows and escape. At length he could not take it any longer and made a dash for the door. "I'll send up mother!" he cried as he ran out. On the stairs he met Sheyne Pessele. He grabbed the *rumkis* out of her hand and set off at a gallop in the direction of the Bundist soup kitchen.

The actual kitchen was now closed, but in the dining room young people were sitting at the tables, a cup of coffee in front of each of them, in case an uninvited guest should come in. They were all members of the Bundist youth organization. The youth on guard at the door informed Shalom of the topic of the meeting. There were actually two topics: one purely organizational, the other about the classic Jewish writer I. L. Peretz. The drama circle was also supposed to participate with poetry readings. At the speaker's table stood Israel. At his side sat Comrade Sender from the Culture Society, and Mucha, the leader of the drama circle. Israel was talking about the five decagrams of bread which each comrade had to contribute to support the sick members of the organization.

Shalom made an unsuccessful effort to concentrate on his brother's speech. In his mind, he saw his father as he had used to be, working with his plane and shaking jokes out of his sleeve. And he saw himself at his father's side, hammer in hand, working over a fine piece of furniture. The image was so life-like, so clear and so absorbing that he did not notice when Israel had stopped talking and Comrade Sender took his place. Israel sat down beside Shalom. "What's new at home?" he asked in a whisper.

"If you came home, you would know what's new," Shalom grumbled. He leaned closer to his brother, "Mother sent along money for a little bottle."

Israel furrowed his brow. "I lost my contact, they've arrested him."

"I'm not going home without a bottle. Get another contact."

"Out of the question . . . and I've a meeting soon. Thirty comrades still have to be provided for today . . ."

"Israel, Father is dying."

"Listen, I've news . . ."

"I know. The Russians have entered the war."

"No. Rumkowski needs a few hundred people to be sent out of the ghetto.

This time we suspect that he'll take party people. He has lists of all our members. He'll probably get rid of the leaders first. Don't mention anything at home. I'm going to the cantor, wait for me here."

Israel left and Shalom turned his eyes to the speaker's table. He could not grasp even one word of Comrade Sender's lecture about Peretz. He did not, however, take his eyes off the bespectacled face of the emaciated president of the Culture Society who never missed an opportunity to read his poems or talk about literature wherever people gathered together. But what Shalom was really seeing was his brother Israel sitting in a garret with the cantor, who had a radio receiver and provided the parties with information. Shalom had no illusions. He knew that the news about the Russians was nothing but bluff. Yet there was some hope cooing inside him too. Perhaps Israel would come back with some good news? Perhaps Itche Mayer would get better after all?

He walked home with Israel. There was not even a bit of news to tease the imagination. At home they met Yossi and Mottle who had also come to see their father. A few neighbours as well as Itche Mayer's regular cronies were also in the room. They all sat around the bed. Itche Mayer's yellow face, freshly washed, shone out from the pillows that Sheyne Pessele had covered with a clean towel. As soon as he noticed Shalom and Israel, Itche Mayer pierced them with his glance, "Another little bottle?"

Itche Mayer's neighbours and cronies were busy discussing Rumkowski and his helpers. Only his four sons joined with their parents in a chain of looks that broke, then linked together, then broke again, linked again, in silence. Mottle was the first to rise and leave. After him went Yossi. The other visitors stayed on for a while and finally they too left. Israel was the last to leave. He pulled Shalom with him. They walked in the yard, in the rain. They had never confided in each other, but there had always been a particular bond between them; even Shalom's resentment of Israel was coloured by respect. It was difficult to justify the thought that his oldest brother did not know what he was doing, or that he should behave unjustly. They kept silent for a long time, then Israel spoke up as if he were reading Shalom's thoughts. "It doesn't seem likely that they will come to search for me tonight ... If you want me to, I'll sleep over at home."

Shalom knew that they might very well come to search for him tonight, yet he jumped at Israel's offer. "Sleep with Father," he said.

Shalom spent the night on the floor in the kitchen. During the hours when he was awake, he thought about the new decree: the deportation of a few hundred people. He saw himself in a train outside of the town, passing fields and forests. He imagined a detention camp where he would work, but be well fed. Then he saw Sheyne Pessele's white head. No, he could not leave her with any of his brothers. She was his. His responsibility, his burden and his comfort.

✦ ✦ ✦

The following evening no one came to visit Itche Mayer. The news of another decree hanging over their heads deprived people of their courage. Only his four sons gathered at their father's bedside. Itche Mayer had been asking for the new little bottle during the day. In the evening he stopped asking. He stopped talking altogether. Shalom was relieved that his father kept silent, thinking this a good sign. However when the brothers wanted to leave, Itche Mayer shook his head and said in an oddly strengthened voice, "Well, children, I'm on my way."

His four sons stood there stunned. Then they recovered and began to laugh at him. Itche Mayer called each of them separately to his bed; he motioned with a finger for each to bend down, lifting his chin so that they could kiss him. Still smiling crookedly, and whispering encouraging words, they obeyed and kissed him. He made an effort to say something to each of them, but what reached their ears was a rattling noise which the sons tried to cover up by talking louder and louder. Sheyne Pessele sat at the foot of the bed; her chalk-white face very much resembled that of Itche Mayer.

That night none of the sons went home. Shalom started to lie down with his brothers on the kitchen floor, but Sheyne Pessele came in to fetch him. Itche Mayer pointed his finger to Shalom's place at his side and rattled, "It won't take much longer."

Shalom forced himself into his father's bed. He tried to lie close to the edge and not breathe too deeply in order to avoid the nauseating odour that filled his nostrils. During the night, as he lay there in the abyss of darkness, not knowing whether he was awake or asleep, he felt a hand manacle his arm. The little body at his side shook and rattled. Shalom heard his name pronounced and a word, a moan sounding like "member . . . remember!" Shalom shut his eyes tight, hoping to vanish deeper into sleep, but instead, his body became stiff, fully awake. He heard Sheyne Pessele's bed squeak, rocking . . . rocking . . . until it rocked him, as if he were lying in a cradle, to sleep. He slept hard, deeply. In his sleep he felt someone's fingernails cutting into his flesh, he heard, "ember . . . remember . . . Shalom."

In his sleep, Shalom tried to free himself of the fingernails and of the hand that held on to him. It gave in. But instead, Itche Mayer's whole body fell upon Shalom's arm with an unbearable weight. Shalom opened his eyes wide. On his arm lay his little father who had finally fallen asleep. It seemed easy . . . light and quiet . . . like nothing. Shalom removed Itche Mayer's head from his shoulder and pushed the body away from him. He got out of the bed and turned on the light. Sheyne Pessele, who was sitting on her bed, stopped rocking. Shalom dressed, unaware that he was dressing. Soon he saw himself running through the yard, to the entrance where Esther lived. He ran up three flights of stairs, but when he reached the door, something collapsed inside him. He sat down on the stairs, curled up in a corner and shut his eyes. He prayed for tears, but they would not come. He leaned his head against his knees and began to dream of Itche Mayer's life in Konska Vola, in the orchard, in Warsaw and Lodz. He dreamed of Itche Mayer's words, his sayings, his wisecracks, his speeches to the hungry masses in the ghetto. When he raised his head and looked around, he was surprised to find himself at Esther's door. For the last twenty-four hours he had not thought of her at all. Going down the stairs, he knew that he was leaving her behind, that his love had expired at last. He felt no sorrow or sadness. All he felt was that he himself had now become Itche Mayer.

Chapter Fifteen

THE HOUSES OF THE GHETTO changed their faces with the caprices of March. One day they were shrunken, shut up behind the frozen windows and locked doors, the heavy roofs with the dark chimneys pressing them down with their weight; the next day they seemed to have grown and straightened, as they laughed with the squeaking of opened doors and windows. The same happened to the people. One day they were depressed, wrapped up in themselves and in their heavy coats and plaids, their wooden rain-soaked shoes dragging the weight of their bodies with their last ounce of strength. The next day the clip-clop of the same wooden shoes resembled the playful clacking of castanets; the light bodies seemed about to soar; the mouths, like melted mountain springs bubbling with lively streams, chatted, and eyes like squirrels woken after the winter, jumped hopefully over God's world: the ghetto.

People had developed a particular sensitivity to the weather, and the longer they were shut in, the sharper, the finer that sensitivity became. It influenced their minds, coloured their moods, led their thoughts and determined the climate of their souls. Only news from the battlefields or, heaven forbid, an evil decree, or a tragedy in the family, or a Jewish holiday was capable of annulling that relationship.

People were almost personally involved with both the sky and the earth. The sky was the sphere free of barbed wire, the only connection between "here" and "there", the sole witness, the eye looking in. In its depth the people searched for secret commentaries, promises, omens. So, if that eye wept, their hearts felt bitter; if the eye smiled, there was light in every human heart. And the earth? The earth meant concreteness: the only tangible lasting thing. Here, on this fenced-in plot of land, the ghettoniks walked. The earth sucked their tears; into it sank their sighs. In the earth rested those who had been frozen to death, those who had expired from hunger and disease. Here crawled hope and fear. Upon this plot of land every single day, every week, every month left its seal like on a calendar, engraving itself on the passage of time. To every Jew walking that plot of land it seemed that his step left a mark, a footprint. The earth was eternal, and here people clung to eternity.

During those days the Jews of the ghetto were like sick children. They possessed not only a sensitivity to the weather, but an overly acute sensitivity to all the changes taking place in their bodies or outside of them. They possessed an additional sense which was capable of perceiving the most concealed vibrations of the space in which they moved. Like sick children, they could sense the impenetrable, the incomprehensible nuances of happenings or of dreams, as these were revealed to them in signs that only they could understand. A kind of fever — kept alive by hunger, by tuberculosis, by despair — devoured their bodies, helping them embrace this impossible life in the only possible manner: as a deep mystery.

And like sick children, the people abandoned themselves to the concealed life, letting their feverish imagination play with all the tones, all the shades possible. Their imagination carried them off into other worlds. It was capable of satiating them with meals they had never savoured, capable of bestowing upon them a happiness they had never tasted. It helped them to escape from their shackles and it embellished their concrete reality. It could blow up the least bit of news to the proportion of a message of redemption. It could fill them with enthusiasm at the sight of a few pieces of potato, of a crust of bread with marmalade, and it transported the physical delight of chewing into the realms of a purely spiritual exultation. It also awoke their gratitude to the hands which made their sickbeds more comfortable. They depended on these hands. These hands freed them of worries about their livelihood, assisted them in forgetting their sick condition and accepting it as normal. These hands allowed them, in the orderliness of that pitiful existence, in its monotonous rhythm, to escape from the present and to occupy themselves with fantastic speculations about a tomorrow which was a blinding, intoxicating light.

There was only one thing which nothing could help the ghettoniks to flee: the intimacy with death that lurked beside them in their sickbeds. And since they were aware that they would not be able to deal with it, with only their crust of bread, or bowl of soup, they began to seek something more powerful with which to arm themselves. During that past hungry winter, a craving for knowledge and beauty awoke within them. They searched for a kind of logical-mystical scheme, into which both their strange kind of life and death would fit. They searched for it in the complicated mechanism of the universe, they searched for it within themselves. One person tried to find it in the pages of the Talmud, while another looked for it in philosophical dissertations, or in the words of historians and scientists. Yet another searched for it in the works of Tolstoy or Dostoyevski, or in those of Sholom Aleichem, Peretz or Leivik. And he who was simpler, or less educated, searched for the same moral support in the words of a long forgotten folk song or a new song created in the ghetto.

They also kept diaries — the children who had just learned to write, as well as the old men with gray beards. They thought that they were writing "for history", but in reality they wrote rather for the sake of their own immortality and for the immediate sustenance of their souls. The ghetto swarmed with poets, with novelists and humorists. The folk singers sold their songs on street corners. Sheets of paper written in pen or pencil wandered from hand to hand. The new literature was realistic, romantic, mystical, decadent, festive, despondent, optimistic.

Mordecai Chaim Rumkowski was no exception. During that time he too was overcome by a craving for intellectual gratification which first expressed itself in his desire to see his name in print. To this end he initiated the publication of the *Ghetto Zeitung*. He quickly found himself a staff that had the talent to dress up their pens with his language, to express on paper not only his thoughts, but even the manner in which he formulated them. It was easy for him to sign his name under such articles. Some of the articles were purely theoretical, containing his personal philosophy: "I have come to the conclusion that our sole salvation is work. Work was the path I chose in the past and the one which

I shall continue to choose in the future. And indeed, with our work, we have proven that we have not lost the capacity to build and strengthen our existence . . . We now have to sit down and ponder deeply on the meaning and value of work. For this reason I have decided . . ." Other articles dealt with concrete events in the Resorts, offices or in the ghetto in general. Every page of the newspaper was full of the Presess' decisions. It was always "my factories", "my workers", "my Jews", and "I have created", "I made", "I order". The *Ghetto Zeitung* also made public the orders and proclamations of the authorities, Rumkowski's own orders and proclamations, as well as the names of those who had been caught stealing. There was also a literary supplement in the paper. It consisted of rhymed panegyrics to Rumkowski, composed by a hungry courtier, a scribbler.

These intellectual activities did not completely satisfy the Presess' sudden craving for culture. Thus he also founded the House of Culture which he located in a building that had once belonged to a Polish Fascist organization. The building harboured a theatre hall as well as some smaller rooms. When the locks to the rooms were removed, a number of musical instruments were discovered. And so, overnight, was created the symphony orchestra of the ghetto, which gave concerts twice weekly. Shortly afterwards, the choir and the Revue Theatre came into being.

♦ ♦ ♦

Esther had become a radiant beauty. Her face, smooth, round, with green eyes fringed with dark lashes, the halo of her fiery-red hair, the full well-shaped body bespoke her young and ripe femininity — as if nature had just put the last dot on its completed work. There was an air of sensuality, of enticement, of concealed magnetism about her that made people restless and drew them towards her. Her step, which had always been light, became a bit heavier, but it retained its elasticity; its rhythm still gave the impression that she did not walk but rather floated on air. When she crossed the backyard or passed through the street, she could feel people's eyes beaming at her from all sides. There was no desire in those swollen eyes, but a light was kindled inside them. It was soothing to look at her. Only now and then, a younger, less hungry man would follow her and talk to her, in order to make her turn her head. She would show him her fine teeth and the green light in the slivers of her eyes — a smile that was not inviting, that was only the acknowledgement of a compliment.

The loneliness which had previously been so unbearable to her, ceased bothering her. Now she felt comfortable with it. It seemed to her that it gave her strength. There was an exuberance which permeated her whole being. More than once would she ask herself what that excitement was all about and reproach herself for being able to feel what she felt, while everything around was so dark and gloomy. She reproached herself for her egotism, her uncommunistic indifference to her fellow man. But she did not take herself seriously with these reproaches. She knew that although her compassion no longer expressed itself the way it had used to, it was of a healthier nature, and that she herself was basically a better person than she had been. Indeed, she no longer had the wish to die with each dying friend, but for that same reason she no longer resented those whom she helped, for torturing her, for devouring her soul with their suffering. Between them and her there was now a demarcation line. It was precisely that demarcation line that allowed her to help them more wisely, to become more direct. She had also come to see the world around her more clearly, to be more aware of the sounds she heard, the sights she saw, as if she had suddenly ceased to be blind and deaf.

Her light-heartedness was something very new to her. In the past, even during the best moments of her life with Hersh, her joy had been accompanied by a heaviness of heart, by a gnawing worry. More than once had she felt happiness the way one feels pain. Now she delighted in every moment, secure in the knowledge that this was all she had: this moment, this present. She was in love with no one, yet felt as if she were. She was not free, and yet enjoyed her freedom. Eye to eye with herself, she no longer felt any repugnance. She became more familiar with her faults and accepted herself as she was.

Her collaboration with her comrades became very harmonious. Not only had she become a more disciplined member of the movement, but her popularity among her friends had grown. Her reluctance to accept a high post in the party and her self-denial and devotion as a "gray sheep" were now considered to be the expression of her modesty. Her relationship with Comrade Baruch and Comrade Julia became more straight-forward, more amiable. And so she was entrusted with the leadership of the newly created group of *gymnasium* students, a function of extreme importance. She threw herself into her work with the youth group with great fervour, eager to share her strength with the young members, to win them with her hopes and carry them along with her enthusiasm. That, however, was not easy.

The faces she saw before her were the faces of young old people whose hungry stomachs held dominion over their thoughts. They could not understand what her excitement was all about. They had become communists in the ghetto, because they were seeking some logical consolation, seeking an optimism based on reality, on facts — and they were brutal to her. Sometimes, when she became carried away by her talk, one of the young people would cut her short without ceremony, at the very height of her fervour: "Your stomach is full and ours are empty, how can you come and tell us what we ought to feel and how we ought to behave?"

Confused, she would defend herself. "I have the approval of the leadership. I am working for the party. I'm helping comrades, the sick, the needy. Would it be better if I resigned from my post at the soup kitchen or renounced the food I am getting?"

"It's the food that makes the difference between you and us. And don't you think that by helping your own comrades you are depriving other people?"

"I know," she would try to overcome the blushing of her face. "And it bothers me too. But if I left, there would be someone else, helping her own people. That is the system."

"It appears, according to you, that we are to make peace with the system."

"The system comes from Rumkowski and his clique, and the Germans stand behind it. We must use it for our purposes. We have to support our cadres, the enlightened segment of the population."

"And where is our responsibility to the apolitical masses of the ghetto? The Bundists are helping their people, the Zionists help theirs, and we ours. But who will care for the community, for the majority? Should we leave them in Rumkowski's hands?"

"We have no choice. What we can do is to infuse the masses with our courage and morally help them to get through the difficult times." During such moments Esther felt very uncomfortable with the young and the best thing to do was as soon as possible to resume the study of Lenin's works.

Sometimes she tried to find a contact with these young intellectuals by touching upon topics closer to their hearts. She tried to talk about culture, to propose discussions on literary works, to invite some of the new poets. But this did not help her much. They still attacked her: "Rumkowski gives us enough culture. And why do the Germans let us participate in such broad cultural activities? Why do they permit us to organize performances and concerts? Do you think that they don't know about it?"

"It's possible," she defended herself. "Maybe they don't care what we are doing, since we are in their grip anyway. But we can use this . . ."

They would not let her finish, but became even more heated. "They don't want us to rebel. That's what it is! That's why they let us drug ourselves with culture. Culture in the ghetto is a sin! It blinds and weakens us; it kills our alertness!" Yet, she knew that these same young people diligently studied their school subjects and never missed a single concert at the House of Culture, that they devoured works of fiction and avidly read the hand-written poems and novels circulating in the ghetto. Only in this group did they refuse to hear about culture. Here they expected something else from her and from themselves. She knew very well what this something else was: active resistance against the Germans — and of that there could be no talk for the time being.

Nonetheless, she did once in a while succeed in carrying the group along with her, through singing revolutionary songs. After the meeting, she would begin to hum a tune softly, while the others, at first apathetically then with more enthusiasm, let themselves be carried away by the words and the melody. Their faces would lose the dryness of old age and become brighter. More than once she found herself wondering how a simple song could achieve more than hours of lecturing.

It was then that she rediscovered her voice. All day long she would hum, taking pleasure in the clarity of tone she was able to produce. She did not miss a single performance or concert in the House of Culture, and she was especially moved by the performances of the choir. Here, dressed up in her prettiest dress, she would run into the boys and girls of her group, also dressed in their best. Here she also met the manager of the kitchen where she worked, and here too she often saw the man who had once held her life in his hands, and who now held the lives of all those present, of all the Jews in the ghetto, in his power: the Presess, Chaim Rumkowski. She would see him arrive with his entourage, notice him cast his glance around the hall, much as he had used to do at the orphanage, to see whether the children were behaving well. Everything inside her would contract when the performance was interrupted, so that the public might stand up and applaud him, until he sat down in the seat of honour and indicated that the show might continue.

Such scenes with the Presess would annihilate her plans of joining the choir. Standing on the stage in the theatre seemed then a crass collaboration with the system. Her *gymnasium* students were right. If her collaboration with the Presess as a *wydzielaczka* in a kitchen could somehow be justified, a collaboration such as this, in the field of culture, had no justification. In her opinion, cultural activities ought to have nothing to do with the Presess. On the contrary, they should be aimed against him and against the Germans. She knew that even when she sat passively as a "consumer" in the theatre, an institution that "belonged" to the Presess, this too was a form of collaboration. But this she could not help. A concert in the House of Culture was a festive occasion for her.

It was a cool evening; on the western horizon there still played some last pink rays left behind by the sun. Swarms of young strollers poured out from all the gates to enjoy the last hours of a beautiful day. Esther was among them. She walked alone, observing the young people. They were neatly washed, dressed in light clothes, as if they wanted to provoke spring in arriving sooner. The girls in their light summer dresses shivered a little in the cool air. Thin and pale, they wore a dream-like solemnity on their faces; their laughter seemed muffled, soft, lacking any aggressive frivolity. An air of calm, of delicacy and modesty accompanied their movements. For their part, the young men, involved in passionate discussions, also appeared delicate and gentle, as if each of them were a young prince deprived of his crown.

As she walked on, it began to seem to Esther that the ghetto did not exist at all, that the barbed wire was nothing but part of a fence around a park where young dreamy people were strolling leisurely in the peaceful silence of dusk. She avoided looking into the eyes of these young passers-by in order not to destroy the illusion. For quite a while she had been noticing something peculiar in the eyes of the people. Framed with violet, larger and deeper than normal eyes, they were dark, as if consisting only of the pupils which cast shadows over the faces. From their depths came glances, tear-soaked, glassy and hot; they seemed to stare fearfully, as if they constantly perceived something awesome in front of them. She also avoided looking at the feet of the strollers. The feet clopped along on the wooden soles, hard and dry. Some legs looked like sticks moving back and forth in the large shoes. Others were swollen and stump-like, moving stiffly, tightly encased at the ankles by the linen of the bootlegs which obviously cut into the swelling.

In front of her, a group of young people strolled arm in arm, barely moving ahead. Among them she recognized Rachel Eibushitz, but it did not occur to her to accelerate her steps, nor to cross over to the other side. Whatever had bound or divided the two of them in the past had no meaning now.

Her ear caught snatches of a conversation. One of the young men in front of her, whom she had often seen in Rachel's company, spoke about the decree ordering pious Jews to cut off their beards. He spoke about the stubbornness and perseverance of the religious Jews, adding, that in his opinion, the latter, in spite of having additional troubles, were more likely to survive the war than anyone else. Then she heard Rachel mention Chaim the Hosiery-Maker, "His two daughters might not have caught T.B., if they had been allowed to eat their rationed portion of unkosher meat . . ." Esther felt ill-at-ease. Rachel was right. It was true: All the help she had offered her relatives had not prevented her two cousins from catching the disease. She too resented her uncle.

Looking over the shoulders of those in front of her, she noticed a familiar figure. Along with the talking, she also heard a singing voice, and recognized the poet Burstin who during his daily evening promenades had become acquainted with the strollers. Half of the ghetto population was on a first name basis with him. Burstin conducted with his hand as he sang. Esther called him over, then tried to push herself through to him. The conversation between the young people had broken off, since they too recognized Burstin. The next moment all of them, Esther included, surrounded the poet, shook his hand and inquired what he was humming.

"The Waltz Macabre from Berlioz's Symphonie Fantastique," he announced in a solemn voice. He was a man in his fifties, but he had the round open face of a child. He also dressed youthfully, his not overly-clean shirt collar lay out over the collar of his threadbare jacket. He let himself be carried along by the group that surrounded him on all sides. "And now listen to this waltz!" he called out, intoning another melody. He did not have a good voice but his humming was faithful to the melody. Again Esther had the illusion of participating in a dream-like promenade. The strolling people were wrapped in the blue and pink of the evening as if in transparent veils. Everything seemed to be moving through idyllic spheres, accompanied by Burstin's warm voice. She gave Rachel a sidelong glance. Had something new sprung to life between them at that moment?

They were now far up Hockel Street, where chestnut trees grew along the sidewalks. Leaning against one of the trees stood a hump-backed man wrapped in a black cape. He had an ugly face with a long pointed nose. His high forehead reached to the middle of his head, where it met with his long artist's hair that fell to his shoulders in long strings. Through the armhole of the cape one could see a huge cardboard folder. At the sight of Burstin and the young people, his mane shook, the ugly face livened up, while his little humped figure disengaged itself from the tree. "*Shalom aleichem*, Burstin!" he hallooed with his hollow sounding voice, and approached the group with an outstretched hand. He spread his sharp claw-like fingers. "What is all this singing about?" He scrutinized Burstin's companions with eager eyes. Burstin pulled him along by the sleeve. "Permit me at least to introduce myself to these people!" the stranger laughed, ready to shake everyone's hand.

"Come, come, no need to introduce yourself. Everyone knows you," Burstin pushed away the man's hand. "Vladimir Winter, the Rembrandt of the ghetto!" he announced, laughing.

They moved on. Winter's gaze halted on Esther. He walked close by her, his hot searching eyes devouring her face, her head, her arms. He leaned over to her. "One thing Burstin and I have in common," he said, "We both love youth. That is because we're artists. Life has no power over the artist, perhaps death doesn't either ..." He began talking to her quickly, heatedly, constantly interrupting himself. Esther had the feeling that his was the voice of solitude seeking its echo.

Burstin invited everyone to come up to his room which was located here, at the end of Hockel Street. The room was actually a shed; the walls were covered with thick brown paper, patched here and there with white. The table and the few chairs were crowded with books and papers, as was his narrow iron bed. The entire shed seemed to consist of nothing but paper. When they had all entered, the room became so cramped, that Burstin himself was barely able to squeeze himself in. He plowed his way through the crowd of his visitors towards the window, opened it wide and proudly spread his hands, "Look, children, here is my freedom!"

Before the visitors' eyes there appeared a huge barren field lying under the vast violet sky. "No barbed wires," someone whispered.

"If you don't see them, they don't exist," Burstin laughed playfully.

Winter sighed, "The wire fence is so close that you cannot see it. Interesting what kind of locations we've fished out for ourselves, you and I, Burstin. At my place the fence is also very near, and that's why I too can see a free landscape from my window." He turned to the young people who stood confused and uncertain in the presence of these two odd characters. "I doubt whether we could work if we didn't have the illusion of freedom before our eyes. I don't say that all of us need it, but those, whose inspiration comes through the eyes, do. Do you understand what I'm saying?" Winter's sharp little eyes darted over the faces before him. "Take for instance Burstin. True he's a poet, but his primary stimuli come from the outside and reach his inside. With others it is the opposite. Those are the most powerful creators. But if you took me, for instance, and shut me up in a cellar, gave me a palette and a canvas, but no contact with the outside world, I would perhaps be productive for a time, painting from memory, but as soon as I lost the recollection of reality, I would stop working. Because even your imagination has to be hooked on to reality. For instance, you paint a man riding on a cloud. The man and the cloud are real, only the combination of these realities is the achievement of the imagination." Winter's monologue was broken by his cough; he felt his forehead with his hand. Around him, people were already sitting on the floor. Carefully wading between their legs, he approached the table, removed a pile of papers from a chair and sat down. A thick writing book came into his hands. He flipped through it, then handed it to Burstin, "Here, read us a few poems."

Burstin did not wait for him to repeat the invitation. He took the writing book and pulled himself up onto the window ledge. He folded one foot over the other, leaned the writing book against his knee and, without checking whether his visitors were ready to listen, he began reading.

At the table Winter sat, playing with his long fingers and moving his lips as if he were repeating Burstin's stanzas. Then he reached into his pocket, drew out a little box of crayons and played with them. He fixed his eyes on one of the paper-covered walls and stood up. Picking his way carefully between the legs on the floor, he approached the wall and scrutinized it from very close. He wiped it with a sweeping gesture of his whole arm as if he were dusting it, then took a little piece of crayon and began hurriedly to draw on the paper. As Burstin recited his poems, on the wall of his shed there appeared clouds and fields, trees and birds — a landscape from which there gradually swam out the shape of a female body. Winter took a red crayon and the woman's body acquired red flowing tresses that wound themselves into the clouds. He moved to another part of the wall and there the head of a sun appeared: again the redheaded woman. She was dipping her hands in a green lake which resembled a mirror. In it a red water-lily floated. Burstin raised his head, silently following Winter's racing fingers with his eyes. Until Winter caught himself. "Why did you stop? Read on, please." Between them sat the young people, aware that they were bearing witness to an experience for which they had no name. The air seemed to be charged with electricity. Winter's hand, its movements on the paper led not only the crayon, but also the gazes of those present.

"You did not even ask me . . ." Burstin, also carried away, whispered.

"Read only airy poems," Winter begged him.

Burstin lowered his eyes to the writing book and began to recite again in his muffled rustling voice. Winter was already at another wall of the shed. On it he was sketching the contours of young men and women loosely holding on to each other's arms. Naked, they soared through a torrential rain; above their heads hung a very low heavily-clouded sky. The entire etching was in gray, only one of the young people's heads was bright, aflame with fire-red tresses. The rain cut into them too like a hail of pins, which below, around the feet of the figures, appeared in the form of barbed wires. On one such wire stood a gray-feathered bird. It bore Burstin's face. With its beak the bird was plucking at a rusty knot in the wires. A bit further, Winter drew a horse with a head resembling his own, and a flying mane that looked like his own artistic hairdo. The horse, flinging its front legs in the air, was galloping over a field where green barbed wires grew. The horse's mouth was open; it smiled a wild smile. Its neck and the black ball-like eyes, full of greed, were turned towards the red woman's clouds of hair.

It became very dark in the room. Burstin stopped reading. Winter, however, kept on working. When he noticed Burstin slide down from the ledge, ready to blacken the window and turn on the light, he stopped him. "Heaven forbid . . . Wait . . ." They remained in the dark, with their eyes following the fantastic world that heaved into sight from under Winter's hand. In the silence of the room only the squeaking of the crayons and the tick-tock of Burstin's table clock were heard.

Then Esther began to sing. She did not know how or why it happened; she was barely aware that she was singing. It was an outcry which, like a thin thread, came winding out from the depths of her throat, of her being. She felt ashamed of her outburst, yet was unable to hold it back. The little room was full of her voice which seemed to penetrate the walls and carry with it the movement of Winter's hand. From the moment when she began to sing, the painter's body seemed to have entered a trance. He raised his arms, threw up his head, dancing and swaying on his legs. As his hand moved to the rhythm of the melody, more and more new lines and new fantastic landscapes appeared, real, unreal, enticing yet devoid of any horizon. Two walls of Burstin's shed had already been covered with Winter's drawings. Someone helped him move Burstin's bed from the wall. "Sing . . . Sing . . ." Winter's wild eyes burnt into Esther.

Through the open window came the sharp cool smell of the barren field. Esther sang familiar tunes. They seemed to be kneaded by her voice, coloured by the mood of the moment, by this strange gathering, by her cravings, by the unknown power that she felt within her. Her hand rested on the shoulder of a young man. Someone else's hand was stroking her hair, while her own eyes and her neck were drawn towards Winter's hand. It seemed to her that it was his hand that was pulling out the thread of tones from her throat, from her heart, modulating and shaping it.

So they sat until the late hour when all four walls were covered with drawings and Winter let the last crayon drop from his hand and commanded, "Put on the light!" Burstin covered the window with a dark rag and turned on the light. Slowly the visitors rose from the floor to stretch their limbs. They looked around as if they had awoken from a dream, or were falling into a dream. There was a land surrounding them, a land of painful beauty, of light and shadows, which enveloped them with the perfume of an unknown life.

"What have you done?" Burstin exclaimed, partly joyful, partly frightened.

"How do you like it?" Winter wiped the sweat off his brow with his fist. He checked his pulse and suddenly grabbed his huge cardboard folder. He thrust the box of crayons into his pocket, saying, "I have fever!" and smiling apologetically, he dashed out of the room.

◆ ◆ ◆

The following day Esther enrolled in the choir. During that evening at Burstin's she had discovered something new about herself — an inner music, a concealed motif, not particularly joyful, not precisely bright; a motif that did not erase the inner shadows but shone through them with a new meaning. As a result of this discovery, her life lost a great deal of the brightness it had lately acquired; it had, however, become more significant, richer. She put out of her mind the words of the *gymnasium* students and the thought that the choir was a partnership with Rumkowski. Singing in the choir gave her back something that had been due her, something which she had been renouncing all her life — a pleasure in serving no ideal; a gratification without any other purpose or intention, except to quench a craving within herself. As she sang, she was like someone who had prepared a feast for herself alone, out of dishes most pleasant to her own palate.

Yet singing in the choir did not completely satisfy this newly awakened need in her. The choir imposed its own thin armour of discipline. She experienced more of the new mood during her meetings with her new friends, sometimes indeed in Burstin's room, but more often still in Winter's. They all wished to meet in order to again experience what they had felt during their first encounter. And it was precisely among these people, who had been strangers to her, that she felt her soul wander about bared and completely liberated. The tunes that at such moments came out of her throat seemed to pour out from the Holy of Holies of her being, with her will or against it, to her own amazement, as if she were a medium through which both the concealed and the revealed worlds were exchanging messages.

She did not, of course, neglect her party work. On the contrary, she worked more diligently and with more enthusiasm. But once she had finished with it, she felt like someone who had done her duty and earned the right to live for herself. And to live for herself meant to sing at the encounters with her new friends, who were like the devotees of a religious sect assembling to join in prayers. With time, however, she gave up her meetings with the group, and maintained only her contact with Vladimir Winter.

Winter was painting a portrait of her and Winter had tuberculosis. But this time it was not as it had been with Friede. She did not feel like a fallen Magdalena at the feet of the Crucified One. There was strength both within her and in Winter's illness. The fever in his body and that of his mind were one flame around which her curiosity fluttered like a moth. If she had the wish to be consumed by the fire, it was a wish not to be destroyed by it, but to reach its core.

She posed for him, leaning against the back of one of Winter's old-fashioned chairs, in the reflection of the light that came from the "cannon" oven. The fine curve of her spine, the half-circles of her hips and breasts, the barely noticeable arch of her abdomen met in space with the circles of the "cannon" burners, and with the contours of its embossed little doors. The "cannon" oven on Winter's canvas looked like a slim altar emitting a red reflection which joined with the red of Esther's hair. The skin of her face and neck was permeated by the glow both of her head and of the oven.

He had difficulties in bringing out the shape of her mouth on the canvas. "Your smile is the smile of a Mona Lisa," he said, "but still more hidden, more internal than hers. Your lips ought not to smile and yet the smile must become part of them. A sensuous smile, but the sensuality must be spiritual. Because your body is soul . . ." He would touch her lips with his long fingers; like a blind man trying to recognize a face, he let his fingers wander over her eyebrows, her temples; he observed her squinting eyes from very close. He felt himself restlessly enslaved to her, yet reigning over her. Sometimes, feeling his hands on her lips she wished to kiss them with gratitude. But he would run off to his palette and canvas.

For her part, she observed his profile, dominated by the long pointed nose and watched his long fingers, fingers like the claws of a bird of prey. She looked at his humped back, at his clumsy crooked figure. There was something of a sorcerer about him, of one who is himself under the spell of someone's curse. She did not see him as grotesque. Rather she saw him as a powerful man enslaved by powerful forces.

Talkative with others, he would keep silent with her. Here she was the talker and her words came from the same source as her singing. She would speak of herself, telling him about Hersh, about Friede, revealing secrets to him which she had never before shared with anyone. It seemed to her that the person who was listening to her was someone outside of him. He was never concrete. Through him she was talking to another. Only once did she speak to him of her daily worries: "I am torn in two. On the one hand I am helping people, on the other, I harm them. It is like a short blanket. If you cover the face, you are cold in the feet. Some people bless me, others curse me. I can barely take either."

He interrupted her angrily, "You talk about yourself, but you mean me. A very pedagogical lesson in morality, whose motto is: you ought not to compromise with the devil. Splendid! But bear in mind, my lady, that in fact my hands are the cleanest. Yes, Madam, I give the bullies from the *Kripo* a smeared piece of canvas and that is all. But it is the ghetto which gives them furniture and clothing; it produces shoes for their soldiers on the front and boxes for ammunition too. And you yourself, yes, you serve the Germans better than I, if you want to know. Because you behave unjustly, and every injustice serves the devil. But to all of you, I am the greatest sinner!"

"I didn't mean that . . ." she tried to defend herself.

He checked his pulse and wiped the sweat from his forehead. His work was interrupted and the next moment he was lying huddled up on the bed, his eyes shut. She approached him and placed her hand on his forehead. He winced, and narrowly opened his eyes, as if he were afraid of taking in the entire light of her body. "You should understand," he mumbled hoarsely. "You are also alone, and you have the strength to be alone, may it bite and burn inside you. We don't seek peace . . ." He pulled her towards him, letting his long thin fingers wander over her back. She surrendered to him. She did not see his monstrous body, nor did she feel his feverish pulse. She did not see him at all. All that was within her became transformed into a passionate search for her own self. Through him she wanted to find herself, through the non-physical power that dwelt in his crippled physical form. He sensed that, and knowing that he was only fulfilling the function of a medium, he mocked her bitterly: "Aren't you afraid of my contaminating you?"

"I don't think about it."

"You don't think, because you're sure that you won't contaminate yourself. You can't catch anything from me. Even my bacteria can't penetrate you."

She covered his mouth with her hand, "You're feverish."

"Yes, and you are cool and white. An icy drop onto the fire. A drop that does not cool the flame, but entices it even more. Hurrah for the fire! In the fire I live!"

The intimacy between them meant nothing else. It did not bring them closer together nor push them further apart. They were like two semaphoric lights searching for the point where worlds meet. They were like two worlds seeking the reflection of their own light in each other. There was a kind of taut hurriedness in their relationship — an intensity. Esther would rush to meet Winter as soon as she was free of her duties. He would be waiting for her in his room where the air was thick, loaded with impatience. They would meet and the air about them would begin to vibrate with the rapid pulsation of his body, with the rhythm of his work, with the ebb and flow of his inspiration, and with his desire for her.

Her portrait was almost finished, and he was dissatisfied with it. She would not allow him to master her and this enraged him. All that he was able to achieve was nothing more than to create a painting of a beautiful female body. The glowing reflection that was supposed to radiate from her was reduced to a reflection of the tongues of flame behind the burners of the "cannon" oven. And the more he erased, corrected and repainted it, the more external she became. Once, he growled, irritated, "What is there about you that I cannot reach?" He threw away the brush and scrutinized her with wild eyes. "May the devil take it!" He grabbed her by the head, locking her face in his claw-like grasp, "Why are you hiding from me like that?"

She replied angrily, "Here I sit in front of you as my mother bore me. Do you think I undress before all the men I meet?"

"You know very well what I mean."

"I gave myself to you."

"To me?" he smirked. "Are you capable of giving yourself at all? That precisely is your power and your tragedy. You are too powerful a female for someone to possess."

She thought of Hersh, of Friede who had each possessed her in a different way. "It is you who made me so powerful," she wanted to tell Winter.

"You haven't met your counterpart yet," Winter went on, "a man who has not burnt up his masculinity by painting, or writing, or thinking; who keeps his total potency within him, for you. Such a man could measure up to you. Then you would explode one within the other like volcanoes, destroy each other's essence and create a new one. But your tragedy is that it is hard to find such a man, just as it is hard to find such a woman as you." She did not know why, but tears filled her eyes. At the sight of them, his hands began to tremble. He let them fall onto her lap, pressing his hot cheeks to her breasts, to her belly. He sat on his knees before her, while she had his hump against her face. Fear and disgust took hold of her, but she was unable to push him away. Pity awoke in her and before long it turned into desire. She embraced his head and caressed him. Later he implored her, "Let's begin all over again." With renewed zeal he rushed to the canvas and everything began again.

Their next encounters were spent in complete silence, until he again exploded, "Basically, Esther, I am much more powerful than you and freer than you, too. After all, you are enslaved to the forces working within you, a slave to what is commonly called love. You carry this within you. You are love. And to me love exists only in my passion for painting. In life I don't acknowledge its existence. In life love is an illusion embellishing youth and femininity. It is nothing but a refined trick nature plays on us in order to sweeten copulation. Understanding through love, through soul meeting soul is hollow bluff. Lovers see each other less clearly than those who are not in love. That's why people say that love is blind. And if love is blind, then what is not? Hatred? Surely not. Only indifference. Yes, life is indifference, and if there is a God, he is the embodiment of indifference. Even a mother's love for her child, or vice versa, is nothing more than a trick of nature. The child needs the mother's protection and her milk; it has to suck out from her her strength and juices. That's why she is there. The child does this with the brutal attachment of a ruler, and we call it a child's love for its mother. But what happens to that love when the little one grows up? Then he has to create laws for himself to remind him: Respect your parents. Because where indifference rules, laws are needed. And that much-exalted motherly love, what is it? What is that readiness for sacrifice, the care and tenderness? Also nothing more than a mechanism that Nature has provided woman with, because her function is to preserve the race. Everyone only fulfils his function. Only the artist, the rebel, destroys this functionality with his work. He is the one who creates love. Therefore, you see, I am stronger than you. Because your power is transitory. It will leave you as soon as you cease to be young, to be able to bear children. Then Nature will no longer need your greatness. A light will go out within you and as far as Nature is concerned you will be as good as dead."

She threw herself at him, "You're a cold fish! Ice flows in your veins!"

He pointed with his hand to the walls covered with his paintings. "If I had ice rather than blood in my veins could I bring out such warmth? You ought to know that we artists are never cold. Love in Nature may be a bluff, a transitory thing; but the love within our creations is a truth, for eternity. That's why they say, 'Ars longa, vita brevis'."

"I would die if I saw the world as you see it."

He laughed. "For the time being the world is for you as you see it, so you will not die. Nature will not let you. You still have a function to fulfil with your beauty. Even the Germans and the ghetto have no power over you." Her eyes filled with tears again, and again he hurried towards her. "Forget what I said," he stammered. "You're eternal."

Thus they spent the hours of those pre-spring days together, shut away from the world, with the canvas between them. Both of then concentrated on the canvas, curious about the struggle taking place on it. Basically their purpose was the same. She also sought to reach herself through the portrait, to know herself. And both sensed that Winter would not achieve that goal. Something within Esther celebrated victory while at the same time it filled her with regret. They both knew very well that the portrait was actually the only thing that held them together. So with trepidation and a sense of inevitability both of them followed the progress of his work, and surrendered to its rhythm, in the firm belief that they were hurrying towards their separation.

The painting was doomed to remain unfinished as the end between them came sooner than they had foreseen. One evening Esther returned to her room, her head buzzing with Winter's talk. Her mind was still fixed on her own incompleted image on the canvas, her skin could still feel the touch of his long sharp fingers. She had to prepare for a meeting with her youth group, but was in no way capable of collecting her thoughts. She sat down at the window and looked down at the cherry tree, her glance weaving it into the chaotic patterns of her feelings. She felt torn apart, cut into pieces. She was exhausted. She hated Winter, hated the choir, hated her new friends. A longing overcame her for the carefree days of not so long ago, for her comrades, for the clarity that had used to hold her together. Suddenly it became obvious to her that she had let bourgeois decadent weaknesses corrode her. She felt that they had completely broken her, and that she would never again be capable of finding peace and inner discipline.

She heard someone turn the door knob. Before her stood Valentino. As she looked at him, a sudden heat rushed through her entire body. "How handsome he is!" It was as if she were seeing him for the first time, as if his appearance had erased everything else within her, making room for his beauty. Her eyes devoured his black hair, his brown face, the heavy sinewy hands, without noticing how downhearted he was. She took a step towards him. She found it difficult to move; her body was awake, but stiff and heavy. Valentino dragged himself over to the table, placed his hands like heavy weights upon it and sat down. "I don't want you to come in here," she said hoarsely.

He raised his heavy gaze to her. "I've come to tell you . . . I've received a 'wedding invitation'. All the toughs have to leave the ghetto."

She felt like choking; her voice broke, "You won't let them take you, Valentino." Suddenly, she had a hopeful thought, "I have protection! You'll be taken off the list!"

He smiled crookedly, "Don't be stupid. If I can't do anything myself . . ."

"Come," she pulled him by the sleeve, "I'm going to see the Old Man!"

He stared at her as if she were a stubborn child. "Of course, now, in the evening, he's just sitting and waiting for you." She took her coat. He remained behind. "I want to talk to you."

She was beside herself with impatience. "Another time!" She waited for him at the door.

Once in the yard, she rushed ahead of him through the gate. The bridge was almost empty, and on Church Place there were few passers-by. It occurred to her that she had no idea where the Presess lived, and at the Vegetable Place she asked a policeman for Rumkowski's address. His eyes lit up with amusement. The madhouse was nearby. The girl with the red dishevelled hair and the wild gaze had evidently just escaped. He put his hand on her shoulder, "You want to see the Presess on the historic date of his birthday, now, dinner time?"

She shook off his hand, "I must see him. I am a ward of his. He will receive me anytime."

"That's a different story," the policeman blinked roguishly and bent over to her, "The Presess is celebrating in Marysin . . ."

As she ran on, she kept the image of Valentino, of his beauty before her eyes. She was full of him. All her life, up to this moment, seemed washed away by him. She did not notice that the streets had become empty, with only knots of people still standing in the gates. She arrived at the fields and houses of Marysin and waded through the muddy uneven paths. It became dark, no light from anywhere to guide her. From the distance the sound of children wailing reached her ears. It reminded her of the "court-martial" the Presess had introduced: lashes for children who stole potatoes. Now she, Esther, was running to him as if she were one of his children. She would fall at his feet and do anything he asked of her, if only he would not deport Valentino.

She noticed a white fence around a white house. Someone was talking very close behind her. Dull sounds of steps in the mud. She looked around. A flashlight shone in her eyes; a hand immediately snatched her by the arm. "Whereto?" She noticed the coloured stripes around a policeman's cap. "Where do you think you're going after curfew?"   .

"I've lost my way."

"Come, I'll take you back," the policeman proposed. Slowly she began to walk by his side. Somewhere in the middle of the field he grabbed hold of her waist. "Do you often lose your way like this?"

Letting him hold her, she lifted her face to him, "I didn't really lose my way. The Presess is inside that house over there, isn't he? I have to get in to see him." She grabbed him by the lapels of his jacket, "Take me back, please, let me in there . . ."

In the dark, all she could see were his teeth as he grinned. "So that's the story," he breathed heavily. "The Presess is waiting for you, pretty young lady . . . and pray, what will he do with you there, at the party? After all, it's a kosher celebration." She felt one of his hands on her bosom, the other around her neck. He dragged her with him deeper into the field. "But for the time being, little one, why shouldn't you have a bit of fun with an ordinary policeman . . . Come, I know of a little spot . . ."

For a split second he loosened his grip on her. She managed to tear herself away and started to run without looking back. His panting laughter followed her. Her heart was jumping, about to burst any minute. She entered the first house she saw and rushed up many flights of stairs, until she ceased to feel them under her feet. It took her a long time to get used to the darkness. She found herself in a garret. Silence surrounded her. No one was pursuing her. She bent down in order not to hit her head against the slanted roof, and moved over to the little window. There she remained sitting, waiting for her heart to calm down. She removed her shoes and wiped the mud off her stockings. Gradually, Valentino's beauty lit up in her mind again. Reaching the Presess tonight was out of the question. She would see him tomorrow, early in the morning, and Valentino would not be on the list of deportees. She was composed. It was after curfew and it occurred to her that it would be wise to get some sleep for a few hours here, and collect her strength. She knew that the race which she had begun would last until Valentino was safe again.

She peered out through the window. The sky was distant and open. Small stars flickered in the navy blue depth. A refreshing fragrance reached her nostrils. Out there, far beyond the line of the roofs, the outlines of the red chimney of a brick kiln could be seen. Between the chimney and the barely noticeable thread of barbed wire she saw a soldier strolling. She did not know why but she felt like singing, overcome with a kind of adoration, with a gratitude to Winter. She could see him now as he was, with his twisted body and the feverish mind of a sick man. It was he who had made her strong. It was he who had cleared her way towards Valentino. Her present running and the running that still awaited her was a race towards him — her man. Her body rejoiced, her soul filled with delight. She thought of Sheindle, Valentino's wife, and was grateful to her too. She thought of the ghetto, and was grateful to it too.

When she came to herself in the gray of dawn and leaned out of the little window, her face felt the sprinkles of a thin rain. She went down into the street. The empty sidewalks silently absorbed the raindrops. She slunk along the walls in the direction of the bridge. Then she hid in a gate to wait for the first people to appear on the wet stairway. Under the bridge a green uniform with a raised collar was marching back and forth. Rain dripped into the open muzzle of his gun. Above the green helmet, the crows living in the turrets of the church were circling very low. It seemed as if they were moving beyond the rain. She crossed the bridge with the first passers-by and entered her own backyard, but not her entrance. She knocked at Mr. Shafran's door and called him out, in his underwear, into the corridor. "I have to get to the Presess!" she told him, not waiting for his sleepy eyes to clear. "I have to see him right away!"

He rubbed his face, trying to rub away his sleepiness. "It's not as easy as you think. They say that he's busy preparing lists and won't let anyone get through to him."

"You have to come with me right away!" she insisted. "It's in connection with the lists he's making."

He stared at her searchingly. "They say that only the toughs will leave, those from the underworld, and the thieves."

How she hated calm delicate Mr. Shafran! How she wished she could shake him out of his complacency. She snatched hold of his hand. "I am not moving away from here, Mr. Shafran, until you come!"

He went in to dress and before long they were both hurrying through the streets along with the workers who were on their way to the Resorts. As they walked, he tried to strike up a conversation. She was indifferent to what he was saying, barely able to restrain her anger. He moved so slowly! In the yard of the orphanage a few hundred children were performing their morning exercises. The teacher directing them blew rhythmically on a whistle. To Esther it seemed that the whistle was a screw drilling in her head. "Good that it stopped raining." Shafran smiled at the sight of the children. He invited her to come in with him. She bit her tongue so as not to scream out with impatience and remained waiting outside.

At length Shafran came out and took her arm. "The director says that it's impossible to get through to the Presess today. After tomorrow it will be easier."

She fixed her eyes on him, "Will it all be over after tomorrow?"

"Yes. Come, the director gave me a letter to Herr Biederman of the Approvisation Department. I told him that a relative of mine is in danger . . ." He was walking by her side, superficially still calm and composed, but his gaze was more serious and worried. "You must tell me whom it is all about, in case I am asked."

"Valentino," she told him.

He did not question her or ask for an explanation. He accelerated his steps, but still she ran ahead of him. In the yard of the Approvisation Department, white heavy-bodied porters were unloading sacks of flour. After Shafran showed him his letter, a policeman led them to Herr Biederman's office.

Herr Biederman was a middle-aged man, clean-shaven and neatly dressed. He gave the impression of a solid merchant who knew the world and knew how to get along in it; a man whose prosperity had not filled him with conceit. He stretched out his hand to Shafran, then nodded at Esther. "Your director is my best friend," he said politely, waiting for Shafran and Esther to sit down at his desk. "Tell me just one thing," he patted the letter that Shafran had handed him. "If such an underworld type as the one on whose behalf you are interceding is indeed a relative of yours, do you still consider him a genuine relation? Don't misunderstand me. The question is purely theoretical. I mean, what can bind a decent human being to a criminal?"

"I am interceding on behalf of a Jew who is about to be deported from the ghetto," Shafran replied calmly.

"So I understand." Herr Biederman moved up on his chair. "This allows us, my friend, to speak quite objectively. I don't have to tell you what we suffer from that kind of Jew, do I? Then the question arises: If to choose whom to deport . . ."

"What do you mean, choose?" Esther jumped up in her seat.

Herr Biederman nodded, as if he were greeting her again. "What do you have to do with the issue at hand, Miss?"

"She came with me about the same thing," Shafran explained.

Herr Biederman took on the expression of an investigating judge. "Then this lady here is your wife, Herr Shafran?"

"No, an ex-student of mine."

"In the letter here, it is said that the person marked for deportation is your relative, and if this lady came with you about the same matter and is not your wife, it follows that he, the deportee . . . excuse . . . the man marked for deportation is her husband?" He waited, his eyes twinkling coquettishly now at Esther, now at Shafran.

"Yes, he is my husband!" Esther gave him a poisonous glance.

"I see," He stroked his chin. "Now, since you are also Herr Shafran's ex-student, and Herr Shafran was for many years a teacher at our magnificent institution at Helenovek, you are obviously also the Presess' ex-ward, and it is very logical that you should try to intervene with the Presess, because the latter particularly liked his female wards. The problem is only that it is very dangerous to intervene with the Presess on behalf of the kind of person your husband is." Esther was about to explode, when she felt Shafran's foot squeezing down on hers. Herr Biederman sank into silence for a moment, to heighten the tension, then he leaned against the table with his elbows. "But a husband is a husband. May he be whatever he is, it is the wife's duty to remain devoted to him. And this proves my thesis, Herr Shafran, that blood relatedness is a secondary issue, because it is a fact that husband and wife are seldom blood relatives. So, going back to our problem, I do understand you very well, dear lady," he nodded to Esther. "But I . . . Although I am one of the few who may approach the Presess nowadays . . ."

.Shafran moved in his chair. "Are you refusing me, Herr Biederman?"

"Who told you that? Your director is my best friend. But in my social position . . . it simply does not suit me . . . Therefore, I will give you a note to Advocate Sirkin. He is an independent man and the Presess takes his opinion into account as well. I will write that it is a question of granting the wife an audience with the Presess."

Esther decided to visit Advocate Sirkin on her own. She took the note from Shafran, and left him before he could manage to say a word to her.

Advocate Sirkin was busy, and one of his office girls pointed Esther to a chair. Through the window of the waiting room was visible a part of the church's tower on Church Place. On the clock the hands indicated ten minutes to ten. Esther's eyes glared at them. There was something brutal, revolting in that seeming stagnation of time which was in fact bringing Valentino's deportation ever closer. The dead clock stared at her with the eyes of fate. She was aware of this deep in her soul, where Valentino, the King of the Underworld, reigned. She was not surprised at her feelings, nor did they appear strange to her. Valentino was her destiny. It was about him that Winter had been talking. Now she understood that the essential within her — all that she had been hiding from Winter, from Hersh, from Friede, all that she herself had not known clearly, she had saved for him, for her man.

The office girl approached her, "Advocate Sirkin is waiting for you."

Advocate Sirkin was a youngish man. He had an open intelligent face and seemed to be of a cheerful disposition. He jovially shook Esther's hand and asked her to be seated. "A difficult task, my dear, to get an audience with the Presess nowadays," he said.

"I know," she replied. "He is making lists of . . . of the underworld."

Advocate Sirkin grinned. "If you like, the whole ghetto belongs to the Underworld, while the Germans inhabit the Upper World. Because, as far as the meaning of that term is concerned, there is no underworld in the ghetto, no great robbers or killers here, nor real criminals. The pre-war brawlers, although they still belong to the toughs, make use of their adventurous spirits to make a living, not so? True, they swindle and steal, but so does everyone else. And if you want to know, they are more just than the others. They don't steal or rob the poor. Their only fault is, that they are afraid of no one." At this moment, the jovial Mr. Sirkin rapped the knuckles of both hands against the table and stretched his body so vigorously, that the bones in his joints cracked. Esther was sure that he was drunk; but she was grateful to him for his little speech. She was almost falling in love with him. They smiled at each other with familiarity as he shook her hand, "Please wait outside for a letter to the Presess' secretary." With the letter in her hand she hurried home to change into the new dress she had bought for two and a half soups.

She had to pass the police control at Baluter Ring several times, before she was permitted to enter the office where the Presess' secretary greeted her like a sister. After all, the secretary too had once been the Presess' ward at the orphanage. She was, however, not overly optimistic. "I doubt whether you'll be able to achieve anything," she declared after Esther told her the purpose of her visit. "The Presess is decided not to remove even one name from the list." The secretary opened her purse and took out a powder case and a little mirror. "Here, fix yourself up in the meantime," she said amiably, as she walked off to the Presess' study. Slightly unsure of herself, Esther opened the powder case. For the first time in her life she put powder on her face. The secretary reappeared, "You may enter . . ."

Behind a huge desk with a shining glass top sat an elderly gentleman with a

full benign face, a silvery halo of hair around his head. A pair of calm friendly
eyes gazed at Esther from behind a pair of gold-framed glasses. This was not the
same Mr. Rumkowski she had known in the orphanage. Before her sat a totally
different man, proud, imposing. The magnetic power that radiated from him
both awoke admiration and froze her heart.

At the sight of Esther, the magnificent old man rose from his armchair and
stretched out both hands to her. He was dazed by her beauty. "Come here,
child . . ." For a moment her head swam; the entire room, with its paintings and
the framed dedications on the walls, went spinning past her tired eyes.
Rumkowski was flattered by her uneasiness. He removed his glasses, came out
from behind the table and stepped forward to meet her. Yes, he remembered
her well and knew her name. She was one of the few of his wards whose image
he carried, clear and fresh, in his memory. He chivalrously took her arm and
with the respect only beautiful women can inspire, guided her to the chair at his
desk and helped her to sit down. He sat down beside her and not removing his
eyes from her face, he exclaimed, "Good heavens, what a beauty you have
become!" He gently placed his hand on hers.

Esther, now recovered from the initial shock, pulled her hand away. "Herr
Presess, I've come about . . ."

The Presess purred with satisfaction, "I know you have come about
something. But we are relatives, aren't we? After all, you are my ward, my child.
Wouldn't it be proper to ask me first: How are you, Mr. Rumkowski? and show
me some attention?" Esther bit her lips and allowed the Presess to touch her
hand again. "Yes, my dear," he shook his head. "No one cares for him who
cares for all . . . And how has life in the ghetto been treating you? Where did
you say you were working?"

"In a public kitchen, Herr Presess."

"You got this position through me, didn't you?" he beamed. "You look very
well. You've blossomed in the ghetto, haven't you?" She suited his tastes which,
in his fortified masculinity, had changed somewhat. He no longer sought very
young budding females. Now he preferred young, but riper ones. He caught the
expression of impatience on Esther's face and gave in, "Well, tell me what you
want me to do for you."

She inhaled deeply and said, "I want to beg you to remove someone from the
list . . ."

Rumkowski's armchair squeaked, a shadow clouded his forehead, but his
voice remained benign, "What have you got in common with that riff-raff?
Hm . . . you always seemed to be a decent child . . ."

"Chone Mekler is his name. They call him Valentino."

The light was extinguished in Mr. Rumkowski's face. There was no longer
any trace of the magnificent kindly gentleman. His flabby mouth moved
agitatedly, two deep furrows appearing around it, like a cut in his chin. He stood
up. "So, you associate with that garbage, with their king himself? What is he to
you?"

"He saved my life . . . during a fire . . ."

The Presess was flabbergasted, paralysed with surprise. He groaned, "That
monster?"

A cold fear took hold of Esther. Valentino was in danger; she had never been
more aware of it than at this moment. "He is no monster, Herr Presess," she
muttered. "I will never again ask anything of you, Herr Presess."

He made a motion as if to shake off her words, and began to pace the room.

"A pack of criminals, robbers, thieves!" he exclaimed. "They undermine everything I build. It's a shame to call such vermin Jews. Yes, let the Germans take them away from me, let them make *mentschen* out of them!" He became increasingly agitated in his rage. It seemed as if he had completely forgotten about Esther. "No, I won't let them destroy my work. I must show the Germans that we are tidy, that we like work, that we are not swindlers or thieves but good and honest people, and only then will they let us survive!"

Esther barely heard his words. Exhausted, she sunk into the chair, her head hanging over the limp hands in her lap. Only her mind was awake with despair; she could not leave this place with nothing.

In the meantime, the Presess' monologue proceeded like a hailstorm. "For me there are no toughs! I am the toughest man here, and I will eliminate all those who stand in my way. One after the other I will remove them!" As he was pacing, his gaze was caught by the flames of Esther's lowered head. He noticed her stooped shoulders and the helplessness expressed by the position of her body. He cut short his torrent of words. Her humility and downheartedness unexpectedly began to strum another chord within him. Pretty weeping women always awoke his tenderness and compassion. With a groan he slumped down beside her. "He really saved you from a fire?" he inquired again. "So, what is this crying about?" His hoarse voice had a ring of indecision. His reasoning was beginning to lose its balance. His mind was still working, thoughts coming and going, but parallel to them a completely different entanglement of feelings was coming to the fore. He placed his hand in her lap, letting it slide down to the roundness of her knee. "He saved you from a fire, you said?"

Esther felt a white frost climbing down her limbs. Each cell of her skin wished to free itself of the touch. Her empty stomach rumbled. "Free Valentino, Herr Presess . . ." she whispered.

The fingers moving around her knees seemed to cut her legs off from her body. The hand slid higher up her leg. All the nerves in it died. Now he took hold of her arms and they too ceased to belong to her. His gray eyes under the glasses were close. Behind their haze lurked shame and confusion. He whispered, hoarsely, almost inaudibly, "This thing is no longer in my hands. The lists are with Herr Schatten . . . He has to deliver them to the authorities."

With a jump she rose. "Give me a note to Herr Schatten!" There was forcefulness in her tone.

It did not seem strange that he surrendered to her command. Slowly he moved his chair back, jotted down a few words on a sheet of paper, tore it up, wrote out another, and handed it to her. From his desk drawer he took out a printed little card. "This is a pass for you . . . I want to see you." He smiled a half smile, not looking at her face.

✦   ✦   ✦

Violin music was playing behind Herr Schatten's door. It stopped as soon as Esther knocked. No one answered. The door knob gave way and she entered a dark room. In a corner, somewhere deep, a candle was burning in a slim candle-holder. A shadowy figure asked from the middle of the room, "What do you want?" The light went on. Herr Schatten was wearing a white sport shirt and black riding pants. He held the violin in one hand and the bow in the other. Esther handed him the note from the Presess. He glanced through it and snickered like a schoolboy mocking his teacher, "The old idiot!" Then the boyish look left his face. He measured Esther with cold eyes which slowly, shamelessly, impertinently crawled over her. He did not move from his place, nor did he say another word. The note dangled from his hand along with the bow as if he were about to let it fall to the floor. A moment passed, then another. At length, he pointed with the bow to the sofa. "Do you want something to eat?" she heard his cold dry voice as she shuffled over to sit down. "You're not hungry, are you?" he asked when she failed to answer.

The electric light in the room went out; the candlelight again became prominent. Schatten sat down beside her, fiddle and bow at his side. Immediately she felt his arms around her bosom and a pair of cold lips on hers. A scream went through her whole body, everything pent up inside was freed at last. With her hands and nails she reached for his cold smooth face and with the tips of her shoes she kicked his boots. She jumped to her feet. Schatten stood close beside her, squinting. Again like a mischievous schoolboy he put his fingers to his lips and, teasing her, chanted, "Tomorrow he'll be in jail!" The screams stuck in her throat, her open mouth refused to let out another sound. "I like you," he said seriously, thrusting his hands into the pockets of his riding pants and spreading his legs. "Had I known that you were in the ghetto, I would have made your acquaintance long ago. Listen. I'll make an arrangement with you. Do you want an arrangement? Sit down." She did not move. "I see you don't want to sit," he picked up the violin and bow and strummed on its strings as he paced the room. "Good, you'll sit later," he spoke as if to himself, placing the violin under his chin. "You're lucky. I'm tired of Jewesses . . . You look Aryan. Your skin is white and you have green eyes. And the nose . . . the chin . . . very Aryan. The Aryan fire is in the flames of your head. I want you. My Aryan soul wants you, *teutonisches* Weib! Sit down and we'll talk about it." He lightly touched her shoulder with the bow. She found herself on her previous place on the sofa. He stood before her, his legs spread apart, his hard boots closely touching her calves. He glided the bow over the strings. Staring at the ceiling, he kept on, "The first time I see such a chaste whore. Hm . . . I shun whores here, but for you I'll make an exception. I'll pay . . ." He was rocking on the heels of his boots, removing the bow from the violin, ready to hear her reply.

"I'm ready," she replied.

Herr Schatten put away the violin and vanished into another room. Soon he reappeared with two glasses of schnapps. "Let's presume, my *Schatz*, that you are indeed as virtuous as you pretend, then this little glassful will help you on the spot." He handed her the glass and poured his own into his mouth. He shook lightly, bursting out into a boisterous laughter which revealed all the strong white teeth in his mouth. "Your beauty is a goldmine, do you know that? You could cash in on your red hair, on the bosom and on all your other properties. You have to fall into the right hands, mind you . . ." He watched her as she copied his gesture and poured the whole glass of schnapps into her mouth. "Another one?" He vanished, bringing back two full glasses. This time they simultaneously gulped down the schnapps. "Get undressed," he said calmly and amicably.

She handed him the empty glass, "Give me another one." She was no longer herself. Her voice belonged to another; she heard the rumbling, the buzzing going on in the other's head.

He began to taunt her. "I'm spoiling you!" He brought her another glass. She no longer felt any burning in her throat. Her tongue felt no taste, only the heat in her stomach grew stronger, more pleasant. She stood up. It seemed strange that she did not know where her feet were. She had become unhinged from them and was swaying in the air. As she swayed, a pair of hands that had once belonged to her, unbuttoned her blouse. She had a dream within this nightmare. The dream was spinning around the candle on the slim candlestick and smelled of grass and sunshine. The dream danced over the shadowy walls of the room which were circling around her, along with the furniture, like four white screens. Sweet violin music was flowing down the walls. As she stood naked near the sofa, she felt like dancing, soaring. She swayed on her unhinged legs. A man's voice was pleasantly singing:

> The silvery moon has deceived me,
> The sun has mocked me with its light.
> Only the shadow keeps its promise
> And visits me night after night.

She danced. But gradually the roaring in her head would not let her hear the tune of the violin. She halted, almost toppling over. A pair of hands caught her. The violin was dumb. The man's voice, no longer singing, honked in her ear, "That was my composition, I am a composer."

"Play some more," she begged him, letting him put her down on the sofa.

He played for her, strolling around the room. The tunes escaping from under his bow were languorous, sad. They seemed like waves in a sea of tears; a sea pleasant and good to swim in, and every time he finished playing, she asked for more. He obeyed her until he stopped in front of her, his voice thundering above her ear. "You are a riddle, redhead. You made me . . . You see, I am giving you my soul for the price of your body."

She became stern. "I hope you remember the price. His name is on the note!" Suddenly she burst out with wild hysterical laughter. "You're an idiot! You think that this is my body, stupid *golem* that you are? All this beauty does not belong to me. I am an ape!" She gasped for breath, then raising her arms to him, made an ape-like gesture. "You'll sleep with an ape!"

He shook his head amusedly, "If an ape tastes like you, then let it be an ape."

"And remember to pay the ape for it, you gorilla!"

"In that case we are a fine pair! So what do you need the other one for?"

"Oh . . . the other . . . the other . . ." she stammered. "Come, and I'll explain it to you. For the other I have as much use as for a thousand plagues. But he belongs to an acquaintance of mine . . ."

"And where is she . . . this acquaintance of yours?"

"Where should she be? With him of course . . ." She raised herself on her knees, interlacing her hands stiffly around his neck. "Swear to me that you'll take him off the list . . . swear it to me . . . by the names of your parents!"

He slowly freed himself from her arms and undressed. "There is nothing easier than to swear by their names," he grinned absentmindedly. "*Mutti* had a heart attack on the *Bahnhof*. Pour soul, she was unable to watch as they lashed

Papa because he had spat at a *Sturmtrupper*. Papa also remained on the *Bahnhof*. Good for them. It's only a pity that they had managed to bring me into this world. But I have an Aryan soul . . . luckily . . . I'm pure here, inside . . . Throughout the nine months that she had carried me in her belly, she did not manage to soil me, here, inside. . . where I have blond hair, blue eyes, and an Aryan love for beauty. Ah, my music, my violin, my culture, my glorious language! I am a German, my dear girl, through and through. My tragedy and my fate are the cursed Jewish semen from which I sprang. And for that I have to be punished. I'm ready . . . ready to let myself be wiped off the face of the earth. But first, I must fulfil my mission. *Ja wohl!* I must help destroy this race of vermin." He made an ugly grimace. "And do you think, little girl, that even one Jew will get out of here? Oho! They and their progeny will vanish from the face of the earth. The world will be free of Jews, and then, with a clean conscience, I will be able to vanish along with them!" He felt something sticky splash his face. He touched it, and realized that the naked girl was spitting at him, over and over again, until she ran out of saliva. He wiped his cheek, somewhat surprised, and burst out with a guffaw. "And if you spat your gall out, Redhead, do you think that you'd hurt me?" He pinched her in the breast. "Within a few years . . . perhaps in a year . . . perhaps even sooner . . . this thing will be rotting in the ground and the man who is pinching it, as well! Come on, let's have another glass . . ."

He brought two more glasses of schnapps. She knocked them out of his hand. She kneaded her fingers into his neck, shaking him with savage fury, "Who made such a monster out of you?" she screamed.

"*Der grosse Herr Gott im Himmel!* He made a mistake, understand? I am a freak of nature. My Aryan soul was supposed to be born from an Aryan seed . . . All mistakes of nature are monsters," he tittered while she pounded her fists against his chest and spat at him again and again.

Suddenly she felt weak. She almost rolled off the sofa. Again she was swimming in a sea of tones — the violin lamenting along with her. It was digging deeply, sweetly inside her, as if it were aiming to dig out her most deeply hidden tears. The violin's voice was becoming increasingly full, heavy, cello-like. It turned into a thick gurgling warmth which was like blood streaming on and on, branching out into thinner and thinner veins. The veins burned, pricking with needles of the thinnest aches which swelled again into thick dull pain. With it, primeval forests seemed to sway on their uprooted broken stems. Suns seemed to burn with hellish fires. Primeval waters were spraying their waves, drunk with their own tempestuous folly. In deep abysses snakes and scorpions crawled over disgusting vipers and clumsy heavy-bodied monsters, multi-legged, multi-bellied, with dangling pointy phalluses, or enormous thick breasts. They copulated, devouring each other, stamping each other out . . . and multiplied . . . multiplied. From their gullets the thick tones, the wailing blood was poured forth ceaselessly, while a multitude of many-fingered paws, long-nailed, hairy, tangled with the roots of the primeval forests, and shuddered along with them in the flames of a sun not yet formed, in the aimless whirlpool of the tempest — in the roaring sea of tears.

Silence came upon her. She no longer heard the lament of the violin. For a moment she felt suspended in that silence as in a hammock of cobwebs, until a blanket of warm human flesh covered her. "I'm not such a villain as you think. If you want to, you can sleep." A warm breeze blew on her ear.

"I want to be awake!" she called out with her last bit of strength and then felt a heavy mass pressing her down into the abyss.

The first thing she did when she returned to her room the following day was to tear into shreds the underwear she had worn the day before. Then she meticulously scrubbed herself. She was not tired, rather she felt festive, filled with self-admiration. She did not want to forget the previous night. She was proud of its gruesomeness, determined to carry its memory to the end of her days. She thought of Valentino and just as she felt renewed after this night, so did her image of him become renewed. She no longer felt any desire for him; what she felt was pure tenderness. She was impatient to see him.

She took out her most beautiful dress which she had been saving to wear for the first time on the day the war was over. Now she dressed herself up in it and rushed down to tell Valentino the good news. As soon as Sheindle, dressed in her flowery housecoat came to meet her, Esther threw herself on her neck, stammering in a choked voice, "He's been taken off . . . taken off the list!"

Sheindle began to hug and kiss her. "Esther, my crown," she sobbed, her body shaking with hysterical spasms. "My angel from the bright sky! We didn't shut our eyes all night. How can we repay you? What should we do for you, golden-hearted Esther!"

"Where is Valentino?" Esther asked.

Sheindle threw back her head. "Where should he be? He's inside. Didn't sleep all night, so he hit the sack in the wee hours. Come, I'll make a *babka* for you. I'll give you a glass of coffee with sugar!" She caught Esther glancing at the bedroom door and smiled, displaying the empty spot left by her two missing front teeth. "I can see that you want to tell him the good news. So why do you stand there like a clay *golem*? Go, go in and wake him up. Let him know. Get a move on, silly cow, what is there to be shy about?" She pushed Esther towards the door.

Esther entered the adjoining room and approached Valentino's bed. She touched the black knot of his dishevelled hair and put her hand on his large body. She buried her head in the pillow near his covered face. "I love you, Valentino," she whispered.

Sheindle came in after her, put herself on the opposite side of the bed and began to shake the sleeping man. "You! Get a move on! Your Virgin Mary has come to announce the good news to you!" Tears the size of peas dripped from her eyes. The bed squeaked heavily as a thunderous moan was heard from under the cover. "Do you hear what I'm telling you, Valentino?" Sheindle continued rocking him. "Esther has persuaded the Old Man to take you off the list!" She lowered her wet face to his and gave him such a loud kiss that it echoed throughout the room.

Some minutes later, Esther hurried to work. The manager received her with reproaches and threats for having been absent the previous day. At the kettle, distributing the soups, she sang, unaware of what she was doing, or of the noisy crowd at her window. In the evening, she brought home her soup and devoured it as soon as she entered her room while standing in her coat. Then she devoured her entire bread ration. Then she again began to wash and clean herself, and again, to dress up. She hated her beauty of yesterday, but rejoiced in her beauty of today. She had barely managed to finish, when Valentino entered. She threw herself at him with her whole body, feeling that every cell was smiling at him.

Valentino's face had changed. He seemed bewildered and absent-minded. Playfully she grabbed the note he was holding in his hand. "A 'wedding invitation' for Sheindle . . ." he muttered, looking at her with a distant gaze. "She is not such a giant as she pretends . . . What will happen to her, all alone, away from home?" His gaze came closer, imploring, "Will you go again, Esther?"

"I will go, Valentino."

Herr Schatten was surprised to see her. "Redhead!" His eyes blinked with amusement. When she told him why she had come, he burst into wild laughter. "Oh God, what a comedy! His wife! Then you will come for the wife's beau, then for the beau's wife, and it will be an end to the lists. Whom will I hand over to the Germans, and where will I find strength for you, Red Devil?"

"For the last time . . ." she implored him.

His manner grew cold. "Out of the question! Firstly, you have nothing more to pay me with. I cannot look at you!" Then, suddenly, he became milder, sadder. "I thought that you were coming because of me. You stole a part of my soul yesterday. I won't forgive you that. And secondly . . . the lists are with Biebow already."

Valentino was waiting for her at the cherry tree. He climbed up to her room with her. She invited him to sit down and sat herself down opposite him. "The lists are with Biebow already," she told him.

He spread both hands on the table. "I know," he said. "I am giving myself up with Sheindle. I haven't got much time. We have to be there today. I thought of hiding somewhere, but that's no business for me. Anyway, all the toughs are leaving with the transport and Lame King and Blind Henech and his wife are coming too. So we will at least be with our own kind. I wanted us to hide because I wanted to be with you . . . But if I become a worm, Esther . . . it won't be good anyway." He stood up heavily and approached her. "For good-bye, I'll give you a kiss, all right, Esther?"

She embraced him. "I love you, Valentino," she mumbled.

With his lips on her mouth, he answered, "I'll tell you a silly thing, Esther. You were my match made in heaven. I am a wild guy, a thief, a piece of dirt. There was no peace in my blood. Perhaps because I was looking for you."

She answered him, "Some people who were meant for each other, never meet. We were lucky."

The following day the transport of underworld men, prostitutes and other undesirables gathered at the prison, was led off to the train tracks — where the red cattle-boxcars were waiting for them.

Chapter Sixteen

PASSOVER WAS APPROACHING and things began to move on the fronts. The Germans declared war on Yugoslavia and Greece, and the ghetto inhabitants, who had the map of Europe engraved in their minds, were sure that salvation would arrive from the Balkans. Moreover, in Africa, great things were happening, enormous battles, huge military movements — while in the ghetto proper the Presess allowed the bakers to bake Passover *matzos* which could be substituted for bread on the rations. There was a large number of non-religious ghettoniks who also took the *matzos* instead of the bread, because nothing reminded them so well of the exodus from Egypt as a piece of matzo.

With the arrival of Passover, people's stomachs became more optimistic, because it appeared that the soil of the ghetto itself would this year become a source of subsistence. In Marysin where the *dzialkas*, the plots of land which belonged to the *shishkas*, had already been in existence for quite a while, the remaining plots of land were divided up, and whoever had a good "back" could receive a few square feet of land. Even some who had no "backs" at all also acquired a *dzialka*, if not in Marysin, then in their own backyards, where the cobblestones were removed and every piece of ground which did not serve as a passageway was transformed into a "field".

The plots of land in the yards as well as the white-washing of the latrines and gutters, at the command of the Presess, added to the festive appearance of the ghetto. Even the monotonous rains, which fell continuously, were unable to tarnish its refurbished face. The arrival of a Jewish holiday, Passover in particular, annulled the dependency of people's moods on the weather. The sun shone in everyone's heart and no one was bothered when the ploughed-up beds of soil were transformed into mud puddles, and the gutters into rivulets. On the contrary. It looked as though the ghetto were cleansing itself to become kosher for the holiday. Because wood had the value of gold, no planks were laid over the waters, which made the houses look like boats. But the people had wooden heels on their shoes, and balancing on these they would step over the puddles. And so, they emerged from the flood on sailboats of hope. All the omens pointed to the unescapable conclusion that the war was nearing its end.

Two days before Passover, beside the posters announcing the food ration for the holidays, other posters appeared, announcing a voluntary registration for work outside of the ghetto, for men from eighteen to forty-five years of age and for women from twenty to forty. Soon through the animated streets there

streamed those who volunteered for deportation, laden with knapsacks and
with kitchen utensils. Moreover, in honour of the first *seder*, bits of news began
to drift in, announcing that the Germans had broken through the front on the
Balkans, that they had had victories in Yugoslavia, in Greece and in Africa, and
the hearts of the Jews in the ghetto began to flutter with fear for the fate of Eretz
Israel. Passover eve itself arrived under a sky full of water, with a grayness in the
air and with cold gusts that lashed the body and froze the soul.

Chaim the Hosiery-Maker and his wife Rivka struggled to sustain their
festive mood. Rivka was now a shrunken little woman who was barely able to
walk. From her dry face the cheek bones struck out, blue, almost violet. Her
lips, crossed over with hundreds of tiny wrinkles which looked like the cuts of a
knife, were no longer able to lie together, and they wound, one lip into the
other, creating a crooked mouth line which expressed indescribable sorrow.
Her nose was always red around the nostrils from cold and frequent weeping,
and her eyes, like those of other ghettoniks, reigned over her entire face. They
shone out from their dark sockets with great deep pupils. But the caressing
warmth remained alive within them.

Nor did Chaim the Hosiery-Maker have the stately appearance of a year or so
ago. The search by the *Kripo* and his visit at the Red House had changed him so,
that even old acquaintances had difficulty recognizing him. Firstly, he was blind
in one eye, the one that had been knocked out during the interrogation in the
Red House. Secondly, his beard had thinned out, his cheeks had become
hollow and an injured nerve in his neck caused him to hold his head stiffly. On
top of that, he had slipped on the ice in the winter, dislocating a joint in his leg,
which left him with a pain when he walked.

Chaim and Rivka now stood in front of the curtain which divided the
kitchen. For days on end Rivka had been trying to talk Chaim into inviting
their neighbours, the Eibushitzs, to the *seder*, or rather to propose to them that
they celebrate the *seder* together, so that at least once they might feel like real
cohabitants. Chaim's inner struggle had not yet been entirely resolved, as he
approached the curtain and called out Blumka's name. She appeared from
behind it, rubbing her back. As soon as she saw the uneasiness painted all over
her neighbours' faces, she began, in order to give them time to take possession
of themselves, to complain about her work in the Ghetto Laundry where she
stood for twelve hours a day, washing bloodstained military shirts.

Chaim wanted to tell her that washing the shirts of wounded German
soldiers should soothe her heart, but instead, he straightened up and staring
with his healthy eye straight into Blumka's face, he proposed, "Perhaps we
should celebrate this year's Passover together, neighbour?"

Blumka, although she had expected the invitation, was at a loss for words; her
face began to burn. "It would be an idea . . ." she stammered. It was not easy for
her to accept the invitation. Ever since Chaim's two daughters had fallen ill, she
and Moshe had been persecuted by the T.B. nightmare, frightened of the Koch
bacteria. They trembled over the health of their own children and day and
night made plans to move out of the apartment into a place of their own. And
who knows whether Blumka might not have refused Chaim, had she not heard
good news from Moshe on the same day. At his work which consisted of the
demolition of empty houses, he had met a former client of his barber shop, now
an inspector of the Housing Department, who had given him the solemn

promise of an apartment which had belonged to a family that had volunteered to leave the Ghetto.

On the *seder* night, everything in the apartment shimmered with cleanliness. All the beds had been made, because even the two sick girls had dressed for the *seder*. The girls wore their daily dresses, the only ones they possessed, because the new things they had bought at the beginning of the war had had to be sold almost unworn, in order to buy food for the two youngest sisters who were spitting blood. But the dresses which they wore had been washed and ironed, and although the healthy sisters had just come home from work at the Corset Resort, where they sewed undergarments for German women, they all looked festive and fresh by the light of the burning candles.

All was ready for the *seder*. Rivka listened for Chaim's steps whose sound was for her always tripled, as if she also heard the steps of her two sons, and she had never ceased wondering that her husband entered the room alone. This time, however, he did not appear alone. A visitor came in with him: an emaciated man in a threadbare traditional frock and a weathered cap, his beard wrapped in a dirty dark-red scarf.

"Good *yomtov!*" Chaim called out aloud, freeing his beard from the cotton stocking in which it was wrapped, since the scarves behind which he used to hide it would irritate his skin. "This is Mr. Zisel Green," he introduced the visitor.

Mr. Zisel grumbled facetiously as he removed the red scarf from his beard, "With these bandages around our beards we look as if we suffered from tooth ache." He handed Rivka a parcel wrapped in a towel, "This is my share of *matzo*."

Before they had managed to move away from the door, Esther entered. She also handed Rivka her share of *matzo*. The news she had to announce to her aunt was not festive at all. Today, before leaving work, the manager had informed her that, by order of the Presess, she was fired from her post. "Woe is me," Rivka mumbled. "Probably because of us . . . the bit of soup that you used to smuggle out." Esther scoffed at this. For such a sin the entire staff of the kitchen should have been fired.

Chaim interrupted them and whispered in Rivka's ear, "Will you have enough food for Green too? His wife, poor soul, left this world and the child is in the hospital. It is written in the *haggadah*. 'Let whoever is hungry come in and eat, whoever is in need, let him come in and celebrate the Passover.' " The curtain in the kitchen swayed and the Eibushitz family emerged. Moshe wore a white shirt with a colourful tie; his jacket was completely buttoned. "Shaven *goy!*" a voice grated inside Chaim at the sight of Moshe's closely shaved face, but, he took Moshe's arm with friendliness. He wanted to beg only one thing from him: that he should not sit at the table with his head uncovered. But before he managed to make his plea, he noticed a gray cap in Moshe's hand.

Moshe covered his head and bent over to Chaim's ear. "That Green . . . I know him. We ought to beware of him. He's been caught twice stealing food rations from people's homes."

Chaim blinked at him with his healthy eye and answered in a whisper, "He won't be stealing any more . . . hasn't got anyone for whom to steal."

Slowly, solemnly, somewhat shyly, they gathered around the table. The white of the tablecloth and the burning candles reflected on the wan faces. Chaim stood between his visitor, Green, on one side, and Moshe Eibushitz on the other. He himself took up the place at the head of the table, on the cushioned chair. His threadbare black frock shone with tiny diamonds of light, as did his red bloodshot eye which stared into distant worlds. His healthy eye wandered from one face to the other as if to tie all of them together with his gaze, to tie them to himself during this evening, when it was given to him to be the head of the Passover table.

He barely felt strong enough to conduct the *seder*. His healthy eye continually darted back to his two youngest daughters, the sick girls with the unhealthy red cheeks, with the glassy hot eyes that were smiling at him, imploringly calling him. The high temperature and their illness made them look magnificently beautiful, so flower-like and radiant, that it cut into his heart. His whole being cried out to the Prophet Elijah, that he should, as he entered, cast at least one glance at his two children. And when he thought of Elijah, Chaim looked at his neighbour, Moshe Eibushitz, the one whose denial of God he could not forgive. But Moshe Eibushitz's creased cap, still wet with rain, itself seemed to express the longing for Elijah the Prophet. Chaim wondered where his own wrath had vanished. He felt weak . . . too weak to sustain the longing of Eibushitz's cap. Would he, Chaim, find the proper words to take this lost man and open the gate of light before him? He cast a glance at his visitor, Zisel Green, whispering to him in his mind, "Brother in faith, comrade in sorrow . . . come, let's go together, crawl together on all fours, call together from out of our straits . . ." Then he cast a glance at the two mothers, the women who had prepared the feast — at his own wife and his neighbour's wife, they who had given birth in pain and whose pains and sorrows were never given him, a man, to experience; those who served His Holy Name with their every action, knowingly or unknowingly. Then he embraced the young faces at the table with his gaze, those for whom this *seder* was conducted. Again he saw his two sick children . . . and the other two, his sons, who were here somewhere, whom he could see only with his blind eye — and his body began to sway, and with it swayed the silence in the room.

With one hand he clasped his beard, as if he wanted to hold on to it, with the other he took the goblet with wine that Rivka had prepared from beets and saccharine, and began the *kiddush*. He said, "Blessed art Thou, O Lord our God, King of the Universe, who has preserved us in life, sustained us, and enabled us to reach this season . . ." He washed his hands, dipping a few parsley leaves in the salt water, then broke off half of the middle *matzo*, hiding it for an *afikomen*. The silence around the table broke. They all began to talk, all the faces seemed younger, more childish. Chaim zestfully lifted his plate, saying in a loud voice, "This is the bread of affliction that our fathers ate in the land of Egypt. All who hunger, let them come and eat; all who are in need, let them come and celebrate the Passover. Now we are here — next year may we be in the Land of Israel. Now we are slaves, next year may we be free."

When the time came to ask the four questions, Chaim's glance halted at Shlamek, Moshe Eibushitz's son, but Moshe smiled calmly, "He doesn't know how."

"Then you ask the questions, neighbour, yourself."

Moshe moved his cap high above his forehead and with a composed dry voice asked the questions. No, in his asking itself there was no question. The question was buried deep in Moshe's eyes; the arrogant, nagging question of all questions. Chaim felt a cold shudder creep down his spine. He decided that tonight he would not lead any Talmudic discussion, nor explain anything. He had no strength. He would stick to the text of the *haggadah*, only the *haggadah* . . .

However, when he arrived at the place in the *haggadah*, where it was said that he who extends and prolongs the story of the exodus from Egypt deserves praise, he became silent for a moment, searching inside himself, until his inner voice laughed out with devotion and faith: No, not for the sake of being praised would he extend the story of the Exodus, but because, after all, they all loved the story . . . Because in the story itself lay the true answer. His heart was full; words rushed to his lips. He heard the loud rumbling of Mr. Green's stomach, saw the young ones devour the matzo with their eyes. Good, to the accompaniment of rumbling stomachs, would the *haggadah* acquire its real taste. He raised the beaker; his whole being swung upward with song, while the rumbling stomachs sang along with him, "And it is this same promise that hath stood by our fathers and by us also. For not only one hath risen against us, to destroy us, but in every generation there have arisen against us those who would destroy us, but the Holy One, Blessed be He, delivereth us always from their hand." Chaim's seeing eye fell on the beaker that stood prepared for Elijah the Prophet. His prayer began to hum inside him, childishly, imploringly. He raised both hands in the air. "And the Lord heard our voice . . ." His voice broke, a shiver took hold of him and he wept, unaware that he was weeping. At his side Zisel Green was swaying and he too wept, unaware that he was weeping. And to the side sat Rivka and she too wept, unaware that she was weeping. The wide-open dark eyes of the young stared in amazement. Chaim continued, "In each and every generation it is a man's duty to regard himself as though he went forth out of Egypt . . . Not our fathers alone did the Holy One, Blessed be He, redeem, but us too . . ."

Chaim heard Moshe say in a half-whisper to his son, "The Jews of Egypt learned something from their suffering. When we get out of here, it will be our duty to head for a new Mount Sinai."

Chaim felt everything turn over inside him, but he mastered himself. What else did he expect Moshe to say to his son? However, his companion, Zisel Green, who also caught Moshe's words, shook with anger, as he pointed his beard at Moshe and said, "And what's wrong with the first Sinai?"

Moshe turned to both Chaim and Green, "I think that every generation has to create its own Ten Commandments, in its own language, in accordance with its own knowledge. What have we achieved with the Ten Commandments? Did they help us avoid a second Egypt?"

"Had we followed them, we might indeed have avoided it," Green said heatedly.

"If so, then the question arises why did we not follow them. What is there within them or within ourselves that does not allow us to become one with the Ten Commandments?" Drops of sweat appeared on Moshe's forehead. His glance caught the expression on Chaim's face. He knew the pain his talk caused him, yet he was unable to hold himself back. He went on even more aggressively. "If you want to know, a cold wind always blew at me from these Ten Commandments; they reminded me of my father's endless chanting, 'You should not! You must not!'. One can follow all that and still remain a villain at heart. And a villain at heart is capable of getting around all these command-ments, killing, sinning, coveting, and yet be left with clean hands. Perhaps if we really cared for one another . . . perhaps then . . . But the principal question is: Why is He, the good, the compassionate Almighty himself such a villain?"

At the table there was an uneasy squeaking of chairs. Blumka, angered, winked at her husband. Moshe stopped talking. In the silence that followed, the loud rumbling of Zisel Green's stomach was heard. He, Green, wanted to answer this *apikores* in an appropriate manner, but on his arm rested Chaim's hand, reminding him that he was a visitor. Chaim himself could not get over the fact that he was capable of listening to Moshe with such complacency — as if the latter were one of his own sons who had been talking back to him. Of course it hurt him, yet, after all, it was his son. Chaim did not know whether it was right or wrong that he felt as he did. Confused, he raised his beaker, intoning the Hallelujah, ". . . Mayest Thou enable us to attain other feasts and holidays in the future, in happiness and peace . . ." He washed his hands. His voice trembled when he said the blessing, broke the *matzo* and distributed its pieces.

Rivka and Blumka along with the two oldest girls served the "fish" made of mashed potatoes, mixed with parsley and onion powder and trimmed with a slice of carrot on top. The fish sauce had fatty "eyes" from the grape-seed oil and had a pre-war taste. The same was true for the *matzo* balls and all the other dishes that followed, although most of them were only concocted from substitute ingredients and embellished with the original names.

At that moment, Moshe's question was of no importance. That moment was beyond any doubt blessed with grace and goodness. The silence — during which nothing but the clinking of the spoons against the plates could be heard — became filled with a heavenly music, as if flutes and drums were playing, as if the Prophetess Miriam herself were dancing over the plates and glasses; as though the spoons, the forks and the knives were the jingling bells of her head-gear; as if they were the earrings in her ears and the cymbals in her hands.

Afterwards, the two youngest girls found the *afikomen*. The third beaker of wine was drunk. In the door which had been opened for Elijah the Prophet, a little man with a long thin beard appeared. "Good *yomtov*, brethren!" he called out, slowly approaching the table.

"The Jewish Dot!" all at the table exclaimed. That was the nickname they had given the toffee vendor who had been living in Itche Mayer the Carpenter's cellar.

"I saw an open door, so I came in," the tiny man blinked familiarly, his eyes darting over the faces at the table. He fixed them on the two youngest girls. "Found the *afikomen*?" He shook his beard with delight and reached his hand into the deep pocket of his frock coat. "That's indeed the reason why I came!" He poured a heap of candies out onto the table. "Kosher for Passover! The grown-ups may taste them too, never mind. Don't we all come under the category of sick children?" His face and beard shone. In his two tiny eyes were reflected the burning candles, emitting sparks. "Have a good and healthy holiday!" he called out, waved his hand and left.

He left the door open, and from outside a neighbour's voice could be clearly heard, ". . . we were like dreamers, our mouths full of laughter, our tongues full of happy songs . . . Those sowing in tears will reap with song . . ." Another neighbour's voice rang out, "Save us thereon for life by the Promise of salvation and mercy, spare us and be gracious unto us, for on Thee are our eyes fixed, for Thou art a gracious and merciful God."

They heard the "Jewish Dot" call out on a neighbour's threshold, "Good *yomtov,* brethren!"

Chaim's body began to sway as he raised his hands, "Out of my straits I called upon the Lord . . . I will not fear: What can man do unto me? . . . I shall gaze upon them that hate me . . . I shall not die, but live and declare the works of the Lord . . . He is the God . . . who guideth His world with loving kindness and His creatures with mercy. The Lord slumbereth not, nor sleepeth. He arouseth the sleepers and awakeneth the slumberers . . . supporteth the falling and ariseth the bowed. To Thee we give thanks."

Only now did the spirit of festivity envelop Chaim completely. His soul was cleansed, devoid of even a trace of bitterness. As he recited, he playfully threw the candies about the table, one for each person. And so he said, "O Thou pure one, who dwells in the Heavenly abode, redress again the countryless congregation of Israel. And speedily lead us, the branches of Thy vine, home to Zion in song. *Hashana habaa b'Irushalayim.*"

✦ ✦ ✦

The following morning they stayed in their beds for a long time. The rain washed the window panes; a monotonous grayness lingered over the part of the kitchen occupied by the Eibushitzs. Moshe was asleep, his head covered with the eiderdown, only his pate was visible. Beside him slept Shlamek; of him too nothing more could be seen but the knots of his brown forelocks. The bed where Blumka and Rachel lay was narrow. Their bodies were squeezed together, entangled in the same warmth. Neither of them was asleep. Rachel kept her knees raised under the cover and leaned a book against them. Somewhat lower lay Blumka's hand, bitten by suds and detergents. The spots on her fingers where blisters had formed were bandaged with strips of rag; a few marks of cured blisters stood out with new pink skin, like the traces of removed rings.

Rachel was aware of the wakeful exchange of warmth between Blumka and herself. So clear was the language of their two bodies, one of which had given birth to the other. But within the younger body there was something awake outside of their common wakefulness; something that was apart, that was uncomfortable. Rachel had not noticed when this separateness had sprung up, when all that intimacy, which had been as natural as the air she breathed, became muddled and the sense of alienation crept into the heart. She was afraid of it. Yet the more she feared it, the clearer it became — a strange duality of love and estrangement. How badly she wanted to call back the times, not so long ago, when she had been able to clearly understand her every emotion. Now everything was entangled and impossible to grasp.

She stretched her feet, letting the book tumble into her lap, then she turned to Blumka and threw her arm around her neck. She kissed Blumka's shoulder through the sweater she was wearing. Immediately Blumka began to rub Rachel's arm, "Like a block of ice!" she whispered. "Why are you so stubborn and refuse to put on a sweater for the night?"

Rachel snuggled up to her, wishing she could wrap herself in her mother, so that the coldness and estrangement would find no room between them. "I'm

not cold," she smiled, putting her face against Blumka's check. "Mama . . .
mama . . ." a voice within her called as if from very far. Deep in her heart, there
was loneliness, darkness. The voice within her was weeping, "De profundis . . .
from the depths . . . Mimamakim . . ." Her Hebrew teacher, the "Karmelka",
had written on the blackboard, "From the depths I call you, God . . ." Chaim
the Hosiery-Maker had sat at the *seder* table, his two hands raised towards the
ceiling. That call had come not from Chaim's lips but from his fingertips, rising
up, up, towards the ceiling, towards the sky. The word "*mimamakim . . . de
profundis*" — this outcry was trapped in her bosom like a fluttering caged bird,
searching for a crack by which it might escape and free itself. Until, stammering,
it found a rhythm to which it could cling:

> "De profundis, I call you, Mother,
> The day grays in the window with fear,
> spreading a curtain of heavy silence,
> dividing my tear from your tear.
>
> De profundis, I call you, Mother.
> Your hand burns me through with its pain.
> Yet although still close, although still together,
> we are strangers, each lost in the rain.

She felt Blumka's hand touch her protruding hips. "How skinny you are!"
Blumka whispered. "Why don't you go down and take yourself a slice of turnip
with sugar?" The rhythm of the poem was broken. Rachel knew that Blumka
would not leave her in peace until she took something to eat. The emptiness in
her stomach, dulled until now, suddenly awoke. She jumped down from the
bed and approached the food box. "Hurry, or you'll catch cold, walking about
barefoot," Blumka said.

"Perhaps this is the reason?" Rachel thought. "Her trembling over me . . .
Perhaps this is the reason for my wanting to run away from her?" She cut a piece
of turnip and measured the sugar jars with her eyes. She had consumed her
sugar ration quite a while before. So had Shlamek. Only the parents' jars were
half full. Her anger swelled. "Why don't they hide their sugar instead of teasing
us?" She dipped the tip of a teaspoon in one of her parents' jars of brown sugar,
and spread it over her slice of turnip. She bit into it, chewing with increasing
greed. Her pangs of hunger had become ferocious. As she stood barefoot
shaking with cold before the cupboard, she devoured the whole piece of turnip,
and yet her palate craved for more. Quickly, she dipped the spoon again and
filled it with sugar. She poured the sugar into her mouth. With one leap she was
back in bed and had pulled the cover over her head. Blumka's warm heels
rubbed against her stiff ones.

"I can hardly wait to get out of this apartment," Blumka whispered. "All we
need is that one of us should, heaven forbid . . ."

Rachel turned to the wall. This animal-like care for one's own brood stifled
her. Pressing herself against the wall, so as not to feel Blumka's body, she fixed
her eyes on the rubbed-off wallpaper. Tiny pictures were printed on it at equal
distances from each other. They presented a highlander motif. On each picture:
a cheerful hut with smoke coming out of the chimney. In front of the hut, a
young couple in colourful dress, their feet raised in dance. Wherever the
wallpaper was rubbed off, the mountain lines were pale and the huts were

erased; but one little picture was unspoiled and clear. She moved into it with her mind.

"How simple," she mused, "a mountain, a house, a couple. The colours: red, green, blue and yellow, a consoling simplicity." It became too narrow for her. "This is a lie, a paper lie," she said to herself. "In reality, there is no such red red, or yellow yellow. In reality everything is mixed with gray . . . with black, one colour dissolved in the other." She was disgusted by the two doll-like faces of the highlanders. Lazily, she began to scratch off the two painted faces with her nail, peeling off the paper with vengeful satisfaction. Then she rubbed off the hut with the smoke and finally the mountain. Now she had the whiteness of the paper before her eyes. "Now there is nothing," she said to herself. "Nothing is not a lie, nothing is the most simple thing." But then she realized that the whiteness of the paper was not nothing. It was creased with lines and wrinkles. She asked herself half jokingly, "Perhaps there is no such thing as nothing? Nothing — also a lie, a figment of one's imagination." She was overcome by a distaste for herself. "Perhaps all that is the fault of the few years of schooling that I have had? The few books that I've read? Perhaps that makes me estranged both from Mother and myself. But why Mother and not Father? He knows just as little about me as she does, yet there is no feeling of estrangement with him. But there is also no feeling of physical intimacy, no language of touches which I understand so well, for instance now, in this narrow bed, at Mother's side. His caress speaks differently to me than hers does, and when I am sick I chase him away, and want only to have her. Her mere presence heals and makes me well. So . . . what is it that goes on between parents and children?"

She saw herself at the *sedar* table of the night before, and remembered the strange relatedness, the entanglement of glances in just as complicated and coiled a pattern as the pattern of lines here on the wallpaper. They were all joined in one. One family. But the ones of that one, each individual — a world unto himself. How well she had felt this yesterday, during the moment when each had sat bent over his plate, spoon in hand, scooping up hot liquid to nourish himself. Only the eyes of the two mothers, Rivka and Blumka, kept jumping away from their bowls to watch their children; as if by this act of mentally sipping along with them, they became doubly satiated. Was it love that their eyes betrayed? How far did it reach? Was it capable of splitting the atom — the ego? She thought of David. Inwardly shrinking, she let her fingernail run along two parallel lines on the wallpaper: They loved each other, they were attracted to each other, but they would never become one line. Here and there, so rarely, they touched, creating a common point; yet the point itself was rather a knot, a coil of question marks. Were they confirmation of the fact that even the closest worlds remain essentially distant from one another? She penetrated deeper into the paper with her nail. The corner between the bed and the wall was full of paper crumbs. She turned to her mother. "Mama . . ." she pressed herself against her, and put her head on Blumka's bosom.

Blumka's soap-bitten hands, with the strips of rag around her fingers, stroked her. "Why don't you sleep some more?"

"I'm hungry . . ." Abruptly, Rachel freed herself from Blumka's arm and got out of bed with a leap. She dressed hurriedly. "I'm going to David's," she whispered. All she had been thinking in bed, just a while ago, seemed silly to her now.

Blumka noticed Rachel tightening the skirt of her fancy blue suit with a safety pin. Her face became overcast, "It hangs on you like on a stick."

"Are you starting that again?" This time Rachel said it with a smile. She approached the cupboard and combed her hair in the glass of its door.

The yard was empty. The thin unpleasant rain which washed the dug-up soil rustled quietly. Over the slice of sky between the roofs, torn clouds were sailing by. In the depth of the yard the cherry tree stood soaked in sadness. Yet, despite that sadness, thin delicate leaves glistened moistly. Rachel recalled when she had seen the tree for the first time: the day she had arrived in the ghetto. Soon she would no longer have the cherry tree. She would be living across the bridge, in an unfamiliar backyard. She gazed at the tree as if it were someone dear and close. "Perhaps the trees have souls too?" she pondered half-seriously. "Perhaps we too have crossed paths in our estrangement, creating a common point. We had passed through each other: the tree through me, I though the tree?"

David was wearing his father's clothes. A pair of pants held together by a leather belt hung loosely on him, falling into pleats around his waist and belly. Tucked into these pants was a sloppy fustian pullover with long, stretched sleeves. His face was yellow and creased; his hair stood upright on his head like strings of wire. He looked very much like his father and almost as old. He was holding a bowl of soup in his hand. When he saw Rachel, he turned around, ill-at-ease, not knowing what to do with the bowl. In one of the beds sat his mother, leaning against a pillow; she was sipping from a bowl. In the bed opposite her, a bowl was steaming on little Abraham's knees. "*Servus*, Rachel!" he called gaily out to her.

The mother too seemed ill-at-ease. She smiled disconcertedly. "Do you have a bit of soup left for Rachel?" she asked David. David deposited his bowl on the table which shook, spilling a bit of soup. "Can't you be more careful?" the mother, irritated, shouted at him, then immediately turned to Rachel with a smile. "He has hands of clay."

The freshness of Rachel's spirit began to wither. It remained for her to choose: either run out as soon as possible, or shut up all sensitivity inside herself and stay with David. She moved over to Abraham and sat down at his bedside. "Here, taste a little eggdrop," Abraham poured a spoonful of soup into her mouth.

"Now you can eat up quietly," she said to him loudly. "I've had breakfast," and gazing at confused David, she added, "I know many people who keep their doors locked while they eat and won't open them when you knock. They avoid embarrassment and spare others the embarrassment too."

David scooped up the spilled soup from the table with his spoon. Then he raised the bowl to his mouth, and gulped down its contents. His Adam's apple moved with every gulp. He scratched together a few eggdrops and pieces of potato at the bottom of the bowl. Dark and shapeless, they vanished between his lips. Greedily mashing them them with his teeth, he shoved the empty bowl to the other side of the table and approached Rachel. "Shall we go down?" He put on another threadbare sweater, his father's, and put his father's jacket on top. Holding hands, they rushed down the stairs. They stopped in the entrance, in front of the curtain of rain. "Everything is asleep . . . everything congealed, rotting," David groaned. "The holiday of liberation . . . There's not the tiniest corner where we could hide in the whole ghetto." He pulled Rachel along with him.

The street was empty. Only now and then someone rushed by them with a clinking canteen in hand. They approached the bridge. "Where are we hurrying like this?" she asked.

"To Marysin."

She looked at him, flustered. "You never wanted to go there. Why today, in this downpour?" They ran through the desolated narrow streets. "Do you remember that once, in the city, we both went running in the rain?" she asked.

"There is a difference between rain and rain," he shrugged. In Marysin, a thin sharp breeze was dancing between the threads of rain, making the boughs of the wet trees sway, and rumpling the new delicate blades of grass which shone moistly. "Where is your *gymnasium?*" he asked. She led him towards the *gymnasium*, to the hut where her classroom was. Its door was locked, but under the part of the roof which stuck out, stood a bench. They climbed onto it and peered inside through the window. "So this is where you're getting smart?" he asked.

She cast a stealthy glance at him, feeling cold all over. "Oscar Wilde says that every person wants to kill the thing he loves. You look as if you wanted to kill me."

"I? I don't love you."

She put her face closer to the pane, so that he would not notice the tears in her eyes. "You are saying that too, in order to kill me."

"There is a girl in your class called Inka. Where is her desk?"

"There, in the first row. How come you know her?"

"Her mother works together with mine at potato peeling."

"Because of her I was almost thrown out of the *gymnasium* for Bundist propaganda."

"I like her quite well."

"The mother?"

"The daughter."

A ladybug, resembling a little red button with black dots, fell on the blue of Rachel's sleeve. Carefully, she took it into her hand, placed it on top of her finger and encouraged it to fly. But the bug, apparently feeling the warmth of her hand, began slowly to crawl up her finger. She pushed the bug over from her hand onto David's. "It's still young," she remarked. "It has probably just been born."

"Born in the rain."

"In spite of the rain," she corrected him. The ladybug spread a pair of tiny transparent wings and after a short moment of indecision soared up and vanished over the dripping roof. Everything around seemed grayer, emptier, without its live spark of colour.

David sat down on the bench, pressing his folded hands between his knees. "And if you think that I got up today on the wrong side of the bed," he rocked himself, "then you are wrong. But she's poisoning my life. She has to shame me even in front of you. She treats me like a rag ever since we came to the ghetto. She wants me to be a man, not a *schlemiel*. Which man is a man in the ghetto, tell me? And what does she mean, anyway, harping that I am not a man? Now at least I know that she never loved me. No one could love me."

"That's not so," Rachel said, "I love you. You only have to be able to make peace with the estrangement. I used to ask too much of love."

A little green frog hopped out from behind the leaves of grass and jumped along on the gravel path in front of the hut. David's face gradually lost its tightness. He pulled Rachel towards him. Sitting pressed against each other, they watched the rain and listened to its quiet rustle — a music of drops, a clip-clop of watery pearls and trembling greenery. An unseen bird warbled on a bough. David unstuck a brown cocoon suspended from the edge of the bench by a thin sticky thread. "Tomorrow this will be a butterfly," he remarked. "A butterfly which came too soon into the world."

"That came just on time," she corrected him again.

"What joy is there for a butterfly without the sun?"

"It seems to me, that even the poorest life creates a sun for itself."

He put back the cocoon on the bench, and turned towards Rachel, lowering his face to hers. Unexpectedly, his moist cool lips fell on hers and his hand, trembling, was tenderly searching for her breast under the warmth of her jacket. Her eyes, open and full, noticed his forehead become tense and veined. She felt the blood in her limbs sizzle, as a warmth spread all over her body; her heart fluttered under his touch. With his tightly shut eyelids he looked like a blind man searching for something, restlessly, avidly. But then he tore himself away from her and jumped to his feet. "There is no place to hide!" he cried out with anger. Then he was back with her, with both hands pinning her by the collar of her suit. "I want to see you naked ..." Hastily, with awkward movements, he peeled the jacket off her and entangled his fingers between the little buttons of her white sweater. The knob on his thin neck moved hurriedly up and down. Behind it, a nerve pulsated. His mouth was twisted and the swollen vein at his temple moved lightly. He was unable to manage the buttons at her neck and she helped him. Their fingers knotted under her chin. His lips, hot and greedy, sucked in hers. She felt his teeth around her mouth. The sweater came unstuck from her skin. Against the grayness of the day appeared the white of her arms and neck. He saw the secret delicate groove between her breasts and took a deep breath, as if he were inhaling the brightness of her skin along with the aroma of the earth, along with the humidity of the rain. His hot fingers, tender, thin, began to lick her arms, her neck, her face, become entangled in her hair. It seemed to her that between his fingers she was a coil of strings shuddering under his touch. He heard her teeth click. "Are you cold? You're shivering," he said.

She wanted to tell him that this was another kind of cold, that in reality she was so cold, not from the air, but from the heat which emanated from him. But her body, drowning in its storm, would not let her talk. Her hands rose to his head and clasped his neck. "I love you," was all she could say.

He freed himself from her embrace and jumped away from her. "Come, let's go back!" he exclaimed, his face angry, unfamiliar. He helped her put on her sweater and jacket and pulled her out into the rain. They set out at an aimless run. The rain soaked them.

✦ ✦ ✦

The Eibushitzs' new apartment was located in the larger part of the ghetto. There was not much furniture in the two rooms, since the previous occupants, who had volunteered for deportation, had used the furniture for firewood, leaving only the beds, a cupboard and a table. The Elibushitzs, however, who, up until now had "lived" on nails in the walls, and in boxes, considered that they had acquired a treasure. But they did not feel at home in the new place and they had the impression that they had moved in only temporarily. It was the corner which they had occupied in Chaim's apartment on Hockel Street that had become home to them.

Their neighbour next door, Mrs. Atlas, took upon herself the role of making them feel at home in the new apartment. Mrs. Atlas was proud of her name, which in Yiddish meant satin. She looked as if she had indeed been "soaked" in silks and satins. She was the descendant of generations of Baluty butchers and was herself tall and sturdy. She carried her massive body with regal pride, fully aware of her feminine beauty. Indeed she looked like a gypsy matron of royal descent. She also dressed in gypsy fashion, with large earrings and copper or silver bracelets. Her full neck and deep décolleté were adorned with a multitude of coloured beads, and when she talked, the adornments moved, jingling and rustling like an accompanying orchestra. The sound that issued from her mouth was however a whisper; it was dainty and accompanied by frequent sighs. She considered herself a fragile person and she liked to fan herself with a handkerchief as she spoke. She never smiled, since she viewed herself as a very unhappy woman. Her tragedy was that her husband was not a husband at all, but a nonentity who was not even worthy of standing in her shadow.

Her husband really was a nothing of a man: a short shrunken creature with the eyes of a little dog. His frame was that of an old man, but his voice, which could be heard through the wall, proved that he was not that far gone yet. The voice was thin and squeaky, but it betrayed strength. Through the wall, Mrs. Atlas' voice could also be heard and it did not sound at all dainty, but rather thunderous. Husband and wife quarrelled frequently, not directly with each other, for they had not been on speaking terms for years, but through the mediation of their only daughter, Teibele, whom they instructed to "Tell him," or, "Tell her."

Teibele was small, pretty, with only a distant resemblance to her mother. Her eyes were also black and enormous, but full of childish naiveté and astonishment. Teibele spoke sweetly; she had cute mannerisms and expressions which caused her delighted mother to press the seventeen year old to her bosom, as if she were ready to breast feed her. "I am so glad, Mrs. Eibushitz," Mrs. Atlas said during her first visit with the Eibushitzs, "that my Teibele will have a girl friend." And she cast adoring glances at Rachel. "I can already see what kind of people you are . . . a daughter and a son, *gymnasium* students, may they be protected against an evil eye. My child, poor soul, had no one to talk to."

The first few weeks, Mrs. Atlas had no luck with the Eibushitz family. To her displeasure, they were seldom at home. It was at that time that Blumka realized that she loved Rivka, Chaim the Hosiery-Maker's wife, like her own sister and that she was unable to miss a day without seeing her. Now that Blumka's own children were out of danger, she was able to help Rivka ease the burden of her heart and to console her. She insisted that Rivka get her two sick girls into a hospital, where there would be a doctor on the spot and healthy meals were offered to the patients. But Rivka refused to hear of it. "God forbid. I won't do such a thing to my sparrows."

"You're jeopardizing the health of the other children," Blumka persisted.

"The other children don't want to hear about the hospital for their sisters."

"Don't hold my saying so against me, but you're giving all your food to the sick girls."

"God forbid . . . only a little bit," Rivka wailed.

"And what will happen if all of you aren't able to keep on your feet?"

"God will have pity on us."

During one of Blumka's visits, Dr. Levine appeared with the news that there were two free beds available at the hospital for the consumptives. With anger, with patience and with Blumka's help, he finally succeeded in convincing Rivka and her family that the hospital was after all the best place for the sick girls. The following week, Malka, Rivka's second oldest daughter went to see Dr. Levine, for she could not rid herself of her cough. Blumka's visits to Chaim's home became less and less frequent.

Mrs. Atlas, the neighbour, did not, however, profit from this development. Apparently the Eibushitzs were not overly domestic people. As soon as they finished their supper, they hurried out into the street, to a lecture or a meeting, or to their *dzialka*. But Mrs. Atlas had a chance for compensation during the day of rest. The Eibushitzs would stay in their beds in the mornings to save themselves breakfast. Then, dressed in her Sabbath best, Mrs. Atlas would come in with a pot full of coffee, followed by Teibele who carried a plate with four black pieces of *baba* made from coffee refuse. Then Rachel and Shlamek would jump down from their "beds", which were constructed of a few chairs placed side by side, and Blumka would enter from the other room, wearing her winter coat on top of her nightgown. She would pull out two chairs from her children's "beds" and invite the guests to sit down. Soon Moshe would come in, in his winter coat, and sit down near his wife and children. They would sip the hot coffee slowly and munch on the slices of coffee *baba*, thanking their good neighbour who followed their every bite with her eyes.

"Don't mention it," Mrs. Atlas said as she watched Moshe's delight in the coffee. "I wish I could offer you a real piece of cake, Mr. Eibushitz. Such fine people as you are, Mr. Eibushitz, don't come a dime a dozen. But what can you do? The riff-raff have grabbed the pot of gold and such people like yourselves have to suffer." She then began to entertain her neighbours with stories about the swindles and thefts that were taking place in the Meat Department and in the butcher shops. She knew what she was talking about, since she was chummy with all the butchers who provided her with the best slices of meat, some of which she sold on the black market, in exchange for a piece of butter for herself and the "child". Her husband, she thought, was not too "sick" to take care of himself.

But Moshe was not polite enough with Mrs. Atlas. He would cut her off in the middle of a story, thank her again for the food, and drag himself back to bed. Mrs. Atlas followed him with her eyes, slightly hurt. But she forgave him. She moved closer to Blumka, her earrings swaying, "Do you at least appreciate your husband, Mrs. Eibushitz? He treats you like a queen. And how refined he is, how he walks, how he talks . . ."

Rachel liked Mrs. Atlas' daughter. Teibele was quite lovable and her shyness made one feel protective towards her. She had a pair of curious searching eyes and she could listen well and remember what she heard. Sometimes, when she came in with her mother, she would take off her shoes and climb up onto Rachel's "bed". Rachel would teach her history and geography and tell her about the Bund. Teibele was the person who inspired Rachel to begin two great projects: to create a study group for young people, and to arrange a public library in their new apartment.

The Eibushitzs were sitting at the kitchen table after supper. The air in the room was gray. The rains had stopped days ago and suddenly spring revealed itself in full splendour. It was a pity to cover the windows through which a refreshing breeze entered the room. As usual, the family was talking about their *dzialka*. Shlamek was impatient. "On the other *dzialkas* things are already sprouting," he said reproachfully.

Rachel was thoughtfully sipping her coffee. It was clear to her that her family was as obsessed with the *dzialka* project as she was with her library project. She envied them their enthusiasm about something so easy to realize. Although aware that the present moment was not a very appropriate one for putting in a few words about her project, she gave it a chance nonetheless. "I've been looking at his empty wall here," she said. "We could put together a few shelves and arrange . . . a library."

Blumka gathered the dishes from the table. "In this weather," she turned to Shlamek, "we might begin to see some green on our *dzialka* within a week."

Rachel took the plates from Blumka's hands. "Mama, what do you say about a library?"

Blumka looked at her absent-mindedly, "What library?"

Rachel turned to Moshe, "What do you say?"

He did not hear her question. He turned to Blumka, "Saturday we all get up at seven o'clock, on the dot."

As they walked to Marysin, Rachel began to nag her parents seriously. Blumka scolded her. "Why can't we have a bit of peace? How long is it since we've been rid of the fear of T.B.? Why live in fear again?"

Rachel tried to calm her. "The Germans don't care what we do inside the ghetto."

"No? And what if Sutter comes to search the house? Have you forgotten Sutter, daughter?"

The field was divided into a multitude of rectangles, each fenced off with cord. Each rectangle contained a family bent over its work. Some were just turning over the soil, while others were already planting or sowing. Here and there, the work was finished and the families admired their beds of soil which looked like graves. Moshe and Blumka were planting potatoes. Rachel and Shlamek, shovels in hand, straightened up the beds of soil and fastened the cord around their plot. Shlamek laughed, "What sense does it make to fence off the *dzialka* with a cord? Have you ever heard of a thief being afraid of a fence of cords? When it starts growing, we'll have to watch it anyway."

Rachel did not reply. Here, in the field, in the light of dusk, with a cool breeze rising from the ground and an unfamiliar aroma reaching her nostrils, strange thoughts were beginning to gnaw at her mind. This was how she had stood at the head of a dug-up heap of soil in the cemetery a few weeks before, when she had accompanied one of her classmates to her grave. Now she was standing before a dug-up heap of soil which would shortly sprout with vegetables, with nourishment. The earth was both a cemetery and a garden. Earth and man belonged to each other. At these thoughts her plans became confused. They seemed both great and insignificant, important and meaningless. She noticed her parents' heads turned towards her, then she heard Moshe say, "Through the party we might perhaps get wood for shelves. Shalom could put them together for you and it would look decent."

Thus began the creation of the library. Rachel was still far from being ready for the shelves. First she had to supply herself with the books. And day after day, after school and supper, she would walk with a shopping bag in hand, from one comrade's home to another, begging for a contribution of books for the library. In some homes there were no books and the people hardly understood what she had come for. In others there were a few books that had been saved from burning in the city — and their owners were not ready to part with them now. But most comrades gladly filled her bag and more often than not she would drag herself home with additional piles of books under her arm. Some comrades had more books than she could carry, and they accompanied her home with the sacks of books on their backs. She indicated the empty walls where the shelves would stand and invited them to sign their names in their books, so that they would feel like partners in the enterprise.

Finally, the time arrived for a conference with Shalom, and Rachel went to the yard on Hockel Street. She had been so busy with her projects, that she had not visited the yard for quite some time, nor had she seen David frequently. Now the big change that had taken place in the yard took her by surprise. The entire yard was dug up, divided into beds and fenced off by stones and cords. From the window ledges, tin cans, pots and boxes stuck out, green and budding. The cherry tree in the far end of the yard was also pink with blossoms. From there, up to the border of the neighbouring yard the soil had been worked, and the tree in the middle of the divided field seemed like a green and pink umbrella. On the narrow paths between the *dzialkas*, the neighbours sat, taking the air, contemplating the tree and enjoying the sight of budding greenery. Here and there someone was watering the beet and potato shoots. Women were weeding or consulting Sheyne Pessele who only now was able to display her thorough knowledge of the problems of "growing". With housewifely care, she paced between her neighbours' plots, praising, criticizing and giving advice. In spite of her bent back and old woman's walk, her voice sounded so clear and loud, that it could be heard from a distance.

Standing in his bed of soil, Chaim the Hosiery-Maker nodded his head familiarly to Rachel and smiled into his beard which was hidden in a cotton stocking. Beside him squatted two of his daughters weeding their plot. Berkovitch, the writer, greeted her from his *dzialka* which was located next to the latrines. He and his wife were surrounding their plot with cobblestones. Their little girl stood nearby watching them. Rachel bumped into Sheyne Pessele, who took her by the hand and led her to her own *dzialka* where the potatoes already had substantial shoots and the carrots had almost completely come out.

"You have the nicest *dzialka* of all, Sheyne Pessele!" Rachel said. Sheyne Pessele accepted the compliment as her due. As she stood there, stooped over her bed of soil, she herself resembled a plant grown out of the soil, its head pulled down, back to the soil. "Where is Shalom, Sheyne Pessele?" Rachel asked.

Sheyne Pessele indicated with her chin, "There ... he's helping the Levines."

Rachel went over to Shalom. From everywhere she heard greetings. People showed off their *dzialkas* to her, and again she regretted that she was unable to participate in the general enthusiasm. "Why do I always have to be apart from the crowd?" she reproached herself, and the projected library again appeared insignificant to her.

Shalom knew immediately what she had come about. "The library, eh? Yes, I heard. The problem is that while I can make shelves for you, wood I cannot make. In the ghetto having books doesn't guarantee having a library."

"That's not so," she protested. "In the worst case we can arrange the books on the floor."

"For that you don't need me."

"Very true. I need you to find a better solution."

"The only solution is the party board. If they want, they can even make a broom shoot real bullets. It would be sufficient for one of our celebrities just to give a wink at the controllers in my factory, for instance."

On Saturday Blumka, Moshe and Shlamek left early in the morning for the *dzialka*, while Rachel stayed behind to watch Shalom transform strips of moulding into shelves. Even before he had finished, she began to arrange the books. She hardly had the patience to wait until all the books were set in order, one beside the other. When the family returned from the field in the evening, the kitchen looked completely changed. From the walls, there peered down at them rows of books, serene and secretive, filling the room with their presence. They made the atmosphere in the kitchen more intimate, more interesting.

The following days, Rachel was busy compiling catalogues and putting on stickers with numbers on the backs of the books. The next Friday night the opening of the library was announced to all the party and youth groups. One week later, the existence of a study group for young people was also announced.

Chapter Seventeen

(David's notebook)

I have become a distributor of "ducks" hatched in people's minds. All my "ducks" are good and fat. In the barber shop where I read the *Litzmanstädter Zeitung* for the customers, I turn the news around so, that the people shake my hand, pat me on the shoulder and leave the shop revitalized. In reality I do myself the greatest favour. I work myself up into optimism, so that no unpleasant thoughts can reach me. Looking with hope at the future development of events is my defence against the fact that neither I, nor the others have the slightest influence upon them, that we are in the grasp of a mighty fist which we cannot even bite. And if all we have left to do is to think, then let us think positively. The bad, if it has to come, will come anyway, without our expecting it. A gloom-and-doom mentality can only weaken our ability to resist. The easiest people for me to fool are those who orient themselves less well in the situation than I do. And if a Jew quotes me Sutter's much-repeated wisecrack, "By Rumkowski you cannot eat, the Germans you cannot outsmart, and the war you will in any case not survive," I burst out laughing and say, "The difference between *har* and *nar* is in one letter!"

Today I walked home from the cemetery with Abraham. A neighbour of ours, a boy of fifteen, died of tuberculosis. We cut through a plot of land where houses had once stood, but are now demolished. The land was black, barren, full of mounds of earth and holes. On these mounds and in the holes, we noticed children and adults with black faces. They were digging in the ground with their hands, with pieces of wood or with spoons. "Coal miners!" Abraham exclaimed, and vanished from my side. By the time I arrived at the earthen mounds, Abraham was already on all fours next to the others and looked like a mole digging subterranean canals. All around lay open rag bags, inside of which were partly burned pieces of coal and clumps of wood. Soon I copied Abraham, and totally immersed myself in the search for the black gold. Hip-hip-hurrah! The Jews have entered a new line of production! Long live the Jewish coal miners!

✦ ✦ ✦

I am so dried up that the doctor who comes to see the children at the school where I work, gave me a note for an X-ray. The result: My lungs are free, but I weighed myself on the scale in the ambulatorium. I have lost twelve kilograms during the time that I have been in the ghetto. Mother responded to the news about my healthy lungs with great enthusiasm, as if the only thing a man could die of were the modern disease, T.B. My calculation is rather simple. If I go on losing weight at the same rate as I have during this past year, I don't have any great chance of getting out of here. But I go on deluding myself that I have a lucky star. My reason mocks this optimism, whispering in my ear that I am an ostrich, hiding my head in the sand. Eh, I must stop thinking. Perhaps thinking also deprives the body of energy?

Not long ago I looked over everything that I had written since the outbreak of the war. I am trying to be sincere with myself. When I read these pages however, I feel the intention, but not the sincerity. What I put down is true, yet it is not the whole truth. It seems to me that by writing, I am descending many stairs into a dark inner tunnel, in the depth of which an important message awaits me. I climb down the stairs as long as there is still some light on them. Then I become frightened of the darkness looming below, and I stop. So I never reach the message. Am I incapable of reaching it, or am I simply afraid of what it will say?

Apparently I am not the only one doing such inner acrobatics. I had a conversation with Rachel. She clearly formulated all that was so foggy, so impossible for me to express. "Even when it seems to me that I say the whole truth," she said, "it sounds like a lie. When I deny the lie, being certain that what I am about to say now will be true, I again feel that it is a lie. How does one dig through to the truth? How can one peel the skin of bluff from its face? What is the truth about life? Perhaps the same thing happens to life as happens to a head of cabbage. You peel off one leaf and encounter another. In the meantime, the head of cabbage shrinks and when you reach the last leaf, there is nothing more behind it; and that's the end and perhaps the only truth."

So, to return to the appraisal of my notes, I arrived at the conclusion, that I have tried to present myself in these pages as a noble unhappy hero who is practically melting with pity for himself. And how much space have I devoted to the people who play a part in my life? Almost none. Because the truth is that no one plays a role in my life nowdays, except myself. I did use to write about Rachel, but that was in the first stage. Of Marek and Isaac I have mentioned almost nothing, although I consider them my best friends, even now.

Before the war we called our threesome "The Flying Brigade". We were inseparable. Now our constellation has changed. Isaac has become an extreme left *Poale-Zionist*, which was a shock to Marek and myself. On the other hand, Marek has become a activist in the party, while I have become completely indifferent to party politics. Why? Because the game of political parties, or the proclamation that we are preparing cadres for the future seems ridiculous to me. In my opinion, there should be only one party in the ghetto and it should be fighting for our survival — the rest can wait until after the war.

Isaac's conversion to Zionism hurt me, so that for a long time I would not meet with him for that reason. But then we heard that he is suffering from decalcification of the bones, the other modern disease of the ghetto, and that he cannot leave the house after work. So Marek and I went to see him. We had a good quarrel with him. That helped. Now when we meet with him, we no longer avoid discussion, yet we feel closer to him. I've come to the conclusion that every opinion a person accepts, even in political matters, its tightly bound up with that person's private life.

✦   ✦   ✦

I interrupted my notes. It has been quite a few days since they announced a ration of carrots and turnips, but the Vegetable Place was empty. Yesterday at last the good news came that the ration would be distributed. When I went there after work today, they were not yet giving it out, so I went home and had time to make a few notes. I got so involved in the notes, that when I went back to the Vegetable Place I found there a killer of a line-up. As I pressed myself into the coil of people, I noticed that our neighbour, the litterateur Berkovitch, was acting as "door-man". This gave me hope and I pressed myself through to him between the two policemen who were keeping the order. But he, the bastard, blew up at me and spattered me with spittle. "I have no neighbours! Here I have no acquaintances!" he yelled. And this, they say is a writer! Woe is us! He screams as if the whole world belonged to him. He has no neighbours, no acquaintances! He no doubt helps himself out quite well. Those who stand at the cauldron, are the greatest moralizers in the world!

The line-up took up half of the street. It was unbearably hot. (Before, we complained about the cold. Now we complain about the heat. No matter how a sick man lies, he is uncomfortable.) It was only after the sun had set, that the line-up became more orderly. The reason: resignation. The good vegetables had been distributed. I went home barely alive — with a bagful of garbage. On the way, I saw a group of people with knapsacks on their backs. Volunteers for deportation. One bright morning I might decide to send everything to the devil and sign up too; for such a purpose I will probably need no "protection". When I got home, Mother gave me a real piece of her mind. People on the street had been telling her that nice vegetables had arrived, and here I bring home a bag of garbage. Abraham made a show of taking the food cards and declared that from now on he would occupy himself with the food rations. As for the supper I cooked, they did not find that to their taste either. I washed up the dishes and left.

I had a date with Rachel. We were supposed to go together to the May Day celebration, but I had lost the wish to see her, or to be with anyone else. (A May Day celebration! *That* will inject us with courage! The bluffing I like to do myself. I cannot bear it when others try to bluff me. From Churchill's speech last week it is easy to infer that the war will last an eternity. He himself admits that England is getting a licking. He says that the final victory will nonetheless be theirs. Perhaps theirs, but not ours, and certainly not mine.)

As I passed through the gate, I bumped into Berkovitch who was carrying a swollen shopping bag in his hand. He grabbed hold of my sleeve, "Listen, I cannot make any exceptions!" he yelled at me, enraged. "There must be at least a bit of justice! And I have to watch my position. I am only the door keeper."

I pointed to his fat bag, "Sure, you'd better watch your position!"

He became as red as a beet. "This is my ration," he said. Look him straight in the mouth! I cannot stand him. A crazy character.

I wandered about the ghetto. A delightful evening. As usual, the streets were packed with young people walking in pairs, in groups, talking, laughing. Aware of my loneliness, I was overcome by self-pity. I thought about Rachel. Why do I avoid meeting her? The entire issue is too complicated. I have even stopped asking myself whether I love her. Sometimes I miss her, but more often I want to run away from her. She makes me nervous. Maybe because she is so damn sure of everything. Even the fact that she is so sure of her love for me, irritates me. She irritates me perhaps because she seems to demand that I should be like her. She asked me, for instance, to lead the self-education group. I refused. She asked me to perform some duties at the library. I refused, to spite her, to spite myself, furious that she is alive and I am vegetating.

A few days ago we were together and quite cheerful. We joked as we walked down Hockel Street. Then she took a little bag from her pocket with perhaps two spoonfuls of sugar in it. She gave it to me and I devoured it on the spot. She looked at me with her familiar gaze, soft, warm. Within myself I wept with gratitude — with shame. She immediately realized that something was wrong with me, and she started to lecture me with pompous words that between the two of us "mine" and "yours" must not exist, that I should accept as natural the fact that she offers me a spoonful of her sugar once in a while. Obviously she was proud of her deed. Small thing! She sacrificed herself for love. At that moment I sincerely hated her.

Yet now, as I walked, I missed her. I wanted to hold her hand, to feel the warmth of her skin, to gaze into her brown caressing eyes. I searched for her amongst the strolling crowd. I passed Isaac's house and saw him sitting with a book in his hand: Lenin's *The State and Revolution*. I sat down beside him. "This book helps to explain even the life in the ghetto," he said to me.

"Did Lenin foresee a ghetto for the Jews?" I asked.

"Lenin analyses the system of the state. Here, in the ghetto, we have a miniature version of a capitalistic, bureaucratic apparatus." I had neither the courage, nor the will to involve myself in a discussion about the bureaucratic apparatus in Soviet Russia. We played a few games of chess, which I won. "I doesn't go," he admitted. "My brains don't work. It all depends on what's going on in your stomach. I didn't go to work and lost my soup." He showed me his swollen legs. I asked him why he didn't try to get a prescription for *Vigantol*, which, people say, is the remedy for the disease. He shrugged his shoulders, "I have the prescription, but who will stand in line for me? Father? My brother? Should they lose their soups at the factory because of me?"

He told me that when his mother was alive there was still some order in their household. His father, who has always had an enormous appetite for food, sometimes goes wild when he is hungry. His mother and sisters would give him five deca of bread daily from their rations. But the mother died last winter and the sisters volunteered for deportation. Now Isaac, his father and brother carry on the household by themselves; a ship without a rudder. As soon as the food ration appears in the room, they devour it and the rest of the week they go hungry. "Even if I divided my food, Father would have stolen some from me," Isaac said. "He keeps grumbling that we don't take good care of him, that we should give him at least two deca of bread from our ration daily, because he is the father, he says. When Mother died, he did not let us report it. For a week he kept her locked up in the other room, while he took out the food ration on her card. In the next room lay my dead Mother, while he sat here at the table stuffing himself. Those are your Bundists for you!" he concluded.

I congratulated myself for having found the reason for Isaac's leaving the party, and also for the fact that my family carries on so well. On the way home, I bought myself a candy from the little Toffee Man. Along with the candy he always tries to sell me a bit of faith. I would gladly have bought some, if I could make use of it. How good it must feel to believe in the existence of God.

✦ ✦ ✦

Today, straight after work, I went to see Isaac. He was in bed. As soon as he saw me, he exploded, "You have no idea how clever the Germans are. For instance, they have arranged it so that we should not see them, and we don't. We only see the injustice done here, inside the ghetto, and forget that it is they who turned us into such garbage. I have a grudge against Father. Yesterday I spoke terribly about him, I couldn't sleep all night. He was a good father, believe me. He cared for Mother. That's why I want to avenge myself on the Germans. I know perfectly well that I won't get out of the ghetto, but I want to live until that one moment . . ."

I scoffed at him, forgetting that I have more than once had similar thoughts. I gave him an injection of my artificial hurrah-optimism which I distribute so skilfully among people. I'm sure that he knew that I was only pretending, yet to my surprise, it worked. For a few hours we let our imagination roam freely, scheming how we could organize a resistance movement.

Later on, Marek came in. He looks better than Isaac or myself. No wonder. His mother and Aunt Sonia share more than one ration of food with him. He is also dressed neatly, and is the only one amongst us who continues his studies; not at all the same beaten Marek I met on the way into the ghetto. He smells delightfully — of optimism. Marek gladly joined Isaac and myself in our cheerful chatter, responding with laughter to Isaac's habitual greeting, "Memento mori!" He drew out a small pencil-drawn map from his pocket and gave us some unimportant bits of news. Later on, he explained a few rules of trigonometry to us and my hurrah-mood dropped about ninety degrees. I could not overcome my envy. Marek is progressing in spite of everything, while I have degenerated. I don't know how we passed from trigonometry to the topic of girls. Both Marek and Isaac stated their physical indifference to the beautiful gender. I did not speak much and what I said was just clowning. Should I have told them about Rachel and me? Or about my visits to a certain woman who has set an accessible price-rate for students?

I think of Isaac and Marek. Before the war what bound us together would have been called friendship. But here there are different standards for friendship. Here one has to prove it. We have not yet arrived at such a test.

✦ ✦ ✦

Hurrah! Hurrah ! My optimism has won! The ghetto is going mad with joy. Rudolf Hess fled in an airplane to England! Nothing else is known yet. The radio listeners spread the news in the streets early this morning. Everyone is sure that the war is coming to an end. I have no patience to write any more.

✦ ✦ ✦

(at night)

The ghetto is "running on wheels". In my enthusiasm I took a decisive, almost revolutionary step. I enrolled at the gymnasium. If the war comes to an end, I must have some document as a student, in order to immediately be able to continue with my education. Mrs. Feiner, the directress, received me very well. I told her that I am teaching in a grammar school and will be able to transfer my work to the second shift. So I will now receive two soups, one at my school and the other at the gymnasium.

How good it is to be energetic! I kissed Rachel today. We were mad with joy. All day long I am running around, unable to sit quietly. For the first time in weeks I went to a youth meeting. The topic of discussion: democracy versus dictatorship. The second topic: the role of youth in revolutionary movements. I actively participated in the discussion.

❖ ❖ ❖

The story about Hess has burst like a soap bubble. He is being kept in England. The Germans say he is insane, and the English have taken a "mouthful of silence".

The announcement of a new food ration has not yet come out; in the kitchens all we get are watery soups. I am beginning to believe in my lucky star. Despite the state of general starvation I am getting two soups a day, so that I personally feel very grateful to Rudolf Hess. Thanks to him, I got my wonderful idea. Studying is a tremendous thing. It helps kill time, doesn't let me brood too much — while at the same time I feel supported by truths which are not transitory. Before I have time to look around, the day is over. Often I forget about hunger and I find it easier to save up my food. I study in the backyard under the cherry tree. I sit in my winter coat. Everyone wears his winter coat in the evenings. People are too skinny to feel warm during these May evenings. Sometimes Rachel comes over to do her homework beside me. I also made the acquaintance of her friend, Bella Zuckerman. I used to look up at her when she sat on the balcony — as if she were a cloud, or a dream. This time I saw her up close. She is indeed dreamy and sad-looking, but also ugly. That's what happens to all dreams when they are seen from close up.

At home I have less work. I don't cook. We all eat our piece of bread with the soup we get — and that's all. Mother leaves me alone. She is glad that I am studying. Abraham too respects me more. Perhaps I will after all become a *mentsch?*

❖ ❖ ❖

All day long a new joyful bit of information has been cruising the ghetto: America has entered the war! No one has heard a confirmation of the fact as yet, but the ghetto is "running on wheels" again. I wasted my whole afternoon, being too impatient to concentrate on my studies. Perhaps indeed . . .?

❖ ❖ ❖

I've just read over my last note. Bluff, of course. Everything is normal again, which means hopeless. But I have no time to brood. My studies keep me captivated. I also give two private lessons. The busier I am, the more energetic I become. And between Rachel and myself everything is fine and clear again. My soul is convalescent.

We got a bottle of *Vigantol* for Isaac. We had to stand half a day in line in front of the *Sonderkommando*. I changed with Marek, he attended half of the classes, and I attended the other half. Isaac took the bottle without thanks or ceremony. That's how it should be.

❖ ❖ ❖

To listen to music with a beloved woman at your side is wonderful! Rachel and I attended a concert at the House of Culture. The musicians on the stage seemed like unearthly creatures. It seemed incredible that all of them, including the female soloist, should be receiving a soup with a slice of bread and a skimpy ration, just like me. They rather resembled a band of angels who had descended into the ghetto directly from the heavens. They performed Mendelssohn's Violin Concerto. I forgot the presence of the people around me and stared at the orchestra and the violinist, and did not even see them. I saw the tunes — young, May-like, silken. I saw flowers and spacious roads. I saw fields of grain and green pastures. Everything inside me was dissolved into a dance — as if all my limbs, my whole being were crushed and splintered, and as if each particle of myself was soaring up separately like a little fly — to sip the juices of life, and then again to join into an entity — and then again to dissolve. My eyes were full of tears. Something deep inside me hurt very much, and yet, I felt happy through and through. For a moment I saw red juicy tomatoes (I have not seen a real tomato for ages.) They soared up and down as if a juggler were juggling them. Then I saw myself, weightless, jumping up into the air and biting into them. The juice streamed coolly down my face; my mouth was full of saliva. I myself became a tomato; Rachel became a tomato. We held each other's hand, we let go of each other. We soared up into the air, then came down. We met and parted — lightly, playfully, sadly, questioningly. Two balls in the hands of an invisible juggler. Ghetto — Rachel — Music . . .

Chapter Eighteen

EVERY INDIVIDUAL is a world that dreams alone, apart from others. Yet when these worlds move in the galaxy of the same day and are bound by the same fate — then a thin thread of relatedness between one dreamer's world and another's winds through them. The same secret wishes, the same fears, coloured by the peculiarities of each one's separateness meet, recognize each other — somewhere, outside . . . perhaps as part of one collective dream?

At last the long awaited moment arrived: The Germans declared war on Russia. The ghetto became a teeming beehive, and for a week people walked about as if they were intoxicated. Then the news of the Russian defeats started to arrive, and the ghetto became ghetto again. At the barbed wire fence, a yellow-haired guard appeared who had received an irritating letter from home; a letter that had had something to do with the number eighteen. As a result, he unloaded eighteen bullets into the ghetto. A bit further away from him stood another guardsman. From the distance, it was difficult to distinguish which one of them was the yellow-haired one. A rock flung from inside the ghetto hit the other. The ghetto police set out to search for the culprit. A day of curfew was declared, from one evening to the next. The public kitchens were closed, the streets were empty and no one was allowed to show himself even in the yards.

That day the Berkovitchs slept late. The shutters on the windows were closed and the only light that furtively flickered in the room came from the large mirror on the wardrobe. It was both an eye which took in the sight of the sleepers and a plate in which their dreams were stirred into one.

Miriam had a cheerful dream. She dreamt that her *dzialka* had had an unusually fine harvest. She, Bunim and Blimele were squatting on the ground, digging out potatoes the size of apples. In her dream, she was saying to Bunim, "Start taking them in." But Bunim, busy digging, did not hear her. So she bent over his shoulder to see what he was digging at so hard, and she saw a fruit appear under his hands — huge, bright. Then she caught herself and exclaimed, "A loaf of bread!" Bunim and Blimele laughed. All three of them dug at the fruit, until it appeared, big and round like a ball, in Blimele's hands. Blimele threw the ball up in the air. Miriam admonished her, "You must not play with a loaf of bread, Blimele." She took the bread and held it near to Blimele's mouth. "Take a bite, my kitten." Blimele touched the bread's crust with her teeth. The crust was hard and slippery and the child's teeth were not sharp enough. But then a huge mouth appeared from somewhere: a mouth without a body, open and deep, ready to devour — the loaf of bread? Blimele? "Run for a knife, Bunim, run for a knife!" Miriam screamed desperately; and while she screamed, she woke up.

Bunim dreamed: He is at work at the Vegetable Place. There are no turnips or potatoes there. The Place is empty, clean. It looks like a fenced off garden where stones grow instead of flowers; the stones are round and crooked, large and small, and come in all shades of gray. Then he sees the gate open and Rachel Eibushitz, who used to live at Chaim the Hosiery-Maker's, enters. She carries a full bag with protruding corners, as if it were loaded with potatoes. She crosses the stone pavement laughing. Her laughter bounces over the stones and comes back in a round clear echo. Each stone separately laughs back. "What neat laughter!" Bunim thinks as she and her laughter approach him. Suddenly he sees himself standing on the scales which weigh the potatoes and turnips. Rachel begins to put the weights on the scale, one after the other. "How heavy you are!" Then they stand opposite each other, her full-bellied bag between them. She opens it, and he sees that it is not full of potatoes, but of books. "If Simcha Bunim will not come to the library, then the library must come to Simcha Bunim," says Rachel, as she hands him a book: "Short stories by Edgar Allen Poe".

He sees himself alone in the Vegetable Place, sitting on the scale and reading a short story about someone, a Simcha Bunim who is really two people not one. Both have unkempt gray hair, small nearsighted eyes and creased foreheads. Both are heatedly gesticulating; each wishes to take a step towards the other, but is unable to. They are far from one another, although both are inside the Vegetable Place. He, Simcha Bunim, is at the gate, surrounded by a wild clamour. The scales are screeching. Mountains of beets, carrots, potatoes and turnips lie about in the black mud. The people at the gate are pressing themselves against him. A million hands scratch him, tear at his clothes, preventing him from going to the other version of himself — who is in the opposite side of the Place, in a dark chamber. Here, in the dark chamber, there are also hands tearing at him. Hands of shadows. He sees the shadow of his father who died two months ago. He sees his mother who left the world a month after. He sees Friede, his friend, sees the sick daughters of Chaim the Hosiery-Maker. Those hands, at the gate, tear pieces of his flesh; they are hands full of hatred, full of envy and terror. The hands in the dark chamber tear at his soul, they are hands full of brutal love, full of smothering tenderness. "Bunim, remember you belong to us!" the crowd in the dark chamber screams at him. "Remember, our day of reckoning will come!" screams the crowd at the gate. "Give us food!" screams one side, "Give us life!" screams the other. He wants nothing. He knows nothing. He only feels amputated from his own self. He only feels the other inside him like an open wound. And his only wish is to become whole again, to rid himself of the division. Suddenly he sees that the street at the Vegetable Place is empty and the dark chamber is empty. Both Simcha Bunims are free. They approach each other, meeting on the scales. Next to the scales stands the weigher, the little Toffee Man. The empty scale levels off by itself. "I no longer have any weight," says Simcha Bunim, the complete man. He sees the little man lift up the glass cover of the box suspended from his neck, sees him pick something up from inside and place it on the empty scale. "I weigh nothing," Simcha Bunim wonders, "then why does he still busy himself with the scales?" He notices a candy instead of a weight on the empty scale. The little man's sparse beard splits in the middle, revealing a mouth which contains one rotten tooth. "Every day of your stay in the ghetto," the Little Man says to him, "you have heroically carried the burden of wholeness through inner division and thus fulfilled the requirements of *Kiddush Hashem*. What kind of special ration do you want as a reward?" Bunim wipes his glasses and replies, "I want a grave with a window, so that I may look out and see what I have achieved!"

Blimele had the same dream that she had had a few nights before. She dreamed about the bogey man; a green man with a green face, with green eyes and green hands. She was pushing her doll's carriage towards the bridge, when the Green Man called her with his green finger, from the other side of the barbed-wire fence. "Come here, Blimele," he said, shaking the green dry bough on his shoulder. He took Lily out of the carriage. "You have a pretty daughter," he said, stroking Lily with his green hand. "I am taking her to school," Blimele told him, and then she asked, "Who are you?" The Green Man bowed before her, "I am the Green King. I live in this palace here," he pointed to the red church on the other side of the fence. He laughed and Blimele saw his green teeth. Then he lowered the green teeth to Lily's body and bit off her little arm and then her little leg. "Give me back my Lily!" Blimele cried. The Green King laughed as if a heavy bell was tolling. "Silly little girl, why are you crying?" he stroked her hair with his green fingers. "I love Lily. She is tasty . . . She is my chocolate." And he ate up Lily. "Mama!" Blimele screamed, as she ran home with the empty doll carriage. Then, all of a sudden, she saw that her mother was pushing the carriage, while she herself, was inside it — but she was not there. So she cried in her sleep a very great cry; such a great cry that she was unable to ask her mother what taste chocolate had . . . because she had forgotten.

✦   ✦   ✦

A morning in June arrived with the promise of a sunny, hot day, although the air was still fresh and cool. Before Bunim opened the shutters, he hurried behind the latrines to have a look at his *dzialka*. The leaves of beets covered with dew blinked at him, inviting him to come over and touch them, but this he could not allow himself to do. He still had a long day to get through. He hurried back and busied himself with the cord that held the shutter together. Blimele appeared on the threshold, barefoot, in her short white undershirt, with Lily, the doll, in her arms. The sun played on her skin, on her hair and eyes, turning her into a little column of light. There was such freshness about her, such brightness, that Bunim felt like taking her into his arms, but instead, he scolded her, "Go inside, you'll catch a cold."

She, however, trotted over to him. There was beauty in her barefoot steps on the stones, in the shape of her feet and of her minute toes. She embraced one of his legs with one arm, "I want to see how you open the shutters, *Tateshe!*"

Bunim opened both shutters. Ever since they had had the *dzialka*, they no longer minded the smell from the latrines. Now Miriam stepped out onto the threshold of the hut. She asked him to dress Blimele and hurried off to the Coffee Centre to bring some coffee. From all over the yard people carrying kettles and pots were rushing to the Coffee Centre. Bunim picked up Blimele and carried her into the hut, where the light of the resplendent morning was spreading over the unmade beds. He pressed the child's head against his unshaven cheek, but Blimele turned away from him. "Your face is not pretty, *Tateshe*, I prefer *Mameshe's* . . . Better tell me a story . . . about a window. A window is a pretty thing." He began to dress her. He liked these few moments of closeness, rounded moments of delight, when the dreams of the previous night had been cut off and the day had not yet managed to reach him.

"Look, I'll show you how to tie your shoelaces," he said, folding the laces of her little wooden shoes. He pushed them between her thin fingers. "You wind them around like this, and then . . ."

Their fingers became entangled. A shoelace dropped from her hand. "Let's do it again," she proposed.

"Yes, let's do it again. You should always try again."

"Sure," she agreed with him earnestly, diligently gliding the tip of her tongue between her lips. "You should also try again, *Tateshe*, to get a better house."

"What's wrong with this house?"

"It's scary."

"What's scaring you?"

"The Bogey Man. He lives not far from here."

He was used to her fears of the Bogey Man.

Miriam arrived with the coffee. They sat down at the table, to eat the few slices of turnip with marmalade and coffee. Miriam told Blimele to play in front of the hut when she arrived back from school, so that no one would have to look for her. Bunim was on his feet. Restlessness had already taken hold of him. He shuddered, overcome by nausea, the usual daily nausea he felt before he threw himself into the yawning abyss of the day. He grabbed his rag bag, his canteen and spoon and hurried on his winter coat.

It was seven o'clock in the morning and the street was full of people racing to work. Wooden shoes clopped, canteens tinkled, empty brick-red *fecalia* barrels drummed, swaying on their rolling wheels; They were pushed by human horses, two in front, two in the back. The hearses too were hurrying to work. The sun reflected on the helmet of the guardsman at the bridge.

It was quiet on the Vegetable Place. The whole space from fence to fence was empty. In one corner only, not far from the office shack where the supervisors and the weighers were gathered, lay a little heap of carrots. Bunim wiped his glasses and held them in his hand for a while. The Vegetable Place seemed like a huge frying pan and the heap of carrots, like scrambled egg yolks. It was good to look at it with his nearsighted eyes. With them he devoured the "yolks", as the saliva gathered in his mouth. As he came closer, he put on the glasses. A light steam was rising from the heap; the carrots were rotten. On the step of the office shack, appeared the young policeman, Mietek Rosenberg. Then the supervisor came out. His elbow leaning on Mietek's shoulder, he turned to Bunim, "You really can't bring yourself to part with your winter coat for even a minute, can you? A bitter frost today, isn't it?" Mietek and the gathering of workers burst out laughing.

Bunim knew that it was not only on account of the winter coat that they were laughing at him. But the coat did make him look funny. How could he wear a winter coat with a fur collar in the middle of summer? In the morning, even at dawn, he could go outside barefoot and without a shirt and still feel warm. But always on his way to work, he felt a shudder, a kind of frost against which only his winter coat could protect him. He shook off the coat with clumsy movements, drew out a large dilapidated broom from a box, and began to sweep the Place. His hands clung to the broom so tightly that his fingers hurt. With the whole burden of his body, of his irritability, he leaned against it, scratching the dust off the cobblestones. Warmth began to circulate inside him. The sun licked his back and began to burn it. The hotter he was, the more tired he felt. The broom began to shake in his hands, lightly smearing the stones.

He cast a glance at the silent scales. During the blessed and cursed hours when the vegetables were distributed, they looked like the scales of fate. They screeched, swayed and trembled, moving up and down under the burden of the weights, while a hellish racket surrounded them. Now the silent scales looked inviting. The sun lay on their empty platforms like a blanket. It made them look not black but brown, like benches with backs to lean against. Ever since the regular transports of vegetables had stopped arriving, Bunim kept hoping for a moment with nothing to do, when the supervisor would be unable to invent any work for him and allow him to rest on a scale.

He turned with his back to the scales. All that he saw now was a stone desert. The tired broom in his hands resembled his chewed-up pencil. It beat out a variety of rhythms — wordless, and yet loaded with content. Bunim felt that in another moment, lines would appear before his eyes on the stony sheet of paper. His mood was heavy with them; he could feel the taste of them on his lips. For the past few weeks he had felt that he was a poet again. He had felt this right after his mother's burial, when he had wandered between the graves of his parents, between the trees of the cemetery. His beginning was now buried in the earth — and from it sprang his new beginning as a poet. There, as he had stood weeping, swaying in his sorrow, he had heard a voice call out within him, "You have the strength, you have the power!" He heard this voice every time he lay on his *dzialka*, close to the earth. He heard it during those moments in the morning, when he went out to open the shutters. And he heard it here, in the Vegetable Place, in the midst of his humiliation, which he did not mind, and of the abuse which no longer hurt him. He wished he could reach that level of detachment during those times when the clamour was the greatest, when the mob was drawing towards him, and he had to hold his fists in check in order not to vent his fury and hit someone. He knew that if he only had the strength now, when the scales were silent, to begin at least the first lines, he would find the courage for those later times which he both awaited and cursed: when the vegetables were distributed.

As he swept the yard near the fence, he noticed a face peeking through the bars, and heard a whisper, "Open the gate, no one is watching." Pretending that he was still sweeping the yard, Bunim approached the gate and let in a porter, a lank agile fellow who was late for work. In the blink of an eye, the porter grabbed a broom. Before he began working he stooped over the heap of garbage that Bunim had swept together and with quick fingers drew out a few foul carrot leaves. These he thrust into his pocket. "It tastes as bitter as death," he said to Bunim, cross-eyedly staring at the tip of his own nose, "but it's not poison. Otherwise we might kick the bucket, before the real merchandise arrives. First we have to wait for them to bring the harvest in from the fields, then the *Yekes* get first dibs on it, then the Poles. Finally, they send us the garbage a month later."

A commotion had started up near the scales. The policemen had let in a few fellows who brought special notes. The supervisors picked out the better carrots from the heap and filled the weighing baskets with them. The fellows who had come with the notes flung their sacks with the chosen carrots over their backs. They were let out through the gate quickly, because a crowd had begun to gather outside, alongside the fence. The weighers replaced the big weights with small ones. The manager winked at Bunim that he should place himself by the gate. Outside, two policemen stood ready, clubs in hand. Their shouts, which were designed to calm the mob, only increased the clamour.

Bunim, took up his place like a condemned man. Immediately, he forgot where he was or who he was. The gate, to which the crowd was glued, opened. People fell upon him and pushed him. He almost lost his balance. He was allowed to let in only fifteen people at a time. His glasses were fogged up, his eyes were tearing and he made mistakes in the count. Those whom he pushed back, clung to him and tore at his clothes. "Why do you let in people outside of the line?" they yelled at him. "There'll be nothing left for us!" they roared. "A crazy door man!" they raged. "He takes bribes!" someone complained to the policemen, "He is letting in his own people. I saw them myself, pushing *rumkis* into his hand!"

The two policemen yelled back, waving their clubs, while they amused themselves at Bunim's expense. He did not see it, yet he knew of it. He felt a strong impulse to throw himself on Mietek Rosenberg, the tall handsome policeman, and jab his radiant face with his fist. There was something immoral, something sinful about this fellow, about his way of walking, his gestures, his arrogance. Bunim hated him with a physical hatred. He feared him as one fears a wild beast with which there is no share of language or understanding — a beast that has no conscience.

This time a crowd far exceeding the number of fifteen broke through the gate. Bunim threw himself at the people, forcing them back with his clenched fists. "Don't force me, brethren! Don't force me!" he howled, beside himself. Sweat streamed down his forehead, burning his eyes. His glasses slid down to the tip of his nose, but he was not deterred even by the fear of losing them. All that he was aware of was the double struggle: with the mob, and with his own fists which he kept stretched out before him. How good it would feel to let them descend onto someone's head! His body, mauled by tens of hands, was torn into parts, each part struggling on alone.

An hour passed, then another. The heap of carrots was already reduced to a flat yellow splotch. The smaller it became, the greater became the despair of the people at the gate. "Please, let in a mother of five fatherless children!" a woman stroked Bumin's face. "It's been two weeks since I've seen vegetables!" another wailed. "We're dying for a bit of food!" another cried spasmodically. "All, all of us are wasting away!"

Bunim was at the end of his rope. He no longer screamed. The last bit of strength he still possessed, he concentrated in his hands which held the gate shut. But the hands on the other side were stronger than his in their despair. Even the two policemen now had to work in earnest to maintain order. And they too were apparently too weak, because suddenly the door was thrown open and the entire mass of people fell on Bunim. He swayed, unable to regain his balance. As he fell, he managed to catch his glasses. People tramped over him. He felt no pain, rather — peace. When the avalanche had passed, he stood up with an effort and put on the glasses. People were running about the Place in all directions. The orange splotch of carrots in the corner had vanished. The gate door swayed lightly. The policemen were no longer there. Today had been an easy work day.

From the office shack the manager appeared and called Bunim over to him. "You're getting worse from day to day, Berkovitch," he said. "You can't handle even such a small ration as today's. I am telling you honestly and frankly, if you were not under the Presess' protection . . ."

Later the kettle with soup arrived. Bunim placed himself in the line-up which formed according to each man's function; the more important the function, the nearer to the kettle. The soup distributor, a lively chap in a white apron, with a white baker's hat on his head, entertained the gathering with jokes, wisecracks and proverbs, assuming, as he did so, the pose of an actor. He mixed the liquid in the kettle, reciting, "You may cook water as much as you like, my friends, but it still remains nothing but water." Or, "You know, my dear friends, I can make the best homemade dumplings, my only problem is that I have no home."

The weighmen and supervisors applauded him and repaid him with wisecracks and jokes of their own. Someone brought out a few big fat carrots from the shack and stuffed them into the soup distributor's pocket. A man in the line-up laughed, and called out, "Idiot, you're giving him carrots? Does he lack carrots? Give him a few cigarettes!" Everyone's impatient gaze hung on the scoop in the distributor's hand. As the soup was poured into the canteens, it was easy to count the pieces of potato. Their number began to diminish, until there was nothing but liquid left. Those before Bunim protested. The distributor tried to calm them. "Should I apologize to you, too, comrades and brothers? You know yourselves that there are no potatoes coming into the Ghetto."

"And the manager, have you given him a canteenful of water too?"

"You saw for yourself, no? The same soup as yours. As far as I am concerned, not even Rumkowski himself . . ." They did not wait for him to finish. Each grabbed his canteen. Some hurried to the side and poured the liquid without ceremony down their throats, others sat down on the platforms of the scales. Bunim occupied an edge between them. It was quiet in the Place. The tin canteens sparkled in the sun. They clinked at the touch of the spoons. Bunim grew tired of sipping. He raised the canteen to his mouth and emptied the rest with one gulp. The cross-eyed porter who sat beside him licking his spoon, jostled him with a shoulder. "God is merciful, isn't He, Berkovitch? If He doesn't give one thing, He gives another. Do you know what has arrived in the ghetto? Yeast! Tell me, do you think yeast is really a remedy for swollen legs?"

Bunim was in the stupor which always befell him after he consumed his soup. He was nothing more than a stomach dissolved in liquid. He felt a jab in his side, "Can't you hear? Someone is talking to you!" This was a young weigher who was playing with his empty canteen, by twirling it on a finger. "Why don't you answer? Are you some great lord or what?"

The cross-eyed man blinked at him with his uneven pupils. "What do you think he is? A nobody? I can assure you that to get out a word from Berkovitch, it is worth your while to wait for hours. Because, dear brother, when Berkovitch does speak up, he offers you pure widsom; pearls pour out of his mouth. Small thing, a writer speaks!"

"A who speaks?"

"I'm telling you, donkey head, can't you hear? A writer! Believe me, you don't know with whom you have the great honour of dealing! That's why, you see, I'm calling you a cabbage head. Sure he's a writer! You think Rumkowski would bother about a nobody?"

"Then what does he write, the writer?"

"Eh, Golem, what does a writer write? Books he writes. Our writer here writes books which no one sees or knows about."

"Then how come you know about him?"

The porter raised a finger up into the air; he crossed his eyes. "That, you see, is a good question. The answer is simple. He himself introduced himself to me. One day he comes to me and tells me his bibliography with a finishing touch; namely, that I should lend him a cup of rice. No more, no less! So I tell him honestly, with my hand on my heart, 'I cannot lend you a cup of rice, but I can lend you a cup of lice!' You should have heard the lecture he gave me!"

"You hear, boys," the young weigher turned to those sitting beside him. "You don't have the faintest idea whom we have in our midst! A writer! The honourable Mr. Berkovitch!"

The group of workers clustered around the scales. The food they had had both enlivened and irritated them. Bunim awoke from his stupor. His mind was clear and sober. He had not missed a word, not one expression of mockery. A painful curiosity awoke within him — as though he had acquired a third eye, a third ear. His gaze was fixed on each man who spoke and he took in the image of each one as he heard and saw him. His lips moved soundlessly, repeating every word, memorizing it. He felt sick, as if he had eaten something disgusting. Suddenly, he was overcome by the need to see Blimele. He tore himself away from his place, and rushed to the office shack for a "pass". The laughter coming from the scales followed him like the barking of a pack of hounds.

✦ ✦ ✦

Blimele was back from school and played with her doll in the yard. A barefoot little boy in torn clothes was with her: Gabriel, Valentino's nephew. As soon as she saw Bunim, Blimele rushed forward to meet him and jumped into his arms. "*Tateshe*," she called out playfully. "Today I painted nabanas at school!"

"You mean bananas."

"Yes, bananas. What taste does it have?"

"I don't know. I never tasted one. Perhaps . . . like sweet potatoes."

The barefoot boy, Gabriel, looked respectfully up to Bunim. "And what taste does a lake have?" he asked.

Blimele laughed. "How many times do I have to tell you, Gabriel, that a lake is not for eating. But it is a big water." She slid down from Bunim's arms and acting the expert, waved her finger at the little boy. "Lakes are on the other side . . . just like chocolate. Chocolate is for eating." she leaned towards him and whispered confidentially, "My *Mameshe* says that I once ate chocolate, but I don't believe it."

Gabriel said proudly, "My uncle also once ate chocolate when he was not in the ghetto. Only me and my mother were always in the ghetto."

Blimele looked at him compassionately. "I was also in another room on the other side. There I ate apples and pears." She sat down on the path between the beds of soil, drawing something on the ground with her finger. "This is how an apple looks. I can't make a pear. Everybody says that pears grow on trees like cherries."

"I don't believe it," Gabriel shook his head like a grown-up.

"I don't believe it either," she agreed with him. "Cherries are light, so a little branch can carry them. But pears are big and heavy, perhaps just like a kilogram, or like a stone."

Bunim followed them slowly and with his third eye, his third ear took in their conversation. They approached the cherry tree which was full of the little red heads of cherries. The tree no longer belonged to Sheyne Pessele or to the people in the yard. It belonged to Rumkowski and the community, and was being guarded by a man with a band around his arm. The man sat on a low stool, his head and sidelocks hidden in a scarf. He swayed over an open volume of the Talmud on his knees. When they passed him, Gabriel pointed at the man's covered beard, "So many fathers have toothaches."

Blimele nodded. "If a new ration doesn't come out soon, everybody will have a toothache. Don't you have toothaches when you're hungry."

"I am so hungry that a few teeth have already fallen out of my mouth." Gabriel opened his mouth and showed her the holes left by his missing teeth.

Blimele had an idea. "Come, let's play father and mother. Lily will be the child."

"I don't like it. I don't know what a father does," said Gabriel.

"Why don't you know?"

"Every day you ask me again the same thing."

She turned to Bunim and looked up at him earnestly. "Every day he tells me that he never had a father, *Tateshe*."

Bunim took her by the hand, "Come, I'll give you a carrot."

"Gabriel, come quickly!" she called.

"I want to be alone with you for a moment, Blimele," Bunim said.

She pleaded with him, "Let him come in." They entered the hut. Bunim took a carrot out of his bag, washed it, and handed it to Blimele. "I will let Gabriel have a bite, yes, *Tateshe*?" she asked.

Bunim groaned, "It's for you. Gabriel's mother probably has carrots too." He felt ashamed and gave in. "Sure, take a bite, Gabriel." he sat down on Blimele's bed, listening to the pleasant sound of the children's teeth munching on the carrot. He felt light. He was smiling broadly.

With that smile he greeted Miriam who at that moment rushed into the hut all heated up. She took both children by their hands and led them outside. Then she shut the door and approached Bunim with her opened bag. "Do you see? Full of potato peelings! No one saw me. Everyone was running to Joy Street. If I'd had a larger bag I could have taken more." She thrust her hand into the bag and lifted a few rolled strips of potato peeling up into the air. "Do you see how thick they are? A lot of potato still left on them, look!"

"What was everyone running to Joy Street for?" he asked.

"They say that the inmates are being removed from the insane asylum. A truck arrived to fetch them."

Bunim stood up, running his fingers through his dishevelled hair. he mumbled something to Miriam and left. he did not return to the Vegetable Place. He ran to the hospital for the mentally ill on Joy Street.

Silence hovered over the street packed full of people who stood pressed against each other. Bunim ploughed into the centre of the crowd. A morbid curiosity pressed him forward. He wanted to be present, to grasp what was going on here — to bear witness with his third ear, with his third eye. By his side, a Jew was prodding a weeping woman with his elbow, "Hush, Madam, one ought not to cry here. We're on Joy Street."

Bunim reached the line of policemen who were surrounding the hospital building. At the entrance stood two trucks like those which transported animals to the slaughter-house, with parallel boards added along their sides. Near each of the trucks stood a German soldier, his gun ready to fire. From the front door of the building the sick exited in slow procession. Some walked with measured steps. Raising their heads to the sky, they looked at the white clouds and deeply inhaled the air of the beautiful June day, as if they were about to leave for an excursion to spacious fields and forests, towards the open arms of the sun. Others shielded their squinting eyes with their hands to protect themselves against the great light. Noticing the crowd that stared at them dumbly, they became frightened and rushed hurriedly onto the truck. Still others were in a holiday mood, waving their hands at the onlookers. There were also some who howled like animals, or called for their mothers. From amid the throng, voices answered them, muffled and choked. The policemen grasped each other's sinewy hands more tightly.

A tiny woman came out of the front door, stroking her head with both hands. "*Mameshe*, please comb my hair!" she mewed like a kitten; her small imploring eyes scanned the faces of those watching her.

Beside her walked a man, his unbuttoned shirt revealing a hairy chest. He hit the arm of the soldier who wanted to assist him in climbing onto the truck. When he had climbed onto it, he grabbed the boards and, facing the crowd, burst into song, "Onto the barricades, ye working people!" He raised his fists, "Down with the bourgeoisie! It is better to die standing, than to live on our knees!"

The tiny woman who had been stroking her hair, was not in a hurry to climb onto the truck. She wandered about the yard, gazing over the knotted hands of the police cordon, searching, imploring, "Mameshe, please comb my hair!" A soldier approached her, and tightly grabbed hold of her arm. She stuck out her tongue at him and let herself be led to the truck.

"A kind German," someone in the crowd sighed. The crowd parted, making a passage for a group of policemen who were coming up from the street, leading those who had escaped from the hospital. Behind them ran the patients' family members. "The *Yekes* have lists of all the sick," someone whispered in Bunim's ear. "No use hiding."

"What will they do to them?" a woman asked.

Bunim's neighbour grimaced, "A *matzo ball* in the head, that's what they'll do to them."

"What else," someone agreed. "What do the Germans need our insane people for?"

"They don't need the sane either."

A woman, her matron's wig sitting crookedly on her head, a plaid thrown over her back and shoulders, came out of the hospital entrance. She looked like some strange bird, or rather like a witch, her fingers cramped up like claws. There was a fire burning in her wild eyes. She practically flew up onto the truck, where her head appeared between the boards, her claws sticking out towards the mob. "My sparrows!" she roared.

A man behind her pushed her away and took her place. The visor of his religious round cap appeared between the boards. From under it his voice called, "Absalom, I'll send you a telegram!"

Two young women emerged from the front door. They held on to each other coquettishly and ogled the policemen in the line-up. Then they fell into each other's arms as if they were about to part forever. A man, his side-locks flying up in the air, walked at their side. Every time he took a few steps, he stopped to consult an invisible watch on his wrist. Then he grabbed hold of his head and cried "Jews, it's getting late! Jews, it's getting late!" In the crowd of onlookers someone giggled hysterically.

A thickset man climbed onto the truck and spat over the boards. "All the crazy fools remain in the ghetto!" he called out.

A girl of about nineteen strode in the direction of the trucks. At the sight of her, the sniffling and weeping in the crowd was abruptly stopped. The people held their breaths. In her white hospital dress, with her long hair falling over her back and shoulders, with her face, milk-white and radiant and the barely discernible pink of her mouth — she looked like an angel created by the crowd's collective hallucination. The innocence of her large eyes melted everyone's heart; her gaze spoke to each onlooker separately, warning, imploring, questioning. Slowly she moved towards the truck, her dress winding around her graceful body. She barely seemed to touch the stones with her feet as she soared up, onto the truck.

"People, what's going on here?" a voice broke into the numbness of the street. "Look at her, she is not insane! She's more sane than we are!"

The girl stood for a while on the edge of the platform. The mischievous breeze lifted her dress lightly, revealing her legs and the whiteness of the flesh above her knees. She did not move to cover herself, but let the revealed parts of her body shine with their living freshness. The light of her uncovered skin too harmoniously, too painfully blended into the light of the day. Now all of Joy Street swayed to a choking lament. But soon the tension was broken by the consoling voices of those who were unable to bear the despairing mood.

Someone gave Bunim a powerful jolt with an elbow, "Have you heard? The Carpentry Resort got an order for a million wooden crutches."

From the side someone asked in a tear-soaked voice, "And have you heard that they are about to give an egg per head for the sick children?"

Further on, people were consoling each other with bits of political news, "The English have begun an offensive in Syria."

The crowd seemed itself to have gone mad. Wailing and odd talk mixed in the air, cutting into each other, contradicting each other. "They're bringing back another one who escaped!" someone cried and the crowd parted to form a passage.

Two policemen were walking ahead of the policeman Mietek Rosenberg, who was leading a woman by the arm. She wore a long oriental dressing gown which colourfully flashed by the dark figures of the crowd. Her face was all bones, a skeletal mask. Instead of eyes one could see two dark deep sockets, from which no glance escaped, as if the pupils of her eyes were looking inward. The red of her painted lips was sharp like a scream. Bunim immediately recognized Mietek's mother, the wife of his former boss, the coquettish trim lady who sometimes during the summer appeared on the balcony. Now she was walking, leaning on the arm of her son, and brushing the nails of her free hand against the lapel of her dressing gown. As she walked, she raised her head to her tall son and stared at him out of the eye sockets which held no glance. A light shone from her small teeth when they were revealed by the red painted lips.

She smiled, "You should follow me right away, Mietek darling. And bring along the basin with water to scrub the floor." She stopped. "How do I look?" Mietek pulled her ahead; her body was beginning to resemble that of a rag doll. Her head wobbled in all directions. As if she had only now noticed the crowd staring at her, she limply waved at it with her free hand, blowing kisses in the air. She laughed; her laughter sounded like the bark of a dog. An opening appeared in the police cordon. Having passed through it, mother and son halted. Yadwiga threw her arms around Mietek's neck and pressed herself against him like a lover. "I'll wait for you at the Hotel Paradise . . . not far from Etoile . . ."

"Quiet, Mama, quiet!" the young man whispered. He shook off her flabby body, and pushed her over into the arms of an approaching policeman. Himself swaying on his feet, he strode over to the German officer who stood in front of the entrance, with a rod in his hand, counting the heads of those who were coming out. Mietek saluted, mumbled something quickly, begged, spread his hands, opened and closed his fists. The police cap he wore was moved up over his forehead to reveal a thick crop of hair. His face shone with sweat. While he spoke, the officer continuously shook his head, until he became angry and pushed the young man away with such force, that Mietek toppled over onto the locked arms of his colleagues. He straightened up and saluted. The officer made a motion with his rod and the police cordon unlocked itself to leave Mietek on the outside; then it closed up once again into a chain of arms. The trucks were packed and the soldier had to force Yadwiga onto one of them. He shut the barrier of boards behind her.

"Good heavens, let there be an end to it!" a woman beside Bunim called out. The crowd looked away from the locked trucks, unable to watch, unable to leave.

"Just wait till America enters the war, then we will be saved overnight," an optimist, not far from Bunim, consoled his neighbours.

The motors of the trucks began to roar. The crowd swayed as a shudder passed through it. The policemen unknotted their locked arms and began to disperse the crowd, in order to clear a passage for the vehicles. The trucks moved heavily. The bodies pressed together inside them swayed backwards like sheaves attacked by a sudden gale. From between the boards and above them, hands flew up into the air, to the left, to the right, to all four corners of the world. In the street a stampede began. People hurried home or back to work. Only the relatives of the departed ran after the trucks, until they vanished behind the barbed-wire fence.

Bunim sneaked into the Vegetable Place. With him came the porters and weighers who had also been on Joy Street. By the fence, near the box with the brooms, Mietek Rosenberg wandered about. He held his hands in his pockets and kicked at pebbles. The police cap still sat high above his forehead and from a distance he looked smaller, almost like a boy, a child playing with a pebble. From the front of the office shack the clerks, the weighmen and the supervisors all watched him. The manager had not come back from lunch yet and some of the employees were sitting on the ground behind the shack, cooling themselves in the shade. No one approached Mietek, nor would Bunim have dared either, if the young fellow had not appeared so small in his eyes, so childlike. Bunim moved towards him slowly, as if he wanted to see him clearer through his squinting eyes. he heard voices calling after him, "Eh, where are you going?" and "Maybe you should leave him alone?"

He stood before Mietek, mumbling, "I saw it . . . the tragedy . . ."

Mietek stopped kicking the pebble and halted. He raised his twisted, glistening face at the sound of Bunim's voice. It seemed that all its muscles had loosened up and an expression of relief spread over it. At the very same moment, the face vanished from Bunim's sight, and a fist appeared aiming straight for Bunim's head. As he lost his glasses, Bunim felt something hurling him about. He heard a sharp squeak come from the chest which was pressed against his. He also wanted to flail about with his fists, in order to free himself of the burden, of the blows falling on him from all sides. But a voice inside him commanded severely, "Heaven forbid!" So he gave in, and his body sank to the ground, and the more he let himself go, the less the blows hurt him. There was a light flashing in his mind. Thoughts sharp as wires cut through it. "Good! Good!" His guilt rejoiced, as he felt a warm clean feeling for Mietek rising within him.

At length, someone tore the young man away from Bunim and helped him to stand up. With trembling hands, Bunim picked up his glasses and looked through them at the sun. Only one lens was cracked. He put them on and saw Mietek being led off to the office shack. The cross-eyed porter approached Bunim. "You're crazier than those whom they deported," he raged as he handed Bunim a glass of water to wash out his bleeding mouth. "How can you get on a man's nerves like that, I ask you? I'm surprised that you got out of it alive. What business is it of yours, tell me? You see a man is broken, leave him in peace, you horsehead!"

A racket had begun on the other side of the fence. "The new food ration has come out!" voices shouted from all sides. People were racing to the corners where the posters had appeared. Women, their plaids flying, rushed to and fro like flocks of birds croaking excitedly. Children skipped out of the houses. Old people trudged over with all their strength, stopped, took a breath of air and moved on. Upstairs, in the house across the street, the windows were flung wide open. From the street someone called, "Two hundred grams of oil, one hundred grams of kasha, one hundred grams of sugar, seventy-five grams of flour . . . coffee . . ."

From upstairs, a voice called down, "How much margarine? How much horsemeat? How much barley? What about potatoes? And the bread ration, how large?"

✦   ✦   ✦

The following day visitors gathered in the bedroom of the Poetess Sarah Samet. The room was small. On the two beds the guests were partly sitting, partly reclining; a few occupied the old-fashioned chairs covered with black leather. On the walls hung photos of Sarah's family, of her children and of groups of writers. A jug of water surrounded by cups stood on a narrow table. The heat and tension of the past day was reflected on the flushed faces of those present. Their shirts were wrinkled and unbuttoned, the sleeves rolled up. Only the poetess looked as usual: cool, her figure dainty and neat. Her girlish-grandmotherly face was covered with wrinkles which ran in all directions, like the net of a transparent veil. She sat in front of the open window. Behind her, like the background of a painting, was a slice of the wall across the street, a black roof with a brick chimney, and above it, a sliver of the sky on which the day was expiring. There was not the faintest breeze moving the shutters which opened to the outside.

This gathering, like many others, had not been planned. They all came, not to read or to listen to poems, but on the spur of the moment, to be with Sarah and to refresh themselves with her friendly coolness. Yet each of them had sheets of paper covered with handwriting stashed away in a breast pocket, or in a pants pocket. The painters Vladimir Winter and Guttman had their drawing blocks beside them, pencils and boxes of crayons peeked out from their pockets.

Bunim Berkovitch also had a few sheets of blank paper in his pocket, as well as his bitten-up pencil, which he lately carried with him wherever he went. This time he did not feel, as he had during previous gatherings, that he had no right to be here because here gathered only those who were creative. Today he felt the poet within him, and the empty pages were already alive with the words which he would one day, in a propitious moment, use to cover them. He needed the air of this room, the presence of Sarah and of the others who were writing. He hoped that his presence here would help him unload his mind, which was like an inflated balloon longing for the pin that would free it of its fullness.

One hour, two hours went by. They drank water from the cups, engaged in occasional conversation and mutterings. Then, a sheet of paper appeared in the hand of one of them, who had had no intention of drawing it from his pocket — and already he was reading a poem composed that very day, about the deportation of the mentally ill; a short-lined, rhyming description. When he had finished reading, the faces of those present became even more twisted and flushed. A long heavy silence fell on the group.

Vladimir Winter was sitting on an old-fashioned chair, the black cape on his protruding hump pointed upwards. Suddenly, his long pale hands burst out from behind the cape like two frightened birds from a nest. He pointed his nose in the direction of Sarah Samet. The two of them, he — a black bird of prey, she — a mild dove, seemed like siblings in the short smile which they exchanged. Their glances, his — a scream, hers — silence, locked into one.

"The reality," Winter said in a voice that seemed to emerge from the hollowness inside him, "that we have been called upon to immortalize, carries a danger for the value of our work. The reality is so sharp in its tragic aspects, so horrible, comrades, that it stands in our way. Understand me correctly, it becomes an obstacle to the work of art, because a work of art cannot be just a photograph. It must be a discovery, a re-creation, a re-interpretation, in a word, a sublimation of reality. Of course, the question arises whether such a work of art is at the same time also capable of giving the authentic breath of our life here. But another question arises as well, whether that is our obligation: to immortalize life in the ghetto as it is? If so, it comes out, that we, the artists, must reduce ourselves to the level of memoirists, of chroniclers, of photographers. Is that the highest mission we have been called upon to accomplish? Is the creation of works of art in these conditions an inferior task? Should the creation of artistic values be left until tomorrow? Then what about our talents as visionaries, as dreamers, as connoisseurs of the human soul? And what about our power to awake, to sweep along, to shape and cure? Must we, who are a head taller than others, cut off that head? Must we who have one more ear than others, cut off that ear? We, who have one more eye than others, pluck out that eye? Must we, who have hearts as large as the universe, cut them down to the size of other hearts? No, and again, no, comrades!" Here Winter thrust his finger in the direction of the author of the recited poem. "That is what misleads us, you hear, Gold? For that reason, works of art will not be created in the ghetto. Because we reduce all these stories, novels, poems, paintings — to mere chronicles. And that is a sin."

Guttman, who had been stirring in his chair, exploded, "Perhaps it is precisely your aesthetic decorations, the cute literary adornments that are a sin?"

Winter sadly shook his head, "Is that how you understand me, Guttman?" He turned back to Sarah Samet as if he were talking only to her. "All right, let's not talk about sin. The question is whether we do this consciously, or whether reality imposes itself so powerfully upon us, that we drown in it? If it does, then we must learn to soar above it. Because our duty is to create, to bring out the core and leave the details to the chroniclers and diarists. Our duty is to reveal another truth, not that of facts, but that which is hidden behind the facts, invisible to the eyes of others. We have to dive deep, rise high, aim far — in order to see better. Of course, this is practically beyond our strength, but so it should be. And don't think, my friends, that I am . . . I am just like you. But the day when I reach that level, I will be satisfied with myself, and . . ."

Guttman interrupted him again. "You really think that we should all have your aims and your ambitions, don't you? I, for instance, think that to immortalize the minutest details of our life is the highest goal. If my work simultaneously becomes what you call art, so much the better . . . But the main thing is to leave a document behind. A precise one, the most precise . . ."

Winter turned his mouse-like frightened eyes on Guttman. "Leave behind a document? And achieve what? Are we sure that what we leave behind will last? But if we will create true works of art, we will bring solace to ourselves and to our brothers, here, on the spot — to the ghetto Jew who is searching for God, whose prayers have grown weary. We must create new prayers, and fortify people with the strength that art is capable of providing. The Latins say, *Inter arma silent musae*, in times of war the muses are silent. But not for us. We have been more than once *inter arma* and our muses were flourishing, nourished precisely by our suffering. Here we might become the humming-birds that sing most beautifully when caged, if we were clearer about the duty that lies upon us."

Gold, the author of the recited poem, jumped to his feet. "To hell with the humming-birds, Winter! I for one don't want to sing beautifully!" His face was purple and sparks shot out from his usually calm eyes. "What are you preaching? You don't like my poem? So you don't! That should be my greatest worry! But is it an outcry of pain or not, tell me! How can you sermonize, as if you lived on the moon? The insane were led away to be executed, to be slaughtered! Let it enter your head! Shame on you . . . shame!"

"Then why did you make your lines rhyme and have provided them with that organ-grinder rhythm, perhaps you can tell me?" Winter would not let him speak. "You should be ashamed of yourself. To make cheap limericks about such a tragedy, in particular during the heat of the moment itself . . . That is the real shame."

"Cheap? This?" Gold, beside himself, slapped his chest with the sheet of paper. "It came out of me like a cry. But to whom am I talking here? You have it too good, and you are too cold to feel it!"

"But that I could choke on your poem, I did feel," Winter shot back.

"That's exactly right! One should choke when one reads about such scenes!"

"Then spare me the pleasure. I want to live and to breathe. If you are not to be merely a chronicler, or rhyme-maker, your poem, even if it is about death, must have air. And here is another inflated phrase for you: It must breathe with eternity. It must comment not only on this horror, but on all horrors, not only on the given moment in the Ghetto, but on human fate in general. Yes, Gold, you," he looked around, "and all of you here, you can turn your noses up at my preaching, my so-called phraseology, but to me it is clear as day that we artists have to see life in general, through the Ghetto, the human condition in general. Out of the blood and pain that this costs us, something should be born, which . . ."

"Eh, you don't know what you are talking about!" Gold waved his hand, thrust the sheet of paper into his pocket and sat down. "The story with you is," he added bitingly, "that not only do you not have three eyes, you do not even have one. As for heart and feelings you don't have even a thimbleful!"

Winter hooted, "You think, Gold, that I don't know what these allusions are all about? Why are you beating about the bush? I work for the *Kripo*, that's what you are driving at. I am surprised that you deign to talk to me at all; surprised that all of you have ceased avoiding me. But one thing you should know, Gold, my account is not with you, but with my own conscience, and even if you spit in my face, you can't touch my pride."

"Why go over to such personal matters?" someone asked.

Winter's hands fluttered in the air. "I didn't offend him personally. He offended me!"

Gold became heated again. "He didn't offend me personally! And the way he tore my poem apart, what was that?"

"It's not my fault that you can't disengage yourself from your poem."

"He is asking me to disengage myself! Disengage myself from my broken heart! Sure, you can disengage yourself from your cold chef-d'oeuvres, they cost you nothing!"

Winter smiled crookedly, "First, I have not yet created any chef-d'oeuvres in the ghetto. Second, Gold, why do you feel so hurt? After all, I didn't mean only you . . . I meant all of us." His smile vanished, his gaze, deep, searching, was again fixed on Sarah Samet. "Do you understand me, Sarah? Suffering alone doesn't make one an artist. That is what I am driving at. Not every chunk of clay thrown into the fire makes a piece of pottery."

The discussion was interrupted, because Sarah Samet did not reply, but remained sitting motionless and serious. A few long moments of silence ensued. Then she reached out for a black writing book on the table and said, stroking her hair, "Perhaps it would be better . . . I too have new poems."

It was strange. No one at this moment felt like listening to her poems. They all regretted that the quarrel between Winter and Gold had not flared with more fire and given the others a chance to release their own pent-up anxieties. Sarah Samet, accustomed to being begged to recite and to being received with enthusiasm, was well aware that today for the first time she was imposing. Nevertheless, she began to read a poem in her soft thin voice: a conversation between a grandmother and her Sabbath candles. It took a while before the restlessness in the eyes of her listeners quieted and they became attentive. Slowly the red in their faces subsided and a child-like dreaminess spread over them. It was as if they had been offered, like tired crying children, a toy that sparkled, radiant and genuine. As soon as she had finished reading, they begged her for more. So she read a poem about her father's slippers, then one about a little boy who got lost on his way to the *heder*, and a poem about a well in a *shtetl*, and a cycle of poems about *shtetl* brides. Unnoticed, the evening covered the window with a navy blue screen. The listeners were even unaware that Sarah Samet had stopped reading from the black writing book and was reciting by heart.

Bunim as usual listened attentively to Sarah's reading. But this time he felt sharply the duality within him. As she read, one part of him saw his mother and felt her hand on his head. There was such sweet tenderness in the sound of Sarah's voice, in her words, that he could barely allow himself to surrender to it. But the other part of him rejected these poems totally. They irritated him, they hurt him. And it was the other who spoke with a shy whisper, after she had finished, "These are not ghetto poems, Sarah . . ."

She gave him a cool glance, "And what would you call poems written in the ghetto?"

The faces which encircled them shone in the dark. Tongues were set free — with praise, with admiration for the poetess. Winter shook his long hair in recognition, "Genuine . . . honest . . . It cures . . . It elates . . ."

Bunim moved closer to Sarah and muttered, "Those poems differ very little from your pre-war ones."

"Really?" she smiled faintly, "I'm glad to hear that."

"You have more talent than all of us put together . . . I think, it is a duty . . ."

"I don't write poems out of duty. It has nothing at all to do with my will. When the mood comes, I write."

"And the ghetto does not create any mood for you?"

"Yes, it does. To write what you have heard."

There was a fog between them. Bunim felt a new kind of solitude envelop him, as if he had once again become orphaned.

He had a restless night. The rhythms of Sarah Samet's poems spun in his head like cold burners over a glowing stove. His own enflamed passions roared within him. They possessed an altogether different sound than that of Sarah's poems. His chewed-up pencil hopped around in his mind's eye. The pencil was a red-hot fire-iron. With it, he slowly removed the burners and for the first time came face to face with the flames within him. He opened his eyes. It was pitch dark in the room. Miriam and Blimele were breathing quietly, rhythmically. He looked up at the ceiling. It looked like a white sheet of paper. The wire from which the light bulb was suspended seemed like a chewed-up pencil, screwed into one point in the middle of the white sheet, stubbornly refusing to move from its place. It was torturous.

He got out of bed and dressed hurriedly. He found the pencil and the piece of paper in his pocket and stepped outside. The air was cool. The *dzialkas* smelled pleasantly. The potato blooms blinked like bright eyes. A thin veil of white clouds covered the sky. Through it swam a small moon and distant pale stars. Under the quietly rustling cherry tree, the sleepy community watchman strolled along the beds of soil. "Maybe you'd like to take a nap, friend, " Bunim proposed. "I'll replace you for a while."

The man looked at him with suspicion. "Replace me, you said?"

Bunim smiled, "Replace you, I said. I want to sit here for a while."

The man wiped his sleepy eyes and in the process wiped away his suspicion as well. He yawned as he picked a couple of cherries from the tree. "Here, say a blessing and wipe your mouth." He patted Bunim on the shoulder. "You see, I am like the Almightly. I sit here guarding the Tree of Life. The Tree of Knowledge remained in the Garden of Eden, but the Tree of Life grows here, in the ghetto." He spread his coat out in the groove between two beds of soil and stretched out on it. "Ey," he groaned. "A few more weeks and the summer too will be gone. Where will you be praying during the High Holidays? I will be praying with my society. Have you heard about the society called, 'Love thy Brother as Thyself?' I belong to it . . ." He began to snore heavily.

Bunim sat down on the box under the tree and turned towards the moonlight which was shining silvery rays upon the yard. He drew out the sheet of paper and the pencil.

The first line of his poem was begun.

Chapter Nineteen

THE SANDY COUNTRY ROAD leading through Marysin was empty. About half way along the road, at its border, a provisional platform had been erected, on which the most distinguished dignitaries of the ghetto were now seated row after row. The seating arrangement, that is, the distance of each person's chair from the central one, where the Presess sat, reflected each person's position in the Presess' heart as well as in the hierarchy of his governing apparatus. They were all dressed in their Sabbath best. The women, unbrellas in hand, wore summer hats with large brims, thus doubly protecting themselves against the glare of the sun. The men perspired profusely in their white shirts and stiff collars which they wore under their buttoned-up jackets. Choking in their tightly fitting ties, they tried to steal some shade from under their wives' umbrellas. Everyone's eyes were turned in the direction of the school buildings from which there issued a muffled clamour like the distant buzzing of a beehive.

The parade of all the children of Marysin was the Presess' own idea, although it came not as much from him, as from his late wife Shoshana who was lying in her grave in the cemetery not far from the school buildings. During the last few weeks the Presess had visited her twice. The first time was during the strike of the nurses, which had aggravated him considerably. The spoiled female eggheads had asked for a ten hour work day and an additional soup for their families. To this unheard-of demand the Presess could only react with a strong fist. So he had thrown out their representatives and warned them through his brother Joseph that he would make the women work with the help of the police, and would not let them leave the hospital buildings at all. The police had indeed occupied the hospitals, seeing to it that, for the twelve hours of the workday, the women did not sit down or take a rest. One after the other they fainted. Then the Presess ordered them to gather and met with them personally. But they, the haughty *prima donnas*, did not respond to his speech, and the Presess lost his patience. He grabbed his stick — he had taken it along not because he lacked strength, but rather in order to release his strength — and began to hit the arms and backs of the women.

The same day, he went to the cemetery. He scrutinized the plot of earth that had been set aside for him. It was silly, but he had a strong premonition that he would never rest here. This feeling strangely confused him and his face twisted into both a smile and a grimace of fear. He placed his arm on Shoshana's tombstone for support. Her voice, her words, revived from their silence by his tenderness, reverberated in his mind. "Feh," said Shoshana. "It doesn't suit you . . . Don't abuse the crown that you wear on your head. You are the leader of a people, not a hoodlum that beats up women." Then he heard her ask, as if with a giggle. "Why do you avenge yourself on women all your life? Are you afraid of them? For how long? You are no longer a milksop — you're a man, strong as a bull. Shame on you, old bones. Go back and mend your ways. Atone for your foolishness with a good deed. After all, you have a heart of gold. Only sometimes . . . sometimes you become one piece of nerve . . ."

The following day, he announced that all the nurses were to receive double soups and that he would do all in his power to help them.

The second time that he visited his wife's grave was a few days ago when he was again in a rage. The Germans had demanded that the death penalty be introduced into the jurisdiction of the ghetto, and that the Jewish judges should pronounce death sentences. But the judges in the ghetto had refused to have anything to do with such sentencing, and the crazy Bundist, Weiskopf, had spoken for them all, when he declared that in the ghetto no Jew would condemn another to death, after which the judges had the nerve to resign of their own free will — as a kind of demonstration against him, Rumkowski, as if it had been he who had given the order, not the Germans. Oh, he well knew what he would do with the rebels. With their declaration they had signed their own death warrants.

He hurried to the cemetery to pour out his heart to Shoshana. He complained to her speechlessly, and his mind responded in her tone of voice, "Against whom are you raging, Mordecai Chaim? Aren't you by chance looking for the wrong address? You yourself insist that a man must know where he stands and there he should stand with both feet. Where are you standing with both feet?" The sound of her voice gave him a gnawing pain in the stomach. She did not understand him. She was on their side. "It's easy for you to scold me, Shoshana," he sighed, "but what would you have done in my place? And what would I have done, if I had been unable to find someone to replace the rebels? Why don't you realize that I am between the hammer and the anvil?" Her voice softened, "I don't say that you have it easy, but how can you punish people who are ready to give up their lives for their convictions? I know . . . I know that the burden you carry on your shoulders is unbearable, beyond human strength. You should allow yourself once in a while to let go. Don't allow your years to be shortened. A person has only one life. You are a king, and at the same time the most miserable creature. You don't even have a family . . . not a soul who loves you without wanting to be paid for it . . . You are kind to others but cruel to your own self. Tell me, is your heart a raisin, or what? Allow yourself a bit of peace . . ." At this moment he was inspired by the idea of seeing the children of Marysin.

Now he sat on the platform, his gray head uncovered, his face relaxed with an expression of tenderness, of warmth. As soon as he noticed the children approaching in pairs, he adjusted his glasses and placed his hand on his brother Joseph's knee, "Look . . . look . . . here they come!" All those present on the platform heard the Presess' voice and obediently turned their heads in the direction of the marching children. Smiles automatically appeared on their sweating faces.

"How sweet they are!" the elegant Countess Helena uttered through her pursed lips.

The Presess threw a glance in the direction of the heavy-set prison chief, who was restlessly fidgeting in his seat, the only spectator who failed to remove the expression of boredom from his face. "Can you hear them, Steinberg, they're singing!" Rumkowski attempted to infect him with his enthusiasm.

But Steinberg was a cold fish, "I can hear them all right, Presess," he grumbled. "I'm not deaf." And he continued to fidget in his chair.

The Presess made an effort not to let Steinberg's behaviour destroy his pleasure. Steinberg was a raw gruff fellow, but he had his good points. He was not lazy and ever since he had taken over his post, the prison had become one of the showpieces of the ghetto; even the Gestapo could not restrain its admiration. Steinberg personally conducted interrogations, personally dealt out what blows were necessary, and thus more than anyone else he contributed to the struggle against thieves and swindlers. Of course he took some slight advantage of his power, in particular with regard to beatings. No one left the prison a healthy person, and he did not even spare the children. But there was nothing that could be done about that. He had the Gestapo behind him and it was not good to order him around too much. The Presess tried not to look any more in Steinberg's direction.

The procession moved by slowly. At the head of the parade marched the smallest of the orphanage: the three- and four-year olds. They trotted unevenly between the grooves in the road, their tiny feet falling in and out of the holes. The little boys wore navy-blue sailor's suits, the little girls white blouses, pleated skirts and red bows in their hair. They waved colourful pennants as they sang a children's song. To Mr. Rumkowski it seemed he was hearing the singing of cherubim. He wanted to hug and kiss each one of them in turn; his fingers longed to touch their bare delicate legs, their velvety cheeks. He felt a gnawing burning joy which made his heart light and heavy with sudden desire: to have one like that for his very own!

That thought hit against his consciousness so unexpectedly, that the Presess remained motionless in his chair. The little ones had already passed; now the slightly older children appeared. Their dress was the same, but the singing was clearer, more uniform. "To have one like that for oneself!" Never before had he felt this desire more powerfully than on the platform in Marysin, during this hot July day. "You are the most wretched . . ." he heard Shoshana's voice. "You deserve a bit of joy." That very joy was given to every beggar, but not to him. He was overcome with self-pity, not a desperate kind of self-pity, but a hopeful one. Did he not have clear proof that here in the ghetto, now that he had begun to take his injections and pills, a tremendous miracle had occurred to him, physically? He sometimes did not recognize himself in the mirror; it was as if he had grown twenty years younger, no, as if he had become an entirely different person, with another temperament, with different appetites.

The ten-, twelve- and thirteen-year olds had already passed by the reviewing stand. "May he live a hundred years, a hundred years!" they sang in the Presess' honour. This woke him from his thoughts. He stood up, applauding and waving his hand. Behind him, the chairs squeaked. The dignitaries stood up as well and applauded. A light dust rose from beneath the youngsters' feet. Countess Helena wiped the dust out of her eyes with a batiste handkerchief and then, with its help, sent air kisses to the children. Rumkowski did not sit down again, and the sweaty dignitaries had to remain standing as well (Steinberg's chair had already been empty for a long time.) They wiped their faces and cast tired glances at their watches. The women in their uncomfortable high-heeled shoes began to rest with one foot over the other. The umbrellas slid down from their hands and leaning on their shoulders, nearly pricked the men with their iron tips. They had all had enough of it.

Only the Presess wished that the parade would never end and, indeed, the three thousand children who were supposed to march that day, marched on and on. When the tots had passed by, the newly awakened desire had chirped in the Presess' bosom like a little bird. But the taller the passing children became, the stronger, the more powerful became his wish. Mordecai Chaim wanted to have a son. He saw him growing before his eyes. His son — he was marching in the parade — increasingly taller, more masculine — an heir to the throne, a young prince. Ah, how great a heritage he would transmit to him! How concrete and attainable would then be his vague dream of immortality! And here — it struck Rumkowski like a thunderbolt. His mind was illuminated by a bright idea: he would marry!

Immediately, he indulged in visions of the new wife he would acquire. Who would she be? How would she look? He must choose slowly, carefully. And there were certainly many from whom to pick. The young women of the ghetto were beautiful. They bloomed like pale graceful flowers, modest, silent, proud and hopeful. Of course there were others too, those who would gladly sell themselves in order to have a good life. But those could be detected easily. He would take one who had feminine honour written on her face; one whom he had never been inspired to woo into his bedroom, an intelligent one. Her aristocratic blood would mix with his, so that their son should have a good head and fine manners. He would know languages, play the piano, and he would possess his, Mordecai Chaim's, courage and strength.

The air was now full of song, well-organized and uniform. The gray-yellow dirt road, full of colour and light, moved like a snake — until it turned about in the distance and came back towards the platform. Now the *gymnasium* students were marching. The girls passed by: partly children, partly women. Mordercai Chaim saw their bare slim legs, their protruding young breasts. Light summer dresses clung to their nimble bodies. Some girls had loose hair, others braided hair, others short boyish hair. Brown, blond and black hair like warm silk shimmered in the sun, framing faces of porcelain smoothness. So many tiny fresh lips! So many bare, perfectly sculptured arms! So many hands like soft waving leaves! It looked as if unknown exotic plants were moving by, gliding on a cool watery surface. Or perhaps these girls, who seemed to be barely touching the ground with their light soaring steps, were a horde of young reindeer? His heart was jubilant. There was not a spark of physical hunger within him, not a speck of the familiar craving to bite into them, to swallow them. There was only admiration, only the urge to bless their beauty, to give praise and thanks for the solace they brought to his soul.

After the girls, came the young men, their white shirt collars were unbuttoned and revealed their slim necks. Again the blood began to hammer in his temples, to pound against the walls of his heart: There . . . there . . . his son was walking — the seventeen year old, the eighteen year old, the *maturist*, the genius. There he marched, looking around with his dark eyes — with a hundred pairs of eyes he was looking at Mordercai Chaim. But why did he stare so arrogantly? What were those sparks of mockery issuing from beneath his brows? And what was the meaning of the unpleasant smile on his lips? The young men were talking among themselves. Why did the teachers allow them to chatter while they marched past the platform? Was this possible? They were laughing aloud. Laughing at him? And here she was walking at their side: the directress herself, Mrs. Feiner. How regally she carried her gray head! How majestically she walked! Why did she not scold that arrogant bunch? And the greeting she gave him, as she stiffly nodded, also contained more of mockery than of greeting. He had clearly seen her pursing her lips, as if to withhold a smile, the same mocking smile. Oh, he would make her pay for this! He would show that dry old cow! She would never be able to put on airs before him again, with her learnedness, her diplomas, the seven or eight languages she spoke. He would take a wife who would surpass her, and on top of it — would be young and have a fertile womb.

After two and a half hours, the parade was over. The crowd of children assembled in the nearby field which began to sway with the multitude of heads like a young forest. The Presess approached the edge of the platform, faced the crowded field and spread his arms. "My dear children!" he exclaimed, as all of Marysin seemed to have sunk into silence. "I gave you a day off from your studies, because I wanted to see you all together, festive and gay! Because all of you surely know that I love you, that I care and worry about you day and night. Yes, day and night I think about how to make life easier and better for you. You are my children and I am your father. I want just one thing in return for my care: that you should study well and diligently, so that I and your parents will be proud of you!" He paused for breath and wiped his forehead. He was speaking well. His voice sounded strong and manly. He could judge this by the echo that rebounded from the partly demolished barns of the liquidated Hachsharas. But now, as he prepared himself to go on with his speech, his ear caught an unpleasant howl coming from the cemetery — and suddenly he realized that there was no sense in prolonging his speech, since he had already said what he wanted to say. He raised his arms once more, "And now, my dear children , you will receive a gift from me! Each child will receive a slice of bread and a piece of sausage!"

Wild applause roared in his ears. Hands were waving. Coloured pennants soared into the air. Hundreds of young laughing mouths let the light of the sun polish their sharp greedy teeth. The teachers made an effort to keep order, each of them leading his class off to the tables where officials stood guard over boxes which contained the prepared slices of bread and sausage. The clamour in the field ceased to be jubilant. It became muffled, loaded with tension.

"Don't push, children, take it easy!" Rumkowski jovially called down from the platform. "Every child will get his share!" Now the children were looking up at him distrustfully, barely paying attention to what he was saying. Their faces were transformed; they seemed adult, old; faces that Rumkowski had seen more than once in the lines in front of the co-operatives. He could not bear to look at them. He stepped down from the platform and waded into the crowd, so as to make order in the queues in front of the tables. "Children, there is enough for everyone, don't push like this," he begged them. He wanted them to remain composed and devoted for at least another moment. But the children neither saw nor heeded him. All their attention was focused on the tables where they were to receive a piece of bread and sausage. He felt useless. Even the children who passed him with the food in their hands did not notice him. Like dogs with bones, they rushed to a corner to devour the tasty morsels.

The Presess went out on the sandy road. Far in the distance he saw his entourage leave for home with their wives, strolling at a leisurely pace. It occurred to him that they had not even taken leave of him and he felt the sting burn inside him. From the pension house for meritorious community officials, came the chiming of a bell, calling the vacationers to dinner. Rumkowksi had to smile: he deserved to be made a fool of, for to be kind meant to be an idiot.

On his way to the droshky, he noticed Samuel Zuckerman approaching. "I was waiting for you, Herr Presess," Samuel stretched both hands out to him. "I wanted to tell you what pleasure you have given me." Rumkowski let him pump his hand. "It's been a long time since I spent such a pleasant few hours. It makes the heart feel lighter to watch the youngsters."

Rumkowski waved his hand, "Peanuts! Do you think they appreciate what one does for them?"

"I'm sure they do, Herr Presess. Children feel who loves them sincerely."

"For a candy, they'll love you."

"Don't say that, Herr Presess. If they don't appreciate it now, they surely will tomorrow . . . And we, their parents, most certainly appreciate it."

Rumkowski furrowed his brow. Waves of conflicting feelings swept through him. "Come, let's sit down for a while," he proposed, leading Samuel back onto the empty platform. "Your girls were in the parade, weren't they? *Matura* ladies, eh? You should see the *matura* diplomas I've prepared. My signature in Yiddish, Hebrew and German. It looks dignified. And your wife . . . did not come along?" Samuel wanted to say something, but the Presess would not let him. "Eh, Zuckerman," he put his hand on Samuel's knee. "You don't realize how good you have it," he laughed falsely. "You have all the good things in life, a wife, two daughters . . . You should go around dancing in the streets, you're so lucky." He moved closer to Samuel and looked into his eyes. He was no longer smiling. "Take me, for instance, yes . . . take me. Does it ever occur to you to put yourself in my place? All alone in this world . . . like a dog, drowning in a sea of hatred. And as for a friend, at least one who would stretch a hand out to me, there is none."

Samuel sat flabbergasted. His relationship with the Presess had long resembled that of a slave to his master and here, all of a sudden, such confidence. "I am your friend," Samuel said.

Rumkowski waved his hand. "What kind of a friend are you? Let's not kid ourselves. Your friendship is not badly paid for." Samuel, ill-at-ease, twisted his face into an awkward smile. But the Presess had said this without reproach. He was serious, downhearted. "I am a cursed man, do you hear, Zuckerman?" he continued. "I am hated by those whom I want to save, hated by those whom I allow to have a good life, and hated by those who want to destroy us all. I know what they say about me behind my back. Don't worry, I know everything. If the war comes to an end, I will be put on trial; perhaps you yourself will be a witness against me." Samuel opened his mouth to deny it, but the Presess would not let him speak. "If there is the slightest trouble in the ghetto, I am considered guilty. From one side the Germans, from the other, the Jews. I may talk my heart out, no one will believe a word I say. Don't deny it, Zuckerman. Yes, I carry a great burden . . . an entire people . . . and am myself the lowest worm that everyone would gladly trample on. Between the hammer and the anvil, that's where I find myself. I need the strength of a devil . . ." The Presess adjusted his glasses, and moved closer to Samuel. "Listen, Zuckerman, a silly idea popped into my head today." He chewed on his lips, then smiled crookedly. "I had an idea . . . to get married." He somewhat shyly scrutinized Samuel's face, expecting to find there an expression of surprise or even mockery. But Samuel remained friendly and serious. So the Presess gathered the courage to speak more openly. "I want to take a decent woman, a quiet intelligent one . . . to have a bit of warmth about me. Before the war, this never entered my mind. But here . . . my heart needs to be strengthened. I need a bit of stability . . . a home, a devoted person. It would make me doubly energetic. I would do great things . . . still greater things for my people." Rumkowski bit his lips. The dream of a son was too intimate, too sacred to bring to his lips; this had to remain sealed deep in his heart. He asked searchingly, "Do you think I am too old for such things?"

"Heaven forbid. On the contrary. A home is a good thing . . ." Samuel stammered.

"So why did you make a face?"

"The sun is burning hot, Herr Presess."

Rumkowski detected a note of derision in this remark. He was already sorry for having confessed to Zuckerman. "Yes, the sun is burning hot," he echoed, then stood up and stepped down from the platform, leaving Zuckerman behind. He made his way towards his droshky. From the nearby barn a young policeman emerged, marching with spirit, his face brown, windswept. The young man's eyes seemed clever, candid and friendly. "That is how he would look . . ." a voice sung out within Mordecai Chaim. The policeman stiffened his body and saluted. "You're on guard, aren't you, my son?" the Presess asked jovially.

"Yes, Herr Presess, I am guarding the barns."

"Are you a good policeman, tell the truth?"

"I do my duty, Herr Presess."

"And what is your name?"

"Rosenberg, Herr Presess."

Rumkowski puckered his eyebrows. "Of which Rosenbergs? What did your father do before the war?"

"The industrialist Adam Rosenberg is my father, Herr Presess."

The Presess' aggravation reached its peak. The perfect son was not his, but the scoundrel Rosenberg's. However, he controlled himself. "And you are a policeman, eh?"

The young fellow laughed, saluting, "At your service, Herr Presess."

The Presess jumped onto the droshky and made a sign to the coachman to move. Samuel was waiting for him on the road. Another time the Presess might have invited him to come along, but now he wanted him to vanish from his sight as soon as possible. He did, however, allow him to jump onto the step of the droshky.

"Herr Presess," Samuel grinned. "I forgot to tell you the most important thing. I want to invite you . . . next week . . . to my home. The comrades wish to spend an evening with you. Will you come, Herr Presess?"

The Presess was impatient. "A lot of water will flow under the bridge before next week. What can I know now?"

"Then I will remind you again, Herr Presess. And . . . come to think of it . . . You promised me a house in Marysin, Herr Presess, last spring."

Samuel's hutzpah was unheard of. "So that's why you've been waiting for me, eh?" He prodded the coachman to move on. Samuel jumped off the step. "To the police station!" the Presess called out.

✦ ✦ ✦

The Presess decided to heed the advice given to him by his late wife Shoshana, to let go a bit and practically force himself to enjoy life somewhat, for his personal benefit — which was after all, for the benefit of those for whom he lived and worked. Never mind, he knew that at this moment he could allow himself this luxury.

His relationship with the Germans and with Herr Hans Biebow, the chief of the *Ghettoverwaltung*, was perfect. In particular, he had Herr Biebow in his pocket. Herr Biebow did not wish to be sent to the front, but wanted to make himself useful for the *Heimat* through the ghetto. And that was a situation to be taken advantage of. Rumkowski had learned how to play on him and how to outplay him in his dealings with the higher authorities, by going to them over his head. It was not only Herr Biebow who needed the ghetto. Berlin needed the ghetto as well. And this made Rumkowski stronger than Biebow. But Mordecai Chaim Rumkowski was wise enough not to let Biebow feel his superiority. After all, they needed each other.

In general, Rumkowski had ceased to fear the Germans so much. At the beginning of the war, he had been afraid of them. To fear the unknown was human nature. But now Rumkowski had come to know the Germans well. He had had the opportunity to watch the Fritzes and Hanses from very close; he often came in touch with the big fish of the German inspecting commissions and had even met Himmler himself, and his fear had vanished. Although he kept on catering to them, he now more than ever felt his intellectual superiority. He possessed a very good eye for judging a person's qualities, or the qualities of a people. He had come to the conclusion that the Germans were creatures whose brains were divided into boxes and each box was labelled like the bottles in a pharmacy. The German way of thinking was based on manipulating these boxes, grouping them in an orderly fashion. *Ordnung über alles!* If they had to deal with something that did not fit into a box, they became confused. Then they waited for orders from their leaders, or from their Super Genius, Hitler himself, so that they might create a new box with a new label. In this way they stacked the boxes with the greatest precision, one on top of the other, both inside their minds and outside them, like children playing with blocks. But they probably suspected that these box towers might tumble at the slightest push, so they fortified them with physical might.

With the box called "Jews", they were not completely sure yet what to do. That was why they continued to wait for orders from the Superbrain, while in the meantime the box shook once here, once there. Nor did Herr Biebow himself — on one hand the head of the *Ghettoverwaltung*, on the other a subordinate to Berlin — have a clear line of thinking. He supported himself with one solid box labelled: personal safety. He knew that as long as the ghetto existed, he would make money and would not have to go to the front. For this reason he rushed to construct new Work Resorts as well as the train line leading to Marysin. He still had other plans for the protection of the ghetto, which he, as a good Nazi and enthusiastic admirer of the Führer, wanted to burn to the ground. Thus Herr Biebow was a man torn by inner conflict. And precisely on this divisiveness did Rumkowski build his own wholeness.

So the ghetto functioned like a German clock. True, the populace was like a wild beast, but Rumkowski, the understanding leader, had transformed it into a milking cow. The ghetto was approaching his ideal of becoming one huge factory. And with the train line and the road that was being constructed to lead up to it, along with the tramway that would soon be running through the streets, it did not appear far-fetched to imagine that one fine day the ghetto would become a mighty industrial centre, a world source of first class products and an essential world community.

As for his position in the ghetto proper, the Presess certainly had no reason to complain. There was no longer any need for him to navigate and play politics with the parties. He could tolerate their meeting and organizing. The Germans did not mind them, neither would he. "Let them stew in their own sauce," he thought, "and leave the population to me." Anyway, they had no power. His commissars sat in their soup kitchens and schools. The party dzialkas had been liquidated as well as the representative bodies of the workers. Once in a while, in order to scare them, he would arrest their leaders and then, with great to-do, set them free. He also had lists of all their members, in case they became too arrogant. And sometimes, to weaken their watchfulness and desire to fight, he threw them a bone and gave one of their people a good position.

He thereby lured them into participating in his "system", as they called it — thus removing the devastating slogans from their mouths. He was smarter than all of them put together. And in this same manner he dealt with his so-called helpers who were swindling behind his back. As long as they did it quietly and modestly, he pretended not to see. After all, they all stood at the brewing pot, and he needed them as well. But if he caught them redhanded, or if they had overdone it, he did not hesitate but fired them or punished them on the spot. The only ones with whom he had to reckon were the Gestapo and Kripo servants, the stool-pigeons. But what damage could they do him? Even Leibel Welner, the bigshot and strongman, the chief of all the informers, was nothing against him, Rumkowski, who had Biebow, the city council and the authorities in Berlin behind him.

In a word, the year forty-one seemed to be the year of Rumkowski's victory. In whatever direction he turned his thoughts, he saw himelf as a winner. He celebrated his vitory, by devoting himself to culture which the mob needed as a tranquillizer, and he himself, as a way to catch his breath, a chance of making a bit of a fool of himself after a day of hard and responsible activity. But for the last few days, after the parade of the children, he wished to celebrate his social victory with a victory in his personal life: with the begining of a new chapter.

Rumkowski disliked playing around for too long with an idea which called for practical action. For him things had to go either one way or the other. His heart had brought up a proposition before the tribunal of his reason and he had weighed and measured it for a short while, and decided to search for a bride. His search led him to the gatherings of those intellectuals who were his protégés and to the homes of the well-bred families that he supported. He kept his eyes open during all the banquets arranged in his honour, waiting for a female face to make him feel: "This is it. This is what I am looking for." These activities were in themselves pleasurable. He undertook them with zest, aware that the search alone made him feel younger and manlier.

It was late in the afternoon, the last hour of the Presess' official working day. Despite the two whirling fans, it was stuffy in the office. The windows were closed, so that the noise from Baluter Ring would not disturb the Presess in his work. With the windows closed, the muffled sounds coming from outside were not only bearable but pleasant — an accompaniment which let the Presess feel that he was holding his hand on the pulse of the ghetto.

On the desk stood a siphon of soda water and a glass from which he took a sip now and then. Nearby stood the telephone which linked the Presess personally to all the fifty Work Resorts and twenty-seven departments in the ghetto. There was another telephone beside that one, by which he could get in touch with Herr Biebow and the *Ghettoverwaltung*. The rest of the desk was covered with files and papers, with boxes of incoming and outgoing mail, and the separate pack of leters and entreaties from the ghetto citizenry, letters which had passed the control of the secretariat and about which the Presess himself had to decide. Apart from that, the table was covered with hexographed reports from the Resorts and workplaces, from the schools and hospitals, all these in several copies, for the Presess and the authorities to study. A folded copy of the latest issue of the *Ghetto Zeitung* lay at the edge of the table.

The Presess was re-reading, for he did not know how many times, an official letter from Herr Biebow. The letter shook slightly in his hand:

> To the Älteste der Juden in Litzmanstadt.
> Herr Rumkowski:
> > Herewith I inform you that according to the order of the *Regierungspräsident*, transports of Jews from *Vartegau* will in the forthcoming weeks be arriving in the ghetto. The first transport of nine hundred individuals from the city of Leslau and vicinity will be unloaded at the new train station, Marysin. I have seen to it that only able-bodied, healthy men and women will be arriving, and your duty, Herr Älteste der Juden, is to make them useful, and incorporate them into the work forces of the Ghetto . . .

Rumkowski was both satisfied and dissatisfied with the news. Satisfied, because the fact that men and women who were able to work were being sent into the ghetto was a sign that the ghetto would grow as a production centre. But he was dissatisfied because these nine hundred people were only the beginning. Probably thousands would follow. They would have trouble with accommodation and would be unaccustomed to the routine of the ghetto. They would not behave in a disciplined manner, not having been re-educated by him. What bearing would all this have on his nerves?

The Presess' secretary appeared in the room to inquire whether he was ready to receive the policeman who had arrived with the second day-report from the streets. He put away the letter and fixed his gaze on the policeman who saluted him and hastily began to spit out his report, like a talking machine: "Herr Presess, I humbly report that there were again shots fired into the ghetto, at two spots. One boy and an elderly man were seriously wounded. A band of Gestapo men went through the streets beating up the passers-by. The police have caught five thieves, a boy of nine amongst them. He stole bread from a bakery. A man in the Tailor Resort stole a spool of thread. A woman stole beets from the community *dzialka*. The other two are from the Carpentry Resort. They stole two sacks of sawdust. On Gabai Street, number seven, the garbage box in the backyard has been completely taken apart. A man was caught passing off cat meat as calf meat on the black market. On the cemetery grounds the German police shot eight people who were from outside the ghetto. A boy threw a rock at the military truck passing by on the other side of the fence . . ."

"Again?" the Presess exclaimed. "Take the boy to the prison, give him fifteen lashes and keep him at the disposal of the Germans. All the other cases, I will deal with tomorrow." Alone again, the Presess nervously tapped the tip of his pencil against the table top. He felt that if he had the boy in his hands at this moment, he could tear him to pieces. For that stupid throw of the rock the ghetto could pay dearly. But gradually he quietened down. Such minor incidences had occurred several times and his intercession had helped. The Germans forgave the misdemeanor. They were not ready to give up a business worth millions because of the action of a child. The guilty one would be punished and the issue would probably be closed. He emptied the glass of its last drop of soda water and stood up. It was time to step outside and have a look at his new carriage.

His new carriage was a closed one, with little windows. Although it did not resemble the carriages of royal majesties, it suggested, in spite of its modest appearance, a certain similarity. Its purpose was to create the proper distance between the Presess and the ghetto streets; a distance to be discarded only when he and not the mob so wished. At no time did it suit him to pass through the packed streets with the crowds running after him like after a fool, attacking him with demands, with cries, with letters and with pleas — a thing which he abhorred. Now he could sit back in the deep darkness of the carriage, see what was going on outside, and not be seen himself.

He decided to try out the new carriage. The air inside was stifling but so was the air outside. He heard frequent thunder claps and saw distant lightning zig-zagging through the clouds. As he rode in the carriage, the Presess saw the waves of Ghettoniks streaming out from the Resorts, while other waves, the second shift, streamed towards them. Women, kettles in hand, were running to the coffee centres, others carried boiling pots out from the gas-centres. Children were carrying pails of water. Here and there he saw someone stretched out on a door step — a half-naked skeleton, leaning his head against a pot, his sharp nose pointing to the sky; someone asleep, or in a faint. At the sight of the carriage, the candy and saccharine vendors quickly hid inside the arched gates. The rest of the passers-by halted, followed the strange vehicle with their eyes for a while, and then hurried on.

The coachman on the seat drove the horse slowly. The Presess had given him an hour's time, and in that time one could pass through the entire length and breadth of the ghetto. But once they got to Church Place, the carriage had to stop every few minutes, and was finally unable to move at all. From all the side-streets, the mobs came pouring out, heading for the bridge. The Presess peered out through the window. Something repulsive and eerie hovered over this place. On one side stood the old houses, on the other, the church, empty and silent. Across from it, stood the brick-red *Kripo* House, the only place in the ghetto over which Rumkowski had no say. And here, in front of him, were the barbed wires with that strange bridge from which the hurried clip-clop of hundreds of wooden shoes could be heard. The Ghettoniks looked like ghosts climbing the ladder of hell; such vertiginous movement of legs, thin as sticks, swollen as pumpkins. The men's shirts were ragged and dirty, revealing skeletal protruding ribcages; their faces were smeared with dirt and sweat, their lips covered with white foam, their eyes like burnt-out coals. The women looked even more repulsive. If not for their hair and dresses, it would have been impossible to distinguish them from the men. Their bodies had not a trace of roundness; what remained of their breasts lay flat — loose empty bags on the claviture of their ribs. Their faces were masculine, sunken, with protruding cheekbones and long pointed noses. Only their eyes were different from those of the men. They were like burning coals, aglow with rage, with impatience and diabolic perseverance. Only here and there in the crowd could one see a normal human figure, a normal face and decent dress. Such a figure did not carry a canteen tied to a coat-button, or to a belt, but the briefcase of a dignitary. Once in a while a colourfully dressed girl would flash by — a sixteen or seventeen year old, one of those who were miraculously blooming in the ghetto.

Rumkowksi noticed the dead clock in the church tower. A clock that had stopped, while the time around it pulsated so feverishly, was a mockery. Yet it made no sense to intervene with the Germans about it. After all, of what importance was the clock? It was a dead thing even when it worked. The real clock ticked in the living pulse of the ghetto. Nevertheless, it was unpleasant to look up at the church tower, not because of the clock, but because of the black crows perched on its top. Only a few of them were flying around, somewhat awkwardly, making a short excursion in the air, then returning. A strange rattle accompanied their crowing, as though muffled human groans were issuing from their throats. And now the Presess noticed: entire piles of birds lay on the roof. What had looked like pieces of tar paper were in fact helplessly spread wings. The entire church seemed splotched with black feathers filling all the ledges, all the holes and niches.

The thunder sounded like wheels rolling through the sky. It became dark in the street and soon he could hear a thin clopping against the roof of the carriage, as though bags with peas were being spilled on it. A still more feverishish hustle and bustle began on the bridge. It was strange to see how such skeletal bodies could move so quickly. The Presess' heart filled with love and pride. A useful diligent people, earning its bread by the sweat of the brow, was hurrying home after a day's work. If only there were not so many old people tangled among them. They, more than anyone else, carried death in their faces. Why did they make themselves so visible? And what were those with the prayer-shawls hidden under their gaberdines doing here in the rush?

As the downpour began to wash the windows of the carriage, the coachman's face appeared at one of them. Rumkowski made a sign that he should stop at the curb. The roof of the carriage clattered like a disjointed orchestra. Once in a while lightning flashed across the fogged-up panes. The earth trembled. On the steps of the pharmacy stood the soaked coachman, his wet face turned to the carriage, ready to catch every order of the Presess. The latter called him over with a knock of his finger against the pane, and opened the door ajar. "What's the matter with the crows?" he asked.

The coachman put his palm behind his ear. There was a curtain of rain between himself and the Presess. "Eh, Herr Presess?" He wiped off the water streaming down his nose.

"The birds on the church, what's the matter with them?"

"The birds, Herr Presess?" The coachman flung his face up towards the sky, narrowing his eyes so that the rain would not fill them. "Oh, those on the church you mean? They're dying out, Herr Presess. They're dying like flies, from hunger, or, some people say, from a plague."

A plague. That was a logical reason. Things like that happened amongst flocks of birds. The Presess slammed the door of the carriage, allowing the coachman to take cover again. He himself remained with his face glued to the window. It was an uncanny sight: the silent church, the dead clock in the tower, the red *Kripo* House, the black cloud of people over the strange bridge, the clip-clop of hundreds of wooden shoes on the stairs, the echoes of distant thunder — and the black spread wings of the dead birds. Rumkowski was surprised at himself. He had never let himself be overcome by superstitions. He, who was always reasonable and logical, suddenly succumbing to such a mood? He had to rid himself of it immediately. If he must be mystical, why not deduce something positive from the signs? The dead crows were a good omen, not a bad one. Live crows foretold bad tidings. Their dying out meant that the ghetto would survive, that he would survive. It was a protective hand that had brought the Presess over here, that he should see with his own eyes the good promise — that the verdict on the ghetto's future had somewhere been pronounced, perhaps at that very moment. He sighed with relief, suddenly overcome by a feeling of gratitude to the same Jews who were hurrying through the downpour with their hidden prayer shawls — to a place of prayer somewhere. He took a resolution to go to a place of prayer during the High Holidays this year. Having reached this decision, he became aware of the emptiness in his stomach. He was as hungry as a wolf.

✦ ✦ ✦

That same evening the Presess had another good omen: he found his bride. The Zuckermans had arranged a little celebration in his honour and there was no reason for him not to accept the invitation. After all, Samuel was the most devoted of all his collaborators, and although he had faults of character and did not always behave as the Presess expected, there was no sense in refusing him the chance to express his gratitude and devotion is such a manner.

The ghetto looked washed and refreshed after the storm. The Presess was after his daily bath and he felt like a child that had just woken up from sleep. He went on foot to the Zuckermans. It was pleasant to take a stroll now. Beside him walked his two guards from the *Überfallkommando* with such thunderous steps, that their boots seemed to be made of iron and concrete rather than leather. The Presess tried to make his steps match the rhythm of theirs; he felt as strong and as vigorous as they.

He was in good spirits and as usual his mood was contagious. The fellow walking on his right told one ghetto joke after another: "Listen, Herr Presess, these two brothers are fighting each other with chairs because of a soup, while the third brother looks on. A policeman arrives and asks the third one, 'Why didn't you make peace between them?' So the third guy replies, 'Because I didn't have a third chair.' And in the courthouse there was this Jew, you know, Herr Presess, one of those swindlers who make fake ghetto money. So this Jew says to the Judge, 'Your honour, how could I have made fake money, if I don't even know how to sign my name? So the judge answers him, 'No one is accusing you of signing your name. You're accused of signing the Presess' name.'" The Presess joined the wag in his laughter. He searched his mind for a joke with which to repay him, but he knew none. All the jokes he ever heard immediately evaporated from his memory.

As they were coming down the bridge, they passed a German guard. He appeared lonely and pitiful in comparison with the merry company of the three vigorous ghetto Jews. On Hockel Street, which was packed with strollers, the people stepped aside with awe, freeing the path for the three marching men. The Presess peered into the backyards through the gates. Everywhere people were stooped over their *dzialkas*, weeding, working the soil. "Do you see what Jews are capable of? Baluty has become one big garden," he beamed.

"This reminds me, Herr Presess," the joker was immediately inspired. "One owner of a *dzialka* asks another, 'How did your potatoes come out?' 'Oh, very well,' replies the other. 'Some are as big as cherries, the others as big as peas and the rest are small.'"

The Presess waived his hand jovially, "It's not so bad. The soil in the ghetto is rich." Once they entered the Zuckermans' backyard, they walked in a single file between the beds of soil. On either side of them, men and women were busying themselves with the growing vegetables. The water pump squeaked gaily. The sight of the Presess caused a commotion. His name could be heard to echo through the yard and the apartments. He smiled and waved at the children. He cast a glance at the cherry tree. Red ripe cherries like mischievous eyes blinked at him from between the boughs. The watchman who had been sitting on his box under the tree, jumped to his feet, nearly dropping a volume of the Talmud from his lap. "Good evening, Herr Presess," he bowed.

"Good evening, good year," the Presess replied. "When will the cherries be picked?"

"The Food Department says next week, Herr Presess."

The Presess admired the tree. He wished he could have it in his garden. "A nice tree," he said, as if it were a personal compliment to the watchman.

The watchman bowed, "Yes, a lovely tree, Herr Presess. We call it the Tree of Life."

From the nearby building, Samuel Zuckerman appeared at a run, a solemn smile on his face. Rumkowski took leave of his companions and allowed Samuel to take his arm. At the open door he was received by Reisel. "Welcome, welcome, Herr Mordecai Chaim Rumkowski!" she exclaimed, spreading her arms as if to embrace him. "Go into the dining room, please."

The Zuckermans had acquired the dining room after Professor Hager and his wife moved out. This allowed the Zuckermans to arrange this first large reception at their home. Matilda appeared on the threshold of the dining room. The Presess had difficulty recognizing her, although he had seen her only the previous New Year at his celebration. A short flabby woman now stood before him. Her full face had a loose drooping goitre. Her belly and bosom created one round mass of flesh and she looked like a deflated balloon from which part of the air had escaped. Above her anaemic cheeks hung two folded tearbags in a net of wrinkles. Her hair was graying above her temples and she looked more like Samuel's mother than his wife. The Presess made an effort to disguise the impression his hostess made on him and feeling Matilda's chubby hand in his, he bent down and chivalrously kissed it.

"I am so grateful to you, Herr Presess," she whispered, "for the House of Culture, for the concerts . . ."

Samuel hurriedly relieved the Presess of her company by guiding him inside the room before he could reply. In the room, the assembled guests sat in complete silence at the set table, respectfully waiting for the Presess to give them his attention. As soon as he approached, they jumped to their feet and applauded. They belonged to the cream of the "ghettocracy" and to the closest circle of the Presess' collaborators. Only one face, that of a young woman, was unfamiliar. "Miss Clara Weinshenker," Samuel introduced her in a special tone of voice; then he whispered in the Presess' ear, "She is a lawyer . . . Before the war she was an applicant at the Court of Trade. A very charming person." Miss Weinshenker sat next to the head of the table where the Presess now made himself comfortable.

The Presess cast not a single glance at the table laden with delicious food. He studied the profile of the stranger at his side. He had been looking for just such a face: open, intelligent, not arrogantly-coquettish nor girlishly sweet, but proud, and at the same time feminine and refined. He moved his chair closer to hers and attempted to strike up a conversation. "How do you come to know the Zuckermans, child?" That was malapropos, calling her a "child," but he was anxious to warm the air between them.

"Mrs. Zuckerman is my friend," she informed him in a voice that was neither friendly nor unfriendly. There was not a trace of servility in her manner, a thing to which he was not accustomed. This bothered him a little at the same time as it pleasantly intrigued him. A royal simplicity — that was what her bearing suggested. He respected her. It was impossible to talk to her the way he usually talked to girls or women. He searched for the appropriate tone in which to address her, but then he heard Samuel's voice.

"My dear guests!" Samuel exclaimed. "I don't wish to bore you by proposing any drawn out toasts tonight. Tonight's gathering is in honour of our Presess, an expression of gratitude, mine and that of my family . . . And may the Presess live in good health and may his heart, which brings solace to all of us, be strengthened by the love we bear for him!" He was obviously moved, since the glass in his hand shook.

The guests applauded energetically. Rumkowski raised his glass and nodded to Samuel with sincere friendliness. He was grateful to him for Clara. "Lechaim!" he said and clinked his glass with Clara's, then sipped the wine with avid lips. He felt very much like putting his hand on the young woman's shoulder, but he restrained himself. He only bent nearer to her. "My name is Chaim," he said, as if he thought it necessary to introduce himself. "The name is the man!" he added, surprised at the clever thought he had expressed. "I mean in my case. Chaim means life in Hebrew."

"Do you think then, that it is not an accident that your name is Chaim, Herr Presess?"

"No, it is a matter of fate."

"Your grandfather's name was probably Chaim."

"That too was a matter of fate. He was given that name for my sake."

"You are a mystic."

"I? I am a realist." For the first time he saw her smile.

Reisel came in with a huge dish full of cholent and the tipsy Mr. Zibert sang out, "Let's not sit like the old babas, let us turn this Wednesday into a Shabbas!"

Reisel dealt out the portions onto the plates. Samuel followed her with a bottle, refilling the glasses. "The taste of paradise!" Zibert put the tips of his fingers to his mouth and kissed them loudly. "Perhaps you come to cook for me a little bit, eh, Reisel, my sweetheart?"

Reisel's face shone with delight and sweat, "Even if you gave me the moon on a platter, I would not do it, Mr. Zibert, darling. I have my masters, may they live in good health!"

"Bravo!" Herr Waldman, commissar of the Department of Finance, applauded. He was a poor drinker and the wine he had downed had loosened his tongue. "That's what I call devotion!" he praised Reisel. "Where can you find such a thing nowadays , my friends? Not even among relatives or husbands and wives, or parents and children. Don't you think, my friends, that we Jews should stand on a higher moral plane in the present situation? The stories one hears! Children stealing the bread of their parents . . . a sister gorging herself on her brother's food . . ." His wife nodded solemnly.

"Horrible, horrible!" the other women agreed, daintily blowing on their hot spoonfuls of *cholent*.

"We Jews who pride ourselves on our ethics . . ." Herr Waldman went on, delighting in the piece of meat between his teeth, "We should be living here like brothers. If we don't, then of what value is our entire *Torah*, if in bad times we put it aside?"

"The people are very uneducated," Countess Helena remarked. "I think that we, the intelligentsia, don't fulfil our duty. We are not active enough socially."

The wife of the police commissar felt offended by her remark. "You cannot reproach me, Madam Helena. For months I have been collecting used underwear and dresses for the children in the schools."

A lively elegant woman, the new wife of one of the lawyers present, coquettishly and reverently turned to Rumkowski, "And what about that ingenious idea created by Herr Presess' genius, that the Jews should cut off half of their winter coats, making jackets out of them, and offer the rest of the material to the needy?"

"Indeed, the main reproach should be directed at us, ladies," the serious Mrs. Waldman agreed with Countess Helena. "After all, the men are busy with their work. It should be our duty to see to it that civilized behaviour in the ghetto improves. We should go into the homes, teach them, if necessary, how to eat. Do you have any idea what the people stuff their stomachs with? The worst kind of filth. And as a result, epidemics and all kinds of diseases are spreading like wildfire. And we ought also to influence the teachers," she turned to the commissar of the schools, "that they should introduce a new subject into the classroom: honesty. The children are growing up thieves and liars. When they are able to steal something from a wagon, or sneak something out of a co-operative, they are proud of their heroism, and the worst thing is that their parents praise them for it."

Rumkowski pushed away his half full plate. He was not hungry. Of the conversation at the table he had heard nothing. He was busy with Clara. The guests were quite aware of the fact and the conversation rolled on without him.

Samuel sat a short distance from the table, lightly rocking on the back legs of his chair. "Apropos the topic of our conversation, my friends." he interjected enlivened. "I once read . . . The famous Czarist Minister Pleve called the greatest rabbis to his office one day, in order to question them. One of his questions was: 'Why is there so much competition among the Jews; one Jew is always ready to tear the food out of the other's mouth?' So our *rav* answered him: 'Simple. It is known that animals of the same species do not devour each other. But there is one exception to the rule. The fish in the river. Why? Because the other animals have the whole world to themselves; they can look for food everywhere, while the fish are limited by the riverbanks. In order to keep themselves alive, one must devour the other. The same is true of the Jews who are imprisoned in the ghetto, while the other people have the entire world to themselves.' And this, my friends, can be said with even more truth about our own ghetto," Samuel concluded.

Matilda buried her face in her plate to conceal the tears which filled her eyes. Samuel could find a justification for everything, she thought. He hoped in this manner to cleanse himself of his own sins, of his own immorality with regard to her. Did he really lack the ability to distinguish between right and wrong? Had he no ethical sense?

Her face buried in her plate, she heard one of the guests deliver a speech in the Presess' honour, "It is thanks to him and only to him, that we sit today at this festive table! It is thanks to him and only to him, that life is better in the ghetto of Lodz than in any other ghetto! Look at our flourishing institutions, the resorts, the schools, the hospitals! There is no corner of our life into which the Presess' eye has not penetrated. May his hands be strengthened! Long live our Presess!"

Applause followed. Matilda controlled herself and raised her head. The drunken Zibert was the next speaker. "What you, my friends, see in the Presess," he called out, "is all true, but I see much more in him . . . much more! Mordecai Chaim Rumkowski, my friends, is a prophet and a visionary. Yes, that's what he is! We look and we see only the ghetto, our minds are fenced in by barbed wires. But not his! He looks backward and he looks forward! All of Jewish history runs through his mind like one very clear road. He knows how to lead us along this road. He is a messenger from God. May he live to see the moment when he can lead us out of here in a good hour and bring us to the Promised Land, the land of milk and honey. Amen!" The guests looked at each other questioningly. As usual there was in Zibert's drunken voice something that made one doubt that he meant what he was saying. But now it was the turn of the tall Commissar of the Police to stand up, a glass cupped in his hand, and begin his speech which he delivered half in Polish, half in German.

Matilda felt Samuel's hand touching hers. The unexpected gesture confused her. How badly she wanted to love him calmly, patiently and not expect anything in return. Did she after all have the right to demand, to expect anything for herself? She felt so little like a woman lately, so little like a person. She wiped her face quickly. She must not think about all these things now. There was a celebration taking place in her home. She had to find the strength to mask her emotions for a few more hours. She clasped Samuel's hand with her fingers. He was both her torturer and the only suppport she had in this world. He leaned towards her. "Clara will have a good influence on him," he whispered in her ear, with his eyes indicating the head of the table where the Presess and Clara were talking quietly.

Tonight Presess Rumkowski did not reply to the speeches overflowing with praise. He had drunk a bit too much and his head was swimming. Now and then Clara's face seemed double to him, and it was only with one of two women that he was having this serious conversation. The other side of the double resembled his wife Shoshana who was resting in her grave in Marysin. So, along with Clara's voice he also heard Shoshana's very clearly. "She won't love you anyway, old bones that you are. Nor will she bear you a son, idiot!"

"She must!" Rumkowski replied in his mind, still moving closer towards Clara.

Chapter Twenty

MISS DIAMAND lived in a yard where there had been a Catholic school before the war, in a house which had been the dormitory of the nuns who had taught in that school. The rooms were tiny, unconnected, facing onto a long corridor. Many teachers lived in that house. Mrs. Lustikman who had become an active communist in the ghetto and had arranged a kind of party secretariat in the two cubicles which she occupied, had offered one of them to Miss Diamand. She and her eccentric husband, the eternally starving professor of mathematics and physics, moved the secretariat to the other cubicle. Their next door neighbours were the directress of the *gymnasium*, Mrs. Feiner and her two daughters, and next to them lived Frau Braude, professor of German. In the house lived also the Professor of Latin, Miss Luba and the teacher of Hebrew, Mrs. Karmelman, whom everyone called "Karmelka", as well as the Professor of Botany, Mr. Hager and his dainty wife.

The teachers lived in a kind of commune. Each teacher kept only his bread and sugar rations in his room, while the rest of the food went into a common pool. An active committee was elected every month, while the actual spokesmen of the commune were the two energetic women: "Karmelka" and Mrs. Lustikman.

The first few weeks Miss Diamand walked around with wide-open eyes. The atmosphere, the way of life was so new and yet so familiar to her from the years of her youth, that it seemed incredible. And the people she came in contact with here were no longer the same colleagues from the *gymnasium*, who had never noticed her. They were no longer the self-satisfied indifferent lecturers who from the dais had thrown pompous phrases at the children, while themselves behaving in the teacher's room with the pettiness and boastfulness of children. They no longer felt secure in their knowledge, but felt rather like beginners. They spent entire evengings discussing what and how to teach. And teaching was no longer a chore for them. It had become the basis for their survival and at the same time their responsibility. Nor was there any longer a difference between Miss Diamand's approach to work and theirs. They seemed as old as she, and she as young as they. In addition, she had their comradeship after work. They would tell her their problems and listen eagerly to her remarks.

Because of this, Miss Diamand's love for her students became stronger still. The change in the teachers, she realized, had come about thanks to the young. Their unusual hunger for knowledge, their insistent questioning and refusal to accept any pat answers had, in her opinion, forced the teachers to respect them and to examine themselves. They themselves had become students, seekers, and in that way, found a common language with the young. How she rejoiced in discovering her colleagues' reverence for work! What pleasure it gave her to see them sitting in the evenings, doing their "homework"! There were of course exceptions such as Professor Lustikman who shouted at and quarrelled with everybody and dismissed everything by saying, "We will, in any case, end with our heads in the ground." But people like this were already mentally destroyed by starvation; they were sick people, who were no longer really alive. And yet, in spite of everything, this same nervous bitter Professor Lustikman managed to transform his lessons of physics into masterpieces. His students more than once gladly sat with him through recess and into the beginning of another teacher's hour.

Miss Diamand had a lot to be grateful for. She did not have to take care to her household or worry about daily trifles. The committee wanted to free her completely from her duties, but she insisted on contributing, and she became the directress of the club for the teachers' children, so that during the day she seldom had a moment to herself. Even when she was resting in her cubicle, her mind was outside. Summertime, all the doors of the little rooms were kept open and snatches of conversations could be heard coming from each one. Now and then someone would pop in for a chat or to unburden his heart a bit. One neighbour had swollen feet, another had the beginnings of tuberculosis. This one's children were constantly sick, and that one was going through a period of misunderstanding with his family. It seemed that she, Miss Diamand, was the healthiest and the happiest of them all.

The longer she lived with her colleagues, the greater became their reverence for her; it was as if she had become transformed into a spiritual mother to them, practically a saint. Thus, they did not mind squandering her time or claiming her attention; she belonged to each of them as if she existed only to lighten their lives and had no life of her own. If there was — in spite of her intimacy with them — also a certain distance between them and herself, it was a physical one. Sometimes she wished that they behaved as had Sheindle of Hockel Street. She longed for someone to inquire how she felt, to touch her hand, to stroke her forehead, to give her a sisterly hug or a kiss. But for this lack she was compensated by the little ones. The moment a tot trotted over to her and embraced the folds of her dress with its hands, or threw its arms around her neck, she felt rewarded for what the parents were too stingy to offer. And the accounts were straightened.

To her own moods, her own thoughts, she devoted herself mostly at night, on her bed. The bed stood by the window, and lying on it, she would turn her face towards the sky. It seemed to her that she actually lay outside, in the soft field. The vines surrounding the window swayed; the *dzialkas* shared their fragrance with her. There was still so much wonder in her, so much zest. There was so much left to be found out, about people, about herself and about life in general. And the sky still had the power to play upon her dreams and desires. It seemed strange that her body was so shrunken, her back bent, her feet barely able to lift themselves off the ground, and yet her being had not grown older at all. There was a freshness within her, as if she had just arrived into this world — with a craving for beauty, for clarity, and most of all, with a love for everything alive and growing beneath the canopy of that magnificent mysterious sky.

At the same time she felt, as she lay on her bed, that she was lying in a grave beneath the sky. And more than once she would at such moments see the face of a baby. She had in the past admired little babies from a distance, as one admires flowers. Now the admiration was of a physical nature, it was intimate and radiated from her entire decrepit body, going hand in hand with her thoughts about death. Death itself, which had used to be an abstract idea to her, a philosophical speculation, became here, in her bed near the window, a tangible presence. She would see them together: the bright arms of life, and the dark arms of death. In her pre-sleep state, they intertwined, while she felt a tenderness and curiosity for both.

But during the month of August, even the nights ceased to belong to her. It was a month before the *matura* examinations at the *gymnasium*. According to her calculations, she had gone through forty *maturas* in her life, but never had she prepared herself for any of them the way she did this year. It happened as if by accident, again because of her students. Never before had she covered so much material, nor branched out into so many fields that were new to her as well. But the difficulty was not so much in the material itself, as in the approach to it. Her usual reasons for reproaching her students — laziness in making their way through a work, or resistance to studying an epoch or a writer in depth — did not exist here. Here the opposite occurred: protests, brutal questions to the authors and a rejection of their approach to life. Each of her students considered himself or herself competent to challenge this or that author's knowledge of human nature and his experience of life. More than once she would find herself in a whirl of critical talk, of laughter and mockery. Lost, confused, she would try to struggle, to navigate through it, searching for the genuine, the eternal in the works of art under discussion — and to cling to it as to a chip of sawdust. Often when she succeeded in controlling the class, she was aware that the question marks remained suspended in the air: What meaning did literature and art have in the light of the present extraordinary reality?

The only thing that saved her was the powerful feeling for beauty that these young people had. Only by evoking that, was she able to win them. They could accept what was most unreal, most impossible, if only it were beautiful. They let themselves be carried away by the music of words, by the playfulness of sounds and rhythms. But their taste was particular and she was never sure what would please them and what would not. And she, whose taste had become clear and stabilized throughout the years, suddenly realized that what gave her aesthetic delight left the young cold, and what enthused them left her indifferent.

This fact worried and frightened her. She had first to be clear with her own self — and she was not. Pencil in hand, she spent her nights at her table, filling hundreds of pages with essays, analyses and thoughts. One day, very soon, all this would have to come together to form an entity. And she was in a hurry. Only at dawn did she allow herself a short nap, and it too was filled with a dance of thoughts which stirred all the knowledge she had accumulated throughout her lifetime, and made it still more difficult for her to come to a conclusion.

In the mornings, she would purposely leave early, to avoid company on her way to school. She had work to do even while walking: to organize the program of her day in her mind. It was pleasant to do one's thinking during these cool bright summer mornings. All was quiet around her. The rays of the pale sun licked at the streets and the houses, making them all look painted. Sometimes her friend Wanda would break into her thoughts, but the memory was vague. Had Wanda ever existed? Miss Diamand wondered about the pale memory of her entire past life on the other side of the barbed-wire fence. Yes, the Ghetto was like a sponge. Thoroughly, tracelessly, it erased the past; it cut through one's life with the barbed wires like with saws, leaving only that part which was inside, between them.

Today she was tired. Her work at school was not running smoothly. She had to run around a great deal. First of all she had her head full of the problem of the students who had stolen fruit from the community trees in Marysin. They had already been caught several times, and now they were arrested. Mrs. Feiner had previously successfully intervened on their behalf. This time, however, the Commissar of the Police was determined to keep the boys in prison, and then to send them off with a transport to Germany. Miss Diamand did not believe that he would do that; what bothered her was that the students were not attending classes now, during the last days before the *matura* exams. She had accompanied Mrs. Feiner to the prison. The arrested boys were quite indifferent to the visit of their teachers. They shrugged their shoulders at Mrs. Feiner's scoldings. "It tempts the eyes," they declared calmly. "It makes our mouths water."

Both women went to plead with the Presess and fortunately the latter was in a bridegroomly frame of mind. He made the necessary calls, and the teachers hurried joyfully back to school. Once finished with that problem, Miss Diamand had gathered her students and left with them on their planned excursion to the hospitals. This was in connection with their course on disease and hygiene in the ghetto. There she found out that ninety percent of the population was infected with tuberculosis. Even the few hours of study she had managed to cram in today, had not gone smoothly. It had been announced that after a long interval, the students would again be receiving a meat ball with their soups, and the young people could barely wait for the moment; they fidgeted in their seats, unable to concentrate.

On her way home, a group of students caught up with her. They discussed their impressions of the visit to the hospitals and spoke about X-rays, about tuberculosis and typhus. They compared their degree of infection among themselves. This one had a mark on his lungs, the other a hole, a third water. One of them flattered himself that he had had a clean X-ray, was as healthy as a horse, but was systematically losing half a kilo weekly. He calculated how many kilos he still had to lose before he was reduced to zero. They talked like scientists, like specialists, arguing about statistics, percentages, taking her, Miss Diamand, both as a witness and a judge. Such days made her feel like crying. Everything lay low on the ground, people seemed like nothing but worms, and that included herself. Truly there was a sky above one's head, but on such a day who noticed it?

Once home, she was greeted with the daily hubbub. The children pounced on their parents with talk, with wailing and laughter. In the yard, beets or cabbage leaves were being washed, while the water pump squeaked. Pots and kitchen utensils clattered. In the corridors women teachers stood over basins, doing their washing. Those whose turn it was to clean the house, were sweeping the stairs. Someone loaded down with bedding, came rushing down the stairs to air it, and almost carried along the tired Miss Diamand. The air was full with heat, with steam and with the smell of perspiration.

When she finally reached her room, she found a visitor waiting for her. Her former student, Clara Weinshenker, greeted her and handed her a jar, "I received a special ration of a half a kilo of curds, so I brought you some." The teacher gave her a tired confused smile as she took the jar from her hand, not knowing what to do with it. "Do you want to wash up, Miss Diamand? Where are your slippers?" Clara asked.

Ordinarily, Miss Diamand disliked being served, but with Clara it was a pleasure, because Clara did everything without a trace of tenderness, or a speck of compassion, as if she wanted to prove that her kindness sprang from her head, not from her heart. Such kindness was easy to accept, just as it had been easy to accept Sheindle's kindness. So Miss Diamand let Clara bring her the slippers and prepare a basin of water for her to wash with. "I have no time for you today," she muttered preoccupied.

Clara did not answer. She sat down on the bed and waited for Miss Diamand to concentrate her attention on her. Finally, the latter sat down beside her and scrutinized her with her red nebulous eyes. Before her sat a young woman who refused to admit that she had any feelings, who never used the word "love", and if ever she grew sentimental, it was when she spoke of her profession. She had an almost sickly passion for justice, the achievements of which seemed as clear and logical to her as the solution to a mathematical formula. "What do you think of Presess Rumkowski, Miss Diamand?" Clara asked unexpectedly.

Miss Diamand puckered her eyebrows, "Why such a question all of a sudden?" Then she replied, "I once thought that he had been sent down to us from heaven. I did not understand his language and thought that great wisdom flowed from his lips. But lately his halo has become somewhat tarnished. His behaviour towards the teachers lacks delicacy. Yet I forgive him everything because of his attitude towards the children . . . towards the school."

"Why do you think the Germans chose him for the job instead of someone else?"

"Clara, my child, why this topic?"

"I am going to marry him."

Miss Diamand had to smile. It was very funny. But seeing Clara's serious face and her stern glance, the spoon which she had been using to eat the curds began to shake.

"If you can forgive him everything, and if it is true that he . . . then it won't be in vain . . . He sends for me every day . . ." Clara spoke in broken staccato phrases. "Yesterday he proposed to me . . . You're right, Miss Diamand, he has a heart . . . a very lonely man . . . Oh, I have great plans."

The teacher's moist tired eyes blinked. "Is this some kind of self-sacrifice?"

"On the contrary. It's an egotistical step. It means I can stop worrying until the end of the war." Clara's eyes grew lively. "Do you know, in a way the ghetto has been one of the happiest times in my life. I have become clear not only about myself, but about many other things; as if up to now I had been suspended in the air, and have suddenly come down on solid ground." She wanted to say some more, but controlled herself. She took leave of Miss Diamand and quickly left the room.

Miss Diamand watched her from the window. She saw her pacing through the yard with measured steps, her dark short-cropped hair shining. Then she saw her vanish into the stream of people in the street. A *fecalia* cart passed through the street; the red tin barrel leaning against the wheels was spilling its brownish contents. A man and a woman were harnessed to the cart in front, while two children were pushing from behind. A third child, very small, was riding on top of the barrel: A family of latrine cleaners.

Some neighbours were already resting in the yard, the Hagers among them; both of them were shrunken and withered. Still it was refreshing to watch that couple, eternally in love with each other. Not far from them, on an old deck chair, upon heaps of bedding, lay Miss Luba, the young Latin teacher who had once declared that women would be stronger in wartime than men. There she lay now, shivering in her tubercular fever, a conquered young woman. Not far from her, Professor Lustikman was strolling with a group of men. He threw wild glances in the direction of the dining room. His wife came out to meet him. In her white blouse and sweater, she looked like a young student. Had she come to tell them that supper was ready? No. From the way the men gathered around her, it was clear that she had brought them the latest news. Somewhere in the ghetto there were a few people, a cantor amongst them, who secretly listened to the radio and distributed the news among the leaders of the parties. In her mind Miss Diamand saw a Jew in a long gaberdine, with a long white beard and sidelocks, sitting bent over a radio receiver. She herself had no interest in the news. It did not seem important to her. She never daydreamed or made plans about her life after the war. If she had plans, if she dreamed about the future, it was in regard to her students. In her class she often repeated the phrase, "When you get out from here . . ."

She went back to her table and sharpened her red pencil, in anticipation of beginning her work. But her mind was not ready. She had Clara's face in her mind's eye. How could she have let her go like that, without giving her the opportunity to bring out everything that lay on her heart? Her own fatigue had blinded her to Clara's anxieties. Realizing this, she became even more tired.

✦ ✦ ✦

Thus the straight thread of Miss Diamand's days would knot and break now and then, preventing her from moving on. Such breaks occurred, for instance, when the bridge was closed for twenty-four hours and her classes were half empty. Or, there was the day when half of her class was missing because potatoes had arrived in the ghetto. Or there were those strange days when the classes were full, the lessons prepared, and yet something was wrong without apparent cause or reason. Then, dull heaviness would hover over the classroom. The young eyes seemed opaque, no light within them; they seemed not even to have noticed the teacher. Miss Diamand felt that she was talking into a void. Such days made her sick. But as soon as they had passed, she forgot about them and rushed ahead.

And so the days of August wound like a thread upon a spool. Miss Diamand barely knew when one week ended and another began. She only felt the rhythm of time — the continous speeding. It hurried her towards achievement, towards the *matura* exams and towards a new start. She already had great ideas for the forthcoming school term. She would introduce daring innovations, try new methods, learning from her mistakes of the present year. In her opinion, the teachers clung too rigidly to the pre-war system of education. Conditions were different here and the teachers should have taken advantage of the children's eagerness to learn; the two last grades should have shifted over to a university system. She, Miss Diamand, would not be shy, but would come out with her revolutionary propositions.

Again a day arrived which stopped the smooth running of her program. It was not raining or cold, but it was dreary outside and this isolated the girls in the classroom from the outside world and helped them to concentrate. The lesson went very well. It was a repetition of the material the students had learned during the past year. But unexpectedly, out of the repetition wound the eternal topic of discussion: literature and life. She should not have allowed that to happen, but the girls were impossible to control. From their seats they exchanged arguments, as if Miss Diamand were not even present.

"Literature does relate to life. Literature makes no sense and neither does life."

"Life makes as much sense as you let it."

"Our fate is not in our hands, but our behaviour is."

"Who cares about behaviour? The question is whether we can change our fate."

"We are not talking about fate but literature!" How heated she became, that argumentative Rose, a girl who lived all alone in the ghetto. "The difference between literature and life is, that life is an inharmonious solemnity while literature is a harmonious game. Those who are afraid of the unexpected in life, cling to the arts, where everything is predictable and is finished off with one of several preconceived conclusions."

Rachel Eibushitz, red-faced, disagreed with Rose violently. "Art is much more than a game. It is a protest, a form of rebellion, a desire to correct life, a craving for something that's missing . . . Every book is a search for . . ."

Little Inka sung out in a thin voice, "Every book is a dream written down. Why do people read so many books? Because they want to dream themselves out of the ghetto."

Again Rose jumped to her feet, "That's exactly the problem! Literature gives us only the illusion that it deals with life, but it only manipulates the facts of life, to make everything appear authentic, so that we might more easily be fooled by the bluff."

Rachel Eibushitz answered her again, "If I have a reproach against literature, it is, that it tries to look like a bluff, and not the reverse. Take the form of the novel, the fact that it must have a beginning, a middle and an end. Life is not like that. Beginning and end are birth and death. But in between, life flows sometimes in waves, sometimes in circles, sometimes it moves forward, sometimes it's immobilized by silence and stagnation, or by deep pits of suffering. There is a lot of . . . of non-narrative in life. While in the novel life must move . . . the story must keep on going. The new novel, of the new times, will have to free itself of that harness. Take life in the ghetto, how ought one to write a novel about the ghetto? Perhaps in such a manner that the reader should throw it away half-read. Or perhaps in such a manner that the reader should not tire of reading it over and over again?"

Rose shook her head, "What makes you think that it is at all possible to write a novel about the ghetto?"

Others agreed with her, "An honest book about the Ghetto could be anything in the world, but a work of art."

Bella Zuckerman spoke up shyly, "The real artist would find his means . . . The Ghetto is not just ugliness . . ."

"Yeah," Rose interrupted her. "And how would you write a beautiful novel about the Germans? The only thing you could write would be a call for vengeance."

"Literature does not make proclamations!" a girl called out.

"That's exactly the trouble. Literature is the so-called art of interpretation . . . of wanting to understand. And to want to understand means to forgive. Yes, forgive! And if you want to know, all the literature that we are studying is a product of Christian culture. That's why . . . Take the Jew, the thousand year old victim of hatred. How many masterpieces about his fate do you find in world literature, tell me? How come the great geniuses, the giants of world literature have not noticed this grandiose topic? And when they do notice it, they give us a Shylock or a Fagin. Because neither they nor their readers want to get to the bottom of the issue. Because this is an issue which calls for judgement, where one has to take a stand and point an accusing finger at the guilty."

Bella Zuckerman shook her head. "There is not always such a distinctive demarcation between the guilty and the innocent."

"You doubt the guilt of the Germans?"

"I doubt our own innocence. Are we innocent only because we are the victims? Is man ever innocent?"

Miss Diamand realized that she would only calm the girls by her own participation in the argument. So she raised her hand as if to ask the class permission to say something too, and after a few minutes of argument, they finally quieted down enough to hear her opinion. and this time she said the same as she would normally say on such an occasion, "*Panienki*," her voice began to rustle, "The French have a painter called Gauguin. He painted a large canvas which expresses the essence of his life's search, and he entitled it, 'Who are we? Where do we come from? Where are we going?' With these questions do religion, science and also the arts occupy themselves. Each of these systems of creative thought searches for the answers through its own means. As far as I am concerned, a work of art, while seeking the answer to these questions, must give aesthetic gratification; it must help me to see life in a new dimension; it must offer me something that intrigues me, stimulates my curiosity and satisfies it. It has both to awaken a spiritual hunger within me and to give me the feeling of spiritual satiation. It has to awaken my reason, my feelings, my senses, in a total conquest of me as a human being. And that is precisely the relationship of literature to life, as I see it. Literature is not a means of escaping from life. It rather helps us to keep attuned to life. That is why you need not be so afraid to indulge yourselves in reading. It will not let you drown in a sea of day-to-day drudgery . . . And when you get out of the ghetto and wonder why you did not become crippled, you will know that it was thanks to the freedom of mind, fostered by your studies of literature, for instance."

The bell rang and Miss Diamand no longer knew whether the lesson had been a success or a failure. The girls left the room. She remained alone steeped in thought. Then she noticed the empty benches. What was she doing among them? Her students were outside, so her place was outside as well.

The blades of grass, still green yet already withering, stood motionless, their brownish burnt tips piercing the grayness of the air. The trees seemed tired of carrying their leaves. Gossamer floated through the boughs. Bella Zuckerman came forward to meet Miss Diamand. "I wanted to tell you, Miss Diamand," the girl muttered, "that to me . . . to me . . . books mean more than life. I mean, they're more real . . . Everybody reproaches me for that . . . It is not true that I don't see what's going on around me. But what goes on in a book I see still more clearly. Is that wrong? Why?"

Miss Diamand, overcome by tenderness, smiled softly. "I will tell you a secret. I am just like you. In general, this is considered a weakness. So what? We escape from life into beauty, and only then do we realize how beautiful life is." Her smile broadened. "However, we have to go and collect our soup, because without it, literature would be no support at all." And they both joined the line-up in front of the soup kettles.

The evening came early and with it a thin rain. In the main building of the *gymnasium* a teachers' meeting was taking place. The Presess himself had come to deliver a speech about the completion of the school term. He announced that the vacations which were supposed to take place in the winter months, would instead begin in September, immediately after the distribution of the report cards and the *maturas*. The school buildings would then have to be cleared for the newly arriving Jews from the districts around Lodz, as well as for the twenty thousand Jews who were supposed to arrive from Germany.

Miss Diamand went home alone. Her head buzzed with the last sentence which Mrs. Feiner had whispered in her ear: "Our careers are finished." Miss Diamand's eyes were dry, but she saw practically nothing before her. A blindness had descended upon her, and she had to hold on to the walls in order not to stumble. She had no idea whether she was moving in the direction of her house or not. It seemed to her that she was stuck in one place, while everything else was turning around her. Somewhere in her room lay her notes, her resumés, her essays on literature, waiting for her conclusions. She raised her head and allowed the rain to drip on her face with its small cutting drops.

Someone accosted her, "Aunty, do you need a good candy, a remedy for the heart?" The unexpected words made her stumble. "Dear Heavens!" the little man in front of her exclaimed. "Don't you see where you are going?" His arm supported her. "Where do you live? I'll take you home . . . Here is a toffee, it'll put a new soul into you . . . Take it . . . try it." She felt something sweet on her lips and opend her mouth mechanically. As the sweetness dissolved in her mouth, the tears in her eyes melted and began to pour profusely down her cheeks. Through her full eyes she saw the tiny Jew who was leading her, and noticed the box suspended from his neck. He pointed the tip of his thin skimpy beard at her, "Woe is me, why are you crying all of a sudden, Aunty? A tragedy in the family, heaven forbid? But in our Scriptures it is written, that God the Almighty heals us by the very wounds he inflicts upon us. So it is written . . . We Jews have a saying that there does not exist a thing more whole than a broken heart. Aunty . . . Don't cry." She looked at him out of eyes from which the blue seemed to have drained completely. "They say," the little man did not shut his mouth for a moment, "that the best cure for sorrow is to have compassion for another person. So take pity on me. Have compassion. Last Sabbath night, my wife passed away . . . may she rest in heaven. She made these same candies with her two living hands . . . from her bit of sugar . . . made remedies for the heart, with her own heart, with her body and her life. Feel with me . . ."

The rain and the dusk enveloped them both in nebulous nets.

Chapter Twenty-one

KRAJNE SHAPSONOVITCH, or Krajne the Gold Digger, was the descendant of a family which had lived in Baluty for many generations. She did not possess any pedigree to prove this fact, since her father had had more important things to do in life than to transmit the genealogy of his long-established family of rag collectors to his heirs. Yet there exists a valid hypothesis that many years ago, when the two enterprising Jews, Blawatt and Birencwajg, set out to outsmart both the Russians and the Germans, by initiating a settlement in the village of Baluty — they had already encountered the family Shapsonovitch there, the "Gold Diggers", who, already at that time, had raised the profession of rag collecting to a high level of efficiency.

Although the Shapsonovitchs had always worked hard at their profession, it is important to state, that throughout all those years they barely earned enough to buy their bread and herring, or to pay the rabbi in their children's *heder*. Only one thing had they always possessed in abundance: hope. Every morning they would rise with the conviction that today Mother Luck would smile at them and they would find a treasure hidden in a garbage box: a diamond or a sack of gold. Because, in general, a rag collector was never just a penniless destitute person. Actually, he was a disguised rich man whose riches were temporarily not resting in his hands. He was a raggle-taggle king, searching for his crown with a long black raking iron.

Contrary to what one might assume, the Shapsonovitchs had good brains. Otherwise they could not have survived in their profession. The profession, simple though it may seem, called for a sharp mind, quick orientation and smart feet which knew where to run even before they received an order from the brain. And the collection itself had to be done with lightning speed; grabbing the truly important rags from out of the filthy piles of trash, that all looked alike in the garbage boxes, had to be done without a second's hesitation. At the same time the ears had to be alert and all the senses awake. First, because competition was tough, and second, because one was a Jew and on all sides lurked the janitors with their brooms and their wives with the full slop pails, while in the street were policemen with their clubs and the Polish boys with their sticks and stones.

Fortunately, the Shapsonovitchs were prepared by nature for their profession. They had rounded backs and sloping shoulders, the better to face the ground while working or receiving blows. Their hands were swift, their legs short and strong, the better to do what was necessary and vanish. They had large ears, the better to hear danger approaching, and they had roving eyes, so they could see a thousand things at once. On top of that, the colour of their skin was gray and the colour of their hair was ashen, a camouflage which rendered them indistinguishable from garbage. That was how the men looked.

Of the women there were several categories. In general there was trouble with the womenfolk until they grew old. In their youth — and they came into the profession before the boys did, because the latter had to attend the *heder* — they attracted too much attention with their straight backs, bright faces and hot eyes beaming out from behind the plaids covering their heads. Later on, when their time for childbearing arrived, they were even worse. They became big and heavy and their alertness was dulled, because their minds were at home with the small fry. Only after the childbearing years would they excel in the profession, sometimes even surpassing the men. They had the fantastic talent of distinguishing, in the wink of an eye, the good merchandise from the bad. And quite often a woman would take over the entire business, leaving the men to play second fiddle. There was however another category of woman who was never suited to the profession. In their youth these women had butterflies in their heads, and in old age — lead in their feet; they had no other talent but to breed and to cook.

Krajne came into this world with one single flaw: she was too pretty. She had a headful of wild black curls and her cheeks were eternally red. Every time she was taken along to work, she brought misfortune. One day, when a policeman twisted her hand out of its joint, the entire gang was almost caught. After that, they refused to take her along to the backyards. But Krajne, who loved the profession and was proud and stubborn besides, refused to accept the verdict of the family. She set out to cover the backyards on her own, and Mother Luck smiled upon her. Before long, she had her own gang of rag collectors and it gradually became clear to everyone that it was Krajne, who had been born under the right star. It was predicted that one bright day the great treasure would fall into no other hands but hers. And who knows whether this might not indeed have been the case, had she not fallen head over heels in love with Feivish Kuropatwa, who was a weaver and had no relationship whatsoever to the rag collecting profession.

Feivish was a gay fellow who always whistled or hummed when he passed Piaskova Street where the rag collectors lived. His small black eyes warmly appraised every girl. Summertime, he usually walked with an ice-cream cone, so that the girls could see his red tongue and moist lips ready for kissing. On his way home from work he, as a rule, passed first through the neighbouring Feifer Street which harboured all the whore houses belonging to the fellows of the underworld. He could sometimes be seen standing there by a gate, talking and gesticulating, surrounded by a bunch of half-naked prostitutes and tough guys. People whispered in each other's ears that Feivish wanted to make a "barricade" out of Feifer Street. What the meaning of the word "barricade" was no one had the faintest idea, but there was no doubt in anyone's mind that this smelled of danger — of "vervolution", which literally meant that all the gals and guys would take up the red flag, march to city hall and set it on fire. It was indeed a wonder that after Feivish's speeches the inhabitants of the street let him leave with all his bones intact. Wintertime, instead of an ice-cream, Feivish walked home with a little harmonica at his lips, or played his comb — until the frost almost let go and the ice almost cracked. The hearts of the girls melted.

That Feivish was a ne'er-do-well, Krajne discovered only after their wedding.

He was a dismal bread-winner who refused to hear about becoming a *mentsch*. At the same time he considered himself a proud "proletariat" and looked down on the profession of rag collecting. He called the collectors no more and no less than "the refuse of Polish Jewry", and warned them that when "socialismus" arrived, rag collecting would cease to be an occupation at all.

Krajne lived with her Feivish in two little rooms on Piaskowa Street. Right after the wedding, they put in a weaving stool, while Krajne began her childbearing period. The harmony between the couple would perhaps have continued, because Krajne, in spite of Feivish's faults, was in love with him. However, the trouble was that he would by no means allow her to join the gang of rag collectors. "I want a mother for my children," he said calmly, "and I will earn our bread and herring!" That was all he wanted: bread and herring! While she would under no circumstances live without the hunt for happiness, without the hope that tomorrow might be the great day, the day the miracle happened. Thus Krajne began to relieve her heavy heart against him, her "calamity". Along with curses, she threw pieces of furniture at him, pounded him with her bare fists and later on she even used the disciplinary whip she had bought for her children. But Feivish did not seem to mind this. If she hit him, he was merely amused, he clamped her hands behind her back until she let him kiss her, then he took her to bed.

Little by little, the fire within her subsided. She saw her children grow up, go to school and learn to write real Polish letters, like the children of the rich. Of course she noticed that they lacked the craftiness, the dexterity of the other rag collectors' children, that they were becoming *schlemiels*, to whom one could not talk without using the whip. But nevertheless she herself began to feel more refined, and sometimes it even seemed to her that she had already found her happiness. Slowly, she began to listen to what Feivish was reading aloud from the newspapers, and the world, which had in her mind been divided into people with raking irons and those without, became divided into rich and poor. She realized that raking irons were not for searching through the garbage boxes, but for bringing down on the heads of the "capitalismus" who lived in the rich streets. She came to the conclusion that the world was no good and that one ought to change it. True, she did not cease quarrelling with her husband who failed to earn even the bread and herring he had promised, but she began to respect him too.

Then the war broke out and all that had so neatly been arranged in Krajne's head, became rearranged again. The world became divided, no longer into rich and poor, but into Jews and Germans. And in the ghetto proper there was Rumkowski and his *shishkas*, on one side, and the *klepsidras* on the other. But Krajne no longer had time to clarify all these things. There was something more important for her to achieve: survival.

As soon as the war broke out, Feivish showed just what kind of a *schlemiel* he really was. There was no work, and the weaver's stool went into the fire. If Feivish signed up for work in the Community House, to replace the rich Jews who wanted to free themselves from working for the Germans, he came home bruised, with black eyes and wounds in his legs. The few marks he brought home were barely enough to cook a pot of soup. But what really made Krajne explode with rage was Feivish's gaiety. Here the world was turning upside down, and Feivish walked around humming, whistling and laughing. "What on earth is this great happiness that has come over you?" she screamed as she bandaged his bruised legs. "Do you ever see a normal person laughing nowadays? That's why the *Yekes* beat you up. Your thievish eyes. You probably laughed straight into their faces!"

Feivish tickled her under the chin, or pinched her full breasts. "They will end with their heads in the ground, and the world will be saved."

"You will end up with your head in the ground before they do, my calamity!" She half pushed him away and half delighted in his hands crawling over her body.

Then the ghetto was established, and hunger reigned over the little rooms on Piaskowa Street. Krajne was unable to sleep at night. Her mind worked frantically, but she could not come up with any solution. The sight of her children cut her heart. In the mornings she wanted to quarrel with Feivish, or throw something at his head, so as to relieve the bitterness of her heart at his expense, but when she looked at him in the morning, her stomach would constrict with compassion. For Feivish was not singing or laughing. The sight of him made here appetite for a quarrel vanish. Now she missed his gaiety. "Feivish, woe is me," she cried, "what has come over you? You are like a block of wood. A man who won't allow himself to whistle the whole day long, or to give a smile? Have you lost a shipful of sourmilk in the ocean, or what?"

"The ghetto . . ." Feivish helplessly spread his hands.

"The Ghetto, the shmetto. So what's the big tragedy? Have they thrown you out of your palaces, or your salons? You have been a *Reichs-Baluter* for generations, after all."

Feivish shook his head, "The barbed wires . . ."

In the meantime they had to fill their stomachs and Krajne set out into the streets. There was nothing left to do but steal from the passing food carts, or walk about the Vegetable Place and pick up whatever she could, or pull the boards out of the fences. And it was true that Krajne had a lucky star. At whatever she undertook, she succeeded. Her strong feet were capable of walking the length and breadth of a city, and they served her superbly when she had to flee from the police. She brought home turnips and potatoes, carrots and beets, so that the family no longer feared starvation. Then another good thing happened. Feivish grew tired of searching for something to do, and began to accompany her into the ghetto; he too brought home whatever he could. It was a kind of second honeymoon for the two of them, even though Feivish no longer laughed and his eyes were no longer roguish and gay; he grew old, and his hair began to gray. But when the children came home from school, the oven was lit, and Krajne and Feivish were cooking and washing the dishes together. Such a sweet life Krajne had never known before, and she grew prettier from day to day, as if for her the years were moving backwards, in spite of the wild war that was playing havoc with the world. On top of that, she began to feel important too. She was now equal with all the other Jews, for better or worse.

But just as Krajne had a lucky star, Feivish had an unlucky one. Three times he was caught stealing trifles, once a board, another time a few potatoes, the third time he was caught as he took out the food ration: he had sneaked through to the sack of peas and thrust a fistful of them into his pocket. When he was caught for the fourth time, he was led off to the jail and was held there.

Krajne had a hole in her heart. She could not live without Feivish. When

Feivish, one bright day, announced to her through the bars of the prison gate that he would be sent to Germany the following morning, the world collapsed for her. She cried and moaned all night, not knowing what to do. She wanted to sign up and join him as other wives did, but she had children and she had to stay. She found Feivish's old mouth-harmonica and brought it to him in prison, along with half a loaf of bread and a coffee *baba*. Feivish looked at her with extinguished eyes while she consoled him, "You see, you're getting rid of the barbed wires." He only had time to tell her to take care of the children, before they tore him away from her.

Krajne remembered well what Feivish had told her, and now the world became divided into herself and her children, on one side, and the rest of the people, her enemies, on the other. Now she really began to show what she was capable of. There were already many Resorts in the ghetto where she could work, but she told herself that she had better things to do than to work for Rumkowski and the Germans. To pluck a hair from a pig's back was also a good deed, and she signed up for an allowance. She also took her children out of school. True, they received a soup there and they studied, but nowadays there was only one thing that children had to study: the art of survival. And for teaching that subject she relied on no one. She wanted to have them near her, so that they could help her, while they learned how to manage. The times were bad, and man like an animal had to keep his nails sharp. So Krajne thought during these sleepless nights when she missed Feivish. Her heart was now full of one kind of compassion — for her children; and she had only one purpose in life — to keep them healthy. Everything else was garbage.

She had never been a thief, and here, in the ghetto, she did not become one either. The real thief was Rumkowski and his clique. She and her children were doing a sacred deed: they were struggling for life. And, indeed the children ceased to be *schlemiels*. They regained the sharpness and dexterity of the Shapsonovitch family. Like little bloodhounds they would scour the Ghetto and they never came home empty-handed. Krajne was delighted. She knew that if, heaven forbid, something happened to her, they would be able to manage without her.

She never tired of teaching her children how a person should be able to navigate through and dodge out from under unfavourable situations, letting them have a taste of both the "hot and the cold". Even when a policeman caught and arrested one of them and she trembled inwardly with fear and knocked at the doors of important *shishkas*, until her child was freed — even then she was satisfied that her brood had passed the test of fire. Apart from that, she herself did not miss a day without treating the children with a couple of wallops, a few slaps, or a lash of the disciplinary whip. That too helped to harden them. And since, for their own good, she would refrain from caressing them, she could at least in this manner show them her love. Only at night, when they were asleep, did she allow herself to set free her motherly feelings. She cuddled the children, kissed them and pressed them to her bosom. But if one of them, on account of these caresses, woke up, she immediately withdrew and scolded him, "Why don't you sleep, you bastard?"

The children were a happy lot. Her oldest, Zipa-Deborah, was ten years old. Zajvel the first born son, was nine, and the two youngest, Shmerl and Berl were six and seven respectively. Krajne spoke to them as if they were her peers. She knew that they did not understand everything she said, but she was of the opinion that to talk to them as one talks to children would spoil them. However, since the children resembled Feivish in their temperaments, they replied to everything she said with a laugh or with "nine measures of chatter".

In the meantime, Krajne became her normal self again, and even more so. She was always in good spirits, as if she had taken over Feivish's pre-war cheerfulness. More than once she caught herself talking like him, and it seemed to her that even her laughter carried the echo of Feivish's voice. In her gaiety, she now longed for him. Sometimes it seemed to her that he was present, hiding somewhere in the room and ogling her with his piercing thievish eyes. She hoped to be reunited with him after the war, and with increasing fervour she moved heaven and earth so that she might live to see that moment.

Last year, most of the fences in the ghetto had been taken apart and the boards stolen. The demolished houses were heavily guarded and firewood was not easy to come by. So Krajne had moved all her belongings to the room where the stove stood, and locked up the other empty one. Unexpectedly, that empty room came to provide Krajne with enough money to pay for an entire food ration. She really did have a lucky star. One day, an elegant gentleman appeared on the threshold of her apartment — rain-drenched and very sad. He asked whether she had an empty cellar and she showed him the empty little room. He said something about a dog, mumbling in an incomprehensible Polish, and finally counted out twenty brand-new *rumkis* on to the table. He left never to return and there was no doubt in Krajne's mind that Elijah the Prophet himself had appeared before her to help her and her children.

She had long believed with unwavering faith that Elijah the Prophet was living in the ghetto. The women who sat outside, on the doorsteps, often discussed him. They said that he had decided that the Messiah would come in spring, but then he had postponed the event until the first frost. He even gave a sign: when the first snow came down with thunder and lightning — on that day the Germans would come to their terrible end. Openly, Krajne laughed at these tales. Feivish had told her that the prophet Elijah had been long dead. But deep in her heart she, along with the other womenfolk, believed in the presence of the blessed protector. More than once would she hurry home from the streets with the premonition that she would again find a wad of money on the table, or come face to face with the prophet Elijah who spoke Polish. She was expecting him. It was the right time for him to come. A day did not pass that she did not think of him in the morning, as soon as she opened her eyes — think of him as she had once thought of finding a treasure hidden in a garbage box.

And he did indeed come again. One day during that summer, he reappeared on the doorstep at dusk. She was alone in the house. The children were running around somewhere, not, heaven forbid, busy with childish games, but looking for some work to do after dark. She herself was standing near the open door, chopping up potato peels on the table. Outside, on their doorsteps, her female neighbours were sitting, chatting about him — Elijah the Prophet. The evening was the best time to talk about him. Sometimes they said that he was disguised as a lame doctor, other times, that he was a vendor of candies. It was said that he performed miracles: that he blew on a sick person, and that sick person immediately recovered and returned to work as if nothing had happened, or if a person was approaching a state of madness due to hunger,

Elijah's breath made him lose his appetite on the spot and feel as well as a newborn baby. Sometimes the womenfolk said that the prophet Elijah was none other than Rumkowski himself who created food with the help of miracles. Krajne laughed inwardly at them. They should have come to ask her who Elijah the Prophet was. Oh, how many times had she been eager to boast! But she bit her tongue. Elijah was hers, only hers and her children's.

So, as she stood there, chopping the potato peels, she cast a glance outside, and the chopper almost fell out of her hand. An elderly gentleman, with a big bald head and dropping flabby cheeks, issued from the depth of the street. He marched vigorously, casting looks at the houses and the women sitting on the thresholds. She wanted to rush out to meet him, but her feet turned into lumps of clay. Then it occurred to her that he might turn away and vanish. With all her strength she conquered the weakness in her legs and stepped forward so that he would notice her. Suddenly, he was standing before her, smiling, his mouth full of metal tooth caps. "I once . . ." he said in broken Yiddish. "Perhaps you remember me? Do you still have the free room?"

Krajne jumped away from the door and let the visitor step over the threshold. In her mind's eye she could already see the brand new *rumkis* on the table, and it did not even enter her mind that he might ask for the twenty *rumkis* back, since he had never used the room at all. "Sure . . . sure . . . Sir." She almost called him, "Mr. Elijah the Prophet".

"How much?" he asked.

"Twenty," she replied. A brand new bill of twenty *rumkis* lay in her palm. And before she had managed to come to herself, the stranger was gone. She was sure that he would not return to move in, just as he had not the first time. Consequently, when she saw him the following morning on the threshold with two suitcases in his hands, she was struck dumb. She moved about as if intoxicated, not understanding what had happened to her. Small thing! Of all the Jews in the ghetto, he chose to live with her, with Krajne!

A few times she entered his little room. She wanted to cover the bed with the only sheets and pillowcase in her possession which she kept hidden, for the wedding-day of her daughter, Zipa-Deborah. She and the children always slept on red pillows full of holes from which half the feathers had escaped; they covered themselves with the torn plaids that she had found in the garbage boxes. But the guest waved his hand, "I'll bring my own bedding." Then he asked her whether she had a key to the room. Surprised, she answered that she did not. He who had chosen to live with her, should suspect her, the saintly woman Krajne, of stealing? But she quickly calmed down. Obviously, he had to be able to lock himself inside, in order to be alone when he carried out his secret important deeds.

He left with the two empty suitcases to bring back some more things, and she could not resist entering his room, on tiptoe, as if she were afraid that he might hear her. She went over to the bed and cast a glance at the things that were heaped upon it. She was dazzled. She saw a man's shirts of pure silk and batiste, thin and fresh as snow petals, and long drawers of the sort she had never seen in her life before, soft as butter and light as feathers, and socks with designs, and fluffy towels, and a suit somewhat creased but of the best English material, and shoes of fresh and shiny leather, and batiste handkerchiefs! On all these things were embroidered flowery Polish letters. No, they were not the monograms of Elijah the Prophet — and yet she was still convinced, that the man who had come to live with her, was an unusual personality. No ordinary person would possess such clothing after such a long time in the ghetto. And if he were a *shishka*, he would not stoop so low as to move into a decrepit shabby place like hers. She had a great temptation to take one of the batiste handkerchiefs for a talisman, but she scolded herself. It was an unclean deed to take without asking.

When he returned with the two suitcases, he saw her hanging up a pair of curtains full of holes which created a complicated design of their own. He opened one of the suitcases and took out an eiderdown blanket, an eiderdown pillow and sheets with pillowcases. Then he opened the other suitcase and took out a pot, glasses and plates. "Perhaps I could cook for you, Sir . . .?" she proposed shyly.

He shook his head, "Not necessary."

He waited for her to leave, which she did as she felt her eyes filling. In her mind, she called on Feivish to assist her. "Look, Feivish, what an idiot your wife has become! Have you ever known the prophet Elijah to walk about without a skull cap, with no beard or sidelocks and as bald as a monk? Have you ever known the prophet Elijah to want to cook for himself?" She felt an even greater rage against the women, the chatterboxes outside, who had turned her head with their tales. And she burst into sobs — inwardly — on account of her loneliness. But in order to help master herself in the emptiness which engulfed her, she put her hand into her bosom, and drew out the brand-new bill of twenty *rumkis*.

So Adam Rosenberg came to live on Piaskowa Street. He was recovering after an experience which had shaken him to the depths of his being. This experience had little to do with his wife Yadwiga's illness, or her stay in the hospital, or even with her deportation. Nor was it related to his son Mietek's loss of his job as a policeman and his abandonment of his father. What had shaken Adam so deeply was his own toothache. The pain in his mouth was a long day-by-day shock which played on his nerves, bit into his brain and crushed the apathy in his bones — so that he had again begun to struggle for his life.

Yadwiga's illness had started imperceptibly a few weeks after Sutckha had died and Reisel the cook had gone back to work for the Zuckermans. At that time, Adam was spending entire days in bed, neither dressing nor undressing; while Yadwiga was forced to get up early, powder her face, smear her lips with lipstick, dress, and with a dainty apron around her hips, begin her work in the kitchen. Through the house rolled the sound of Reisel's dry voice which gave off a metallic echo. Then came the crash of broken dishes, followed by Reisel's short laugh which sounded like a faucet spitting water on a tin surface. And then, more talk, louder, more vehement. Then, a weird little laugh, sharp and squeaky, reminiscent of the yelp of a dog on whose tail someone had stepped. After that, the smell of something burning began to permeate the house.

One day, Yadwiga appeared in the bedroom, carrying a bowl between her manicured nails. The bowl was steaming and the steam wrapped her head in a transparent fog. She lowered her humid shiny face to Adam; the fresh powder she wore was full of grooves, the red of her lips was smeared around her chin and under her nose. Her protruding eyes shone through the steam with an alien light. She sat down beside him, stirring the soup and blowing at the steam. The smell of burnt soup mixed with the smell of Yadwiga's perfume was nauseating. Adam let her feed him. After all, it was all the same to him whether he ate or not. He felt no taste in his mouth. Between one spoonful and the next, Yadwiga tucked him in and caressed him over the blanket, smiling at him with her smeared lips — an eerie, servile smile. He did not know what disgusted him more: the sight of the soup or the sight of her.

Finally, he chased her away. The next moment he heard her open Mietek's door, then Mietek's exclamation, "I don't want to eat such dung!" Adam could hear a jingling of plates and spoons. A dish was broken. Squeaky laughter followed, then Mietek's shouts carried over from the kitchen, "I bring home enough money for you to make food I could swallow!"

Then again he heard Reisel's tinny voice ring out monotonously, followed by the squeaky bark-like yelp. The utensils clattered. The house was already awake. The water in the washroom hissed. Doors were being opened and shut. Samuel's bootsteps thumped. Then Adam heard Yadwiga through the wall, calling her son, "You haven't kissed me, my baby!" The next moment she was back with Adam, and still wearing her dress and apron, got into his bed. Her hands slid under his shirt. With her sharp nails she combed his hairy chest. "Kiss me, Adam, please," she squeaked.

It seemed to Adam that he was clamped up by a pack of snakes. Her fingers were ice cold. The feel of her breath against his ear was disgusting. He turned his head away, so as not to see her submissive dog-like eyes. Yes, Reisel the cook was right. Sutchka was peering out from Yadwiga's eyes. The memory of Sutckha awoken in him by Yadwiga's gaze was unbearable. "Leave me alone!" He tore her hands away from him.

She removed her clothes and stood naked before him. It was cold in the room. She began to shake, her drooping empty breasts resembled two undulating pouches of leather. "Look, Adam, I am still pretty." She turned about before him, barefoot, on the cold floor. Then she doubled up beside the bed. "Take me back in, Adam, I am cold . . . I'm shivering." She slid under the cover and hugged him with her ice-cold legs and her stiff frozen arms. Her cheeks were moist and cold; they stuck to his face. It seemed to him that it was death taking him into its arms. He tore himself away from her and moved over to the other side of the bed. "Warm me up . . ." she whined. He felt the burnt soup inside his stomach. Salty water came up to his mouth. He sat up, took his head between his hands and scratched his scalp. He shivered. His teeth chattered, until the despair threatened to overwhelm him. He tried to push Yadwiga out of the bed, but her arms manacled his neck. "Love me, Adam," she squeaked "Love me, because I will die . . ." He began to hit her on the shoulders, on the chest and belly with all his strength, but her face began to clear with his blows. She even smiled, as if each blow were a caress. At length, he tore himself away from her and jumped out of the bed. He began to dress hastily. She too jumped out of the bed and dressed. She approached the mirror and began to paint her face. Then she found the food cards and hurried on her coat, hat and gloves. She threw him a kiss from the door, "I'll bring the food ration!" Immediately he scrambled back into bed. His mind was blank. He fell into a deep sleep. Lately he had acquired a heavy sleepiness in his bones. He could sleep days and nights in a row, if they let him.

These scenes with Yadwiga were repeated often. Little by little he had become used to hitting her with his fist every time she slid naked into his bed.

He stopped doing this in rage — but rather did it matter-of-factly, in order to have peace. After such a scene, she usually became full of energy. She would dress, and rush about, bringing in basins of water and scrubbing brushes. Day after day she scrubbed the floor, while singing or giggling to herself; she seemed to take a demonic delight in crawling on all fours. Then she scrubbed the floors of the other rooms, the corridor, the kitchen, the toilet and the muddy staircase. One day Mietek moved Yadwiga's bed back into the bedroom. "Here is your place!" he shouted enraged. The eyes of father and son met in a knot of gazes: venom against venom. Adam had long since become indifferent to all the people in this world, except his son — him he had sincerely begun to hate.

So Adam slept in the same room as Yadwiga. Sometimes he was woken up by the feeling that Sutchka was lying near his bed, howling. When he opened his eyes, it became clear to him that this was Yadwiga howling. He pulled the cover over his head and went back to sleep. Sometimes he felt her fingers creeping over his body. She seemed to remember the caresses which she had given him many years ago; now she replayed them on his body. At the remembrance of his bygone passions, everything would shrink inside him. Fear overcame him; her caresses awoke in him a revulsion towards any female body.

One day in May, she returned from the street, wearing one of her full summer dresses which he had once bought for her in Paris. The dress was blue with huge red flowers embroidered above its hem. Once this dress had fitted her well. It had enhanced her graceful figure and made her appear both slim and well rounded. Now, of course, the dress hung on her. The large décolleté revealed her protruding chestbones and the bare shoulders displayed her joints in the minutest detail. But the colours of the dress had remained lively, completely erasing the effect of Yadwiga's waxen complexion. This was a walking dress, above which hung a red smeared mouth. Adam's eyes drank in the freshness of the flowers around the skirt, without noticing the two large holes in the material above her knees. Was she really so pale? No, it was the dress that made her pale. She held a scrap of paper in her hand. One of her cheeks stood out as if swollen. She smacked her lips as if she were kissing something, and in this way she approached her bed. Her protruding eyes were opaque, dead; she seemed to be cross-eyed or blind. It was precisely this gaze that caused him to divert his eyes from the dress and concentrate on her.

"You see," she said, and her voice was changed as well. "He loves me, and he gives me candies." She fell down on her bed and remained prostrated on it, with her arms spread out. Sweat appeared on her forehead. She said nothing more. He listened but could not hear her breath. This brought him out of his apathy. He shook her. Then she gave him a glance from out of the corner of her eye, and her voice, strange, hollow, seemed to be coming out from deep inside her. "I put on this dress," she said. "Spring outside . . . People turned their heads to look at me. Then I saw Him looking at me from the other side of the fence . . . Handsome like a god, in His uniform with a shiny buckle on his belt, in the riding pants . . . the gun . . . the helmet. I sent Him a kiss. He hurried over and asked me to walk along the wire fence with Him. He on the other side . . . I on this side. We strolled. He devoured me with his eyes and led me away from the bridge . . . to be more intimate. Then He stopped, He stared at me . . . God stared at me. He asked me to raise my arms and turn my face to the wall. I felt the wall from head to toe. The gun jingled. I was grateful to Him. I wanted to give myself to Him, like this . . . in *extase d'amour*. But I wanted Him to remember me . . . my name. I let myself down to the ground and on all fours crawled over to Him . . . to the fence . . . to his boots. Now He stared at me with one big eye . . . in the muzzle of the gun. So I said straight into this eye, 'My name is Sutchka, Herr Gott.' That's what I said, and He was surprised to hear that. He took out the scrap of paper with the candies from his pocket, and threw it to me over the fence. He chased me away . . . I refused to move. I wanted Him to love me . . . with the muzzle. A policeman pulled me away . . ." Her talk became incomprehensible. The candy jumped lightly between her teeth before it stopped. Unexpectedly, Adam's long-dead sexual urge awoke in him with such power that it almost blinded him. Without delay he mounted fainting Yadwiga.

A few times during that afternoon Yadwiga opened her eyes, rattling incomprehensible words, as if she wanted to convey something to the ceiling. Adam lay covered up in bed, sleeping. Only at dusk did Mietek storm into the room with a yell, "Where is my food?" He noticed Yadwiga lying prostrate on her bed, her open eyes showing only the whites. His voice stuck in Mietek's throat. For a moment he stood there, stunned, then he burst into the kitchen with alarm.

Reisel came running in. "The woman is gone!" was her verdict, as she began to slap Yadwiga's face so hard that her cheeks turned red. Reisel sent Mietek to fetch some water. She splashed Yadwiga's face with it. This brought back the pupils from behind her eyelids. They were like two black suns appearing from under two horizons. With the tip of her tongue she threw out the remainder of the candy from her mouth and smiled at the ceiling. "Call me Sutchka," she moaned.

All night, in his sleep, Adam heard Yadwiga's dog-like whining. In the morning she got up fresh and lively, made herself pretty before the mirror and entered the kitchen. Soon there came the sound of barking, along with Reisel's screams, "A *dybbuk* has entered her!" A noise arose in the corridor. Then Mietek appeared in the bedroom with Yadwiga hanging on his arm. She dropped on the bed like a block of wood. Her son stood over her, his face gray, his lips trembling. He resembled the little Mietek of years ago, as he had stood by the open door of their little palace, watching his parents leave for a trip abroad. Adam tried not to look at Mietek. At this moment he was afraid of him.

Yadwiga would go through a few phases during the day. Either she stood in front of the mirror, dressing, or she crawled on all fours, barking, or wailing, or she would faint. She no longer cooked any meals, so Reisel came to Adam with the proposition, "For twelve marks a week I'll cook for you . . . and about your wife you have nothing to worry. Mietek will support her until the doctor finds a place for her in the madhouse." Adam drew out his pocketbook from under the mattress and handed her the twelve marks.

Adam did not know why, but he began to lock himself up with Yadwiga in the bedroom. This reminded him of the days when he had hid with Sutchka. He even kept the windows shut, as he had before, so that Yadwiga's howls would not be heard outside. His bond with her at first consisted of one single thing: their fear of Reisel. Their existence depended on her. At every knock at the door they would both shudder. The clip-clop of Reisel's slippers sounded like the steps of an ogress, treading over skulls and crushing them. Her talk was like burning pellets poured over one's head. When she appeared in the room with the precious food in her bony hands, they both, like dogs, stretched their avid muzzles out to her, their master, as if she had brought them a good bone to chew on.

Imperceptibly at first, Adam let Yadwiga drag him into her macabre games. He would fondle her as he had used to fondle Sutchka, and when she lay down beside him in his bed, he sometimes responded eagerly to her caresses. He felt that his manliness was returning to him in an unmanly, unfathomable manner. He was sleeping not with a woman, but with a bitch, while he himself was a dog. That awareness brought an enormous fright upon him. He became convinced that Yadwiga was pulling him down into her dark pits, that like a spider she was entangling him in her web, which he both desired and feared, choking on his anxiety.

He had weird nightmares. He was falling into an abyss from which he tried to climb out with tooth and nail. But the walls were slippery. His tooth and nail had nothing to hook on to, and he fell back — down — deeper still — into a gruesome state of oblivion. Sometimes, while awake, when he watched Yadwiga during her attack of crawling on all fours, he would throw himself at her, pommel her with his fists and kick her with his feet. Her smiling face, her inability to feel pain made him wild, bringing him to the verge of insanity. He had a mighty desire to clamp his fingers around her thin loose neck, in order to break through her insensitivity to pain. With her scream of agony he wanted to tear apart the nets in which she had enveloped him.

In the evenings Mietek would remove Yadwiga from the bedroom, leaving Adam with her smell, with Sutchka's smell in his nostrils. From the other side of the door, the sounds of a lively commotion would reach his ears. Yes, they all seemed united against him, by a bond of hatred. They blamed him for everything — and made a great fuss over Yadwiga. She had become their plaything. She made them feel kind. From all sides Adam heard them calling his son, as if thanks to his crazy mother Mietek too had become a more important personality. Oh, he did not give a hoot about them anyway. The only one about whom he cared was Mietek. He hated and feared him.

Once, during the night, the sound of Mietek's sobs reached Adam's ears through the wall. Adam's fear of him became so powerful that it tore him out of his bed. He hurried on his clothes and ran out of the house as if someone were chasing him. Outside, the fresh night air made his head turn. Like a drunk he began to trot about the soft dark beds of soil. His dizziness almost knocked him off his feet. He fell towards the cherry tree, embraced its trunk with his arms and put his hot cheek against its cool bark. A man wearing an armband came running towards him. In the dark the man's eyes multiplied into hundreds, thousands of dancing eyes.

"My head is turning," Adam groaned. The man moved a box towards Adam who slumped down on it, holding the treetrunk in his embrace. Then he leaned his back against it and looked up. Above him the boughs were spread out low, like an umbrella. White blossoms were strewn over the ground like pieces of a torn white tablecloth. Petals like snowflakes fell noiselessly from the boughs. He swept a few off his pate. The shadow of the Jew with the white armband moved among the beds of soil, as if that Jew were the watchman of the surrounding silence. From there came a soft singing voice, half spoken, half hummed words, soothing, like the rustling of boughs. The tightness around Adam's head relaxed, the hoops pressing against it disintegrated. Adam's memory went blank. Even the tree vanished. Calm like a sponge erased the world. When he opened his eyes, it was dawn. He noticed the night watchman pacing energetically, stamping his feet and making rowing movements with his arms. Adam thrust his hand into his pocket. He wanted to pay the man, though he did not exactly know why. His pocket was empty. He had left his pocket-book upstairs under the mattress, unprotected against Reisel! He raced towards the stairs.

Upstairs, he was immediately trapped in the nightmarish cobwebs weaving around Yadwiga. They enmeshed his brain, his eyes, his ears and nostrils. He longed for the mild perfume of the cherry tree which he saw when he looked down at it through the closed window. He was amazed. What was the power of that nothing of a tree that it could so calm a man's mind? But he did not linger at the window for more than a few minutes. His thoughts, his cravings were disrupted by Yadwiga's crying or laughing, disrupted by her hands clasping his legs. Again he let her drag him away from the light, spin him into her forsakenness; he allowed himself to sink along with her into her abyss. But when he found himself in the same pit the following night, he saw a bough high above him, like a hand with white fingers. Sometimes it seemed to him in his nightmare that a moment would soon come, when he would be able to climb up and grab that bough.

Finally, the day came when Mietek took Yadwiga to the hospital for the insane. Adam stood at the window, following them with his eyes. That was the last he ever saw of her, because for these few hours when Mietek tried to save her from deportation by sneaking her out of the hospital, Adam was already preoccupied with his toothache.

The night after she left, he went down to the cherry tree. As he sat there huddled up, he noticed a long double shadow near the stairs to the cellar. The shadow jumped over the wall and vanished in the entrance. Adam said to himself, "That is death coming for me too, but I am not at home."

He was completely alone. His only link with life was Reisel. It was she who every once in a while disturbed the rhythm of his agonizing existence, an existence filled with sweaty trepidations, with the echoes of Yadwiga's howls and with the reflection of little Mietek's eyes following him from a thousand thresholds. Mietek himself, Adam no longer saw or heard. Sometimes he wanted to ask Reisel about him, but after all it did not matter. The weeks rushed on while time stood still, congealed in the air of the room, transforming it from light into darkness, from darkness into light. A few more times he made an effort to go downstairs and sit by the cherry tree. But the tree had changed with the passing of time. The snow petals had vanished. Red shiny cherries beamed above Adam's head like tiny red light bulbs. Then the rains began to sprinkle the tree, and the cherries began to resemble Yadwiga's red protruding eyes. The drops dripping down from them were her tears. After that he never went down to the tree, and so lost even that pleasure.

Apathy held him so strongly in its grip that he felt or remembered nothing. His mind was a void filled with dullness. Yadwiga and Sutchka had never existed, neither had Mietek, nor the cherry tree. He even ceased to fear Reisel. He felt no hunger, nor did he know what he was eating. He forgot to smoke his cigars. The only thing he did was go to the washroom, and accomplishing this feat became increasingly difficult for him. His legs refused to carry him. Sometimes he wondered whether he had any legs at all. When he looked at them, he did not recognize them — no more than a pair of sticks which shook at the knees as if broken.

During one of those days, Mietek appeared before him. He seemed taller than Adam remembered him. His hands also seemed enormous. He approached the bed and pounced on Adam. "It's all because of you! Of you! You!" he roared. Adam had no idea whom Mietek had in mind or what it was all about. Then it became dark and everything vanished. He had no notion whether this had happened while he was awake or asleep.

He ceased to realize who Reisel actually was. A mouth talked to him and he obeyed its orders. She would come for money and he would pull his pocketbook out from under the mattress. Until one day he was unable to find anything in the pocketbook and the mouth said to him, "We are quits." The mouth suggested to him that he sell Yadwiga's things and retain only the most important of his own belongings. For a time the strange normalcy of his existence continued. Then Reisel appeared with a bowl of food, and the mouth was saying, "Mr. Rosenberg, you're kicking the bucket," and quietly it added, "You have a mouth full of gold, Mr. Rosenberg, sell the caps on your teeth and save your life . . . I know of a technician . . ."

Then he felt that he was lying with his mouth open, while someone was scrubbing, digging inside it, drilling and pounding in his gums and in his entire skull.

And so it all started. In the paralysis of his mind, Adam began to feel the thin needles pricking inside his mouth as though a sewing machine were sewing together his gums with slow deep stitches. With surprise and curiosity he waited from one stitch to the other. They arrived, now from one side of his mouth, now from the other. He tried to guess where the next stitch would come from and, to his amazement, the stitches became increasingly bigger. Now they threaded through his nose, then they reached his eyes, or pinched him suddenly in the temples. He was fully awake and no longer amazed or surprised. And so he surrendered to the stitches which spread over his whole face and his head, stretching from his hands down to his feet, pulling a sharp thread through his very heart. He had never thought that such a state of wakefulness could exist. The needles woke up every nerve in his body, each nerve becoming sensitive to every breath he inhaled. All his being had turned into a nerve-like surface which in turn began to prick the surrounding air — not him. When he gave a shudder, it seemed to him that the air itself was shuddering. He stopped feeling.

Then, at a certain moment, he caught sight of the moving mouth. "So, what's new?" it asked. Reisel's voice was sweet; the hands adjusting his pillow were motherly soft. "I'll feed you, Mr. Rosenberg," the mouth said. "You're weak." She sat down at the edge of his bed and placed the bowl in her lap. "He has a pair of golden hands, this technician. You didn't give a peep. And do you know what a treasure you had in your mouth? Don't ask. Now you'll be able to live like a king and I'll put you back on your feet, rely on me. If Reisel says so . . . So, open your mouth." He opened his mouth and she poured in a spoonful of food. He burst out with a roar. His entire body jumped up in the air.

Having swallowed the spoonful of food, he calmed down somewhat. Then he heard his own voice, "Where is Mietek?" he asked.

The mouth above him smiled, snarling, "You don't know? He moved out!"

She pushed another spoonful between his lips. He jumped again as if all the nerve threads in his mouth were on fire. "And my wife?" he asked, howling.

"The whole hospital on Joy Street has been deported. Yes, our tragedy is great . . . But she tortured you good and proper, Mr. Rosenberg. Such a diseased person could suck the marrow out of one's bones . . . Don't worry . . . I saw everything." She fed him another spoonful. He pushed her away. "The heat doesn't agree with you?" she asked delicately. She did not insist. "If you listened to me, Mr. Rosenberg, you'd go to the ambulatorium and let them put in new caps, metal ones. The war will come to an end, with the help of God, and then you will get yourself a new mouth full of gold. The main thing now, you understand, is to have something to put into your mouth. But don't worry, when Reisel takes someone into her hands, you know what happens . . ."

All morning long she busied herself in the room, sweeping, dusting, opening the window. Adam was taken apart by the pain, but he also noticed the light of the day. Something had flown out through the window, bringing him a lightness of spirit, in spite of the pain. Yadwiga was gone, Mietek was gone. The chain which had been choking him for a long time had finally let go. He did indeed jump up in his bed when the pain gripped him, but there was a delight in feeling it. Every pricking nerve cut into his mind, calling out to him, "You are alive!" And it was good to look at Reisel. He was in love with her. He worshipped her. He was ready to kiss her dry hands which were putting him back on his feet. He was not a goner yet. He would get out of bed and go to the clinic to get new caps put in his teeth, and best of all: he was free! Free of Mietek, free of Yadwiga, free of the dread of dying. He knew that he had met death eye to eye, he had already been in its sombre embrace — and he had escaped! That was why every spasm of pain should be greeted with enthusiasm. It was wonderful to feel pain, good to moan in aching delight!

Reisel brought him a sweet potion and a cachet. "To quiet the pain, Mr. Rosenberg." The pain was not quieted, but in spite of it, his appetite for food revived. Reisel brought him cool soups with morsels of bread, with oats, with pieces of sliced horsemeat dipped in it. He swallowed avidly, gratefully. He creased his forehead with pain, puckering his eyebrows, but he emptied the bowls.

Then his face began to swell. The dulled pain hammered inside him; as if wrapped in cotton, it pulsated with the heat of his body. Yet he dressed every morning and took a walk around the room. He invented a game. He endlessly wrote long columns of numbers, adding them, multiplying, dividing, finding their roots and elevating them to a given power. He also designed a small chess board for himself, using pieces of paper for figures, and played short games with himself. Yes, his head was working. His former freshness of mind was returning to him. This encouraged him, and he went out to pace the corridor. The neighbours avoided him, which amused him. He also entered the kitchen. If someone happened to be there, Reisel pretended not to see him, but when she was alone with him, she blinked at him with her cold eyes, "What do they need to know, eh, Mr. Rosenberg? It is our secret, and that's that."

One day, he saw through the window Professor Hager and his wife, carrying their few belongings with them. He was triumphant, "I chased them out! They are fleeing from me!" Then it occurred to him that he too should leave the house and begin a new life. "And I shall take Reisel away from them!" he decided. "Without Reisel they won't be such hotshots," he laughed and his pain laughed along with him.

From day to day he felt stronger. He was no longer afraid of the backyard and he took a stroll through it in the daylight. He also went out into the street. He saw the bridge in the distance. It looked like the skeletal jaw of a crocodile. "When will I be able to conquer this giant and have the strength to raise my feet over its stairs?" he asked himself.

Then the pain returned stronger than during the previous weeks. Now, however, Adam was no longer dumb in his torture. He hollered so that the house shook. He danced around the room like a drunkard, his head buried in both arms; with his fingers he stroked his own bald scalp and gasped. Once, in the middle of such a wild dance, Samuel appeared before him. Adam's gaze, burning with pain, took in the latter's tall figure with the dark-brown stern face. A well known fear grabbed him by the throat. Death itself was standing before him, aiming to destroy him. Adam called upon his suffering to assist him, clinging to it like to a shield. Thanks to the pain, which made him feel alive, he did not surrender. He would struggle on! He took a step towards Samuel, fixing his twisted face on him like a child who wanted to scare someone with an ugly grimace.

"We can't stand your hollering," Samuel said.

Adam burst into such guffaws that a foam appeared on his lips. He displayed his swollen gums and the tiny remains of teeth left in his mouth. His laughter hurt him, burnt him, yet it was worthwhile. "You prefer me to be silent, don't you?" he roared, "Ha-ha-ha! I intend to yell so loud, that you will hear me like Titus heard the fly in his ear!"

"Then I'll throw you out."

"So I'll follow you through the streets!"

"What have I done to you, that you want to torment me like this?"

"Nothing. Only that you are my Angel of Death." Samuel shrugged his shoulders and left. Adam yelled after him, "There is no room for both of us in the ghetto! It must be either you or me! And you have lost your round, brother. I'm alive! Alive! I'll trample you!" He burst into the kitchen to see Reisel. "Come with me to the clinic!" he ordered.

Reisel looked at him as if he were a drivelling idiot. "Are you out of your mind, Mr. Rosenberg? Such a *klepsidra* like you?"

"Come I said!"

Reisel folded her arms over her flat bosom, "Look at him! Who are you in this town to order me around? Bigshot! If not for me, the black coach would have taken you away long ago!"

The next word remained suspended on Adam's lips. What had happened to her? With her impatience she removed the ground from under his feet. His overcast face was pitifully twisted, "I'm bursting with pain!"

A few days later she went with him to the clinic and left him in the sultry narrow waiting room. It was quiet in the room. The patients pressed together in the crowded space, each coddling his own ache, as they listened with acute sensitivity to the faintest noise issuing from the dentist's office: the squeaks of children whose teeth were being pulled, the groans of adults, the buzzing of the drilling machine and the clank of the dentist's instruments. With their tired starved bodies they barely had the strength or the courage to face what was awaiting them inside.

Adam, however, was master of himself. He was proud that he had conquered the bridge. He discovered something new about himself. Before the war he had lived only with caprices, with a feeble will which was subordinated to his petty whims. Now, however, he had arrived at a state of concentrated perseverance. What power there was in suffering! How capable it was of digging to the very bottom of a man's being, crumbling the weak, cementing the strong, making the will power as hard as granite! He looked around. There was no end in sight to his waiting. Suddenly an idea came to his mind and he realized what he had to do. He began to moan aloud, then to scream, then to roar. His ache was both real and faked. The bandaged faces surrounding him turned to him with compassion and also with obvious satisfaction that they had not arrived at such a level of torture. "Not enough misery in the ghetto? So here you have toothaches on top of it," people moaned along with him.

Someone said, "Yes, but for that reason we will go straight to heaven, because hell we have right now."

Others pulled Adam by the sleeve, insisting that he show them the exact place where it hurt him. They gave him advice. Others chided him. How could such an old man lose control of himself? A man with a swollen cheek showed him the sole tooth left in his mouth. "I am worse off than you, you see? It's about me they invented the curse that goes: May you lose all the teeth in your mouth, and have one left for a toothache." Others carefully watched Adam's every move to check whether he was not faking. But they let him through to the girl in the white apron who distributed the numbers. She decided that his was an exceptional case.

Adam sat in front of the dark-haired angry-looking woman dentist, who without much ado began to run her cold fingers over his heated gums. She yelled at him, "How can a man let his mouth rot like this?" He could not reply, because she was already probing his mouth with her cold sharp tools. "We have to cure the abscesses, pull out the rot and the rest we'll cap," she announced.

He felt good. She was taking him into her hands. She would put him back on his feet. He worshipped the dark-haired woman dentist, just as he worshipped Reisel. When she had finished with him at last, he thanked her meekly. She wrote out a prescription and asked his name. When she heard it, an unbelievable amiability smoothed out the creases of her dry face. "Adam Rosenberg, the industrialist?" She stretched out her hand to him as if they had just been introduced, "My name is Felicia Nadel. Delighted to meet you, Herr Rosenberg. Come every day around six and I'll see to it that you don't have to wait." In the meantime Adam was feeling for his pocketbook. But she placed a comradely hand on his shoulder. "Here one does not pay for the visit." He remembered that his pocketbook was empty anyway.

He went down the stairs of the clinic, feeling practically no pain. "I am Adam Rosenberg!" he called out to himself, as if he had just recalled his name. He had noticed that unbelievably friendly smile that his name had charmed onto the dentist's angry face.

He followed her orders. He rushed to his visits at the clinic like a lover to a rendezvous with his beloved. Oh, how he wanted to kiss her cold hands and put a banknote into them. And the empty pocketbook in his pocket began to make him feel very uneasy. So, one day, he decided to ask Reisel about the money she had cashed in for his golden tooth caps. But instead, when he came home, he took out his last box of cigars. How charitable life was, after all, he mused. Another time he would have gone out of his mind on seeing that he was running out of cigars. And here he was looking at the box as at something foreign, and with a triumphant gesture he handed it to Reisel. "I've weaned myself of them," he said. "Perhaps the boss will buy it."

This immediately made Reisel livelier, "Heaven forbid!" She grabbed the box. "To deal with someone so close is no business. I will 'sugar' it for you, don't worry."

When, after his last visit to the clinic, he pressed two *rumkis* into the dentist's hand, she pushed them away, whispering with a smile, "If you would instead get some office work for my daughter . . . She is going through hell working in the Ghetto Laundry. She is a ballet dancer with a diploma."

After he left the clinic, he began to pace the street with light carefree steps. It was the last time he was taking that route. His mouth was full of metal tooth caps. Every bite still brought a little shudder to his body, like the screeching of a knife against glass. But he was cured, he was healthy. He looked about the lively streets and began to distinguish faces. He was amazed. What strange faces these were! Like slabs of wax. And their eyes, so deeply set under the eyebrows! And how these people were huddled up in their coats, today, on such a magnificent September day! Reisel was right. They were all *klepsidras*. He smiled mockingly to himself. And they wanted to survive?

He noticed an old-fashioned streetcar pass through the street. The ghetto had become motorized. It seemed strange, but only for a moment. The streetcar was loaded with merchandise and was followed by loaded trucks heading for Baluter Ring, the seat of the *Ghettoverwaltung*. There sat Rumkowski, the almighty King of the *Shnorrers*. Adam passed Church Place and saw the Red House. Reisel had told him a lot about it; of the *Kripo* one should beware as of fire. Near the bridge a youngster wearing a *Hasdic* cap was singing before a cluster of people:

"Rumkowski Chaim has God-like power.
He will shower the ghetto with sugar and flour."

As Adam climbed the bridge, Samuel entered his mind. "I called him my Angel of Death". Adam smiled to himself. "The hallucination of a tormented mind! The man who will become my Angel of Death has not been born yet. I will trample him!" That thought gave him pleasure; a delight, like that aroused by trampling a worm. He looked down from the bridge and thought of Mietek. Mietek was here somewhere, in this anthill. Perhaps he too already had a *klepsidra* face? Good for him! "It's all your fault! You're guilty of everything!" that bastard of a son had said to him, while he, his father, was writhing in pain. Guilty? Of what? Of the ghetto? Of the war? Of Yadwiga's madness? He, Adam, would become guilty now. He would be guilty of having survived the war. The most noble guilt of a ghettonik! Here was the barbed-wire fence. It wound around and around the ghetto. That was the cobweb that he had seen in his nightmares. But he would never again be a fly caught in its net. He nonchalantly thrust his hands into his pockets. In one of them he touched his pocketbook with the thirty rumkis that he had received for the cigars. He was glad that the dentist had refused to take the two *rumkis*. Anyway, she no longer existed for him and two *rumkis* had their value. He would not throw his money about to the left and to the right so recklessly any more. He had too soon turned such wealth into naught. All of Yadwiga's jewellery, all the wads of dollars he had had, where had they all gone? And here, something stung his mind like a fiery needle: Reisel! He accelerated his steps. His suspicion of her made his entire body burn. Rage grew within him. Yet he controlled himself. First he had to eat.

Reisel greeted him with a maternal smile, "So, show me your furniture." He opened his mouth to let her see the metal tooth caps. "A pleasure to look at you!" she purred, as she handed him his bowl of oat soup.

"Have you got a piece of horse for me?" he inquired jokingly.

She fixed a pair of large eyes on him, "Where from? What do you think, I'm God? I can create horsemeat for you?"

"Witch!" Adam muttered to himself, as he devoured the soup with great relish. He was gay. A youthful mischievousness took hold of him. *Homo himini lupus est*, he recalled the proverb from his student lessons in Latin. He corrected the saying in his mind, "One man is either a wolf or a lamb to the other." He approached Reisel and put his hand on her shoulder. "Reisel, you deserve a medal!"

She beamed, "At least one hears a good word. As they say: A good word costs nothing and is worth a lot."

He bowed to her, "For what you have done for me, you deserve more than a good word. Starting from today I shall ease your burden. I will cook for myself. Give me the money left from my gold caps and . . . A man able to care for himself should not trouble others. You were my good angel, Reisel."

Her face began to change as if illuminated by colourful reflectors. First it went white, then blue, then pink, and suddenly — red. In her eyes green panther lights went on. She folded her arms over her bosom, and emitted a sigh as if something had broken inside her. "My, I did not expect such a slap in the face!"

Adam scruntinized her with pleasure. He was curious to see how she would behave, what she would say. "I didn't want to offend you, Reisel," he modulated his voice, trying to make it sound delicate.

She was desperate, "Big thing to offend me! Whoever has a hand and a foot spits at me. Why not? All the goats jump over a bent fence!" She grabbed her cheeks with both hands.

"Is it now your turn to get a toothache?" He was amused. "You yourself used to tell me that the heaviest thing is an empty pocketbook."

For a moment her face became kindly again, "Have you squandered the thirty rumkis for the cigars?"

"Heaven forbid. But the pocketbook is too big, they don't show . . . Give me back the remainder of my money."

She was beside herself. "The remainder? Of What? Of the bread I bought for you on the black market? Of the cachets that I gave you? Go out into the streets and ask how much it is all worth. But my heart told me right away that you would suspect me; me, the one person who sacrificed herself for you! I didn't sleep whole nights while you squealed and yelped. I deserve it, my, do I ever deserve it! I should have let you kick the bucket and die like a dog!"

Adam remarked that her performance was not convincing enough. "Why were you so kind to me?"

"Why was I? Good question! How can a cold-blooded brute know what it means to have a Jewish heart? How can a man who slaughters his own wife, who chases out his own child, understand this?" Suddenly her gaze halted on his hand and concentrated on one of his fingers. She immediately regained her affectionate tone of voice, "Why don't you sell the wedding ring, eh!"

Now it was Adam's turn to be stupefied. Reisel was a genius, an absolutely wonderful genius. The thought of the wedding ring would never have entered his mind. He almost worshipped her again. With his former gratitude painted all over his face, he stared at her, "Sell where?"

"If you want me to . . ."

"No, I don't. I'll do it myself."

This time she was not angry at him. "Walk about the bazaar. People will approach you . . ." She sighed with relief as she watched him dash towards the door. She called after him cheerfully, "The last cow gives milk, Mr. Rosenberg! And if you need another favour some day, don't be shy to ask me!"

Adam smiled to himself. The game of spying on Reisel had begun. He would steal from her the remainder of the treasure that she had stolen from him.

Walking about the bazaar awakened Adam's sense of the ghetto. He plowed through the crowds, while people accosted him from all sides. They proposed to sell him old shoes, pieces of coats, broken stove pipes, bags with feathers, saccharine, potato peels, spoonfuls of butter, crumbs of cheese, shoelaces, pieces of paper. The street singer whom he had seen the same morning on the other side of the bridge, was now here. Adam approached the circle of listeners and caught the words of the song:

> Rumkowski Chaim, he gives us manna,
> he gives us barley, he gives us bran.
> Once the Jews ate manna in the desert.
> Now every woman eats her darling man.
>
> The first Chaim was Chaim Weizman
> who wanted to take us to the Holy Land.
> But with our Chaim of the cemetery
> the Angel of Death is walking hand in hand.

A man pulled Adam by the sleeve, "Perhaps you have 'noodles', hard ones or soft ones?" Adam understood that the man meant foreign currency and showed him his wedding ring. Right away a cluster of people surrounded them. Someone pulled him aside and slapped his palm to make a deal. Adam was enjoying himself. Instead of lowering, he constantly raised the price. When at length he became hungry and the sum offered was about two hundred, he slapped the buyer back, sealing the deal. The excited short man took him by the arm and led him away from the bazaar.

The man snivelled as he said to Adam, "You think I am the buyer? Heaven forbid. I'm taking you to a Resort director. How does the saying go? The ghetto resembles an egg. Whoever hatches it, to him it belongs." A cold thin rain began to fall. The preoccupied little man wrapped and re-wrapped himself in his gaberdine, which hung so large and loose on him, that the yellow Star of David appeared in the middle instead of at the side of his chest. He walked with little jumps and the large leggings of his pants fluttered. From his red nose dribbled a rain of his own. "You must be soaking in troubles good and proper, Mister, that you're already selling your wedding ring. For my part, I would have kicked the bucket long ago . . . Because a man, you understand, has to know how to trick fate. If he doesn't, fate tricks him. Of course, brokerage is not a very honourable occupation, but how do they say? Better a shame on my face, than a disease in my stomach. Oh, our sweet little ghetto . . . our darling ghetto! How do they say? May we never be tried by the things we can get used to." He wiped his nose with his sleeve. Apparently incapable of keeping quiet when he walked at someone's side, he went on talking, "Did you see the prisoners the Yekes were parading today past Zgierska Road? People say Voroshilov himself is among the captured. Others say Stalin's son passed by in a cart with wounded. I don't believe it, do you? I believe that our hour has not come yet. Things are not yet dark enough. Do you consider me a pessimist? Heaven forbid. It is you, who seem to be a pessimist, Mister . . ."

"You are wrong!" Adam burst out laughing. "I am the greatest optimist in the ghetto!"

The man pounded his fist against the Star of David on his chest, "There cannot be a greater optimist than me. As soon as the High Holidays are over, with the coming of winter, the Yekes will freeze to death on Russia's steppes. Do you already know where you will be praying during the holidays? You see, with the fasting there is a problem. Jews are fasting every day of the year, so in what way will the Yom Kippur fast be different?" They entered a backyard; the man led Adam to a door and whispered in his ear, "Wipe your shoes . . . We're going to meet with the ghettocracy . . ." He piously blew his noise. "They must be at their feast right now. How do they say? A ghettonik wants meat for his stomach, while a shishka wants a stomach for his meat. You better wait here a minute. I'll call you in." He knocked a few times in the air with his finger before daring to knock at the door. It was opened by a tall woman with a round puffy face. She wore glasses, had black eyebrows and her hair was pulled back and knotted into a bun at the back of her head. She looked familiar to Adam, but before he had a chance to scrutinize her more closely, she had vanished along with the broker on the other side of the door.

Adam, with his hands in his pockets, paced in front of the closed door. His nostrils were full of the ghetto air. Only today had he really noticed this little world in which he had to start a new life. It did not frighten him. It challenged him. It reminded him of a chessboard on which all the figures were moving towards one goal, each figure hoping to remove the other, to free the way for itself and to checkmate Death. And what chess figure was he? He was a knight. He would become one. He would jump, but not in a straight line, for to jump in a straight line in the ghetto meant to break one's neck. He would jump like all the chess knights: sideways, increasingly closer to his goal. He smiled to himself. The comparison pleased him. For instance, the little king on the chessboard whose name was Rumkowski. He led the good life and had the say over everything. But could he walk? Only one step to one side, one step to the other, and no more. And what if he had to run, to take cover and hide? What would he do then? With all his castling, it would be easy to mate him. There was no reason to envy him. And, for instance, the man who lived behind this door? What was he? Probably a rook, forced to move in a straight line, to be dependent. And the little broker? Quite clever and shrewd, but nevertheless in trouble — no more than a little pawn. Which meant that cunning alone was not enough. What then was necessary in order to climb to the top and yet not be noticed too much, and still feel free? For a split second the Red House of the Kripo flashed through his mind.

Through a crack in the door the broker beckoned to Adam with a finger. Adam entered a dark corridor. "He'll be out right away," the broker whispered. "Take off the ring."

A beam of light burst into the corridor from the room across. Before them stood Mr. Zaidenfeld. Adam immediately recognized his general manager who had for so many years directed his factory in the city. He had not changed an iota, had only become a bit slimmer, but this made him look younger. And after he turned on the light, Adam also noticed that Zaidenfeld still had his fine bushy crop of blond hair.

"Let me see the ring," he turned matter-of-factly to Adam. Adam stared at him provokingly. Was it possible that his former subordinate, the man with whom he had spent so many days throughout so many years did not recognize him at all? Zaidenfield took the ring from Adam's hand and moved it closer to the light. He turned the ring around, studying its inside, then said calmly, "I'll take it." He reached into his pockets, which just as in earlier years were packed with papers, rulers and measuring tapes. From one of them he drew out a wad of paper bills. Deftly, he counted them out and handed Adam the two hundred *rumkis*. He also shoved a few bills into the broker's palm.

Adam pushed the money between the folds of his pocketbook and looked Zaidenfeld straight in the eyes. "You don't recognize me, do you, Zaidenfeld?"

Zaidenfeld focused a pair of indifferent eyes on him. "You remind me of someone . . ."

"Forgotten your boss, Zaidenfeld?"

Zaidenfeld gave a jump backwards. With a kind of bitter satisfaction Adam watched his confusion. "You're not in Switzerland?" Zaidenfeld stammered, unable to absorb the shock. "Two years in the ghetto . . . and I haven't run into you . . . God, what can become of a person!"

The broker also got involved in the scene. "How do they say?" he shook his head, "The ghetto is as big as a yawn and yet as big as the whole world."

Zaidenfeld sent him off. He took Adam by the arm and led him into a spacious room. He did not take his eyes off his former master, as if he could not believe that he had the same Adam Rosenberg before him. "Zosia!" he called in the direction of the kitchen.

Adam's spine stiffened. Before him stood Zaidenfeld's wife, Zosia, the bespectacled stenographer. It seemed as if she had been transported, as she was, directly from his office into this room. "Good evening, Mr. Rosenberg," she said and her voice sounded just as it had used to, pale and monotonous. But the eyes which she had used to keep lowered were now fixed on Adam with the same sombre hatred in them as in the past.

"Look how she recognized you right away!" Zaidenfeld wondered. "So what's new with you?" He was gradually beginning to recover. "An acquaintance with the Presess comes in handy, doesn't it?"

Adam swallowed. "I don't have recourse to that *shnorrer*."

"Who then? Leibel Welner?"

"Who is Leibel Welner?"

Zaidenfeld, whom it had never been easy to surprise, again fixed bewildered eyes on Adam. In the meantime Zosia appeared hunched over a tray, in the same way as when she had used to bring Adam his second breakfast. Three bowls sat steaming on the tray. Zaidenfeld informed him, "I am manager of the

Tailor Resort and Zosia of course works for me." Adam avoided looking at Zosia. He knew that it was appropriate to thank her for her hospitality and for the soup that she was offering, but the words of thanks refused to come to his lips. Instead, he picked up the spoon and waited for Zaidenfeld to begin eating. The taste of the soup increased his impression that he was living a dream. Was it the ghetto that he was dreaming about, or the past? They kept silent for a while, busy with the food. All three of them gulped loudly, hurriedly. Only after the bowls were empty, did Zaidenfeld raise his face to Adam, "How come you don't know Welner? What are you doing in the ghetto? Is it a secret?"

"Why a secret? I do nothing."

"And you are already at the wedding ring?"

"Hm . . . my wife is dead."

"Tuberculosis?"

"Yes, tuberculosis."

"Oh, that's like fire. Gets in through doors and windows. And your son?"

"He's all right."

Zaidenfeld gave him a glance, as he had used to do in the office, when Adam had a capricious moment. "And if one still has some valuables to live on, Mr. Rosenberg . . . How can a man not be attached to a post nowadays? At least nominally be registered somewhere? Don't you see what's going on? The Jews of the provinces keep on arriving. Transports from Germany are expected. There will be a terrible scarcity of food." Zaidenfeld stood up. Adam understood that it was time for him to leave. He nodded to Zosia. His thank you could by no means escape his mouth. Zaidenfeld accompanied him to the door. "Listen to my advice, Mr. Rosenberg," he added in his matter-of-fact voice.

Adam waveringly proposed, "Perhaps at your Resort . . .?"

"At mine? By all means. Of course. Bring a letter from the Presess. I will put you on the staff list. You'll receive two soups, a few *rumkis*, and be as free as a bird. You'll be better off than I."

Adam walked through the evening lights of the street, his mind digesting the strange encounter and Zaidenfeld's words. Yes, Zaidenfeld was right. Nowadays one had to be connected with a Resort. Food would soon become very dear. He touched his pocketbook which contained the two hundred *rumkis*. "All goats jump over a bent fence," he recalled Reisel's saying. Then the broker's words entered his mind, "Better a shame on one's face than a pain in one's stomach." These lowly creatures really were very clever and strong. One had to learn from that scum. When one found oneself in a pit, there was no sense in copying the lions or the tigers, the eagles or the swans. From the snakes and worms one ought to learn, and to remember that the end sanctifies the means.

At night he was unable to sleep. The past day's experiences disturbed him. He turned and twisted in his bed. Suddenly, it seemed to him that the bed was squeaking strangely. He told himself that the noise in his mind was producing the noise outside it. Yet he grew more and more surprised at what he was hearing. The squeaking seemed to come from under the floor. He recalled that his ears had often caught such sounds before, but he had not paid any attention to them. Curious rather than frightened, he jumped out of bed and dressed. He went out of the house and approached the cellar on tiptoe. It was quiet inside. He tried the door. It did not give, but immediately he heard a screeching. He withdrew hurriedly and hid behind the corner of the house. Someone unbolted the door of the cellar and came sliding out very carefully. Adam immediately recognized Samuel and one of his daughters, he was not sure which.

All night he lay awake, pondering. These were the two shadows he had seen that night when he had sat under the cherry tree. He had taken them for imaginary shadows of death, and here the truth was so prosaic. Prosaic? No, it was a mystery. What had Samuel and his daughter been doing in the cellar in the middle of the night? At dawn, the first rays of light shot Adam in the eyes with the answer: the radio receiver! He dressed and went down into the street to wait for Samuel. The sleepy Samuel and wide-awake Adam stared at each other for a while, making talk superfluous. But Adam was seeking a bit of entertainment.

"I will accompany you to work," he said. "We never have the opportunity to have a good conversation, and so, I'll save you time."

Samuel cut him short. "I don't want to have anything to do with you. Butt out."

"I will soon butt out. Only one minute. I want you to take me into your resort. I want to be registered on your staff list."

"I have to want to do it, don't I?"

"I will make you want to. When should I come to see you at the resort?"

"Never."

"Oho! So categorical? Fine, then I'll make another deal with you. I mean, you don't have to be afraid of me . . . I haven't stooped so low. But I want to survive the war, and in the name of our friendship, you ought to help me. I don't want much. Only twenty-five *rumkis* a week, and safety of the radio will be assured."

+ + +

It was during one of these days that Adam searched out Krajne the "Gold Digger" and moved in with her.

It did not take long after their first encounter, for Krajne to recover from her belief that a holy man was living with her. After she had slept through a few restless nights, her head began to work with more clarity. Feivish had said that the prophet Elijah had been dead for a long time, and if Feivish said so, so it must be. But even in her dreams he was unable to deny a thing which the entire Piaskova Street and the entire ghetto knew, namely, that among the inhabitants of the ghetto there lived disguised holy men who were called the *lamedvovniks*. This fact she had surely not invented. And so, Krajne came to the conclusion that if her visitor was not the prophet Elijah, then he was another disguised holy man. And the fact that he was walking around with his head uncovered and had no beard or sidelocks, she now understood, was because he was disguised; or he was just a modern saint who laughed at such things, just like her Feivish.

And the miracles were not long in coming. Before the eve of *Rosh Hashana* the mailman distributed five deca candies for every child. True, on the packages it was written, "In honour of the holidays — a gift from your Presess." But Krajne was not so stupid as not to know who was really behind the candies. For nothing in the word would she believe that the Presess had such a kind heart for children, when he had the nerve to so torment their parents. Aside from this, potatoes began arriving in the ghetto and her children started to bring home bags of vegetables which they had stolen from the passing carts, and they were not even once beaten for it. A loaf of bread suddenly had to last six days instead of eight, which came to a portion of thirty-three decas and three-tenths per head, so that Krajne could afford to sell half of the bread with interest and treat her children to a whole loaf of bread for the holidays.

The eve of *Rosh Hashana* an autumnal rain poured down on the ghetto. Humidity came down through the walls and up from the floor, as usual in autumn. Krajne kindled the fire in the stove early, to prepare the holiday meal, and so that the children should be warm when they came home. She was alone in the house. The "visitor", or Mr. Rosenberg, as he asked her to call him, had disappeared for the whole day. She stood at the table making "herring" out of beet leaves. She also prepared a *baba* from coffee dregs, and it was the *baba* that was cooking now in a pot of water on the stove.

Today Krajne had been particularly careful about kindling the fire. Usually, she laughed at the bad omens associated with starting a fire, which the neighbours had enumerated for her. But today was the eve of *Rosh Hashana* and she did not want to take any chances; there was always some truth in what people said. For this reason she had picked straight dry pieces of kindling wood, so that they would all catch the fire at once and the flames would rise evenly and smoothly. Because if one piece of wood failed to light up, it was a sign that someone would, heaven forbid, not live out the year. And if the flames were not smooth and even and did not rise straight upwards, but fluttered sideways, it was a sign that something would happen to a mass of people, perhaps to the entire ghetto — an epidemic, or deportation. That was why she had been so very careful this time. And although her hands had trembled, all the kindling wood had lit up together. Later however, the flames had begun to dance on the side. She assured herself that this was due to the weather, and that, after all, the women did not know what they were talking about. Yet, in spite of the fact that she concentrated her thoughts on the visitor, her protector, something had begun to gnaw and dig at Krajne's heart.

Apart from that, the quacking of the pot seemed suspicious to her as well. As a rule, when she put the little pot with the *baba* in the big pot with water, it bubbled quietly. Now however she could by no means figure out the right spot for it. If she removed the pot from the burners, a frightful silence came over it; if she moved it closer, it began to hiss, pounding the cover and lifting it into the air as if with the hands of a band of demons. She had no doubt that in this pot were cooking the fates of herself, her children and Feivish. She shuddered and rushed to warm her hands at the pail of water which she had put on the stove for the children to wash themselves with.

She often looked out into the street. It was gray, wet and awesome outside. Anxiety nagged deep at her heart. Was something about to happen to her children and herself? "God Almighty," she sighed, "Bring a good year for my sparrows and for their mother. Ruler of the World, even if I do not talk to you, because I don't know how to pray, you do understand . . . even a sigh, don't you? Hear my sigh, dear God. For some reason I am frightened . . . very frightened. I, Krajne, who never knew what fear was, don't know what is happening to me . . . Have mercy . . ." She burst into sobs. Her tears dripped onto the glowing top of the stove, turning into sizzling little balloons. She clung to the thought of her "visitor". Yes, at this very moment he must be at a house of prayer somewhere, probably praying for her, or at least mentioning her name. She decided to invite him to the holiday meal. But this failed to ease her heart. She tore herself away from the stove, put on her plaid and rushed outside.

The street was desolate. It seemed to lie bare before the rain, letting itself be pricked by its needles. Krajne noticed a little dot in the distance — a tiny figure which moved hastily on a pair of bare little feet. She spread out the tails of her plaid as if they were wings and dashed forward to meet Berish — her youngest, her greatest *schlemiel*, who so resembled Feivish. Although she was not in the habit of caressing her children, she now swept down on the little boy, embraced him and pressed him to her bosom, making him shake with the feverish shudders that had taken hold of her. "Woe is me, you're soaked, my little wretch! Where have you been in such a downpour?" She entered the house with him and helped him out of his soaking clothes. "Where have you been rambling around?" she insisted.

Berish slid his thumb into his mouth and began to suck it vigorously as if he wanted to suck away his mother's questions. At length there was no way out but to answer her. "You'll give me the whip, if I tell you . . ." he stammered and burst into tears.

His crying aggravated her and she gave him a slap on the behind. "Answer when a mother asks you."

"I . . . I was in the theatre . . . I was . . ." he panted, covering his face with his sleeve.

"What put the theatre in your head again?"

"I pushed myself in."

She pointed to the slop pail. "Go, blow your nose and stop wailing." Her heart was melting with tenderness at the sight of the dark little creature who was blinking at her with his full black eyes that so remind her of Feivish. She took the pail of water off the stove and filled a washbasin.

Now the little boy began to cry seriously. "I don't want to wash my hair!"

She took a piece of soap and moved the basin closer to the stove. "Of course not. You want to walk around with a scabby head, don't you? Today . . . Do you know that today is *Rosh Hashana*, you *sheigetz*?" Through his tears Berish was now throwing strange glances at her. His face turned into a mask of anguish, of fear, not of her, his big strict mother, but of something still more fearsome. He began to undress hastily and obediently put his head into the water. His submissiveness began to make her feel uneasy. He seemed like a little chick stretching its neck for the butcher's knife. She began to scrub his head, scratching the skin on his skull with her fingers. The little boy did not utter a sound. When she at last let go of him, his face was as pale as the white foam that remained on the surface of the dirty water in the basin. She grabbed the ash-coloured towel and pulling the boy closer to the stove, wiped him energetically. "It's a sacred day today. All Jews are cleansing themselves of their sins," she explained, "so that we may deserve to survive the war. Take off the shoes. We'll wash your feet too."

She felt even more ill at ease at the touch of his ice-cold heels and began scrubbing them with a hard brush, both in order to cleanse him and to warm him up. "I too have sins, Mother?" the boy asked, chattering his teeth.

"What else? Are you God? Everyone sins. You know it yourself."

"I don't remember . . ."

"And what are such filthy feet, do you think? Also a sin."

"The Jews in the theatre have even more sins," the boy remarked. "They cried like someone was hitting them. And you know . . . Guess who was there? The Presess Rumkowski. He said a speech. He said that bad things are coming. And everyone cried even more." Krajne stopped wiping him. Her heart froze. Yes, she had known that something was cooking. All those signs had not been for nothing. The boy looked at her with his wise sad eyes. "If you want to, you can wash me every day," he said, giving a chew on his finger and adding, "I don't mind. You can spank me too, so I won't have no more sins."

She jostled him. "Shut up, will you. Go and get dressed."

"And the pants?" he asked uncertainly. "They're wet . . ."

She grabbed the pants from his hand and hung them up on the hot pipe over the stove. "Come, sit down here, near the fire," she ordered, sitting the half-naked child on a chair near the stove. She looked at his thin bare legs, at his wet head. He again resembled a soaked miserable little chick. His eyes, wise and sad, Feivish's eyes, looked searchingly into hers. She could not bear his gaze. "What are you staring at me like that for? Don't you know me?" she scolded him. She handed him a cup of hot water which she had scooped up from the pot with the bubbling *baba*. "Here, drink it. I'll give you a spoonful of brown sugar to lick." He greedily grabbed the cup from her hand, then thriftily began to lick from the spoonful of sugar that she offered him. She removed the rag cover from a bed and wrapped it around his legs. As she did this, she had an impulse to kiss his wet head, but she controlled herself.

The sound of a lively clamour could be heard outside. Soon the other children burst into the room. They were soaked, but their wet faces shone with gaiety. They all talked at once, displaying their full bags, jostling each other and making such a hullabaloo, that Krajne had to grab for the whip. "Look at the mud you've brought in, bastards!" She shook the whip over their heads so energetically, that each of its separate "noodles" stretched in a different direction. "And shut up all of you once and for all! And don't you know that a sacred holiday is arriving in the ghetto? Don't you see the floor is freshly scrubbed?"

The children were too excited with their achievements to pay sufficient attention to their mother's talk. Zipa-Deborah, the oldest, opened her coat and brought forth a substantially loaded knapsack. The other children displayed the treasures they had in their bags. A mish-mash of turnips, boards, pieces of wood, paper, pulp, nails, potatoes, a few matches and rags were heaped upon the table. "And *Mameshe*," Zipa-Deborah flushed radiantly, placing the knapsack at the edge of the table and undoing it. "I have a new dress for you . . . and perhaps a blouse for me . . ." The children became silent. They wiped their noses and stared tensely at Krajne.

Krajne grabbed herself by the head, "Where, the blazes, did you get this knapsack, bastards?"

Zajvel, the oldest of the boys, explained. "From the Vloclavek people. The policemen put them into a school and they sit on their bags and they cry. One was fainting. So Zipa-Deborah went over to revive her and in the meantime Shmerl and I took the knapsack."

Krajne wrung her hands, "You took? You stole! Good heavens, regular thieves . . . today, the eve of *Rosh Hashana!*"

"Try on the dress, Mother," asked Berish, who came over to the table wrapped in the bed cover.

"I will give you such a 'try on', that it will get dark before your eyes!" Krajne was beside herself. "Take this knapsack back right away! I don't want any stolen things on the eve of *Rosh Hashana!*"

Zipa-Deborah was already parading around the room in her new blouse. Krajne seized the whip and began to wallop the behinds of the children one after the other. As she did so, her eyes fell on the brown material on the table. At least she could try on the dress. Then she looked at Zipa-Deborah. The blouse fitted the girl like a glove. Suddenly Krajne realized how pretty her daughter was, resembling her mother like one drop of water resembles another. She could barely remember when her daughter had tried on something new. Everything that ten-year old Deborah wore reached far above her knees. It was even beginning to look indecent; after all, a big girl. But Krajne's anger would not subside. "Take it back! Take it back straight away!" she pointed in the direction of the door. "Not enough that the woman was fainting, you robbed her from head to toe? Today? On the eve of *Rosh Hashana?* Do you want to bring a calamity on our heads? Quick, Deborah, take back the knapsack, and the rest of you, scabheads, undress and we'll wash your hair."

"Don't be so stupid, Mother," Zaivel said courageously. "Take the dress at least."

The whip shook above his head. "Whom are you calling stupid?" She became thoughtful for a moment and turned to her daughter. "Did you hear what I said? Take back the knapsack! But you can wear the blouse; you've got nothing to wear."

Zipa-Deborah jumped into the air. She hung on to Krajne, whooping with wild triumphant laughter. The boys laughed with her and also pressed themselves against their angry mother and grabbed hold of her skirt. With all her strength she tore herself out of their hands. "You're out of your minds, woe is me! To laugh on the eve of *Rosh Hashana?* Who ever heard such a thing?" But she herself felt light and gay; delight was spreading all over her. Now she was sure that nothing could happen to them. "Go already, Zipa-Deborah, shake a leg!" she chased out the daughter, waving with the whip in the girl's direction. "Hurry up, because it's almost curfew. And don't stop to potter around on your way. I'm frying herring for the feast!"

✦ ✦ ✦

All the children were washed and combed. Krajne herself also took time to dress herself festively. After all, one felt good on the inside when one looked good on the outside. She sat with her children at the table, feeling completely cleansed, almost like a holy woman. On the stove stood the meal, ready to be served. Now it was only a pot of coffee that was cosily bubbling — not devilishly wild, as it had before, but quietly, pleasantly, just as it should to signify a good omen. The table at which they sat was covered with one of the white bed sheets which Krajne kept for Deborah's dowry. Even the broken tin dishes looked more festive on such a tablecloth. And then there was the glow of the lit candles which reflected in the children's eyes, as they embraced the table with a bright circle of light.

They waited a long time for Mr. Rosenberg. Krajne was sure that he was at the prayer house. He had a lot to pray for, she thought. She had already given instructions to her brood, commanding that as soon as the door opened, they should call out all together, "Happy New Year, Mr. Rosenberg!" and in order that the children should not become impatient as they waited, she offered them slices of turnip in the meantime. So they sat around her, munching on the turnip and casting avid glances now at the stove, now at the door. To be honest, the children, did not care too much for Mr. Rosenberg. He behaved as if he did not see them, never said a word to any of them, and he ordered their mother around. They could not grasp why she made such a fuss over this "visitor", as she called him.

The children tried to overcome their impatience, their sleepiness and boredom by telling Krajne about their adventures of the day. "When she saw me bring back the knapsack," Zipa-Deborah said, "she began to kiss me and cry so that I was afraid that she would faint again. They are rich, the people from Vloclavek. They have bags full of food. They have straw mattresses already to sleep on in the school. Then I passed by the place where they pray, and the men were crying . . . With the prayer shawls over their heads they looked like women. The Presess was speaking to them. People in the street are saying that even worse decrees are coming."

"Quiet! Shut your mouth!" Krajne could not bear to listen to the bad news. "There will be no evil decrees. All the Jews will pray for a good year and after the holidays, the plague will come down on the *Yekes'* heads."

"And then what will happen?" Zajvel asked. With his clean face and wet combed hair he already looked, in spite of his nine years, a bit like a man.

"Then we shall be saved," Krajne replied earnestly.

"So what will happen?"

"What do you mean, what will happen, donkey-head? Father will come back."

"And after that?"

"We'll be rich," Zipa-Deborah echoed her mother's tone of voice. "We'll live on the first floor. We'll be dressed nicely. We'll have the best things to eat and we'll get out of the ghetto."

"Get out of the ghetto?" Zaivel shook his head discontentedly. "What for? All the goyim live on the other side."

"You're stupid. There will be no goyim then."

"Why? They'll all die out?"

Little Berish's eyes lit up, "They'll become Jews!"

At long last the door opened. Mr. Rosenberg entered and the children greeted him, calling out as instructed, "Happy New Year, Mr. Rosenberg!" The "visitor" halted in the middle of the room, obviously ill-at-ease. For the first time he saw them all together with their eyes turned on him. It was impossible to go straight to his room and pretend not to see them. Krajne felt a lump in her throat. She wanted to stand up, step forward to greet him and lead him over to his assigned chair at the head of the table, but she lost all the strength in her legs. She saw the "visitor" take a parcel out from under his wet raincoat. Through the rips in the paper there peered out the brown crust of a bread. She was not surprised, although she had expected him to bring home a more unusual thing, such as a *hallah*. But she was becoming used to the fact that her "visitor" should do the most usual things and make them seem unusual. The sight of the bread encouraged her. "Mr. Rosenberg," she muttered, "in honour of the holiday, I invite you to kindly eat with us . . ."

He was half way to his room and he could have entered it, pretending not to have heard her, but something forced him to turn his head to that robust woman, whom he now really saw for the first time. He noticed that she was not at all like the other ghetto women. She was massive; her face was full; her cheeks, flushed from busying herself around the house and from excitement, were red like apples. And she had a pair of lively clear eyes, unlike those of the other ghetto-women who had a sharp animal-like stare. She also had a rich head of wild thick hair which was half-wet and fell in waves around her face. He had to take another look at her. And as soon as he embraced her once more with his eyes, his heart became restless. He dashed into his room. In his confusion however, he forgot to lock the door.

Krajne came in and stood before him. "Mr. Rosenberg, in honour of *Rosh Hashana* . . . perhaps . . . you'd honour my table . . ." she stammered.

Adam made an effort not to look at her. "I've told you a thousand times that you should knock on the door before you enter."

She whispered humbly, "Yes, I'll knock . . ."

"Don't come in here at all. This is my room."

Her eyes overflowed. "Yes. The food is getting cold . . ." He showed her the door. She went out but returned immediately, with a plate in her hands. "Try at least a piece of my fried herring, in honour of *Rosh Hashana*."

He grabbed the plate out of her hand and waited for her to leave. Without feeling the taste of what he was eating, he swallowed the dish along with a chunk of bread. He was tired. He had a difficult day behind him. Today he had again knocked at the door of his former employee, Director Zaidenfeld, the only person who made him no reproaches. But Zaidenfeld talked patronizingly to him and, to tell the truth, his attitude enraged Adam even more than the open talk of his other acquaintances. And he hated him more than the others. Today, during Adam's visit, Zaidenfeld had been dressed up. He was solemn. Lighted candles stood on the table in the dining room. "Happy New Year, Mr. Rosenberg," he shook Adam's hand, but he had not invited him to sit down.

"You must help me!" Without delay, Adam made his plea. "You must give me a position. I haven't got a pfennig to my soul."

Zaidenfeld was obviously put out. "Today is a holiday. I know that you don't care much for Jewish holidays, but I . . . In the Ghetto one willy-nilly becomes more of a Jew." Then he said, "And I thought that you brought at least half of your fortune into the ghetto. What kind of work could you do in my Tailor Resort?"

"I'm ready to do anything, I'm telling you."

"What do you mean by anything? Would you become a janitor, for instance, and clean the halls?"

"When should I come?"

That was the finale of Adam's day, which had begun with his realization that the two hundred rumkis he had received for the ring were almost gone. And on top of that, his craving for food had lately grown enormous. Night after night he dreamt of Feldman's restaurant on Piotrkowska Street. He grew envious of the people who walked in the streets with their canteens of soup. He had tasted these soups. They were watery, but delicious. And now Jews from Germany were supposed to arrive. The ghetto would become even more crowded and the prices would rise sky high. He felt like a trapped animal. He had to hide his pride and save his life. Before a man could set free his great ambitions, he had first to act humbly, submissively. Like a mole he had to dig underground corridors, before he could throw off the heap of earth and emerge into the light of the day.

He hurried first to wait for Samuel, to nag him about a job at his resort. Samuel, without uttering even one word, pushed twenty-five rumkis into his hand and turned away from him. Adam looked up his acquaintances from before the war. But instead of getting their help, he got bitter words and abuse. He never knew that he had had so many enemies before the war. It seemed that the entire world was conspiring against him — and all he could do was to accept the "position" which Zaidenfeld was ready to offer him: to become a janitor. Having left Zaidenfeld's home, Adam headed for the bazaar where he bought the loaf of bread. Now he sat on the bed, cutting one slice after the other. His desire for vengeance was so great, that it seemed to him that he was gnashing Zaidenfeld with his teeth; that he was tearing into pieces the servant who had done him the favour of employing him — as a servant.

The gay chatter of the children, the clinking of spoons against the tin dishes reached Adam's ears from the adjoining room. These sounds inflamed his nerves even more. He devoured the entire loaf of bread.

Chapter Twenty-two

Dr. Michal Levine,
Litzmanstadt-Ghetto,
October . . . 1941.

(Fragment of a letter)
. . . I am desperately searching for the cause of all that is so difficult to bear and still more difficult to understand. Who is the culprit? It is easy to cast the entire blame on the Germans. But this blame has deeper roots, reaching further back.

Life here is autumnal. The rain-soaked ghetto drowns in gloom. There is not a straw of hope to hold on to. All of us in the ghetto are like flies wriggling on the deadly glue of the flypaper. The more we try to extricate ourselves, the more we stick to it.

I would like you, Mira, to appear in my dreams, but you never come. Perhaps I have banished you myself? I have torn you out of my guts, because the remembrance of things past hurts so much. I am even unable to recall your face properly, or your body. Who are you . . . you? If you exist somewhere as a woman, as a person — then you are a stranger whom I never met. Because I am a stranger, and I'll be damned if I know who I am: perhaps the incarnation of a man whose name is Michal Levine.

Sometimes when I think about myself, I see myself as a mite, as a kind of biological cell. In its middle there is a concrete core: I. Around that core there is a floating plasma, which is also I, expanding over time and space. For that I-core, you, Mira — who are, like myself, nailed with your Star of David to the dart board — are the symbol of physical freedom. How appropriate it is to paraphrase here the song of Yehudah Halevi, which my father liked so much! However, I am in the East and my freedom is in the West, and we both are in chains. You, Mira, are the name of the meaning life promised to have. Mirage. What deep inspiration whispered this new name for you into my ear? We shall never meet again. "Never" is an abysmally dark concept. But my external, my protoplasma-like "I" which lives in eternity is calling you, greeting you — it is with you. And what unites it with you is called "Forever".

If I am amusing myself with such queer terminology, let me proceed a bit further. It is clear that this "I-core" of mine is desperately pessimistic. Even to say pessimistic would not be exact, because pessimism possesses an emotional colouration which still affirms life, while that "I" of mine is bereft of any emotion. If something stirs me up now and then, it is when I cast a glance at Mother, or when I roll up my sleeves to save a child. Of course, I still manipulate the phrases: "I hate, I love." But as far as hatred is concerned, it is

327

the superficial feeling of an impotent; and as for love, I experience the cheapest form of it: pity. Through pity for others I feel basically pity for myself. Because this "I-core" of mine is a dry mathematician; his calculations are simple. He knows that the world will not perish, nor will mankind become extinct — not even the Jewish people as such. His pessimism is therefore only in regard to himself and the ghetto. A question of time. Hunger and tuberculosis are slow blunt axes, but they are sure ones. If hunger or tuberculosis do not get me, then I will succumb to the tortures of Sisyphus. Eighteen, nineteen hours a day I wrestle with inevitability. I am like our firemen who pump the water out from one flooded cellar, at the same time as the rain is flooding another. I extinguish a fire with a spoonful of water. My beautiful, magnificent profession — how absurd!

So actually all my "philosophies" could end here. If there is no future for us, ghettoniks, then our destruction is the destruction of the world (for us). And yet I never thought so much about the future as I do now. My extended, eternal "I" is thinking these thoughts. Probably this "I" is an invention of the perishing one — a kind of defence, created by the still functioning mind which refuses to make peace with nothingness.

You will laugh, but I have constructed an entire system of thought based on this senseless kind of logic. I say to myself that every form in the universe is more or less the form of a circle or elipse, that the straight line does not exist; it is nothing but an illusion created by the segment of an enormous circle. This means, there is no beginning or end. Why then should life exist in a straight line — with a beginning and end? Why could it not be considered a segment of a huge circle? This question is posed by me, the man with the scalpel, who has studied and analysed the disintegration of organic life. However, only the "I-core" in me is a doctor. My broader "I" refuses to accept the former's judgment. It is full of a blind clairvoyance, full of proto-emotions, of proto-longings. And so are all of us. That's why we live with thoughts of the future.

I think of the future on two levels. One: how I wish it to be. Two: how I imagine it will be. How do I wish it to be? I wish that man would learn something from this experience and draw the proper conclusions. I wish that the aggressive nature of man should consciously be made use of in the fight against the elements which destroy mankind's well-being. That the highest ideal should be: to let every single living creature live its life undisturbed, according to the possibilities that it has, in the frame work of the conditions which nature and accident have created for it. That is actually my religion. Because the existence or non-existence of a godhead is a mystery, and all one can do is speculate about it. I personally am mainly preoccupied with man and his life — and with the idea of God only insofar as it is related to man. All I know is that there is no justice or injustice in the universe, no beauty or ugliness. All I know is that life wants to be lived; that both man and animal crave for "happiness". An animal is "happy" when it is free, has enough food, a lair and someone with whom to serve the "law of multiplication". Man, because of his spirit, needs something more. In order to be "happy", that is, to be in harmony with himself and his surroundings, he must have the awareness that he is living his life to the fullest. He must first say "It is good" to himself, before he can say "It is good" to the world. And we can say "It is good" to ourselves, when we feel that we are good. To the universe, it makes no difference whether we are good or bad, ethical or unethical, but it is important to us. Because we possess, in my opinion, both a moral and an aesthetic sense, which we long to satisfy. We long for an aesthetic and just atmosphere in which we feel that we could enjoy our existence to the fullest and could perhaps become physically healthier. (That is why I consider the Germans to be the most miserable creatures in this world.)

I know that you could call me a naive dilettante, totally unrealistic, unscientific, illogical. Easy to say all that about me, because I have not studied philosophy, economics or psychology, nor have I deepened my knowledge of any religion. My only true experience of life I glean from the ghetto. And the only knowledge I have about life is gleaned from medicine. And yet, as an individual, I permit myself to arrive at my own conclusions.

And so I arrive with my wishful thinking at the problem of our people and of races and nations in general. You could have expected that here, in the ghetto, I should have felt sanctified, so to speak, in my Jewishness, and united with my brothers in fate — in the pride of the oppressed, in the self-love of the under-dog; that I should now feel what I never felt before, that we Jews are better than the others, if only because we are the victims, not the torturers. But this does not happen to me. I see the ghetto not merely as a concentration camp for Jews — but as a concentration camp for people. And this leads my mind in an entirely different direction. Because I also believe that each nation has a hidden or overt inclination to consider itself superior to others, and I believe that the ambitions and passion, the pretentions and the pride of entire peoples are more dangerous than those of individuals. Therefore I am for the conscious abolition of any national framework. Do you think that would be a loss? That national characteristics are interesting, lending each nation a regional or folkloric charm and beauty of its own? True, but I would sacrifice these particular characteristics of nations for the sake of peace — and for a superior kind of beauty which is that of every individual. The great spiritual leaders of the world, the prophets or artists, are in my opinion the prototypes of the future man. At the highest level of their achievements they become universal and their language is understood by all.

I am for the abolition of borders between countries. I am for one government, one collective culture, the characteristics of which should not be national or racial — but personal, gleaned from the fascinating uniqueness of each man. No child should be able to pride itself on its fatherland; its fatherland should be the entire free world, and he should look upon his most distant neighbour as one of his kin. When there are no nations, one nation will not fight against the other, and the swords, no longer needed, will be forged into plows. Anyway, I am convinced that the development of science and technology will erase local characteristics. People will travel more and transmit and transform their particular ways of life. If however this does not go hand in hand with fostering the freedom and individuality of each person — we will arrive at a single-faced society which will become so bored with itself, that it will destroy itself by its own design. So, as you see, Mira, I have not changed as much as I tried earlier to make you believe. This is my dream, my *chalom* which rhymes so well with *Shalom*.

But how do I imagine the future world to be in reality? How much more will it have learned from this war than from the previous? Probably not much. We people learn little from history, and are liable to repeat our mistakes. If we concentrate our will power, acting radically in order to change our surroundings, we do it only when we feel the noose around our throats. The impact, the magnitude of an experience depends on how close we are to it, on how much it concerns us personally. For us Jews, the present tragedy is the greatest in history. For others, it is only a part of the picture of war. Therefore I don't have any illusions. Our suffering will be no moral lesson for the world.

Then how should I bind my dream about the future with the reality that I am convinced will be our share of the future? I hope for action on the part of all those who have been touched by the present experiences to the marrow of their bones, of those who will not be able to forget — of the Jews who will survice, of the soldiers saved from destruction, of the mothers who have lost their sons. How gladly would I leave behind a will for them: the wish that one man should try to hurt the other as little as possible. That man should at long last answer God, "My brother Abel is alive and I am his keeper".

✦ ✦ ✦

(Fragment of a letter)
. . . Mother fasted *Yom Kippur* and cried the whole day. I let her fast and cry. I had the feeling that it did her some good. I feel the same way with regard to the ghettoniks who are overcome by the wailing hysteria. The gatherings of the praying people shaking in tearful spasms made me realize that they have more strength than I imagined. In their prayerful humility they seemed to be giants; their hands raised in prayer seemed like pillars of stubbornness supporting the sky, to prevent it from collapsing over their heads. Many of the worshippers are not religious. They have, just like Mother, come to cry themselves out in a "legal" way. Each of us is loaded with that cry. That is why such a day gives us relief.

Sometimes I walk around, stunned by the miracles which can happen to some people. According to the rules, not only the body, but also the mind should have succumbed to apathy. Some of us look like puppets consisting of mere bones. Others are swollen and puffed like pumpkins. They lose their hair, their teeth, they see badly, hear badly, their nails break. Some walk around with stomachs which no longer digest food. Others have decalcification of the bones or disintegrating lungs. And you should see how they hustle and bustle. They put in ten-twelve-hour days at the Work Resorts. Afterwards, you see them carry pails of water, fight for a place in line in front of a co-operative, trade food in the gates and work on the *dzialkas*. Of course they collapse after a time, but much later than you would expect. Even afterwards, when they can no longer get out of bed and you have for the tenth time given up on their lives, they welcome you enlivened, their deepset eyes aflame, as they demand that you give them back their health — with such hutzpah! They lie on their deathbeds and talk about going to work the next day. They are already disintegrating, and to them it only means that a man has the right to rest for a day. They don't even recognize the Angel of Death. For instance, one day I sat with a patient during his last moments, and he said to me, "Doctor, do me a favour, write me out a referral to Rumkowski's vacation house."

And the worse it becomes and the longer this war drags on, the more stubborn they become. They make me think of weight lifters in a circus who, despite the increasing heaviness of each weight, conquer them one after the other. They are involved in a kind of match with the Germans: who will hold out longer, the Germans who inflict the tortures, or they who resist them? I should be ashamed of myself for having given up on their lives so soon, and for having pronounced my verdict on the ghetto. Perhaps the ghetto is indestructible? Perhaps people, who see in their struggle for life a struggle for something more than life, are the true heroes? And yet, I don't believe in miracles. When death is in one's own bones, it willy-nilly achieves its goal.

In the meantime the ghetto has diminished in space. People say that gypsies are supposed to arrive and occupy the empty houses. Besides them, the German Jews keep on arriving as do Jews from the provincial towns. And now an order has been issued that men from fifteen to sixty years of age must register, no one knows why or what for. Rumkowski has delivered a speech to the directors of the Resorts, saying that he is unable to provide for everybody, and that we will have to leave the old and weak to die. And to the newly arrived German Jews he said, "You may be doctors, lawyers or other members of the shmintelligentsia, but don't look for privileges. I am the head of the Jews. If you submit, you'll be able to live here; if you resist orders, I have a strong fist." And in the meantime, the other, the real "Head", Herr Hitler, has announced a major offensive in the East. People say that the Germans are breaking through the front lines and are heading for Moscow; that the Führer himself has taken over the command of the front.

It is evening now. A storm is raging outside. Rain lashes the window panes. It is good to sit between the four walls of a room. I prefer the autumnal storms to the monotonous rains. They make the blood circulate. They carry me off somewhere, like for instance now — to you.

I forgot to tell you: We are living in a new apartment — at Nadia's place. The Housing Department wanted to place five newly-arrived people with her, so we decided to move in instead. Her apartment is warmer and in a better condition than ours. Apart from that, my friend Shafran's wife has moved in with us. Yes, he has graduated from bachelorhood with flying colours. His wife is a teacher, a honey of a girl. So now we are six adults and one child, Nadia's little girl. How long the harmony among us will prevail I do not know. I see destructive elements in Guttman and myself, while capacity to keep us together I see in Mother and in Mina, the baby. By the way, Shafran is writing a paper on family life and the relationship between men and women in the ghetto. As for me, although I am healthy and well, I have become completely indifferent to the opposite sex. I sleep with Nadia and I am cold as a rock. Lately, I seek the company of men. With them at least I feel that my mind is not yet altogether impotent.

I am curious about Guttman. I know that he once had a weakness for Mrs. Zuckerman. He painted quite a good portrait of her. But that was related rather to his fantasy life than to reality. Sometimes I catch him following Nadia with his eyes. Why not? She walks gracefully and dresses with taste. The expression on her face, the eyes of a beaten fawning dog, begging for warmth can attract the attention of a man. Are you curious how I feel about it? I feel absolutely nothing. It does not fill me with pride that she pleases others, nor does it make me jealous. I wrote you that the only kind of love I am capable of offering nowadays is pity. That is what I feel towards her and the child; perhaps also some gratitude. It would not bother me a bit if Guttman "stole" her from me, freeing me of the burden of her devotion, which sometimes feels like a rock suspended from my neck. But I cannot push her into his arms, can I? That would offend her as a woman. Have you noticed how conceited I am — I, the lame impotent male? At least I am sincere here, on paper.

I do know however how Guttman, as an artist, feels among us. When evening comes and he wants to work, he begins to drag himself from one corner to the other with his palette, his easel and his paintbox. Little Mina seeks him out immediately and begins to daub everything with paint. I too long for a corner of my own. I can be alone only in the street, or at night when I sit at the edge of the table, writing to you. Right now little Mina is pulling my trouser legs, while Mother interrupts me every minute with some remark. How can I be angry with them? Mina is a curly-haired mischief of a year and a half, who is all over the place, and into everything. What this little woman does for me is unbelievable. She has six white shiny teeth and when she displays them, the world lights up. If I could choose a God (Goddess) for myself, I would choose her. And Mother? In comparison with her, we are all shallow, helpless, poor. I watch her in amazement. What kind of a creature is she? Who is she? Oh, I don't understand her and don't wish to understand her, or explain her. She is our nest.

✦ ✦ ✦

(Fragment of a letter)

. . . As soon as Guttman comes home from the Resort (he works at the Saddle Resort), he eats and picks up his brushes. The only paintings he completes are the ones made to order by either Rumkowski or one of the *shishkas*. He endows his sitters with kind faces and adds highly "symbolic" backgrounds. While he is working on such a painting, it is impossible to talk to him and if I want to have a look, he is ready to tear me to pieces. His other paintings remain unfinished. The latter he usually begins with great solemnity. He no longer paints scenes from the ghetto. He paints Spain, recollections of the Civil War, vineyards and the soldiers, male and female, of his brigade — most of the faces resemble his own. "You see, that's how I looked," he points to an unshaven fighter with a machine gun under his arm. "Eh, Michal," he pats me on the shoulder. "Those were the times when I really lived, when I was a whole person." I ask him, "That firearm you carried made you so whole?" So he replies, "Sure, a gun in your hand, to help protect what is sacred to you, makes you a complete person. It gives meaning to your life. Life becomes dear to you and yet you're ready to sacrifice it. If you only knew what a weapon is capable of straightening out, how it simplifies everything, how easily it erases all pettiness, leaving you only with the essentials."

At such moments he is friendly, approachable. His face glows dreamily. He almost caresses the canvas, as he populates it with his comrades. I see him move his lips as if in a greeting, flaring his nostrils as if he were inhaling the air of Spain. Sometimes he hums tunes, pleased that he can remember them, as he waits for us to ask what he is humming. But one careless remark from one of us is enough to make him dip the brush in black paint and smear a black cross over the canvas. I once asked him why he does not paint the battles, but always quasi-idyllic scenes of the hinterland. Right away he burst out with fury. "Because the beauty of fighting can only be experienced. On the canvas it comes out obnoxious." And the brush with black paint appeared in his hand.

Another time I asked him why he no longer painted the ghetto. So he answered me, "The ghetto is painting me . . . black." Again his black brush attacked the canvas.

When we decided to move into this house, Guttman was excited. "We shall live in the same house as Vladimir Winter. You know, he is a great artist," he said to me as we pushed the wagon with our belongings. I looked at him surprised. Never before had I heard him say a kind word about Winter. "Why do you stare at me like that?" he smiled, ill-at-ease. "Because I was always speaking derogatively of him? That was the dilettante inside me, protecting himself against jealousy. The truth is that I don't reach to his ankles. I should become his pupil, that's what I should do. Perhaps we should establish a kind of painters' colony, with him at the head. Van Gogh dreamed of such a colony but it was a fiasco, because he and his colleagues had their freedom which such a colony is liable to limit. Here the reverse would happen." We had barely finished unloading the things when Guttman vanished. The following day I did not see him at all. So the first few days passed. I left him alone, until one evening as I was about to fall asleep, he sneaked over to my bed and sat down beside me. "It's working out!" he whispered. "Winter wants me to move in with him. He's all alone in a huge room. Don't misunderstand me. I must work, if not, I'll go out of my mind. Here . . . You know for yourself . . . Winter's room has such a wonderful atmosphere. After all, we'll live in the same building. What do you say, Michal?" I told him to wait another few days and see how things go. "Why wait . . . waste time?" he asked. "I must grab inspiration by the hair."

A few days passed. He did not move his things out. Every day he disappeared, but came down to sleep. Finally, one day at suppertime, we heard screams coming from upstairs. Then Guttman appeared with his tools. His chapter called Winter was closed.

But for me it was precisely at that time that it began. I became a frequent visitor to Winter's studio. The fault was Mother's. She insisted that I eat a morsel of meat once in a while. "In the ghetto everybody is a vegetarian," she said. "But if there is a piece of horsemeat in the house, it is your sacred duty to eat it." And right away she burst out crying. The others mixed in, and the discussion began. I became disgusted. How could I explain to them that I consider this my sole means of resistance against the Hunter whom I saw last summer from this same backyard, saw him with the gun at his eye, taking such accurate aim at the naked deer — the boy on the water pump? What a sportsman! What a marksman! He made no distinction between one animal and another, because everything which carries a spark of life is a worthy object to test the sharpness of his eye, the deftness of his finger on the trigger. The Hunter aims with heart. His heart is the hard leaden bullet landing in the depth of shuddering guts. I bend my head before him, the Hunter — with disgust. He is a stranger to my being. He is a Nazi. Perhaps my protest against him, by refusing to eat my portion of horsemeat, is ridiculous — but it gives me satisfaction to be in solidarity with the cattle, with the horses, the deer and rabbits, with everything that is chased through the dark recesses of the forest. When I do that, I have the strength to raise myself to the level of pity for him — for the Butcher. So, I sometimes leave the table and go up to visit Winter, to inhale a bit of "freedom" at his window. I look out at the city, into the depths of the distant sky, and more than once do I feel a craving to liberate my lame body and unite it with the infinite Nothingness.

As soon as I come in, Winter begins to busy himself playing host to me. He prepares coffee, cuts up slices of turnip and talks on and on like a radio. Most of the time I don't listen to him. But now and then he drops a word which penetrates, buzzing into my head. I prick up my ears and realize that his monologue is weirdly interesting.

Lately he conveyed to me the basic principles of his theory on art. He insists that he himself is not an artist, that he is only the medium through which the external Creative Inspiration — supposedly existing in the space around us — expresses itself. He, himself, is only a kind of prism in which the rays of Inspiration concentrate, projecting colour and form-schemes through him onto the canvas. He is only the hypnotized paint-mixer, the brush's guide, who, in his trance, materializes the will of that outside Power. Therefore he believes that he will live as long as this External Inspiration continues to use him as its medium. The entire theory is too complicated, too symbolic for such a dry mind as mine. But as far as the care for my patient is concerned, I am glad. His theory does him some good — and this again is *my* "medicynical" theory. Really, I admire that hunchback Winter. How loaded he is! He works like a devil, burning up the rest of his energy on incessant talk (fed by the high temperature which is consuming his body). Apart from that, he has begun to write poetry. He just finished reading a dialogue to me between a *Yid* and a *Jude*. (The *Yid*, one of ours; the *Jude*, a German Jew.) He sometimes tires me out. I feel like running away from him. Yet I stay on for many many hours.

I asked him what had happened between him and Guttman. He shrugged his shoulders, "Nothing happened. He is an honest fellow in every respect, except in his own self-evaluation. Basically he is in love with pettiness. He is the intelligent draftsman of every day, a man of workaday qualities. He seeks clarity and order in the images presented by reality, and that's why he paints. But he does not have the ability to soar, nor the élan or intuition with which only true creativity is blessed. He is not an innovator. He is part of the ghetto and as such he paints it. I understand his tragedy, but I cannot help him. He suffers. Of course he suffers. But suffering is not enough to make an artist of you. Perhaps I shouldn't have told him that, but he asked me for criticism. So I gave him what he wanted. I said that the painting he made was only a photograph under an impressionistic camouflage. That's why he became so heated."

I looked at Winter and a kind of fear of his ugliness took hold of me. A monster. The voice which comes from his throat is hollow, simultaneously loud and distant, as if it were emanating from a deep cave with long dark corridors. Sometimes he looks like a diabolical bird which has set up its nest in this room. So it seems odd that the eyes, glaring out of the face of that bird of prey, give no sign of bloodthirstiness. They are moist, filled with acute torment, and wise with some superhuman wisdom. Sometimes his eyes seem like those of a lost prematurely saddened child. At other times they suggest the loneliness of universes that wander about seeking God. Sometimes his very hospitality seems uncanny, and I fear his kindness; he is always ready to share his food. Occasionally, a fear befalls me that I am trapped between his claws, that he is secretly plotting something. The cup of coffee which he offers me begins to shake in my hand and I become almost too terrified to take a sip. But then my eyes meet his and I feel guilty for the strange impressions I have of him. I cast a stealthy glance towards the door — but I stay on . . . and on.

Don't think that Winter is the only one of my male friends who is an artist.

Most of them are of Winter's category. Perhaps it is my concealed "artistic soul" which seeks out their company. Perhaps all my letters to you are nothing but a game of "art". But it is precisely with the literati that I am the least in accord. I feel a kind of disdain for them — for myself? Words are the most helpless tools in the ghetto. The musicians, the painters rise above words. The wordless language of the paintbrush, of the violin reaches further than any words could. The ideal would be to leave behind masterpieces of silence, but this would at the same time be nothing. And we fear nothingness. Everyone wants to leave a trace behind: a child, a painting, a letter.

The name of one of my artist friends is Mendelssohn. A violinist. He arrived with the transport from Hamburg. A hundred percent *Yeke*, punctual, pedantic. But as soon as he picks up the violin, this superficial mask falls off him. I met him, that means he found me, as soon as his transport arrived. My cap with the red cross on it attracted him.

"Herr *Sanitar*," was his greeting to me, "What are the hygienic conditions like here?"

"Deplorable," I replied, not without a trace of irony in my voice. I noticed the fiddle in his hand and asked, "Musician?"

He tried to repay me with the same amount of mockery, "It would have been wiser not to have dragged this along, wouldn't it?"

"No, on the contrary," I replied. "It can be of some use to you." Then he introduced himself. "Of the great Mendelssohns?" I again half-mockingly inquired.

He replied in the same tone, "Of the greatest."

He also introduced me to his family, his father Herr *Vonrat* Mendelssohn, his *Mutti* Hanna and his older brother Rudolf. I searched my heart for the feeling of brotherhood. I looked at their faces, trying to read the mark of two thousand years of diaspora in them. I searched their eyes for the *Pintele Yid*, the Dot of Jewishness — in vain. What I did discover was both the expression of superiority and a tiny bit of fear, of us. But they spoke sweetly and politely. Within a few minutes I learned about their glory in Hamburg; about the houses they had left behind, the diplomas they had brought along — as well as the *Sehnsucht* that they already felt for their *Heimat*.

I had rushed to await the transport of Jews from Germany with an open heart and a readiness to warm and console them. All this became frozen inside me. Perhaps I had wished to see them downhearted, humble — and their conceit, their puffed-up self-satisfaction and hopefulness, mixed with a kind of slimy calculating self-pity, cooled me off? And perhaps our disdain towards them was the disdain towards life itself, to which they so tenaciously clung? It was we who were already ghosts, who had come to greet those who would soon turn into ghosts.

What a grotesque sight that train station was! From all sides the newcomers called to one another, "Herr Doctor! Herr Vonrat! Herr Professor!" A European breeze blew from these politenesses. And a few steps away were the heaps and holes that the "coal miners" dug with their hands, searching for some flammable material. Had the newly-arrived noticed them? Perhaps they had, but they refrained from asking what it meant. And those who understood what they saw, did not need to ask; they committed suicide on the spot, (out of courage or fear?). Aside from that, there was only one heart attack and a few attacks of hysteria.

Every day I spend a few hours with the newly arrived transports. The representation from all parts of Europe is increasing, in particular from central and western Europe: Vienna, Berlin, Prague, Hamburg, Luxembourg, Frankfurt, München. Hundreds, thousands keep coming, bringing along with them the air of universities, of diplomas, of the most distinguished professions. One's heart grows with pride. So much culture! Doctors, like borscht; engineers, like sand; professors, like dust, not to mention the world-famous chemists, dentists, artists, lawyers. They are mostly elderly people, but they look fresh. Some of them greet us with an artificial "*Shalom!*" and quote passages from the prophets in German. In their eyes always the same expression of servility and conceit.

When I meet them a week after their arrival, in the schools where they have been put up, they are already partly freed from their illusions and the *Pintele Yid* begins to peer out of their eyes. They live twenty or thirty to a room; their beds are wooden bunks. In some places it is already un-Germanly dirty, and here and there they are already fighting over a bit of food; the *Kultur* has been left on the other side of the ghetto. They specialize in trading the clothes they have brought along, in selling their *Familien Andenke*, marriage and birthday gifts, rings and watches. The first snows have fallen already, but it is not cold yet. They, however, are already shivering in tens of sweaters and coats. The art of suicide blossoms in their midst. Apparently this is all that they can put their education to use for. They do it well, aesthetically and thoroughly.

I had forgotten about the Mendelssohns after their arrival. But Kurt searched me out and waited for me at the gate. A thin snow was falling. Kurt wore a heavy coat with a raised collar, a hat with ear-muffs and a scarf wrapped a few times around his neck. His hands were thickly covered with about ten pairs of gloves. "Please, Herr Doctor," he said to me, "You are the only person I know in the ghetto." His voice had the ring of suicidal determination, his teeth chattered, "I have a violin for sale . . ."

I was dead tired. I asked him impatiently, "Are you at that point already?"

"No, but the violin is the least necessary object. I want to find a place of my own. I cannot stand living in a crowd, Herr Doctor. *Ich werde crapieren* along with the violin. I must live alone. Schopenhauer says that the great are most powerful when alone. You understand, Herr Doctor, I am a composer. The violin will not be with me, but music will."

I told him to bring the violin and left in a hurry. The following day, he was waiting for me and immediately pushed the violin into my hands, as if he were in a hurry to be rid of the burden. He asked me when he should come for the money. I told him that on the Sabbath I would look around for a buyer. He wrung his hands, desperately. He had found a shed, he explained, where a lone man had died, and he had to move in there before others grabbed the place for themselves. He wanted to buy a little stove with the money; he had to take care of his hands.

I wanted to rid myself of him as soon as possible and proposed that he meet Winter, who knows all the artists and musicians, and could be of more help to him than I. I led him upstairs. Winter, of course, received us with exaggerated hospitality. He poured out his well of words as he began to dance about us. "So . . . So . . ." he kept repeating. "From Hamburg . . . a musician . . . a composer, how extraordinary!"

I left Mendelssohn and his fiddle in Winter's hands and rushed down to my apartment to eat. Nor did I afterwards feel like going upstairs to find out what happened to Mendelssohn. Guttman was stuffing the windows with rags, Shafran was repairing the stove which had been giving off fumes, and I had to lend them a hand. Mother had a long story to tell me, little Mina was pulling me by the finger and Nadia was fawning on me with her eyes, expecting something. Yes, as soon as they see that I have a free hour, they attack me like locusts. Not bad to feel so important, yet it is an unbearable burden. The more I am aware of belonging to them at such moments, the more I feel like escaping. At length I did get away, fleeing upstairs, to my neighbour's, or rather — to his window.

I was stopped at Winter's door by a thin sound, like a line broken up by silence. Mendelssohn was playing the violin on the other side of the door. On this side — I remained nailed to my place. How long was it since I had heard the sound of a violin? I think I was at a concert last with you. There are concerts being given at the Culture House, but who has time for them? Mira, I have probably turned into stone during these last two years. It seemed to me that each thin sound was a little file trying to file through the stone, and I became frightened — of Mendelssohn. I hurried back home. I played with Mina, helped Mother wash the vegetables and listened to her story. I laughed with the women, while all the time that thin file was sawing away inside me. The memory of you attacked me with such force that I was literally present in two worlds. Worry about your safety hammered at my heart. So I grabbed this letter which I keep on writing to you and added a few paragraphs to it . . .

Let us not kid ourselves, I write so much to you, but in fact my writing has been empty of you for a long time. How can I find again the language by which I could fit you back inside me — the way you returned to my memory, called back by the pale musical sounds? No, it was not from outside that you came back. You were always chiselled into my inner stoniness, but I did not know it. How shall I manage with you? Should I allow Mendelssohn and his violin to free you inside me? This must not happen. I must not live in two worlds. The brightness of the past must vanish, so that I can concentrate completely on the sombre present. I am useful here both with my instrument bag and without it. You must not disturb me. I don't want you, nor the light that surrounds you.

The next day, I met Mendelssohn at Winter's place. There was no music this time. The violin, like an alluring female body, lay bare, without its cover, between them on the table. Mendelssohn himself, without his coat or his scarves and gloves, or his hat with the ear-muffs, only now made me realize how handsome he is. His face is fine, manly, there is stubbornness in his eyes. His hands do not seem to agree with his massive structure: delicate pampered hands, a feminine chubby softness in the fingers. "Herr Winter will get me a stove," he announced, so that I immediately felt the reproach in his voice, that it was not I who was helping him.

Winter jumped to his feet, "He had the idea of selling his violin! How do you like such foolishness? Do you know whom we have here, Doctor? Small thing! A virtuoso!" On Mendelssohn's lips there appeared the smile of a child kissed on the head by its mother. Winter spoke heatedly, "I'll get work for him at the House of Culture. We must help him. We must move heaven and earth. Such a talent! He must not go back to that hell. Tonight he will sleep at my place. And don't worry, Mendelssohn, you won't waste your time here. You will create masterpieces, symphonies greater than the Eroica, more powerful than the Fifth, and finer violin concertos than all those created up to now. Oh, Doctor!" he suddenly grabbed himself by the pulse. "If you only knew how Mendelssohn has elated me today! If I were not feeling so miserable, I would right away put myself to work for the whole night . . . a musical vision of colour and form . . . vibrating . . . exploding." He began to throw about his long fingers, drawing forms in the air. "Oh, if only I were a musician! Where music can reach, the paintbrush will never reach! We are stutterers in comparison to the musicians, do you hear, Doctor? We are stutterers!"

That evening I did not talk much with Mendelssohn. Actually I rarely have a decent conversation with him. He is not much of a talker, and I unload all my verbosity here, on paper. Besides, what is there to talk about? He looks me up only when he needs something. I don't mind it any more. I rather expect it from him. At the same time he is a *schlemiel* and a coward, afraid to walk the streets near the fence and shaking in his pants even when he sees a Jewish policeman. And he worries about his "golden" fingers. He speaks of them like a father of his children. Winter got him a good room, found work for him in the symphonic orchestra and, in addition, provided him with a few private students of German. Apart from that, Winter gives him the soups he receives at the Resort where he is registered. So everything seems under control. Yet whenever Mendelssohn sees me, he never misses a chance to complain that he suffers from cold and hunger. In Hamburg, he told me, he never paid any attention to food. Nowadays, he constantly needs to have something between his teeth. He spends entire days with Winter, waiting for the latter to offer him some food. A week ago he met me, overjoyed. He had learned to smoke; hunger does not bother him so much after a cigarette. Now he begs me and Winter to get him cigarettes. He holds them between his dainty trembling fingers; he coughs, then smiles triumphantly. That expression of triumph in his misery glows through his face like light through a fog, and it makes me give in to his demands.

✦   ✦   ✦

(Fragment of a letter)

Last night Winter organized a "party" in honour of Mendelssohn and although there was a bitter frost outside, a considerable crowd of writers, painters, musicians and just friends gathered in Winter's room. People sat wherever possible, but mostly on the floor. Mendelssohn gave a concert. He stood against the backdrop of the blackout plaid on the window, violin in hand, dressed in his black suit. With his head bent sideways, he seemed to be listening to the wind outside. He hovered over those of us who sat on the floor, like a colossus, a hypnotist. All the grotesqueness and meekness belonged to another Mendelssohn.

He played Wieniawski's Violin Concerto and the blizzard outside seemed to accompany him both with the clinking of the panes and the whistling and roaring of the wind in the pipes of the "cannon" stove. It was quiet in the packed room; the guests, motionless, listened to Mendelssohn, to themselves, to the wind outside. Warm faces. Glowing eyes. They played along with the violin, constantly changing from light to shadow — as if Mendelssohn's bow were a magic wand. Eyes and ears seemed to have become one. I noticed that

Mendelssohn was not completely carried away by his music. He stared at us, letting his gaze wander over the paintings on the walls, the stove and the coffee pot warming on it. Was he playing Wieniawski, or himself, or the wind, or the ghetto?

I was afraid of the violin and had promised myself not to listen to it but think of something else. However, as soon as he started, my decision burst like a soap bubble. It was not like the first time, when I caught the few tones from behind the door. Now I had Mendelssohn before me, and also the other faces. And this time too I thought of you, saw you. The will to defend myself against you — against the violin — was gone. You shall come to me, not in order to break me, but to make me whole. You are part of me and thus we both belong to these surroundings. Your fate and mine are one. That truth was played out for me by the mighty meek Mendelssohn, my brother.

And so we listened to him while he played Wieniawski. Beside me sat Winter, his head leaning against the side of the sofa, a board with a little paper block on his raised knees. He was working with his crayons. Awkward lines and circles flowed from under his hand in rhythm with the music. Across from him, with his legs stretched towards Mendelssohn, sat Guttman, leaning against the back of his neighbour. His gaze jumped over Mendelssohn's fingers. Then it fell on Winter with an expression of painful jealousy, then on me, with wild questioning. Beside me sat Nadia, searching for my gaze with her caressing eyes. I pretended not to notice it. "Don't leave me alone," her eyes seemed to beg, as if she felt that at this moment I was seeing you, the distant one. I took her hand in mine without looking at her. "Don't be afraid," I tried to tell her with my touch. "I shall never leave you. The bond with you, Nadia, who are a stranger to me, is sacred and final." Beside Nadia sat Shafran and his wife, all four hands knotted in his lap. Their fingers laced and unlaced to the rhythm of the music. Only then did I become aware that what was going on between them is called love. Near them sat Winter's friend Burstin, a poet who knows entire symphonies by heart. Carried away by the music, he threw his head about, conducted with a finger and swayed as if he himself were nothing but music. A contrast to him was his colleague, Berkovitch, who seemed to be carried by the music into himself, so that he perhaps did not hear it at all.

Afterwards Mendelssohn played Sibelius' Violin Concerto. He wittily apologized for playing without orchestral accompaniment. At first his bow seemed like a needle threaded first by a thick, then by a thin thread. He sewed with it, until it was transformed into many needles, thick and thin, making big stitches. Then there was silk. A silken cradle rocking. Above the cradle goddesses wrapped in white flowing shawls began to dance with demons in black plaids. Under the silken cradle I saw darkness coiling up with full foamy knotty tones. Then again, a broken lullaby; then, thunder crushing the cradle. The two kinds of tones, the black and the white, fought, quarrelled, came together in a hateful love which tore the silk and made the broken cradle heavy, until together with the lullaby it began to sink deeper and deeper. The violin was sawing up a dry rock. The thick sound of a horn echoed through a forest, rolling down from mountains over rocks as if on wheels. From the abyss the silken lullaby called, torn and hopelessly lost, until it became nothing but a thin fluttering thread. The white goddesses and the black demons danced between the thinness, back and forth, trying to wipe out the last trace of the lullaby with their wing-like capes. Again and again the song surfaced — until it could surface no more. Silence. The goddesses and the gods fell asleep on top of the lullaby. Rivers rested congealed upon the lullaby. Then the goddesses and the devils awoke, dragging the dead motif behind them, while the mountains and the abysses looked on, but not the sky. Because this was the dawning of a night. A morning for devils and gods — but not for a dead lullaby. There was the void of space. An icy desert. Emptiness. Then the silence was broken by a playful dance, knavish, young, whimsical. Horses galloped through pastures. A mocking mirage of charm, of youth and hope. The dead lullaby lay prostrate under the horses' hooves. The young horses were but a herd of pre-historic gigantic animals. Somewhere, over a steaming cauldron, over a bleeding sun, over the open wound on an operating table, a wound from which life poured extravagantly, Eternity was twirling on a broken axis in chaos. Pitilessly the lullaby was burnt on the flames of blood. And that was the end.

We remained motionless in our places, taken apart, pressed down by an unspeakable sorrow. The powerful meek Mendelssohn wiped his forehead with his handkerchief and looked at us as if to say, "That's it." We barely applauded. The wind outside was applauding much louder. Nadia helped Winter distribute the cups with coffee. I looked into the steaming blackness of my cup. In it, I saw your face and sipped slowly. I felt a sweetness in the bitterness and force in our despair. Before I had managed to finish my coffee, Mother came for me. I was called to a very sick patient. I set out into the blizzard.

Who said that we have no contact with the rest of the world? Baloney! The entire world has joined us in the ghetto — even the gypsies. They are separated from us by triple rows of barbed wire, apparently electrically charged. Between the wires are moats of water. A kind of ghetto within the ghetto. The Tzigans are however considered a part of our society, which brightens the feeling of international brotherhood. Gypsies, small thing! The free birds of the roads, of the fields and forests! The fiery dancers, the singers and story-tellers! In the evenings they would play on their harmonicas at the fence, and our girls would sing back to them, "Play a song for me, Tzigane, with green leaves on your fiddle." Woe to Tziganry! Instead of harmonicas and fiddles, we hear tones not at all musical coming from their side at night; the squealing of pigs being slaughtered. Perhaps it is true what they say, that these are no gypsies, just insane people called partisans, freedom fighters from the mountainous Balkans: Bulgarians, Yugoslavs, Greeks? We should be grateful to them for making us realize how well we Jews are being treated. On our side, marriages are taking place! The Presess gave his blessings today to twenty-five couples. And amongst us, German journalists walk about, filming the Work Resorts. And here people still read books and listen to music.

There are about five thousand gypsies with their wives and children. Fresh snow covers the empty yards between their barracks. The wind's ravages are worse there than on our side. The frost has painted the wires white and everything there is empty and clean. Even the barracks there are divided from each other by wire fences, like in a zoo. Those of my patients who live nearby are themselves half crazy. The screams coming from across the fence drive them out of their minds. Once I looked across through a window and saw a rifle moving from house to house, knocking out the panes. No people in sight, only the screams seem to have a body. My patients advise me to come in the morning, so as to see the corpses being loaded on wagons. My hysterical patient — I cannot find out what is wrong with him — likes me to ask him about the gypsies. Telling me about them seems to give him the same sort of pleasure as his detailed accounts of his illness. He tells me that every night a carriage arrives full of drunken Germans, who proceed with their entertainment in the Tzigane camp.

The blizzard was still performing its concerto. I rushed, not back home, but to the hospital. I stretched out on a cot in the corridor. It must be wonderful to be sick, to let go the reins and surrender to the bed, to the earth. But they would not let me surrender, even to sleep. Evidently, disturbing me gives pleasure to both the patients and the nurses. The major part of the night I promenaded among a forest of beds. Is it strength that makes me carry on, or weakness?

Chapter Twenty-three

LIKE HIS FATHER, Mietek Rosenberg was not one who surrendered easily. At first his dismissal from the police seemed to him a cruel trick of his colleagues, or just some devilish mistake. It never entered his mind to link this event with his encounter with the Presess that Sunday of the children's parade. The encounter itself he, of course, remembered well, cherishing the memory of the Presess having called him "my son". He compared this friendly old man with his own father and wondered whether the world would not be a much better place, if children could pick their own parents. His own father was a bitter egoist who had never loved his only son, whereas Presess Rumkowski had a big heart and every child was dear to him. It was after his encounter with the Presess, that Mietek revised his attitude towards him, reproaching himself for having previously mocked him, or told jokes about him and, like everybody else, having called him 'King Chaim the First'. Only now did Mietek realize how hard the Old Man's road was and how many rocks his own Jewish people were putting under his feet. Consequently, he decided to take his job as policeman more seriously.

He had always been a first-class policeman. The officers praised him and singled him out as an example, while his own colleagues respected him. But he had been a good policeman out of egoism, the egoism that he had inherited from his father. He had considered his policeman's cap as his passport to survival, and his motto had been: climb over others in order to keep yourself at the top. And climb he did, unscrupulously, without any pangs of conscience, without seeing whom he was hitting, chasing, arresting and dragging to jail, to Steinberg and his whip. But after his historic encounter with the Presess, Mietek realized that the life for which he had been struggling was empty and aimless, because it was so petty. During his mother's illness he had succumbed to the habit of analyzing himself and thinking of the mystery called human nature. He had wanted to help her, as he now wanted to help people in general. Being a policeman began to mean being a guardian of the ghetto, a watchman in the service of the community.

His dismissal was a blow which blinded him. At the police station he cursed and shouted, throwing himself at his colleagues with his fists. He had the suspicion that it was they who had tripped him up and squealed on him on account of some minor sins. But they themselves were not free of sin. He hissed that out at them from between his gnashing teeth, while the innocent fellows tried to appease him. So did the commander, who was himself also afraid of him. He too tried to calm Mietek with kind words and promises to find another good position for him. But Mietek jeered at him, stamping his foot and slamming his fists on the commander's desk, a thing which was unheard of. When he heard that the order to dismiss him had come from the Presess himself, he burst into guffaws. "The Presess is my best friend, Herr *Kommandant*, in case you don't know!" The commander swore by the names of his wife and children, while Mietek looked down at him. "Then I want to see the order!"

The commander spread his hands, "There is no written order. He told me . . ."

"So, he told you? That we shall soon see!" And Mietek dashed out of the commander's office, running in the direction of Baluter Ring. He was still laughing inwardly. Soon the truth would come out and the commander would shake in his pants. He, Mietek, would advance in the ranks. With time he himself might perhaps become commander, because it was no secret that the present commander was a nincompoop, a coward and a lazybones, who had only his fat rations on his mind. He, Mietek, would build a real police force, a just and honest one. And as he made his way to see the Presess, Mietek managed to see himself in even more important roles than that of commander of the ghetto police. Handsome guy though he was, with his fine muscular figure, with his straight legs and calves of steel, he was by no means merely vain like a movie actor. He was a man of brains, of intellect. As he ran, he saw himself as a hero, accomplishing acts of unusual, almost super-human bravery, in which both his mind and his physique played a part. He saw himself decorated with medals, his picture hanging on the walls of offices and schools. He saw his name in black print on the front pages of newspapers, both Polish and foreign. He read many-columned articles about his heroic deeds, each sentence full of praise . . . praise . . .

It was not difficult for him to get into Baluter Ring. He winked familiarly at the two policemen on guard at the Presess' office, and they let him through to the Presess' secretary. She immediately went in to announce him, because there was no doubt in her mind that what Mietek had to convey to the Presess was of extraordinary importance. She read it on his face. It was not long, however, before she reappeared with astonishment in her eyes. "The Presess refuses to see you, Mr. Rosenberg."

Mietek smiled confusedly, "He refuses . . . or is unable to?"

"Refuses."

A thought lit up in his head: they had squealed on him before the Presess, perhaps mentioning some of his insignificant trespasses. His blood began to boil. He insisted that the girl ask the Presess to give him at least a few minutes. But she had already nodded to the two policemen at the door and all traces of amicability had vanished from her face. He hurried back to the police station, ready to raise hell. They were waiting for him there. His police cap and armband were taken away from him, and his career as a policeman was over. And since during that ceremony, Mietek managed to throw himself at the chief himself, he was sent to prison, where he was held at the disposal of the police chief who was personally interested that Mietek be punished as he deserved.

In prison, his pants, jacket and boots were taken away from him. He was given a shabby suit with short pants and a jacket full of holes; the shoes he received were practically falling apart. But he was well treated. The supervisor of the jail wanted to send someone to Mietek's home to bring his own clothes, but Mietek forbade him to do this. He was ashamed lest Mrs. Gurecki and her family, with whom he had been living, should find out what had happened.

The Gureckis respected him and considered him one of their own. They had washed his laundry, shined his boots and cleaned his room. And all that, they did in return for a few turnips or for his help in getting them into the food co-operatives without having to stand in line. For Mietek, such trifles had required no effort, so that he had acquired a real home for himself for practically nothing. The old Gureckis not only treated him like a son, but they did not even utter a word when every once in a while he took their only daughter, Stefcia, to his bed. On the contrary, they were delighted. "After the war, we'll celebrate with a lavish wedding," said Mrs. Gurecki. Stefcia herself was head over heels in love with him, and to make love to a girl who loved him was delightful. It was thanks to her and her parents that he soon forgot his own mother, whose memory he pushed down into the nebulous world of his nightmares, which he seldom recalled. Thus, the Gureckis were on no account to know what had happened to him.

The commissar of the prison, Herr Steinberg, was also favourably inclined towards Mietek. Commissar Steinberg had long ago learned what had gone wrong for Mietek, and he was against avenging oneself on the sons for the sins of their fathers, especially since he doubted the sins of old Rosenberg himself. It was clear that the whole story was nothing more than an expression of the Old Man's pre-war envy of the rich, and Steinberg washed his hands of the business. "May the old fool have such a year, as the way he leads our little ghetto," he thought. Here was a young fellow, fiery, with a good head on his shoulders, with the bearing of an athlete and on top of that, fluent in the German language, and he gets thrown into the garbage bin? Steinberg was ready to take him in and give him work in the prison office. Such a fellow would look good to the German commissioners as well. Such a fellow would also serve devotedly; he had seen Mietek's excellent record in the files of the police. But it made no sense to talk about it to the Old Man. In such cases, the latter's reason stopped functioning at all, and to quarrel with him because of the affair was not worthwhile.

However for this reason, Mietek had every comfort possible in his cell: good soups, meat, and even cigarettes. From the other cells could be heard the screams of the flogged inmates, the wailing of men, women and children. But him the guards were ready to keep company, to come in and play *bellote* with him, and once they even gave him a thimble of vodka.

But Mietek did not appreciate the good treatment. He bucked like a young stallion that felt a rider on his back for the first time. He had attacks of fury, when he cursed the guards with the entire foul-mouthed lexicon he had acquired in the police force. He refused to play cards with them and accepted the good soups and meat as if he were doing them the greatest favour. And the guards were real angels. But they amused themselves on Mietek's account, whispering among themselves about their chief's weaknesses for him, or saluting him every day with pretended earnestness, saying, "To us you are still the policeman."

Sometimes, when Mietek screamed too loud, Steinberg himself would pay him a visit, carrying the whip with which he personally treated the inmates. He was a head shorter than Mietek, but what he missed in height he gained in width. His body was tightly kneaded, the meat on him pressed under the skin to such an extent that it looked like rock. His round face was also one hard mass, which at the sight of Mietek grew red with pleasure. One day, he approached

Mietek slowly, massively, as if every step nailed him to the ground, "What are you hollering for? The soup's not to your taste?" he asked.

Mietek snarled, "I want to get out of here."

"Why? Has someone offended you? Spoken impolitely to you?" Steinberg put one booted foot on Mietek's bunk. "Idiot!" He played with the whip. "Anybody else in your place would already be covered with red marks from head to toe. Don't you see that I'm sparing you?" Mietek sat on the bunk, unkempt, wild-looking. Steinberg moved his boot closer to him. Yes, he had a weakness for the fellow. Mietek's arrogance gave him pleasure. "You know, Rosenberg, that here, in this prison, I am king and you're in my hands. But, you see, I'm telling you openly: I like you, the plague knows why. You want to thrash around, thrash as much as you want. But why against me? What have I done to you? I didn't arrest you, nor have I treated you badly. I would even make you my adjutant, may I live so long . . ." he let his heavy hand down on Mietek's shoulder.

Mietek wanted to shake off Steinberg's hand but could not. It weighed him down so heavily, that it was impossible to gather strength under its pressure. The feeling of total helplessness was shocking. How could he bear this reversal of fate? From freedom to imprisonment, from policeman to prisoner, he, the best member of the police force! How was it possible for a man to survive such injustice? Such injustice could drive a man out of his mind!

Another time he again said to Steinberg, "If you like me so much, why don't you let me out of here?"

Steinberg again gave him a short lecture, "Idiotic ox that you are! The ghetto is divided into two parts: one is this jail, the other is the rest of the ghetto. Here, in jail, I have the say over everything. Outside, the Old Man has the say. So the thing is that I would let you out of here with pleasure, but he refuses to let you in there. Got the message? You have to sit here for a whole month. That's your sentence. On the other hand, what's the hurry? You can take a rest in the meantime. You don't suffer from the heat. Food is put in front of your mouth. Worries about making ends meet you haven't got, and you don't have to put your hands into cold water. But one thing I promise you, Rosenberg. I will do something for you later. I like you, bother that you are, and only God knows if I know why. After I let you out, I swear to you by the Holy of Holies . . . You know to whom I'll send you? To Leibel Welner, I'll send you. He'll know what to do with you. Anyway, one fine day the Old Man will come down from his throne so fast that he won't know where his head is. Welner has the Gestapo behind him, and, say what you will, Welner is a just fellow. He won't play such crazy games. He could trick the old idiot into a sack, you hear me? You'll get such a nice little job from him that you'll kiss my hands for it."

Mietek shook his head capriciously, "I don't want to work against the Presess."

Steinberg's neck became stiff and red, "What? What did you say?"

"It's not the Presess' fault. Someone squealed on me."

Steinberg began to shake with laughter and to prod Mietek with his knee so hard, that Mietek almost fell off the cot. "Idiotic ox, he told me himself that he has an account to settle with your father!"

Mietek jumped to his feet. "It's a lie!"

Steinberg straightened up. This young fellow had gone too far with his arrogance. "What did you say? I am a liar? . . . I?" His whip wound around

Mietek's body once and then once again. Then he pushed Mietek away from him, "Get out of my sight! And I thought that you really had some marrow in your head. A fellow like you, to be such a rounded cretin? Whoever heard of such a thing?" And he left the cell.

The two lashes did something to Mietek. It was as if he had received them not on his body but rather on his head. He dragged himself over to the low window which was covered with boards. He found a crack between them and put his puffy eye against it. He could not see much, only a slice of earth, half-brown, with a few wild clumps of grass of a juiceless wan green. Along with that sight, clarity shone into his mind. He was indeed a thorough-going cretin. He was no hero, and not at all the master of his fate. He was a born ghettonik, a dry blade of grass. He was a mite, a nothing, a rounded zero which did not even have a place to roll off to. Sharp pangs clamped his body like a hoop. They pressed down on him with the fresh scars left by the whip. He took off his shirt, let down his pants and observed the red scars. He looked at his muscular chest, the hard belly — crossed over, crossed out. He burst into sobs. He was a little boy whom his parents had abandoned. He was an adult in the ghetto, lying at the foot of his insane mother's bed. Through his tears he saw Yadwiga on that day when he had led her to the truck. He heard her talking the wise talk of a mad woman.

He clasped his knees and buried his head between them, moaning, "You weren't even a mother . . . You didn't even love me. Mama . . . Mama . . ." he repeated tens of times. Fear engulfed him. He felt that he was going out of his mind. In his panic, he threw himself on his cot and buried his head in the straw mat. "That's what I've inherited from you . . . your madness is your heritage . . ." he bleated. He thought that he had already crossed the borders of sanity. The image of Yadwiga refused to vanish. He jumped off his bunk. His body hurt and he became curious about it. He had never felt anything like this before. Again he had the impression that the pain in his body was really in his brain, and again he looked at the red marks on his chest — to convince himself that it was not so. He began to pace the cell, taking pleasure in the difficulty of doing so. His body had been crossed over with a red pencil, not his mind. The mind was intact. He had proof of it. He began to multiply numbers, add, subtract. Then he began to recite poetry. "Dark everywhere, cold everywhere . . . What will now happen? What will now happen?" He cut short his recitation and searched his mind in vain for some more cheerful verses. Suddenly, he had a wild craving to sleep with a woman. It was more powerful than ever before. He threw himself back on his cot. Sharp clear images began to rush past his mind. He felt smells . . . tastes. He gave himself to them until he stopped feeling the scars of his body or the fear in his heart — losing himself in an all-effacing pleasure.

The two routine lashes from Steinberg's whip did indeed work wonders on Mietek. It became a delight to have him as an inmate. Not only did he no longer stamp his feet, but he became friendly with the guards, was ready to play cards with them, or to tell and listen to jokes. He did anything to get them to stay in his cell as long as possible, because he had become afraid of being alone. He tried to entertain them with spicy tales, true or invented, about himself as a policeman. It was not difficult for him to talk about his past. He was not ashamed of himself and regretted nothing, although he would never again, for any price in the world, go back to being a policeman. He wanted to use his brains, apply his intelligence. But the guards were evidently losing interest in him and they came less and less often to visit him. In vain did he wait for them, killing time by playing games with the bedbugs, or in vague daydreaming, or by replaying his recollections of the roof window in the Gureckis' apartment.

Steinberg also seldom came to see him now. The more submissive and obedient Mietek became, the more uninteresting he found the young fellow. Besides, Mietek had also become physically less attractive. He had grown skinny. His face lost its fresh healthy glow, becoming sallow under the cheekbones; a face which incited Steinberg to swing his whip. When Steinberg at last paid him a visit, Mietek received him with joyful awesome respect. He whispered shyly, "I have only five more days to go, Mr. Steinberg."

The prison commander was indifferent. "I see you can count."

"You . . . you . . . promised to find me a job . . . brain work . . ."

Steinberg had no sentiment left for the pitiful creature. He yelled at him, "Why don't you stand up when you speak to me, idiot?" Mietek jumped to his feet. "And your shirt, why is it so filthy, my great prince? The lice are probably crawling all over you! My, do you ever deserve another lesson from me!" Confused, Mietek began frantically to arrange his dress. Steinberg was not pacified. "Still another five days to go, you said? Then I'll have to hurry up and give you some training . . ."

During the next five days Steinberg invited Mietek to his office, and treated him each time to a number of lashes. When they were finally about to take leave of each other, Steinberg gave Mietek a few kind words, "Just your luck that the transport for Germany is complete. And hurry, scabhead, sweep up the cell and turn over the straw mat, so that someone else won't have to eat your lice!"

✦ ✦ ✦

On his twenty-first birthday, Mietek was released from prison. He fell into the ghetto as into a boiling kettle, shaking on his feet because of the clamour and the blinding light which engulfed him when he stepped out into the street. Like someone who was leaving his sick-bed for the first time after a long illness, he stumbled ahead towards the Gureckis' house to fetch his belongings. He was about to lose the place he had called home. Now that he was no longer a policeman and did not have any rations of turnips to give away, or the ability to help them out in the lines, it was obvious that the Gureckis would refuse to keep him.

The Gureckis were at work, Mr. Gurecki at the Paper Resort, Mrs. Gurecki at the Millinery Resort and their daughter Stefcia at the Knitting Resort. As he stood behind the locked door, it occurred to Mietek for the first time that the Gureckis were locked up in a jail for ten hours of every day. He would still have to wait many hours until they returned. He had his own key, but had probably left it in the pocket of his police uniform. Slowly, he went down the stairs and passed the yard with his head lowered, in case he should meet a neighbour. He was ashamed of his appearance. Once in the street, he still kept his head lowered, in case he should meet an acquaintance. After he had crossed the bridge, he peered into the backyard on Hockel Street where he had once lived. "I don't want to see him," he mumbled to himself at the thought of his father.

As he was about to move on, he heard someone call him. Before him stood Bella Zuckerman. Her summer coat was unbuttoned and revealed a white blouse with a stiffly ironed collar. She was pale; the wings of her irregular nose fluttered. He avoided her gaze which was both sad and acute in its astonishment. Nor was he able to look at her mouth which was twisted into an awkward smile of surprise. "I haven't seen you for so long," she whispered, looking to the side.

"I've come to see Father," he said, in spite of himself. They passed through the backyard in silence, at a distance from each other. His heart was pulling him backwards, as his feet carried on.

Reisel received him as if he were a Purim clown. "I am going to faint!" She folded her hands over her chest. Mietek cast an uncertain glance in the direction of Adam's room; he had the impression that Yadwiga was still locked inside. Reisel shook her head, "My, my, what clothing can do to a person! What happened to you?" She saw that Mietek's gaze was fixed on Adam's door and announced, "He's not at home; suffering on account of his teeth, poor soul; spends his days at the clinic."

Mietek felt his knees give way under him. His head swam. Bella's voice reached him as if from very far, "Come into my room . . ." He followed her, entered her room and sat down on a bed. It seemed to him that he was seeing the room for the first time: the shelves with books, the dry autumn flowers in a vase on the table, cut out reproductions of paintings on the walls, and the open balcony door. A shaft of light, a yellowish-pink reflection of the sun, was cut into the floor and expanded over half the bed. Wearily, he turned his head to Bella. There was something alien between that ugly girl and himself, but it was a kind of alienation which was warm and bright. "You are not with the police any longer?" she asked.

The air in the room was soothing. He inhaled deeply, inhaling simultaneously the sight of Bella. "No," he replied, observing her navy blue pleated skirt and the spotless white blouse trembling lightly over her bosom. His gaze was trapped in her eyes and was unable to extricate itself.

She reached out for his hand, "Congratulations!" The coolness of her hand penetrated his. He was unable to let go of her, and he pulled her closer to himself. She sat down beside him.

Words began to bubble on his lips, "You must help me, Bella. Talk to your father. I want a job . . . brain work . . . You know that I have a good head, don't you? I was an ace in maths, algebra, trigonometry . . . I could be the head of an office. You know I am not . . . so shallow." She made a move to bite her nails. A noise came from the corridor. Mietek jumped to his feet, "I don't want to see him!" he burst out. "I must run. Come to see me." He gave her his address, waited until it became quiet in the corridor and dashed out of the room. He wandered about the ghetto, his head hanging. It seemed to him that everyone was watching him, that the entire ghetto was laughing at him behind his back. He decided to wait in front of the Gureckis' door.

Mrs. Gurecki received him joyfully. Stefcia clung to him, kissing and hugging him. Only Mr. Gurecki twisted his face as if he had a belly ache. Mietek changed into one of his suits and sat down at the table. He had not eaten all day and was disinclined to wait and see whether or not they would invite him to join them in their meal. Mr. Gurecki's face twisted even more. But the two women accepted his presence at the table. They asked him no questions. He wondered why, but was glad. As soon as the meal was over, however, he wanted to find out where he stood with them. "I am not with the police force any longer," he announced.

They did not seem surprised. "Stefcia could not get in to see you," Mrs. Gurecki said. "That dog Steinberg refused to let her in." She gave a maternal chuckle. "You, Mietek, have helped us for so long, now it is time for us to help you a bit." She turned to her husband consolingly, "With his 'protection', he can come by something better than work with the police. He can become the head of an office, or a manager of a co-operative." Mietek agreed with her. They struck up a conversation about the position Mietek should choose. At night Stefcia paid a visit to his bed. He leapt on her greedily.

Three days later Bella came to see him. When he saw her radiant face, he fell upon her in the presence of all the Gureckis, and carried her off to his room. He was not sure whether it was the good news he read in her face that so overjoyed him, or whether it was the mere sight of her.

"You are to be a foreman at the Metal Resort!" Bella made haste to calm his curiosity. His enthusiasm subsided immediately. Slowly he let go of her and collapsed on his bed. She approached him. "I quarrelled with Father because of it . . . Why aren't you satisfied?"

"I told you that I want to be the head of an office, or a manager."

"I cannot make you a manager."

"Your father can."

"Do you think it's so easy?" She sat down beside him, shyly touching his hand, "You will go to work tomorrow, Mietek, won't you?"

Her touch calmed him. He was silent for a long while before he answered, "I'll go. I'll work myself up to the top. I'll advance. You'll see. They will find out what I am capable of." He got up from the bed. "Come, let's go down," he proposed. It was a mild evening in early fall. Mietek had his arm around Bella's waist. "A few days ago was my birthday," he whispered in her ear.

At night Stefcia came to his bed. She cried, while he consoled her with a compassion which he had never suspected himself of having. "Silly girl," he whispered. "I've never even kissed her." This straightened something out inside both of them.

"She is ugly," Stefcia stated, completely reassured. "But you have to be nice to her. Her father is a *shishka*." She cuddled up to him, proud of herself, of her pretty face and her shapely body.

Mietek's work at the Metal Resort went well, just as he had decided it would. During the first days he became chummy with the other foremen and *Meisters*. Office girls noticed him immediately and ogled him shyly. The manager was also friendly towards him. Although he had no idea about metallurgy, he took over his hall with self-assurance, and the young metal turners who worked under him treated him with respect. He often stayed on at the Resort after work to learn the secrets of the trade. The machines fascinated him. He admired their construction, their precision. He liked their loud metallic roar which made the floors of the entire building shake. It was good to pace between these steel giants on the swaying floor. He felt himself to be strong and gigantic, because he was master over such giants. He introduced a police-like discipline in his hall. He tolerated no late coming; towards the sick he was fair, but not lenient; if necessary, he let his fist fly. The boys feared him, but did not dislike him. He demanded what he was entitled to, yet he was a *mentsch*.

Unexpectedly, Mietek's hall began to turn out the largest production of the Resort. The other *Meisters* and foremen would come in to watch and learn how he achieved such results. In the other halls the foremen could not step out even for a second, because the workers would immediately slacken their tempo and gather between the machines to chat about food and politics. In Mietek's hall this never happened. Food and politics were discussed only during the lunch break, when he left his workers alone; he did not care for these topics of conversation. The only thing he cared for was production, discipline, the double soups and the food premiums. He cared for praise from the manager, for the compliments of the foremen and *Meisters*. He felt good, calm. He had no enemies in the Resort and no one envied him. He did not use any devious tricks, resorted to no flattery and if he could, did a favour when asked. Such was the person he was and such was the person he wanted to be. He was a grown man now. Somewhere in the ghetto there was a girl with an ugly nose and a clumsy figure. Did she have anything to do with the great change in him? He saw Bella rarely and often forgot that she existed. He had his family: the Gureckis.

When he did remember Bella, he would cross the bridge. He did not go into the house on Hockel Street, but rather called her down through the balcony. With her also came out the slim and pretty Junia. She would chatter away, while he admired her fiery eyes and her bosom which winked down at him through the railing. But it was Bella he wanted to see. She came down to him and he embraced her entire clumsy ugliness with his eyes. In his heart a voice sang out; he could barely wait to lock her in his arms and take her cool soft hand in his. They strolled along Hockel Street together with the crowds of other young people. He told her about his days and weeks, about his achievements at the Resort, about his new friends and the boys who worked the machines. He was also curious about her life. She was in the middle of her *matura* exams. It was wonderful, she said, to be passing one's *matura* and to have him, Mietek. She had no fear of the green table and the long row of professors who bombarded her with questions, without giving her time to catch her breath. She told him in detail the questions she had been asked, the tests she had taken and how she had handled them.

He listened to her attentively. A desire to absorb information took hold of him, the same eagerness to learn that he had had as a boy. But then he had wanted everything to come easily to him; he had hated the boredom of studying. Bella's talk kindled his craving for knowledge, his craving to work for it — the more difficult the better — to aim at reaching intellectual gratification. Sometimes as they chatted, they would leave Hockel Street, cross the bridge and arrive at a place which Bella called 'The nicest corner in the ghetto' — the cemetery.

✦ ✦ ✦

One day the news spread like lightning through the Resort that Presess Rumkowski had arrived with a German commission for an inspection tour. A feverish nervousness took hold of all the floors and halls. Mietek himself did not know what was happening to him; never before had he experienced such tension. There was no fear mixed with it, but an almost joyous anticipation of praise. He was informed that his hall would be the last inspected, and that he should see to it that everything was in order. He felt flattered. They wanted to show him off, so that the commission would leave with a good impression. He marched past his boys, patting them cordially on the shoulders, unable to conceal his excitement. "Hold on to yourselves, boys!" he encouraged them, laughing aloud, distractedly, enthusiastically. How good it was that he was no longer a policeman, a do-nothing, someone who attacked the unprotected! Now he was a productive useful person, the best foreman in the most important Resort in the ghetto! He felt that the fate of the entire ghetto depended on his hall.

Then he sensed rather than heard a commotion in front of his hall. A few uniformed decorated officers stood in the entrance. Automatically, Mietek snapped to attention, like a policeman knocking his spurs together and called out, "*Achtung!*" His voice came out somewhat hoarse, but sounding courageous and military.

The German officers began their walk between the rows of machines. A few steps behind them came Presess Rumkowski and the manager of the Resort. Mietek cast a sideways glance at Rumkowski. He recalled him being much taller and more broad-shouldered than he seemed now; as he followed the officers his head stooped forward. One of the officers beckoned to him with a finger, as one beckons to a boy, and the Presess ran over, followed by the manager. They meekly answered the questions put to them, and then all faces turned to Mietek. A gloved finger now beckoned to him. Mietek pulled himself together, marched over to the officers with a military step and halted before them with his head proudly raised. He caught the mocking sparks in their eyes, but would not allow his heart to sink. He was questioned about the work, the production. He answered calmly, in correct German, and the sparks in the officers' eyes gradually went out. Instead, they listened attentively to his explanations. He lucidly and precisely described the function of each machine, its advantages and disadvantages, displaying the screws and machine parts being produced in his hall. Then it was all over. The officers left, followed by the stooping Presess.

But it was not completely over yet. Two days later, a big order arrived at the Resort, along with a letter of praise from Herr Biebow. As a result, the Presess himself gave a banquet for all the *Meisters* and specialists of the Resort. Mietek was given a place of honour at the banquet. Assigned to receive a prize, he was seated between the Presess and the commissar of the Resort, at the head table. Friends had insisted that Mietek deliver a speech in the name of the *Meisters* and foremen when he received his prize, a signed portrait of the Presess. But he had refused. He did not like speeches. His friends praised his modesty and liked him even more.

There were enough speeches without Mietek. The commissar, the representatives of the *Meisters*, the director of the Labour Department, the Presess' personal friend Herr Zibert, all spoke, after which the Presess himself stood up and spoke about the importance of the new order. He praised the Resort, in particular Mietek's hall, while everyone applauded. The Presess was in good spirits (he was in love), and he spoke with feeling. While the meal was being served, he turned to Mietek with a friendly remark, "Too bad, my son, that your parents are not here. They would have been proud . . ." Mietek's face flushed a fiery red. He began talking fast, hoping to take the Presess' mind off the subject of his parents; somehow he felt it was wiser not to mention them. But the Presess did not take his eyes off him. Their gazes met. The Old Man's face suddenly became alien, repulsive. "You . . . you are that Rosenberg?"

A few days later the raw materials for the order arrived. The Resort turned into one wild roaring machine going full steam. Mietek, perspiring heavily, rushed back and forth with blueprints and schemes. He conferred with the engineers and the manager, so that they might explain to him the new type of screws which his hall had to produce. After work, he stayed on at the Resort, not yet clear on all the details. He would not let the engineers go home; he demanded explanations, discussed methods, pondering how to raise the output of the machines. When he came home it was late in the evening. The Gureckis were not at home. As he changed his clothes, he noticed a card on his table. It was a summons for him to appear within forty-eight hours at the prison, in order to join the transport of men being evacuated to Germany for labour.

Unlike the event of his dismissal from the police force, there were now people to intercede on Mietek's behalf. There was the Resort commissar and his friends, as well as the Labour Department. Had some mistake again taken place? Mietek was calm. He tore up the summons and went to work as usual, waiting for the problem to be cleared up. At the end of the day, the commissar declared, "The Old Man has something against you and there is nothing I can do about it.".

But there was still Samuel Zuckerman and there was still a day left. Bella rushed with him to the Carpentry Resort, to Samuel's office. Samuel calmly declared to Mietek, "The Old Man does it all on account of your father. He's just waiting for the opportunity to send him too out of the ghetto. Your father once called him a *shnorrer* and refused to contribute to the orphanage." Something began to buzz, to swim about in Mietek's head. Samuel added, "I cannot risk my neck. The best thing would be for you to hide out for a certain time."

"Go to the Presess, Papa," Bella implored him.

Samuel jumped to his feet with rage, "I told you, I cannot risk my neck!"

Mietek left father and daughter behind and rushed home. "I must hide!" he distractedly declared to the Gureckis and scoured their faces with his glance, impatient for them to come up with some advice.

Mrs. Gurecki spoke up first, "During the day you can stay in the house and we'll lock you in."

"And at night," Stefcia jumped to her feet, "If they break in, you can climb onto the roof through the roof window!"

Twice the police came to look for him and the roof window saved him. After he had hid for a week, his ration cards were annulled. He lost the right to pick up his food and Mr. Gurecki began to grimace and to quarrel with his wife and Stefcia. At length, he told Mietek not to show up at the table.

Every evening Bella arrived with a bag of food. She brought warm soups, and sometimes meat and sugar. The first day Mietek was wise and patient, dividing his food and leaving a bit for the following day. But after a few days, hunger had him snugly in its grip and he could barely wait for Bella to leave, before devouring his next day's bit of food. Sitting locked up brought back the taste of his days in prison, but this time he felt no rebellion or rage. A hollowness nestled within him. He lay on his bed for entire days, his eyes staring upwards, to the roof window over which he saw the clouds sailing by. He would wait for Bella. In his imagination, she became one with the bag of food. He longed for her, counting the hours to her arrival.

When she did arrive, everything inside him stirred, as though a wind had swept through his blood. He rushed to meet her and took her hurriedly into his arms. He wanted to look into her big dark eyes. But while he held her pressed against his chest, he could not remove his eyes from the bag in her hand. It was difficult for him to eat in her presence. He wanted to hide like a dog with its bone, and he sat down to his meal with his back turned. She talked to him from behind his back, pleasant whispers, to console him. He swallowed her words along with each bite of food, and without the slightest idea of what she was talking about.

At night Stefcia would come in. She too would bring him a part of her food. He would throw himself both at the food and at her. During his first week of hiding, he would tear her out of her sleep each time he awoke and felt the hollowness inside him. Then all his hunger for her body dried up and the forsaken Stefcia would sob at his side. The sound of her sobs mingled with the sound of the rain against the panes of the roof window. Somehow the nights passed. The days were worse. Bella brought him books. He could not read, his thoughts being wholly occupied with food, and the greater his craving for it became, the longer the day seemed to him.

One day, as he lay in bed counting the hours until Bella's arrival, the thought of Junia entered his mind. He once used to flirt with her, to fool around. There was a playful cameraderie between them, and she was brave, energetic and clever. He imagined her arriving every morning with a bag of food, then Bella coming in the evening, and Stefcia at night. Then the hunger would not bother him so, and he could collect his thoughts and analyze the situation. He pondered how to reach Junia without Bella's knowledge, and the strangest idea possible in the ghetto occurred to him: he would write her a letter. He immediately sat down to it. Then he called in a boy and for ten pfennig the problem was solved.

When Bella arrived the same evening he had more patience for her. After his meal, he allowed himself to look at her and take her hand in his. He felt the mild vibration that started inside him as soon as he touched her. Always when he was near her, he had a desire to embrace her with his entire body, to protect her. He felt the taste of a soothing silence, of a new kindness in his heart. Words would rush to his lips, but refuse to come out. All that he wanted to tell her he could do only by stroking her hair and by holding her hand in his.

The following morning — he was still in his pyjamas — Junia arrived. She dashed into his room, dishevelled, unbuttoned, immediately making a lively noise around him. She came close; they looked at each other with the familiar expressions on their faces, mischievously, amiably. "Why did you send for me?" she asked. He bluntly came out with his plea. She spread apart the tails of her coat, and stood with her hands on her hips. Tall and graceful, she made him think of a gazelle. Her glance was sharp, "Bella brings you nothing? She feeds you only poetry?" She buttoned up her coat and vanished before he could manage to utter a word. Within an hour, she was back with a basket of food, but immediately she turned around again to leave, calling out to him, "I'm already an hour late . . . I've become a police woman!"

He rushed after her, grabbing her by the sleeve. "Stay and talk to me for a minute."

"You didn't send for me to talk with you," she laughed, tearing herself out of his grasp.

The next time she came, she informed him, "I found out about you. The transport to Germany left a few days ago. Nothing would happen to you if you go down into the street. For the time being there is no talk about another evacuation. That's one thing. Secondly, I have connections in the Registration Office and we shall see to it that your ration cards are unblocked." Then she ordered, "Take off the pyjamas, lazybones, and wash up. Tonight you're going out with me."

In the evening he waited for her at the gate. He felt as he had on the day he was freed from prison. His head swam. The air was intoxicating. The wind seemed unable to make up its mind through which side of the gate to blow him. He almost toppled over into Junia's arms when she arrived, so weak was he on his feet. She took him by the arm and they walked up the street, the wind blowing in their faces. She turned her dishevelled head to him, "We are going to a meeting of the *Shomer Hazair*," she informed him.

He stopped short, "I don't want to go there."

"Then I won't bring you food tomorrow." She laughed, displaying her tiny teeth. "That's how it goes in the ghetto. Nothing is for free." She led him up to a room which was crowded with young people sitting on the floor around a glowing "cannon" stove. She introduced him and from all sides hands reached out to shake his. A place near the stove was freed for them. Junia pulled out a fat writing pad from her purse and whispered in Mietek's ear, "I'm the secretary."

The change from the loneliness of his room to a room full of people and the walk with Junia through the windy streets was so confusing and unexpected, that Mietek barely knew what was happening to him or around him. Junia was reading something from her pad; some young men were talking heatedly, while firewood was constantly being added to the stove. It was hot, yet the crowd squeezed even more tightly together. An older member of the group gave a lecture, repeating every few minutes, "The fifth Zionist Congress in Basel . . ." Then a sentence cut into Mietek's mind, "Not in vain did Max Nordau begin his speech with the words, 'knowledge is might!'" Who was Max Nordau? What did the Zionists go to Basel for? Mietek did not want any knowledge. Knowledge was powerlessness, not might. Better to know nothing. Better to be blind and deaf and dumb. The speaker finished and a heated discussion began about the ghetto, about Palestine, about a free Jewish homeland that would be established on the other side of the fence. What did it mean: the other side of the fence? Suddenly, the people around him began to sing. They removed their wooden shoes and began to dance a *hora*. Where did they get the strength to dance? A girl pulled at his hand, inviting him to join the circle. He made himself heavy. He was sleepy. Good thing that they did not insist, and left him alone. Good that they danced so lightly, sang so quietly — not to wake him up.

They left the room by couples, so as not to draw any attention. The wind woke Mietek from his numbness. He deeply inhaled the cool air. Junia held snugly on to his arm, laughing at him with her eyes, "So, will you come again?"

"No," he cut her short. "I don't give a hoot for all that stuff."

"Why? Aren't you a Jew?"

"The Germans say that I am."

"Wouldn't you fight the Germans if you had the chance? Don't you hate them?"

"Bullshit. I'm afraid of them."

"And whom do you like? What do you like?"

"I used to like sleeping with girls. Now that is bullshit too."

"Then what are you alive for?"

"I am not alive, my hunger is!"

"And when the war is over, what will you do?"

"I don't think about it. I will probably eat . . . drive around on a motorcycle, swim . . . I'll buy myself a canoe. Or I'll become an officer in the foreign legion."

"What will you fight for?"

"For money and fun. And after I win, I'll drive around on the motorcycle and row my canoe."

"And that's all?"

"That's all."

Junia tore her hand out from under his arm. "Do you know what? You're bullshit yourself!" She let go of him and vanished in the windy darkness.

The following morning she came with the basket of food and announced to him with her usual busy cheerfulness, "Tomorrow your ration cards will be unblocked. And do you know what else? You'll get a job, thanks to my father. He quarrelled with the Presess because of you."

Mietek's eyes opened wide, "I don't believe you. Your father is just as great a pig as mine."

At this, all of Junia's inner fire was stirred, lighting up her eyes and exploding on her lips. Her hand flew up towards Mietek's cheek and came down on it with a smack, "Don't you dare abuse my father!" She made ready to slap him again, but he grabbed her hand and wrestled with her playfully as if she were a little animal. She bit his fist and he let go of her. "You don't deserve that anyone should lift a finger to help you!" she screamed.

He unwrapped the food that she had brought him. "Forgive me," he said good-humouredly. "You are really great. Why do we have to fight because of your father or mine? All fathers are garbage. Look at the paradise that they have made for us. On the other hand, if it's true that your father fought with the Old Man because of me, then please give him my thanks."

She was still angry at him. "He didn't really quarrel because of you but because of my sister. You should thank Bella." Before she left, she added, "You'll work at Zaidenfeld's Tailor Resort."

The sky was bright again. He would be free and he would work. That thought however gave him no particular pleasure this time. He felt like doing nothing. Instead of diminishing, his apathy grew. He could go down into the street, but did not go. Nor did he dress, but rather spent the whole day in his pyjamas. He did not even wait for Bella with any particular anticipation.

She arrived, radiant, happy. "Tomorrow you're going to work at the Tailor Resort!" she announced. "Come let's celebrate! There is a concert tonight."

He shrugged his shoulders, "I would have to be crazy . . ."

"Come down just the same," she insisted.

He obeyed, to please her. Phlegmatically, indifferently, he got dressed. He led her past the Gureckis' room, saluting clownishly to Stefcia. In the street they walked for a long time in silence; at length he put his arm around her shoulder. "Say something."

She smiled sadly, "Stefcia is jealous. She loves you. I am jealous of her too. I live only for the time that I spend with you."

He recited mockingly, "*Eifersucht ist eine Leidenschaft die mit Eifer sucht was Leiden schaft.*"

She bit her lips, "Come with me to the concert. Music soothes . . ."

"You are music . . . You are the most beautiful woman I have ever met . . ."

Tears filled her eyes. "Don't make fun of me."

"I swear to you." He became serious. "I used to think of you as an ugly little bird in a cage. Now I see you as the freest, most beautiful bird. With no one else do I feel as good as with you." Her tears melted something within him. He tightened the embrace of his arm around her shoulder. In this manner they walked through the streets, oblivious to what was going on around them. "Believe me . . . Do you believe me?" he muttered.

She smiled wistfully, "Sometimes we find ourselves in more than one cage. We look at ourselves through bars. We harm ourselves and each other through bars, because we're helpless . . ."

He did not like her to talk like that. Her thoughts were his own and therefore doubly painful. Despondency engulfed him again. "I didn't know that you are almost as desperate as I am."

"Almost? I built a tunnel under the cage and I hide inside it. Dreams . . . books . . . studying. The tunnel leads nowhere. Those who have forgotten the aim of life . . . the meaning . . . the ideals . . . are lost, doomed. What should they do?"

Her words made a noise in his head. The longing of his heart whirled like a merry-go-round while standing fixed in the same place. It was unbearable. He wanted to run away from Bella, but was unable to tear himself away. "Yet, you are my free bird . . . We are in the same cage."

"Oh, let me be. What will you do with a bird that is ugly and cannot sing?"

✦ ✦ ✦

The following morning when he opened his eyes, he knew that he had to report to work at the Tailor Resort. It even occurred to him to jump out of bed and dress, but instead, he turned over and went back to sleep. In his sleep he smelled toasted bread and his stomach woke up. Stefcia came in, dressed in her coat and shawl, ready to leave for work. "Mietek, have you forgotten? You're supposed to go to work!" she shouted.

He blinked his eyes. "I'm sick . . . Lend me a slice of bread . . ."

"I don't have any."

"And the toasts?"

"They're gone. You can take out the bread ration if you're staying home. Take out ours too."

She brought him a few slices of turnip and left. He lazily munched on the turnip, then fell asleep, but not for long. Something made him jump to his feet. The silence in the room? The noise in his stomach? The first thing that entered his mind was that Junia and Bella would no longer bring him food. He dragged himself into the Gureckis' room and began to nose around in their bread cupboards. They were all empty, except for one, where a jar of marmalade stood. He grabbed it and dipped his finger into it. Quickly he licked the finger and dipped it in the jar again. He had a great desire to finish the entire jar, but the thought of Stefcia entered his mind. "I have not fallen so low," he said to himself. "I will no longer be at the mercy of women." He went on dipping his finger in the jar until only half of the marmalade remained. Inside, in his long body, there burnt a craving for the jar. It roared in his head. His fingers, on their own, continued to dip into the jar. On its own his mouth licked his fingers hastily, greedily. He no longer felt the sweet taste — only regret that the contents of the jar were diminishing so rapidly, that the empty jar was nothing but a glass which he could not swallow. He put it back deep into the cupboard and ran into his room to dress. On the plate beside his bed he noticed a piece of turnip peeling. He put it into his mouth and chewed on it as he dressed. The peel was dirty, juicy and tasty. He grabbed the bread cards.

There was a big line in front of the bakery, mostly women and children. He was ashamed to put himself behind them. At the door stood a policeman whom he knew. He was ashamed before him too. Such humility, such a feeling of having fallen overcame him, that he gagged on it. In the meantime the first people were being let into the bakery. Women and children reappeared with brown loaves of bread in their hands. They patted the loaves, weighing them in their palms. When he saw the loaves of bread, Mietek forgot everything and dashed towards the policeman at the door. "*Servus!*" he said as he patted him on the shoulder.

It took the policeman a while before he recognized Mietek. "They've freed you?" he asked.

"You bet!"

"Good 'backs', eh? Are you registered somewhere on a staff list?"

"You bet!" Mietek leaned over to the policeman, "Be a good friend and let me in." The policeman cast a quick glance at the front of the line and let Mietek enter the bakery.

The air inside the bakery was permeated by wonderful smells. Never before had Mietek realized how wonderful the smell of bread could be. His eyes danced impatiently over the loaves. An old woman receiving her loaf twisted her face into a frown, "More chestnut flour than anything else . . ." Mietek felt like killing the old witch for offending the magnificent loaves. Soon he felt the warm touch of bread in his own hands.

As he passed the exit, the policeman grabbed him by the lapels, "Maybe we can do a little business together?"

"You bet!" Mietek laughed, tearing himself away. He ran home, rocking the treasure in his arms. "My bread, my own bread!" his stomach sang inside him. Again a voice began to toll in his head, "I am a man. I will no longer live at the mercy of women." He solemnly promised himself to pay back the jar of marmalade he had devoured, with a half of a quarter of his loaf.

Having entered the apartment, he put the Gureckis' loaves into their cupboards, snatched a knife and approached the table where his loaf lay. He spoke to himself: "A ghettonik divides his loaf so that it will last for five or six days . . . sometimes eight. Am I a respectable ghettonik, or am I not?" He sat at the table. It was quiet in the room, except for the air that was buzzing in his ears. The bread, dark and sticky, crumbled under the touch of the knife. He was devouring not a warm loaf, but a body warm with life . . . life itself. Imperceptibly, it vanished inside him along with the crumbs, and the table was empty. The knife glistened, bright and immobile.

It was difficult to stay in a room which harboured a cupboard with three untouched loaves of bread — and a glistening sharp knife on a table. He could go out somewhere, wherever he liked, but it semed to him that someone was standing on the other side of the door, watching that he should not run away.

He climbed onto a chair in his room, opened the roof window, climbed out and sat down on the roof, his feet dangling down into the room. He was not making ready to hide. He was only afraid of staying in the Gureckis' room alone with three loaves of bread. As he sat there, he congratulated himself on his endurance. He was no longer a boy; he was a man who was responsible for his actions. He thought of the Gureckis in a way he had never thought before. They had done him extraordinary kindnesses and this was how he repaid them: devouring their marmalade, without even leaving them a piece of bread as compensation. No, he was not yet a man. He only had the wish to become one. He should have gotten up in the morning and gone to work at the Resort. But he would not go there tomorrow either. He could not. It all made no sense whatsoever . . . Yet he would not touch the Gureckis's bread; that he would not . . .

He stretched out the upper part of his body on the tar-papered roof and leaned his head against his arm. In the pane of the open window he saw the lopsided reflection of a pale autumnal sun setting, and a slice of blue sky. A cloud reflected in the pane acquired a similarity to an Olympian mountain. Against its background Mietek saw his own askew reflection. The sun polished his thick knots of hair with its sparkling rays. His arms and shoulders were framed in light. He saw in the pane a reclining young god — himself — created in the glorious likeness of a man. What mockery! From somewhere downstairs rose the muffled distant clamour of the bustling ghetto. What senselessness! He shut his eyes and, in his mind, he saw Bella with her neat hands outstretched. Her ugly face was alluring, enticing, radiant. He felt ashamed before her — because of his unkempt hair? His sloppy shirt? No, not because of that.

He was sleepy, yet he forced himself to jump down from the window. He entered the Gureckis' room, avoiding the bread cupboards. He snatched the two empty pails and went down to fetch water. As he worked the wheel of the pump, he whistled to himself. With a pail in each hand, he headed back towards the entrance, his whistling cut short because of the load he was carrying. His knees gave under him a few times as he walked. He felt like laughing. Such a new funny feeling. One walks on stiff straight legs and suddenly — bang — the body sinks. Having made it to the room, he drank a cup of water. A coolness spread over all his limbs but could not wake him up inside. He slumped down on his bed and immediately fell asleep. In his sleep, he saw himself at the roof window. In the pane he saw not his own reflection, but Bella's. He desired her, not only her face, not only her clumsy body with the bulky hips, with the heavy shapeless legs, but also her neatness . . . her crystalline light in the pane. He wanted to break through to her, to reach her glass-like core and become as bright as she.

He did not notice when he woke up. He lay on the bed with open eyes, staring at the ceiling. Nearby on the table lay his watch. He was not curious about the time. Yet he knew that he had to do something. Yes, he had to sweep the floor in the Gureckis' room. He stood up to do the chore, slowly, clumsily scratching together the dust with the broom. When he finished with that, he took the empty coffee pot and washed it. Then he took the knife and split some wood to kindle the fire and laid it out on the stove. That done, he put the knife into his pocket, as if it were a pencil, and began to pack his belongings. He left the apartment, locked the door and shoved the key back into the room through the crack under the door.

At the house on Hockel Street, he was received by Reisel as if she had been waiting for him. "What do you know! So you've come back to live here!" she exclaimed angrily.

"Where is Bella?" he asked in such a low voice that Reisel did not hear him. She went on talking, moving straight towards him. He retreated, stepping back, until he turned and ran away from Reisel's hard voice. He ran through Hockel Street, with the feeling that Reisel was following him. There was no longer a corner for him to hide in, there was no longer a house which would shelter him. Bella's face swam past his eyes. What meaning did houses have after all? Another person's heart was the sole place where one could live, where one could be at home. Move into Bella's heart? That would again mean being at the mercy of women, if he did not let her move into his. And this he could not do. He had nothing to offer. His granaries were empty. He never wanted to see Bella again. She was the embodiment of ugliness. She had a disgusting figure, a hooked nose, stumpy legs and broad hips. He would not sleep with such a woman, not even out of pity. In his imagination he undressed her in order to mock her ugliness, to torture and hurt her. O, he would arouse the wildest desires in her. On her knees she would offer him her virginity. Then he would leave her.

He noticed that he was at the bazaar. He was being accosted from all sides; his suitcase was patted by many hands. He was offered quarters of loaves of bread, pieces of butter, potatoes, carrots, in exchange for the suitcase. A nagging spindly man, thinking that the unresponsive fellow with the suitcase was hard of hearing, finally shouted into his ear, "I have the real thing for you!" Before Mietek could punch his face, he noticed a piece of paper on the man's palm, and on the paper a red shiny lump of sausage. He grabbed it, stuffing it into his mouth so quickly, that before the man had begun to realize what was going on, Mietek was already at the other end of the bazaar. He ran through the street, knocking the suitcase against the passers-by. The lump of sausage between his teeth had no taste, giving only a little pleasure to his tongue and palate.

When he crossed the bridge, the street vendors on the other side accosted him. He thought of repeating his trick, but lacked the energy. Instead, he allowed himself to be dragged into a gate, so that a vendor might investigate the inside of his suitcase. The vendor picked what he wanted for himself and Mietek received a slice of bread, a bit of sugar, a few carrots in exchange. Then he let himself be dragged into another gate and sold his underwear, shirts, socks and sweaters. Thus he walked from gate to gate. It seemed a fine game — until the suitcase was emptied of all his belongings and filled instead with packages of food wrapped in all kinds of paper.

He found himself in Marysin and wandered among the houses, finally sitting down at a water pump. He opened the valise, took out the knife from his pocket, but did not use it. He stuffed his mouth with whatever came into his hands, tearing the food with his teeth. Before long the suitcase was empty. He wanted to leave it on the water pump, like that — open and empty — like a ripped-open belly, but it occurred to him that someone might find it and make use of it. He picked up the knife and little by little began to cut the valise to shreds. It was the game of a boy, a little Mietek, amusing himself with a toy which let itself be destroyed so nicely. With precision he cut straight strips of leather, diligently sawing through the hard borders. He eyed his knife with friendliness. There were two kinds of neatness in this world: the neatness of the knife and the neatness of Bella. One neatness was cutting up the suitcase, the other was cutting up his insides, as if his being were nothing but an empty useless suitcase. He left behind the heap of shredded leather strips and began to walk from tree to tree, cutting off pieces of bark and carving the shape of a heart crossed with arrows on the trunks. He carved his name, Bella's name, then crossed them both out with one slash of the knife.

The air was already cool and dark when he returned to the smaller part of the ghetto. He entered the familiar backyard on Hockel Street and looked up to the balcony. He threw a pebble at the pane of the balcony door and saw Bella in it. She resembled her reflection in the roof window, in his dream. She came running down to him and fell into his arms, attacking him with the enormous wealth of sadness in her eyes and with the heavy warmth radiating from her. As if on their own volition, his arms locked around her; his mouth fell upon hers. He had an urge to devour her.

"I was worried about you." She fluttered in his embrace. All of his face was buried in her hair. They hurried out into the street like two blind people. "I love you," she moaned into his chest. He pressed her so tightly against himself that she could barely catch her breath.

He laughed, "Did you notice how well we played the balcony scene?" She laughed with him. How rich was the laughter of the sad Bella! So contagious, that he had to burst out laughing with her again. They could not stop laughing. Where were they? What was going on around them? And so, as they laughed, free and loud, Mietek said to her, "Come with me to the nicest corner of the ghetto, the cemetery. Do you see what I have?"

"A knife."

"Are you scared?"

"No."   •

He carried her along with him, surprised at the strength in his feet which had not rested the whole day. He carried her along with such impetus that she was almost soaring through the air, barely touching the ground with her feet. The night, prickly and wet, came on early. The streets became empty and dark. The windows covered with black-out curtains isolated the houses from the outside, cutting them off from the two of them. Mietek and Bella listened to the slapping of their shoes against the sidewalk; his, rhythmical and strong; hers, light and scarcely audible. Heavy Bella had almost no weight.

The houses of Marysin came into sight in the dark. Mietek and Bella stopped running. The firmness of the sidewalk under their steps vanished. They were treading over soft paths, which they lost, then found again. They entered the softness of plowed soil and could not find their way out. It was cold and windy in the field. Bella began to shiver. He unbuttoned his coat and folded her under its wing. Glued together they walked in the dark, their heads flung up towards the dark sky where the clouds were sailing very low. It was on their softness that the two of them seemed to be walking. It was quiet. They were satisfied. No hunger, no desire. A dazzling calm in the awareness of finality.

Silently, they searched for the path leading to the cemetery. It seemed to have sunk into the ground somewhere, drowned in the darkness. The beds of soil in which their feet sank, became wetter, muddier. Mietek and Bella had no idea whether they were moving forward or returning to the same place. No houses or barns were in sight, only pitch black space — a pit with no beginning or end. Something whisked past their heads. A metallic hard sound issued as if a huge nut-cracker had cracked open the darkness. Mietek and Bella fell into the mud, body upon body. Another shot followed. Mietek and Bella dug themselves deep into the slimy ground, pressing against its frosty surface. For a moment they lay like that, listening to their hearts pounding against each other. Mietek was the first to jump to his feet. He grabbed Bella by the sleeve and pulled her backwards. Another bullet swooshed past their ears. They hurried to where the outlines of the houses and barns began to reappear against the sky. Mietek muttered through his chattering teeth; "Soon we'll come to Marisinska Street . . ." Now they were running at a distance from each other. The distance and the darkness between them grew. They could no longer see each other and ceased to hear each other's footsteps. Bella arrived alone at Marisinska Street. She let herself sink down on the first doorstep she saw, and leaned her head against the wall. It took a long time before Mietek found her and sat down beside her. "Perhaps here?" he proposed uncertainly.

She threw her arms around his neck, "It no longer makes any sense . . . can't you see? . . . Why didn't the sharpshooter hit us? It would have been *deus ex machina* . . ." She felt Mietek's tears on her hands. She did not move. From behind closed doors came the clink-clank of kitchen utensils, of people talking, of children whining. Someone was singing an old folksong, pots and pans clanked. Mietek stood up. Bella grabbed him by the hand, "Mietek, I love you . . . Perhaps that makes some sense after all?"

He left her where she sat and walked away into the darkness.

✦ ✦ ✦

By the time winter came, Mietek had turned into a full-fledged ghettonik. He worked at the Tailor Resort, but instead of advancing, he went downhill. At first he was put at a sewing machine, but he was unable to grasp the skill of sewing and so spoiled a lot of material. As a result, he was assigned to pull out the stitches from the finished products. But he worked too sloppily for that too. At length he was ordered to join a group of ten to twelve year old children who collected the empty spools.

He was tall and thin, had a *klepsydra* face and dark deeply-set eyes which seemed to consist of only the pupils. He wore an old winter coat that reached to his knees and was full of holes. The coat was held together by a leather belt from which his canteen and spoon dangled. On his feet he wore big wooden shoes, filled with machine refuse and with pieces of rag and paper.

He was now living with an old couple not far from the Resort. The couple had one room and Mietek slept on a straw mat on the floor. The old people were living on an allowance. Their daughters and sons were dispersed all over the world, one in Palestine, another in America, a third in Argentina. The walls of their room were covered with photographs of their children and grandchildren. Both old people spent the entire day holding long conversations with these pictures, talking now to one of their daughters, now to another, or repeating by heart the names of their grandchildren. The old man and the old woman were childishly carefree and seemed not to have a worry on their heads. A triumphantly spiteful light glimmered in their eyes as they looked at Mietek, as if they were delighted to see him in his misery. More than once did the old woman shamelessly comment in Mietek's presence: "Right now our Yankele is driving around in an automobile with his four treasures, may they be healthy . . . And our Feigele is probably sunbathing at the beach in Tel-Aviv."

The old peoples' room was well heated; the fire in the oven was never allowed to die out. The old pair seemed to have endless reserves of rags which they fed to the fire with enthusiasm, day and night. They barely slept. Whenever Mietek woke up in the middle of the night, he would hear them whispering or scratching at the oven as they fed the fire, cooking something for themselves at some unearthly hour. They did not eat much; they cooked in a tiny pot, then spent hours sipping their soup. Their food cupboard was locked up. Mietek knew that inside there was bread, flour and sugar. What of it? They never left the room.

Mietek would devour his whole bread ration as soon as he picked it up. The rest of the food he ate raw. A few times he had tried to cook a bit of water with flour drops for himself, but it had no taste. He was not a good cook and the old woman was so busy with her children, who smiled down at her from the photographs on the wall, that she barely had time to notice Mietek's helplessness. She had taken him in not out of pity, nor for profit, but simply because she was afraid that the Housing Department would assign some Judes from Germany to the room, people who in her eyes had the same worth as all the goyim.

Mietek would not have paid so much attention to the doings of the old people, had it not been for the lice which plagued him, making their nests under his skin, in his arm pits and on his hairy chest. The lice did not let him sleep at night, and he spent the evenings playing cat-and-mouse games with the old people. He wanted to delouse himself so that they would not see, in order to be able to sleep better, and he was also waiting for an opportune moment to be able to attack their food cupboard. But the old people were always there, and although their eyes were rarely fixed directly on him, Mietek felt that they watched over him like devoted guardians. If there did happen to be a moment when they were completely absorbed by something else, Mietek often lost his chance because of his own wavering: should he attack the cupboard, or take care of the lice, or steal some water from the half-empty pail which the old man brought up every day.

Mietek had stopped washing himself a long time before. Nor did he shave. He did not feel like it. Lately he had begun to suffer not only from hunger, but also from the cold, and his obsession was to search for old paper bags and for rags to wrap himself in, because the only shirt that he had left was falling apart, and he had sold his jacket before the frost arrived — on the day when he had run into his father.

There was a head of a sewing machine that needed to be fixed at the Resort, and the Meister had sent Mietek to the machinery repair shop on the other side of the Resort yard. It was cold outside and Mietek quickly ran across the wind-swept yard. As he ran, he noticed the janitor at the garbage box with a broom in his hand, and he was glad that he did not have to work outdoors in such weather. He entered the machine room, gave the head of the machine to the repairman, and as he waited for it to be fixed, he wandered about between the rows of machines. He noticed the janitor come in with a pail full of refuse and some spools which he was about to empty into the oven. Mietek ran over to him, hoping to save the pieces of material to help fill his wooden shoes. Their eyes met, and a choked scream escaped both their throats. Mietek fell upon the shrunken wrapped-up man. For a moment they stood shivering, until the janitor raised both his hands which were clad in a pair of torn gloves through which the tips of his fingers peered out — and pushed Mietek away from him. He picked up the pail without emptying it and dashed out of the machine shop. That day Mietek sold his jacket for a bit of marmalade.

Sometimes Mietek would wait for Bella at the gate on Hockel Street. He would stand on a corner, stamp his feet to keep warm and blow at his frozen hands, while he followed the passers-by with his eyes. As soon as he saw her, he jumped towards her and asked her to bring him down something to eat. She would become flustered, stammer something, run upstairs, and return with a canteen full of food. He devoured it on the spot and before she could manage to utter a word, he would dash off. He heard her call after him, but he would hide somewhere until she lost his track.

After a time, he stopped waiting for her. Sometimes she would pass him on the street without recognizing him. He did not stop her even when he was very hungry. It required too much effort and he was cold. He had trouble with his nose. It ran uncontrollably and during the cold days the mucus would freeze, hanging down in an icicle from the tip of his nose. The tip of his nose was in any case frost-bitten and the more he rubbed it, the more it hurt. Apart from that, something urged him to get off the streets as soon as possible, and head for his straw mat. He had the feeling that there was something invisible but enormous crawling through the streets of the ghetto, which made his heart stiff with fear.

During those nights when the lice and the whispering old people did not let him sleep, he lay on his straw mat, staring at the fire which shone through the cracks in the stove. He saw red dancing tongues of flames, and when he got back to sleep, they would dance into his dreams. He dreamt that he had set the ghetto on fire, house after house, kindling the poles of the barbed-wire fence. Nor did the fire spare the wires themselves. It swallowed them, sweeping over to the other side, to the city and embracing it with red arms. It ate up the houses, the necks of the streets, the squares and parks, gorging itself on the chimneys of factories as on tasty cakes. Then the flames rushed on further to the fields around the city — towards Warsaw, Cracow, to the mountains, to all the corners of Poland where he had once driven around on his motorcycle. Until all of Poland was roaring like one joyous fiery kettle, which spread out its flaming tongues towards Russia, towards Germany, towards Czechoslovakia — through mountains, fields and forests, jumping across the Baltic to Scandinavia, gorging itself on all of Europe, and still not satisfied, passing with its torch over the Mediterranean to digest Africa, crossing the Red Sea, the Black Sea to lick up Asia Minor, running to the steppes, the taigas, as it devoured Asia, drank up the Pacific, emptied the Atlantic, carrying along America and Australia, north and south, east and west. A flaming geographical map, a torch-like globe which was as beautiful as a round glowing bulb, as a balloon, as a red ball fringed by the night's violet aureole. Mietek was asleep inside the core of the ball. He was naked, but not cold. He slept the sacred sleep of a young god.

Chapter Twenty-four

THAT WINTER NO ONE dreamed of summer; but only of food. At night people played with these fantasies alone. In the daytime they would dream in groups. The ghetto seemed like one big stomach, covered with ice on the outside and empty inside. The streets were like frozen throats and intestines, dying for a hot flood of soup that would inundate and melt them. However, these were not the hungry streets of the previous year. These were streets wise in their passivity; streets no longer screaming their throats out in protest or rebellion.

Cleanliness reigned. This was not only the cleanliness of winter, that aesthetically covered the ugliness and dirt with the dazzling whiteness of snow, nor was it only the cleanliness achieved by the disciplined army of janitors. It was mainly the cleanliness of a clear dagger-sharp fear which had at least cut through the air of vague premonition. Its cause still concealed, it ran through the streets wrapped in inexplicability, back and forth, in a frosty whirl. The fear behaved as though it were the incarnation of a rat unable to get back into its hole, because it had grown so huge, so unrattishly white, that it was doomed to scour, all-exposed, in front of everyone's eyes — not knowing whether it was searching for its place of origin or escaping from it.

New Year's Eve.

Clara, Mr. Rumkowski's young wife, lay in bed, wearing her silken nightgown which was fringed with lace around the neck. It was warm in the room and her arms lay over the covers, pressing around the form of her body. She was suffering from insomnia, from the white rat of fear that was gnawing at her heart and considerably embittering the sweetness of her honeymoon with Herr Rumkowski. The restlessness had actually attacked her before the wedding, during the days when the gypsy camp was being decimated by the typhus epidemic, to which even the camp's *Kripo* chief had succumbed. Three physicians from the ghetto had been sent into the camp to fight the epidemic. One of the two who had died as a result was her cousin, with whom she had been raised, while the third, Dr. Michal Levine, who was now struggling for his life, had been his class-mate. The gypsy camp was quickly liquidated, and Clara was overcome by a curiosity, which she was unable to control, to find out what the Germans did with a camp of people infected by typhus; people, who, rumour had it, were partisans from the Balkans. She constantly had the image of her deceased cousin before her eyes, as if it were he who was asking her the question and sending her around to investigate. There was, however, no one to give her an answer.

364

One evening, when her fiancé had without warning failed to meet her as arranged, the usually composed cool-headed Clara felt a pang in her heart. She hurried to Baluter Ring where she met him. He had just arrived from an extraordinary conference with Herr Biebow. During that conference Herr Biebow had informed the Presess that the number of inhabitants of the ghetto must be a fixed one, and that since a great flow of incoming population had taken place, it was now time for the ebb. The housing supply in the ghetto was at a critical low anyway, Herr Biebow said, and to worsen the situation would clearly be detrimental to the health of the Jewish community. Therefore the Presess was told, with the assistance of all the necessary bodies at his disposal, to prepare a peaceful evacuation of twenty thousand Jews within the following few weeks; he had to create an apparatus to take care of that project; lists had to be compiled, the train station prepared, the police mobilized and the means of transportation kept ready for those unable to walk.

The Presess was not surprised. For weeks he had felt that something was coming, he told Clara. Did she not remember that he had warned the ghetto ahead of time? To her question about where the evacuated people would be sent, the Presess did not answer right away. When she insisted, he looked aside, saying that he had forgotten to ask about it.

It was a week of culture and entertainment in the ghetto, another project which had not been entirely the Presess' idea. The inspiration had come rather from a cultured Gestapo inspector who had visited the ghetto. However, the Presess was the one who had proclaimed the celebration. Each Resort arranged its own performances, its own evenings of song, and all these activities were crowned by those arranged at the House of Culture where magnificent concerts were given, in which soloists from 'abroad' participated; great European artists, piano and violin virtuosos appeared with the first-class symphonic orchestra of the ghetto.

To some of these concerts Clara accompanied the Presess. Inspired by the music, he often whispered in her ear that she was his crown, his solace and his support. After the concert, members of the "ghettocracy" would surround him, thanking him and pumping his hand with enthusiasm, as if he himself had been the main performer in the wonderful program. Now and then, he delivered a speech after the concert. "Our passport to life is work, brothers!" he would say. He spoke of the German order: "They demanded twenty thousand Jews from me, but I've successfully interceded, reducing the number to about ten thousand. And they are allowing me to decide who should leave the ghetto and who should not."

At night, he would study the lists of those who received allowances, of the Jews who had arrived from the provinces and of the German Jews. He counted, added, subtracted — each number — a person. He decided not to break up families, but to deport first the wives and children of those who had previously left the ghetto. What could he do? The ghetto had become a pool, with clean water pouring in, dirty pouring out.

The ghetto would awake in the morning with a shudder. Over the Resorts and offices, in the lines in front of the co-operatives, over the slippery streets and backyards the question hovered, "Who . . . Whereto?" It grew from hour to hour, and one evening when people were pouring out of the Resorts, it turned into panic. The white rat of fear swelled. It had already found its cause and was now chewing on it. Little by little people began to learn against whom the evil decree was directed and a race began to the doors of important *shishkas*, for "protection", everyone hoping to provide himself or a near one with the best passport to life: work. Gradually the fear began to shift, remaining only with those who felt the Presess' finger pointed directly at them. The others assured and reassured themselves with the Presess' arguments: The ghetto would continue to exist and they would continue to exist. Proof: the Jews who had been sent in from the provinces and from abroad. Only the useless would have to leave, the parasites, those taking allowances, the lazy, the thieves of wood, of thread and of potato peels. With their behaviour they had brought this punishment upon their own heads.

It did not take long for those with whom the fear remained, to make peace with fate. With stifled hearts they packed their knapsacks, consoling themselves that they were leaving for the country where the supply of provisions was easier. They might perhaps work the fields, be on the fresh air, since the Polish men were in Germany, working in German factories. So, after all, they would not lose much. In the ghetto they were barely alive. Nor would they lose their few belongings, which could be sold to the Carpentry Resorts or given away for storage until their return.

As the Presess and Clara prepared for their wedding, she nagged him with her misgivings. How could they go through with it during such times? He comforted her by saying that it was precisely for this reason that he had to be with her, in order to have strength. He looked at her with the eyes of a martyr, promising her that it would be a quiet wedding. He told her about his sleepless nights, and that he had lost all appetite for food. He told her about his conference with the Rabbinate, whose members had warned him that it was a sin to evacuate women and children, in particular during such cold days. Yes, they had come to preach to him, the tireless father of the children of the ghetto. And whom should he, in their opinion, evacuate? The workers of the Resorts? The rabbis washed their hands. He called the Zionists to a conference, and they supplied him with lists of their people who were not to be deported, and they washed their hands. So he called the Bundists who did the same, washing their hands, too. Never before had he felt so lonely, so in need of a close person — as during this time in his life.

Two nights before the wedding, they both drank a glass of schnapps. The Presess drank more than usual and Clara was sure that although his words were clear, he was in fact very drunk. He told her about a dream he had had. His dead wife whom he called Shoshana appeared before him, saying that he had not divorced her, that one had to divorce a deceased person too. So he told her, in his dream, that whatever the law may have been before, it was now as he, Mordecai Chaim, wanted it, and that there was no one who had any say over his life. Warmed by the schnapps, Clara and Mordecai Chaim went out to stand in front of the door. In a fraction of a second the frost had them in its grip. Clara asked again, "Where are these people being sent in such a cold?"

Their wedding was indeed a quiet affair, taking place on an evening at the end of December. Outside, a mad wind was wailing. In the room where the guests, only two dozen people, assembled, it was warm and bright. Six wedding cakes stood on the table as did numerous platters containing fruits and sweets. The wine bottles shimmered in the light of the candles. On a separate table were piled packages and albums, partly unwrapped from their silken ribbons and velvety paper coverings — part of the wedding gifts which continued to arrive. Tiny Mr. Zibert would not move away from that table, flipping with curiosity through the pages of the albums filled with inscriptions, good wishes and wise sayings about the Presess. Zibert smiled his clownish smile as he read them.

The guests glittered in the light of the candles. The women, wearing gowns made especially for the occasion by the best seamstresses of the Resorts, with their hair waved and faces painted, smiled enchanted and enchantingly. They looked like beautiful dolls. The men in their ironed suits with the white cuffs and stiff collars, wearing their shiny boots, looked like some doll-like landowners. The bridegroom himself looked regal. His gray, neatly combed hair seemed to surround his head like a kingly diadem. Hot sparks beamed out from his eyes through his shiny glasses. With boyish grace, he moved among the guests, while not taking his eyes off the group of women who like the petals of a flower surrounded his bride. The bride herself, in her white dress and white veil, was sitting stiffly, absentmindedly. She was pale, her lips were tight, her eyes were dry. The dull expression on her face did not invite any familiarity. She exchanged not a word with the women who were gathered around.

The marriage canopy was set up and the *rav* began the ceremony of uniting the couple in wedlock. All around him reigned a solemn silence. The candles flickered. There came a hissing sound from the firewood in the oven. Tears washed profusely down the *rav*'s face as he finished. "May we live to get out of here in a blessed minute, in a lucky hour!" he exclaimed heartily. Neither the bride nor the groom cried.

Later on, as they sat at the table, Clara noticed clever Zibert prod Samuel Zuckerman with his elbow. Samuel had not touched the food. "Why are you sitting as if a ship with sour milk has gone aground?" she heard Zibert ask. "Drown the worm, idiot, there's no hope anyway. So let's live it up at least. We won't get out of here alive, no matter what we do. No one will know a thing about it . . . It will be quiet . . . Shush . . ."

Samuel asked, "Is that any way for a Zionist to talk?"

"What has Zionism to do with it? Zionism, you understand, is a personal sentiment . . . the same as I feel for my wife and children. Zuckerman, listen to what I am telling you. We must hurry and lick the platter, because the end of the ball is approaching!"

Clara and the Presess were riding home to their new apartment. They sat snuggled up in the coach. The Presess held both of Clara's hands in his, blowing at them to warm them. "I would ride with you like this into eternity, Clara my life," he sighed lovingly.

. . . Now Presess Rumkowski was asleep in his bed, in the new bedroom. He had taken a sleeping pill because for the last few nights he had been unable to shut his eyes, upset and confused on account of the deportation and the chaos which had come over his daily routine. Tonight he had drunk *lechaim* with his wife, and wished her a happy New Year. "You look tired," she had said to him. He should be grateful to her for her attention. But her remark pricked him inside. She had said "tired", probably meaning old. And this was supposed to be their honeymoon. He was supposed to be youthful and virile. His personal hopes which had been crying out for realization were now supposed to celebrate their victory. And here he barely had time to do something about them. Every day at dawn, when he lay exhausted on his bed, he felt sapped to the marrow in his bones. The only thing he could do was look at the sleeping Clara. And to tell the truth, he preferred her asleep rather than awake. She had the unpleasant habit of poisoning his every moment of relaxation. During the very middle of a good meal, she could ask him something that made him choke on his food. It was for this same reason that he had taken the sleeping pill tonight — because she was lying awake.

Clara stared in front of her, her eyes wide open. She knew already how little she would be able to achieve. But she did not regret her action, nor did she pity herself. She made no account of her life. She smiled at herself in the dark, the bitter sardonic smile of a clown.

✦ ✦ ✦

New Year's Eve.

The backyard on Hockel Street was white and empty. Between the crooked bumpy piles of earth which during the summer had been the *dzialkas*, a white path branched out towards the entrances of the houses, like the tributaries of a river. High above, the moon peeked out from under a cloud like a thin milky horn on the head of a stag. It seemed like the reflection of another stag's head, down on earth: the cherry tree standing half-buried in the snow.

Shalom stood inside his entranceway, wrapped in his winter jacket, with Sheyne Pessele's plaid on top of it. He was on guard for the comrades who were presently gathered at an extraordinary meeting in his apartment. As he stood, leaning against the wall, his eyes fixed on the yard, it seemed to him that he saw something moving inside the archway of the gate, and he made a dash in that direction. In the gate, at the cellar where he had used to live, someone stood with his ear against the door, humming. Shalom touched the stranger's shoulder. "A neighbour?"

The stranger gave a jump, then answered, "They are studying the Talmud down there . . . I'm on guard."

"Who are you afraid of now, at night?"

"Did you just drop from the moon? Don't you know that with this evil decree hanging over our heads, the police are nosing around looking for victims?" The shadowy figure began to shake piously, "The Jewish people are like millstones. Just as millstones should never stay idle, so the People of Israel should never stop studying the Talmud, not by day, nor by night . . ."

Shalom hurried back to his post. It was good to know that there was someone else in the yard on guard too. But how superior to this *yeshiva* boy did he feel! That fellow was guarding a place where Jews studied the Talmud. But in Shalom's apartment, the situation would be discussed and appropriate steps will be decided upon. Again something flashed before his eyes. This time it seemed to him that he saw a face in the entranceway across from him. He thought it was an optical illusion, and leaned against the wall, letting himself be carried off by his thoughts.

He was thinking about himself. He had changed a great deal. The first weeks after his father's death he had felt apathetic. He had clung to Sheyne Pessele and she was his only worry. Thanks to that worry, he had come back to himself. So had Sheyne Pessele. She had even become cheerful, vivacious. She talked a lot with her sons about Itche Mayer. Her tone was as respectful and proud as in the rare old days when Itche Mayer had brought home a satisfactory pay. Yet Shalom could not bear her talking about him. It became too stifling to absorb so much of Itche Mayer: to feel him inside oneself, to see his resemblance in Israel, and to hear about him from Sheyne Pessele. It seemed as if Itche Mayer had grown into an invisible giant who filled the world with his presence. Shalom would have preferred Sheyne Pessele to utter a sigh or shed a tear, and thus make the father more mortal. But she, who had used to cry with dry tears, sniffling through a wet nose, would not do even that. She had no time for it. She was taking care of the household, fetching the food rations, doing the laundry and the mending. And when she had nothing else to do, she would unravel Itche Mayer's old sweaters, knitting jumpers for her grandchildren, the babies of her two middle sons, Mottle and Yossi. Apart from that, she was busy with the neighbours. Now, that Dr. Levine had left the yard, people would first come for her. She was also called upon to be a judge in family disputes. Apart from that, she knew how to explain politics so that even a child could understand, and she spoke as if Itche Mayer himself had put the words into her mouth.

Ever since Israel had moved in with her and Shalom, his comrades would frequently visit the apartment; they had meetings there and often stayed on for a cup of coffee. They would discuss the situation in the ghetto, or politics in general. Sheyne Pessele paid great attention during these discussions and more than once threw in a word of her own. She oriented herself well with regard to the political situation in the ghetto, and knew exactly the ideologies and arguments of each party, as well as what was cooking in Rumkowski's kettle. But mostly she was attracted by world politics. She knew the strategic positions on the fronts down to the minutest detail, as if she herself were a general. And indeed she had sound military advice to offer the headquarters, being certain that if they followed her instructions, the war would have been over long before. She had the complete map of Europe and the world in her head, and her map had the advantage of not being as chaotic and complicated as the paper maps of her sons. In general, she was now a convinced Bundist, both as far as world politics and ghetto politics were concerned, although her feeling of competition and her jealousy of the party remained. She was never sure whom her sons put in the first place in their hearts: herself, or the Bund.

Shalom looked up at the moon hanging over the yard. From Sheyne Pessele his thoughts wandered off towards the snow-covered field at the Russian border. Then, too, the moon's silver had poured down from the sky. Then he had lost his bride, Flora, and it had also been at the end of the year. An eternity had elapsed since then. He asked himself whether Flora was still alive somewhere, but his heart was estranged from her, indifferent. Again he noticed something in the entrance across from him. He crossed the yard, holding his clenched fists ready before him. He expected someone to jump out on him and to grab him by the throat, but nothing moved. Then suddenly, he saw a face. "A neighbour?" he asked.

"Yeah, a neighbour," he heard a young resonant voice.

Shalom calmed down immediately. However, when he tried to pull the stranger by the coat, a fist slammed him painfully in the arm. They wrestled. Shalom was trying to keep his strength in reserve until he could find out who the fellow was. He pulled him out into the backyard. In the light of the moon he saw a wan youth in a threadbare *gymnasium* cap which came down over his ears. It was clear that this creature presented no danger for the meeting in Shalom's apartment. "What are you doing here?" he inquired.

"And what are *you* doing here?" came the reply. They eyed each other, each unable to decide whether to throw himself on the other, or burst out laughing. The young man moved closer to Shalom, "I thought that you were a *Kriponik* following me, but you don't look like one."

"Neither do you. And why are you afraid of the *Kripo*?"

"Aren't you afraid?"

"Perhaps you can tell me what you are doing here. In case you don't know, there is a policeman in the yard at the fire station who is a friend of mine."

"I know. He is my comrade from the *Shomer*."

"Are you having a meeting?"

"And what are you having?"

"Also a meeting."

"Of whom?"

"The Freeland League!" Shalom laughed. "Good night, enjoy your guard duty!" and he crossed the yard back to his entrance.

There seemed to be no end to the meeting. After many hours of waiting, Shalom, stiff, frozen, ran upstairs to warm up. Sheyne Pessele offered him a cup of coffee and told him what Israel had said when he came in for a moment from the other room. The main thing they were discussing inside was the question of why Rumkowski, who had never reckoned with the political parties or with the Rabbinate, was so afraid this time to take responsibility upon himself. It was true that he had never before had to send so many Jews out of the ghetto, yet if he were sure of their fate, he would have behaved differently. Inside, at the meeting, Sheyne Pessele told Shalom, they were debating what to do, and they did not know what to do. That was why it was taking them so long. The only thing that was clear was that the kind of Jew who was now being deported was incapable of being of any use to the Germans and therefore, wherever he may be sent, he would be worse off than in the ghetto.

✦ ✦ ✦

New Year's Eve.

The young fellow in the threadbare *gymnasium* cap had not, after all, revealed the truth to Shalom. He was indeed on guard, however he was not guarding a meeting of the Zionist *Shomer* but a small conference of the two communist party veterans, Comrade Baruch and Comrade Julia, with Comrade Esther. The two party leaders had lately come to suspect that they were being followed and for this reason they were accompanied by a bodyguard of the Communist Youth members.

Upstairs, in Esther's little room, all three of them were sitting on her bed, exchanging glances more than words. Comrade Baruch was restless and worried. Comrade Julia looked sorrowful and somewhat ashamed. At this moment, there was nothing in her bearing to indicate that she had been a seasoned prisoner, an exalted fighter. She looked rather like a tired ghetto woman, a neighbour who had come in, shyly to ask for a favour. Esther, exhausted as she was, sat stiff and indifferent. She listened to their talk, aware of both the commanding and the begging in their eyes. The longer they sat with her, the more she clammed up inside and the more aloof she became. And now they seemed ready to spend the night with her. She knew very well that they were trying to awaken her courage — and that they would achieve the opposite; that they wanted to bring out the best in her — and would achieve the opposite.

"To be a communist is not to play a game of pretty words," Comrade Baruch said nervously between one silent interval and another. "The three of us know that well enough. Yes, you too, Esther. It is our duty to find out, first, where the evacuated people are being sent; second, to make contact with the underground KPP; third, to organize a core of our comrades at the place where you will arrive with the transport."

"And we trust you," Julia added in a whisper. "We know you better than you know yourself."

Comrade Baruch went on in his nervous voice, "We could send a comrade who is willing to leave, but he has no experience and he has a wife and a child. We don't want to break up families. And we also have another candidate who wants to leave the ghetto with the transport, but we need him here; an officer and a military expert, he would be an important asset in case we fight. I'm telling you too much . . . but you may as well know . . . We want to send out someone who, first, has experience and intelligence; second, has no family ties; third, is not absolutely indispensable for our future activities here; fourth, is, preferably, a woman. You fit all these qualifications."

Comrade Julia added, "Don't misunderstand us. We also took your character into consideration. For instance, I knew of comrades who, when free, were wonderful personalities, active, self-sacrificing heroes, but in jail they gave up, became despondent, demoralized. Free again, they again became their usual selves. The same with you. The ghetto affects you like that . . . But once you get out . . ."

"This is true," Comrade Baruch agreed. "Each fighter needs his post. Each person has his role to play. Normally . . . yes, normally we should have simply said to you: this is an order. But it seems that the ghetto makes us sentimental. Anyway, we are talking to you, we want to convince you, because we want you to leave the ghetto morally strong. We don't want you to feel that you are a sacrifice, nor should you do it out of despair, or even because of party discipline. We want you to be fully aware of the meaning of your mission. Only then will you be able to accomplish it properly."

Comrade Julia remarked, "We talk on and on and you haven't said a word."

Comrade Baruch smirked crookedly, "She doesn't have to say anything . . . It is clear . . ."

"Explain to us," Julia begged Esther. "We are comrades. Perhaps your situation is such that we ought not to send you? Are you ill? Are you frightened?"

Esther raised her head, but her eyelids remained lowered, "I'm tired," she said quietly. "Tired of everything and of you too."

Comrade Baruch wrinkled his forehead, "Eh, Esther, to live in such ugly apathy, to be rotted through with such resignation must be worse than death itself. Stand up on your feet, comrade. Believe me, it is not easy to put this demand to you. But neither Julia nor myself would ever have refused such an order. Therefore we have the right . . ."

Esther fell backwards and stretched out on her bed. "To give such an order?"

she whispered. "Who has the right to order whom?" She rubbed her eyes. "I'll be late for work tomorrow and will lose my soup . . ."

✦ ✦ ✦

New Year's Eve.

In the cellar where Itche Mayer and his family had once lived and where the writer Friede had died, young men were now studying the Talmud. New inhabitants now occupied the cellar. Lame King, the pre-war burglar and safe-cracker, the director of the school for thieves, had kept his eye on the cellar for a very long time, and as soon as it was vacant, he occupied it by establishing his uncle's family in it. This very uncle had many years before taught Lame King the profession of thief, along with its moral philosophy — and had thereby made a thief with principles out of him. Thanks to that uncle, Lame King fought all his life against social injustice, actively assisting in its eradication. He became a burglar of safes because safes were the symbol of wealth. That was why he had attacked them, but throughout his career he never touched anyone who had no safe of his own.

In the ghetto, Lame King immediately sniffed out on what foundations life had beeen established and began to wage a holy war against Rumkowski. He now began to attack — not safes, but the warehouses of food and merchandise. He considered each warehouse to be the private property of one or another of its directors, so that to rob the warehouses was nothing but a good deed. Thus he himself needed a kind of warehouse in the ghetto, to be able to put through some broader enterprises, because he had never been a man of petty business deals.

The carpenter's cellar had a loose floor. To remove a few of its boards was the easiest thing in the world, and one could dig beneath it as wide and as deep a hideout as one wished. And such a warehouse had still another advantage: one could keep food fresh for a longer time, thus suffering less of a loss. And this was the reason why Lame King had put his foot into this cellar — his uncle's foot that is — and soon work began. A team of Lame King's students gave him a hand and in the course of a few nights they dug out a cellar beneath the cellar. They carried the dug-up earth out in pails to the *dzialkas*, so as not to arouse a trace of suspicion. The cellar under the cellar was finished off properly, complete with a special hiding place for the money and jewellery that the booming business was bringing in.

When Presess Rumkowski set out to rid himself of the so-called underworld, Lame King did not even bat an eye. What did he have in common with the underworld? Perhaps only the fact that he had a warehouse under a cellar and carried on his business under the world, so to speak. Besides, the warehouse was never discovered and Lame King and his family felt the ground quite securely under their feet. The smart guy had not yet been born, they thought, who could manage to pull a board out from beneath their feet, or cause them to fall into the pit of tragedy.

The cellar had indeed been built for eternity, while Lame King himself was evacuated from the ghetto, an innocent victim. But Lame King had left the ghetto with his head raised high. Overnight he had sold all his merchandise and before he set out into the world, he did his last good deed, namely, he saw to it that the cellar should fall into the hands of someone who deserved it — and his choice fell on the tiny Toffee Man.

Lame King had sometimes bought a few toffees for himself from the Toffee Man, but he actually struck up a conversation with him only on the day that he received his "wedding invitation". The little vendor had the habit of inquiring from his customers what was new with them, as if each customer were his nephew or his cousin. Lame King, on the other hand, loathed people who had the habit of crawling into one's soul with their 'dirty shoes on', and more than once had he given the little vendor a 'smear under the nose', so that the latter might lose the appetite for asking him any questions again. But the tiny Jew apparently had a tiny memory, and he went on asking questions. And this last time something had happened to Lame King, when the Toffee Man raised his wispy beard — he was the only one in the ghetto who did not disguise his beard and sidelocks — fixing on Lame King a pair of hazy little eyes and inquired, "Have you lost a ship of sour milk at sea?"

Lame King thrust the candy into his mouth and sucking on it, replied, "Congratulate me. I've received the 'Wedding Invitation'!" On the Toffee Man's face appeared an expression of such sorrow, as if Lame King were not only his nephew but his own flesh and blood as well, practically his very own son from whom he was about to part. He emitted such a sigh, that Lame King was shaken by it down to the marrow in his bones. A need to complain about his fate took hold of him. "Have you ever heard of such a story? They made an underworldnik out of me."

The Toffee Man nodded, "And what are we, all of us? We are all underworldniks . . . each human being. Here, have another candy, it won't cost you more. What do you think is the Upper World? That is of course the world of the angels, which the souls of men enter after one hundred and twenty years . . . The bright Paradise."

Lame King could not make up his mind whether the Toffee Man was simply an idiot, or was pretending to be an ignoramus. "What are you yammering?" he boiled. "Don't you understand the simple meaning of our mother tongue? I have in mind the thieves, the whores, the swindlers and the toughs. The Old Man has included me in their party. That's what underworld means, donkey-head that you are."

The Toffee Man tilted his head, "Then the name is ridiculous. Conceited people have invented it. Here, on our earth, there is no difference between people . . . And if you want to know, one can say that each of us carries both the underworld and the upper world within him. The heavenly and the earthly. The fact that one seems to be a villain and the other a holy man is a question of luck. Because you should know, that the Yetzer Tov, the sense of goodness, and the Yetzer Harah, the sense of evil, both play tricks on us. They mask and disguise themselves, exchanging their weapons. He who seems a saint can sometimes be ninety percent villain, and the villain, ninety percent saint. The difference between one person and the other is not as clear as we think. Therefore, you see, a man ought to watch out day and night for one thing: his actions. Not to harm another person. One may have good or bad thoughts, good or bad intentions, but the main thing is what one does. Because if one thinks evil thoughts, there is still hope; but if one does evil things, one gives oneself completely over into the hands of Satan."

To his surprise, Lame King began to feel that everything inside him was filling with light from the Toffee Man's words. All this he himself had used to think, and it was now being confirmed by the words, no, not of an idiot or a dotard, but of a man of *Torah*. The difference between one man and the other was in the deeds. One's ideal had to be not to hurt anyone. And he, Lame King, had a clean conscience in that respect. Thus he had just received the keys to paradise directly into his hands, from the Toffee Man. And out of great enthusiasm, he pulled the Toffee Man into the gate, and led him down into the cellar. "Here you must move in right away!" he proclaimed categorically. "I offer you this cellar, so that you will remember Lame King for the rest of your life."

Now it was the Toffee Man's turn to think that Lame King, poor soul, had lost his mind. Because Lame King removed the boards in the floor, and compelled the Toffee Man, who carried his box of candies on his belly, to climb down the ladder. He lit a candle, displaying the whitewashed walls and even the empty secret hole for money. The usually talkative Toffee Man inhaled a mouthful of silence. Now he in turn began to experience the same brightness as King had felt up there, in the street. Yes, Lame King was a messenger from the Almighty, from the One who would not let a man go under, but follows with care his every step. Three things became clear to the Toffee Man at once. First, the cellar was underneath the bakery and there would perhaps be less need for heating material during the winter. Second, that into the under-cellar he could store the candies he was producing, to let them harden. And the main thing: that the under-cellar was a precious hideaway, precisely such a place as the Talmud students from the society 'Love thy Brother as Thyself' needed.

Having climbed back to the top, the Toffee Man wiped his eyes with his sleeve and bowed, together with his candy-box, before Lame King. "Let's not be afraid of anything," he said. "It has be written down, up there, that your road leads out of the ghetto, whereas mine leads here . . ." For Lame King any other words of consolation were superfluous.

A dirty bulb was lit in the cellar, casting a weak light on the walls and avoiding the corner close to the stove where, covered with rugs and huddled together, the Toffee Man's children lay asleep. He himself stood over a clay pot at the stove. With a wooden ladle he was stirring the sugar and honey out of which he prepared the toffees for the following day. Steam was rising from the pot, enveloping his head, then rolling away to the panes of the window. The Toffee Man's eyes were on the pot, but his ear was pricked up towards the side, where a stubborn *yeshiva* youngster was asking him foolish questions. With the same ear he caught the *Germara* lilt as it reached him from the table, where a few other scrawny *yeshiva* students were swaying over the open volumes of the Talmud. His other ear was concentrating on his other side, where a few neighbours from the backyard were sitting.

The youngster standing beside him belonged to the group of students who barely saw the light of the day, eating only what the members of the society provided for them. The Toffee Man cared for them like a hen for her chicks. He made them feel as if the entire world were supported by them; as if by their studying they were capable of saving the ghetto from annihilation. They, in turn, considered the Toffee Man to be no more no less than one of the thirty-six holy men who justified the existence of the world, or in the worst case, a holy rabbi. They could discuss with him everything under the sun, could blaspheme to their heart's content without fear, and could vent their doubts without feeling sinful; it only eased their hearts. However, if one of them forgot himself and called him, "Rabbi", rage would boil up in the little man. He would yell out, as if someone had stepped on the most painful corn on his toes, "What kind of rabbi am I to you, for heaven's sake? I won't let you make a laughing stock out of me, not on your life, not of me and not of *Rabones.*"

Tonight the stubborn youngster calling him "Rabbi" refused to leave him alone. Staring him straight in the face, he asked, "Then why do you have so much strength, eh?"

The Toffee Man wiped the steam from his face. For some reason this stubborn boy was incapable of shaking him out of his composure this time. "What strength, *Golem?* Can't you see that if you gave me one blow, I would fall?"

"I see that you are as strong as iron, may you be protected from an evil eye. And how much you eat, we all know."

The Toffee Man was patient, "In that case, I'll tell you. The man who knows what he wants can manage almost with nothing."

"What is it that you want, tell me."

"Look at you. Do I have to tell you everything?"

"Is it a secret?"

"Heaven forbid, silly head. The problem is, you understand, that it is not so easy to tell. Inside me I know it. All my limbs know it. Let's say, to console . . ."

"What do you mean, console? Console whom?"

"Console God, who bewails the sorrows of man. Console man, who bewails the sorrows of God. If you really want to know, I'll tell you more. You understand, between Him and ourselves it is like between a father and his children. They love each other with all their hearts, but suddenly a misunderstanding sets in between them, and the heartache of both is great. Because one is tied to the other. So both need consolation. And now move away and stop nagging me."

The young fellow refused to stop. "Tell me only one other thing. How come, as the week is long, you never look into a volume of the Scriptures, and yet . . ."

"What 'and yet'? To you, who are a little goat, I seemed to be a learned man. And if you insist on knowing, I will not be ashamed before you and tell you that I don't have behind me more than a few terms in the *heder.* And the fact that you sometimes catch a little saying from me only means that it has rubbed off on me, from spending time among the Sacred Books, from holding them in my hands and absorbing their sacred dust."

"Then tell me another thing. Why does your face shine like that?"

The Toffee Man had to chuckle, "It shines you say? Put yourself here, over the pot, and let the steam surround you, and your face will shine too." He raised the wooden ladle at him. "If you don't go back to the table, I will give you a smack good and proper, so that you'll remember me all your life!" At length, the youngster returned to the table, transmitting to his friends in a whisper what the Toffee Man had told him. There was no doubt in their minds that the little man who had risen to the highest level of modesty was far from being a usual man.

Among the neighbours who visited the Toffee Man sat Chaim the Hosiery-Maker. His two youngest daughters were in the hospital and another two were also sick, in bed at home. He had been nervous and confused lately, afraid that the two healthy daughters, as well as his wife and he himself would collapse, since they were giving most of their food to the sick children. At the same time Chaim was unable to handle his craving for food, and he was also unable to step out of the house because his family needed him. On top of that, he had to be careful not to explode, heaven forbid, with a bitter word or a shout, for he knew that it would be like putting a knife to their hearts. So the world seemed to be choking him, particularly since he felt that God had forsaken him, that he was a base, unneeded and sinful creature. He had become even more pious and observant in his comportment, and when he saw that Rivka was cooking an unkosher piece of horsemeat for the sick children, he had a desire to prostrate himself before God, imploring him for consideration — if not for himself, then for his wife. But he was unable to sit down to the Holy Scripture, and barely had enough patience to say his prayers. When he stood up to pray, he felt like sobbing, like striking his chest for his sins. But as soon as he began, all became locked up inside him. He had his wife before his mind's eye, and the more he chased her image away from him, the clearer it became, putting itself between God and himself.

After such a day, when his family had gone to sleep, he would come down to the Toffee Man whom his children called "The Jewish Dot". He came to hear the voice of the Torah. If he could not do it by himself, he thought, perhaps his locked-up heart might open through the mediation of the *yeshiva* students. Sometimes it seemed to him that this was indeed happening. His tension would subside and it would become easier for him to breathe. At such moments he could absorb the talk of a neighbour, realizing that he was not the only one who sinned and suffered.

Near Chaim sat Hersh Beer the Shoemaker who worked in the Saddle Resort and was an activist in the society 'Love they Brother as Thyself'. The other neighbour present was Simcha Bunim Berkovitch who lived in the latrine-man's hut and who was considered by his neighbours to be an odd fellow. He had the habit of strolling about the backyard at night, frightening the women when they went down to the latrines.

Having freed himself from the questioning of the stubborn student, the Toffee Man was now able to turn all his attention to Hersh Beer the Shoemaker who was endangered by the evacuation decree, since his son had once spent time in jail for stealing a wooden board. With a rustling, whispering voice, Hersh Beer set free his memories, describing the long life he had spent in the same room on Hockel Street which he would probably have to leave any day. Chaim and the Toffee Man helped him with the reminiscences, with sighs and mournful words. Had not they themselves been citizens of Baluty for many generations?

Simcha Bunim Berkovitch who could sit there for hours without saying a word, absorbed the talk of the neighbours, along with the sounds coming from the table. When he could not take in any more, he stood up and dashed out of the cellar.

Upon entering his hut, Bunim stopped, listening. With his ear he caught the sleeping Blimele's barely audible breathing; he spread his nostrils as if to inhale her light breath. He heard Miriam calling him, and on tiptoe he approached the bed and took her warm hand into his. Then he took off his coat and spread it over her blanket. Quietly he placed a chair near the bed, put a plate with a lit candle on it and pulled out from under the bed a pack of loose sheets from a used bookkeeping register. On the reverse sides, the sheets were covered with his handwriting: the eleven chapters of the poem which he was in the middle of writing.

He undressed quickly and got into bed. Stiff, frozen, he delighted in the warmth of Miriam's body. For a moment he lay like that, then he turned away from her and reached out for the pencil and the sheets of paper. He placed them on his raised knees. As soon as the pencil and the paper met — as in a first kiss — they could not tear themselves away from each other.

In the late hours of the night he began to feel the stiffness of his fingers. He pulled his gloves out from his coat pocket and put them on. At first the wool between his fingers bothered him, but then again the lines wound out smoothly from under his hand, one line pairing off with another, multiplying into stanzas, while the dance of singing letters seemed to carry over from the paper, filling the room, the world. Bunim was no longer in his bed, nor was Miriam or Blimele. He was taking them along towards the streets and yards. They were naked just like he and he dressed them in song, with fear and hope, with sorrow and stubbornness. They wept in the rains, froze in the snows, glowed in the suns. At the same time both Miriam and Blimele enveloped his rhythmic lilting sighs in warm shawls of tenderness.

For years he had been wondering why he had been offered so much love throughout his life. Sender, the friend of his youth, used to say that Bunim deserved this love because he was capable of paying it back a thousandfold. For years it had seemed to him that Sender had been wrong, that he did not deserve it. Now he knew. His way of repaying this love a thousandfold was through his song, his poetry. He was filled to the brim with devotion. That was the great poem which he had undertaken to write, the monument which he wanted to erect to his father, his mother, the Toffee Man, Hersh Beer the Shoemaker, to himself. His writing was both a singing from the abyss and a singing about the abyss. It was a call to distances of time and space. And it was the whisper into the nearest ear at his side, on the pillow.

However, overflowing with emotions though he was, bubbling with melodious rhythms which tore themselves from his insides, he was not intoxicated by them. He struggled with the overflow, bridling it with sober borders, measuring it with clear cold reason. He crossed out and erased, avenging himself on his verbosity, hammering it out the way a smith hammers out a glowing iron in the fire. He shaped his stanzas like a potter who discards superfluous clay, in order to reach the form of the vessel he wants to create.

It was almost daybreak. The candle at Bunim's bed had burnt down to the last bit of wick, the fingers in his gloves had become like icicles from between which the pencil slipped. Bunim fell back on his pillow. He removed his glasses and put his cold hands to his burning eyes. He felt satisfied and empty. Then he leaned on his elbow and gathered the written pages into his hands. Through the closed shutters the pale gray of dawn was sneaking into the room. It was impossible to read by that light. Yet with an inner lilt, Bunim sang his stanzas to the frozen window, to the mirror in the wardrobe, to the breaths of the sleeping Blimele and Miriam. Now he could allow himself the luxury of drowning in his poem, of descending into a well which was his, yet no longer his. Over the edge of the well perched a white dove cooing mildly: the grateful humble joy of creation.

◆ ◆ ◆

New Year's Eve.

(David's notebook)

To mark the occasion, the party has distributed a small leaflet: "The year 1942 is the year of liberation!" This time I don't ascribe it to hurrah-propaganda. I believe in it, not because I want it to happen, but because everything clearly indicates that it is going to be so. I am glad and proud that I have endured; that most of the Jews have.

I have not noted here the two most important events: Russia's entry into the war and very recently, America's. Pearl Harbour, although it cost so many lives, we consider our victory. Brazil, Mexico, Columbia and the republics of Central America have also come over on our side. Then why not be hopeful? Don't we know that America enters a war only in order to finish it? And lately Russia has also shaken off its lethargy. Zhukov and his heroic boys have stopped the *Yekes* twenty kilometres from Moscow and General Timoshenko gave the Germans the first blow, by taking back Rostov. On top of that, the Napoleonic winter and Stalin's proclamation of a great offensive, as well as Hitler being forced to take over the command of the *Wehrmacht* — aren't these facts obvious proof that the end of the war is approaching?

My team of the "Flying Brigade" arranged a modest party at Marek's, and we invited a few of our closest friends, amongst them the pair of tubercular lovebirds, Manik and Gittele. We drank big jugs of hot water with saccharine and evaluated the political balance of the past year. Naturally, I was the main speaker and I got drunk on my own words. Then we invited Gittele, who is our traditional reader of poems, to recite something. She is a chubby girl with pink cheeks, blue eyes and shining white teeth. I have the impression that she is joking when she speaks of her illness. She must not be very clever, because she chose, precisely at such a moment, to recite a poem called 'Grammar' which begins with the words 'I die, you die, we die.' Of course, this poem has a social connotation and could be a good comment on the situation in the ghetto. But it was not appropriate to our mood. And besides, as she recited, she smiled her angelic smile, displaying her white teeth as if she were making fun — of the poem, of herself, or of us?

When I came home I began to cheer up my own family, a feat which, as far as Mother is concerned, is not easy to accomplish nowadays, particularly when the danger of deportation hovers overhead. Mother still works at peeling potatoes in a public kitchen. She spends her days in a dilapidated shed among a heap of frozen potatoes, surrounded by a swarm of women with pails between their legs. They look like witches in the power of an evil sorcerer who forces them to peel, on and on, through eternities of darkness and cold.

I try to be obedient to Mother, accepting her angry words in silence. Stoically. She can call me all kinds of names now, I don't mind. She has chosen me to be her scapegoat, an object on which to unload her rage. If this helps her, so be it. Sure, I sometimes feel that she has never loved me, yet lately I take it philosophically. In the the ghetto people are afraid to love — even mothers.

Mother made a *baba* of the coffee dregs mixed with frozen potato peels. A delicacy! We added wood to the stove to keep the heat longer. Then I warmed

Mother with the good political news. Abraham took a pot and drummed on it with a spoon. Mother clapped her hands, and I, seeing Mother in such a good mood, grabbed her into my arms and we kissed. It is good to feel hopeful. May this damned war be over at last and may we be liberated soon!

Today it would be appropriate to make a few resolutions and oblige myself to see them through: 1) Observe my decision about the consumption of bread, eating an equal portion of it every day. 2) Find a booklet with health and sanitary rules and stick to them to protect the family against illness, mainly typhus. (Delicately remark to the fellow who works with me at the Resort about the lice I saw promenading on his collar.) 3) Wash every day down to the waist and see to it that Mother and Abraham do the same, no matter how tired or how cold we are. 4) Wash my socks every evening and begin seriously to learn how to mend them. 5) In spite of the fact that the schools no longer exist and I work in a Resort, continue with my studies, in particular maths and languages. Begin to study English on my own. 6) Register in Rachel's library and begin to read books again. 7) Try to get reliable political news every day and recount it to the neighbours and co-workers at the Resort, with the purpose of keeping up their spirits. 8) Become more active in party and political life. 9) Try to clarify once and for all my relationship with Rachel. 10) Write in my notebook as often as possible.

The point about Rachel is stupid, just a wish to be logical and rational about an issue which neither thoughts nor words can disentangle — a knot which is there, yet not there. Why, instead of seeing Rachel, did I go to visit Marek today? I don't want to dig into it. Not today.

◆　◆　◆

New Year's Eve.

The blackout curtains were removed from the window and the skimpy light of the young moon cutting through the frozen panes met with the shimmer of four open canteens on the stove. Under the stove stood four pairs of wooden shoes with muddy tangled shoelaces. The stove itself was embraced by a cord on which hung rags to wrap the feet, gloves and socks. The stove looked like the belly of a housekeeper wrapped in a torn apron. On the cold pipe, Moshe Eibushitz's jacket rode like a wounded rider on a horse. Beneath it, on the frame of the stove, lay pieces of "jewellery" on a rag: two frozen potatoes, a carrot, half a turnip and a few damp pieces of wood.

Near the stove stood two pails full of water covered with a glassy skin of ice. It was on that corner that the shadows and the moonlight played. Further up in the room the walls looked odd. The shelves holding books looked like parted lips, between which stood the rows of books like teeth. A figurine of a girl, the size of a dwarf stood on one of the shelves, like a character out of the covers of a book. The tiny girl, made of mashed paper and flour glue, held a *cholent* pot the size of a thimble in her tiny hands. With her bead eyes she stared at the room and at the cots made of chairs. On one of the cots Shlamek was asleep. On the other slept Rachel, half of her face sunken into the pillow, the other covered by a net of hair.

In the reality of her dream, Rachel saw herself as a doll kneaded into the events of the past day as into a fantastic puppet show. Scenes from her life flickered past her mind like an uneven jumpy film, full of talk, clear and muddled, full of symbols and dancing colours. They were all inspired by the project that she had been working on lately: scenes of a Friday in the streets of a Jewish *shtetl*. That was her new occupation.

After her *matura* exams she, unlike her classmates, had not felt the void following her sudden freedom from school. She liked to study, but preferred to do it without an imposed discipline. After all, she was involved over her head in the impetus of her life. The library, now a fully functioning institution, was devouring a great deal of her time, while it also influenced her in a particular way. She liked books, not only their content, but also their unread presence. They intrigued and incited her curiosity. They both urged her on towards something and imposed a majestic calm. More than once would she think about the power of books and of their papery weakness. She herself, in her inner being, felt just as perishable and just as enduring as a book.

Here, in the kitchen — the library room — she was leading a self-education group twice a week. Here she also began to write poems, short stories and essays on literature. Here, during the cold gray hours of dawn, the festive hours of her day, she studied difficult trigonometric problems, logarithms and the laws of logic and physics. Sitting snuggled up on her bed made of chairs, with gloves on her hands, she flipped the pages of her notebooks, and of the disintegrating history textbooks which were passing from one student to another. And every evening she would go to the barn near the bazaar where an army of *maturists* and graduates attended the university which had sprung up practically by itself.

It was good to sit among the wrapped-up young men and women, squeezed together, filling the barn from one end to the other. It seemed as if secret rites were being performed here, while the professor who had single-handedly founded the university, a young man with a face as open and clear as a mathematical formula, performed the functions of a priest. With the lump of chalk in his hand he deciphered formulas, opening great vistas; he reached into dark wells; he split the skies and filled everything with light. Along with him his listeners built scaffoldings of thought, put in posts of rules, destroying in the process the silly old axiom that hungry stomachs do not want to know of anything but food. Yes, even to be hungry was easier there.

Until recently, Rachel had been working at the Millinery Resort, cutting out felt forms with large scissors which left their imprint on her fingers, so that holding a pencil became painful. Then one day in December something happened. She was hurrying home from the Resort. A mild thick snow was falling, creating a curtain between the passers-by and herself. Tired as she was, she was making plans for the following hours of the day when her real life began. The thoughts she used to have during her walks through the streets, all her self-analysing — the eternally nagging question: Who am I? — had vanished. Somehow she had already found the answer. In her femininity of an eighteen-year-old, out of the labyrinths of restlessness, out of her hunger, which was not only physical, little by little the awareness of her self began to emerge. It did not lend itself to any formulation in words, and yet it was clear. This allowed her thoughts freely to turn towards the future, towards the hours and the days which awaited her.

As she walked on, she noticed a strange sign: "Scientific Department". Near the sign there was a narrow glass door, and at the side — a window. Through the crack in its ice-covered pane she saw a room containing a few tables, and around them, men and women bent over heaps of paper. Amidst the paper stood pots, boxes with pencils and around them, heaps of colourful rags. The people at the tables held small figurines in their hands. Grown-ups playing with dolls? Someone was walking around the tables, someone who himself looked like a fantastic doll; an oriental patriarch, a Jewish prince. He was tall, slim, wore a three-quarter length gaberdine and a black silken skullcap on the tip of his head. The paleness of his delicately shaped face and the expression of mystery fading into his well-trimmed beard reminded her of Jesus. It warmed and attracted her so powerfully, that Rachel forgot where she was heading, and, as if by an order of the kindly prince inside, she opened the door and found herself in a warm room, beamed on by the light of a pair of eyes which seemed to know that she was meant to come.

The people at the tables raised their heads as the quaint man stepped forward, arms outstretched, and greeted her as if she were someone dear whose arrival he had been impatiently awaiting. "Have you come to see the exhibition?" he asked in a voice which perfectly matched his appearance. He headed for the neighbouring room where the light was dim. She followed him. They stopped in front of a few illuminated showcases. Approaching the first one, he explained, "A Jewish wedding in a *shtetl.*" He glided his finger over the glass, "The groom, the bride, the musicians, the in-laws . . . Here is the street: the water carriers, the Sabbath-goy. The wedding is the theme, but we're trying to give a picture of the *shtetl* in general. How do you like the goat at the well? And this is the town fool . . . And here are the *heder* boys." The man's voice flowed out with a lilting wistful sound. His bright eyes were fixed on Rachel's face, as if he were trying to read there the effect of the scenes. He led her over to another showcase. "A *Simchat Torah* scene in a synagogue," he said, then consulted his watch. "You've come too late . . . We're closing."

She raised her head to him and muttered, "I would like to work here."

He did not seem surprised. He smiled faintly as he led her back to the front room. "Artists, sculptors and painters work here," he explained calmly.

"I could help . . ."

His eyes beamed at her, "Good. We can try."

For one week she came in after work, to watch. The next week she was allowed to try her hand at something. The third week she became a full member of that odd little Resort, under the direction of *Rabiner* Wolman. To work there was a pleasure. The hours flew past feverishly. They were filled with Rachel's struggle, as her own inexperienced fingers attempted to conquer the papier mâché. And there was the companionship of her co-workers, a completely different kind of Resort people, who had clever sure hands and spoke to her in a language she understood easily. And besides, there was the presence of the director, the *Rabiner*, who was an entirely different kind of magician than the young professor at the university barn. The young professor evoked enthusiasm for the truths which he revealed. The *Rabiner* Wolman evoked curiosity for the truths which were concealed. The lights in his eyes constantly flickered alluringly, like distant stars.

Then there were the visitors, the accidental and the habitual. And there was also the mute exchange, the unspoken conversations of the finished figurines among themselves — on the tables, the shelves, and in the showcases. There was an atmosphere both of the grotesque and of sanctity in these few rooms, keeping the mind and heart on constant alert. However more than once Rachel heard the voice of her young professor at the university, asking a question of her which gnawed at her mind: "At whose command, in whose service does this museum exist?"

But the figurine of the girl which Rachel had created was simple and uncomplicated. She had taken it home, firstly, because she could not part with it, secondly, to finish it during her free moments at home. She also wanted to show it to David, perhaps hoping that the figure of the girl, so primitive, so modest, would help them find the straight path between themselves and bring their love back to its former simplicity. David had not come to greet the New Year with her. However, he had appeared in her dream. In her sleep she moulded him with her fingers, as if he were a figurine which had to match the figurine of the girl.

✦ ✦ ✦

New Year's Eve.

For Miss Diamand the space between the state of wakefulness and sleep became increasingly smaller. Most of the time she stayed in bed, often not knowing whether it was day or night, let alone the day of the week or the date. There were only rare hours when she was fully conscious of the passing of time.

As soon as the *gymnasium* had closed down, an unwillingness to walk befell her. The bed attracted her, and it was easy to submit to its luxury and to respond to the call of the pillow. Her mind, like her body, was indifferent to her surroundings; having become lazy, it turned into a capricious mechanism which worked one moment and stopped the next. Her memory began to play with comic anachronisms, mixing up or displacing important events in her life. "Before" and "after" ceased to have any meaning, while she had no ambition to put back the images coming to visit her into their chronological order. She was more comfortable with things as they were. She felt no cold or hunger. If occasionally someone walked about her room, she would not know who it was. She smiled with her thin lips, spreading them and tying them together like an accordion of wrinkles. Someone pushed warm spoonfuls into her mouth. She thanked whoever it was, while her eyes which had used to be blue and were now like two bloodshot dots, would flood, wetting her cheeks. When a child of the club which she had directed came in, she would stretch her hands out to it, moving her body towards the edge of the bed. But she could not see the child clearly. The smile on the little face shone into her heart through the prism of the tears in her eyes. She heard the child's words from very far and at the same time as if they were coming from her own heart. When the child sat down on the bed and she felt its delicate freshness through her dulled fingers, she would respond to the child's chatter with her own, as one responds with a hum to the memory of a tune. Long silences interrupted her chatter. Her eyelids would droop and she would sail off to where it was day and night at the same time.

But she was not left alone so easily. There were those who begrudged her silence; those tactless, demanding, brutal creatures who came to tear her out of the pleasant state of stagnation and kept her awake for hours. These were her former students, the *maturists*. They had taken to storming into her room daily, making her feel ill-at-ease and unhappy. They even made her sit up and talk aloud — long and forcefully, as she had never talked before. They, who had just received the paper confirming their maturity, noticed nothing. They arrived loaded with books and note-pads, demanding that she read their essays, correct their mistakes and answer their questions. They besieged her bed, handing her her glasses, forcing her memory, which had recently been so lazy, to become taut like a bow. Arrows were aimed at all the locked cells in her mind, attacking the deposits of knowledge which she had collected on her long road. And these boys and girls whose names she no longer recalled demanded more and more. So she gave them more, submitting herself to their will, in order to unload herself faster — and so be free to return to her peace.

However, these private meetings with their former teacher convinced the cruel visitors that she had never been as great a teacher as she was now. That precisely now, lying in bed, she had reached the perfection which she could never achieve in the classroom. So they delivered themselves into her hands, ready to absorb every word she said. It was as if she had at last mastered an instrument which resounded at the slightest touch of her fingers. That was indeed an achievement. In spite of her resentment she realized that. It was another proof that she had arrived. However, it was precisely this fact that did not permit her escape into peace. It forced her to react. And in her nervousness, in the discomfort of her tired body, she had to smile, curiously and proudly, whenever one of these sadists lit up her mind with a brilliant thought which had never entered her own mind. Or she would exclaim with pleasure, when she read an essay or a passage that awoke her sense of beauty. Against her will and to her regret she had to admit to the absurd — that she was learning again. Instead of emptying her granaries, she was pitilessly filling them again.

Today they arrived in a big crowd — an army of pale gay devils, who penetrated into her timeless silence. Their arrival seemed to make her room sway. Their breezy words, their clamour made her head swim. It was unbearable. What they were saying was impossible to grasp. Today was the last day of the year, they said. "We have come to wish you a happy New Year!" they yelled, bending down over her like birds of prey over their victim. They pumped her dry hands, forcing her to sit up. Bells tolled in her ears; huge, swaying, pitiless bells, pouring lead and steel into her limbs, armouring her flabby body. These young devils, against her will, awoke her will. Finally, she showed them the door, so that she could dress to receive them properly.

It was a strange feeling to touch the floor on her spindly legs. But to her astonishment, her two legs, thin as twigs, supported her body, leading her to the door where her mauve dress hung. She had no idea when and how the dress flowed down over her. She washed her rutted dry face and to her surprise, took great delight in the touch of the cold water against her cheeks. She glided her comb through her silvery feather-thin hair, then opened the door to let her tormentors return.

They scrambled towards her, prodding her with their elbows, and the amazing thing was that she did not topple over. They carried her along to the bed, made her sit down on it, then seated themselves on the floor at her feet. She heard herself talk to them: "I wish you a happy New Year, children." There was strength in the sound of her voice. "Soon you will leave the ghetto, and you will know where to go from there. That is the most important thing: to know the direction. There are no straight roads . . . Everyone is doomed to blunder. But those who know what they want feel lead and steel within themselves. One day they will know what it means to be satiated . . . just as I . . . who have arrived . . ." She was surprised that she spoke with such conceit about herself, yet she did not feel guilty. On the contrary. She began to tell them about her life. Yes, that too was knowledge which they should absorb. Everyone's life was a tapestry with a design of its own, with its own rhythm, its own repetitions, riddles and symbols of Fate. Not to everyone was it given to find the key to its code. Like a blind person one followed the paths of one's predestination. However the wish to be able to decipher onself, was present in everyone. Then let these young people, the eternally curious, know that it is just as wonderful to discover the world within oneself, as the world outside. So it was right to display her tapestry before them, in order to enrich them with it, now that the last knot had been tied. She knew that she was taking leave of them.

When she had finished talking, the noise broke out anew. She was offered gifts: scarves, little bags, candies and fat pads filled with their handwriting. It seemed that they were mocking her with their sweet talk. America had entered the war, they told her. Russia had begun a great offensive. She nodded impatiently, confusedly. She felt as she would during a lecture which had turned into a failure. And then, out of the blue, they started a discussion about *War and Peace*, quarrelling about its literary worth. They asked for her opinion on Tolstoy's truthfulness to life. They talked about the new forms that art would acquire after the war. She sat there, smiling absent-mindedly. The subject was of no interest to her personally; not that subject, nor any other. But the longer they buzzed around her, the better she began to feel. That was how it should be. They did not have to understand her. They were supposed to flash past her in their heated impatience, searching for what they needed of the past, of the future — for their own use. Only in that way could they respond to her. She no longer even heard what they were saying. She was too busy absorbing drop after drop of bliss.

They left her in such good spirits, that she did not feel like going back to bed. She wanted to celebrate. A sudden whim carried her mind to the sole name alive in it: Wanda, her friend. She took the volume of Slowacki's poems into her hands and sat down at the table. She flipped the pages. Her eyes caught a line, "I am sad, my God . . . Before me, in the west, you have spread a rainbow of radiant lights . . ." She did not read the poem through to the end. For the first time it left her cold. If she still admired it, it was from a distance. Wanda's face was also distant. Miss Diamand was not sad, nor was she merry. She felt festive, as festive as a colour which partook in the rainbow of beauty. The feeling of festivity was beyond the old or the new year.

✦   ✦   ✦

New Year's Eve.

The New Year's celebration for the Resort commissars and directors had been arranged with pomp. Samuel had planned to go there early. However, although Matilda and he had begun their preparations on time, it took them a long while to get ready. Matilda put on a white brocade creation with a low neckline; a dress she had ordered for herself years ago on the occasion of an important charity ball. However, as soon as Samuel saw her in it, with her face smeared with powder, rouge and lipstick, he made an ugly grimace. Without a corset Matilda's belly stuck out, immense and ballooning, while on top of it rested her heavy flabby breasts which in the tightness of the bodice could find no place for themselves but, flattened, overflowed the edge of her décolleté. The same was true of her behind. It jumped from side to side at her every step like balls in a tight bag. In this way she paraded past Samuel, begging with her eyes for a compliment.

He had long since stopped paying attention to what she wore or how she looked. In general, he avoided looking at her. This time, however, he could not allow her to appear in such a state before his friends and make a fool of herself. "Put on something else!" he said sharply. She squirmed at his remark, yet went over to the mirror and put on her hat. "I won't go with you dressed like that!" he warned her. She bit her lips, fastening the hat with a long pin. He exploded, "Don't you remember that it's wartime and that there's an evacuation threatening the ghetto? What are you so dressed up for?" Ready to leave, dressed in a neatly-pressed suit and shiny boots, he made for the door. "Quick, change into something else!" he ordered, stepping out of the room.

He paced the corridor, rage boiling inside him. He was unable to handle his messy private life. He could not bear his wife, but the girl with whom he had been spending time lately gave him peace only for short moments. And the guiltier he felt towards Matilda, the more difficult it became to live with her under the same roof. At the beginning of his "carefree" life, he simply had not talked to her. Recently however, he had begun to force himself to be friendly with her; but this only led him to explode more violently during his frequent attacks of rage. At the same time, the lack of solid ground under his feet, of a close woman, of a home, made him feel unsure of himself, especially since his relationship with the Presess had stopped running smoothly. With increasing frequency the Presess would treat him to moralizing speeches and less and less praise, having long since forgotten the debt of gratitude he owed the Zuckermans for having found such a fine wife for him. On the other hand, Samuel's attitude towards the Presess had also become more complicated on account of his activities in the Zionist Party and of his daughters pressing him to oppose the Presess, as he had done in the case of Mietek Rosenberg. Altogether, there was quite a turmoil in Samuel's head, and he had no courage to make order out of the chaos of his feelings.

At length, Matilda came out of the bedroom, putting herself in front of Samuel with her face painted and wearing her housedress. He was appalled and felt himself capable of tearing her into pieces. "You want to wear these rags to the party? Are you out to spite me? Do you want me to go by myself?"

"Yes, go by yourself!" she broke into sobs.

He turned his head around and noticed Bella and Junia. Over their shoulders, Reisel was observing the scene with amused mocking eyes. He adjusted his jacket and, pushing himself through between his two daughters and Reisel, dashed out of the house. He did not go to the Presess' party, but went to another: at Miss Sabinka's place.

At Miss Sabinka's there was not just a New year's party. Her friends had gathered in her house to drink "lechaim" to the good news from the fronts, to the quick end of the war and to the liberation of the Jews. The party had been arranged discreetly, modestly, for a little group of hand-picked people. After all, there was an evil decree threatening the ghetto and Sabinka's friends were people with feelings, with a sense of responsibility and an awareness of the role they had been called upon to play. Assembled there were a few Resort commissars, two *Sonder* policemen, a judge and two members of the Deportation Commission.

Miss Sabinka's little house resembled the chocolate-and-candy hut of Hansel and Gretel. It stood hidden between the bigger houses of Marysin and would hardly have been noticed between the mountains of snow, were it not for the blue ribbons of smoke winding from its snow-hugged little chimney, as from a white top hat. Inside, the rooms were tastefully arranged in a modern style. The floors were covered with an assortment of rags made at the Tapestry Resort to Sabinka's specifications. The furniture and sofas came from the Carpentry Resort, while the felt flowers in the vases came from the Millinery Resort.

Sabinka herself also looked like a magnificent blond flower. She still had her long silken tresses, but now she wore them wound around her head, braided in a double crown which revealed her marble-like forehead, the tiny perfectly-shaped shells of her ears and her bright statuesque neck. She hoped that this hairdo would make her appear older and more mature, but in reality it did not help her much. Now, more than ever, she looked like a young girl in a painting done by a Dutch master. The winsome sadness of her eyes beneath the butterfly lashes and the sweetness of her mouth like deep-red cherries, along with her teeth which like two strings of pearls could light up with the most alluringly innocent smile — had the power to make anyone who looked at her feel cleaner, more honest and noble.

Mr. Rumkowski had kept his word. All that he had promised her during that long-forgotten evening when Herr Schatten had brought her, frightened and trembling, into the Presess' bedroom — had come true. It was the Presess who had given her this little house and permitted her to furnish it to her taste. And it was thanks to him that she had blossomed, nourished by the good extra rations and gifts of food. Miss Sabinka even now wondered what had happened to her. All she could grasp was that the ghetto had saved her. And in the deep secrecy of her heart she hoped never to have to leave the ghetto. She was happy here and needed nothing more. True, she had fears that she might again be deserted and fall back into the pits of loneliness and hunger. However, these fears were deeply hidden within her and the bit of them that shone out from her eyes, only added to the mysterious sweetness of her appearance.

It was true, that Presess Rumkowski had quickly forgotten about her and that the extra rations had begun to arrive at greater intervals, but the ghetto had been kind to Sabinka. Her other good angel, Herr Schatten, reminded himself of her, and in fact she had much more to thank him for, than the Presess. Because it was he who had transformed her into the independent lady that she now was. He had helped her in her intellectual development, so that she could shine like a jewel in any company. The educated Herr Schatten had played Pygmalion to her flower girl, but unlike Henry Higgins who strove to transform the flower girl Eliza into a refined lady of the salons, Herr Schatten had no intention of destroying the former Sabinka. On the contrary, his purpose was to preserve her freshness while developing her intelligence, to transform her into a courtesan in the French style, one who practised her art with knowledge while remaining angelically innocent — thus giving a man pure delight from every point of view.

He did not occupy himself directly with her education. He sent her tutors and books for that purpose. He himself taught her only the German tongue, because he was of the opinion that there was no one in the ghetto capable of speaking it with such a perfect accent as he. And Sabinka was an enthusiastic student. He would perhaps have fallen in love with her himself, but he was no Professor Higgins. He could not fall in love with his own masterpiece. He had rather fatherly feelings for her. She did not inspire him to play the violin for her, yet he played it in order to train her ear. And in bed he instructed her with a cool head, sometimes until the small hours of the morning. Wise pedagogue that he was, he did not try to wean her from her fixed ideas about marriage and children. She would tell him that the ten unborn children which she had promised herself visited her in her dreams every night, demanding that she bring them into the world. And he left her to cherish that dream. It contributed to the enhancement of the hours spent with her, making them lose every trace of cheapness. The way she cried and implored every man who went to bed with her, that he should give her a child, transformed each moment spent with her into a real love scene.

When his work was completed and touched up to the last detail, Herr Schatten, with generosity and fatherly pride, offered it as a gift to his best friend, the chief of the *Sonderkommando* who immediately took Sabinka under his wing, giving her a job in his office. She, on her part, kosherly deserved the post. She had mastered the German language, was diligent and orderly, and it was a pleasure to be with her and to look at her. She advanced rapidly, and recently, although the chief had to leave her because he suffered hell from his wife, she had been given the task of supervising the food and medicine reserves which were at the disposition of the *Sonder*. From there, she moved ahead automatically, with her will, against her will, passing from hand to hand — innocently, lovingly, intelligently. The men were grateful to her. They were kind and respectful in their behaviour. Yet, although they so much liked to hear her pleas, they would not respond to them. They all had wives and children.

Sabinka had learned from Herr Schatten how to arrange a pleasant and cultured reception for a few select guests. On such an occasion her living room was lit discreetly, which allowed the guests to see each other, but not to look into each other's eyes. The guests sat on low sofas, or on pillows on the floor, around the low tables on which plates with sweets, wine bottles and glasses stood. Herr Schatten had taught his student not to overload the tables with food, because food and wine were only supposed to serve as stimulants to the mind and the senses, and were not meant to transform the guests into gorging drunken swine. Herr Schatten also provided her with an old gramophone with a pretty blue tube on which she played recordings of Martha Egerth and Joseph Schmidt.

Tonight's party was not, however, proceeding as Sabinka wished. Her most recent lover — and she was unable to overcome her weakness of having only one lover at a time — Samuel Zuckerman, for whose party she was stealing medicines from the supplies of the *Sonder*, had appeared unexpectedly, bringing along a little bottle of pure spirit. He sipped from it, selfishly refusing to share it with anyone. Besides, he refused to let Sabinka out of his arms, kissing her incessantly, not tenderly, but rather brutally. Moreover, her other male friends, her ex-lovers, had brought along their most recent girl-friends and notwithstanding the fact that Sabinka was not at all jealous, that feminine presence introduced a clear dissonance in the harmony of the group as such. Sabinka felt ill-at-ease, and was shy and withdrawn, as if she were not in her own home. The noisy girls with their drunken giggles and silly talk destroyed the atmosphere of intimacy. Behaving too familiarly with her, they insisted on telling her stories that she did not feel like hearing. They sat in the laps of their patrons, which made her own sitting in Samuel's lap appear cheap and vulgar. The girls flailed about with their bare arms, crossing and recrossing their legs and chattering so loudly that she was unable to catch a word of the men's serious conversation about the Eastern Front and the Western Front.

But what bothered Sabinka most was Samuel's strange behaviour. Instead of amusing her, he made her sad. That was the kind of person that Sabinka was. Each man who was good to her became her own, her child. Her heart was always full of worry about them. Just like they, she feared that their wives would find out about her. She wanted her lovers to have no trouble at work. When they felt good, she would feel good too; when they laughed, she would laugh, and when they sighed, she would sigh. And they, for their part, liked to take her on as a partner in their worries. It felt good, before one went to bed with Sabinka, the angel with the sweet smile and the sad eyes, to open one's heart, to sigh oneself out, to share with her one's secrets and doubts, one's pangs of conscience, which one experienced because of her and because of other sins. She would feel guilty along with them, and this made it sweeter still to sin with her.

But Samuel was in all respects different. His peculiarity consisted of the fact that he never confessed to her, nor spoke seriously to her. That could have been insulting, but it was not, because he would burst into the room like a lively breeze; with his arrival all the corners of the house lit up. He was boisterous, playful and charming like a little mischievous boy. His childishness evoked both the mother and the child within her. Their particular relationship set him apart from all her other friends, making her forgive him his greatest sins. And these were, firstly, that he came to her only in the daytime, leaving her all alone at night, and secondly, that he would not supply her with firewood from his Resort, but insisted on giving her *rumkis*, something that, with other friends, would have offended her.

Tonight Samuel was drunk, and she had never seen him so serious before. He did not utter a word to anyone, but holding Sabinka in his arms, he kissed her non-stop and shamelessly kneaded her body. Sabinka burned with shame. She felt like crying. She waited impatiently for her guests to leave, as she had one consolation: it was too late for Samuel to cross the bridge and she hoped that he would stay with her overnight.

She heard a voice call out, "Midnight!" and the lights went out. For a moment it was so quiet that it seemed to Sabinka that she could hear the snow falling on the roof outside. Then she heard a kind of kittenish mewing and squeaking. Suddenly she felt Samuel's arms loosening. He pushed her away from him and ran out of the house. The mewing stopped. Sabinka's heart was pounding; her head was spinning. She stood up with an effort, the darkness whirling past her eyes in colourful circles. She ran out after Samuel and saw him lying in the snow, face down, half-buried. With a scream she ran back to call her visitors. It took them a while before they managed to drag Samuel back into the house.

He stayed with her overnight. So did her other guests. Sabinka did not sleep alone — and yet she cried all night.

✦   ✦   ✦

New Year's Eve.

Adam Rosenberg's heart pounded strongly, rhythmically, drumming out the

Latin phrase, "*Pecunia non olet.*" Money does not smell. That phrase followed him day and night. Sometimes he heard it, at other times he was not aware that he was hearing it, just as one hears one's own heart, without realizing it: Money does not smell . . . bread does not smell . . .

To the *fecalia* people were often "sent" as a punishment, just as people in other countries are sent to slave labour. One could be forced to work there for a week or two, or for a month, depending on the gravity of one's offence. There were, however, also *fecalists*, entire families, who chose that occupation voluntarily, because of the double soups, the glass of milk and the extra ration they received. Adam was one of the volunteers.

Like certain sects in the Orient, the *fecalists* were a closed caste and were considered untouchable. They performed to perfection the holy service of cleaning the wooden "temples" in every backyard: the latrines. The *fecalists* also had their own priestly garb: brown stained overalls. Their sacred vessels consisted of a large wooden scoop with a long handle, and a pail. With these they would draw the excrement out of the cesspools and fill the long brick-red barrels which lay horizontally on the framework of a wagon. Usually, it was the men who pulled the shafts in the front, while behind, the weak and the women and children pushed with outstretched arms, faces down. Often on top of the barrel, a child or two could be seen riding like on a red pony. The "sacred" *fecalia* wagon was quite picturesque. Not with chiming bells nor chants was its passing announced to the passers-by, but rather with the "incense" which preceded it, and hung in the air after it had passed. Instead of cymbals and flutes there was the clank of the wheels against the stones and the drumming of the pail and scoop against the shaking tin walls of the barrel. The lucky by-passer, who found himself near such a sight, could feast his eye on the brownish shimmer of the sacred liquid that dripped from the barrel, "anointing" the middle of the road.

It would be wrong to say that Adam had left his post as janitor in Zaidenfeld's Resort for so called economic reasons, for the double soup, or the extra rations that one received working at *fecalia*. Nor was it for the family reasons created by his unique and sudden encounter with his son Mietek. He had been forced to go to *fecalia* by another encounter, weeks later, with his former servant, Reisel.

Tired, bent, wrapped in his coat, he had trudged home after a day's work at the Resort, pressing a canteen with soup to his chest. The canteen was hot. He had warmed it up on a heap of garbage and he was in a hurry to reach his room before it cooled. But as soon as he had descended the bridge, he came eye to eye with Reisel. She straight away pulled him aside and launched into her tirade, "Look at this face you've put on! The blazes! A real *klepsidra!*" She moved closer to him, so that the steam rising from her mouth crept into his nostrils. "You've lived to see fine times, haven't you? But on the other hand, with all your lack of luck, you're still lucky. There's been a search in our house. The *Kripo* was looking for you. So, between you and me, where do you really live, eh?" Adam tore himself away from her, and ran off at such a pace that the soup in his canteen began to spill over his coat.

All night he shuddered under his blanket. It seemed to him that he would hear steps under the window at any minute and that Sutter and his *Kripo* people would come in, to drag him out of bed and lead him off to the Red House. The next day he signed up for *fecalia*. And in order to better erase his trail, he gave himself a new name: Adam Neiman. He had intended also to part with his first name, Adam, but that name was too intimate. To renounce it would have given him the feeling of walking around without a shirt.

Today, New Year's Eve, Adam sat in his little room scrubbing his toes with a hard brush, until they hurt. He could never bear any dirt under his nails and now it seemed that no matter how much he washed, the stench coming from behind his nails remained, and it was impossible to get rid of it. Adam had already taken his daily bath of ice-cold water, and although it was not too warm in the room, since the heat from Krajne's oven could not penetrate through the closed door, he was not cold. He had just finished his daily gymnastic routine which he had taken up along with his new occupation and his new life-style. Reisel had told him that he looked like a *klepsidra*. She should have seen him now. The four weeks at *fecalia* had done wonders for him. He ate good soups, drank a glass of milk daily and had fine extra rations. He lacked nothing.

He put away the brush, stood up, put out the light and plunged into his bed like a suicide plunges into the sea. Because, despite all these good things, the stench of his body almost made him sick — not during the day, at work, when he did not smell it, but at night, in his bed. Then his nostrils became particularly sensitive. He was filled with disgust for his hands and no matter where he hid them, their stench would persist. He blinked at the blue window to which, stiff and frozen, the torn curtains were stuck. From the distance, the curtains and the frosty flower design of the panes looked like a silvery tent. It made him suddenly think of Krajne. It was odd . . . He wanted her. He was dying to have her with him in his bed, to calm him down. Oh, he could not bear the sight of her, he had no doubt of that. Yet she was one of the rare women in the ghetto who still had breasts and hips. When he sometimes saw her in the morning walking about her room, half-dressed, he would shudder with bitter-sweet remembrances, like someone to whose memory a familiar smell, a pleasant one for a change, had returned. Krajne possessed a heavy kind of beauty, the kind he used to like. Given the life that he was now leading, his encounter with her had taken on the aspect of a miracle.

Lately, he had tried to be friendly with her, even humble. He helped her in her housework, kindling the stove and bringing in water. He let her scream at him, or order him around as if he were one of her children. He was waiting for a moment of courage. He, the once self-assured Adam, who had used to take a woman as one takes a piece of dough, without ceremony or consideration, was afraid of Krajne, the Gold Digger — not so much of her, as of her refusal, because he not only craved the warmth of her body, but also the warmth radiating from her eyes. However, it happened that the meeker he became, the angrier she grew. Sometimes a fright would even come over him, that one bright day she might throw him out of his room. And this room was the last station. There was nowhere to go from there.

The problem with Krajne was quite simple. It was not the stench that she minded. She was used to such smells and they did not bother her. Where had she spent her childhood if not near the latrines? And where had she lived through her youth if not near the garbage boxes? On the contrary. The smell should have brought him closer to her and made her feel familiar with him. The problem was a different one. What had upset her equilibrium was her disillusionment. A holy man, one of the Holy Thirty-Six, might be anything in the world but a *fecalist*. Why? She did not exactly know why. All she knew was that the two professions did not match, and that was that. Of course she had already had her doubts about Adam's holiness before, and more than once had she pounded her fists against her head for being such a stupid cow as to delude herself with such idiocies. Yet, the note of hope would persist in taking the upper hand. Perhaps, in spite of everything, she did indeed have a private protector watching over her, who would not allow anything to happen to her children and herself? And she went on hunting for signs and hints in Adam's behaviour, finding them everywhere and thus acquiring solace for her soul.

But the smell which attacked Krajne's nostrils the very first day that Adam came home from his *fecalia* work, was the smell of truth. It became pitch dark in her heart and she then realized how forsaken she and her sparrows really were. So, the following day, she began to unload her despair and bitterness on the head of the "visitor", as if he were responsible, not only for her tragedy, but for the tragedy of the entire ghetto. She could by no means forgive him for not being a holy man.

Nowadays, if Adam left the door of his room open, so that a bit of warmth from her kitchen might reach him, she would slam it shut with such force that its hinges squeaked and its frame groaned. Yet, in his room which had once been a Holy of Holies to her, she now reigned freely. She took whatever seemed useful to her, not scrupling to grab a potato or a carrot from his drawers. Nor would she have spared his bread or his marmalade, if he did not carry it with him in the big pocket of his overalls. Even the fact that he obeyed her orders did not incline her more positively towards him. More than once she was overcome by a desire to throw something at his head, or to throw herself at him with her bare nails and scratch his face, or in general to give him a proper going over. But she did not want him to move out from his room. Because now she needed him in another way. Her heavy heart needed him as a scapegoat.

This New Year's eve, she was lying awake just like he. She, on one side of the wall, he, on the other side. He — restless in his craving for her; she — involved in fantastic plans of how to kill, choke and destroy him. Tonight her fury was doubled. Three of her children had caught a "draft" in their ears and had blisters on their tonsils. All night she had to keep the oven going, because she had put a dozen cupping glasses on each one's back and rubbed the last bit of butter she had into them. They were all perspiring and might, heaven forbid, give up their souls if the slightest chill came into the room. So she was lying in bed, shuddering, as she listened to her children's breathing. Normally, she would not take such slight cold to heart. Children had to harden their constitution and the less one fussed about them, the better they were able to get over their illnesses. But this time the situation was not normal at all. Krajne expected to receive a 'wedding invitation' any day now. She was in the first line of fire, since she was the wife of a deported man and also was one of those who lived on an allowance. And she did not know whether she should wail or be glad. On the one hand, she shuddered at the thought of setting out with her children into the unknown in such a cold. On the other hand, she hoped to meet with her Feivish for whom her heart still yearned. And she had never felt so alone before in her life.

From under the table the knapsacks packed with her few belongings stared at her. The knapsacks — did they resemble angels or devils? What were they ordering her to do? Set out in search of Feivish into the strange icy world which was not Baluty or even Lodz? Or stay in the ghetto and hide with her sparrows?

The sick children were moaning restlessly in their sleep, twisting and groaning. She jumped down to attend them every few minutes. She felt their foreheads, pressed them to her loose bosom and added some wood to the fire. She was moving barefoot around the table, around the knapsacks, wringing her hands, when she heard Deborah's voice. Her daughter sat up on the bed and swayed slowly, mumbling feverishly. Krajne ran towards her, embracing her with her entire full body. She laid her back on the uncovered pillow and whispered, "May what you've dreamed this night and the other nights come down on our enemies' heads." She spat three times to ward off an evil eye, and hurried to the stove to cook a bit of *tzimmes* out of one carrot. With a spoon she pushed it into the big girl's mouth. "Eat, eat, my little lamb. It's good . . . it melts in your mouth." Big tears dropped from her eyes, washing the girl's face which gradually relaxed. Deborah's breathing became lighter, escaping more evenly from between her dark red lips.

Krajne went back to bed in tears. Her teeth chattered, and in order to compose herself and become stronger, she revived the fire of hatred in her heart. Oh, how angry she was! Oh, how she raged against the wrong done to her children and herself! The fury grew inside her, swelling her bosom, tightening her limbs. "I will finish him off! I will finish him off!" She gnashed her teeth in fury — against Hitler? Against the Presess? No, against her visitor! Her nails cut into her palms. She pressed her clenched fists against her thighs and bit her lips, until she could no longer stay in bed. The quiet warm room swayed with her anger. She did not know what was happening to her. And in an attack of maddening pain she threw open Adam's door.

At that moment, Adam's craving for Krajne had reached its culminating point. He forgot all his fears and waverings. The fire in his body lifted him off the bed and when Krajne opened the door, they fell into each other's arms.

✦ ✦ ✦

Michal Levine,
Litzmanstadt-Ghetto,
New Year's Eve, 1941.

New Years's Eve.

My Dear Mirage:

Here I am writing to you again as if nothing happened. Don't be mistaken. This time it is a letter from someone who has come back from the Other World, but only partly. When the typhus epidemic broke out in the gypsies' camp, I volunteered to go in, along with two other colleagues. It was not a question of courage in my case, but rather an uncontrollable curiosity about what was going on there. There are, in my opinion, two kinds of curiosity. One is the kind that draws together a crowd of people who seek the satisfaction of watching a catastrophe, so that they can assure themselves, "It is someone else's misfortune, not mine." The other kind of curiosity is the one that looks for the opposite, for the discovery, "If it is someone else's, then it is mine too." To which category my curiosity belongs, you may judge for yourself. You would perhaps have found an additional reason: a subconscious drive for self-destruction. So I leave that to your judgment as well. I personally shall stick to the facts.

I will not describe to you what I've seen or experienced. Neither I, nor even the paper could bear this. Everything I saw there has wound itself into the fever of my typhus illness, giving flesh and blood to my wildest hallucinations. They tell me that twice I fell out of bed. I was moving over to make room for my comrades, the gypsies and their children. When I returned to consciousness, all that had happened seemed like one feverish nightmare. But as soon as I took the first step with my lame foot, a brutal light cut through my mind: the truth about man. Difficult to accept it, to continue with it. But as far as I know myself and human nature in general, I will probably begin to protect myself against that truth — by returning into the darkness, into ignorance. My body will force me. It wants to live.

For the first time today, I climbed a flight of stairs. I visited my patient, Winter. Strange, isn't it, that it was precisely with him and not with Mother or Nadia, nor with Guttman or Shafran that I felt like spending this evening. The thing is, that in spite of the devotion of my near ones, they have become strangers to me. My personal experience, which is only mine and not theirs, has created a division between us. Today I am more related to Winter than to them. Today I am not his doctor, nor is he my patient. We are two burnt-down stumps. Two equals.

We sat at the window of his dark room. Winter scratched the frost off the pane with his painter's knife, as if he were scratching off a superfluous coloured stain on a canvas. With his breath he blew away the ice on the glass and the night view of the ghetto appeared before our eyes. A bright night outside. A thin moon illuminated the houses, the streets; you could even see the bridge on Hockel Street.

"What splendid indifference!" Winter's voice reached my ears. My eyes sucked in the cold beauty with delight. But when the image reached my heart, it began to burn and sizzle like coal on an icy surface. It hurt. Winter said, "Night in the ghetto is a white slaughtered hen. Her two spread wings cover the black chicks, the houses of the ghetto, with cold feathers, with frozen fuzz. And there, can you see the bridge? That is the white neck of the hen, stiffly arched in its last spasm. And can you see the black Zgierska Street stretching beneath it? That is the butcher's knife, sticking in the hen's neck. There is no blood oozing from the neck, nor from the knife. The blood has coagulated into a red and black blood clot: the red-brick church nearby. From the very top of the tower the dead hen's eye stares out: the clock with the motionless handles. The red empty church in the middle of the ghetto, what a manifold, multi-faced symbol! There, in the niche stands the figure of the Holy Mother, the weeping wax doll in a blue dress. It is the eve of her child's birthday. She stands there with the cold snow heaped in her arms, with the cold snow in her halo and in the folds of her blue dress. What relation does she have to the dead hen? Sometimes . . . when I pass her, I feel like tearing her off her pedestal, and taking her under my cape. I want to crumble her idol's body and with my breath melt the cold tears shining in her glass-bead eyes. From her crushed waxen limbs I want to extract the live image of a Mother of the World, a Mother who guards us, who embraces us with tenderness, who leads her erring children not towards Golgotha, but away from it. I want her to become the Universe, become God. The wish of a child, of an artist. But, Michal, the truth is different. Indifference is the truth. Sometimes a loathsome indifference, another time one of splendour . . ."

As he talked on, Winter constantly checked his pulse or felt his forehead. As if in jest, he stretched his hand out to me, so that I could check whether he had a temperature. I felt a vein trembling rapidly between my fingers. In my fingertips something also pulsated, hot and fast. I was unable to distinguish which pulse rhythm was his and which mine. I told him that. And the touch of our hands again ceased to be the touch of a doctor's hand on that of his patient. It became a handshake of two brothers. He smiled at me, apparently feeling the same.

"New Year's Eve," he turned back to the window-pane. "Look how quiet. Everything huddled in the white innocence of the snow. Do you feel the festivity in the air? The snow is a white tablecloth and above it there flutters something shimmering: jewels, diamonds, emeralds, rubies, sapphires; a suggestion of huge bouquets of everlasting flowers, of sweeping trains of gowns, of milk-white partly-revealed female breasts, of eyes glowing like beakers full of rum, of hot grog, of *aqua vitae*. Or perhaps the outside world is on vigil, awaiting only the clink-clank of quiet sleigh bells, or a soft mewing of white cats, or a rustling of snow dust sparkling on its way down from a bough . . . from a roof? And perhaps the contrary: It is awaiting the drums, the trumpets, the brass cymbals that will splash the world with sparks of white restlessness and carry off the blood in one's veins into a wild dance? Look, feel . . . Can you hear the longing of innocent whiteness? What kind of cravings are hidden inside its dumbness? What gnawing pain runs through its covered depths? What does it want, this last night of the year? Does it long for eternity, or for the arrival of the day and its own annihilation?" Winter fell silent. He coughed for a long while before he caught his breath. Then his cough turned into laughter, Winter's hooting, rumbling laughter — the laughter of a bird of prey, "Indifference is the only truth."

Glossary

Ab damit!	Take it off! (Ger.)
Achtung!	Attention! (Ger.)
afikomen	Piece of matzo hidden during Passover feast, for children to find.
Aguda	Political party seeking to preserve orthodoxy in Jewish life.
ahava	love (Hebr.)
Alle Juden raus!	All the Jews out! (Ger.)
Älteste der Juden	Eldest of the Jews (Ger.)
Am Israel chai!	Long live the people of Israel! (Hebr.)
angst	fear (Ger.)
apikores	heretic (Gr.)
arbeiten	to work (Ger.)
Aufmachen!	Open up! (Ger.)
Aufschnitt	cold cuts of meat (Ger.)
baba	a kind of pastry (Slav.)
bellote	a card game (Fr.)
brodyage	riff-raff (Yidd.)
beschlagnahmt	confiscated, requisitioned (Ger.)
Bund	Jewish socialist party
chalom	dream (Hebr.)
cholent	dish served on the Sabbath (Yidd.)
chutzpah (or hutzpah)	impertinence, nerve
Das ist er!	That's him! (Ger.)
Das stinkt doch!	This stinks! (Ger.)
Der hat eine Nase wie ein Horn	He has a nose like a horn. (Ger.)
Du sollst arbeiten, jüdisches Schwein!	You must work, Jewish pig! (Ger.)
dybbuk	soul of dead person residing in the body of a living one. (Hebr.)
dzialka	plot of land (Pol.)
Eifersucht ist eine Leidenschaft die mit eifer sucht was Leiden schaft.	Jealousy is a passion which with passion seeks to inflict suffering. (Ger.)
Einkunftstelle	In the ghetto: post for turning in forbidden items, in exchange for some ghetto money (rumkis). (Ger.)
eintreten	line up (Ger.)

395

Eine jüdische Hure mit einem jüdischen Hurensohn	A Jewish whore with the son of a Jewish whore. (Ger.)
Eintopfgericht	stew, all the courses in one. (Ger.)
Ersatz	substitute (Ger.)
Familienandenken	family souvenirs (Ger.)
farbrokechts	vegetables for a soup (Yidd.)
Folks-Zeitung	the people's newspaper. Name of Yiddish socialist daily in Poland. (Yidd.)
Gemahl	husband (Ger.)
Gemara	the Talmud
gemütlich	cosy (Ger.)
Gettoverwaltung	German ghetto administration (Ger.)
golem	dummy, artificial man (Hebr.)
goy, pl: goyim	non-Jew(s) (Hebr.)
grober yung	person with no manners (Yidd.)
hachshara	preparatory training farm for Zionist youth.
Haggadah	text recited on Passover night (Hebr.)
Halacha	legislative part of the Talmud (Hebr.)
halah	white bread eaten on the Sabbath (Hebr.)
har . . . nar	master . . . idiot (Yidd.)
Hasid	follower, member of Jewish religious movement (Hebr.)
Halutza	female pioneer settler in Palestine (Hebr.)
hosen-kala	groom and bride (Hebr.)
Hashana habaa birushalayim!	Next year in Jerusalem! (Hebr.)
heder	Jewish religious school (Hebr.)
Himmelkommando	commando of the heavens (ghetto expression)
Holzschuhe	clogs (Ger.)
Hutzpah (or chutzpah)	nerve, arrogance (Hebr.)
Ich liebe dich, mich reizt deine schöne Gestalt.	I love you, I am tempted by your beautiful form. (Goethe: "Erlkönig")
Ich möchte dich nur für mich haben.	I want to have you only to myself. (Ger.)
Ich werde krepieren.	I will kick the bucket. (Ger.)
infolgedessen	consequently (Ger.)
Ja, ich hasse dich, kratziger Jude, mach das du fortkommst.	Yes, I hate you, mangy Jew, get lost! (Ger.)
Jude	Jew (Ger.)
Judenrein	clean of Jews (Ger.)
Junker	Prussian aristocrat, member of reactionary militaristic political party (Ger.)
Junkerheimat	Junker homeland (Ger.)

kaddish	prayer for a dead parent (Hebr.)
kalinka	Barberry tree (Slav.)
kibbitz	watch a game, offering unasked-for advice to players (Yidd.)
kiddush	the benediction over wine (Hebr.)
Kiddush-Hashem	to be martyred for being a Jew (Hebr.)
klepsidra	announcement of death, ghetto expression re someone's face
Kohelet	Book of Ecclesiastes
Kommst du vom Reich?	Are you from Germany? (Ger.)
kosher, kashrut	Jewish dietary law (kosherness. Hebr.)
Kripo (Kriminalpolizei)	Criminal Police (Ger.)
lody	ice cream (Pol.)
Los aber schnell!	Vanish, but quickly! (Ger.)
Lechaim	To life! (Hebr.)
Lech-lecho	Go forth ("The Lord said to Abraham, 'Go forth . . .'" Genesis. Hebr.)
mameshe	endearment for mother (Yidd.)
matzo, matzos	unleavened bread eaten during Passover (Hebr.)
mazal-tov	good luck (Hebr.)
menorah	a candelabrum (Hebr.)
mentch	a person, a decent human being (Yidd.)
meshuga, meshugas	mad, madness (Hebr.)
mezuzah	small tube, containing blessing, attached to doorpost (Hebr.)
Mishna	part of the Talmud (Hebr.)
mitzva	good deed (Hebr.)
Morgen . . . nächste Woche	Tomorrow . . . next week (Ger.)
Nach oben!	Up there! (Ger.)
Napoleonkis	a kind of French pastry (Pol.)
panienka, panienki	young lady, young ladies (Pol.)
Pardes	pleasure garden, paradise, according to esoteric philosophy (Hebr.)
Passierschein	a pass, a permit (Ger.)
pintele Yid	the dot of Jewishness
Poale-Zion	Zionist workers' party
Polizei	police (Ger.)
Presess	chairman
pshat, remez, drash	three methods of interpretation (Hebr.)
Rabiner	non-orthodox rabbi
Rashi	commentator on the Bible and the Talmud
Ressort (Arbeitsressort)	name for factories in the ghetto (Ger.)
Sehnsucht nach der Heimat	longing for the homeland (Ger.)

sheigetz	non-Jewish boy, Jewish boy who misbehaves (Yidd.)
Shalom-aleichem	greeting: Peace be with you.
Sejm	Polish parliament (Pol.)
servus	students' greeting
Simchat-Torah	A holiday celebrating the completion of the year's reading of the Torah.
Shishka	privileged person in the ghetto
Sitra-achra	the forces of evil
Seuchengefahr	epidemic, danger of infection
Sonderkommando (Sonder)	special unit of the Jewish police in the ghetto
Sperre	ban, house arrest or curfew
shlimazl, shlimiel	unlucky person (Yidd.)
shnorrer	beggar (Yidd.)
shochat	ritual slaughterer (Hebr.)
shtetl	small town (Yidd.)
Siehe mal diese hübsche Dame im Pelzmantel!	Look at this pretty lady in the fur coat! (Ger.)
Sie sollen . . .	You should . . . (Ger.)
So was!	such a thing! (Ger.)
Sperrkonto	blocked bank account (Ger.)
tateshe	endearment for father (Yidd.)
Torah	the Pentateuch (Hebr.)
Totenkopf	death's-head (Ger.)
treyfa	unkosher food (Hebr.)
tzimmes	vegetable or fruit dessert (Yidd.)
Überfallkommando	raid commando (Ger.)
Übersiedlung	resettlement (Ger.)
Vertrauungsmann der Kripo	confidence man of the criminal police (Ger.)
Volksdeutsche	a German born in Poland (Ger.)
Warthegau	Polish territory incorporated into the Third Reich
wirklich	really (Ger.)
Wissenschaftliche Abteilung	Scientific Department (Ger.)
Wohngebiet	place of residence (Ger.)
Wo ist das Brot?	Where is the bread? (Ger.)
wydzielaczka	woman distributing soup in the ghetto (Pol.)
Yeke	a German, (derisive) (Yidd.)
Yid	a Jew (Yidd.)
yeshiva	institution of higher Talmudic learning (Hebr.)
Yom-Kippur	the Day of Atonement
yomtov, or yom-tov	holiday
Zukunft	the future (Ger. Yidd.)

Library of World Fiction

S. Y. Agnon
A Guest for the Night: A Novel

S. Y. Agnon
In the Heart of the Seas

S. Y. Agnon
Two Tales: Betrothed & Edo and Enam

Karin Boye
Kallocain

Martin Kessel
Mr. Brescher's Fiasco: A Novel

Chava Rosenfarb
The Tree of Life: A Trilogy of Life in the Lodz Ghetto
Book I: On the Brink of the Precipice, 1939

Chava Rosenfarb
The Tree of Life: A Trilogy of Life in the Lodz Ghetto
Book II: From the Depths I Call You, 1940–1942

Aksel Sandemose
The Werewolf

Isaac Bashevis Singer
The Manor and *the Estate*